Saker smiled wryly at the thought of himself keeping out of trouble.

He seemed to *attract* trouble, swinging towards it like a compass needle pointing north.

A moment later, right on cue, he knew he wasn't alone in the warehouse.

He wasn't sure what had alerted him. A faint inhalation of breath? The almost inaudible scrape of a shoe against the rim of a cask? Something. While counting the cargo, he'd circled the whole warehouse, walked down every narrow alley between the stacks. *And I didn't see or hear anybody.* The hair on the back of his neck prickled.

He eased himself down into a crouch, holding his breath. No one shouted an alarm. The silence remained as intact as the aromas saturating the air, yet every instinct told him he was being stalked. It wasn't a mouse or a warehouse cat. It wasn't the creak of timber warming up as the sun rose. Someone was there, in the building, following him.

Va rot him, he's good, whoever he is.

By Glenda Larke

The Mirage Makers

Heart of the Mirage

The Shadow of Tyr

Song of the Shiver Barrons

Shadowdance

The Last Stormlord

Stormlord Rising

Stormlord's Exile

The Forsaken Lands

The Lascar's Dagger

THE LASCAR'S DAGGER

GLENDA LARKE

www.orbitbooks.net

Orbit
Hachette Book Group
237 Park Avenue, New York, NY 10017
HachetteBookGroup.com

First U.S. Edition: March 2014

Orbit is an imprint of Hachette Book Group, Inc. The Orbit name and logo are trademarks of Little, Brown Book Group Limited.

The characters and events in this book are fictitious. Any similarity to real persons, living or dead, is coincidental and not intended by the author.

Library of Congress Control Number: 2013952803
ISBN: 978-0-316-39966-1

10 9 8 7 6 5 4 3 2 1

RRD-C

Printed in the United States of America

For my agent
Dorothy Lumley
to whom I owe more than I can possibly say

The Va-cherished Lands

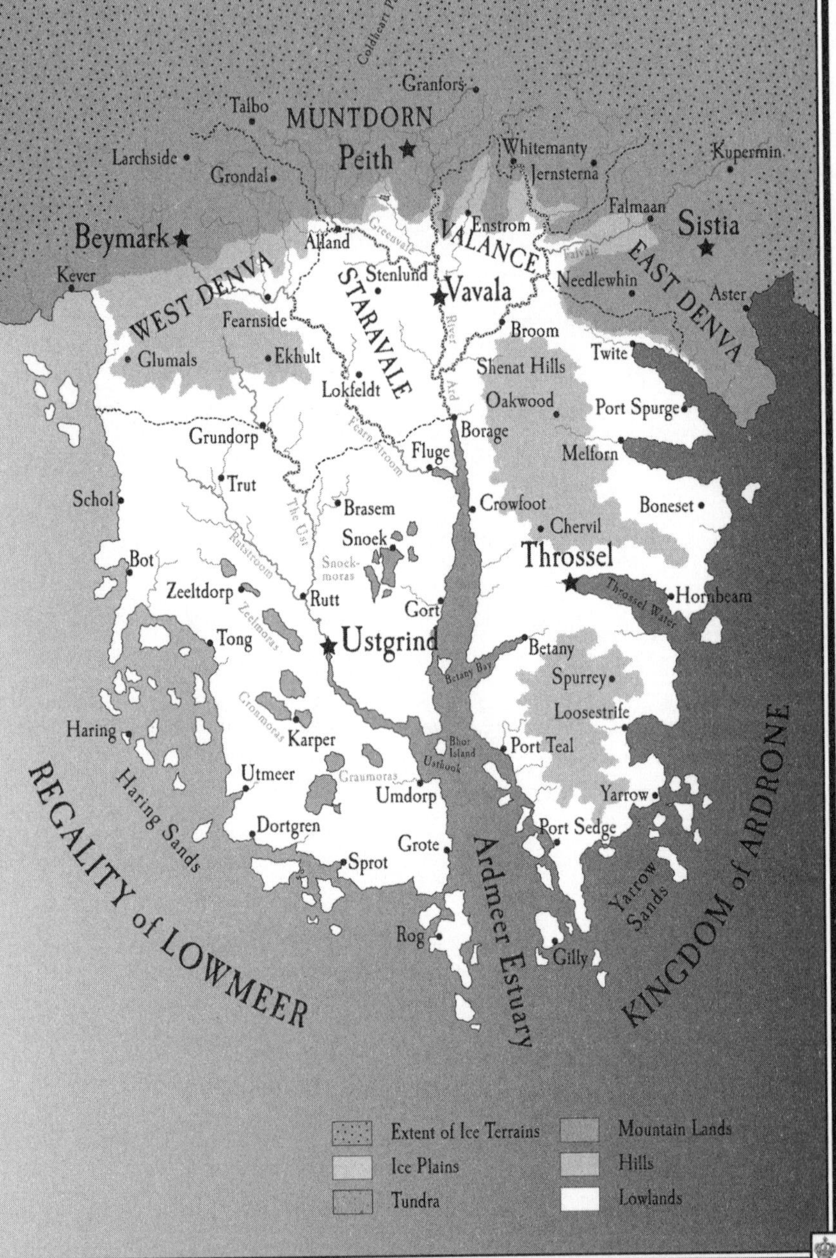

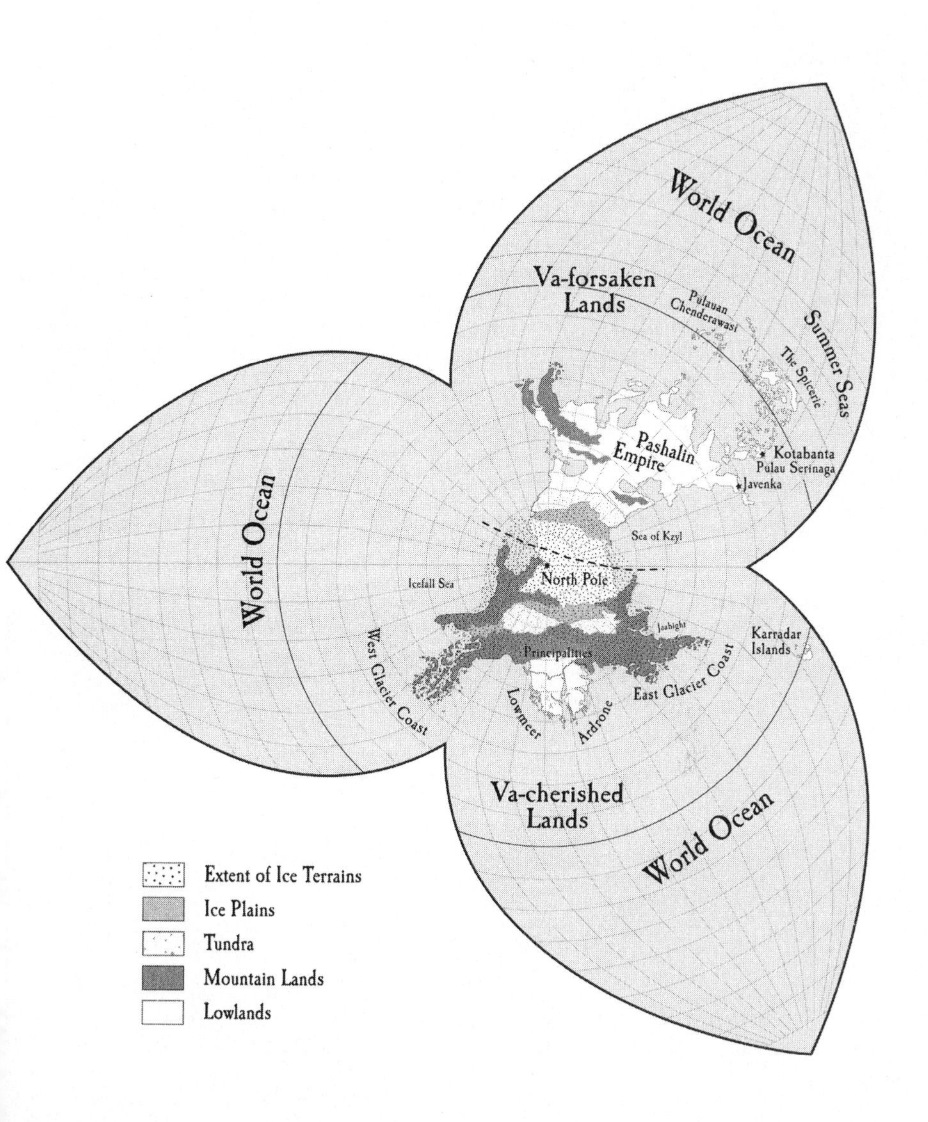
World Ocean
Va-forsaken Lands
Pulauan Chenderawasi
Summer Seas
The Spicerie
Pashalin Empire
Kotabanta
Pulau Serinaga
Javenka
World Ocean
Sea of Kzyl
Icefall Sea
North Pole
Jaabight
Karradar Islands
Principalities
West Glacier Coast
East Glacier Coast
Lowmeer
Ardrone
Va-cherished Lands
World Ocean
Extent of Ice Terrains
Ice Plains
Tundra
Mountain Lands
Lowlands

One year before

The youth ran, running as he'd never run before, racing time itself down the beach. White coral sands scudded under his bare feet, muscled arms pumped, breath laboured. He raced, yet his mind screamed at him all the while, *You'll be too late . . . too late . . .* He sailed over the fallen trunk of a coconut palm, leapt the sun-whitened driftwood of a forest giant, splashed through a stream trickling to the sea.

Too late, too late . . .

Out of the corner of his eye he glimpsed the ship anchored in the lagoon, sails furled, prow swinging to meet the incoming tide. His mind refused to consider it. Refused to absorb the significance of the rowing boat drawn up on the sand of the far curve of the beach.

My fault . . . all my fault . . .

At the edge of Batuguli Bay where the coastline was heaped with marbled boulders, he turned away from the sea, his feet flying from sand to forest track as if speed could halt the disaster his foolish words had nudged into motion.

Air rasped into his lungs; pain lanced his side.

Don't give up . . . There's always a chance . . .

The path curled upwards through the trees. The canopy thickened to dim the light and block the breeze. Roots knobbled the path, but his footing was sure. He laboured on, sweat pouring over his bare torso to soak the waist of his sarong.

The burst of a gunshot. A single explosion splintered into tens of echoes, each reverberation a promise of horror. Startled birds rose around him, bursting from the undergrowth and branches, their calls spreading their panic.

He sped up, not knowing until then that greater speed was possible but taking hope from the lack of any further gunshots. And then, much later, a scream, a human scream of anguish. It crushed him, that anguish, as it disintegrated all hope.

Too late.

Yet still he ran, long past his normal ability to endure. He burst into a clearing ringed with warriors and came to a halt.

Too late.

All my fault.

Raja Wiramulia lay on the ground, blood still seeping from his breast. The regalia proclaiming his ruling rank had been torn from him, part of it scattered on the ground around his body, part of it missing. Plundered. The prize the murderers had sought.

Rani Marsyanda crouched at his side, her forehead bowed to his cheek, her grief a tangible thing spreading around the gathering, scarifying them all. The Raja's only son, too young to fully understand, stood at her side, his body trembling with shock. The Raja's warriors, some spattered with blood, stood in a semicircle around them, stunned, disbelieving, leaderless.

Slowly the Rani raised her face, to look not at them, but at *him*. Her glance swept up over his sweaty heaving chest, to linger on his wild look of horror.

Was it you? she asked. *You who betrayed us?*

He knelt, touching his forehead to the ground, acknowledging his guilt, aware that she could order his death, knowing it would be justice rightly dispensed. He heard the rustle of the warriors unsheathing, but when he glanced up, it was to see her stay them with a gesture.

Who better than he to avenge this death? Who better to bring back what was stolen? The questions were asked, but she expected no answer.

They shuffled and glanced away, not meeting her gaze, as she turned to him once more. *You, Ardhi, with your foolish hubris, you will make this right, or die.* She picked up one of the blood-spattered plumes from the regalia now lying on the ground. Glorious in colour and splendour, it had adorned her husband. Now she held it out towards him like an accusation, her gaze implacable.

Helpless, knowing what she was doing, knowing what it meant for him, he took it from her and shuddered at the sticky wetness on the shaft.

You will go to the krismaker and have a blade wrought. This I command. The hilt – the hilt I will make myself.

He bowed his head.

Then you will bring back all that was stolen from us, no matter if the quest takes you to the end of the world. Do not think of returning until you succeed.

A sigh whispered around the circle of warriors like a flutter of leaves on the wind. They knew what she asked of him. Perhaps they even pitied him, a little. Or perhaps they were just glad she had not selected one of them.

You know why this is necessary. You know the horror this theft can bring. You cannot change what happened. This is the closest you can come to atonement.

Her words faltered and faded, showing how tenuous her hold on her grief was. He wanted to weep. "I know," he whispered. "If I could undo . . ." Pointless words. He halted and said instead, "I know what must be done and I will do it. How – how many were taken?"

Three. Only when you have all three will you return. Now go.

He turned and stumbled away, his shame and grief driving him forward when his legs would have failed him.

When he reached the beach once more, the ship was already unfurling its sails, the sailors just distant spiders in the rigging. And Lastri was there on the shore, watching. Her long black hair shone in the sun, and the sea wind whipped strands across her face. He stopped, arms hanging like lifeless driftwood, one hand clutching the cascading golden feather. She regarded him in silence, her eyes filled with fear. She'd heard the gunshot, she'd heard the birds. Her gaze dropped to the bloodstained feather. She would know that it meant more than a death.

He said, "You – you tried to tell me, but I was foolish and would not listen." *The frog under the coconut shell, thinking it knew the whole world.* "The Rani has bade me leave."

"Then . . . then go with the spirit of the wind, and pray that the same wind brings you back." The words were ritual, but her voice shook with anguish and he saw the tears on her cheeks.

"Will you wait?" he asked. But he was the one who waited, in agony, for the answer she did not give.

As she walked away, he knew he'd lost everything. Home, family, love, honour, the life he had led until now. Perhaps even life itself. No way to change anything, only a chance, a sliver of hope, to prevent further wrongs.

He sought the krismaker, knowing he was taking the first steps on a journey that could lead him to the other side of the world.

1

The Touch of Spice

Saker paused, nose twitching. Good Va above, the *smell.*

No, not smell: aroma. The intense, rich aroma of spices saturating his nasal passages and tickling the back of his throat. Gorgeously pervasive fragrances, conjuring up images of faraway lands. Perfumes powerful enough to scent his clothes and seep into the pores of his skin.

He recognised some of them. The sharp tang of cloves, the woody snippiness of cinnamon, the delicious intensity of nutmeg. Saker Rampion, witan priest of the Faith, was privileged enough to have inhaled such fragrances wafting up from manor kitchens, but never had he smelled spices as pungent as these. Never had he been so tantalised by scents redolent of a world he'd never visited.

Crouching on the beam under the slate shingles of the warehouse roof, he inhaled, enjoying the richness of an olfactory decadence. Any one of the bales beneath him could make him a rich man, for life.

Enough of the daydreaming, Saker. Witans are never wealthy . . .

His early-morning breaking and entering into merchant Uthen Kesleer's main warehouse did have a purpose, but it wasn't theft. He'd come not as a thief, but as a spy for his employer, the Pontifect of Va-Faith.

Several hours remained before the city of Ustgrind would waken to another summer's day, but slanting sunbeams already filtered through the ill-fitting ventilation shutters to illuminate the interior. In one corner, ledgers were neatly aligned on shelving behind the counting clerks' desks. The rest of the warehouse was stacked high with sacks and casks from the holds of the thousand-ton carrack *Spice Dragon,* recently docked with a cargo purchased halfway around the world.

Narrow aisles separated the rows of goods. Seen from his perch on the beam, it was as confusing as a hedge maze.

He had already seen – or rather, smelled – enough to glean some of the information he'd been sent to obtain, but he wasn't about to leave without proof.

Tying one end of his rope to the beam, he lowered the other end on to the burlap of the bales. He rappelled down the wall until his feet hit the top bale. Leaving the rope where it was, he crouched to examine the sacking beneath his feet.

He peeled off his leather gloves and tucked them into his belt, then used the tip of his dagger to tease apart the strands of burlap. The hole he made was just large enough to insert the tips of two fingers and pull out a sample. In the dim light he wasn't sure what he had. It felt like wood and was shaped like a star, no larger than his thumbnail. He lifted it to his nose and inhaled. A tantalising smell similar to aniseed, but stronger and subtly mixed with a hint of . . . what? Fennel? A spice obviously, but not one he knew. He slipped several of the wooden stars into his pouch, smoothed over the hole in the sacking and moved on to another bale.

After quarter of an hour he'd extracted samples of eight different spices and done a rough count of sacks, bales and casks. In the interests of secrecy, he'd resisted the temptation to break the seal around the bungs on the casks to see what they contained. His instructions had been explicit.

"Just for once, no one is to know what you are doing, Saker," the Pontifect had said with weary sternness after giving him his instructions. "No adventuring, no brawling, no sword fights, no hair's-breadth escapes. You're supposed to gather intelligence, not be a one-man army."

"Not so much as a bloody nose," he'd replied cheerfully. "I swear it, your reverence. I find out if Lowmeer's merchant traders have found the Spicerie and, if they have, what their intentions are, then I return with the information. No one will know the Pontifect's witan spy was even in Ustgrind. Simple."

"Somehow nothing is ever simple if you're involved." As this was said with a sigh that spoke of a long-suffering patience not far from being shattered, he'd had the wit to stay silent.

Now, however, he smiled wryly at the thought of Saker Rampion keeping out of trouble. He seemed to *attract* trouble, swinging towards it like a compass needle pointing north.

A moment later, right on cue, he knew he wasn't alone in the warehouse.

He wasn't sure what had alerted him. A faint inhalation of a breath? The almost inaudible scrape of a shoe against the rim of a cask? Something. While counting the cargo, he'd circled the whole warehouse, walked down every narrow alley between the stacks. *I didn't see or hear anybody.* The hair on the back of his neck prickled.

He eased himself down into a crouch, holding his breath. No one shouted an alarm. The silence remained as intact as the aromas saturating the air, yet every instinct told him he was being stalked. It wasn't a mouse or a warehouse cat. It wasn't the creak of timber warming up as the sun rose. Someone was there, in the building, following him.

Va rot him, he's good, whoever he is.

The warehouse doors were barred on the outside, and the street was patrolled by arquebus-toting guards of the Kesleer Trading Company. His only escape route was the way he'd come in, over the roofs.

Edging down a narrow canyon between stacked casks on one side and layers of bulging sacks on the other, he headed back to the rope. Each step he took was measured, silent, slow. As he moved, he ran through possibilities. A thief? A spy for another trading company? A warehouse guard? The thought of someone skilled enough to stay hidden and quiet all this time sent a shiver tingling up his spine. His hand dropped to the hilt of the dagger at his belt. Confound his decision to leave his sword back in his rented room! He'd feared it would hamper his climb to the roof; now he feared its lack.

He'd almost reached the rope when a soft slithering sound gave him a sliver of warning. Too late, he threw himself sideways. A man dropped on him from the top of a stack of sacks, his momentum sufficient to send them both sprawling. His heart skidded sickly as he tried to roll away, but there was no escaping the grip on his shoulder. Face down, his nose ground into the floor hard enough to start it bleeding, his dagger inaccessible under his hip, he was in trouble.

So much for his promises . . .

He relaxed momentarily, allowing his muscles to go soft. The hand jamming him down to the floor was powerful, yet the body on top of his felt surprisingly slight.

A *woman*? Surely not. His assailant had the muscles of an ox. A strong smell of salt, though. A sailor, perhaps. Yes, there was the confirmation – a whiff of tar from his clothes.

He arched his body up and over, reaching backwards with his free arm. Clutching a handful of hair, he wrenched hard. The fellow grunted and punched him on the side of his face. He let go of the hair and they separated, rolling away from each other and springing to their feet.

The young man facing him was at least a head shorter than he was, but the real surprise lay in his colouring. Black eyes stared at him out of a brown face, framed by black hair long enough to be tied at the neck. Not Lowmian, then. Pashali? A Pashali trader from the Va-forsaken Hemisphere? He was dark enough, but his clothes were all wrong. He was dressed in the typical garb of a tar straight off a Lowmian ship. In the dim light it was hard to guess his age, but Saker thought him a few years younger than himself. Nineteen? Twenty?

Not much more than a youth, crouching, arms held wide, body swaying slightly. The stance of someone used to hand-to-hand combat. Bare feet. *A brown-skinned sailor and no shoes.* He'd heard about them: skilled sailors from the Va-forsaken half of the globe, but not from Pashalin. They were recruited from the scattered islands of the Summer Seas and their reluctance to wear shoes in all but the coldest weather was legendary.

What did the Pashali call them? Lascars, that was it.

But what in all the foaming oceans was he doing in Lowmeer? Lascars crewed Pashali trading vessels half a world away. They didn't turn up in warehouses in chilly, wet Ustgrind, capital of Lowmeer, though he'd heard they occasionally reached the eastern coasts of his own nation, neighbouring Ardrone. He'd never glimpsed one, though.

He dropped his hand to pull out his dagger, but barely had it free of his belt before the young man sprang at him, turning sideways as he came, his front leg rising in a kick. Confused by the move, Saker hesitated. The man's heel – as hard as iron – slammed into his wrist. The dagger went flying and he was left gasping in pain. Consign the whelp to hell, a wallop like that could kill. And with bare feet too – his heels must be as thick as horn!

He ducked away and, to give himself time to recover, said with all the calm he could muster, "Can't we talk about this? I imagine you don't want to get caught in here any more than I do."

That was as far as he got. The youth came barrelling at him again, his speed astonishing. Saker reacted without thinking. He slid one foot between his opponent's legs, laid a hand flat to the floor to give himself leverage, and pushed sideways. His legs scissored around the youth's right knee, pitching him over. The lascar fell awkwardly, grunting in pain. Saker threw himself on top, and for a moment they wrestled wildly on the floor.

The sailor might have been small in stature, but he was all sinew and muscle. Worse, he was a scrapper. He head-butted Saker's face, sending fierce pain lancing through his cheekbones. His nose gushed fresh gouts of blood. Only a lucky blow using his knee to jab the fellow's stomach saved him from further ignominy. They broke apart, panting. Saker cursed. His shirt was torn all down the front, so he used it to wipe the blood from his face.

His opponent had scooped the fallen dagger up from the floor and drawn another from his belt. His blade was oddly sinuous. Saker's mouth went dry. Sailors said there was sorcery in blades like that.

Fobbing damn, Fritillary will be furious. Sorry, your reverence, I think trouble has come calling again . . .

Sometimes life just wasn't fair.

He back-pedalled away, fast, relying on his memory of the configuration of the cargo heaped behind. The lascar leapt after him.

Saker grabbed a barrel balanced on top of another and pulled it to the floor between them. The metal rim rolled over his attacker's bare foot. He didn't flinch. Saker tumbled another after it, and then a third, a smaller one, bound around the bulge with cane. The cane broke when it hit the floor, splitting the staves apart to release a cloud of bright yellow powder which billowed up around him. Disorientated, he tripped over one of the staves and fell face down into brightly coloured ground spice. He pushed himself up, blinded, utterly vulnerable, dripping blood and sneezing, blowing out clouds of gold-coloured powder.

He blinked away the spice and found himself looking into twinkling black eyes. His assailant's amusement didn't prevent him from pricking his ribs with the point of his wavy dagger, or twisting his other hand into his torn shirt to haul him to his feet.

Pox on the cockerel!

Saker could have said any number of things. Instead, he wiped bloodstained powder from his face and selected the most harmless question he could summon. "What *is* this stuff?"

"*Kunyit.* Here, men say turmeric."

"A spice, I hope, and not a poison."

The grin broadened. "Maybe you no live long enough to be poisoned, yes?" The fellow jabbed the point of his dagger a little more firmly into his side.

Saker sneezed again, a series of explosive paroxysms. Each time, the point of the dagger jabbed unpleasantly through the cloth of what was left of his shirt. Va help him, he was as helpless as a featherless squab!

The side door of the warehouse swung open with a loud creak. Light and the sound of voices flooded in. Both of them froze, then – as one – ducked down below the level of the stacked cargo. The lascar eyed him warily, keeping his wavy blade at the ready, even as he slipped Saker's knife into his belt in a deliberate gesture of ownership.

Their danger was now a shared one. If the newcomers wanted to inspect the cargo, there was no way they'd miss the broken cask with its contents spilled. Any man caught in an Ustgrind warehouse could expect no mercy. Lowmian law protected trade and traders, and punishment of transgressors tended to be lethal.

Va-blast, we could soon be as dead as soused herrings in a firkin.

Silently he shrugged at his unwelcome companion. The lascar leaned forward, until his mouth was almost at his ear. "Betray me, my blade stick your heart. You understand, no?"

Saker rolled his eyes to signal his lack of interest in continuing the fight. He glanced at his rope where it hung against the wall. It suddenly looked all too obvious. Carefully he reached for his gloves. The lascar watched, alert, as he pulled them on.

Footsteps rattled floorboards at the entrance. He counted the number of shadows cast across the light as men entered the door one by one: five. Five people. Only one spoke, directing the rest to the desks. Relieved, Saker breathed out. Clerks, then?

No, too early for clerks. This was a clandestine meeting.

Chairs scraped, more murmured conversation. Then one voice, authoritative, irritated, spoke above the rest. "Well, Mynster Kesleer, what's all this about, then? Dragging us out of our warm beds at this Va-forsaken hour! I trust you have good cause."

Kesleer? Kesleer himself? The Ustgrind merchant who not only owned the warehouse, but who possessed the largest fleet in all the Regality of Lowmeer.

The idea that such a powerful man had called a meeting at five in the morning in a dockside warehouse was startling. Saker's astonishment paled, though, under his growing fear. If he was caught and identified as an Ardronese witan working for Fritillary Reedling, the Pontifect of the Faith, he would not only be hanged as a thief and a spy, but his involvement would drag the Pontificate into an international incident. He winced. The repercussions would be horrendous.

He strained to hear the conversation, but the men had dropped their voices to a murmur. Beside him, the lascar peered around the edge of the bales to see what was happening. His frown told Saker he wasn't having much luck either.

The next audible words were uttered by a different man, his tone incredulous. "That's a preposterous proposal! Your skull's worm-holed, Kesleer, if you think we'll agree to that!"

Once again, the reply was muffled. Saker gritted his teeth. What proposal? To do what? Between whom? Without a second thought, he hoisted himself up the side of the bale until he lay flat on top. He was nowhere near the front row of the stacked cargo, and stuffed sacks on top of the bales still hid him from the Lowmians, but there was a gap between them, several inches wide.

A slit he could look through.

He had a narrow view of the counting table near the desks, now scattered with papers and charts, and the face of a man seated there. A lantern on the table provided more illumination, and there could be no mistaking him: Uthen Kesleer. Although they'd never met, the merchant had been pointed out to him on the street, and a bulbous growth on the side of his nose made for a distinctive visage.

A soft scrabbling behind told Saker the lascar had followed him. The young man, baring his perfect white teeth in a grin that might have been infectious in another situation, burrowed his way between Saker and the sacks, until he was sharing the same view.

One of the men raised his voice to growl, "Profit? Not from this recent venture of yours, I think, Mynster Kesleer. I notice neither of your other carracks followed the *Spice Dragon* up the Ust estuary home to the berth outside."

"Scuttled in the islands. Shipworm. Three in every four men in the fleet died, so there weren't enough to man all three vessels anyway. Those still alive sailed the *Spice Dragon* home. The dead were no loss. More profit for the rest, in fact."

The lascar drew breath sharply and his muscles tautened against Saker's torso. His hand groped for his wavy-bladed dagger, now thrust through the cloth belt at his waist.

He was on board, Saker thought with sudden insight. *He sailed on the* Spice Dragon *to Ustgrind.* Those poor bastards who'd died had been his shipmates. Scurvy-ridden fish bait, probably, or dying of bloody flux and fever in strange ports.

"Come now," Kesleer was saying, "you know how it is, Mynster Mulden. Since when have any of you rattled your brains about such things? It's the way Va has ordered life. There are always plenty more tars willing to take the risk and seek their cut of the trade. I'm sure Mynster Geer and Mynster Bargveth agree with me."

The shoulder muscles of the youth rippled like a cat about to spring. Saker gripped him, shaking his head. The fellow turned to glare, dark eyes flashing, daring him to say something.

He kept silent.

The conversation mellowed, the softer words unintelligible, but he had gleaned the identity of three of the other four men. Geer, Mulden and Bargveth, all merchant families with shipping interests, families not just wealthy, but influential at the Regal's court. The Geers hailed from Umdorp, the second largest port of Lowmeer. The Muldens controlled the docks and fleets of Fluge in the north, while the Bargveths had a monopoly of trade out of Grote in the far south.

That they were talking to one another astonished him. Competition between ports was a normal part of the country's commerce. Lowmian shipping merchants didn't cooperate; they prattled the whereabouts of rival merchantmen to Ardronese privateers instead.

Cankers 'n' galls, what's going on? The Pontifect won't like this, whatever the truth. When rich men played their games of wealth, they endangered the independence of Va-Faith and the neutrality of the Pontificate.

He strained to hear more, but caught only fragmented snatches. And he still didn't know the name of the fifth man.

". . . new design of cargo ship. They're called fluyts . . ." That was Kesleer speaking.

". . . the Regal will want a privateer's ransom!"

"Well, we can't succeed without him, that's for sure."

". . . I have just such a tasty bait . . ." Kesleer again. The words were followed by a short silence, then a rattling sound.

"A piece of wood as a bribe for the Regal?" someone asked, tone scathing.

"This is bambu," Kesleer replied, "from the Summer Sea islands. It grows like that, with a hole down the middle."

The lascar jerked, the expression on his face an odd mixture of both pleasure and fierce rage as the conversation murmured on.

Oh, Va save us, what now?

"This hollow stuff is valuable?" someone else asked, incredulous.

"No, no. The value is in the contents." That was definitely Kesleer again. The next few words were indecipherable. Then, also from Kesleer, "Here, take a look . . ."

Saker couldn't see what Kesleer was showing them. He pulled a face, frustrated.

More muttered words, then, "I agree, they're certainly magnificent, yes, but what value can they have?"

What the rattling pox were they looking at? With a sudden movement the lascar pulled himself away from the crack and hauled himself up on to the bulging sacks to see better.

In horror, Saker leapt upwards to grab his ankle before he'd crawled out of reach. He yanked as silently as he could, trying to draw the young man backwards. What in all the world was he trying to do: get them both hanged?

The lascar kicked, but Saker was below him, well away from his flailing foot. Infuriated, the young man turned back and slashed with his dagger. Saker released his hold before the blade connected and the lascar wormed his way out of reach, heading across the sacks towards the merchants.

And the Pontifect thought *he* was reckless? He was a model of circumspect decorum compared to this idiot of a tar. At that moment, he could have cheerfully murdered the fellow. Instead, he slipped down to the floor. Stepping over the shattered cask of turmeric, he headed through the maze of cargo towards the back wall of the warehouse and his dangling rope.

Kesleer was saying, ". . . but Regal Vilmar is a jackdaw, hoarding pretty things. He'll love the idea that King Edwayn will have to watch and fume while Ardronese court women clamour after goods like these, at our price. Huge profits for Lowmian merchants . . ."

Every nerve in Saker's body told him that in a moment, the relative quiet of the warehouse would vanish. These men would react violently when they realised their secret meeting had been overheard. What if they were armed with pistols, those new-fangled wheel-lock ones that didn't need a naked flame to ignite the powder? If he climbed up on the bale to seize the end of his climbing rope, he'd be visible to anyone who looked his way. Worth it, or not?

The Pontifect's words echoed in his ears. *You're a spy, not a one-man army. In Va's name, try subtlety, Saker Rampion!*

Best to wait until the lascar was seen, then escape in the ensuing confusion. No sooner had he made that decision than a child's voice echoed through the warehouse. "Papa! Papa! Someone's been here. There's a broken barrel and yellow footprints! Come see."

He winced.

The fifth person. A child. At a guess, Uthen Kesleer's ten-year-old son, Dannis.

He had no choice now. He hauled himself up the wall of bales, gripping with his knees and digging his fingertips into the burlap for purchase. Behind him, chairs scraped, enraged voices shouted. Kesleer called out the boy's name, but it sounded as if he wasn't sure where the lad was in the maze of aisles.

And then, a gasp behind him, just as he pulled himself on to the topmost bale. Lying flat, he looked back over the edge.

He'd never seen Dannis Kesleer, but this had to be him. He was dressed in black, a miniature merchant, with silver buckles on his shoes and belt, his broad white collar trimmed with lace.

They stared at each other. He hesitated, reluctant to use force to stop the boy yelling for his father. But Dannis was silent, staring. Not at Saker's face, but at the medallion around his neck. It had fallen free through his torn shirt and now dangled over the edge of the bale. His cleric's emblem, the oak leaf within a circle. His immediate thought was that the lad would not recognise it, for it was the symbol of an Ardronese witan, not a Lowmian one. Ardrone and Lowmeer might share the same Va-Faith, but there were differences in the way they practised it. The oak leaf was not used in Lowmeer.

Beyond Dannis, he caught a glimpse of the lascar fumbling among the papers on the table on the other side of the warehouse. Their gazes met as the man found and snatched up what appeared to be a wooden rod. The merchants had scattered and were nowhere to be seen.

Saker looked back at the boy to find that Dannis Kesleer knew the oak symbol after all. He was making the customary bow given to all clergy, with both hands clasped under his chin. Saker smiled down on him and raised a conspiratorial forefinger to his lips in a sign of silence. Briefly he thought of directing the lad's attention to the lascar to make his own escape easier, but dismissed the thought. Instead, he made a gesture of benediction. Obediently, the lad laid his hand over his heart in acceptance. Then he turned and walked away.

Saker let out the breath he'd been holding, but his heart refused to stop thudding. He leapt for the rope and clawed his way up. The skin between his shoulder blades tingled as he imagined lead shot ploughing into his back. He scrambled on to the beam and hauled the rope up behind him, frantic.

How can they miss seeing me?

But the merchants were still shouting at one another, their voices coming from all over the warehouse as they looked for Kesleer's son. No one looked up.

Kneeling on the beam, he untied the rope with fumbling fingers, his mouth dry. A movement low on the opposite wall near the desks caught his attention.

The lascar was on top of the ledger shelving. Even as he watched, the youth began to climb. Saker froze. Va's teeth, how was he doing that? He knew sailors could climb rigging in the roughest of seas, but that wall was sheer, built of rough wood planks, and all the man had were his bare toes and fingers. And his dagger. He was carrying the stolen wooden rod too, which he'd shoved down the front of his shirt so that the top of it poked up over his shoulder. Even that didn't seem to faze him.

That must be the bambu they were talking about.

Fortunately for the lascar, that corner was deeply shadowed and so he remained unseen. Incredibly, he paused to look at Saker, who was keeping an eye on him as he slid back the loose shingles where he'd entered the warehouse. Their gazes met, and the lascar removed the bambu and waved it, grinning hugely, as if to say, "*Look what I found!*"

Saker winced, convinced the overconfident tar would plummet to the floor, or be seen by the traders. Yet his luck appeared to hold. He scrambled up to the top of the wall where he pushed open the ventilation shutter. The gap would be just wide enough for him to squeeze through, but the morning light now slanted in to illuminate him.

Va favours the bold, Saker thought. Still, on the other side there was a sheer wall dropping straight on to a narrow walkway along the canal, and near certainty of being seen by the outside guards.

Saker pushed his rope through the hole he'd made and prepared to wriggle out. Out of the corner of his eye, he saw one of the merchants rush past the table. His action scattered papers and something else lying there, something wispy. Gold-coloured filaments fluttered in the air, as bright as sparks. Yelling, the man pointed a pistol at the lascar, and pulled the trigger. The noise was deafening.

Looking over his shoulder, Saker saw the unharmed sailor one last time through the opening of the shutter. He was outside the warehouse, hanging on to a beam of the overhang. He made some sort of hand gesture just before he swung up on to the top of the roof, as agile as a squirrel.

Saker thought it was a wave of farewell, but then he saw the flash of a dagger blade flying through the air.

Not at any of the men below, *but at him.*

Impossibly, it spiralled through the air, its point always facing his way. It whirred noisily as it came, and the merchants below swivelled to follow its passage. Saker hurtled himself upwards on to the roof.

Something tugged at his trousers and scraped his leg. Grabbing up the rope and the coat he'd left there, he set off at a run up to the ridge of the warehouse roof. He heard doors crash open below, followed by shouts in the streets. He didn't stop.

He was already on the roof of the neighbouring warehouse when he heard the second pistol shot, followed almost immediately by the bang of an arquebus.

He didn't look back, but he did look down.

The wavy dagger was firmly stuck through his trousers below the knee, and his leg was stinging.

2

The Lascar's Legacy

"Oi, you! What are you doing here? This here's Kesleer property! Be off with you."

Saker, standing on the dockside not far from the warehouse he'd broken into eight hours earlier, turned without haste to confront the guard hurrying towards him. "Pardon?" he asked politely, setting his velvet cleric's cap firmly on his head to stop it being whisked away by the wind.

After cleaning himself up and snatching a few hours' sleep in his cheap port-side doss house, he'd dressed in a witan's robe before venturing out to have something to eat. The long skirt irritated him, but the clerical garb gave him instant respectability – and it could cover a multitude of uncleric-like items, such as the wire hooks and lock picks in its deep pockets, and the sword swinging at his side underneath. An arbiter's warrant recognising his years of study had earned him the right to dress as a witan; his only lie was the Lowmian medallion around his neck, which he'd just swapped for the Ardronese symbol recognised by the Kesleer boy.

Va only knows what the Pontifect will say, if I mention that incident . . .

He'd been careless, and Fritillary Reedling didn't like carelessness.

"Pardon, witan," the guard said. "Didn't see as you were a man of Va, like. But you're treading wrong here. This here's a private dock, and you need permission to gawk."

Saker took in the wickedly sharp pike the man carried. "Then it's me who should be apologising," he said with an assumed accent he knew reeked of the southern Lowmian provinces. "It was just that I heard a heathen lad drowned here this morning at cockcrow." That was true enough, although the gossip at the pie stall he'd patronised had been confused as to why the man had drowned. "Was I misinformed? I thought to say a prayer for his unshriven soul. Although blessed is he who dies by water." He fingered the wave-shaped curves of the Lowmian medallion, feeling only mildly guilty. Lowmian faith emphasised connections to water and aquatic life, and Lowmians adhered to the religious precepts they called the Way of the Flow, but they recognised the supremacy of Va the Creator and the religious leadership of the Pontifect, just as he did.

"Was there indeed a drowning here?" he asked.

"Ay. Saw him die with my own eyes. One of them darkish Pashali heathens."

Interesting. They hadn't recognised the man as a lascar. "Then all the more important he is remembered with a blessing."

The guard grunted. "He stealed summat from the warehouse. Bit o' furrin wood, looked like. Tried to escape over the roof. One of our Kesleer men shot 'im and he fell still holding it. Just missed the walkway and went straight into the water. Kept me eye on the body. Watched 'im, floating face down, till he was out of sight. He was a deader, right enough. T'ain't no one can hold their air that long."

"Did anyone salvage the stolen property?"

"Not as I heared. Went into the water clutched in his mitt, and by the time they roused sailors to get a boat after him, both the corpse and the bit o' wood bobbing alongside were out o' sight."

"Alone, was he?"

"Don't rightly know. Some said there was a second fellow, but nobody got a good gander at him."

Saker shook his head in genuine sorrow. "A poor way to end his days, a thief in a foreign land. Still, he deserves a prayer in the hope that Va grants him mercy." Resisting a desire to roll his eyes at his own unctuousness, he raised the medallion towards the estuary instead, murmuring the standard prayer for the dead. He spoke the words, but found it hard to believe the lascar had died. He'd seemed so . . . vital.

I don't even know his name.

If the guard hadn't been there, he would have reached into his pocket for the lascar's dagger, and dropped it into the water in homage.

There seemed little point staying in Ustgrind any longer. He already had the information the Pontifect wanted. The Kesleer Trading

Company had found a route to the spice islands in the Summer Seas of the Va-forsaken Hemisphere.

He sighed as he contemplated the upheaval *that* would cause. *Talk about jiggling a sore tooth . . .*

A map of the Va-cherished Hemisphere had graced the wall of one of his childhood classrooms, and he'd thought the land mass resembled a molar extracted from the mouth of some gargantuan monster. The crown was set in the polar ice. The body of the tooth was cracked by the borders of the five Principalities, otherwise known as the Innerlands because they lacked viable warm-water ports. The two roots of the molar, dangling southwards under the Principalities, were Lowmeer and Ardrone with their ice-free shores and thriving sea trade.

For centuries, trade into the Va-cherished Hemisphere had been at the mercy of the Va-forsaken Pashali caravanners, because only they possessed the mastodons capable of the brutal ice-cap crossing over the North Pole. Now Lowmians had proven it was possible to bypass the Empire of Pashalin via an ocean route to reach the spice islands and the Summer Seas. And the politics of *that* were about to give everyone the commercial equivalent of a colossal toothache.

Ardrone will be wickedly overcharged by Lowmeer, instead of by Pashalin . . .

Ardrone could at least attempt to compete by searching for the sea routes, but what about land-locked Muntdorn and the other Principalities? They'd be worse off, and the Pontifect, responsible for the spiritual health of the hemisphere, would not be happy.

Saker sighed and headed along the dock to purchase a berth on one of the coastal flat-boats that plied the western shore of the estuary separating Lowmeer from Ardrone. This one was due to depart with the tide early the next day, sailing for Borage at the head of the estuary. From there, he would take a barge up the River Ard to Vavala, the seat of the Pontifect in the Innerlands, to report his findings.

With the ticket token in his pocket, he headed back to the doss house to catch up on his sleep, but his thoughts were with the lascar. He couldn't dismiss the memory of that broad, mischievous smile, or the way the fellow had so casually swarmed up a straight wall to escape. And why in all Va's world had he thrown that dagger? To kill him?

No, more likely in the mistaken belief that drawing attention to my presence would diminish interest in his own.

And then there was the mystery of the bambu. The lascar had risked his life to obtain it. Or to obtain what was inside it. Well, it mattered little now that the man was dead. He pictured him floating out to sea, face down, the bambu bobbing beside him.

Bobbing . . .

His line of thought was abruptly broken when he turned down a side alley leading to his lodging, to find it blocked by a hand cart. As he came closer, wanting to squeeze past, his stomach heaved in recognition of what it was.

A death cart.

He swallowed the bitter taste that welled into his mouth, prompted by his memories of a spotted fever epidemic when he was a student at the university in Grundorp. For years, the call of the carters had haunted his nightmares. *Bring out your dead!*

As he approached, two men emerged from a nearby hovel, their lower faces wrapped in cloth. They carried a middle-aged man by the shoulders and ankles. With casual indifference, they heaved his body into the cart as if he was no more than a dead rat found on a midden heap. When they turned and re-entered the hovel, a smell of spice lingered in the air. *Nutmeg*, he thought. And yet it wasn't a well-to-do neighbourhood whose inhabitants could afford such luxuries.

He squeezed past the cart as best he could, glancing down at the corpse. A player's grotesque demon mask looked back at him, a face no longer human. Eyes bulged, bull-like nostrils flared. Horns sprouted from a bulbous skull, the sharp tusk-like prongs curling backwards to dig into the top of his head. Not a mask. A man, once, that much was obvious.

Saker stared, his mouth dropping open in his astonishment. *Sweet Va! What botch of nature is this?*

Horror became terror as one of the man's hands shot out and clamped tight around his wrist. Unnerved, he squawked an appalled protest. He tried to jump backwards, only to crack his head and right elbow against the outer wall of a house.

The supposed corpse, very much alive, held him in a crushing grip, pulling him off balance until his face was inches from the slobbering mouth. "Surprise!" the man cried.

Saker reeled from the foul stench of diseased breath.

"Not dead yet, am I? Lookee here, witan. Lookee on the work of A'Va, and despair! Is he not called A'Va the devil? See my devil's horns?" He gave a demented cackle. "And you thought you was under Va's protection!" He was still grinning as he vomited copious black bile, before collapsing on to the floor of the cart like an emptied sack. His smile died, his eyes clouded, first with despair, then with the approach of death.

Head spinning, gagging on the smell, Saker wrenched his fingers free. He was still standing there, gasping and trembling with shock, as the death rattle sounded. He ought to have been murmuring prayers for the dying; instead he was thinking, *Thank Va, merciful Va, he's dead.*

When the two men emerged from the hovel, they carried a second body, a woman this time. She too was growing horns and animal teeth. She was more obviously dead, her limbs already as stiff as planks.

"I'll be blistered," he stammered, looking at her face as they laid her in the cart. "What do they suffer from?"

One of the men re-entered the dwelling; the other looked at him, sunken eyes bleak. "Well, well, a witan of the Faith and this is yer first taste of the Horned Death, eh? Get used to it, young'un! You'll see plenty more, I'm thinking." He dug into his clothing and brought out a pomander stuck with nutmeg. Holding it up to his cloth-covered face, he inhaled.

The first man returned with a half-grown child. This one was also dead, and he tossed the body into the cart with scant attention to the sickening squelch it made as it landed. Saker wrenched his gaze away, swallowing back the contents of his stomach. He looked instead at the carter. "Treat the dead with respect," he snapped. "They may no longer be of our world, but their dignity means something to the living!"

"Not this lot," the man drawled from behind his face cloth. "A'Va got these. The devil's work now. Your business, I s'pose, brother witan. Not mine, fer sure. But you mark me words, reverend sorr: there's too many twins being bore. The Way of the Flow is doomed, lest you lot tackle the sprout of evil!"

What the beggary has twins to do with anything? Or A'Va of all things?

The whole question of the existence of a demonic antithesis of Va, a being called A'Va, was moot, and in another situation he might have argued the point. However, the two men wrapped filthy gnarled hands around the handles of the cart and trundled it away down the alley at surprising speed. Saker gaped after them. "Where are you taking them?" he called out. Neither man looked around or answered.

A tendril of memory brushed his thoughts, something about the Lowmian attitude to twin births, but he couldn't recall it to mind. He sucked in a breath of fresh air and strode after the cart, but by the time he reached the end of the alley, it had vanished into the throngs of people pouring out of the local Va-Faith chapel.

None of his business, he supposed, but the weirdness and the lack of care for the sick bothered him. Pox 'n' pustules, the man hadn't even been dead!

By the time he reached his lodgings, he was almost inclined to believe he'd dreamed the encounter. He was certainly too tired to think about it. Once in his room, he barred the rickety door, hooked his robe and his sword belt over the peg on the back, and lay down to sleep.

When he woke, the sun had already set, the room was dim, and there was something horribly wrong.

He lay still, alert. Moonlight shafted in from the street through cracks and knot holes in the walls, and he could hear the chattering and laughter of passers-by. Both the door and the shutter were still barred. He was definitely alone. But something had . . . changed.

He rose, fumbling for his tinderbox, steel and flint. His fear built as the tinder refused to catch. By the time he finally had the wick of his candle alight and could see what was out of place, he was sweating.

The lascar's dagger. It was lying on the floor halfway between the door and the bed. He stared, his mind trying to make sense of the impossible. He'd left it inside the capacious pocket of his robe. He had, he was *sure* he had.

The evidence said otherwise. He must have been half asleep and careless. He shrugged, picked it up and turned it over and over in his hands. He'd studied it earlier, and it was no different now. Beautifully wrought, the curved handle was crafted of polished horn inlaid with silver filigree. The cross-guard was not part of the handle, but an extension of the top of the blade. Even odder for a throwing blade, the guard was asymmetrical, with a long and a short side. The rest of the blade was double-sided and sinuous, but the curves weren't of even length. He wasn't sure what metals had been used in its crafting, but they'd been forge-melded – folded and refolded – and patterned throughout with orange-gold filaments he couldn't identify. The overall appearance was of an ornamental work of art, rather than a weapon.

And yet that had to be a faulty assessment. It wasn't designed for cutting or slashing, but rather for throwing or stabbing. He'd seen – and heard – it whir through the air, spiralling as it went. He'd tried it himself, tossing it at the door. It wasn't easy to throw straight, but it could be done. The workmanship and the balance of the dagger had surprised him. With practice, it might be a formidable throwing weapon. Moreover, he thought if it was used point-first to stab something, it would slide in with the ease of a hot needle jabbed into soft candle grease.

He shook his head, smiling ruefully. *You're an arrogant cockerel, Saker Rampion. Just because something is from the Va-forsaken lands, you want to scorn it, and look for proof that it's inferior.*

He stood and dressed in order to go out. He was starving.

It took the flat-boat three weeks to sail to Borage, where ramshackle buildings clustered around a small bay at the mouth of the River Ard like herd animals gathered to drink at a waterhole. The fishing fleet were out to sea, so the ship crawled into port on a light breeze at dusk and docked at an empty wharf covered in fish scales. In the distance, the last rays of the setting sun bathed an ornate manor house on a distant hill in a golden glow. Saker watched the light fade as the first passengers disembarked.

"That's the Foxheim Palace," a voice said at his elbow. "The Ardronese Prime belongs to the Shenat branch of that family. Rich as oysters, that lot, they say."

Saker turned to find the captain leaning on the railing beside him.

"You can't get to Vavala tonight, so you might want to think about staying on board, witan. There's plague in Borage."

His heart skipped a beat. "Va above, how can you know that?"

The captain pointed over Saker's shoulder. "The plague flag is flying from Signal Hill." He shrugged, indifferent. "Probably the Horned Death. Naught to worry about. The Death pops its ugly head up a lot these days, but never seems to get much of a hold. Some folk blame

A'Va and his twins. Hogs-piddle, I say. I know what happens to twins. Still, you're welcome to stay on board."

He opened his mouth to ask what he meant about the twins, then realised the captain expected him to know. If he didn't, then he might be betraying his disguise as a Lowmian. He could do without the complications. "Thank you," he said, "but I'll stay at the Borage Va-Faith cloister tonight." He'd been dreaming of having access to a cloister bathhouse and their herbal soaps to deal with the infestation of lice he'd picked up on his travels.

If I don't rid myself of this itch, I'll go mad, he thought as he strode down the gangplank a few minutes later.

He should have slept the night through. He was clean and free of vermin, well fed, in a real bed again, not swinging below decks crammed in with snoring travellers. He'd even been reassured that the outbreak of the Horned Death was confined to two families on the outskirts of the port town.

Yet he woke barely an hour after he'd retired. The room was rocking and his head spun as if his body was trying to convince him he was back on the boat. Groaning, he rolled over. He'd forgotten he always felt like this for at least a day after disembarking from a ship.

The room, actually a cell for a Lowmian monk, had a glassless window slit, and moonlight streamed in. A movement on the floor caught his eye, and when he turned his head to look, he felt he'd been turned upside down. His stomach rebelled, and dizziness prevented him from seeing straight. He struggled to regain a sense of physical equilibrium, but had to battle with the idea that he'd just seen a sinuous silvery creature slither across the floor. Like a snake. Or some kind of large worm. No, just a figment of an imagination confused by the giddy spinning inside his head, surely. Yet when the world settled down once more and his vision cleared, he stared at the patch of moonlight in disbelief. There, lying in clear view, was the lascar's dagger. It hadn't been there when he first woke up. He *knew* that. Just as he knew it'd been buried deep in his pack when he went to bed.

And yet there it was, lying on the stone floor.

His mouth went dry. He lay without moving, stilled by his terror of the unknown, unable to wrench his gaze away.

Va-forsaken witchery.

If I look at it, perhaps it won't move again.

If I don't look at it, perhaps it'll kill me.

He sent a prayer for guidance to Va, even though experience told him Va rarely answered prayers.

With his gaze nailed to the dagger, he realised that the gold threads in the metal catching the moonlight glowed as if they were alive. He'd seen something like that not long ago.

Where?

He struggled to remember, then it came to him. On the counting table in Kesleer's warehouse. A heap of charts and papers, the bambu rod and yellow-gold gleaming. Not coins. Not metal. Fluffy, flyaway filaments. Like sparks. Like silken threads. No, not quite . . .

He concentrated, remembering.

They'd been so light, moving in the slightest breeze, like goose-down from a pillow . . .

They'd been feathers. Soft, downy feathers.

What the pox?

He had to have it wrong. Feathers weren't valuable to a man like Kesleer, or the Regal; the idea was ridiculous. And of course, no one put feathers into a knife blade. If they did, the heated metal would frizzle them.

Shivering, he drew the rough wool blanket up under his chin. He would have taken on an intruder without a second thought, but nothing, nothing at all, was going to entice him out of bed to pick up that dagger with its wicked, sinuous blade. Not when he was damned sure it could slither out of his pack and cross the floor like a snake. He'd stay awake till morning, staring at the thing.

Half an hour later, he dozed off.

When he did wake, it was in horrified panic as he realised that the first dawn had already pierced the dark, and the monks were ringing the bell for prayers. He sat bolt upright even before his eyes were fully open. The first thing his gaze sought was the dagger on the floor, but the flagstones were bare. He drew in a deep, calming breath. Obviously it was all some horrible nightmare, none of it real. He chuckled. What an addle-pate he was! The blade was still buried at the bottom of his pack, and always had been.

He stood and went to grope for the piss-pot under the bed. And halted halfway, shocked.

Lying on his pillow, next to the indent of his head, was the lascar's dagger.

3

The Haunted Woman

The house was cold. It always was, even in the height of summer, and now it was well into autumn. Perhaps it was the pretentious size of the rooms and the lofty corridors that made it that way. Perhaps it was just that there was no warmth in this household for the wife of landsman Nikard Ermine.

Sorrel Redwing pulled her shawl tighter around her upper body and shivered. *Loggerheaded fool that you are. This place is squeezing the life out of you, one drop of warm blood at a time. One day you'll wake up to find you're no more than a dry husk lying on the bed . . .*

A murmur of conversation reached her where she sat, Nikard's voice recognisable, although the words were indistinct. Drunk again, of course. He always was, when dicing with his friends, especially if his brother Hilmard was there, as he was tonight.

Nikard and Hilmard, confound them both. Pretentious brothers with pretentious names for a Shenat family. And they *were* Shenat, born of the northern folk even if they no longer lived in the hills. Unfortunately, as landsmen rich enough to employ others to till the land, the Ermines believed they were better men than mere yeomen. Their parents had turned their backs on Shenat customs when their sons were born, eschewing names derived from nature. More recently, Nikard had even called their daughter Antonya.

A pompous name for her little Heather. She'd never used it, of course.

Va rot them all! Because of them, she'd sunk this low, sitting upright in an uncomfortable chair in a cold passageway – just in case her gambler of a husband, or his sot of a brother, called her into the withdrawing room. The relative warmth of the adjacent ladies' parlour with flames dancing in its marble fireplace taunted her, yet it wasn't worth the risk to wait there. She might not hear his summons, and experience told her Nikard Ermine didn't like being kept waiting.

I should leave him, of course I should. But if I do, I lose everything of Heather . . .

Silly, but true. Heather had been born here. Her baby gurgles still lingered in the nursery; her toddling footfall sounded in the corridors; her childish laughter echoed from behind the hedges of the gardens. How could she leave the only place that contained any memory of her child?

Besides, where could I go? I have nothing.

No money, no property, no family who cared what became of her.

Va, but it was chilly tonight. She sat on her hands in an attempt to warm them. If Nikard didn't call her soon, perhaps she could risk going to bed. She tilted her head to listen, but heard nothing she could interpret. Only the two brothers remained in the room now. The other men, all from neighbouring estates, had ridden off about an hour earlier, around midnight. Before that, Nikard had made a point of calling for her every hour or so, to ask her to pour the drinks, or put some more wood on the fire.

"She likes to do these little things for me," he'd explained to his guests. "She thinks the servants should go to bed early, don't you, sweet mistress mine?" And he would smile at her, that benevolent smirk of his that was a lie through and through. All because she'd once remarked, early in their marriage, that it was unfair to expect the servants to stay up late when they had to rise with the dawn to start their chores for the day. He'd accused her of interfering with the ordering of his household. *His* household, never theirs. Since then, he'd found a hundred different ways to punish her for her offhand remark, and this was one of them.

He'd never hit her, she'd give him that much. She suspected his restraint might have come from his tacit acknowledgement that she'd have scratched his eyes out if he'd tried, at least in the early days of their marriage. She'd been feisty then. Rebellious. Now, though, her courage had eroded under his relentless despising.

Like water on a stone, it wears you out.

It was easy enough to identify when her defiance finally crumbled: the moment she'd knelt beside the limp body sprawled at the foot of the stairs and seen the blood seeping from Heather's ears and mouth and nose.

In that moment she had ceased to live as well. Oh, she spoke and smiled and listened, but none of it meant anything.

Her heart, her joy, her precious daughter. Just three years old and gone for ever. Heather, who'd never heard her mother's voice, never heard the sound of her own laughter. Heather Redwing Ermine, born deaf, destined to be an object of scorn to her own father.

Six months gone, and the agony of the loss was still raw with the power to claw her insides, to shred her sleep. Her equilibrium was as fragile as spun sugar, shattered half a dozen times a day by a word, by a memory.

She was twenty-two. She knew she must start living again, but had no idea how.

A bark of contemptuous laughter interrupted her thoughts, and then Heather's name was mentioned as if to parody them. Startled, she rose to her feet to approach the door. Nikard never spoke of his daughter, never gave any indication he ever thought about her death. Why would he mention her to his brother?

She laid her ear to the panelling. Her action was enough to crack the door open, startling her. Apparently she hadn't latched it properly the last time she'd left the room. The voices within changed from an indistinct murmur to clarity.

". . . didn't know better, I'd have said she wasn't mine. Can't have been my blood that caused her to be born gummy-eared! Better off dead than being feeble."

Nikard. He couldn't even cease his bile now Heather was gone.

Hilmard replied, his voice slurred with drink. "Prob'ly would've died without any help from you. Thin-blooded. What if someone'd seen what y'did? You could've been hanged! Va's blood, Nikard, you always were the boil-brained one. 'S'time you learned to control your temper."

"Blister your tongue, Hilmard! Why must you bring it up again and again? I was fed up with her mewling. Forget it!"

Sorrel reeled, aghast, shrinking against the wall. *Had Hilmard just said that* Nikard *killed Heather? Murdered his own daughter?*

Va above, let that not be true!

Her heart hammered wildly; her knees gave way until she slipped down the wall into a crouch. *This can't be true, this can't be true . . .*

She heard Hilmard's next slurred words, but they barely registered. "You shouldn't have wed that common country milkmaid in the first place, just 'cause she has pert tits and good teeth. She's a clod-hopper's daughter! Might've known a yeoman's get would whelp a wrong'un . . ."

"Shut your mouth, Hil! I didn't marry her because of her flirtish milkmaid looks."

"'S'right, I 'member now. You wed her 'cause her sire forced it on you. He wanted your guildeens and he had the evid'nce you killed that yeoman in Barment Green. So you had to take her off his dirt-grubbing hands – *and* pay him mightily for his silence." He guffawed. "Might be Va's truth, but result's the same. You're stuck with her, and looks like her womb's shrivelled."

Clutching her middle, she retched, bent over, heedless of the need for silence. Propped up against the wall, shaking, her shoulders heaving, she could think of nothing but the horror.

Nikard killed Heather.

No one had questioned the death; no one had considered the unthinkable – that a man had murdered his own daughter, thrown her from the top landing to the foot of the stairs . . .

The searing hell of that moment, engraved for ever in memory. She'd come running out on to the landing when she'd heard Heather's single scream, cut brutally short. Nikard had been standing there at the top of the stairs, unable in his horror – so she'd thought – to move. Later, he told her that Heather had run down the stairs ahead of him, tripped and fallen to the bottom.

She'd never doubted him.

And now the truth was just too much to bear.

A sob caught in her throat and emerged as a hiccup. A moment later, the door was wrenched open and Nikard was standing there, staring at her, his gaze and jaw hardening. She saw the danger. Felt it, like a rabbit sighting a fox. Every instinct told her Hilmard would be no help. And hadn't he said something about *another* murder? Nikard had killed someone before they were even married . . .

Sweet Va, I'm dead. She turned and fled, picking up her cumbersome skirts as she ran.

In the middle of the hall, she had to make a choice: run for the front door and hope she could undo the latches before he reached her, or flee for the scullery door through the empty kitchens – or race upstairs? None of them good choices. The servants would all be sound asleep in the attic, and Nikard was hard on her heels. She tore across the empty space of the hall, losing her silken slippers.

The stairs.

Perhaps she could barricade herself in her bedroom. Once there, she might have a chance to think how to escape with her life. Maybe he'd calm down, maybe Hilmard could calm him.

She took the stairs three at a time, skirts clutched in a bunch at her waist. She made it to the top, but before she could cross the landing, Nikard reached out and grabbed her wrist. He might have been drunk, but fury had fuelled his pursuit.

He swung her roughly around, pushing his face into hers. His breath stank of ale.

Her rage bubbled up from inside, a cauldron of ire that would no longer be confined. "You *murdered* Heather. *Why?* She was a *child*, your child. It wasn't her fault she was deaf."

He swayed, trying to catch his breath. "What did she ever matter?" he asked. "She was damaged goods. Useless, a runt who'd bring my house nothing but shame. Better off dead. Come to think on it, what use is a woman who can't give me an heir, eh? A fall down the stairs is so . . . easy."

The slight twitch of a smile at the corner of his mouth revolted her. Her terror should have been building; instead it was her rage that burgeoned, a black wave of it swallowing her from without, bitter ire bubbling up from within, until she was nothing but elemental fury. Her whole marriage had been a lie. Her father had sold her. Her husband had never wanted to marry her. He thought their child a burden.

At the bottom of the stairs Hilmard had paused to look up at them. "Nikard," he said in warning. "Don't be beef-witted."

Nikard half turned to look at him. "Keep out o' this, Hil. 'S'my business."

In her anger and revulsion, she flung up her hand, and twisted her arm away from his grasp. Unbalanced, he teetered drunkenly at the top edge of the stairs. Without thought, without even considering what she was about to do, she said, "This is for Heather."

And pushed him.

He toppled, falling backwards, arms flailing in vain. He fell hard, his skull cracking on a step. Momentum carried his unconscious body downwards, banging his head on every tread. She glimpsed the appalled look on Hilmard's upturned face. Whirling, she fled to her room without waiting to see what happened.

Temporarily safe inside, she barred the door and pushed a chest across it. Anything to buy a little time. Panting in reaction, she dragged in deep shuddering breaths. She was shaking so badly she could barely move.

I've killed him.

Maybe he didn't die.

She didn't know which was worse.

Either way, she had to escape or she'd be gibbet bait. She looked across the dark room to the window, where a twig from the oak outside scratched at the glass in the wind, beckoning her. *A summons,* she decided, her thoughts wild in her fear. When she opened the casement, the muted whisper of leaves swelled to a rustling song.

I am Shenat. In the name of oak and acorn, I beg forgiveness and mercy . . .

She climbed on to the window ledge and reached for the nearest branch.

4

The Pontifect and the Spy

"Let me see if I have the story straight." The Pontifect's drawl was heavy with sarcasm. "In spite of your promises, you chose to indulge in a brawl under the noses of Lowmeer's most powerful and richest men, endangering your mission and risking scandal to this office."

"It wasn't exactly my *choice*, your reverence."

"It never is."

"I do try—" he began mildly.

She cut him short with a sound best described as a derisive snort. She was famous for them.

Her birth name was Fritillary, after a pretty, fragile-winged butterfly, but Pontifect Reedling was neither fragile nor pretty. She stood taller than most men, with a build to match. Invariably dressed in the dull green robes of her office, she wore her iron-grey hair caught up in a net snood at her neck designed for convenience rather than beauty, and her lined face was always devoid of paints or powders. Most people, taking their cue from her hair and wrinkles, guessed her to be about sixty years old; Saker was not so sure. She moved with the supple ease of a much younger woman, and the backs of her hands were smooth, unmarked by age.

"I do my best," he said, attempting to stare her down. Tough, when she was taller than he was. Not for the first time he wondered if her intimidating height had anything to do with how she'd ended up elected as the Pontifect of Va-Faith, with authority over all its primes, arbiters, witans, seminarians and prelates, right down to the humble shrine-keepers throughout the Va-cherished Hemisphere – especially as she'd not had a promising beginning. She'd been born to a poor farming family scratching out a living in the Shenat Hills, just as he had been.

"Let me make one thing quite clear, witan," she said. "Maintaining balance in the Pontificate's relationship with Lowmeer and Ardrone, and between their Way of the Flow and our Way of the Oak, is a matter for the most delicate diplomacy. In spite of being Shenat and Ardronese, I must be seen to be utterly neutral in purely political matters. Yet by your own admission, you wore our clerical oak medallion on a spying mission in Lowmeer – and allowed Kesleer's son to see it!"

She was pacing the room like a caged wildcat, spinning on her heel every so often to fix him with an icy stare. He might have known she'd worm that slip of his out of him. She always homed in on the very thing he was trying to hide.

I swear she reads my mind.

"Your reverence, I *do* know it would cause trouble if Regal Vilmar thought you sent Ardronese witan spies to check up on his merchants. He would consider it a deliberate insult to both his person and to the sovereignty of the Basalt Throne. The medallion was a careless mistake on my part."

"Keeping the unity between the duality of the Ways is like walking a thin crust of ice over a frozen lake," she said, "and you nearly put your foot through the surface. It is particularly difficult for me because I'm Shenat."

He knew she was right. The Way of the Oak had begun in the Shenat Hills, where the first shrines had been erected to the unseen guardians of forests and oaks and fields. Shenat witans had taken these beliefs to Lowmeer, where Lowmians had adapted them into the Way of the Flow, proclaiming this to be the purer form. There had even been several wars fought over the matter.

Centuries later, a much-blessed witan from Vavala – after receiving divine revelations – unified the two Ways under the umbrella of the one true god, Va the Creator, but the unification had always been an uneasy one. To keep the peace, pontifects were usually elected from clerics of the Innerlands, where shrines followed an eclectic mix of the two Ways. Fritillary Reedling was an exception.

With an exasperated sigh, she waved her hand towards her work table. "Sit down, sit down. Here's hoping the Kesleer boy kept his mouth shut after you left." She took the chair opposite him, her gaze fixed on his. "Explain about the lascar."

"Lascars come to Ardronese ports from time to time, as crewmen on ships from Karradar, but they're not common in Lowmeer. I asked around and found out there'd been one on board the *Spice Dragon*. A young man called Ardhi. I suspect my lascar was that man. The description fitted him."

"And now the poor fellow is dead."

"I . . . well, yes." *Perhaps.* Something in the account of his death bothered him, and he hadn't put his finger on it yet.

"Let's move on to this meeting of traders. Why would Kesleer want to cooperate with his business rivals?"

"The fluyt he mentioned is a new design of ship, suitable for large cargoes and long journeys. I think this meeting was about raising more capital for shipbuilding."

"Between rival trading companies?" She pondered that. "Just possible, I suppose. Shipbuilding is an expensive business. But then, would Regal Vilmar allow such an alliance? He raises money selling separate trading licences to all the different companies."

"What if they cut him a percentage and sweetened the deal with a costly present?"

Once again she paused to consider, then said slowly, "The Regal *is* indeed a jackdaw hoarding pretty things, as Kesleer said. Vilmar Vollendorn loves baubles, especially ones no one else has. He's a vain and acquisitive ruler. But there's no value in feathers."

"I think they were just the soft packing for something breakable." *And of course the gold feather-like strands in the dagger were something else entirely.*

"So, something precious," she was saying, "intended to buy the Regal's support, was packed in feathers inside the – what did you call it? Bambu? And you saw the lascar steal it. So this valuable gift is now at the bottom of a port waterway, or floating out of the Ardmeer estuary on the tide?"

"I suspect Kesleer still has whatever was inside, and the lascar took the bambu not realising it was empty."

Her eyes narrowed. "What could be so valuable that Kesleer thought it would buy the Regal's support for a trade monopoly?" She tapped his written report, now on the table next to the sample of spices he'd stolen.

"A new spice is possible, I suppose," he said. "Something with curative powers? Kesleer made some remark about Ardronese court women clamouring for something only Lowmeer would be able to supply. But a new spice doesn't fit with the idea of baubles and pretty things."

"Pity you didn't hear more of the conversation."

"At the time, I was rather more worried about my skin. Per your previous instructions, of course."

Her eyes narrowed still further to indicate she was not amused. "What was the lascar doing in the warehouse?"

"Stealing," he said promptly. "Obvious, surely."

"I'm not so sure. Assuming he was this Ardhi from the *Spice Dragon*, he'd just been paid. Why would he steal?"

"Greed?"

She made an exasperated sound in her throat. "Put yourself in this sailor's britches." She stood to walk over to the window. With her back to him as she gazed out, she asked softly, "What sort of a man sails halfway around the world, under the command of people he doesn't know, with men who speak a different tongue and follow a different faith, to arrive at a destination unknown to him?"

"A madman? A slave?"

She was silent, her back an eloquent rebuttal of his flippancy. "An adventurer," he suggested, serious this time.

"I would have thought the word 'hero' might be closer to the truth. Or at least a very *brave* man."

Pickle it, she was right. The man had indeed been brave. "Someone passionately in search of something. Enlightenment. Knowledge. Something precious to him." At last he saw what she was ferreting out. "Ah. A man who thinks he's been robbed of something precious."

"Exactly. Perhaps he came to take back what had been stolen from him by Lowmian traders. Whatever was inside the bambu." Her next words were said so quietly, he had to strain to hear them. "This spice trade will not be good for any of us."

"You fear Lowmeer ascendancy."

"Yes, but not because I'm Ardronese."

"I never thought that was your motive," he said hastily. "An overly rich and arrogant Lowmeer will mean a fearful Ardrone, and that's a volatile combination that could lead to yet another war."

"Possibly, but not even war motivates my concern. There are deeper evils in Lowmeer than that, and they may be exacerbated by an excess of trade wealth."

The tremor in her voice took him by surprise. *Fear?* The Pontifect was *frightened*? No, he must be mistaken. Nothing scared Fritillary Reedling.

"Tell me," she said, "did anything odd catch your interest while you were in Lowmeer? Anything that seemed unusual?"

His hand dropped to his knife sheath, where he now kept the lascar's dagger, intending to show it to her. He had tried to rid himself of it. He'd tried to leave it behind in the cloister. Later, he'd offered it to an itinerant knife-grinder he'd passed on the street, then he'd attempted to sell it to a blacksmith. Each time, at the last moment, he'd been unable to follow through the intention.

Now his fingers spasmed when he touched the handle, refusing to clasp it. He opened his mouth to tell her about it, but couldn't form the words. And he couldn't move his hand. A moment later, he was struggling to remember what he'd been about to say.

When he hesitated, his thoughts scrambling after something just out of reach, she added, "No matter how uncanny or inexplicable it may have seemed at the time?"

For a moment he saw again the way the lascar had smiled just before he'd thrown the dagger. Not a smile of malicious intent, or of enmity, but of . . . hope. The act of throwing the knife hadn't been an attempt to divert attention, and the lascar was more than just a tar; he saw that now.

Once again he opened his mouth to tell her, but couldn't remember the words.

He choked, stammering, then thought, *Oh well, it couldn't have been important,* and relaxed. He said instead, "There's the Horned Death. I'd heard of it before, vaguely, but this time I *saw* it. A man died in front of me, speaking of A'Va."

"Oh? And what were your thoughts?" She came back to her chair and sat.

"You know the victims grow horns? Reverence, they *change*. They look more like animals – and not particularly *nice* animals, either. It was . . . horrible. Inhuman. Insane."

"I've had it described to me."

"One other odd thing. Twice people mentioned twins to me when talking about the Horned Death, hinting they were somehow to blame for the plague. Which seemed . . . weird, as well as ridiculous. I've been thinking about it and I recall Lowmian myths about twins being evil. They called them 'devil-kin' in the past, didn't they?"

"Superstitions are tenacious things. I suppose any plague is so horrible that people feel it must have an origin outside of Va-Faith. Then of course, if A'Va the anti-Va exists, he must have his minions. Devil-kin, or whatever name one wants to bestow on them. Although I've no idea why they settled on twins to fill that role and I'm glad the rest of us had more sense. Anyway, no need to concern yourself about Lowmian twins. It's just silly superstition."

The back of his neck prickled. She was hiding something, and he decided to challenge her secrecy. "Scuffing leaves across a trail doesn't eradicate the scent of prey. What's worrying you? What's wrong in Lowmeer?"

For a moment he thought she might avoid answering, but after a short pause, she said, "I don't truly know. Something the Regal himself knows about and yet conceals. The Horned Death, twins, the Regal's men – there is a link."

"Do you want me to go back to Lowmeer and investigate?" Even as he asked the question, he remembered the death cart and had to stifle a shudder.

"No." There was no hesitation in her answer, no hint that his return was negotiable. "I have others there working on this and I have other plans for you. I'm sending you to Ardrone. Specifically, to King Edwayn's court in Throssel. Of course, if you hear of any outbreaks of Horned Death in Ardrone, I want to know about it, but I don't expect that. So far, Ardrone has been spared."

Saker blinked, taken aback. In his mind's eye he remembered the misty, ethereal beauty of the vales of the Shenat Hills where he'd grown up. But the *court*? He suppressed a desire to sigh. Too much stone and too little forest or field. Besides, he'd have to behave himself.

Protocol. I hate *protocol.*

She continued, "King Edwayn has asked for a spiritual tutor for Prince Ryce and the Princess, Lady Mathilda."

"Oh?"

"So I'm sending you."

He gaped at her, now completely thrown. "Me? A *spiritual* tutor? To the King's children?"

"And now you're going to tell me you're more oak-shrine inclined, so you'll make a dreadful adviser to palace-dwelling, chapel-attending young who've never set foot in a shrine."

Va-damn, there she was again, reading his mind. "So why me?"

"Because, at nineteen and seventeen respectively, they'll relate to a tutor not much older. And because I want the royals to understand the importance of shrines, of witchery, of field and forest, of the true Way of the Oak. They get far too little of that at court. The Prime of Ardrone, Valerian Fox, doesn't favour close affinity with the natural. He'd like to replace shrines and shrine-keepers. Replace them with his town-based clergy and their rituals."

"You want me to counter the influence of the *Prime*?" He was incredulous. The Prime was the most important cleric in any country, and in Ardrone, he or she was appointed to the post by the King, not the Pontifect.

She smiled. "You're dying to ask why I have such faith in your abilities."

Pox on her mind-reading! Was he really so – so transparent? He said carefully, "Young clerics are as common as daffodils here in Vavala. So why me? Come to think of it, I've never understood why me. Not from the time I was ten and you came to my father's holdings and arranged to send me to university." She'd been the Faith arbiter of the district at the time, but she'd had no connection to his family. At least, none that he knew about.

"Your courage. You lived in a house where your father ignored you and your stepmother actively worked to send you away because you were a threat to the inheritance of her own sons, yet you still managed to look them proudly in the eye."

"Did I? I just remember feeling about as low as a mudworm all the time because I didn't understand why I wasn't loved." He wanted to shiver, just thinking about it. "There has to be more to it than that."

"Well, I did know your real mother."

He stared at her in shock. In anger. *Why did you never tell me that?*

She shrugged. "I decided to look you up when I was in the district."

He hesitated, searching for the right way to draw her out, to be polite and not show his rage at her secrecy. No one had ever spoken to him about his mother; his father had forbidden it. And now she was telling him she'd *known* her?

He was still framing his question when she added, "You impressed me. I could see you didn't belong on that farm, so I bargained with your father. He allowed me to send you to university. In exchange I swore to him that I would never speak to you about your mother. I'll keep that agreement while he lives. One day you'll know all there is to know, I promise."

He pushed aside the fury he felt towards his father for imposing such a condition, and thought instead of his mother. Only one memory remained: a dark-haired woman, kneeling on the floor beside him where he stood. No memory remained of her voice, or her face, or what she'd told him. He'd been upset because she was crying. He couldn't have been more than two or three at the time.

"I didn't send you to university out of sheer sentimentality," she said. "I'm always on the lookout for acolytes who have a love of nature. People to whom worship at a shrine is more natural than adoration inside the stone walls of a chapel. Too many of the bright young clerics are more fond of doctrine and rituals than what is real. You're true Shenat, like me. You know what I mean."

He did, too.

"Our lands are in danger when the old beliefs are neglected," she said. "Never, ever forget that. It's easy for the nobility and rulers to lose sight of what is important. I have no faith in the Ardronese Prime to remind the King and court."

"You think they'll take any notice of *me*?"

"The court? No. The Prince and the Princess? I hope they'll respond to your sincerity. There are bad times coming, and when they do, it is old ways and the witcheries that will save us."

Bad times? He didn't like the sound of that. "May I ask what your witchery is?" He was sure she had one. How else could a woman of no particular family or history come to be Pontifect? Va, via a shrine's unseen guardian, must have gifted her.

"What do you think it is?" she asked, amused rather than offended by the question.

"You read minds?"

"Nothing so simple or so invasive, thank Va! I just have a talent for knowing the general essence of what someone is thinking, if those thoughts are important to me. I doubt I would have become Pontifect without it."

Oh, fobbing grubbery. She can *look inside my head.* "A convenient talent, I imagine."

"Not something I would wish on anyone." She paused, then added softly, "A witchery lays a terrible burden on whoever possesses it."

He glimpsed a bleakness in her as she spoke, even as she changed the subject. "But to business. Your real mission in Ardrone. As you must have guessed, it is not just to give spiritual advice. I thought you might be the person to give Prince Ryce a nudge in the right direction every now and then – and that he might listen to you."

"On the false impression that such advice would be disinterested?"

She silenced him with a glare. "If Lowmeer dominates the spice trade, there'll be huge disparity in wealth between Ardrone and Lowmeer. The price of spices will spiral to ridiculous amounts if there's a bad outbreak of the Black Pestilence or the Rose-Spot Fever. You are aware that many people believe carrying a pomander of spices and hanging wreaths of them in the house will ward off pestilence?"

He nodded, remembering the men with the death cart.

"It's nonsense. But the belief could result in outrageously rich merchants in Lowmeer. That would not be in the interests of peace or of Va-Faith. I hardly need to point out to you that townsfolk are the sector of the population that most ignores our sacred guardianship of nature. Especially very rich townsfolk."

Ah. It was all about keeping the balance between the differences within the Faith, as well as between the two largest countries within the Va-cherished lands.

"Keep your wits about you, and let me know if you hear anything," she added. "Prince Ryce won't be nineteen for ever, and King Edwayn has already appointed him to take charge of the royal interests in the trade routes and the merchant navy."

That sounded like a fine way to ensure disaster. What on earth would a young pleasure-loving prince – with a penchant for boar- and bear-hunting, or so he'd heard – know about trade and shipping? "Do you really think I'm the person for the task? I can't say I know much about court manners. Or giving spiritual guidance, if it comes to that."

"You'll learn. The Ardronese merchant fleet should match that of Lowmeer, and that's the way I'd like you to turn Prince Ryce's thoughts."

For the next hour, as they sat at her work table, she filled him in on all she knew about the Ardronese court, its royal family and the state of the kingdom's finances, trade and politics.

She concluded the briefing with a warning. "Be careful with Prime Valerian Fox. I did not choose him for the post, remember. And I have never been able to sense his thoughts. Send your most private reports to me without going through his office and use code words where appropriate. I have a trusted courier. His wife runs a tavern called the Three-Horned Ox. She sits at a cash desk just inside the tavern door. You address your letter to me, and give it to her. The courier – or one of his many sons – gets paid when it's delivered here."

He nodded thoughtfully. Things must be worse than he'd imagined, if she couldn't trust the office of the Prime.

Picking up a handful of the spices he'd brought, she lifted them to her nose and inhaled. "I don't trust anyone," she said. "Not even you. I worry about your conceit, Saker. Remember that the cocksure rider falls harder. And I expect you to behave at court with all the decorum of a true witan. Keep your gambling and your whoring—"

"I beg your pardon, your reverence, I do not *whore*."

"Your tupping of willing taproom serving girls, then. Keep *any* unwitan-like behaviour discreet, or better still, non-existent. Is that clear?"

He resisted the temptation to say he had no particular love of gambling either, and wondered what he was missing. Something. It was as if she was looking inside him for something she couldn't find. He kept his reply devoid of expression. "As you wish, your reverence."

"I wish I could believe you," she muttered, exasperated. "You may go. On your way out, ask Secretary Barden for your letters of introduction to the King and Prime Valerian Fox. And see the counting house about your expenses." She looked him up and down. "You need new clothes. A king's court, witan. Priestly robes, good quality, not clothes for tavern crawling and brawling. Understand?"

He tried desperately hard not to think of anything at all.

* * *

The merchant in Gort cradled the spices in the palm of his hand. Twenty cloves, five anise stars and six candlenuts.

"Where did you steal these?" he asked, and the look he gave was as hard as the nutmegs and the cinnamon sticks Ardhi still had concealed in his pack.

"Not steal," Ardhi said firmly, submerging his annoyance under a veneer of polite neutrality. If the man wanted a reason to justify his purchase, the truth would suffice. "Bring from island mine. Er, from my island." *Splinter it, I need to practise this pesky language more.*

The suspicion in the merchant's eyes didn't vanish, but the tension across his shoulders eased. "Five guildeens for the lot."

It was an insulting offer, but Ardhi hid a smile. In the Chenderawasi Archipelago, children learned to bargain the moment they picked up their first cowrie shell from the reef. "Five guildeen, one piece," he said, knowing that price was just as ridiculous.

When he left the merchant's much later, coins were jingling in his purse, and the rueful tone of the man's farewell was satisfying.

Outside in the street again, he paused as needle-sharp pain lanced his eye, as real as the jab of a sea urchin's spine. He knew that pain. It was the prick of the kris, coming from a long way off. Usually it was faint, tantalising, a reminder of all that was familiar – then suddenly it would jab him, becoming a reminder of the horror that had sent him halfway around the world.

And always, always he asked the question: why had it left him? He hadn't thrown it. It had *abandoned* him. Flung itself at that unknown man in the warehouse. *Why?*

He still had no idea.

And he had no idea if he'd done the right thing after he'd fooled the warehouse guards with a child's bambu trick. His first actions – to swim ashore and retrieve his pack – were obvious enough, but to decide to follow the traces the kris had scratched into the air, instead of seeking the stolen regalia on his own without its help? That was a dubious decision.

Until the warehouse, the kris had been leading him like a villager leading his pig on a string; afterwards, he was lost and lonely, with panic perched on his shoulder like a mischievous *gawa* spirit uttering teasing whispers in his ear.

He sighed, and the bitterness of bile rose into his throat, searing him with the memory of his splintering failure. He'd grabbed the empty bambu instead of the contents. So close, so very close, and he'd bumbled it, bleached bonehead that he was! And he hadn't even realised it until it was too late.

The ultimate dilemma was still lodged somewhere in his gut, a churning, sickening quandary he had no way of resolving: he couldn't find the regalia without the kris, and the kris had deserted him because he'd failed to seize the one opportunity he'd had.

I have *to find that man and the kris.*

The man's name he didn't know, but by the time he'd reached the port of Gort, he'd discovered that the medallion the fellow had worn meant that he was Ardronese. If necessary, he'd follow him all the way to Ardrone. He'd kill him to obtain the kris if he must, then start his hunt for the regalia all over again.

He had no choice. Failure not only meant his eternal exile; it would mean the end of the Chenderawasi Islands.

5

Gift of Glamour

"This weather is ridiculous! We should have stayed in Twite." Lady Mathilda, Princess of Ardrone, glared at her elder brother where he sat opposite her in the coach. She was irrationally irritated that he was there at all. The moment it started to rain, he'd abandoned his horse for the interior of the lumbering vehicle. A sensible decision, for though the coach might lurch and sway, at least it was dry, but his presence annoyed her anyway.

"This trip," she continued, knowing she was whining and not caring, "has been a disaster from beginning to end. I mislike it when Father decides we're to do our royal duty and display ourselves to the Kingdom."

"Like a pair of well-bred whelps being shown to the houndmaster to see if they're suitable for the pack?" Prince Ryce, heir-apparent to the throne of Ardrone, grinned at her. "I've quite enjoyed myself."

"Yes, you would. It must be *so* convenient to have every pretty – or even not so pretty – marriageable woman under thirty paraded for your edification and, I have no doubt, with half of them quite prepared to warm your bed if they thought it would get your attention."

"And you mislike having so many young men pay attention to you?"

"Don't look so insufferably smug. There's not one man I met whom Father would consider eligible, so what's the point in even looking their way? And has it escaped your notice that for the past few days I've had no lady-in-waiting and no maid? It's been horrible having to rely on women I don't know, and maids I've never seen before in my life."

"I'm sorry, Mathilda. That was rotten luck."

She glared at him, knowing he really didn't care that her two ladies-in-waiting and her maid had been taken sick with the ague and she'd had to leave them behind in Oakwood.

"With a little luck," he continued, "we'll be on board ship tomorrow, sailing for home. Once we arrive at Redpoll Manor tonight, Lady Frytha will supply you with whatever you need."

With an audible sigh and a slump of her shoulders, she changed the subject to what was really bothering her. "Last night Kenda Rosse hinted she'd heard rumours that Father had sent my portrait to Lowmeer, at the request of the Regal. Have you heard anything about that?"

He stared at her, shocked. "Regal Vilmar Vollendorn asked for it? For himself?" His tone was so hushed she barely heard him over the sound of the rain and the rattle of the wheels.

She nodded. "Ryce, he's so *old*. And he's buried three wives!"

"Oh, pox! Thilda, I'm sorry. But maybe it's just a rumour. Vilmar was last widowed only a few months ago, so he can hardly wed again yet. It would be unseemly not to observe the mourning period. Besides, you've only just turned seventeen and he's got to be fifty if he's a day! Kenda Rosse is a silly ninny; she's just passed on gossip as truth."

"She said Lady Rosse told her—" Her words ended in a squeal as the horses were hauled to an abrupt halt and she was flung into Ryce's lap. "Oh, vex it!" she said, pushing herself upright. "What now?"

Ryce, oblivious to the rain, pulled aside the leather blind and stuck his head out of the window. "I can't see anything. I'll go and find out."

"Not if you want to ride with me, you won't. I'm not having you coming back in here covered in mud and with your coat smelling wet! Besides, it's – it's inappropriate. You wait for the servants to come and tell you what's happening, you don't go to them."

"Have I ever told you how irritating you are?"

She pulled a face, and he subsided, resigning himself to waiting. Nineteen years old, and he still didn't know how to assert himself for more than five minutes at a time. *Oh, Ryce,* she thought, *if I were you, I wouldn't listen to my little sister. I'd do what* I *wanted . . .*

But Ryce was Ryce. Swaying like a reed in the wind, following his pleasures without thought. It wasn't *fair*. He was always addressed as "his highness Prince Ryce", whereas all she merited was "milady the Princess Mathilda". He was a prince, and one day he'd be king. She was a princess, and one day she'd just be someone's wife.

But I'm the one who would make the better monarch . . .

The sergeant of the Prince's outriders, Horntail, rode up a moment later to inform them what had happened. "Naught to fret about, your highness," he told Ryce. "A wench ran out on to the road straight under my horse like she had a wolf nipping at her heels. She was knocked down, but got up and fled through the hedge on t'other side of the road. The coachman has bad news, though. When we stopped so sudden like, a coach shaft cracked. The lads are binding it up now as a temp'ry measure, but we're going to have to get it fixed proper in Melforn."

Ryce grimaced before replying. "Is he sure it won't get us as far as Redpoll Manor?"

"'Fraid not, your highness. There's a coaching house on this side o' the town, and they'll be able to mend it proper. There's a tavern nearby, with an oak shrine opposite. P'raps Lady Mathilda could rest there while we get the shaft fixed."

How I loathe being spoken about as if I'm not here, Mathilda thought. *As if I don't exist. As if I can never have a say in my own life. And isn't it just typical to pack me off to some horrible cold shrine while the men sit around a warm fire in a taproom and drink ale?*

Just then the Sergeant's mount plunged as a pack of hounds appeared out of nowhere, flowing around the coach and the horses, sniffing and snuffling and yipping. Horntail swore and yelled. "Away with you, you slubbering mongrels! Coachman, put your whip to the curs!"

"Fellhounds," Ryce said in surprise. "That yipping means they've lost their prey." He stuck his head out of the carriage to have a look, but hastily pulled it back in as the rain gusted. "Difficult for them to keep the scent in a downpour like this. There must be hunters around somewhere."

"Over there beyond the stile," said Mathilda. On the other side of the coach, riders were strung across the hillside, all of them angling to where a stile cut through the hedge.

"After a fox, I suppose," Ryce said.

Mathilda blinked, surprised he was so obtuse. "No, Ryce. The woman." She called to the Sergeant. "Tell your men not to say anything about the woman to the hunters. You didn't see her."

Sergeant Horntail switched his gaze to Ryce, raising a questioning eyebrow. Mathilda gritted her teeth and glared at her brother. For a moment she thought he was going to argue the point, but in the end he just gave a curt nod. The Sergeant rode off to issue his orders.

"It really is none of our business, Thilda," Ryce grumbled.

"Hunting a woman down with dogs is none of our business?"

"We don't know what she did."

"I don't care what she did; she shouldn't be hunted like vermin."

"I think I'll tell Horntail we've changed our minds."

"Don't you *dare*!"

The leading rider reached the stile, but his horse baulked at the coach drawn up so close on the other side and refused to take the jump. The huntsman circled around, yelling for the coachman to move the vehicle. Several other riders arrived just as the rain was beginning to slacken, and one of them spoke hurriedly to the first man, gesturing at the coach. The angry expression on the first man's face disappeared into an ingratiating smile.

Sergeant Horntail spoke to him and then came to talk to Ryce. "They *are* hunting the woman," he said. "She's the wife of a landsman from a nearby manor. Apparently she murdered her husband last night. That's the husband's brother, Hilmard Ermine, leading them. They saw her cross the stile. I told him we didn't see which way she went." His expression was blank, but the set of his shoulders expressed his disapproval.

Mathilda ignored him and glanced again to where the riders in the field still milled around, waiting for the coach to move. They were wet and angry and too cowed by the coat of arms on the coach door to complain. She smiled. Perhaps she'd saved a life today. She rather liked the idea that a woman who'd murdered her husband was still running free because she, Mathilda, had intervened.

I'm not helpless, she thought. *I'm not as helpless as everyone would like me to be.*

A secretive smile curved her lips. One day she'd show the world what she could do. She was the daughter of a king, and she knew how to rule men, even if Ryce didn't.

One day, one day . . .

The Melforn shrine was outside the town limits, but not by much. The spreading branches of the oak shaded an area the size of a large farmyard, and the leaves – now turning yellow and orange – glistened wetly as wan sunlight poked through a gap in the clouds. The outer branches draped down to the ground, and the shrine, a circular building surrounding the trunk, nestled comfortably under the protection of the tree's vast spread. Its outer stone walls, topped by a thatched roof, were pierced by a line of narrow, glassless windows. The trunk of the tree poking out of the centre of the roof was so huge it would have taken five or six men holding hands to surround the base.

Mathilda stared sourly at the doorless archway that led into the shrine, and shivered. Ryce and their escort cheerfully delivered her into the charge of the shrine-keeper and disappeared into the tavern on the opposite side of the road, while the two coachmen saw to the repair of the shaft. The tavern was busy; the hunters and their hounds were there already. Idly she wondered if they'd caught their prey and wished she could talk to them herself to find out. Va pox on't, why did women always have to be so proper, while men had all the fun?

With a sigh she turned to the shrine-keeper, who'd given her name as Marsh Bedstraw. Tall and slim, narrow-hipped and broad-shouldered, she was dressed in a simple woollen gown. Her age was impossible to say. Forty? Fifty? But then, shrine-keepers aged slowly and lived, some said, for centuries. In Ardrone, they all had Shenat blood in their veins, without exception. It was said that the unseen guardians would not accept the non-Shenat. Not, Mathilda thought, that people from elsewhere complained. After all, what normal person would want to spend all their life under an oak tree?

Her spirits sank when she realised there were no servants at the shrine; she and Marsh Bedstraw had the place to themselves – along with the unseen guardian of the shrine, or so she assumed. She huddled into her cloak and gave another shiver.

Fortunately this was sufficient to goad Marsh into action, and in a short time Mathilda was seated on cushions piled on the shrine's single bench, in front of a burning brazier of red-hot coals, with a feather-down quilt over her knees and a pewter mug of steaming fruit punch cupped in her hands. Ryce had said he'd ask the tavern to send over a hot meal, but Marsh had snorted at that, commenting that the tavern food was even worse than their rotgut.

"I'll fetch bread and cheese from my kitchen," she said, and disappeared into the only private part of the shrine, a tiny partitioned area which was evidently where she lived.

Mathilda glanced around. Although the shrine was built in a circle around the tree, the massive trunk in the centre was free-standing, towering through its central hole. Nowhere did the building come close to touching it. There was no inner wall to the shrine, just stone pillars holding up the beams of the roof, which meant that no matter where one stood, the trunk was always accessible and visible.

She'd never been impressed by shrines. Cold, windy places, with beaten earth floors and no furnishings except stone seats for those coming to pay homage. They might each have had an unseen guardian, but who could tell? This one, she had to admit, had an exceptionally impressive oak.

Just then she heard again the baying of excited fellhounds and turned to look out of the main entrance. It was no longer raining, and the dogs were pouring out of the tavern yard. A woman was clambering over the stone wall of the field adjacent to the shrine. Bedraggled and filthy with mud, with her hair loose, and not even wearing a cloak, she looked like a mad bawd, some poor village lackwit cast out into the streets. When she saw the stream of dogs bounding her way, she raced for the shrine, lifting her muddy skirts like a wanton.

The murderess. This has to be her.

Mathilda knew she ought to be frightened. She knew she should call Marsh Bedstraw. The fugitive was desperate; she might also be crazed and dangerous. Instead, Mathilda revelled in the thought that she was about to have a real adventure at last.

The woman was terrified. She was closer to the shrine than the dogs, but they were bred to run and eager to reach her. Fixing her gaze on the shrine archway ahead, she flew across the yard. The first of the hounds nipped at her heels. She was crying, tears streaking dirt on her cheeks. The hound grabbed the back of her skirt, its teeth ripping through the cloth as she lunged away. She made one last desperate leap for the shade of the oak, as if even its shadow could save her.

Her feet hit the yellow carpet of autumn leaves. A mere breath behind her, the leading hound wailed in pain.

Startled, the woman looked over her shoulder. The animal skidded to a halt, the leaves banking up under its feet. It yelped. The hounds behind tried to bypass it, but the moment they trod on the fallen leaves, they lost all interest in their quarry. They leapt and twisted and howled. Then, as one, they tore away, tails down, in abject distress.

The woman halted by the shrine entrance, staring back at them, her face a picture of amazement. She'd not expected this.

This is better than any theatrical, Mathilda thought, jumping to her feet and clapping her hands in her own excitement.

Roused by the hounds' fervid barking, the men from the tavern poured across the road. Not just the owners of the fellhounds, but Ryce and the royal guards as well.

The woman took one look and dived into the shrine. She raced past Mathilda and brushed Marsh Bedstraw aside as the shrine-keeper emerged from her dwelling, mouth agape. Her headlong dash took her through the covered area to the base of the trunk. She laid her hands on the rough bark and said in a firm, clear voice, "I, Sorrel Redwing, beg sanctuary from the guardians of oak and field, from Va above. Should my plea be answered, I pledge service to Va from this moment forth."

Turning to press her back to the trunk, she placed the flat of her palms to the tree on either side and fixed her gaze on the main entrance. Fear blazed in her eyes, and she shrank back as if she could disappear into the bark. Her chest rose and fell like bellows and she dug her fingers into the oak so ferociously Mathilda winced.

"Va, in the name of oak and field, save me. Save me and I am yours," Sorrel said.

Marsh Bedstraw laid a warning hand on Mathilda's elbow. "Say nothing. This is in the hands of the Way of the Oak."

Mathilda looked towards the men now at the door. Two of them stepped inside, and once they were no longer backlit by the sunlight, she recognised one as the leader of the hunters. What had Sergeant Horntail said his name was? Ermine. Hilmard Ermine. Behind the landsman, Ryce and Horntail came running up.

"Are you all right, Thilda?" Ryce asked, his face a ludicrous mix of remorse and alarm.

"Of course I am," she said.

Hilmard Ermine concentrated on the shrine-keeper, apparently not noticing his quarry against the tree. "We're looking for a runaway, a criminal. She committed the foul murder of her husband, my brother, and then fled his home. We've had the hounds after her half the night, nearly caught her several times, but lost her an hour ago. We know she entered the shrine just now."

"Rest assured," Marsh Bedstraw said, inclining her head in polite deference, her voice low and husky and calm, "no one of black heart is ever sheltered by the shrine, or by Va. Search if it please ye, and if y'find the person y'seek, she has no place here."

Mathilda turned to look at the woman to see how she reacted, but there was no one there. She stared at the trunk, her mouth gaping. There was no way Sorrel Redwing could have moved without drawing attention to her presence. Marsh Bedstraw's hold on her arm tightened. Mathilda shook her off, torn between scolding the shrine-keeper for daring to lay a hand on a member of the royal family, and asking her what in Va's name had just happened.

Hilmard doffed his cap and made a sweeping bow in her direction. "Forgive me, milady, I'd not disturb you if it weren't urgent. The miscreant we seek needs to be apprehended for your safety, and to see justice served."

Mathilda tilted her head in acknowledgement. Her mouth was as dry as dust.

"With your permission, milady, may I ask my men to enter to search the building?"

Ryce interrupted. "You may, now that I am here to maintain the safety of the Princess. Please do what you must and leave us in peace."

For once, Mathilda was glad of his intervention. Everything had suddenly become confusing and frightening. Surreptitiously she glanced back at the tree. Out of the corner of her eye she could see a blurring of the bark. Sorrel was there, she was sure she was, but when Mathilda looked straight at the oak, she saw nothing. No one did, except perhaps Marsh Bedstraw.

As Ermine's hunters filed into the shrine, the shrine-keeper leaned over and whispered in her ear, "'Tis in the hands of the unseen guardian now. If the lady's heart is pure, the men'll not see her, and their blindness is Va's will."

Mathilda shivered with pure delight. She was seeing a Va-inspired miracle at first hand! Superbly pleased, she seated herself and allowed Marsh Bedstraw to tuck the quilt around her once more.

The hunters, together with several of the liveried men from the outriders, scattered through the shrine looking for their quarry. Outside, the hounds howled and yipped their frustration. Hilmard strode around the tree trunk, his features distorted with rage and determination. By the look of him, he'd been drinking in the tavern. His gait was unsteady, his face flushed. He even stopped to stare at the trunk of the tree, frowning.

"She's close," he muttered. "I can smell her. Smell her fear. She's here somewhere, the slut." Slowly he raised his head to look straight up the trunk into the tree canopy. "Comfrey," he said to one of his men, "that's where she is. Climb up and have a look."

"The tree is sacred," the shrine-keeper said in an implacable tone of prohibition. "'Tis the realm of birds and bats, squirrels and butterflies and the unseen guardian. No one climbs it. Ever. And that includes the woman you seek."

"How dare you question my decision," Hilmard Ermine said, his tone close to a snarl. "This shrine is mine as much as it's yours, woman. And I'll search it until I find the murderous whore who attacked my brother. One of my men saw her enter this place and you must have seen her too! Unless you tell me where she's hidden, I'll see you charged with the crime of aiding a felon."

Mathilda rose to her feet, drawing herself up in a way she had practised in front of the mirror to appear older and more imperious. She made sure her next words ripped through the air like an executioner's axe. "Are you going to charge *me* as well? Do you accuse a princess of Ardrone of aiding a felon? It is impossible for me to have failed to see someone entering the building! What do you accuse me of, Hilmard Ermine, *landsman*? I'm sure my brother here would be delighted to relay your accusation to our royal sire the King."

There was a startled silence. Everything stilled, as if everyone had stopped breathing. Ermine's face turned ashen. Even Ryce was speechless, although he was the first to move, to stand protectively at her side.

When Hilmard did find his voice, it quavered like that of a sick old man. "Milady, I abjectly beg your pardon. Of course you would have seen someone enter had they done so. I did not think. My grief for my brother has disordered my senses. Forgive my foolishness." He bowed his head.

"Begone from this place," Mathilda said coldly. "There is no one here who is not under Va's guidance and protection."

The men filed out, leaving her standing with Ryce and Marsh Bedstraw.

"It's all right, Ryce," she said brightly. "You can go back to your tavern now."

"No, I'll stay," he said. "Who knows where that mad woman might have got to."

"Va will protect me. This is a shrine! Did you not see how even the hounds could not enter? 'Twas amazing! They couldn't bear to put their paws on the fallen oak leaves. Truly, I need to pray and sit at peace for a while. Mistress Bedstraw here will take care of me."

He glanced out of the doorway towards the tavern. "Well, if you're sure . . ."

"Of course I'm sure."

He kissed her on the cheek with unusual solicitude, and left.

"Those fellows will be poking around outside for a while, I reckon," Marsh Bedstraw said, addressing the bare bark of the oak. "Best I get you into my cuddy, lass, out of sight. Then y'can clean up a bit."

"What happened to her?" Mathilda whispered. "She disappeared!"

"That's oaken witchery," Marsh Bedstraw said. "She's been granted the gift of the glamour. You're still there, aren't you, lass?"

Mathilda stepped over to the oak. With a hesitant hand she reached out, her fingers groping. When her thumb tip touched the woman's shoulder, she gave a laugh of delight. "You *are* there! You were there all the time, but invisible! How did you do that?"

Slowly Sorrel Redwing reappeared, still standing with her back to the tree. Her eyes were closed, her face unnaturally pale. In spite of the autumn cold and her wet clothes, perspiration had beaded on her forehead. When she opened her eyes, she blinked and took a deep, calming breath. Her gaze held traces of horror, as if she had seen the inside of her own grave.

"Y'are safe now," Marsh Bedstraw said. "The men have gone."

The woman stepped away from the bark, looking from the shrine-keeper to Mathilda. Her gaze focused and settled on the Princess. "My thanks, milady, for your protection." She spoke quietly, with a soft country accent, and sank into a deep curtsey. "And yours too, mistress," she added to Marsh Bedstraw.

Mathilda watched her, assessing. Her curtsey was practised. Her dress with its overskirt was without lace or brocade, but even covered in mud and soaked with rain, it was clear the material was fine velvet and the bodice was embroidered. Her stockings were torn and she'd lost her shoes and her coif, but she held herself well.

And she'd apparently committed a murder.

"Did you *really* kill your husband?" Mathilda asked.

Marsh Bedstraw intervened, scolding. "What's past is past. This lady is under the protection of Va, and what happened is no business of yourn."

Mathilda, unused to being thwarted by anyone outside her family, was about to remonstrate, but something in Marsh Bedstraw's face stopped her.

"Va's business," the shrine-keeper said. "The Way of the Oak. No right of yourn to question."

Chastened, Mathilda nodded. Having seen an example of witchery, the idea of angering Va and his shrine guardians was unnerving.

The shrine-keeper hustled the woman away into her dwelling, came out again with the promised bread and cheese for Mathilda, then disappeared once more.

Mathilda spent the time deep in thought. If this trip with Ryce had proved anything to her, it was how powerless she was. She was royal, yet had no say over her own destiny.

I have to change that, she thought. *I have to, or I'll go mad. I have to use whatever ways are available.* And perhaps, just perhaps, she now had the means to do it.

Half an hour later, seeing Sorrel Redwing's new appearance, she was shaken once again. Somewhere the shrine-keeper had found her a plain grey gown and matching coif, hose and some battered shoes. None of that surprised her nearly as much as what had happened to Sorrel's face.

The woman who'd disappeared into Marsh Bedstraw's cuddy had memorable, strong features; rich ebony hair; startling eyes, deep and blue. The person who emerged was of indeterminate age, a grey-eyed, plain-faced woman with greying fair hair.

"Oh!" Mathilda exclaimed. "How . . . Is . . . Are you Sorrel Redwing? But you look so different!"

"That's the glamour," Marsh Bedstraw said. "A glamour can make the lass appear to be what she wills."

"She doesn't look too glamorous," Mathilda said doubtfully. "She looks like a – a meek grey mouse!"

"That she does," Marsh agreed. "And now she can leave the shrine without them men hunting her down like game."

"She must leave under my protection. It is quite obvious to me we were Va-fated to cross paths today. I am momentarily in need of a lady to attend me, and you, Mistress Sorrel, obviously need to leave this place. You shall come with me to Throssel!"

"Milady, that's very kind of you, but—"

"Oh, tush! Va protected you. How could I possibly do otherwise? I will tell my brother you're the shrine-keeper's niece. We'll think of a new name for you."

"That's a generous thought," Sorrel said quietly, "but milady can't have considered the complications. I'm wanted for murder. If—"

Mathilda waved away her protests. "Where else can you go? What else can you do? Do you have relatives who will take you in?"

Sorrel was silent. Marsh Bedstraw looked from one to the other and said nothing.

"Va planned for me to be here in the hour of your need," Mathilda said. "The shrine's unseen guardian would not have aided you unless you are a virtuous woman. Am I not correct, Mistress Marsh?"

The shrine-keeper inclined her head in agreement.

"Then that's settled!" She creased her brow in thought. "If I make you a lady-in-waiting, there will be far too many questions about your lineage. Yet you're too genteel for a maid. So you have to be somewhere in between. A handmaiden. You shall be my handmaiden. Now, let's see what we can call you. Your present name means you are Shenat, does it not? So a flower and an animal, I think. Celandine is pretty. You shall be Celandine Marten."

6

A Witan Goes Home

He ought to have taken passage on a flat-boat south to the Ardronese port of Betany, where he could hire a hack and ride to Throssel. That was the quickest route.

Instead, Saker had bought a horse in Vavala, an old and staid animal which was all he could afford, and headed through the principality of Valance, and so into northern Ardrone across the Shenat Hills. Had she known, the Pontifect would not have approved. He didn't care.

Pickle it, he needed to go home.

He was so riled. He was furious with both his father, whom he hadn't seen for eight years, and with Fritillary because she'd made that ridiculous bargain not to tell him about his mother. And she'd *kept* the bargain, kept it even though it was made with a man who knew nothing of honour.

But most of all, he was enraged by his younger self. How could he have been so *feeble* as to never demand information about his mother? Iris Sedge Rampion had died when he was three, and he'd never paused to wonder why nobody spoke of her. That was too much to expect of a young boy perhaps; what shocked Saker was that he'd never insisted on knowing more once he was older. What had she done that merited being so obliterated from his life?

He sighed, remembering his ten-year-old self. Arbiter Fritillary Reedling had dangled the idea of a university education in front of him and he'd grabbed the opportunity without a second thought. At fifteen he'd returned to the farm for a short visit, then gladly turned his back on that life forever, walking away from his inherit-ance rights.

On that last visit, he'd asked his father a vaguely worded question about his mother's family, the Sedges, only to be told none were still living, and they'd all been worthless layabouts anyway. Now he wanted better answers.

As his elderly mount plodded its way south into Ardrone five days after leaving Vavala, he expected his heart to rejoice. These rugged hills framing long valleys of farms and fields, those rippling stony rivers and soughing pine-forested slopes – this was the landscape of his childhood. Here nestled the heart of Shenat belief. At each shrine he was welcomed as a witan, offered food and wine, the company of local people come to hear the latest news, and a bed for the night. He expected to feel at peace, suffused with the calm of being back in the world of forest and field and fell.

Instead he was uneasy, anxious. The lascar's dagger at his belt was still a brooding presence, reminding him of Ardhi. Often it stirred in its sheath, like an animal stretching in troubled sleep. He didn't quite believe the blade was malevolent. No, it was more . . . watchful. Not alive, but not quite inanimate either. It *spied* on him. And he couldn't understand why he hadn't told the Pontifect of its existence.

When he crested the Branchwood Pass and gazed down on the valley he grew up in, the thoughts that came were not memories of childhood, but nebulous worries of a future that brooded, promising turmoil and plague. Sometimes he thought he could feel the dying man's grip on his wrist, and hear his voice speaking of A'Va the devil.

Absurdly, he found himself looking behind from time to time as he rode, as if there was some dark menace there. *You're as bad as a child waking up from a nightmare, imagining the horrors under his bed,* he thought. *What's the matter with you?*

He was still half a day's ride from his father's farm when the weather turned bleak and miserable. By its lacklustre pace, his mount was registering its disapproval of the muddy track and driving rain. Sympathetic, Saker pulled into a wayside inn. After stabling the horse, he ran for the inn door through the rain, lugging his saddlebags. He scrambled inside shaking the water from his cape and hat, before realising he had walked into the middle of an altercation.

A woman was standing on one of the tables. Pewter mugs and plates were scattered at her feet, liquid dripped on to the floor. She held a sword as if she knew what she was doing, but Saker doubted it would do her much good. Surrounding her table were three men of varying ages, all armed with staves. They were poking and swinging at her feet, and there was little she could do except dodge. The inn's patrons had backed away from her and were now arranged around the walls, some watching, some inciting the men, some protesting the attack.

Galls 'n' acorns, he *knew* her. Gerelda Brantheld, by all that was holy. He couldn't begin to imagine why she was here and in this predicament. He dropped the saddlebags and his cloak and hat without a second thought. As his hand sought the hilt of his sword, he asked the ploughman standing next to him, "What's it all about?"

"Those Primordial fanatics don't like city women," the fellow said. He eyed Saker up and down, and his gaze settled on his witan's medallion. "Might not be over fond of you, either. Watch your step." He took another bite of the pie he was holding, and turned his attention back to the fight.

Saker drew his sword and picked up a wooden stool in his other hand. "Enough!" he roared, addressing the men with the staves. "Is this any way to behave?"

Their apparent leader, a thin man with long tousled hair and the intense gaze of a zealot, scowled at him. "Keep your witan nose out of our business lest you want it bloodied," he said, and swung his stave at Gerelda's ankles. She jumped over it with ease.

"Three men harassing one woman?" Saker rejoined. "Where is Shenat chivalry? Leave her be, or answer to me!"

"Blister your tongue," Gerelda said disgustedly. "When did I ever need saving by a witan?"

One of the other men stepped towards Saker, waving his stave. "Witan of Va! Befouler of true Shenat faith! Begone from the heart of Shenat country, you perverter of our ancient—"

Saker threw the stool at him.

The man ducked, his stave dipping. Saker leapt forward to stamp hard on the wood. Unbalanced, the fellow let it go.

Saker raised his sword and his opponent backed off. Gerelda leapt down from the table to pink the neck of the leader while his attention was diverted. The third fellow, a young lad who looked vaguely familiar to Saker, retreated towards the door with an appalled expression.

"Take your men and go," Saker told the leader. "Believe what you will, and naught will be said, but if you can't live peaceably with your neighbours, you'll find yourself in trouble with both Va and the earthly followers of the Faith."

The leader snatched up his stave and headed towards the door. "Stone-lover! Street swain! Cobble-fancier! Your chapels will fall to rotted ruin, mark my words."

As the three disappeared outside, the patrons of the inn drifted back to their tables and the potboy began to clean up the mess.

"Street swain?" Saker asked, raising an incredulous eyebrow at Gerelda Brantheld. "*Cobble*-fancier?"

"They hate town-dwellers. Primordials have brains pickled in vinegar." She shook her head in a gesture of disgust and thrust her sword into its scabbard. "Hello, Saker."

He righted a couple of stools and offered her one. "Good to see you again, Gerelda. Sit down and I'll buy you a drink. I had heard there was a resurgence of Primordial idiocy, but I didn't know it was a problem around here."

"Ah, there's always some Shenat hothead who decides Va doesn't exist and our interpretation of the Way is wrong, so we should all return to the purity of the bucolic paradise of a thousand years ago. Va preserve us from that, and a pox on the Pontifect for asking me to investigate." She sat down opposite him.

He blinked. "The *Pontifect*? I thought you were a lawyer."

"Yes. I'm her roving legal proctor, didn't you know?"

"No, I didn't." He hadn't seen her since their university days. She'd read law while he studied Va-Faith, but they'd conducted a passionate affair when they'd both been seventeen or so. It had flamed brightly, then burned out just as fast as it had flared.

The tapboy passed by bearing ale, and she snagged a couple of brimming mugs from his tray. "I'm not paying for this," she growled at the hapless lad. "Fat lot of help you were when those giddy hedgepigs attacked me." She pushed a mug over to Saker as the boy flushed and fled.

"The Pontifect sent you – a Lowmian – to deal with that lot?" he asked, disbelieving.

"Not exactly. I was in Twite to solve a legal matter, but her reverence suggested I sound out the Primordials if I came across any on the way back. It was just my luck to meet one who thought any woman not dressed like a farmer's wife offensive." She grimaced. "You're from around here somewhere, aren't you? No wonder you skedaddled young! Was that one of your loving family there?"

"Huh? Who?"

"The youngster of the three stavemen. His name's Rampion too. Gromwell Rampion."

"Fobbing damn. That's my half-brother."

"And you didn't recognise him?"

"Haven't seen him in eight years. He was just a boy in a smock when I left."

"If you're going to see your family, you might try to straighten him out. Primordials worry the Pontifect."

"Probably because Prime Valerian Fox might hang them for apostasy. They're misguided idiots, not evil men."

She looked at him over the rim of her mug as she sipped the ale. "Is it family that brought you back here?"

"I'm on my way to Throssel to tutor the King's offspring."

"Sounds hideously boring." She was silent for several moments, fiddling with her mug handle. "Saker, you know me. About as imaginative as a hunk of wood, right? Remember how I used to fall asleep at university theatricals?"

He nodded. "You said you couldn't think of the actors as being anyone other than your fellow students."

"That's me. So when I tell you there's something nasty going on in the Va-cherished Hemisphere, you'll know I'm not seeing things that don't exist."

"Like what?"

She didn't answer directly. "People are suddenly anxious about the future. People talk to us lawyers when they're scrambling to secure their money, or their property."

"What's making them anxious?"

"Well, that's just it. With one man it might be fear of this Primordial resurgence. With another, it's fear of war with Lowmeer. Over in Lowmeer, it's the Horned Death, or evil twins. Rumours, gossip, superstition. It's coming from twenty different directions, and yet . . ."

He waited, not prompting her.

In the end she just shrugged. "Forget it. Maybe I am finally fanciful after all."

"You think it has a common origin." *A'Va?*

"Ridiculous, huh?"

"Perhaps. Haven't folk always worried?"

"Yes. But not like this. This – this *intensity*, it's new." She made no attempt to hide her anxiety.

He resisted a sudden desire to put a comforting arm around her shoulders. "I did hear strange whispers about twins in Lowmeer recently," he admitted.

"Sweet Va, you too?" Words came tumbling out, rushed, as if she didn't want to give him time to think about them. "You know it was Lowmian law a couple of hundred years ago that twins were killed at birth, along with their mothers? They're supposed to be evil. They call them devil-kin. I've heard it still goes on, drowning them at birth, like unwanted puppies."

"Codswaddle, that's – that's *sick*!" He stared at her, appalled.

"What did you hear, Saker?"

"People linking twins to the Horned Death."

"The devil is supposed to have horns, isn't he? Devil-kin. A'Va, the devil, always trying to bring Va low."

"It's the victims who have the horns, not twins. All superstitious nonsense anyway." But nauseating nonetheless.

"If twin murder continues, it's hidden and illegal," she said. "What worries the Pontifect is the lack of overt condemnation on the part of Regal Vilmar Vollendorn. By all reports, he's a pragmatic ruler, not a superstitious one. Yet on this matter, he and his royal guards appear to turn a blind eye to murder."

"I'm glad it's not an Ardronese problem. Killing *babies*? I don't remember hearing anyone doing that when we were students in Lowmeer. Do you?"

She shook her head, smiling faintly. "But then we had other things on our minds."

"They were good times, that year we spent in Grundorp."

"They were indeed."

"Tomorrow we go our separate ways. Tonight, though – are you up for some nostalgic revisiting of the past?"

"They say it's a mistake to go back." But she was still smiling as she added, "I have a room upstairs."

An hour later, sated and relaxed with Gerelda curled into his side, he remarked, "You've learned a lot since we last did this." He traced a finger idly over her breast to her thigh, appreciating the hardness of her muscles as much as he admired the femininity of her curves.

She laughed softly. "So have you."

"And I don't remember you being as . . . um, so *strong*. Do lawyers always carry swords?"

"I don't recall you having all those muscles, either. Would you be more than just a witan, by any chance?"

They exchanged a glance and said as one, "Fritillary Reedling."

"She employs the damnedest people," Gerelda said. "Be careful in Throssel, Saker. The Ardronese Prime makes my fingers curl and my skin crawl. I met him when Fritillary sent me to solve some legal problems about religious taxes. He was as polite as can be, yet . . ." She shrugged. "He won't like your strong adherence to the Way of the Oak."

"His family is Shenat, surely? He has an oak-and-field name."

She propped herself up on one elbow. "Being from a Shenat family doesn't guarantee love of the Way of the Oak. His father was Harrier Fox, Ardronese Ambassador to Lowmeer, and his mother was Lowmian, so he was brought up in Ustgrind. At court. I doubt he's ever been to the Shenat Hills."

"Didn't I hear his mother committed suicide when he was young?"

"Yes, but his father stayed on in Lowmeer. He's dead now too, leaving Prime Valerian Fox huge estates in every country of the Hemisphere, a rich man who favours chapels over shrines."

"And who prefers chapel clerics over shrine-keepers. Perhaps because a three-hundred-year-old shrine-keeper can be remarkably recalcitrant." He respected shrine-keepers, but had no illusions about them. He began to trace out patterns around her nipple.

"Last week in Twite," she continued, "I was told he's been raising money from merchants and landsmen to build chapels. Not, mind you, in towns, but in places where previously everyone went to the local shrine."

"Va above!" He was genuinely shocked. Shrines and their unseen guardians and keepers were the protection for waters and things wild, for fields and forests, for crops and livestock. It was one thing to have stone chapels in towns, quite another to replace age-old shrines in the countryside. "The Pontifect knows this?"

"Not yet."

"Why would the King appoint such a man to be Prime?"

She had no answer to that. "Just be careful," she warned. "I wouldn't like to make an enemy of Fox."

"I'm not likely to do that. I'm just a lowly tutor, after all."

She snorted in disbelief, sounding much like Fritillary Reedling. "You? If there's a beehive, you'd kick it just to see what'll happen." Leaning into him once more, she asked, "Shall we try for another bout of nostalgia?"

When he woke the next morning, she'd packed and gone, leaving behind a note written on the linen paper she used for legal documents. If that extravagance was supposed to impress him with the importance of the words, it succeeded.

> *Not a mistake after all, was it? Thank you for the nostalgia. But beware, Saker. I fear the menace that threatens is greater than us all.*

He destroyed the note, but coming from her, it left him with a sick anxiety in his gut, made worse by how nebulous it was. How could he be wary of something no one could even put a name to?

By noon he was riding up to the farmhouse where he'd been born. The double-storeyed stone house was shabbier than he remembered, the vegetable garden more unkempt, the flower garden dead. The once busy farmyard drooped in the midday heat. Even the hens seemed unkempt and cowed. The prosperous farm had fallen on hard times.

His father emerged from the stables when he rode up. Even he seemed smaller, less imposing than the tall, handsome man Saker remembered. His growth of whiskers was greying and untrimmed. There was no sign of anyone else about, although Saker could see several men working in one of the distant fields. His half-brothers?

"Hello, Father," he said.

Robin Rampion stared, frowning, before his eyes finally widened in recognition. "*Saker?* What're *you* doing here? Never thought I'd see you again."

"Just passing through. Don't worry, I've no intention of staying, or asserting any rights I might have." He dismounted, but kept his hold on the reins.

"You've *no* rights here."

"Debatable. But I want nothing from you except information. I want to know more about my mother."

A tiny pause stayed him, then he growled, "She was a whore. What else is there to know?"

"She was my mother. I have a right to know about her, and her family, and how she died. Where was she from? Who were the Sedges?"

"Who cares? Though if names are so important to you, I'll tell you this. I've always doubted you had a right to mine."

He digested that. It made sense. If his father had suspicions about his first wife's fidelity, it was no wonder he'd refused to allow her name to be mentioned. "I see. Well, I wouldn't regard the loss of your name as any great tragedy."

His father shrugged. "You think I care?"

"What's the secret? Why won't you tell me about her?"

His father glared at him in silence.

"What was her relationship to Arbiter, now Pontifect, Fritillary Reedling?"

"Ah, so that's it, is it?" He grinned, revealing several missing teeth. "Now you're a cleric wearing your pretty medallion, you want to know how cosy you can get with the Pontifect on the top of the heap, eh?"

"Don't bother to tell me lies."

"Oh, I'll not do that. She'd have my guts on her platter if I told you what I know."

"She? Fritillary Reedling?"

"Bitch made me swear I'd never utter a word. Not to you, nor anyone else. And that's the way it's going to be. You don't mess with the bull in the herd, and she's the snorting bull in this case, for all that she lacks a pizzle. Forget it, Saker. You're never going to find out about your dam from me."

Fritillary had forced his father's silence, not the other way around? He stared, trying to decide who to believe. *Fritillary, of course. When was your da ever honest with you?*

Before he could say anything, his father added, "Your ma left you, you know. Ran off and left you here with me. That's how much she cared. And then word came she was dead." He laughed.

Saker drew in a sharp breath. "Blister your lying tongue, Da. I don't believe it!"

"Believe what you will, you ninny. She didn't care enough to stay, or to take her mewling son with her. I didn't want you, but she left you anyway."

Just then, the door of the house opened and his stepmother came out, carrying a pail. She stopped dead when she saw him. "My, the brat is back again. What the hog's piddle do *you* want?" She put down the pail, placed her hands on her hips and thrust her chin out in his direction.

Va-less damn, he thought. *They* have *come down in the world.* There'd been a time when she would never have lugged a pail. They'd had servants to do that.

"Naught to do with you," his father said to her. "Go back in the house and mind your hearth."

For a moment, Saker thought she might defy her husband, but in the end she shrugged and went inside. His father turned to him, saying, "Get going, you botch of nature. Clear out, and don't come here again. You'll learn naught from me. You want the truth, go talk to that Pontifect of yours. She's the one who knows and she's the one who'll feed me to the pigs if I utter a word she don't approve of." With that remark, he stomped away across the yard.

Saker hesitated, wondering if there was anything else he could say that would make a difference. In the end he decided there wasn't. His mother wouldn't have left him. His father was lying, of course he was.

On his way back to the village road, he crossed the stone bridge over the stream where he'd learned to swim. The rushes still grew along the bank and the ducks still dabbled there. He led his horse down to drink, his mind drifting back to his boyhood. His favourite game had been to hide under the water, breathing through a hollow rush stalk, until his young half-brothers had been scared out of their wits thinking him dead.

. . . the corpse and the bit o' wood bobbing alongside . . .

Not *floating*, flat on top of the water, but bobbing, like a floating bottle. He stood still, mouth falling open. *Sweet Va, that bloody lascar.*

Bambu was hollow. Ardhi was no more drowned than he himself had been as a boy.

7

A Witan at Court

When Saker entered the Prime's office in the Ardronese royal city of Throssel for the first time, Valerian Fox was seated behind a table at the far end of the room. As he approached, trying to soften the noise of his footsteps on the wooden floor, Fox said, without prior greeting, "I fail to understand what sort of service you'll be providing the Prince and Princess that they don't already receive."

How in all Va's world am I supposed to answer that? He decided not to say anything.

He'd expected to see someone of fifty or sixty, and was surprised to find Fox couldn't have been much past forty. His habit was unadorned, but it was fine velvet; gold buckles shone on his shoes and the lace of his undershirt frilled at his wrists and neck. Two fingers on either hand were decorated with ornate rings. His Va medallion was gem-studded.

He leaned back in his chair and stared at Saker. "You're not old enough to have suitable experience or maturity, and your family is of modest origin, yet you presume to be the spiritual adviser of the man who will one day be king?"

Oh, sweet swill in a trough. I think I loathe him already. "I don't presume anything, your eminence. Least of all to question the orders of her reverence the Pontifect." He tried to sound respectful. "If I had to guess why she chose me over others more polished, I'd assume it is because of my university learning."

Fox picked up a letter from the table and scanned it with a frown. The lascar's dagger chose that moment to wriggle in the pocket of Saker's robe. Surreptitiously he clamped a hand over it, jamming it against his thigh. *Pox on the damned thing!*

"Yes," Fox said, mercifully oblivious to his squirming, "she has listed your credentials here." He shrugged and laid the letter back down. Then, with a charming smile, he added, "And of course you're correct: neither of us should question the decisions of the Pontifect. A woman is entitled to her little foibles, is she not? Welcome to Throssel, Witan Rampion. My secretary has arranged your accommodation in Throssel Palace, rather than here in Faith House with my clerics and administrative staff, so you can be closer to your charges. You'll report to me in person once a week, and supply a written report for the Pontifect once a month."

The next half-hour was a tedious lecture on how to behave at court, covering everything from what was appropriate for him to discuss with the royal offspring, to the depth of his bow to the various levels of courtiers. The Prime remained seated while he had to stand uncomfortably, his stance made awkward by the need to press the dagger flat against his leg.

By the time he made his escape, he knew two things for sure: the Prime was a condescending pizzle of a man, and he – Saker – was going to buy a thicker leather sheath for that fobbing lascar blade.

As he looked about the crowded hall of Throssel Castle at his first official function, Saker felt a chill of isolation. He was surrounded by people, yet couldn't see anyone he knew, not even the Prime. Valerian Fox had departed for the north, saying the Shenat Primordial heresy needed his attention, which had left Saker regretting he hadn't told his father to discourage his half-brother from mixing with those muckle-headed zealots.

King Edwayn was present, sitting up on the dais with several of his councillors and courtiers while the remains of the meal were being cleared to make way for the entertainment, a troupe of itinerant tumblers.

I feel I'm dressed for a funeral while everyone else wants to look like a Pashali parrot, Saker thought as his gaze swept the crowd of courtiers and liveried servants. *Loathsome, confining garb.*

He was obliged to wear a cleric's sombre dark green gown and matching velvet hat. The robe buttoned under his chin fell to precisely a thumb's length above the floor, as dictated by the office of the Prime. The only adornment a witan was permitted was the silver medallion, so the whole ensemble was definitely funereal, in stark contrast to the courtiers surrounding him. The array of colour and glitter within shouting distance would have cast even Pashali parrots into gloom, and left him with the feeling that the court of the King of Ardrone was more alien to him than the docks of Ustgrind. Among the women, feathers seemed to be in fashion, and each elaborate hairdo was decorated with shimmering plumes.

"Tell me, what is a witan doing at a licentious revelry such as this?"

The voice behind him did not belong to anyone he knew, but he didn't need a name to realise he was being mocked. He turned, and found himself looking up into the tanned features of a lean but well-muscled man who was taller than him by a hand span, and older by ten years or so. He was definitely dressed like a parrot, with a heavily embroidered doublet, sleeves trimmed with lace cuffs, velvet pantaloons, and numerous items of ostentatious jewellery scattered about his person.

The twinkle in his eyes as he raised his wine goblet to his lips told Saker the mockery was possibly more friendly than otherwise, but before he could decide, the man continued, "Don't tell me you are here to chastise us for our extravagance and wanton behaviour, because I'm sure you'd have no success. And I would be forced to mock you with my sharp wit."

"I'm sure I have far too much sense to try," Saker replied, "even if it was my inclination. Perhaps my gloomy plumage deceives you."

"Hmm. The garb *is* somewhat sober. Or do I mean sombre? Forgive me, I have imbibed too much wine. A poor habit of mine when on shore."

"May I ask which neither sober nor sombre courtier I have the pleasure of addressing?"

The man grinned at him and sketched an extravagant bow. "At last! A cleric with a sense of humour. We have need of such. Lord Juster Dornbeck, younger son of an obscure family, ne'er-do-well on land, successful privateer on the high seas, trader to Karradar in the Summer Seas. At your service."

"I assure you, my lord, being a cleric does not necessarily preclude possession of a sense of humour. My name is Saker Rampion. I am the recently appointed spiritual adviser to the Prince and Princess."

Lord Juster threw back his head and roared with laughter. When he'd finished wiping the tears from his eyes, he said, "I wish you luck with that, witan." He leaned closer, lowered his voice and added, "The Prince has few interests outside horseflesh, hounds and light-skirt wantons. He has to be dragged to the chapel on holy days."

Taken aback by the candour, he said nothing.

"The Lady Mathilda on the other hand," Lord Juster continued, "appears pious. Intelligent and well read, but cunning and conniving, too, for that is the only way a maiden has power in a man's world. You may have met your match in the pair of them."

"And to think that I thought a year or two at court would be boring! Why, already I have met an interesting nobleman who must be foolishly in his cups, if he is bold enough to make personal remarks about the royal family to a complete stranger."

"Ah, a riposting cleric! But I've not said anything that is not known to the entire court, including His Majesty the King. Have you met your charges yet?"

"Not yet. I thought it would be easy, but they always seem to have something else to do. I know the Prince is not here tonight."

Juster glanced around. "He's more likely to be out carousing with some of his young courtier friends. The Princess, however, is yonder, the lovely fair-haired lass in the blue dress surrounded by her gaggle of nattering ladies."

He turned to look in the direction Juster indicated. At first, all he saw was a dozen women, varying in age from twenty or so up to fifty, dressed in gowns with absurd skirts too large to pass freely through a doorway. Then, in the middle, he saw her, clad in a less ornate style. More a neatly elegant bluebird than a Pashali parrot. The blue of her kirtle repeated the blue of her eyes, and her featherless snood did not quite cover a head of fair curls. She was laughing, her eyes dancing with amusement.

His heart lurched up into his throat. *That* was the Lady Mathilda? Fobbing damn, but she was the loveliest woman he'd seen all evening, a waft of fresh air amidst all the pomp and posing.

"Delightful, isn't she?" Lord Juster said. "But not for the likes of us, witan, so it's no use looking so smitten. She's destined for greater things, is our beloved Princess."

"They have a marriage arranged already? She's only seventeen." Smitten? It would be easy enough with someone so lovely. Banish the thought. It'd be enough to earn a rope around his neck.

"So? Her mother married at fourteen. I've heard whispers the King thinks Regal Vilmar Vollendorn of Lowmeer a suitable groom, since his third wife died a few months back. Or was it his fourth? He does run through spouses at *such* a pace! But a pending betrothal may well be rumour; I'm not close enough to the seat of power to know the difference between faulty tattle and well-founded gossip."

Bile rose in his throat. That fresh young woman to be the bride of an old and raddled monarch? The idea was nauseating! "Well, I hope the rumour is indeed faulty. Regal Vilmar is far too old for her."

"Here, my lad," Juster said to a passing potboy. "More wine!" As the lad topped up his goblet, he asked, "And when does age matter in royal marriages? What counts is the accounting, don't you think? In short, how much is a virgin bride worth to each contracting party when they sign the documents?"

The remark was flippant, but Saker felt the man was more cynical than unkind. He said, "I can't imagine what Ardrone would gain by such a marriage." His stomach churned at the idea. What was it the Pontifect had said about something deeply evil in Lowmeer that the Regal deliberately concealed? He glanced across the room again, where the Princess now chatted with several courtiers, flirting outrageously with her fan.

Seventeen years old. Va above.

"Who understands the ways of kings? The idea that the royal backside on the Basalt Throne one day in the future would have his blood might appeal to King Edwayn." Dornbeck raised his goblet, grinning, and downed his wine. Saker was beginning to think there wasn't much the man took seriously. His hobby was doubtless making cynical comments on life's idiocies, and he'd homed in on Saker because he thought that in a naive witan he'd found a good subject to goad.

"Tell me," Juster asked, "what do you do when you're not advising young royals on what they ought and ought not to think? Do you hunt?"

"Not a pastime open to witans, my lord. Hunting as a sport is at odds with the Way of the Oak."

"But you do ride, I assume?"

"Of course. But I've just sold the nag I used to get here."

"May I persuade you to invest in a good mount? I'll take you out to my cousin's place. It's not far from the city and he breeds fine horses. He's also a terrible gambler and always in need of money. You *will* want a horse, believe me. Without one, you'll never get close to Prince Ryce. Nothing he likes better than risking his neck jumping hedges. Don't understand it myself. I *much* prefer the deck of a ship underfoot than a saddle beneath my arse."

"That's very kind of you. Unless you're thinking to sell me a spavined nag. I should warn you, I do know my horseflesh."

"Alas, to think so ill of me after such short acquaintance! I'm wounded. But still, I think I like you, Saker Rampion. Are you interested in ships and sailing?"

There was invitation in his glance, which Saker ignored. "I fear I believe a ship is merely a piece of wood to get me from one place to another, preferably without sinking," he said diplomatically.

"Sacrilege! I hereby rescind my affection for your person."

"I think perhaps that's wise, Lord Juster."

"Oh dear, again you disappoint me. But if you're not interested in swinging in a berth in the captain's cabin, may I offer you a word to the wise about avoiding the enticement of the fairer sex? Beware the lady who is approaching right now, because a maiden's innate predatory charm is hard to combat."

Saker turned to see who he meant. The Lady Mathilda was heading their way, her bevy of attendants trailing in her wake. As she came up, both he and Lord Juster bowed. Juster took her hand and raised it to his lips.

"Lord Juster," she said, her gaze fixed on Saker, "please present your companion."

"With pleasure. Milady, this is Witan Saker Rampion, whom I understand is to be your spiritual adviser. Witan, may I present your enchanting pupil, the Lady Mathilda, Princess of Ardrone."

She dimpled and held out a hand. He brushed her fingers with his lips and smiled at her. "I look forward to being of service, milady."

"I hope you are not as dull as the chapel priest."

"I hope I'm not dull at all."

"I was expecting some elderly wizened cleric with a hearing problem, or a dribble. When I saw you across the room I did not dare hope *you* were my new adviser. Whatever possessed the Prime to choose somebody not yet decrepit?" Her eyes sparkled at him over her fan.

Va above, she was indeed charming. "I suspect you have the Pontifect to thank for that, milady. I trust I will not disappoint. Youthfulness in a teacher can mean lack of both experience and wisdom."

She tilted her head and looked at him from under her lashes. "Do you know, I suspect you do not lack experience, Witan Rampion." She tapped him on the wrist with her folded fan. "Come to my solar at ten o'clock tomorrow morning and we shall talk." She smiled and walked on with her ladies.

Saker's gaze followed her. "I think you maligned her, my lord. She is delightful, hardly predatory."

"Oh dear, I do believe she's already caught you in her net, so baited with an overload of sweet wiles. Beware, my friend, the court is no place for the wide-eyed innocent."

"Lord Juster, I wonder your wine-pickled tongue hasn't been the cause of the parting of your head from your neck before this."

"Money, witan, money. If one is rich and dutifully pays one's taxes, one can get away with being audacious."

"Buccaneering pays?"

"You are looking disapproving again, witan."

"The fact that a buccaneer carries his ruler's letters of marque doesn't make him any less of a thief and pirate."

"Oh, you wound me to the quick! So swift to judge – I believe you're a true witan after all. The word is privateer, not buccaneer, or worse still, *pirate*. My *privateering* career is a way to redress the present imbalance. Lowmians dominate the spice trade. They buy spices from one of the Pashali ports, a place called Javenka, but Pashalin won't allow us the same privilege. So we must steal Lowmian cargoes on the open ocean." He shrugged. "The law of both our nations recognises the legitimacy of privateering."

"Lowmeer is now building more ships capable of sailing all the way to the Summer Seas, bypassing Javenka. Wiser, wouldn't you think, for Ardrone to do the same?"

The mocking smile disappeared from Juster's face as if it had never been. His gaze, now thoughtful, held Saker's for a long moment. When he did speak, his tone was serious. "The Pontifect appointed you to this post? Not Prime Fox?"

"As I mentioned to the Princess."

"Ah. Over Fox's head, I imagine. I begin to see. My friend, we need to talk more seriously than this revelry allows. And I want to take you to buy that horse."

He nodded. "Very well. Can you tell me – what's a solar?"

Juster laughed. "Oh, the fancy word royalty give to their personal apartments. 'Solely' for them, not us common folk. Except their body servants. And their chosen favourite ladies, of course."

Of course.

8

The Princess and her Spy

The Lady Mathilda, Saker discovered, had been granted her own solar in the royal wing of the palace, which she shared with four or five of her fifteen ladies-in-waiting and, he guessed, numerous body servants.

The woman who opened the door to his knock on his first visit was too modestly dressed to be a lady-in-waiting. She kept her eyes downcast and stepped aside for him to enter. Her plain dress was entirely grey, as was her hair covering. He would have taken her for a chambermaid, except that the neckline of her gown was low enough to display a simple silver chain, dangling a silver oak leaf. She escorted him through the solar to the Princess, then curtseyed and withdrew to a corner of the room.

With a wave of her hand, the Lady Mathilda dismissed the rest of her ladies-in-waiting, leaving only the grey-clad lady to chaperone.

"Witan," the Princess said with a smile that made him think of warm sunshine and had him swallowing his saliva. "I am glad you're here. I *so* look forward to your lessons and advice."

"I am flattered, milady. I trust neither will disappoint."

"I know far too little about the Way of the Oak. Prime Fox discourages anyone at court from going to shrines."

Pox on the man! "I hope I can help you, milady. What is it you would like to know first?"

"Come sit beside me here, and tell me all about witchery!"

Out of the corner of his eye, he saw the lady in grey jerk her head up to stare at them. By the time he turned to look, she'd already dropped her gaze, her face an expressionless mask, to stare at her hands in her lap.

Interesting.

"Witcheries," he said as he seated himself, "are a gift from Va to the worthy. Each oak shrine has an unseen guardian serving Va's wishes, and they choose the particular witchery granted."

"Can I ask for a witchery? What sort of people are granted one? Tell me about glamours!"

"Witcheries can be many things. Glamours are very rare, however."

She smiled and clapped her hands as if the answer delighted her. "Go on."

"I knew a woman whose witchery was to mend broken bones. And a man whose witchery was to be trusted by all animals. In Lowmeer, I've heard of men who can attract fish to a net and others who can tell when a storm is coming. Witcheries are usually useful things like those. They often fit the people who gain them – it will be a fisherman who has the skill over fish. Shrine-keepers always have a witchery, sometimes more than one, usually something to do with growing things." He smiled at her. "But I've never heard of anyone asking for a witchery and having their wish granted. It doesn't work that way."

"Then why are some people chosen to receive such a gift?"

"Perhaps those who have witcheries know why they were chosen; but if they do, they don't speak of it."

"So what do these people have in common?"

A sensible question. "Nothing that I know of, except they all dedicate their life to Va and the Way of the Oak. Or the Way of the Flow, if they are Lowmian. Or to a combination of both if they are from the Innerlands. But that often happens *after* they have the gift, not before. Forgive me if I am blunt, milady; I don't think you'll ever have one. A princess is destined to marry and raise a family, not dedicate her life to serving Va, or an oak shrine."

Her sparkle vanished. For the briefest of moments her eyes appeared flat and hard. Then she pouted prettily, so he wondered if he'd imagined the hint of a different emotion. "You disappoint me, witan. But you are right, I don't think I want to devote my life to Va and become a cloistered nun or a shrine-keeper! Tell me, what can someone with a glamour witchery do?"

Something about the way the lady in grey tensed up told him she was listening carefully. He wondered if she was a spy. The King's?

The Prime's? When he glanced at her, she reddened and quickly looked away.

Sweet Va, what is it about the court that makes me suspicious of everyone? "A glamour enables a person to mimic something or someone else. Such a witchery carries a great responsibility. Imagine the damage that could be done if a thief had the power of glamour!" *Or what a wonderful advantage it would be for a spy . . .* "Perhaps that's why a glamour witchery is so rare."

"Can someone who has a glamour disguise themselves and somebody else as well?"

"I don't believe so, milady."

"Do you have a witchery, Witan Rampion?"

"I'm afraid not."

"I'll wager Prime Fox doesn't either. He's always so sour!" She sat back in her chair and sighed. "You're right, I'll never be granted a witchery. I'd use it to play tricks on my brother, or some other silly thing. And Va would be angry with me." She dimpled, and he smiled back.

As they chatted on, he was touched by the way she slipped between youthful exuberance and a maturity beyond her years. At times he was sure her charm was assumed and aimed to stir his sympathy and concern, but then he'd glimpse a girl afraid of her own future, a young woman who had no mother to guide her, and who was surrounded by courtiers who cared more for their position than for her reality. He had not expected to be so moved. He wanted to pat her hand, and tell her that she shouldn't worry.

And he couldn't, not just because she was a princess, but because it wouldn't be true.

After a while, she turned the subject away from the shrine and witchery aspects of the Faith, and said, "Why is it we can have a woman Pontifect, but never a woman monarch?" The hardness had crept back into her gaze. "Were I the eldest child of the King, I'd still *never* rule. Ryce gets to be king, he can choose when and whom he marries, he can come and go as he pleases. But because I'm a woman, I can't do any of those things. How can Va allow that?"

He was taken aback. A woman ruler? The idea was ridiculous! Then he thought of Fritillary Reedling. She'd make a better king than Edwayn was, and she hadn't been the first female pontifect either. In the end he said, "I think history has given us kings, and somehow we're stuck with the custom being law."

"And what about a princess and her marriage?" she asked softly. "Is it just, or right, that I have no say in who I shall wed? Or who shall sire my children? Or even what country I'll live in?" A single tear ran down her cheek and she turned her face away as if she didn't want him to see.

Her sketch of her future brought a lump to his throat. Put like that, it was not only unjust, but something much, much worse. He said huskily, "No, it's not fair. But it *is* something you can do for your country, for your people. Perhaps your marriage will unite another country with this one. It is a way for you to be the mother of kings, a way for you to be a woman of influence."

She turned back to face him, her tear-filled eyes an accusation. "Do you think that's sufficient compensation?"

"If you make it so," he said. In his heart, when he thought of Regal Vilmar of Lowmeer, he knew he was lying.

When he stood to go soon afterwards, he felt he'd failed her, and in doing so, he was complicit in a crime that was to rob her of choice and freedom.

The grey lady escorted him through the adjoining room to the outside door of the solar. Before she opened it to let him out, she said, "And is it sufficient compensation if she is powerless and friendless in a land not her own? If her chosen husband is old or cruel or diseased?"

"It's not your place to comment on such things," he said, astonished at her effrontery.

"Then who will, sir? You? Where does a princess turn when her position of privilege becomes a cage?"

"Mistress, I do not know your name. Are you one of the princess's ladies-in-waiting?"

"No, merely a handmaiden. Handmaidens do not have names. We are even lower than princesses." She swung open the door, and the stare she gave him cut off the possibility of any further conversation.

He stepped out into the stone-vaulted passage beyond, disconcerted.

* * *

Mathilda looked up as Sorrel returned after letting Saker out. "So you were right. You can't weave a glamour that will change *my* appearance. Never mind, you can continue to be my spy at court."

"Milady, I may be able to blur myself so people don't really notice me, but I'm still there. All it would take would be for someone to bump into me and they'd know. And it's my head that'd be forfeit."

"You haven't been caught yet!"

"No, but it's difficult to blur into the background if I'm moving." With practice, she hoped to perfect it.

"Are you lying to me?"

"I don't lie."

"No, you just kill people."

For one sickening moment it all came flooding back. Pushing Nikard; watching his astonishment that she would dare to do so turning to utmost shock as he tumbled backwards. *I wonder if you remembered Heather as you fell?*

She clasped her hands behind her back to stop them shaking. *You have to cease thinking about this, Sorrel. It's done; you killed a man. You killed the murderous father of your daughter.*

And then the little voice in the back of her head said, *And he deserved it.*

The witan had intimated that only trustworthy people were chosen to have witcheries. She didn't feel like a particularly *good* person. She just felt trapped. Mathilda had her exactly where she wanted her. She said stonily, "Are you sure you want a murderer living in your solar? Perhaps you should turn me in to the King's magistrate."

Princess Mathilda appeared abashed. She said contritely, "Celandine, forgive me. I should not have spoken so. It was mean-spirited. But you *have* to aid me: I need to know whom I'm to wed, and when. You don't know what it's like to be so powerless. You don't know what it's like for other people to decide the whole rest of my life, even where I will live until I die!"

Don't I? Oh, pretty princess, I know exactly *what it's like.* But she already knew it was useless to explain that to Mathilda. The Princess didn't put herself in another's shoes. She'd never had to. "You're wheedling, and it is unbecoming," she said. "I think I prefer you when you're blackmailing me."

Mathilda laughed. "And that's not unbecoming of a princess?"

Sorrel shrugged. "Not if you get away with it."

"All right then. Let me say it differently. Celandine, my dear, will you please try to help me, in exchange for the help I have given you? After all, we both know you swore to serve Va. And surely what Va intends is for you to aid me. Why else would you be here?"

Sorrel opened her mouth to utter a sharp retort, then changed her mind. "Of course," she said. "What other reason could there possibly be? I'll help you by being the person no one ever notices. And I'll listen. But I won't risk my life to go places where I'd be hanged if I were found."

And with that much you'll have to be content, milady. But, vex it, the woman couldn't be *right*, could she? She couldn't have been granted a witchery for the sole purpose of serving a spoiled princess for the rest of her life!

Inside, something shrivelled at the thought.

9

The Spy at Work

"So, how do you think you'll enjoy court life?"

Saker was inclined to ask himself the same question from time to time, but this was Lord Juster Dornbeck enquiring. They were on their way to his cousin's manor, and Saker was enjoying the feel of good horseflesh under him again. He was mounted on one of the nobleman's spare mounts and, after an easy canter followed by a gallop, they were now riding side by side at a walking pace. Around them, autumn vibrancy had succumbed to the onslaught of winter drab.

I don't trust you, Juster, he thought. *You're always fishing for information.* And he would have loved to have known why, of all the people at the court revel, Lord Juster Dornbeck had been the only courtier to approach him.

He said vaguely, "It's not what I'm used to."

"Watch your back, my friend."

"Listening to you, I'm beginning to think I should watch out for everybody in Throssel! Are they *all* after my blood?"

Juster laughed. "Probably. It's a monarch's playground, after all, and when games of influence and power are played, everyone vies for the King's favour, because it can lead to lucrative sinecures. Disfavour or perceived disloyalty can lead to the chopping block. Pox on't, sleeping with the wrong woman can lead to the gibbet! Fortunately King Edwayn is not his grandfather, whose idea of festive entertainment was chopping off heads, or burning Primordials at the stake, but even so, there's more nastiness at a royal court than there'd be in a dungeon for the land's worst rogues."

"I doubt my role as a cleric is of much interest to the court."

"After what you let slip the other night about fluyts and Kesleer shipbuilding, I'm supposed to believe the limit of your interest is religious?" Juster shook his head in mockery. "Your real concern is the Ardronese spice trade. Or lack of it."

Saker didn't reply.

"I have a vested interest in privateering," Juster said, "but even I can see we'd all do better competing in legitimate trade. To be fair to King Edwayn, that was the initial intention."

"And what went wrong?"

"The King awarded the shipbuilding contract for a merchant navy to the grandson of the Earl of Twite, but he sold the rights to someone else, who then sold it on to a third person, a shipbuilder in Port Spurge. The trouble is, the shipbuilder paid so much that his contract wasn't profitable."

Saker sent a look of disbelief his way.

"Because the cost of suitable timber shot up," Juster explained. "The Lowmians bought all last season's cut from the Innerlands."

"So the first two people made a wonderful profit and did absolutely nothing. Va above! That's ridiculous! Were you involved?"

"I'm not that daft. I finance my own ships and my own voyages. The risk is mine, but so is the profit. Fortunately, I'd already bought the timber for my new vessel."

"You're building a ship? To search for the Spicerie?"

"No. I pounce on the Lowmians as they leave Karradar on their way home, pregnant with all that lovely cargo I don't have to pay for." He glanced across at Saker. "Don't look so disapproving, witan."

"Privateering is war by another name. We're all Va-cherished, and good men die when you loose cannonballs at their ships."

Juster shrugged. "I could be one of the dead. All sailors know the risk. They also know a successful voyage will make them a fortune."

"Tell me, do you have lascars on board?"

"One, at the moment. I'd like to have more."

"Why?"

"They know how to sail, those people. Practically live on the ocean, trading and fishing in open boats from island to island. A lot of them sign on to Lowmian ships between Javenka and the Karradar Islands. Not so keen on coming here from Karradar, because they've heard about how cold it is. On my last voyage, though, there was a fellow who wanted to look for himself. Unfortunately for him, it's going to be a long time before he gets home again. My ship was badly holed in a battle with a couple of Lowmian traders, and it was only by the grace of Va that we managed to limp into port. I'm not venturing out again until my new ship is finished."

"Did you know Kesleer's ships to the Spicerie lost three in every four sailors?"

Juster gave him a sharp look. "How do you know? Did his fleet really find the Spicerie as rumour claims?"

"Yes." He was silent for a few minutes, gazing at the track ahead as the horses ambled on, while he pondered what to say.

Wisely, Juster said nothing.

"Let's do an exchange." Saker made up his mind. "I tell you all I know about the Lowmian trade to the Spicerie, and you give me access to your lascar."

"Why?"

"I want to learn the language of the Summer Sea islands." Which wasn't the whole truth, but it was explanation enough. "Would he teach me, do you think?"

Juster shrugged. "Pay him and I'm sure he would. But why would you want to do that?"

"I like learning languages. I speak fluent Pashali, and I'm familiar with most of the dialects of the Principalities."

"I'll introduce you to him, then. And now you can tell me all you know about Kesleer and his ships."

After Saker had finished relating the bare bones of what he'd learned in Ustgrind, Juster's only comment was a laconic, "You need to tell all that to the Prince. You do know he's in charge of the royal naval interests?"

"He's avoiding me. I've been trying to set up a meeting, but all I get from his attendants is that 'the Prince is busy'. I think he probably equates a spiritual adviser with someone who's going to tell him he shouldn't go whoring when he wants."

"Easily fixed. Last night Prince Ryce stayed at the manor we're visiting. He's waiting for us."

"And you neglected to tell me? What bait did you use to get him there?" *What game are you playing – helpful new friend, or something else?*

Juster was offhand. "Told him you needed expert judgement for your purchase of a horse. Told him if he wasn't there, you'd have to rely on mine, to which he replied he couldn't bear to have anyone mounted on an animal resembling a rowing boat."

"I gather he doesn't think much of your judgement in matters equine?"

"Saker, take my advice, and *always* pretend you know less than a prince or a king."

And at a guess, Lord Juster, you love manipulating us all . . .

Saker took Juster's advice to heart, and after meeting the Prince, begged him for his opinion on the mounts Juster's cousin, Orrin Dornbeck, was offering for sale. Prince Ryce proved to be an excellent judge of horse flesh, and Saker was pleased with his choice, a dapple grey named Greylegs.

They adjourned to the manor house for lunch, and after the meal Orrin offered to show Juster the latest puppies dropped by his favourite fellhound bitch, a ploy Saker guessed was designed to give the Prince a chance to speak to him in private.

"Lord Juster tells me you've some information about Lowmeer and the spice trade," Prince Ryce said the moment they were alone. "I need to know everything you've heard." There was no doubt that was an order.

So for the second time that day, Saker repeated all he knew about Kesleer and his schemes. He ended by saying, "Lord Juster told me shipbuilders here were having problems obtaining reasonably priced timber."

The Prince nodded. "Our present fleet isn't capable of returning with sufficient cargo to make such long voyages profitable. Their capacity is too small. We have an improved design; we just need the timber."

"I might be able to advise you . . ."

"I hardly think shipbuilding is any concern of my spiritual adviser!"

Saker inclined his head respectfully while he sorted out the politest way of expressing what he needed to say. "Your highness, I'm sure the Pontifect is aware that you've already received sufficient instruction in the ways of Va-Faith. Her reasons for sending me here were not, therefore, to tell you what you already know, but rather to explain how the Way of the Oak can be of value to the Crown."

The Prince's eyes widened. Saker could almost see his thoughts turning over as he wondered how the Way of the Oak could be relevant to shipbuilding.

He continued, "Your highness, forests are never static. Trees of great age die and are replaced by new growth. If a large tree is needed for the well-being of the Kingdom, then of course it may be cut. You don't need to go to the Innerlands for a mast or a keel. It's up to local shrine-keepers to say which tree or trees can be removed without damaging a forest. Such is the true Way of the Oak."

Prince Ryce began to smile. "You mean to tell me there'll be no tedious poring over sacred texts with you when I'd much prefer to be out hunting?"

Saker schooled his face to a bland mask to hide his exasperation. "That's exactly what I mean, your highness. I can, however, advise you on how the Faith can help achieve the task the King has given you."

"In that case, I think we will do very well together, Rampion," Prince Ryce said.

Saker wasn't so sure. If the Prince was more concerned about his hunting than his country's merchant navy, it didn't bode well for the Kingdom of Ardrone. His thoughts returned, reluctantly, to Mathilda. He'd hoped to find in her brother someone she could lean on. Now he doubted Ryce would be much support for his little sister.

Who can she turn to? he wondered. *She deserves so much more than she'll ever receive . . .*

"Demon! Demon!"

The farming lads pounded after Ardhi, hurling their stones and their words with equal ferocity.

Just ignorance, he thought, attempting to quell his panic as he leapt over a stile barely breaking stride. *They've never met anyone like me before.* People in the ports had been more tolerant; they saw the odd trader from Pashalin or sailor from Karradar. Even a lascar like him, occasionally. But here in the Shenat Hills, far from the coast? Here, with his long hair, his seaman's clothes and his bare feet, he was as exotic as a Lowmian merchantman sailing into the Chenderawasi lagoon.

And as feared.

A stone grazed his cheek, pushing him to greater speed as he headed up the track through a cow pasture. His pack bounced on his back as he tore over the roughness of the hoofprints in the dried mud. He was fast, but his pursuers knew the short cuts; worse, all they had to do was draw close enough to hit him with a lucky stone.

It can't end this way, can it?

A solitary tree grew alongside the track ahead, but its leafless branches offered little shelter. Seri defend him, here even the plants were perverse! Chenderawasi trees were always tall, striving towards the sky and clad in leafy foliage, but the broad-spread, drooping boughs of this tree offered no refuge. It was bare of leaves, and yet it drew him.

Without thinking, he left the track and raced towards it. Behind, the pack of young men hooted and yipped like dogs sensing the flagging of prey.

He hurled himself upwards on to a broad bough. Without effort, he pulled himself higher and higher, revelling in the joy of climbing, but all too aware that the tree offered no cover and he was as vulnerable as a fish stranded in a rock pool by the tide.

Below, one of his pursuers, intent on following him, hauled himself on to the lowest bough.

Another of the lads immediately pulled him off, cursing. "Are you mad, Hobby? You want to scramble up there, risking a choiceless soul? 'Tis an oak! What if it has an unseen guardian?"

"Ay, he's right," another agreed. "Anyways, we got this brown rat treed. Sooner or later he'll topple."

"'Specially a freaky one like him," another agreed. "Be there a guardian, he's a dead'un for sure."

Ardhi listened, struggling to understand their accents, so unlike the familiar cant of Lowmian tars. He knew nothing about any guardians, but he didn't feel threatened. He felt safe – until the youths began to hurl stones and rock-hard clods at him. He dodged and twisted and ducked, pulling himself from one side of the trunk to the other. When they surrounded the tree on all sides, he chose a place partially protected from below by interlacing branches, where he could place his back to the trunk and hug his pack to his chest like a shield. Fortunately, most of their missiles bounced harmlessly off the branches.

From his perch, he was the first to see another man top a nearby rise and plod across the field, a black and white dog trotting at his heels. When the man was close enough, he raised his voice and shook the gnarled stick he carried. "Be off with you, you lazy layabouts! What ails you that you tree a man? 'Tis disrespectful to the Way of the Oak. Hobby, I might have known 'twould be you! Get off back home and help your da!"

The lads faded away in several different directions, abruptly cowed. The man, grizzled and lined, looked up at Ardhi. "Come you down. They won't be back."

He swung himself to the ground. "I thank you, sir," he said. "Not want to hurt foolish boys."

"You, hurt that lot? Looked more like they were about to give you a drubbing!" He looked Ardhi up and down and gave a grunt. "Funny one, you be. All dark like dust. Pashali, are you?"

Ardhi shook his head.

"And barefoot like 'twere a summer day! Have you no wits about you, lad? Got no money for clogs even, then wrap y'feet up in summat!"

"Feet not hurt." Anyone from the islands of the Summer Seas had soles tougher than leather.

"Hmph." His grunt was both disbelieving and contemptuous. "You best be going. Folk in this here valley don't like strangers. 'Specially not witless ones. You ask to be stoned, a dusky fellow like you, looking so daft with your long hair and funny garb." He grunted again. "Shoeless in winter, 'tis unnatural! Where y'heading?"

Ardhi pointed in the direction the kris had taken on its journey. He'd no idea who carried it now, and the trace it left behind was faint, but he still felt it. "That way."

"To Oakwood?" The old man nodded as if that made sense. "Townsfolk!" He spat. "Be off with you, and best not stop till you've hit the town walls."

As Ardhi walked on, he considered the rough wisdom behind the man's insults. As an islander from the Summer Seas, he stood out like a pigeon floating on the ocean. He looked down at his feet. Money wasn't a problem as he still had spices to sell; no, it was his own stubborn pride that was the problem. He was Chenderawasi and hadn't wanted to look like these people.

Shoes, he thought, with a sigh. *Splinter it.*

10

The Geese in Winter

Prince Ryce and his closest friends spilled out of the playhouse into the square, laughing and joking. Saker, following behind the Prince, wrapped his coat a little tighter against the cold of the wintry afternoon.

He'd earned an occasional place in Ryce's company because of his swordplay and his riding skills, the two things the Prince and his inner circle admired above all else, and he had to admit there were any number of compensations. Having a front-row seat at the first public performance of a new play, with the planking padded with a cushion, was definitely one such.

"And so what did our witan think of the lad playing Saucy Sallie?" one of the party asked. "Nice pair of tits he conjured up from somewhere! Enough to twitch one's pizzle, eh, Saker?"

Ser Rossland Burn, of course. Nothing he liked better than to chaff one of the clergy. "I'm sure you would know, Ser Ross," he replied with a faint smile. "As a witan, I just wonder why we do not allow women on the stage, rather than paint and powder up lads to titillate the audience."

They all looked at him then, in surprise. "Women on the boards? Surely you jest, Saker!" Prince Ryce said. "No woman of good name would lend herself to such a dubious profession!"

"Do we make assumptions of a man's moral worth when he chooses to be a player?" he asked. He wasn't sure why he was being perverse. It was not a subject he'd ever given thought to, but there was something about their casual acceptance of their privileged positions that riled him.

There was a puzzled silence, as if they couldn't comprehend what bothered him, but they were interrupted before they could respond.

Irate voices bellowing down the street made them all turn their heads, and a moment later a man tore through the square, pursued by several others shouting, "Stop, thief!"

The Prince whooped, drew his sword and cried, "Stop him, men!"

For a moment Saker felt he was back in the playhouse, watching a drama unfold before his eyes. The courtiers spread out across the square, unsheathing their blades in readiness. *The careless arrogance of the privileged*, he thought. *Like players who risk nothing.*

The accused thief stopped, appalled. He took in the array of armed courtiers and the remainder of the playgoers pouring out of the theatre behind them, glanced over his shoulder at his pursuers, then back again. In what was now a wall of people milling around, he singled out the only one wearing religious garb, and raced to sink to his knees at Saker's feet. "Mercy," he begged. "Mercy on a wretched sinner."

One of his pursuers ran up. "He stole . . . from my . . . master's kitchen!" he panted, doubling over as he gasped for air. Ryce and his courtiers closed in.

"You are in the presence of your prince!" Ser Rossland snapped at him. "Show your respect!"

The accuser's jaw dropped as his gaze alighted on Prince Ryce. After a moment's stunned shock, he bowed deeply. "Y-y-your highness."

Ryce raised an eyebrow at him. "What's the story?"

"I'm one . . . one of the cooks in Merchant Cornbatch's kitchens, your highness." He pointed at the kneeling man. "This here fellow . . . delivered us some wine, he did, an' the kitchen skivvy saw 'im pinching some spices while he was in the pantry."

"You can have them back!" the thief cried. He fiddled in his fob purse and extracted a scattering of cloves and a single nutmeg, which he held out on his palm towards Prince Ryce.

"Is that all you took?" Ryce asked him. He waved a languid hand at Saker, to indicate he should take the spices.

"By me oath, that's all. Wouldn't've took that if it weren't for my babe being sick with the plague . . ."

As one, everyone except Saker took a step back. A number of the wealthier folk in the crowd reached into their purses for pomanders, and the scent of spice on the air doubled.

"Fodder for the gibbet, then," Ser Rossland remarked from a safe distance.

Saker looked down at the pitiful heap of spices now in the palm of his hand. "For *this*?"

"Them's worth five guildeens!" the cook said indignantly, and snatched them back.

Prince Ryce beckoned to one of his personal guards in attendance. "Gerth, send the thief along to the city jail." He looked around the assembled crowd and added loudly, "Thieves have no mercy granted them in our kingdom. Be not worried, good people, there's no plague in Throssel. Believe me, your prince would be the first to know!"

There was laughter, and the crowd began to disperse.

The thief, still kneeling, looked up at Saker with pleading eyes. "My babe has the plague, Master Witan. Have mercy!"

"Your fate's already sealed," Saker told him, his heart a hard lump in his chest, hurting. "The Prince has spoken. I will see your family taken care of, if you tell me their direction."

"Me name's Trewbridge, master. I live by the Watergate in the basement of the wine merchant's . . ."

He cried as he was led away.

Prince Ryce bent to speak softly in Saker's ear. "Do not go to that man's house, witan, under pain of my severe displeasure. It may not be the plague, but who knows what might ail his child? You will *not* risk bringing contagion into the palace."

Va-damn. For a wild moment he had indeed been contemplating putting his witan's concern for someone down on his luck before his obligation to the royal family. A grievous error that would not have been forgiven.

"Of course not, your highness." He'd send someone with money for the wife and child instead, if they existed.

He was puzzled, though. Why had so many people already been carrying pomanders, when there had been no pestilence – of any kind – reported lately in Ardrone? Someone was spreading rumours, arousing fear. Stirring the erroneous belief that a pomander stuck with spices would ward off the illness . . .

Someone perhaps who wanted the price of spices to rise?

Five guildeens for ten or eleven cloves and a single nutmeg. Sweet cankers. An obscene price, all for something that cured nothing.

"Don't tell me it's my pretty lady's keel you've come to see!"

Saker looked up from where he was leading Greylegs through the building debris of the dry dock. Lord Juster waved from under the stern of his half-built ship, and came over, grinning and full of joyous pride in the progress of his vessel. He was also decidedly three sheets to the wind. "I know she doesn't look much at the moment with her innards exposed, but when she heads out to sea with her swan-like neck forward of the bow and her hair flying . . ." He glanced affectionately up at the ship. "I'm having the best woodcarver in all Throssel make her figurehead. Did you come to meet my lascar?"

"I came to see you. But yes, I'd like to meet him too."

Juster grabbed a passing sailor and asked him to stable the horse and find the islander. When the man had led Greylegs away, he added, "I've just had a most unpleasant visit from the Secretary to the Fleet's lackey. Apparently a Lowmian galleon and a couple of carracks were seen sailing down the Ardmeer estuary, possibly heading to the Spicerie. They were flying the Regal's flag and Kesleer's colours. King Edwayn was not pleased."

"Ah. He wants you to make sure no spices get back to Ustgrind?"

"Yes. No way I can sail again soon, of course, not even for a king, but doubtless the Lowmians won't be returning for well over a year anyway, not if they're bound for the Spicerie. I'll be waiting for them. What puzzles me more, though, is why Lowmeer is willing to risk sending a fleet out at this time of the year." He glanced up at the sky, heavy with clouds. "The worst of winter may be over, but I wouldn't want to take a wager on that."

Saker thought of the Horned Death and spice pomanders, and wondered if merchants might think the risks worthwhile.

Juster cocked his head slightly, frowning. "Why do I always get the idea you know more than you tell?"

"I'm sure that applies to you more than me."

"*Me?* I'm a full sail billowing in the wind with nothing hidden! I understand the Prince has had some success sourcing timber from shrine-keepers for our shipbuilders. Makes me wonder why Prime Fox didn't make that suggestion a long time ago. Fellow knew of the shipbuilders' predicament, wouldn't you say?" Juster raised a questioning eyebrow at him.

"I would think so." But he couldn't think of a single logical reason Fox could have to sabotage the King's plans.

"Ah, here's the lascar now." Juster introduced them, concluding, "The witan would like to learn the language of your islands, Iska. Could you teach him?"

The man looked startled. He was older than Saker had expected; his face was weather-beaten, his body all sinew and muscle. A few grey patches sprinkled his hair. "Yes, but not understand why," he blurted, puzzled.

"Our ships are going to your islands to trade," Saker said. "We need people to speak your tongue."

Iska opened his mouth to say something, then closed it again.

His frustration was obvious, and Saker realised he didn't have the language to explain. "You don't happen to speak Pashali, do you?" he asked in that tongue.

Iska brightened. "Of course! Many islands. Many tongues. Much trade with each other and with Pashalin. So all coast people speak Pashali! No need you learn my tongue." His Pashali was heavily accented, and not perfect, but it was understandable.

Juster sucked in his cheeks, folded his arms and leaned against a bollard to listen, obviously at home with the language himself.

"Oh," Saker said, surprised. "I think I am not wise, er, knowledgeable, in this." *Damn it, my Pashali is rusty. I should practise more.* He pulled out the lascar's dagger. "Do you know what this is?"

Before he finished the question, the man was backing away, his gaze fixed on the blade. He stopped three paces off and said quietly, "A kris. Every lascar has a kris. Gift from father when he become man." He tapped his own dagger sheath, but didn't draw the blade.

Saker couldn't decide whether Iska was scared or just respectful. His tone didn't waver, but his stare didn't either.

"Yours is like this one?"

Iska shook his head. "That a Chenderawasi blade. Only Chenderawasi make throwing blades."

"Chen . . . Chenderawasi?"

"Not my island. Far-off island." His nervousness was more obvious and he was groping for the right words.

"You're afraid?" The taint of the man's fear swept over him. Of course the man was afraid, and he ought to be. A dagger that could move of its own accord? *It's like keeping a serpent in the sheath on your belt.*

The lascar said quietly, "Strong magic lives in Chenderawasi kris. Wise man, he full respect such thing."

Saker swallowed, hard, wanting to halt the fear that threatened to close his throat. "Good magic or bad magic?"

Iska finally shifted his gaze to meet his own. "*Powerful* magic. Each Chenderawasi blade belongs to one man. Real owner find Witan Saker to take kris back."

"The man who owned this one is dead." Not that he believed that any more.

Neither did Iska. "Bah!" His snort was contemptuous. "He still alive! Chenderawasi kris always buried with owner. Magic says so. Kris still here, so owner still live."

Va rot you, Ardhi. "What is this gold colour in the metal?" he asked, holding out the blade so Iska could see it better.

This time he held up his arms as if to ward off an attack. "Powerful *sakti*! Not for me to touch!" Addressing Lord Juster, he begged, "I go work now. Witan Saker in big trouble." He sent a sidelong glance towards Saker, and when he spoke, his tone was one of concern. "Sorry, master witan. Much trouble, pain come to you if you keep kris."

"Perhaps he'd better throw it away?" Juster suggested.

Iska gave a hollow laugh that contained no humour. "Can try, yes," he said. "Chenderawasi kris has . . ." He frowned, hunting for the right Pashali word. "It has soul. Like – like it lives. He who holds Chenderawasi kris, he serves Chenderawasi." He looked straight at Saker. "Chenderawasi control you. Your fate not your own, not now. You be cursed." He turned on his heel and walked away.

"Well," Juster said brightly, unfolding himself from the bollard, "I guess when one stirs up things one doesn't understand, one does tend to get kicked in the teeth. I wonder if I should spend any more time in your cursed company. Do you think curses rub off the cursed person on to others?"

"Oh, puddle it, you long-nosed loon!"

Juster grinned and clapped him on the back. "Ah, don't look so serious. I'm sure you, as a witan, don't believe in curses from the Va-forsaken Hemisphere. How did you come by the dagger?"

"It was thrown at me."

"And obviously missed! Not such a great weapon after all, is it? Besides, the things that threaten you – us – are much closer to home. And much more tangible."

It wasn't the words that sent a stab of cold into Saker, it was the way Juster uttered them, with a bleakness foreign to his usual banter. "You can't mean Lowmeer and the edge they have on the spice trade?"

Juster was scornful. "Of course not. That's hardly so dire, is it? Lowmeer has been richer than us before, and we've survived."

"So what then? You know spices are useless against the Horned Death? And we haven't had a single case of the Death on our side of the border anyway."

"No, and I'm not worried about mysterious daggers, either. Come, let me buy you a drink . . ."

"Not until you tell me what you think threatens us." He stayed stubbornly still, refusing to move as the nobleman began to walk away.

When Juster realised he wasn't following, he stopped and regarded him with a sober stare. His next words were said so quietly they were hard to hear. "The greatest danger is always the closest. The hound guarding the crib, the man carrying the lantern to light your way, the worm eating its way into the ship's hull, the woman lying beside you. You've already seen the seeds of your downfall."

"Oh, a pox on that. I hate riddles. Say what you mean out loud."

"I will, when I'm sure of the truth and when you're ready to hear it. Neither of which is so yet. Right now, I'm going to have that drink. Are you coming?" This time when he walked away, he didn't stop.

Saker ground his teeth, exasperated. Who or what did he mean? *Patronising fobbing bastard, speaking in riddles like a stage player!*

Standing there in the sea wind, he shivered. First Gerelda, then Iska, now Juster. All spouting warnings. It was enough to make him want to curl into a ball and hide under his bedcovers. He looked down at the kris, unresponsive in his hand. Alive? In the sunlight, the gold strands shone brightly, the metal unmoving.

Don't be stupid, Saker. All these warnings are about as tangible as a wisp of mist, like tales of ghosts told to children. Still, he'd feel so much easier if he could find a way to rid himself of the fobbing Va-forsaken blade. He slipped it back into its sheath with a sigh; even *thinking* about throwing it away was difficult, damn it.

Briskly, he walked after Juster, trying to leave his vague unsettled feeling behind. He could do with a pot of ale.

"Va's balls! Where did you learn to do that?" Prince Ryce, disarmed and shaking his fingers to relieve the sting of having his sword spun out of his hand, regarded Saker in exasperation. "How many times have we sparred over the past moon? Four? Five? And every single time you've disarmed me at least once! How the curdled damn does a witan learn to use a blade better than a prince?"

Saker bent to retrieve the Prince's weapon from the floor of the palace's Great Hall. He returned it, hilt first, with a placating smile. "He starts as a university student. Nothing students like better than fighting one another. Then he serves as a cleric to the border patrol, up near Coldheart Pass in the Principalities. Nothing much to do there all winter long except fight. That particular trick came from a Pashali caravan guard when we were snowed in," he added truthfully. "Would you like me to show you the secret of it?"

"Indeed I would! But not just now. I have to dress and be on my best behaviour. There's a delegation from West Denva, and Father wants me looking suitably princely." He flung a sweaty arm around Saker. "You know what I like about you, witan? You don't make a mat of yourself for me to tread on. You're the only person I know who dares to make a fool of his prince by disarming him with a trick like that."

"It's all part of being a prince's spiritual adviser – making sure he remains humble."

Ryce laughed and hit him on his shoulder with a balled fist. "Addlepate! Ah, I wish I could dine with you tonight. Instead I have to listen to the Denva delegation extol their heir as a suitable groom for Princess Mathilda."

"Isn't he only, what, six years old?"

"Five, I believe."

"Well, I suppose that's an improvement on fifty," he said, but remained doubtful.

"Mathilda would eat him alive. But I don't think it'll happen. What can a piddling border principality offer us, compared to the Regal of Lowmeer? If Regal Vilmar wants Thilda enough, he'll meet Father's terms."

Saker, feeling sick, turned away to pull off his sweat-soaked undertunic. He was reaching for his clean shirt, wondering how much he could say to Ryce about the marriage without risking his position, when a burst of feminine giggling made them both turn and look upward. Movement behind the carved screen of the minstrels' gallery told them they were observed.

Ryce frowned. "Thilda, you wretch! Who said you could spy on our sparring practice?"

One of the carved wooden casements opened and the Princess leaned out, waving. Behind her, Saker glimpsed several of her younger ladies-in-waiting, still giggling. His face reddened at the thought of Mathilda observing him stripped to the waist, and he struggled to pull on his shirt over a torso sheened with sweat. Thank Va, at least she couldn't have heard their conversation.

"You shouldn't spar in the Great Hall then!" she called down to her brother. She lingered a moment longer to watch Saker as he battled his shirt, her lips curling upwards in a teasing smile. Then, after another wave to Ryce, she was gone with her ladies. Her handmaiden, the grey mouse, appeared, po-faced, at the opening to pull the casement shut.

"That one's like a cloud about to drop a cold shower on us," Ryce muttered in his ear. "Damned if I know what my sister sees in her."

"Who is she?"

"Celandine somebody-or-other. Mathilda had need of a maid when we were travelling up in the north. She's the niece of a shrine-keeper. I call her the grey ghost." He slid his sword into its scabbard. "Poor Thilda. We neither of us are more than cooked geese served up to the Crown of Ardrone. And folk *envy* us?"

He strode away, and as his footsteps echoed through the hall, Saker looked up at the minstrels' gallery again. All was quiet, but he thought he caught a lingering whiff of Mathilda's perfume. Va, it was hard to think of her being married off to the highest bidder. He'd always known such marriages were normal in wealthier families, but now it was more than just knowledge; he could put a face to the woman involved. He could see her tears, know her grief, picture her future.

It was so *wrong*.

He wondered if she had any real friends, any ladies, who would accept exile to be with her when she married. She needed a trustworthy confidant.

He thought, *I hope I can be that for her, at least while she remains at court. Better me than her colourless handmaiden, who's about as joyous as a wet dishcloth.*

Just as Saker was leaving the Great Hall, Princess Mathilda arrived with Celandine.

The Princess pouted when she saw he was alone. "I wanted to catch Prince Ryce. Never mind, you shall escort me back to my solar instead, and we'll have a game of Fox and Geese. And you can tell me the latest court gossip."

He stepped forward, bowed and offered her his arm. "I fear my knowledge of gossip is meagre. No one tells a junior witan anything."

"Nonsense, of course they do." She rested her hand on his arm as they turned to leave the hall. "Does the West Denvans' visit pertain to my marriage? The heir to the throne there is but a child, I know, but perhaps . . ."

Her words trailed away, and he was disturbed once again to see tears lingering on her lashes.

In his dismay, he was at a loss for words. One part of him wanted to take her in his arms and brush the tears away with soft words, a longing that was appallingly inappropriate. He swallowed and said carefully, "I'm not privy to discussions on your marriage, I fear." Hastily, he added, "It's years since I played Fox and Geese. I feel sure you will outwit me in the first few moves."

"I shall play the Fox. One person against all others, for that is how I feel."

"Ah," he said, striving for lightness, "a fox can eat many an unwary goose."

When they reached her solar, he hung back to allow her to enter the apartments first. Celandine followed her in, saying under her breath so only he could hear, "Indeed, foxes have very sharp teeth, and they love geese. And ganders can be so very, very stupid."

Pox on her, he thought. If ever something was fraught with double meanings, that was.

11

The Fox in Summer

Prince Ryce galloped across the meadow with scant concern for his safety, pursued by Saker lying low to the neck of his dapple grey. Hooves scattering sods of earth, the horses thundered towards the laden tables and gaily coloured tents erected at the other end of the field, where courtiers gathered for their midsummer revelry.

No matter how much he urged Greylegs on, Saker was still staring at the rump of Prince Ryce's roan.

Just before reaching the first of the fires with kitchen boys turning the spits of roasting fowl, the Prince drew rein and waited for him, grinning. "I trust you were not allowing me to win, witan."

"You jest, your highness. I think you know me better than that." He patted Greylegs' neck. The loss wasn't his horse's fault. Prince Ryce not only rode a faster animal; he rode like a man who didn't think of the possibility of breaking its legs – or his own.

The Prince's reply was sober. "True, I do. I wonder if you have any idea how good it is to have a friend who tells me exactly what he thinks, instead of what he thinks I *want* to hear?"

Friend? He was moved. "Then may I tell you what I think, your highness? You should have more respect for your neck. You are the only prince we have."

"Saker, if I didn't get to risk my princely neck sometimes, I could never sit through all those boring councils." There was no hint of amusement in the statement. "When I am King – and please Va let that not come until I'm old and grey – you shall be my Prime. And then you'll understand!"

"I knew there had to be a disadvantage to friendship with a prince! I would make a *terrible* Prime."

Ryce grinned again. "I know. We can be incompetent clodpates together."

They rode into the heart of the revelry, and handed their mounts over to the grooms. The King was not there, but Lady Mathilda was, with all her younger ladies-in-waiting. Saker even caught a glimpse of Celandine, looking bored as she threaded her lone way through the crowd behind the other ladies. He felt a moment's pity for her. It couldn't be much of a life, always trailing after her mistress, clutching a pair of gloves, or a fan, or a cloak, for when the Princess might need it.

The Prince rejoined his courtiers, including Lord Juster, so Saker headed for the refreshment table. He was sitting on a stool eating a meat pie when a familiar voice grated in his ear, the last person he'd expected to be present.

Prime Valerian Fox stood at his shoulder, asking, "You really do not understand the position of a spiritual adviser, do you? *Racing* with the heir to the throne? For a *wager*, I believe? Is that the kind of example you wish Prince Ryce to follow?"

Scrambling to his feet, he hurriedly wiped the gravy from his mouth with the back of his hand while debating what to do with the rest of the dripping pie. "Your eminence." *Blast you.*

"Do you think the King would be pleased if his son were to take hurt in a fall from his horse?"

There was no good way to answer that, so he tossed the pie to a nearby hound and stayed silent.

"You should wear your witan's robe at all times, both figuratively and actually. And your monthly report is late."

Sure that Fox had chosen his words carefully to make him feel like a schoolboy again, he was about to give a sarcastic reply when the kris jabbed his thigh. "Argh . . . Ah, I'll – I'll write it this evening. My apologies."

Fox's gaze fell to the hand he had clamped over the dagger sheath at his belt. "What is that thing you're wearing?"

Va's teeth, at least when I wear the witan's robe, no one sees the blithering blade. He strove for nonchalance. "A lascar dagger." He pulled it from the sheath, keeping a tight hold to the hilt. "Weird thing, and not all that useful, but I like it. Beautifully crafted."

He held it up, and Fox took a step backwards, his expression pinched.

"Totally inappropriate for a man of the Faith! Heathen-made. Get rid of it!"

"As you wish," he said lightly. He turned and detained a passing serving lad by the arm. "Throw this away, will you?" he asked, and dropped the kris on to his serving tray.

The lad stared at it, his surprise robbing him of speech.

Fox gave Saker a narrow-eyed look of fury and waved the lad away. He scuttled off, and Fox said, "Mock me, witan, and you'll find out there's always a price."

"Try not to treat me like a half-witted acolyte and we might rub along together a little better."

"You overstepped a line today." A cold malice saturated the stare Fox directed Saker's way before he stalked off, brushing past Lord Juster as he went.

Saker remained where he was, cursing his too-quick tongue.

"What the fobbing hells did you just say to the Prime?" Juster asked. "If looks could curdle, you'd be no more than soured cottage cheese right now."

"I don't think he likes me much."

"My friend, you need to be a lot more careful. That man is dangerous."

"More of your dire warnings, Lord Doom?"

"Bad things happen to people who upset the Prime." He glanced over Saker's shoulder, then looked away hurriedly. "Uh-oh, and here's more trouble on her way."

Princess Mathilda, her full skirts held high, stepped daintily through the grass towards them, Celandine at her shoulder like a permanent shadow. Saker, annoyed with Juster, said under his breath, "That's a gratuitous remark." When someone momentarily detained the Princess, he asked, "Have you heard anything more about her impending marriage?"

"Not a word. I assume that means there is much negotiation in the process."

"Have you any idea what bride price could be offered that would tempt the King?"

"I'd conjecture something long-lasting. A trade advantage, perhaps?

Especially if Lowmeer is involved." When Saker failed to hide his distaste, he added, "Whoever the Princess weds is no concern of yours. It's the price nobility pay for their power and their luxury."

"The price women pay is higher than men's, I imagine."

"We all marry for reasons that have nothing to do with personal happiness."

"You've managed to stay single. You, at least, appear to have had a choice."

"I have three older brothers, all prolific in their breeding, fortunately. No one in my family cares if I wed or not. Which is fortunate for me, considering I enjoy my life the way it is."

He fell silent as Mathilda and Celandine approached. Mathilda acknowledged their bows and lifted her skirts far enough to display her ankles and embroidered slippers. "Look!" she said. "My best pumps are sopping wet!"

"Milady, we can't have that! You may catch ague." Juster, without asking her permission, picked her up by the waist and sat her on the table.

She squealed. "Lord Juster! I am sure that is inappropriate behaviour!"

He laughed at her. "Not mine, surely. I am saving your life." He waved to Celandine. "Put her slippers in the sun to dry. We mustn't allow our princess to catch the ague. Oh, did you mean *your* behaviour, milady? Sitting on a table amongst the food?" He turned to Saker. "What do you think, witan? Quite reprehensible manners on the part of a princess?"

"I think it is you who are incorrigible, my lord," he responded lightly, trying not to stare at Mathilda's stockinged feet as Celandine removed her pumps.

"Quite incorrigible," Princess Mathilda agreed, wriggling her toes, "and I'm sure no one else would dare treat me so cavalierly, except you, Lord Juster. Go disport yourself elsewhere, if you please. I wish to speak with my spiritual adviser."

"Milady," Saker said when Juster had left, "how may I serve you?"

"Oh don't be so formal, witan. Especially as I know you wish to chide me, for being either too indecorous or too imperious, when a princess should be above reproach on both counts."

"I must lack daring. I have not the courage to chide a princess." He couldn't stop his lips curling at the corners. No matter what she did, she could always make him smile.

She was suddenly sober. "I just wanted to tell you that the King has rejected the marriage proposal from West Denva."

"I hadn't heard that. Did Prince Ryce tell you?"

She pouted. "No, he wouldn't. But I have my methods."

Behind her, Celandine tilted her chin, a small movement, but full of meaning. *Celandine* had found out? There was no way of confirming that, though, so he asked instead, "Are you pleased?"

"I – I think the alternative proposed is not one that pleases me. Witan, if you have any compassion for me, any concern for this loyal servant of Va, you will intercede if – if . . ." But she couldn't continue.

Sweet Va, he thought. *She's heard more hints it's to be Regal Vilmar.* Bile rose into his gorge, stinging his throat. *Don't let that happen. Please don't let that happen.* He'd never felt so helpless. So gutted. How would she ever be able to stand it? "I will pray that the final decision is one you will find . . . attractive," he said.

She sat there wriggling her toes in her damp stockings, her face a mask of disappointment and loss. Her next words were whispered so low he almost missed them. "Never attractive. Never. I cannot marry him to whom I'm drawn. Passable is all I can hope for. Or kind. Will he – will my husband be kind?"

Her words were a whip flaying his conscience.

"Witan Saker, is there nothing you can do? Intercede for me with the Pontifect?"

He was overwhelmed by a desire to say he'd do anything – but the words died before they reached his tongue. He had no say in the affairs of princes or kings. "The Pontifect has said she can do nothing if both parties agree to a marriage."

"How can I refuse if the King insists? He threatens to confine me to my solar until I agree. Who is there to prevent that?"

"You . . ." He caught the informality, swallowed it back. "The Princess is always in my prayers."

She looked away from him, swinging her feet. "You disappoint me." The side of her foot brushed his thigh. He stepped back abruptly, as if she'd burned him.

"Doubtless I ask the impossible," she said bitterly, "and I have no right to do so. Celandine, put my slippers on again. I have little heart for these revels."

He watched her go, sick to the stomach, and wondered at the depth of his sorrow for her. Her predicament had lodged in his flesh like a wound he could not heal. When he was back in his room, he'd write to the Pontifect and ask again if there was some way to discourage a union between the Princess and Regal Vilmar – although he could almost hear the derisive snort Fritillary Reedling would give when she read his request.

And he must tell Fritillary all about the lascar's dagger. Thinking back, he wasn't even sure why he hadn't told her already. Keeping silent seemed asinine in retrospect; she might have been able to explain its power. And now he had another reason for her to know: he was certain there was something consistently odd about the way the kris reacted in the Prime's presence.

"Master Witan?"

The serving lad was back, nervously holding the dagger out towards him. "Did you really want this thrown away?"

Saker smoothed away his frown. "Somehow I don't think you could, even if you tried." He held out his hand. "Give it here."

Relieved, the young server surrendered the blade and scampered away.

He replaced it in the sheath, only to find it had managed to cut a hole through the leather, and the point was poking into his thigh. *Pox on't*, he thought. *Is there no way I have any control over this wretched thing?*

That night, as he sat in his room penning his private letter to the Pontifect, which he would send through her courier, he included his concern for the Princess. He suspected, however, that if Ardrone received some trade advantage as a result of her marriage, Fritillary would be pleased, not upset, and the thought depressed him. *Everything's always about monetary advantages and politics.*

He dawdled over finishing the report. An odd feeling niggled at him that there was something else he'd wanted to say. Something that had occurred to him during the revelries. The more he tried to remember, the more the idea of it skipped out of reach. It was a weird feeling for someone who prided himself on his memory.

Finally he gave up, and signed and sealed the letter.

12

The Glamoured Woman

Sorrel Redwing stood with her back to one of the stone pillars that held up the roof of the Great Hall of Throssel Castle. The stone was hard and cold, but at least it was something to lean against. She expected to stand there for several hours. Her appearance blended in with the stonework, until she was as well camouflaged as a bittern among reed stalks. If she was noticed, she hoped that she'd be of no more consequence than the menservants scurrying to and fro to put the suckling pigs and the roasted swans on the table for the evening meal.

She'd have preferred to do almost anything else, but this was now her life. Mathilda's spy, feeding the Princess the gossip of the court, the truths people uttered when they didn't know they were overheard.

Another autumn come, and she still didn't know why she'd been given a witchery, or how she was supposed to be serving Va. She was waiting, still waiting for some kind of revelation. Some Va-sent vision. Something, anything not this. She was so *bored*. Worse, she was shackled in place by her lack of resources. It never occurred to the Princess to *pay* anything for her services.

I think this is worse than living at Ermine Manor. At least there I could remember Heather so easily. I could hear her laughter. She'd escaped from the Ermines, only to end up as the Princess's penned goose. *Va, I dedicated myself to your service. Isn't there something more important that I'm supposed to be doing?*

An unpleasant thought followed hard on the heels of that: perhaps this was penance for having killed Nikard. If so, how long for the murder of a man who'd deliberately killed his own child because she was born deaf?

Oh, Heather . . .

She shivered. *I'll never cease looking for a way out.*

Her next thought surprised her: she wanted so much more of life than she would once have thought acceptable. In Ermine Hall, her life had *plodded* from one day to the next, the only bright window in her years there being Heather. Now she wanted more. To be loved, yes. Someone, somewhere. A man like Saker Rampion. Strong, honest, caring. *Why does he never look at me?* She almost snorted. Why would he? She was just the grey nonentity, always fading into the background.

But even love wouldn't be enough. She wanted to find joy in life, to experience hope, to be *challenged.*

She glanced around the room. Knots of courtiers formed and re-formed as they laughed and drank and gossiped and waited for the King to arrive. Her gaze moved on until she located Saker Rampion. He was standing next to Lord Juster, talking quietly with a seriousness at odds with most of the others in the Hall. *If I could have married someone like him*, she thought, *I might have been happy. He'd have been a wonderful father to Heather.*

As chaperone when the Princess was with the witan, she listened to all their conversations. There was something about Saker's watchful eye, his quiet, thoughtful air, that both attracted and intrigued.

He and Lord Juster Dornbeck were an unlikely pair. She knew Dornbeck was a buccaneer, a man whose passions always seemed larger than life. Gossip said he loved too well and too often, drank too much and too frequently, played too hard and too dangerously. By contrast, in all the time Rampion had been at court, she'd never heard gossip about him that linked his name to any woman, or to any kind of excess. And yet his friendship with Lord Juster appeared genuine.

Silly, she guessed, to think a man as handsome as Saker, with such a gentle, winning smile, would not bed a willing tavern lass occasionally. Often. Maybe he had a regular lover. Someone he wanted to marry. The thought caused her a stab of pain, and she sighed. Pox on't, she was *such* a fool.

Just then, the King entered with the more important courtiers and made his way to the main table. Once they were settled, everyone else sought places at the trestle boards that ran the length of the hall. On their way to their seats, Lord Juster and Witan Saker halted only two paces away from the edge of her skirts.

They were too close. One false step and either of them could trip over her feet. She began to sweat, but didn't dare wipe the moisture away as it dripped down her brow and into her eyes.

"You're sure? Those money-grabbing Lowmian merchants managed to make their consortium *work*?" Lord Juster was asking.

Saker nodded. "The Lowmian Spicerie Trading Company, with the Regal as patron. I'll wager he's been playing off one merchant family against another, one port against another."

Juster nodded. "And collects the gifts bestowed by those striving to reassert their privileged places. One can only wonder how the most frugal and austere of men often seem also to be the most covetous! What in all damp and watery Ustgrind does Vilmar *do* with his gold? Sit on it, like a mythical dragon on his hoard?"

"Well, he certainly doesn't wear his wealth. He dresses like a shipping clerk."

"I heard the Lowmians have already laid the keels of three new fluyts."

Flights? She wondered if she'd heard the word correctly. Ships of some kind, that was obvious.

Saker nodded.

"While our penny-pinching merchants continue to bicker like children with the King and the shipbuilders," Juster said in disgust.

"My sources in Lowmeer tell me Kesleer's carrack the *Spice Dragon* is being refitted to bring the new fleet up to four. All only lightly armed."

"No match for my *Golden Petrel*, then!"

"Is it rigged yet?"

"*She* is indeed," Lord Juster corrected. Casually he leaned an arm against the pillar, his hand resting just a finger's length from Sorrel's shoulder. "I wouldn't be surprised, though, if one of the Regal's galleons didn't sail with them to provide more fire power."

She almost screamed. How could they not see her? Her heart was pounding. She concentrated, pressing herself into the stone. *I am not here, not here . . .*

Intent on their conversation, neither of the men noticed her.

"I'm looking forward to seeing how the *Petrel* matches up to these fluyts," Lord Juster continued.

Through the blur of sweat trickling into her eyelashes, she saw a golden haze around Saker, misting the air from a point at his hip. They didn't notice that either. She eyed at it uneasily, mystified.

Dornbeck said, "Don't look at me like that, Saker! My ship is the only chance we have of being able to obtain spices without paying through the nose for them."

She heard the words but hardly absorbed their meaning. The space around Saker was filling with golden light, cascades of orange and vermilion, as soft as rolls of satin. Her terror grew. Smells filled her nostrils: the tang of salt borne on a sea wind, the musty damp of a forest floor after heavy rain. Song filled her ears, birdsong, but of no bird she'd ever heard, unearthly, bell-like notes beautiful almost beyond bearing.

Rampion and Dornbeck moved to be seated at the tables, and the colours and sounds faded, leaving Sorrel shaking and wet with sweat. No one was looking at her. No one else had noticed anything unusual.

She stayed where she was, her fright gradually fading. Some kind of vision, she decided, caused by the fear of being caught. *Nothing more, please Va. Nothing more. I couldn't take on another burden to worry about.*

After dinner was over, as the tables were dismantled and the hall was prepared for dancing, Sorrel caught sight of Saker again. He had ensconced himself behind a pillar, and to her amusement he was eavesdropping on a conversation between Tonias Pedding, the Prime's secretary, and the palace resident prelate, Conrid Masterton. Well, two could play the same game, she supposed. Without further thought, she crossed to stand where she could both watch and listen. Blurred into the wall, she went unnoticed.

". . . Horned Death," Pedding was saying.

"The Lowmian disease?" the prelate asked.

"Not just Lowmian. Prime Fox has sent word from the north. Quite a few deaths up in the Shenat strongholds of Ardrone, near the border with Valence."

Prelate Masterton was appalled. "Va above! I trust the Prime has left the area."

"His letter said he thought it was his duty to stay," Secretary Pedding replied, shaking his head. He was a nondescript man, dour by nature and dull in dress. His support of Fox was so devout that courtiers joked he worshipped the Prime rather than Va. "We're not to say anything. He doesn't want any panic."

"The Prime is brave, but he ought to put his safety first." Masterton was unable to conceal his anxiety.

"He never does that," Pedding said proudly. "He's a man of courage. I should be with him, but he refuses to take me on his travels. Says that being responsible for his own affairs prevents him from being too prideful. But this plague has me worried."

"I've heard it's been spreading in Lowmeer, too. Pestilence doesn't take any notice of borders, after all."

"Spice pomanders protect you." The secretary sounded hopeful, as if he wanted reassurance.

"Have you heard what that belief has done to the price of spices? Only the wealthy can afford nutmeg or cloves in the kitchen these days. And who benefits? Lowmians, drat their waterlogged hides."

The conversation ended there as the musicians started up and the two men went their separate ways.

Saker vanished into the crowd, and Sorrel doubted she'd hear much more that was interesting, so she left the festivities and headed for the Princess's solar, hoping to snatch some sleep before Mathilda and her ladies-in-waiting returned.

Her sleeping quarters did not merit being described as anything except a cupboard. Containing only a truckle bed and a wooden trunk, the tiny room had a single door leading into Lady Mathilda's bedroom, which eliminated any chance of Sorrel being seen by other servants while asleep and unable to control her glamour.

Sleep, however, did not come easily when she returned that night. *Even here I'm not really safe,* she thought. *If I upset Mathilda, I could be dismissed and she wouldn't even realise how hard it is for a woman alone to survive . . .*

She wished she could talk about her problem with Saker Rampion, but how could she embroil him in her tangles? It wouldn't be fair to him, and Mathilda would be furious. Besides, perhaps he'd think it his duty to hand her over to the assizes for murder.

When she finally slept, she dreamed of lying naked, warm and protected in Saker's muscled arms. When the dream faded with her wakening, she grieved its loss.

13

A Touch of Dusk

When Saker was ushered into the Prime's office not long after Fox had returned from the north, he thought the man had lost weight. Sunken cheeks gave him a gaunt appearance.

Remembering his own brief view of a victim of the Horned Death, he wasn't surprised. If Fox had been attempting to succour the ill, he'd had an experience that would drain the vitality from any man.

"You asked to see me, your eminence?" As he took the hand the Prime proffered and raised it to his lips in the ritual kiss, Fox's fingers tightened around his own in a gesture he couldn't read. An acknowledgement of their mutual status as clerics was unlikely, so he took it as a gesture of dominance. "We've heard rumours of the Horned Death in Shenat country."

"Two hundred deaths that I know of," the Prime acknowledged, with a flat neutrality.

He blanched. *Far more than any single Lowmian outbreak . . .* A tickle against his thigh under his robe made his heart skip a beat. That dammed Chenderawasi blade was rippling in its sheath again. Would that he could rid himself of the wretched canker of an island sorcery! Yet he couldn't even bear to leave it in his room when he went out.

"Odd, isn't it, that the plague now strikes at the heart of Shenat," Fox said. It wasn't a question.

Saker shrugged, but his chest tightened. "Quite logical if it's an A'Va-inspired illness. Where better to attack than at the heart of the Faith?"

"The heart of the Faith lies in the Pontificate, not the wastes of northern Ardrone, among ignorant farmers and shepherds," Fox snapped. "More to the point, why does Va do nothing when it strikes where Va-Faith was supposedly birthed? This disease has shaken my belief in the authenticity of the Shenat-based Way of the Oak. Twenty-five of those who died were shrine-keepers. Not a single shrine-keeper who fell ill recovered, in spite of the heartfelt prayers of the shrine's adherents."

He was dizzy with shock. "What – what are you saying, your eminence?"

"Shenat is no more than a withered root to a much greater faith. We city clerics worked among the sick with impunity. The shrine-keepers died. Va rules, not the Way of the Oak. We must learn to bend our knees to the greater deity, not to an oak tree and its supposed unseen guardian! The Horned Death is indeed sent by A'Va, and he attacks our weakest point, an old and crumbling idea that barely scratches the glory of Va's creation."

Saker stared at him, horror rising like bile. Against his thigh, the dagger twisted and turned, as if trying to free itself from its containment. He held his arm flat to his side to subdue it. It was a moment before he could give voice to his strangled protest, "You can't be serious! The Way makes Va's wishes comprehensible to mankind. By adhering to the Way of the Oak and the Way of the Flow, we protect all of Va's creation. You can't separate one from the other!"

"I've seen the proof that says otherwise. Our generation will oversee the death of the Ways." He turned to face Saker. "This is your chance, Witan Saker, your only chance to choose the true path. I beg you, think deeply on this."

"You're out of your mind," he blurted. No sooner were the words said than he knew he'd made a terrible mistake. He should've dissembled; he should have done anything rather than outright contradict the Prime. He said, more carefully, "Your eminence, perhaps we should discuss this another time, once you have rested from your long and arduous journey and I've had time to think on your words."

There was a long silence and then Fox said, "Perhaps." His voice held a world-weariness in its tone that might have moved Saker if it hadn't been matched by an implacable look in his eyes as cold as wind-borne northern snows – and far more frightening.

"One other matter, witan," Fox added. "The King is concerned at signs of rebellion in the Princess. Please remind her that it is a daughter's bounden duty to obey her father, just as it is a father's duty to do what is best for his daughter. I have counselled him to that effect; you must do likewise for the Lady Mathilda. See to it that she accepts with regal grace and dignity whatever decision King Edwayn makes, knowing that it will be in her interest. You may go."

As he walked away from the Prime's door, his thoughts seethed like an agitated sea. For once he wasn't interested in the numerous clerics scurrying through the corridors with their files, all part of Fox's administration of Ardrone's Va-Faith.

What he wanted most of all was to speak to the Pontifect. With a sinking heart, he realised that all he believed to be true – Shenat, the sanctity of shrines and the Way of the Oak – was tumbling towards disaster. There was something at work here that was deeper, more sinister than he knew how to tackle. A pox on Fritillary for tying him down to this post when he could have done so much more as a spy!

When he reached his room, he sat down and wrote to her using their long established codes, detailing all that Fox had said. Dressed in the drabbest of undistinguished clothing, he walked into the city to deliver the missive to her courier, using all his normal ways of ensuring he wasn't followed. He dived unexpectedly into a crowd, changed direction once and doubled back twice. He saw nothing unexpected, no one who seemed out of place, and yet, halfway to the courier's house, the lascar's dagger started to writhe in its scabbard.

As an added precaution, he then stepped into a baker's through one door and immediately exited through the back kitchen. Lurking in a nearby alley, he watched the kitchen entrance. No one emerged.

The dagger still refused to lie quiet, but this time he decided to ignore it. He continued along to the Three-Horned Ox, where he ordered a slice of roast duck with apple sauce dumplings. Afterwards, as he paid the courier's wife for the meal, he dropped his letter surreptitiously into her lap.

Back in his room, he unsheathed the dagger and turned it over and over in his hands. It lay there, quiescent, the gold filaments dulled. He placed a fingertip on the blade and then snatched it back. The metal had *burned* him. A blister was forming on the skin of his forefinger.

"You swag-bellied whelp of a haggard!" he swore. In a futile expression of his anger at his powerlessness, he removed the kris from its sheath and flung it through the window opening into the gardens below.

Useless, of course. It would be back.

The following morning, he resisted the urge to visit the gardens under his window, and walked to the port instead. There he found Juster striding off his ship, now tied up quayside as the final varnish was applied and the rigging tested. He waved when he saw Saker and came across to clap him on the back. "Well met, my friend. Come, let's wipe that frown from your brow! I was just about to head to the Wharfside Rats to have an ale or two. What's niggling you this time, you inveterate worrier?"

"Valerian Fox."

"Ah, our beloved Prime, the snake. Never trusted that man. Always been too . . . Lowmian."

"That's hardly a crime. Or a sin. Or even something nasty. I have some very good Lowmian friends." With a pang, he thought of Gerelda, and missed her sharp wit and analytical intelligence.

"I know, but I love poking at the purity of your witan's soul. Tell me what he's done now."

As they walked the length of the wharf, dodging the longshoremen trundling barrows and hefting sacks, Saker recounted his conversation with Fox. The buccaneer said nothing until they were in the tavern and had their ales in front of them. Then he leaned back against the wall behind and said, with a grimness in his steady gaze, "Well, there's something I can tell you immediately. Fox told you for a reason. Certainly had nothing to do with wanting to convert you to his way of thinking. If there is anything he must be certain of, it's that you're dedicated to the Way of the Oak.

"The other thing he must know is that you'll tell the Pontifect. Maybe that's why he told you. Or maybe he just wants you to accuse him of denigrating the Shenat so he can deny he ever said any such thing, and squash you like a bug beneath his elegantly shod foot."

Saker rolled his eyes. "Thank you for that image. Doubtless it will return in a nightmare sometime. Somehow, though, I don't think I'm big enough to be more than a stingless gnat as far as Fox is concerned. Whatever his plan is, I'm only incidental."

"So he has something bigger in mind. Sounds as if he's planning to rid the Faith of both Shenat influence and the Way of the Flow beliefs."

"The sick feeling in the pit of my stomach has just grown larger," Saker replied. "I was hoping it was me seeing a monster where there was none. Was it the Prime you meant when you spoke of the danger close to home?"

Juster took a long draught of his ale, and wiped his mouth with the back of his hand. "What do you think?"

Saker said slowly, elaborating on his thoughts only with reluctance, "He wants to divide the Faith and ultimately unseat the Pontifect. To take her place." The idea of the Pontificate without Fritillary to lead it was bad enough; the thought of Valerian Fox instead was unspeakable disaster.

"Very possibly."

"Va forbid." Saker played with his mug, still trying to make sense of the unthinkable. "When he was in the north, maybe he recognised an opportunity in the Horned Death, and seized it. The Shenat are dying up there. The very people who support the Pontifect most. Without shrine-keepers, what will happen?"

"He's not a fool. Wouldn't do this unless he has substantial backing elsewhere," Juster said.

"He wouldn't have much from the Innerlands. They've always supported Fritillary Reedling." But city clerics in Lowmeer and Ardrone? He wasn't so sure.

Juster leaned forward and lowered his voice. "Any new candidate must have the support of both King Edwayn and Regal Vilmar. They are the real power in the Va-cherished Hemisphere. They can promote a change, or hinder it. If you're right, no wonder Fox wasn't happy when the Pontifect sent you, a Shenat-born cleric, as spiritual adviser to Edwayn's heir, Prince Ryce. Which might be a good reason for him to bring you tumbling down."

"I don't know why either Regal Vilmar or King Edwayn would support him."

"They might do it for monetary gain. Commercial advantage."

He rolled his eyes. "*What* monetary gain? The Pontificate is always scrounging for money just to keep charity work alive. No cleric is rich, and shrine-keepers are downright poor!"

They were silent for a moment, both of them deep in thought, before Saker added, "We know King Edwayn supports Fox – he chose him as the Ardronese Prime, although I've no idea why."

"The King went to shrine-keepers for help when the Queen was dying. Their prayers didn't help. Edwayn was bitter. He turned away from shrines, and when the Prime's seat fell vacant, there was Fox, with his emphasis on chapels and praying direct to Va. But I want to know why Fox revealed so much to you."

"I don't know."

"Careful, Saker. Put one foot wrong, and you'll end up getting yourself unfrocked, or worse. Like dead."

"You exaggerate, surely."

"Listen to me, my friend. I don't *know* anything. But I've been sailing the seas since I was twelve. Been from here to Karradar and Javenka. Visited every tavern brothel and low dive on every wharf in Lowmeer and Ardrone, and there's not much I haven't seen of reeky scum and craven curs. And every now and then among the wretches and the flea-bitten varlets, I meet someone who sends a prickle down my spine and dries out my mouth with fear. Not because they're scurvy, or because they're murdering mongrels, but because they are *evil*. Some charming, rich, even generous, but there's always something in the back of their eyes that tells me what is in their black hearts."

He stopped talking to drain the last of his ale, then added, "Prime Valerian Fox is one of those men. Don't know how I know. Never done anything to me, but I *know*. He's an evil man. Not just dishonest, or untrustworthy. *Evil*. He'd not only squash you under his heel, but he'd walk over your dead body and hardly even notice, let alone care. There's something about Saker Rampion *in particular* that he doesn't like."

"And you don't know what it is. This sounds like a silly riddle to me."

"Ah yes, riddle me, riddle me, riddle-me-ree. 'Person who makes it sells it. Person who buys it never uses it, person who uses it doesn't know it. What is it?' That's exactly why I wouldn't say anything earlier. You wouldn't have listened, because it would have sounded so silly. Now perhaps you will, because it doesn't sound quite so stupid, does it?"

Saker was silent. Juster continued, "And I'll tell you one more thing. Almost all those evil men were Lowmians."

"Fox isn't Lowmian."

"His mother was Lowmian, and Fox himself was born in Ustgrind. There's a darkness growing in Lowmeer."

"Va damn it, Juster! Must you be so ambiguous?"

"Did you know that one of my relatives on my mother's side was the Regal's first wife?"

"No. No, I didn't."

"She was also a cousin of King Edwayn's. Ten years married to the Regal, and she was childless and unhappy. Then she died. Her father always thought the Regal murdered her. She smuggled out a hurriedly scribbled note to him, saying she feared for her life because she'd found out the truth about the Dire Sweepers."

"What are they?"

"She said they were a band of assassins under the Regal's orders. That was all she had time to write. She died of a stomach complaint the very next day. The Regal said her illness made her irrational, and King Edwayn chose to believe that. Perhaps it was even true."

"But you don't believe it."

He fiddled with his tankard, not meeting Saker's eyes. "I tell everyone I'm a privateer because I'm a born greedy adventurer. Untrue. Ah, well, let's say *partially* untrue. The other part is because there is something in Lowmeer that frightens me. Not the ordinary citizen, who's just like you or me, but something deep and dark. I want to keep that land bog-weak, and privateering is my way of doing it." He looked up. "No matter what happens in the future, remember that. Juster Dornbeck is scared of something at the very heart of Lowmeer. And you ought to be frightened, *because Valerian Fox told you his plan*. A man shares that kind of secret only with a fellow conspirator – or someone easily cozened into doing something stupid. You don't want to be either."

He stood, tossing some coins down on the table for the ale. Saker sat and watched as he walked away, slipping a coin into the cleavage of the barmaid on his way out. From the grin she gave him, she was an old friend.

He remained, nursing the last of his ale, until he'd worked out the answer to the riddle.

A coffin.

* * *

Back in his room that evening, he lay on his bed with his hands behind his head, deep in thought. His mind kept churning up the same indigestible fact that he couldn't explain: the Prime had displayed courage and compassion by staying in the north during an extended epidemic of the Horned Death. He'd worked tirelessly with no thought for his own safety.

Fox himself had said little about his part; the details had come from the servants who'd accompanied him – the coachmen, his manservant, his scribe, his page. The idea of doing something like that himself scared Saker witless, but every account he'd heard included fulsome praise of the Prime. He was already doubting his own interpretation of events, but it wasn't Fox's words that had sowed the seeds of his uncertainty. It was the nobility of the man's actions.

A knock roused him from his reverie. When he opened the door, one of the footmen was standing there. "Begging your pardon, witan," he said, "but I was wondering if this was yours. One of the gardeners found it under your window."

He held out his open hand. The lascar's kris lay on his palm.

There was nothing Saker could do but reach out and take it back.

14

The Dagger by Night

When Saker delivered his next official report to Faith House, late one afternoon, he did not return to the palace afterwards. On each previous visit to the House, he'd studied the layout of the building carefully. Several times he'd pretended to lose himself in the labyrinthine corridors, so that he had a ready explanation for being discovered where he had no right to be. No one had made much of it, merely laughing and saying they'd got lost too, at first.

He'd found what he was seeking, a room that was little more than a cupboard, empty and dusty and forgotten, tucked away under the eaves on the top floor in the same wing as the Prime's office.

Now, after giving his latest report to Secretary Pedding, he headed upwards, walking purposefully with a sheaf of papers in his hand, ignoring the clerks and clerics scurrying by on their own errands. He'd learned long ago that a man could get away with much if he looked busy. Once he reached the cupboard without anyone remarking on his presence, he shut himself in, jamming the door so it could not be opened from outside. He already knew that although all visitors were vetted by clerical guards on entering, no one checked afterwards to see if a visitor had actually left.

He took off his witan's robe and used it to block the gap under the door. Underneath he was wearing his working clothes: dull and dark and comfortable, containing numerous pouches and pockets to hide useful items. From one such he drew out his tinderbox, flint and steel; from another a four-hour candle inside a small collapsible lantern of his own design. Once it was lit, he reduced the light to little more than a glimmer by manipulating the lantern shutters.

He settled down to wait. From time to time footsteps passed the door, and he heard occasional laughter or snatches of conversation. At nightfall, those sounds ceased.

When the candle was almost done, he lit another. When that was half burned, he opened the door and stepped out into the silent building. He stood for a long time, listening. Faith House was home to the Prime and most of his numerous staff, but they lived in a different wing. He was still in the administrative side and, he hoped, at this time of the night the offices would be empty.

When he was sure no one moved anywhere nearby, he reached back into the cupboard and picked up his discarded robe and the lantern. His sword and the lascar's dagger were both sheathed at his waist, one on either side. His shoes were his soft leather ones that made no sound on the boards.

He made for the stairs, but did not descend the treads. He already knew they creaked. Instead, he slid down the banisters. From the bottom, it wasn't far to the Prime's office, and it was the work of moments to pick the primitive lock on the door. Obviously the Prime was supremely confident that no one would ever dare to break in.

He stepped into the outer office where Secretary Pedding usually sat, relocked the door from the inside and threw his robe over the back of the secretary's chair. The lascar's dagger writhed at his hip. He cursed it under his breath, drew it from its sheath and laid it down on Pedding's desk before he began to search.

His task was made all the more difficult because he had no real idea what he was looking for, and he needed to take scrupulous care to leave no clues behind. Pedding's office yielded nothing except ledgers of data on Ardrone's numerous clerics, religious establishments and shrines.

The second room was the office where Valerian Fox received visitors. He spent an hour there, but once again found nothing that indicated anything except meticulous record-keeping, much of it in Fox's bold hand. Every time the Prime had a visitor, he'd recorded the name, the date, the topic discussed and decisions made. Sometimes there were more personal observations on the character or appearance of those visiting. "Slovenly," said one comment. "Capable and unimaginative," said another. Saker could not resist looking up his own name, only to find there was no comment at all, not even on his first visit, or his last.

And that was a curious omission.

When he moved on to the third room, he found the door locked.

This time it took him almost half an hour to conquer the locking mechanism, which he took as a sign that there would be something worth hiding within.

At first glance it appeared to be no more than a pleasant sitting room with a large fireplace, rugs, chairs and an embroidered banner, twice his height and four paces broad, hanging on the wall. The embroidery portrayed an oak tree, its twigs in full summer leaf, and its root system branching below the ground.

And that was a curious decoration to have on the wall of a man who despised everything about the Way of the Oak. He lifted it to look behind.

A number of shelves were recessed into the stone wall, and they were filled with more ledgers. One by one he opened them and read a few pages of each. Some were lists of names and payments; others were labelled "Resources". He could make little sense of what he saw, but it appeared to be no more than more information-collecting. Yet . . . why hide the ledgers under the banner?

He was running out of time. He committed some of the names and amounts to memory, hoping that when he had time to think, he might be able to see some kind of pattern.

Letting the banner drop, he was about to return the way he'd come when a flash of silver slithering across the floor caught his eye. His first horrified reaction, that it was a snake, gave way to an almost equally appalled realisation that it was the dagger. It wriggled – fast – past him, the blade as sinuous and supple as any serpent, dragging the more static hilt behind it like an unwanted cart, and stopped two paces in front of the banner, where it coalesced back into a dagger once more, just metal and bone.

Saker gathered his scattered wits and bent to pick it up. Before his fingers could grasp the handle, it shot upwards, spinning, to bury itself point first into the base of the embroidered tree trunk. Aghast, he raised his lantern to look.

Pox 'n' pustules, you misbegotten offspring of a lascar!

He pulled it out carefully, then jammed it savagely back into its sheath. His heart sank when he examined the cut it had made. It was all too obvious, and the threads around it had begun to unravel. He groaned. So much for secrecy.

In the slim hope that he might be able to disguise some of the damage by pulling threads through to the reverse side, he lifted the banner once more, this time to look at the back. When he raised the candle to see better, he was transfixed. The embroidery on the wrong side bore no resemblance to that on the front.

He was staring not at an oak tree, but at a family tree, an embroidered lineage diagram. At the top was a crest, not one he ever remembered seeing, featuring a pizzled red fox running across the field of the escutcheon, a white goose gripped in its mouth. The fox was grinning.

Underneath were the embroidered names and dates and linking lines that made up the family ancestry. The top entries were faded, as if they'd been made long ago; the final name at the bottom, sewn with bright red thread, was Valerian Fox – and the dagger had neatly sliced through the Prime's first name.

No sooner had he absorbed that much than the candle guttered and he was blinking in a blackness so deep he could have been rendered blind. The darkness was total because all the windows were tightly shuttered.

He swore. He didn't have another candle. Groping, he retraced his way to Pedding's office. Once there, his questing fingers found his robe. Then, still cursing, he remembered he hadn't relocked the door to the inner sitting room. He had to go back.

While he was still feeling his way through the doorway into the Prime's office, he heard a key inserted into the main door. Horrified, he shut the office door, then blundered across the room, mercifully without noise, despite bruising his shins on a chair and knocking his elbow on the side of the Prime's desk.

Creeping his way along the wall, he found the entrance to the sitting room, slipped inside and closed the door. His fingers fumbled with his lock picks, as he tried to remember the sequence that would lock it again. Fortunately it was something he did by feel rather than sight, and he let out the breath he'd been holding when he heard the lock click into place.

If the newcomer had heard it, or if he wanted something from the sitting room, he was doomed. There was no hiding place. The only exit was through a shuttered window three storeys above the ground.

No, wait. There was a fireplace. Va, what he wouldn't give for a light! He crept across the room, his robe tucked under an arm, until his shoe stubbed on the iron fireguard. He ducked down into the empty fireplace, glad that the grate was newly cleaned. Feeling around with his fingers, he pushed open the iron damper until it lay flat against the back of the bricks of the chimney flue. It was a wide opening, allowing him to stand up inside the actual chimney. He looked up. Far above he could see the light of a moonlit sky filtering in through chimney pots.

He fumbled around at the wall in front of him, until he felt a chimney sweep's climbing rung. Good, he could climb out. Hurriedly he pulled his witan's robe on over his head; it was easier to wear than carry, and he couldn't leave it behind.

And just then he heard the unmistakable sound of a key turning in the lock of the door behind him.

Gripping the rung, he hauled his knees and feet up. With infinite care, hanging by one hand, he reached his other hand down to close the damper, and to do it in utter silence. Just before he edged it shut, the room beyond flooded with candlelight.

He only relaxed when the chimney plunged back into darkness as the damper slotted into place. Taking a deep breath, he began to climb. The chimney flue was narrow, the robe was cumbersome and the dust of ash and soot made him ache to sneeze or cough. Every now and then he dislodged a shower of soot. Because he'd closed the damper, none of it would billow out into the room, but he worried that the noise of its fall would signal his presence. He hitched up his robe between his legs and climbed as if someone was about to light a fire under him.

At the top of the chimney, he found his exit blocked by four chimney pots. Fortunately, the lime mortar was old and cracked, and when he scratched at it with his dagger, chunks of it fell away. Even so, no amount of pushing and heaving on his part budged the pots from their place. Swearing under his breath, he continued scraping and shoving until one final heave sent them crashing down on to the roof. They exploded on the copper surface like thunder, the pieces clattering down the pitch towards the guttering loud enough to wake every sleeping cleric in the building.

He levered himself out of the chimney, jumped on to the roof, hitched up his filthy robe and began to run. At least it was a bright moonlit night and his footing was sure. Somewhere below people shouted, wanting to know what was happening, but he took no notice. He couldn't see anyone and guessed they were calling out from their windows after hearing the crash of the falling chimney pots. Somewhere ahead he'd find a way down to the ground; the Faith House roof connected to other buildings along the street.

Tarnation, he thought. *How am I going to enter the palace when I must look like a chimney sweep?* He'd have to find a bathhouse that was open . . .

The night that Ardhi decided to reclaim his kris was a dark one, moonless and wet. Rain – birthed in storm clouds and borne on cold winds – gusted in drenching bursts. Any sensible person was inside, tucked up in a warm bed. Ardhi, however, was scaling the outer wall that circled the grounds of the King's palace in the heart of Throssel.

At last it is within reach . . . I can feel it, so close now. His eyes misted over, with rain, or tears of relief and anticipation, he couldn't tell.

It had taken him more than a year to arrive in Throssel. In Oakwood, he'd lost several months to illness, holed up in a Shenat hospice coughing his lungs inside out. Once he was on his feet again, the trail was cold and he'd taken the wrong road south. Forced to backtrack, he'd sold his hoard of spices little by little, marvelling at how high the price spiralled, until at last he found traces of the Chenderawasi *sakti* again. After he'd arrived in Throssel, his search had been no easier: there were traces of the kris everywhere. His problem had become to sort out which were the most recent. In that, he'd failed. He'd criss-crossed the city, but all he could determine for sure was that the power of his kris pooled thickest somewhere in the King's palace, and the palace was the best guarded building in all Throssel. And so he'd bided his time, waiting for a night when the darkness was deep, and the weather a friend.

Now, finally, the time had come. As he clawed his way up the wall, the touch of the kris in the air overwhelmed even the bitter chill of the rain; it drowned the moan of the wind, subdued the smell of salt swept in on the spume from the sea. He shuddered under its spell.

The year had changed him in ways he'd not expected. He'd finally accepted the need to be inconspicuous, to wear Ardronese shoes and clothes, to trim his hair to a shorter length, to appear more like one of the Va-cherished. He'd worked hard at mastering the language, and understanding a way of life not his own. He'd watched and learned and remembered. But through it all, the loss of his kris haunted him.

Now the anticipation of holding it once more was as painful as a fist around his heart. Soon he would have protection once again; soon he'd be enveloped in the safety of a familiar magic. He would once again smell the beaches and forests of home.

His bare toes and fingertips gripped the rough stones of the wall, his body perfectly balanced, his strength effortless. At the top, he lay flat on the stones for a moment, careful not to offer a silhouette against the sky, even though he thought it unlikely he would be seen in this rain. Still, there'd be guards about. He'd already dodged those outside the walls on their endless trudge around the perimeter.

Inside the wall was a garden. It wasn't a concept he truly understood; in the islands, if you wanted beauty and a place to walk, then you entered the forest, you didn't plant a garden. Planting was for food. He looked beyond the long hedges and the patches of lawn to the building beyond, looming huge, large almost beyond his comprehension.

How many people must live here! He couldn't fathom why any raja or king would need so many people about him, but it didn't matter, so he pushed the puzzling thought away.

Before dropping down into the garden, he pinpointed the section of the building that held the kris. The windows there were smaller and, he guessed, shuttered rather than glassed. He slipped down the wall and scuttled low through the hedges until he was crouched on the ground as close to the concentration of Chenderawasi power as he could get without another climb. There, he froze. Someone was coming.

He resisted the urge to run. Instead he lowered himself slowly, edging down until he was no more than a dark ball at the base of a bush. His view was restricted to what he could observe by peeking out under his armpit. He eased out the dagger thrust through his belt until it was in his hand.

Head down, a guard plodded his way between the hedges. A stream of muttered curses was testament to his hatred of the weather and his fobbing guard duties. He was holding something Ardhi guessed might have been a flintlock arquebus. He knew about those; on the

Kesleer ship all the tars had been taught how to aim and fire them. He also knew damp weather could make them misfire. With his memory of Raja Wiramulia's shattered chest, he loathed them with a bitter hatred.

Squinting against the driving rain, the man brushed by, oblivious to his presence. When he was gone, Ardhi slowly unwound himself, took a deep breath, and began to climb the wall of the palace.

Even in the dark, his fingertips and his bare toes were attuned to every roughness, to every tiny crack and crevice, to every unevenness. He used friction and balance with the instincts of an animal, without thinking. Walls were tougher than the rock or trees of his island home, but his natural skill and strength were enhanced. *Sakti.* It was with him yet. That, at least, had not left him.

He'd hoped the first-storey window was the one he wanted, but the touch of the kris drew him on, beckoning him still higher. It was the third window up that led into the room that housed the kris. The shutters, made of perpendicular wooden planks, were barred inside against the weather. In front of it, the window ledge – a wide stone block – was exposed to the elements.

He sat hunched over on the ledge and contemplated what to do next. He had no idea what was on the other side of the shutters; for all he knew, the room beyond could have been filled with guards.

Drawing his dagger, he began picking at the bottom crosspiece of the left-hand shutter, loosening the wooden nails. In the dark, it was mostly guesswork, aided by the fact that he'd examined similar windows. Since his failure at the Kesleer warehouse, he'd become obsessive about things like that. Right then, he was glad.

The rain stopped; the wind dropped and then blew with renewed vigour. In a brief appearance, moonlight broke through the cloud cover and then disappeared. He worked on, ignoring the guards who periodically crossed the gardens below, ignoring the distant sounds of drunken revelry somewhere in the palace. The shavings of wood whisked away on the wind as fast as he created them. It was three o'clock, as tolled by the bell on the palace tower. Such regimented timekeeping was foreign to the Chenderawasi, but right then he appreciated its usefulness. He had another two hours before the first stirrings of the city would make his escape hazardous.

A single vertical board from the inner edge of one shutter came loose in his grip. He lifted it free of the inside bar and pulled it through the opening to the outside. Peering into the room, he could see nothing, although the sound of steady breathing told him the room was occupied. His other senses told him the dagger was there, unharmed and unsecured. His exultation almost stopped his breath.

At last.

His loneliness was over. The long months when he'd been powerless, helpless, unable to pursue his quest to seize back the stolen regalia, because without the kris he had no idea where to look. He stayed where he was, secure in the knowledge that the kris would come to him, that he would find out now why it had left him in the first place.

Inside the room the sleeper stirred, made restless perhaps by the wind entering through the gap in the shutter. Ardhi held his breath, but the rustle of a body turning in the blankets settled down once more and the sound of regular deep breathing resumed.

Ardhi waited.

Nothing happened. Nothing stirred in the room. The kris did not move. The scent of its power remained exactly where it had been when he'd first arrived at the window. As the time passed, he decided the weapon must be constrained after all. Or maybe it was essential for the good of the Chenderawasi that the sleeping man die by his hand and the kris was waiting for him to enter and perform the deed.

He subdued his exasperation. Instead, he slipped his arm back into the room and edged the bar to the shutter upwards. He had to contort himself to pull it free without dropping it to the floor, but finally the shutters opened and he slipped inside the room. He closed them behind him to shut out the worst of the wind, but laid the bar down on the floor. He might need to disappear out of the window in a hurry.

Gradually his eyes adjusted to the increased darkness. A fire had been banked in a fireplace, so with delicate care he parted the coals, allowing them to flame. By their light, he examined the room, ignoring his desire to go straight to the kris. He needed to find out as much as possible about the man – and it was a man, he could see that much – who slept in the bed. The clothes hanging from the knob on the back of the door he recognised. He'd seen those on his journey through Shenat country. A witan's garb.

Silently he knelt beside the bed, to stare at the man's face. In the dim light he couldn't be absolutely sure, but he thought it was the fellow from Kesleer's warehouse. He wore the same medallion around his neck. Ardhi knew the meaning of it now: the oaken symbol of Va-Faith as worn by an Ardronese man of religion.

He bent to look under the bed. A chamber pot. A pair of boots, a pair of buckled shoes. Nearby, a chest. He prised it open: some neatly folded clothing. Books. He eased it closed. He stood to look at the things on the table in the corner. A jug, a washbasin, a towel. A flagon and a pewter mug. Some writing materials. A candle, tinderbox, steel and flint. A sword in a scabbard. An ordinary dagger – and the kris, separately sheathed. A cloak draped over the chair.

He reached out to the kris, fingers trembling, pulled it gently from its sheath. Closed his hand over the hilt and felt again the raw power of Raja Wiramulia's bone beneath his fingers. Shards of memory splintered in his mind, stabbed him to the marrow with the tragedy his stupidity had initiated.

Raising the weapon, he touched the hilt to his forehead in obeisance and grief. His cheeks ran with tears.

"Come," he whispered in the language of his island, and headed to the window once more.

The kris twisted savagely in his hand, forcing his fingers apart, wrenching his thumb backwards. He gasped as it fell free. It clattered noisily on the floorboards. Even then it refused to lie still. It skittered across the room, before sliding deep under the bed. He stood stock still, so utterly shocked at his rejection he almost didn't react when the man on the bed erupted upwards.

At the last moment, Ardhi flung himself backwards, hitting the floor hard. And under his leg felt the bar for the shutters. His hand groped for it, and when the man came at him again, he lashed the bar sideways into his knee. His assailant fell backwards against the stone of the wall, and was eerily silent. And motionless.

Seri save him, I think I've killed him.

He stood up, still in shock. Gathering his scattered wits, he took the candle from the table and lit the wick by holding it against the glow of a coal. The fellow was lying on the floor, unmoving. He knelt beside him and lifted one of the man's eyelids. There was no reaction, although he was still breathing.

Perhaps I should *kill him. Perhaps the kris wants him dead.*

No, that couldn't be right. The kris had *warned* the witan that he, Ardhi, was in his room.

The bitterness he felt at the betrayal was acid in his throat. Was it punishment for his failure? He doubted that. The *sakti* of a Chenderawasi kris was never petty. He might have deserved punishment, but the kris was only ever motivated by concern for the greater good of the Chenderawasi.

The message was clear. When the kris had flung itself across the warehouse, it had been a deliberate act of abandonment for him and a new bonding for it with the witan, for reasons he would never be able to fathom.

Desolated, shattered, he knew now he should have accepted that. Instead he had crossed these strange lands for nothing. He had wasted more than a year of his time. He covered his face with his hands and dragged in a shuddering breath.

Outside, the wind bore the sound of the four o'clock bell. He sat back on his heels, gutted. Why did the kris no longer want him? His task was still undone!

So what do I do now, Sri Kris?

Under the bed, the kris was silent and still.

He supplied the answer himself. He must return to Lowmeer, to Ustgrind. He must go back to work for the Kesleer Trading Company. He must find out what had happened to the stolen regalia and retrieve it without the aid of the kris.

He bit his lip, brushed away the tears, accepted his fate. As gently as he could, he hauled the unconscious witan back towards the bed, then heaved him up on to the mattress. The man did not wake, not even when Ardhi covered him warmly.

He blew out the candle and replaced the holder on the table. He left the kris under the bed; it did not need him to move. Pulling the shutters closed behind him, he put his arm through the gap and manoeuvred the bar back into its place. There was nothing he could do about the board he had removed, so he left it on the windowsill.

He scanned the garden to make sure there were no guards around, then began to descend.

In the morning he would go down to the port and seek a sailor's berth on a ship bound for Ustgrind. Tars could always find work.

Saker awoke into a grey morning light, feeling cold. For a moment he lay still, wondering what was wrong. Then he sat bolt upright.

Va curdle me, what the fobbing . . .

His head spun and pain shot from the back of his skull through his brain to his eyes. He swayed and had to put out a hand to stop himself from falling back on his pillow.

There was a gap in his shutters, and a puddle of rainwater on the floor. Moving his head slowly, he surveyed the room. The kris lay in the middle of the floor and its scabbard was empty on the table. His candle had been moved.

Oh, spittle damn, I wasn't drunk *last night, was I?*

He vaguely recalled a nightmare. There had been a brawl, and rain, and pain in his knee . . .

For the life of him he couldn't remember anything more. He groaned and swung his feet to the floor. He was late for morning prayers.

15

The Buccaneer's Wager

Life at court continued without change as autumn crawled its way towards winter. If the King and his courtiers were worried about the plague to the north, they didn't show it, although Saker heard that King Edwayn had sent guards to block the main roads entering Throssel to anyone who appeared sick or weak.

If there were ever any repercussions about the dagger cut on the Prime's embroidered banner, Saker never heard about them. When he returned from that adventure, he'd written down all he could remember from the ledgers he'd seen. He mulled it over, put it away, then considered it again. So much of what he remembered had been abbreviations. What, for example, in a ledger labelled "Resources", did *Mi.For.Okwd* mean? Abbreviations like that had headed columns of tree names, followed by a number and then a value. Some kind of code, he assumed.

Another ledger had been labelled "Lances". It had contained lists of people grouped into tens, each group headed by the name of a place, most of them in Ardrone, although he recognised villages and towns from all over the Va-cherished Hemisphere. He estimated there could have been as many as five thousand people listed.

He'd thought about sending his notes to the Pontifect, but had ultimately decided against it. She'd only be angry that he'd taken such a risk for so little coherent return. He'd tell her about it when he knew more.

As for the night the lascar's dagger had apparently tried to dig the nails out of his bedroom shutter . . . He *thought* he remembered fighting someone, but in the morning the door and the window shutters had still been barred from the inside. His window was three storeys up, and the gap made by the single missing board – which he'd found on the outer sill – would not have allowed entry to anything bigger than a cat. In fact, the events were so bizarre, and his blurred memory of them so weird, he thought it all better forgotten. *Just the kris up to its usual tricks . . .*

He remained alert and watchful, more cautious about his personal safety than usual, while he waited for a communication from the Pontifect. As a result of his conversation with Juster, he'd sent another letter after the first, with an even stronger warning. As time passed, he wondered at the lack of reply, and sent a third communication, even though the courier's wife assured him coldly that all his letters had been delivered to Vavala. He'd never warmed to her, but her frigid reception of his last letter made him wonder if she was furious with him for involving her husband in something she thought clandestine.

While he waited, it was the Princess who diverted him, who brought both joy and inspiration to his days. Trailed by her grey mouse of a handmaiden, she kept him constantly at her side, although it was her future that concerned her most, not her religious life.

"Amuse me, witan," she said one day. "Tell me what it's like to go to a university and study." The next day it was a request that he tell her tales of his boyhood on the farm; after that she wanted him to relate the tales told by the Pashali traders, and describe the mastodon caravans that rode into Muntdorn through Coldheart Pass. She laughed at his silly jokes, teased him about his childhood escapades and his first love, and listened wide-eyed when he described his adventures as a sixteen-year-old acolyte taking foolish risks for all the wrong reasons.

Every now and then, his breath would catch as she fought tears at a mention of her marriage, or lifted her chin when someone spoke of the Regal. Once, when Prince Ryce carelessly told her she would bring brightness to the Lowmian court if she married Vilmar, she'd clutched Saker's arm so tightly, her fingers bruised him. The terror that flared in her eyes tore his heart to shreds, yet there was nothing he could do. His counsel was trite, and left the taste of ashes in his mouth. He tried to imagine what it could possibly be like for her to have a father using her as a commodity in a business transaction, to be refused any information about her future until it was settled, to know she was to be traded away to a foreign country, to be made aware that she had to accept whatever others decided for her.

Worst of all, he was the one who had to guide her to acceptance and submission. He agonised over whether to tell her what Juster had said about Regal Vilmar's first wife, torn between warning her and making her acceptance of her fate even harder. Inside, he wanted to spit at the injustice of it all.

As the days shortened and the colours of the oaks peaked, there was more news from Lowmeer about the preparation of the Lowmian Spicerie Trading Company's new spice fleet. There'd been delays, according to the Prince, probably something to do with the shortage of cladding for the hulls against shipworm.

"Terrible little beasties, those worms," Juster told Saker with a grave shake of his head as they walked through the city in search of a tavern to have a midday meal. "In warm seas, they can turn good strong oak planking into wet sawdust. The Lowmians were well advised to clad their ships. Pity they had trouble finding the right metals for the job."

"By which I take it your ship is cladded against these worms and perhaps you had something to do with the shortage of the cladding?"

"Me? Tush! True, my cousins do have an interest in the East Denva copper mines, but how could I possibly have had anything to do with delays?"

"Indeed." The man was incorrigible.

"Witan?" someone asked at Saker's elbow. He turned to see the ten-year-old son of the courier who took his letters to the Pontifect. "My da said I was to give you this." He handed over a slim packet wrapped in canvas and quickly disappeared into the crowded street.

He knew the handwriting scrawled on the cover; it belonged to the Pontifect's elderly secretary, Barden.

"From the Pontifect?" Juster asked. "Open it up. I know you've been waiting for it."

It contained a short note from Fritillary. He read it twice, stabbed through with surprise. It contained no thanks for his intelligence, and no instructions about what to do next.

I have considered your information and will be taking action. In the meantime, you're to confine yourself to advising the Lady

Mathilda to marry as she is instructed, and to continue to bestow your spiritual advice on her and his highness Prince Ryce.

She'd signed it using her full title, not as she usually did with her initials. Deeply annoyed, he folded the note and tucked it into his sleeve, unsettled. He'd just been put very firmly in his place. Fritillary was going to use other agents to deal with the matter. When it came to an affair of real importance, he was being relegated to the role of spiritual nursemaid.

The following week, Lord Juster Dornbeck feted his friends aboard his new galleon, *Golden Petrel*, to celebrate the ship's completion.

The vessel rode at anchor on Throssel Water within sight of Throssel Palace, bobbing gently in the middle of a cluster of river barges like an elegant mother swan surrounded by fussing cygnets. Saker lounged against the taffrail, observing another crowd of bejewelled courtiers being rowed across on the royal galley to join the party. The flag at the stern told him they included his two charges, Prince Ryce and Lady Mathilda.

Watched by a nervous riverman, the Prince – having commandeered the sweep – was standing in the stern doing a reasonable job of keeping the vessel heading in the correct direction. The Princess, shaded by the silken canopy, ignored the antics of her brother and sat chatting with her ladies-in-waiting in the prow. Celandine the mouse, grey-eyed, meek and dull, dressed as usual in her grey widow's weeds, watched expressionless.

Saker wondered how much longer Mathilda was going to stay compliant and accept she had no say in her future. When he'd tried to draw parallels between her and her mother, who'd been a Staravale princess sent to marry Edwayn, she'd given him a flinty stare, saying, "Yes, my mother was sold too. After all, a princess is never more than an offering made by one *man* to another, never more than a cynical gift from one monarch to another, all to secure a bargain that is rarely kept!"

He'd been unable to hide a wince.

Her laughter came to him now as she clambered up the ladder on to the deck, hampered by her copious skirts. He watched as Lord Juster bowed over her hand and raised her fingers to his lips while the grey mouse busied herself straightening the hem of her mistress's kirtle. He looked away quickly, knowing how easily he could love Mathilda, if he allowed himself that liberty. Knowing how sometimes she looked at him, and the corner of her mouth would quirk upwards as if she, too, could have loved . . .

Those were thoughts better forgotten.

He ran a finger around his collar, not enjoying the last warmth of autumn on the windless deck. *What I wouldn't give to be back in the nondescript, comfortable garb of Saker Rampion, spy, with the comfort of a sword at my side.*

Damn the Pontifect.

"Beautiful, isn't she?"

He jumped, unaware until then that his private corner on the aft deck had been broached by Lord Juster, who'd abandoned the two royals to their courtiers. He waved a flagon of wine at Saker, and continued, "She's my maiden, my virgin, my about-to-be bosom companion, everything a man could want in a wife. Look, Saker, at her slim elegance. And think of the dowry she'll bring . . ."

"You forgot to mention the sharp angles of her rump and the rope wig of her hair. She's a paunch-bellied *ship*, you moldwarp." He grinned, though. Juster might play the fool, but his idiocy concealed a mind Saker appreciated. Pity he drank far too much. And whored too much too, either side of the bed depending on whether he was on shore or on board ship, by all reports. At least he was never *boring*. And boring was what his own life threatened to become if he was confined to his spiritual role.

"Tut-tut, such language from a witan. Can't you at least admire her lines? That squared stern you speak of so disparagingly offers me more cabin room. Her sleek lowness, her narrow lines – they make her faster and more manoeuvrable. No high fo'c'sle that used to make the carracks such a bitch to sail close to the wind." The slight slurring of his words and the extra care he took to enunciate more clearly betrayed his drunkenness. "Come, my clerical friend, put that empty goblet aside and toast the success of her maiden voyage." He handed over the flagon.

Saker raised it and drank. Swallowing, he said, "Here's to your safe return. If you have more of this wine on board, I'll admit that a voyage would have much to recommend it." He took another draught, savouring its rich, tangy tartness. "When will you be sailing?"

"Before the winter storms arrive, I trust. I already have the King's signature on the letters of marque, but I'm still hunting for good officers. Can't bear the thought of sharing a table with ignorant idiots for months on end. Don't mind what a man's ancestry is, but he must have good conversation."

His quick frown didn't escape Juster as he took the flagon back. "You aren't going to get self-righteously Va with me, are you, my friend? Privateer, remember; not pirate."

His tone was edgy, and Saker hid a sigh. A drunk Juster was more belligerent than he liked, yet he himself wasn't in the mood to be conciliatory. "You could have the *Golden Petrel* sunk beneath you."

"Bastards do it to us whenever they have the chance. 'S'truth, we've both been at this for nigh a hundred years. What's the matter with you lately? You act as if you have prickles in your hose!"

"It's called maturity."

"Va forbid I catch it, then! No, I suspect you have a secret desire to escape to adventure and sail aboard the *Golden Petrel*." He drained the last of the wine and flung the empty flagon over the stern. One of his servants hurried up with a newly opened replacement. "Tell the truth now! Aren't you hankering after adventure in exotic lands?"

"No. My sailing is confined to the role of a passenger who prefers to arrive at his destination in the shortest time possible."

"Look up there," Juster said, pointing to the crow's nest. "Imagine those masts straining under full sail, with ocean on all sides, the crew hauling on the sheets."

Saker looked up and grimaced. "Imagine climbing up there in the rain, with the wind howling. I prefer *not* to imagine it, I think."

"You could do it now, easily," Juster said, and drank again. "We're at anchor."

A hand reached over his shoulder and took the flagon from him. "I dare you, witan!"

"Your highness," Saker said, and bowed to Prince Ryce. "I believe I'm too old for dares."

Juster pulled a face in his direction.

"Nonsense!" Mathilda had followed her brother up the ladder from the quarterdeck, her ladies-in-waiting giggling behind her as a gust of wind whipped at their skirts. "You could do whatever you put your mind to. Is not Va watching over you?" She dimpled at him, holding out her hand. Her overskirt, looped with panels edged with pearls, was so wide the men had to move away to give her room on the aft deck. Her only concession to being out in the open was a gauzy kerchief to protect her neck and shoulders from the sun.

She rested her fingers on his as he bowed low, and he resisted the temptation to kiss them. "Milady, I cannot imagine that Va is concerned with such trivial matters as my safety while performing a dare."

"Witan, your safety is no trivial matter! However" – she clapped her hands, still smiling – "if Va is not disturbed by trivial matters, the antics of one of his witans indulging in a harmless bet will be of no import!"

"Why don't you and I have a race to the top?" the Prince asked him, grinning.

"I can hardly race anywhere dressed in clerical robes," he said, hoping that would be the end of it.

"That's easily remedied," Juster cried, grabbing the arm of the servant who had been passing out goblets of watered wine to the ladies. "Tarker, go down to my cabin and fetch the britches lying on my bunk, will you?"

Alarmed by the turn of the conversation, Saker said, "Your highness, I can hardly race against your person. The King would rightly hold me responsible for endangering your safety."

The Princess pouted. "He's right, Ryce, you know. You can't be clambering about those ropes like a common sailor." She looked up at Juster. "*You* can, though, can you not, Lord Juster? A race between you and Witan Saker!"

"I'm not racing anyone," Saker protested.

"Oh? Not even if I make it worth your while, witan?" Juster asked. "I'll tithe my first captured cargo, and give it to a charitable cause of your choice – if you win a race to the topgallant yard and back here to this deck."

"I don't even know which spar that is," he said truthfully, although he could guess. "Really, Juster, I—"

"See the third yard on the mainmast? The smallest, highest spar above the middle mainsail?" Juster pointed upwards.

They all looked, and the Princess gave a gasp of dismay. "Oh! I thought you meant just as far as the crow's nest."

Saker grimaced. The crow's nest, an easy climb up the rigging to just beyond the lower mainsail, was not even halfway up. After that, it was straight up the mast, past the main topsail to the top gallant. No climb for a man not entirely sober.

"That must be a hundred feet!" someone exclaimed from the crowd of courtiers listening to the conversation.

"More," Juster said. He and the Prince were now handing the flagon backwards and forwards between them. "From the waterline to the top of the mainmast is over two hundred feet . . ."

"You're drunk, Juster," Saker said amiably.

"Not a bit of it! On a single flagon of wine? One I've been sharing around?"

He forbore to point out that this was the second flagon. "My lord, I'm not afraid of heights. You might lose your bet, and I won't go scampering around that spider's web of ropes up there risking *your* life because you're too drunk to hold on."

"I resent the implication, witan. A tithe of whatever the *Golden Petrel* brings back."

He shrugged. "I'm not interested."

Prince Ryce, waving the flagon, intervened, saying, "But I am, master witan! And you shall not gainsay your prince – I insist. You and Lord Juster shall race to the topgallant yard! You would not dare to oppose a royal command, would you?"

He felt the blood leave his face. *You idiot, Ryce.* The Prince was far drunker than he'd thought. Refusing a royal command, when it was named as such, could give rise to accusations of treason.

Lady Mathilda spoke into the startled silence before anyone reacted. "Oh, that's naughty of both of you – Lord Juster and especially you, brother – to tease my spiritual adviser. Is there no end to the foolishness of men in their cups?" She turned to Saker, undoing her kerchief and handing it to him. "Pay no notice to such wild words from the Prince and oblige *me* instead. Take my favour, and tie it to the topgallant when you arrive there." She gave him a brilliant smile and turned, laughing, to her ladies-in-waiting. "Which one of you will bestow their favour on the oh-so-wicked tease Lord Juster?" Several of her ladies instantly untied their kerchiefs to oblige and the awkwardness of the moment dissolved into good-natured banter. *Ah, Mathilda, bless you . . .*

He still worried, though. Juster was definitely drunk. *One day, my buccaneering friend, I'll throttle you. If you don't kill yourself first in a drunken wager like this one.*

"Your britches, witan," someone said, and thrust a pair of Juster's trousers into his hands.

"Am I to pull these on in front of the maids?" he asked. As he intended, this led to ribald comments, teasing and laughter. The Prince held up his cloak in front of the ladies-in-waiting, and Saker dressed himself more appropriately for a climb. Fortunately, his undershirt was clean; unfortunately, it was sleeveless, which led to more feminine giggles and teasing about his muscles when the Prince whipped the cloak away.

When there was enough chatter to cover a remark to Juster, he said, "Why don't we do this some other time when you've drunk a little less?"

Juster gave the faintest of shakes of his head. "Too late. Don't worry, I just sobered up." He moved away to take up his position at the foot of the main shrouds, where he removed his gold-buckled shoes. Realising that climbing in his stockinged feet would be easier, Saker followed suit.

The Prince offered to start the race. Saker moved after Juster, sure that the man was not as sober as he thought. Around the deck, he heard bets laid. From the suggested odds, it was clear Juster was favoured to win.

Juster pulled on a pair of leather gloves brought for him from his cabin. He grasped the rigging and grinned at his opponent. "You're pompous enough to sour beer sometimes, my friend. You deserve what's coming to you."

Saker sighed. "And you're a tipsy bilge rat who sails far too close to the wind on occasion." He lined up beside the lord, and the Prince waved them off with his hat.

The first few feet were easy climbing, side by side. The shrouds narrowed in width as they approached the crow's nest; and only then did he realise why Juster had chosen to climb on his left. The rope ladder to the lookout was on that side. They reached the top of the shrouds together, but it was Juster who had access to the crow's nest.

Saker, seeing him fumble drunkenly with his feet for the new ladder, readied himself to grab the man if he fell. A moment later, however, Juster was safe, grinning at him over the edge of the lookout.

"You've lost the race, my friend," he said. "There's no way you can pass me now!"

"Crowing from the crow's nest, my lord?" Saker asked sweetly. "I believe the race doesn't end until one of us has his feet on the stern deck again."

"That's the poop deck, you lubber. Now, how long shall I leave you hanging there?"

"As long as you like." He turned his head to look straight down at the deck. "The view is spectacular. Why, I believe I'm looking straight down the cleavage of Lady Sevaria's ample bosom . . ."

Juster laughed and turned to climb from the crow's nest on to the ropes leading upwards.

Saker hauled himself into the vacated lookout and studied the way up. He saw what Juster meant now. The rope ladder up the mast was narrow all the way to the tiny platform of the trestle trees, from where it would be possible to tie the favour on to the topgallant yard.

Damn. Juster was right: the first person to reach the crow's nest had the race won. No, wait a moment. He had to come down again, but he couldn't pass Saker, who'd be on his way up. So how was he intending to descend?

Only then did he realise how well he'd been tricked. The mainmast itself, and the area between the masts, was a thick forest of ropes of varying thickness and purpose, some taut, some slack, some looped, some tarred. Vaguely he knew they all had names: clewlines, buntlines, leech lines, bowlines, halyards, stays . . . He could only guess at their varied purposes, but Juster would know – and he'd know exactly which one he could slide down, all the way down, until his feet hit the deck.

The gloves. That was why he had wanted to wear gloves.

Damn, damn, damn. He'd been well and truly outwitted.

Odd, at first he hadn't cared a whit about the race; he'd just wanted it over, with the drunken Juster down safely. Now that he knew he'd been so easily duped, he wanted to win.

He started up the ladder towards the trestle trees as fast as he could move, glad to see he was actually overhauling Juster, whose feet kept slipping on the ratlines between the shrouds. While he climbed, he eyed the numerous ropes. The logical one to use ran from the mast at the trestle trees to the aft hull. It was, he guessed, a fixed stay for the mainmast. Tar-covered and taut, it would be ideal, as long as the person sliding down it had a pair of tough leather gloves.

He caught up with Juster as the man was tying his favour. Juster gave him a delighted grin and bent to grab the stay rope. "So long, ninny," he said, and dropped, using his momentum to swing his legs upwards and wrap his ankles around the tarred hemp. Secure, he hung there for moment while Saker ruefully tied on the Princess's favour. Then, loosening his hold a tad, Juster began sliding towards the deck.

Saker watched him go. Juster's weight made the rope dip a little, enough to bring it in contact with a stay for the aft mizzenmast.

The idiot, Saker thought, suddenly alarmed. *He's going far too fast . . .* "Look out!" he yelled, appallingly aware that Juster's feet were going to hit the second stay as he picked up speed.

Juster, oblivious, let go with one hand to wave.

With the horror of inevitable disaster unfolding before him, Saker began to slide back down the way he'd come up. His gaze riveted to what was happening below, he didn't notice the friction that burned the skin from his hands.

One of Juster's feet was jerked above the second stay. His other foot slipped below it. The taut rope from the mizzenmast slammed into his crotch and all Saker could do was watch. When Juster screamed, a hideous, searing scream, Saker heard the collective gasp from the deck.

His own feet hit the topsail yard as Juster, still yelping in agony, was jerked from his hold on the mainstay. Saker crouched there, unable to think of anything he could do to stop Lord Juster Dornbeck plunging to the deck and certain death below.

16

Witchery and Taint

Juster didn't fall. One foot remained jammed in the V where the two stays crossed each other.

Kept taut by his weight, the ropes passed in front of his ankle. He was left hanging precariously upside down, midway between the two masts, high above the deck. Below, courtiers scattered and screamed.

As Juster was both silent and unmoving, Saker guessed he'd blacked out. The thought of having the most vulnerable part of his anatomy sawed into at speed by a hard, tar-covered rope had Saker shuddering.

He glanced around. Ropes everywhere, and he had both his own dagger and the lascar's. He loosened the cover on the sheath to his own knife, his thoughts racing. If Juster struggled, if the wind blew, if the ship heeled – the result didn't bear thinking about. The end of the spar he was on was directly over Juster's body, but how to reach him? He dared not use the same rope. The slightest movement of the stay and Juster's ankle could slip out of the V.

Using the footropes just below the furled sail, he edged his way to the end of the yardarm. Once there, he seized the ropes dangling from the end. A cursory glance told him that one had something to do with the sail; the other held the spar in place. His hands were sore and bleeding where he'd skinned them, but he swung under the yard and began to let himself down the ropes, grabbing both with his hands and hooking his feet around one. Agony stabbed through his fingers. He ignored it. He halted when he was level with Juster, who was groaning as he regained consciousness. "Don't move, my friend," he said calmly. "Don't even open your eyes."

Juster said nothing. His breath was ragged. Grimacing in pain, Saker switched his hold to only one of the yardarm ropes he'd descended, twisting a foot into its slack. He tried not to think about how precarious his hold was. Breathing deeply, he groped for his knife and began sawing at the other rope, now hanging loose. After an age, the bottom half dropped to the deck, and the dagger fell with it as he lost his hold on its handle. From the end of the piece still dangling from the spar, he made a noose with a slip knot.

When he looked down, he saw that courtiers had scrambled out of the way of the falling rope and blade. Sailors swarmed up the shrouds towards the crow's nest. Good: he'd have help soon.

His hands were slippery with blood, and the pain grew worse as the hemp fibres ripped deeper into his fingers and palms. An agonising ache dragged at his arms and legs as he swung himself to and fro, until one arc of his swing brought him close to Juster.

Va's teeth, I hurt.

Holding the loop of the cut rope, gripping his own rope with his legs and his other hand, he tried to flip the noose over Juster's free leg. He missed the first time and had to swing back to try again. Pain brought tears to his eyes as his bloody hands slipped and he was forced to grasp even tighter.

This time the noose slid over Juster's foot and he pulled it tight around his ankle.

Juster was now groaning louder than ever. Saker's action had spread-eagled his legs, hardly the most comfortable position for a man who had just had a rope sawn across his genitals. He jerked and muttered, with more coherence this time. "What the flaming fucking *hell* . . ."

"I wouldn't suggest you do too much moving, Juster."

"Saker?" The word was as much a squawk of pain as anything else.

"Yes."

"I fucking *hurt*!"

"I know. Try not to move."

Prompted by his agony, Juster screamed invective at him.

He ignored the words and grabbed hold of the nobleman's belt. He looked up, wondering just how long he could hold on himself. Every muscle was screaming. He twisted his other foot tighter into the rope, trying to take more of his weight from his arms and shoulders. It would be ridiculous to crash to the deck now.

The first of the sailors arrived above him, on the yardarm. They seemed to know what they were doing, and when he felt the rope he'd attached to Juster begin to rise, he let him go. Pulled from above, Juster's trapped foot came free and he swung upwards suspended by his other leg, still upside down, uttering a number of imprecations about Saker's parentage as he went.

Relieved and exhausted, Saker sagged against the rope for a moment. Up, or down? Up was closer, but he doubted he could haul his body weight upward. He headed for the deck, hand over weary hand.

He was the hero of the moment. The Prince clapped him on the back, others crowded around to praise him.

It was Mathilda who noticed his bleeding palms and torn fingers. "Oh! You're hurt!" she said. She raised her face to look at him in concern and beckoned to the grey mouse. "Celandine – you must bind his hands. He's bleeding! Tear up your kerchief."

Celandine gave a bobbing, graceless curtsey of acquiescence to the Princess before coming across the deck to him, already untying the linen kerchief from around her neck. When she did speak, her tone was matter-of-fact, lacking any of the artifices he'd come to expect from Mathilda's entourage.

"May I see your hands, witan?" she asked. Around them, the courtiers turned their attention to what was happening above. Sailors had safely hauled Juster on to the yardarm.

"There's no need to sacrifice your ke—" he began.

"Are you about to question the decision of the Princess?" she interrupted. "I'm sure you would not want me to be scolded for failing to obey my mistress." With her strong, long-fingered hands, she was already tearing the linen into strips.

He wondered if she was making fun of him, then decided that was unlikely. He'd never seen her laugh, and her smile was never more than a tight upturn of her lips for the sake of politeness. She snatched a flagon of wine from a passing servant, and with scant concern for the expensive quality of the alcohol, poured it over his torn palms.

Pox and pustules, that hurts!

"There is tar in the wounds," she remarked, picking out the largest pieces.

"From the ropes," he said, looking up to distract himself from the pain. Juster was now being lowered safely to the deck in a sling.

"Have someone pick out the small bits when you return to the palace," she said as she began to bind his hands.

He let out the breath he had been holding as Juster reached the deck and the courtiers cheered and crowded around. "I will. I'm sorry about your kerchief," he said, returning his attention to Celandine. "I'll buy you a new one."

He half expected her to simper, or protest. She did neither. "That would be kind. I certainly cannot afford to buy another." A statement of fact, said without rancour or inflection, but odd nonetheless. Not the type of comment one usually heard from a court lady, but then Juster had told him she was from a shrine-keeper's family, not an aristocratic one.

Her hands were deft, and she soon had her linen strips neatly tied in place. One long piece of cloth dangled. "I think I'd better cut this off," she said. "May I borrow your knife?"

Without waiting for a reply, she reached for the kris and pulled it free of its sheath. She sawed at the loose end until it parted and fell to the deck. For a moment her fingers lingered over the kris, stroking the blade with interest. Then she raised her gaze to look at him. Her eyes were a deep, dark blue, the colour of spring gentians, and quite, quite beautiful. Why had he never seen that before?

No, wait. He *had* noticed her eye colour. Grey. To match the rest of her. Well, they weren't grey now. Something shifted, even as he watched; a subtle blurring, as if he was looking through gauze. No, more as if there was a reflection of a woman imposed on the features of the real person. One was strong-featured, not beautiful, but certainly memorable. The other was grey and sallow, unattractive at worst, boring at best. He couldn't decide which was real, and which was false.

A tremor ran through the hands that held his, and then her eyes changed again as she panicked. She dropped the kris, her face an image of appalled shock. Clumsily he caught the blade with his bandaged hands, wincing. She stumbled away, a hand clamped across her mouth as if to hold back a scream.

Disorientated, unsure of what he'd just seen, he blinked and shook his head to clear his confusion. He called after her. "Mistress Celandine!"

She half turned, but didn't look at him. The grey mouse once more, she was reluctant to meet his eyes. She had her trembling under control as she replied in a whisper. "Witan?"

"Thank you." He lifted his hands to indicate her bandaging.

She inclined her head in acknowledgement and joined the Prince and Princess and the rest of the courtiers still crowding the quarterdeck to see how Juster was.

He watched for a moment, relieved to see the nobleman, still prone and ashen-faced, accepting a drink. No one was looking his way. He thought wryly that his moment of glory was over; a lowly witan was of no interest to the average courtier. Deciding it would be better to disappear, he pulled on his robe and shoes, checked that his purse was safe, then walked to the railing to call a wherry over to the ladder.

"The palace dock?" the riverman asked when he dropped down into the boat, grimacing as he used his hands to steady himself.

"No – the tide is coming in, isn't it? Take me to the shrine upriver instead."

"King Oak? That'll cost you, master. Two coppers and a brass bit."

He nodded and counted out the coins, too tired to bargain. He wanted peace, a quiet time to calm himself. For the first time in years, he desperately *needed* to pray at a shrine, needed it the way a thirsty man needed water.

As the boatman pushed away from the ship's side, Saker looked up. Celandine stared down at him from the railing. The grey of her dress and coif framed her face like a shroud. An aura of sorrow clung to her like mist. Her grey eyes regarded him with a troubled gaze and she wore her dignity in a way that was utterly foreign to the grey mouse he'd thought her to be.

Yet he'd seen her with blue eyes. A skewing of the world around him, creating a lie. The lascar's dagger to blame, of course, this time catching an innocent woman in its wanton magic, scaring her witless. She'd not deserved that. His anger at the thought of its arbitrary power roiled inside him.

Halfway between the ship and the shore, he took it out from its sheath. He turned it over and over in his hands. It had witchery, and it was Va-forsaken.

As he felt the smooth polish of the bone handle, he thought of Ardhi. For a moment he felt his presence there, at his side, as if any moment the lascar was going to drop a hand on his shoulder and say something to mock him.

In that moment, he had no doubt whatever that the man was alive.

He bit his lip. *I don't want this.*

Without another thought, he dropped the dagger over the side into the water. With luck, it would sink to the bottom of the estuary, and disappear forever in the mud. *See if you can return from this, you misbegotten twist of metal.*

Buoyed by the handle, it floated. He stared at it as the wherry drew away from where it bobbed in the water, handle uppermost, the sun glinting on its silver inlay. Then, slowly, it slid beneath the waves.

If someone else finds it, he thought, *it'll be their problem, not mine.*

He'd finished his prayers and was about to leave the shrine when Penny-cress, the shrine-keeper, entered. She glanced at him, then came forward to rest her hand on the fissured bark of the oak, the living pillar that pierced the centre of the otherwise unpretentious building. From the base of the trunk, roots crawled over the earthen floor and burrowed beneath the shrine's stone walls.

Penny-cress was old, rough-skinned and as crenulated as the trunk she touched. For a moment he had the fanciful idea that she and the oak merged into one entity.

"Witan Saker Rampion," she said. "A sight for my rheumy eyes. Too rare, your visits. Your connection to what's true grows as weak as an old man's pizzle." In spite of her age, there was nothing frail about her voice.

"I visit the palace chapel twice a day, you know." He sounded as defensive as a schoolboy and almost laughed at himself.

"Pah! Y'think to sup on truth up there in the palace with its dead stone an' rotting wood? This" – she slapped the flat of her hand to the bark of the tree – "is where the real power is. Wild power."

"I know."

"No, you don't. When I say wild, I don't mean pretty 'n' green. True oaken power is *savage*. It comes from the wild of nature and rips 'n' tears the heart out of you, if you was brave enough to use it."

"I don't have a witchery."

"Yet. Listen, witan. You 'n' me, we know we go back to the land when we die. We'll be there, part of it, lookin' on the world for all eternity. If we live well, we'll get to choose what part of the land we become at our rest. Me, I want to be right here, with my ancestors, my essence in a tree like this, shining in the leaves in summer, sleeping away the winter . . ."

He resisted a desire to tell her he did know the basic tenets of the Way of the Oak.

"But town people?" she continued. "That don't mean naught to them. So they don't care. They just want to lead grand lives. So they cut down them woods, catch them hares, cage them birds, tame them lakes 'n' shores."

"That's why there are shrine-keepers and witans. To protect the land."

He suspected that no matter what he said about the need for people to have wood to burn, she wasn't going to believe in anything that implied the necessity of the death of a single living tree. *She'd freeze to death rather than kill an animal for its skin to make a coat.*

Lord, he was tired! *I need to go back and sleep.*

"T'aint enough, I'm thinking. There's summat nasty afoot. Why y'reckon there are them as want us gone?" She paused for dramatic effect, then waggled a bony finger at him. "'Cause they want the wealth of slaughtered forests, of dug-up mines, of hollowed-out quarries."

The hairs stood up on the back of his neck. "Who wants us gone?" he asked.

"Folk died of the Horned Death up in Shenat country. That's A'Va. A'Va is always at the back o' things. But A'Va has a human face, never forget that."

The idea was appalling.

What if she was right? Right there: the reason he and Juster had not considered because they'd been thinking too small. Rid the Faith of those who protected the natural world, and who would benefit? Those who were greedy – on a huge scale. Those who wanted not one tree, but an entire forest. Those not hankering after a few stones from a single quarry, but planning to dig up a whole hill. Mine-owners, shipbuilders, landowners, merchants. Not all or even most of them, of course. Pain gripped his heart. But some of them. *Or a single someone planning the end of the Way of the Oak . . .*

Fox?

Oh, sweet Va. The ledgers behind the banner in his sitting room. Mi.For. Okwd. So obvious. Middle Forest, Oakwood. The headings were the names of all Ardrone's finest forests. And the lists recorded the tree species, their number and their monetary value. Fox had been using his clerics to catalogue the natural wealth of Ardrone.

Nothing wrong with that . . .

Not if your motives were pure.

Oblivious to his seething thoughts, she said, "What if us shrine-keepers, us with the knowledge and witchery to protect the sacred heart of the wild, what if we all die of the Horned Death? Do y'think them forests have stood sacrosanct through the ages all by themselves?"

He caught the horror that tinged her voice, and slowly, oh so slowly, all the hair on his body rose. *No. No, it can't happen, surely?*

Her hand shot out without warning to grab his wrist. "Who marked you?" she asked.

He didn't understand. "I beg your pardon?"

"Your hand."

He looked down. Celandine's bandages were still neatly tied across his palms so that only his fingers were visible. "I scraped the skin off . . ." he began.

But she was pointing to the fingers on his right hand. They were blackish, as if he'd smudged them with ink. He frowned, puzzled. They hadn't been like that when he'd left the ship. Tar, he supposed. Even his clothes had picked up the horrible stuff from the rope. "It's only tar," he said.

"No. A servant of A'Va touched you."

"No, it's just—" he began with a smile at her superstition, preparing to argue the point.

"I can prove it. It shows only when you're in the shade of a shrine oak." She pushed him towards the entrance. "Go outside, till the tree no longer shades you. Look at them fingers there."

He shrugged and did as she asked. In growing horror, he watched the black marks fade and disappear as he stepped away from the oak. For a long while he stood in the sunshine and stared, shocked, at his clean fingers. He tried shading them under another tree, but his skin remained unstained.

He looked back to where Penny-cress watched from the doorway. He thought he read pity in her eyes.

As he returned to the oak-shaded building, it was an effort to put one foot in front of the other. He fixed his gaze on his right hand and watched as the oak tree canopy cast its shade on them, and blackness rippled and smudged across his fingertips.

Whatever it was, it wasn't tar.

Cold fear shivered him, and he remembered the man with the plague in Ustgrind, the way he had gripped his hand with his disease-ridden fingers . . .

"The Horned Death," he whispered. "Sweet Va, I have the Hor—"

Penny-cress patted his arm in comfort. "No, no. That's not any pestilence! *He* has marked you as a danger. A'Va's servant on earth. Followers of A'Va can see or feel that mark any time, 'n' know you as a danger. You must take care, witan. The evil has its eye on you."

Inwardly he groaned. "Mistress Penny-cress, I'm just a lowly witan."

She tapped his fingers. "You best ask yourself why you are seen as a danger to *him*. To us, this mark's only visible when you enter a true oak shrine. But to those who follow him, they see it any time. And it leaves a taint behind wherever you go."

"I've never heard of such a thing!"

"Maybe not, but any ageing shrine-keeper'll tell you the truth of it. So who could've left that mark on your fingers?"

"Lately?"

"It fades in time. That's been done, oh, in the past year or so. Course, if you could be sure your hands were unmarked the last time y'entered a shrine . . . ?"

But he couldn't be sure. He might not have noticed.

Who could it have been? *Just every noble lady whose fingers I have bowed over, from the Princess downwards. Celandine, when she bandaged my hands. Gerelda, when we made love. The Pontifect, whose hand I kissed. Likewise Fox. The man dying of the Horned Pestilence. Ardhi, he gripped my hand. Prince Ryce, when I was showing him a sword stroke.* And Va knew how many others in the ordinary transactions of a normal day.

"A devil-kin, maybe?" she suggested. "One of them Lowmian twins? You'd not have felt anything at the time." She sighed, and seemed to age still further even as he watched. "S'pose it was inevitable. Some things y'can't run from. After all, you were given the name of a hunter at birth."

He shook his head, tired, irritated. "Saker?"

"Ay. The saker, the hunter falcon, a swift killer. We need the hunters like you to keep us strong."

"How? By culling the weak and the sick, as the falcon does? To kill men, even though you wouldn't consider killing an animal? Wonderful. Just what a witan needs to hear."

"To cull the sick with evil at their heart, or deep within their mind, just as we put down a rabid dog," she said. "Evil – or the devil or whatever name y'like to use – has no power without the helping hand of his human devil-kin."

That word again.

She waited for him to digest that before she added, "Some'ud have us reject the wild. But then justice'ud dwindle. Choose your prey wisely, witan, or we all suffer."

He snorted rudely, too tired even to be polite. "Are you a seer now, Mistress Penny-cress?"

She shook her head. "Nay, but 'tis a time-honoured truth I utter. And perhaps the truth of the very old. This tree 'n' me were birthed together."

"This tree must be four hundred years old." The shrine-keepers were indeed long-lived, but they all exaggerated their longevity. Perhaps it was a matter of pride.

"Summat like that," she agreed cheerfully. "Take an acorn on your way out, an' keep it close by. Never hurts to remember where you came from. You want a witchery to help you in the final fight, witan? You've got to suffer 'n' surrender. T'aint easy, gaining a witchery."

He thought of the lascar's dagger and the odd change in Celandine when she'd been holding it. Aloud he said, "No, I don't want a witchery, Penny-cress. I've had enough of magic forces to last me a lifetime."

"They come in handy, times. You watch your health if you meet a devil-kin or a Lowmeer twin," she concluded darkly.

He wanted to throw up his hands in exasperation. Why was he plagued by people who spoke in riddles and warnings? "Have you ever

met the Pontifect, by any chance? You have a lot in common. If you have something to say, say it so I know what you're talking about!"

"If I knew, I'd tell you. I can say a great evil is coming out of Lowmeer, 'n' twice in my mem'ry there's been a twin's hand therein."

And with only that much explanation, he had to be content.

17

The Fox, the Falcon and the Princess

The day after the incident on the *Golden Petrel*, Fox instructed Saker to meet him in Faith House. Not wanting to give the Prime any cause for complaint, he obeyed the summons without delay, but, as he expected, was then left to cool his heels in the anteroom for more than an hour.

Most of the time he stood looking out through the narrow slit that passed for a window. Faith House, built on a hill, provided fine views over Throssel Water, and he could see the *Golden Petrel* still anchored among the other ships littering the waterway like children's toys in a puddle. The bare masts appeared of less significance than fiddlesticks, the rigging as fragile as fine sewing thread.

Such flimsy vessels to sail halfway round the world . . .

Juster had guessed correctly; he'd have liked to sign on to one of them. Anything would be better than court life. He shoved his hands into his robe pockets and his fingers encountered the acorn he had taken from the grounds of the King Oak shrine. He took it out and rolled its patterned perfection between his fingers.

"Witan Rampion."

He turned away from the window to see Tonias Pedding emerge from Fox's chambers, saying, "His eminence will see you in a moment."

"That's what you said half an hour ago, Secretary Pedding."

The man gave a thin smile.

He held up the acorn. "Tell me, do you ever go to the King Oak shrine on the river?"

"No, witan. The Prime would not approve. The chapel here is more than adequate for prayer and contemplation. My grandmother used to pray at that shrine, though; I think the old folk find the old ways more familiar."

"Especially if Penny-cress the shrine-keeper is as old as she says she is."

Pedding laughed. "Penny-cress was already ancient when my grandmother was a girl, or so Gran told me. Gran also told me that *her* grandmother said the same thing." He shrugged. "But there are all kinds of stories. Did you know old women say if a young wife places an acorn in her womanly passage just before she gives birth, the baby will live to be as old as the oak that springs from the acorn if she plants it together with the afterbirth?"

Saker smiled. "Yes, I've heard that one too. It carries the disadvantage that some oak saplings don't live very long."

"Superstitious lot, shrine-keepers. The sooner they die off the better. Then we can replace them with trained clergy."

He wanted to protest, but Pedding was prattling on. "Shrine-keepers are troublemakers. There was a nasty incident last month, up near Twite, when legitimate woodsmen were—"

A bell sounded in the Prime's room and the story stopped abruptly there. "His eminence will see you now, witan."

"Thank you, master secretary." He dropped the acorn back in his pocket and schooled his face to careful neutrality as he opened the door. At least this time he didn't have to worry about the lascar's dagger. It hadn't found its way back to him, thank Va.

Valerian Fox was sitting at his table, a pile of documents in front of him. He pushed them away, closed up his inkwell and reached for the carafe and pewter goblets to one side. "Rampion, please be seated. I've instructed Secretary Pedding we are not to be disturbed. Some port?"

"Thank you, your eminence. It would be a pleasure. Your Staravale port is much sought after." *I'll try not to choke on it.*

"Indeed. I regret we don't do this more often. I should see more of you." He unstoppered the carafe and poured them both a drink. "It seems you are in need of closer guidance."

"Oh?"

"Come now, Rampion. I'm sure you must be aware that yesterday's incident was hardly one that sets a good example to your royal charges, or indeed to the court."

"I don't know what you've heard, so I can't comment."

"Accepting a dare, encouraging gambling, endangering the life of a courtier from a prestigious family . . ."

"None of that seems to quite fit my recollection."

"Are you saying you didn't accept a dare to climb the mainmast to the top, against a man who was patently drunk? He could have been killed! Almost *was* killed. In front of the Prince and Princess, what's more. It was up to you to stop such behaviour, not encourage it."

"Your eminence, you were not present. Accept my assurances that I did my best to defuse a situation which could have been much worse."

"Defuse? You should have stopped it!"

"I am a lowly witan, not a noble. I did my best. Va be thanked, there were no catastrophic results."

"No? From what I heard, Lord Juster was almost castrated!"

"I imagine he will be sore for a time. I understand he has gone to his country estate to recuperate."

"I will hold you responsible if he takes any permanent damage from this affair."

I wonder what you are up to now. He was so fed up with the politics of court life. So sick of having to use the formal language of court protocol. So tired of the necessity of thinking through the nuances of everything he wanted to say before he said it. If the Pontifect didn't send him somewhere less tedious soon, he'd go mad.

The Prime's eyes flashed with annoyance as he added, "I hope your ascendancy over the Princess will not be affected by her viewing of your infantile behaviour. How can you influence her if she has no respect for you?"

"Lady Mathilda is all a princess should be. Kind, obedient, pious, wise beyond her years." Va blast it, he sounded such a pompous rattler.

"Hmph. Really? Heedless and foolish, with a love of dancing and play-acting is closer to what I've observed." Fox handed over one of the goblets, his smile far from benign.

Saker returned an equally false smile as he took the proffered drink. "She's only just turned eighteen, your eminence. If she did not love such pleasures, if she were not at times thoughtless, would we not wonder at her extraordinary rectitude?"

"Possibly. But she's the King's only daughter and much is expected of her."

Pox on this, we're dancing our words around like it's a game. "Perhaps that's the reason for her love of things other than her studies. She's heard whispers of a marriage that would entail leaving her home, her friends and indeed her country. Unsettling thoughts for a girl of her age."

"True. And that is the very subject I wish you to broach with her. A marriage proposal has been accepted and you will inform her accordingly."

"Me? I'm just her tutor in things religious. Hardly the person to speak to her of nuptials." And he was appalled at the thought.

"The King requests you be the one to break the news to her."

"The *King*?"

"He has decided that she is to marry the Regal of Lowmeer. In fact, negotiations have been ongoing for the past year or so and the matter is now settled." He took a sip of his port and looked at Saker over the rim of his goblet. "You look shocked, Witan Rampion."

He strove to repair his shattered equilibrium, without showing anything of the depth of his feeling. "I *am* shocked," he admitted. So shocked he felt physically ill. In his heart of hearts he hadn't really believed they'd give her to the Regal. "I had heard the rumours, but hoped they were false. The Regal has not long buried his third wife, and he is old enough to be the Princess's grandfather."

"Barely. He's fifty, I believe. And desperate for an heir. King Edwayn is aware the Princess will not be happy with this match, which is why he asks you to explain the matter to her. He wishes to avoid dealing with his daughter's tears."

You're lying. The King hardly knew of his existence. No, His Majesty had asked the Prime himself to deal with the Princess, and Valerian was passing on the distasteful task to him.

Saker inclined his head. "And what explanation am I to give her? Forgive my blunt speaking, but the King is selling her to an ageing, unpleasant man who rules a foreign land with a court unfamiliar to her. A man who has, what's more, buried three wives and produced no children after thirty years of married life. Can we hope then that there is a reason for this marriage? One imperative, at very least, to Ardrone's prosperity? Not, mind you, that I can think of any reason that will appeal to an eighteen-year-old princess, especially not one who would be both beautiful and desirable even if she were a seamstress from Calico Street."

His tone was level, amused even. Anything to conceal his outrage. And let's be honest, his pain. *Mathilda, I admit it. I care more than I should. I've cared about you for months. And it's taken this for me to understand just how much . . .*

It took all his control to sit there with a stupid smile on his lips as if it meant nothing to him, when all the while he wanted to plant his fist into Fox's smug face.

"Oh, the price is substantial. I wonder, did you hear what happened to Lord Denworth's expedition to the Pashali port of Javenka, some years ago?" Fox asked.

"Yes, although I hardly see the relevance." He frowned, trying to recall the details. "He set sail with five ships, wanting to establish a sea trade route to Javenka. He returned four years later with one ship and a pitiful cargo of a few mouldy spices. Apparently the Pashali didn't take kindly to Ardrone bypassing their mastodon routes. They detained his fleet and sailors, and only released the crews and one of the ships on payment of a substantial ransom. When Lowmeer tried the same thing, they were wiser. They paid off the Pashali rulers of the coastal ports beforehand."

"Exactly so. Then they used that foothold to explore the Summer Seas and finally found a way to sail all the way to the Spicerie. Now they apparently sail direct from Karradar, bypassing Javenka and the Pashali coast."

"So I've heard."

"The King is not happy, nor are our merchants. We may not be at war, but it was a Lowmian privateer that actually fired on and sank one of Denworth's fleet. If this continues, the money that once went to the Pashali traders could soon well be going to Lowmeer. Think what that would mean, Rampion!"

"It will certainly affect our commerce. I'm still puzzled, though, your eminence. What has that to do with the upcoming nuptials?" *Damn it, they've sold her.*

"Everything." Valerian smiled, a smile of self-satisfied pride. "My Lowmeer counterpart, Prime Mulhafen, has been a veritable fount of helpful information. It seems that the Regal, in his declining years, has a frequent problem related to, um, rising to the occasion, shall we say? On being shown a painting of Princess Mathilda, however, his uncooperative member sprang to instant attention. Ever since, desperate for an heir, he's been sending out feelers to King Edwayn. And finally he made a suggestion that tempted the King and our merchants. Equal rights to the port of Kotabanta on Serinaga Island in the Summer Seas, which Lowmeer has leased from a local island prince. Rajas, they call them. Not quite the Spicerie, but a hub for tropical trade from the spice islands nonetheless."

"And that is to be the Princess's bride price?"

"Yes. It's all agreed upon. The final documents will be signed when the Regal arrives. He will be on the ships that will escort the Princess to Ustgrind."

"The Regal is coming *here*?"

"Well, not to Throssel. To Betany, I understand." His thin veneer of sarcasm made it clear he thought Saker's unthinking remark less than intelligent. Betany was on the west coast, a short sail across the Ardmeer estuary from Lowmeer, whereas a ship coming to Throssel would have a long sail around the south of Ardrone. Depending on the winds, that could take many weeks.

"He will not land on our soil, though," the Prime continued. "The protocol is too problematic. They will be married on board the Regal's vessel within a matter of weeks, and then sail for Ustgrind."

"She's been sold for a cargo of spices." *And you are not a disinterested party, are you, you bastard? I heard you bought shares in the new trading company being set up here . . .*

"Not one cargo," Fox said, unfazed. "Many. A fifteen-year agreement with Lowmeer, plus a land-based concession area, shipping berths and protection, all granted by the raja of the island to us and Lowmeer, at Lowmeer's insistence. Doubtless backed up by their guns. Not to be sneezed at."

He thought, *Juster will be furious. The King will be revoking his letters of marque once the agreement is signed, I'll wager. Ardrone can't sign a treaty of cooperation on one hand and have privateers thieving Lowmian cargoes on the other.* "One wonders what the inhabitants of Kotabanta think about their commerce being part of a dowry to a princess they can hardly have heard of."

The Prime shrugged, indifferent.

"Well, I hope I can persuade Lady Mathilda that the trade is worth her sacrifice," Saker said, even though just considering the idea made him ill. He clamped his jaw tight to stop himself speaking the angry words that hovered on his tongue.

"I rely on you to do that, Rampion." Valerian lifted his drink in toast. "Here's to a profitable commerce in spices!"

Saker raised his goblet in turn. The sip he took almost choked him.

Poor Mathilda.

He pushed that thought away and dug his nails into his palms as Valerian Fox began to tell him exactly what to say to the Princess.

Celandine the grey opened the door to the Princess's apartments in answer to Saker's knock. No hint of a glamour, or of blue eyes, or of beauty. Just sallow skin, a dull expression and a silent tongue. She was dowdy, always unadorned, so insignificant. He felt a pang of guilt. This surely was the kind of person a witan should reach out to in case they needed help. Instead he'd ignored her, disregarded her occasional astringent wit.

Looking at her now, he saw nothing to hint at the illusion he had glimpsed on board the *Golden Petrel*. It must have been lascar magic. Nothing to do with her. She had been holding the dagger . . .

He smiled at her and handed her a woven gift basket with a lid. "A new kerchief," he said, "with my apologies for the ruin of your last one."

She smiled then, but he thought it was more in surprise than in delight. "My thanks," she replied. "I hope your hands are healing."

He showed her his newly scabbed palms. "Sore still, but no signs of infection, thanks to you."

"More thanks to the wine I put on them, in all probability." She ushered him in and closed the door. Taking the lid off the basket, she peeked inside. He'd chosen a grey kerchief, guessing she wouldn't wear any other colour, but he couldn't resist one with white lace edging depicting oak leaves. It had cost him more than he'd expected, and quite a bit more than he could comfortably afford.

The corners of her lips twitched up. "Lace," she said, and her cheeks flushed pink. "Are you tempting me away from my widow's weeds and into the frivolous, witan? Reproaching me, perhaps, for my lack of ornamentation when in the presence of a princess?"

"Mistress, I would not presume to do either. Besides, the oak leaf is a symbol of the Va-Faith. It can never be considered frivolous." He smiled so she wouldn't think he was chiding her.

"I stand corrected, and will wear it with that in mind. Thank you, sir." She inclined her head, and effaced herself like the mouse she was. When he noticed her next, she'd faded away into a corner of the room like a shadow, to sit with her head meekly bowed over a book. Probably her prayer book, although he was beginning to wonder if it was wise to make assumptions about her.

Princess Mathilda was sitting on a window seat surrounded by others of her ladies. She was examining something in her lap. She looked up as he crossed the room towards her. His heart jumped. She'd never looked so lovely, or so openly glad to see him.

Dear Va, what I wouldn't give to have her look at me like that every day of my life . . .

"Witan Rampion! I am so glad you've come. Look what we have." She indicated the heap of feathers that struggled in her lap. "It's a finch that flew into the room, but it broke its wing against the window in its attempts to escape. Is there anything that can be done for the poor thing?"

He heard resignation in her tone, but when she raised her face to him, her eyes were pleading.

He took the bird from her and examined it. "It may be Va's mercy if we were to kill it painlessly."

"They are such beautiful songsters. I cannot bear the thought that it will never sing again." She stroked the head of the bird with her forefinger. "I have an empty cage right here . . ."

Knowing what he did about her future, he was unable to refuse her anything. "Very well. We can try. First, does anyone have a kerchief I can use to immobilise the wings?"

One of the ladies immediately produced a piece of fine linen that probably cost enough to support a working family for a month or more. Carefully he wound it around the finch's body and tied it firmly. Celandine brought the cage and Mathilda placed the bird inside, where it sat unmoving, traumatised.

"Everything should be free," she said. "I hope it knows we are only trying to help."

Va have mercy, how could he tell her she was about to lose whatever freedom she had? Postponing the moment, he said quietly, "I'll ask the gardeners to supply you with a selection of seeds and nuts, for I doubt it will eat much else. Keep it bound like that until the wing is healed. Then we'll see if it can fly and be released back into the wild."

One of the ladies cried, "Oh no! We must keep it in a cage so we can enjoy the song!"

"Birds sing more sweetly without bars," Princess Mathilda told her firmly. "Should it heal, I shall let it go."

"Truly spoken indeed," Celandine said, coming forward to take the cage and set it back on its stand.

"Right now, it's better covered, to keep it still and quiet," he said.

Celandine placed her own shawl over the cage, then retreated again in silence to her corner. The others giggled and lifted the edge of the shawl to see what the poor thing was doing in the dark.

Under the cover of their chatter, he turned to the Princess and said, "I must speak to you in private. Could you send your ladies away for a while?"

Her mouth tightened as she absorbed the seriousness of his request. She shooed the women from the room, telling them the bird needed quiet and she wished to pray. They left without a murmur, although being alone with a man, even a cleric, was a breach of protocol for a princess. Luckily, none of her older ladies-in-waiting were around. One of them would have insisted on staying, for sure.

With a gesture, Mathilda granted him the privilege of being seated in her presence. She herself sat upright, her back straight, her hands neatly folded in her lap, her eyes round with foreboding. Still she did not speak, and he felt his heart twist.

He said, "I am here at the request of the King, through the agency of Prime Fox. His Majesty wishes you to know that he has settled on a husband for you. He asks that you accept his choice and remember your duty." The words choked him. *You bastard. How can you even* say *them aloud?*

She paled. "So very formal, witan? I think you have ill news for me."

He ploughed on, each word bruising his soul. "The Regal of

Lowmeer has asked for your hand and his offer has been accepted. Your dowry has been agreed upon and the monetary amount in jewels and gold has been received. The rest of the dowry concerns – concerns a trade agreement, as yet to be signed."

She was quite white now, and her hands twisted in her lap. "How long do I have?" she asked in a low whisper.

"The announcement of the nuptials will be made tomorrow. You are expected to leave as soon as we have word that the Regal's royal barque has been sighted at the entrance to Betany Bay. I believe you will be escorted there by Prince Ryce. The wedding will be performed by our Prime on board ship because the Regal does not wish to set foot on Ardronese soil. That could be as little as two or three weeks hence."

For a long while she sat silent, her face hardening in a way he'd never seen before. "And you?" she asked at last. "What do you think?"

"Need you ask?" The huskiness of his voice betrayed him.

"Yes."

He chose his words carefully. "The marriage of a princess of Ardrone is a matter of duty, not pleasure. Your late mother was sent from Staravale to marry your father. I doubt anyone asked her if it was what she wanted. Yet by all reports, she was content, even happy."

"No one married her to a man more than thirty years older than she was."

Oh, blister my tongue. "Ah . . . that's true."

"Can you save me from this?"

"I? I have no power at this court." Her lack of guile surprised him, even as the request ripped him apart. She couldn't think he could offer her a way out, surely?

"Would you save me if you could?" she asked. She stretched out her hand and laid it over his fingers. The touch was soft, but it sent waves of tension rippling through him.

"That's not a fair question." He swallowed. "You know I think of you kindly and desire your happiness."

"I know you love me."

He was stilled, appalled at having been so transparent, terrified that she was outraged by his presumption. Fool that he was, he'd thought he'd hidden the depth of the affection he had for her. She sat regarding him with her lovely blue eyes, no sign of tears now. Her face could have been carved from cold marble.

He said, carefully neutral, relying on the formality of language to maintain his distance, "You are the daughter of the monarch to whom I give allegiance. As such, you have my deepest respect."

"You love me. And I do not speak of your duty, but of your heart. I am not blind. Your eyes tell of your longing. Your body speaks to me of your desire."

Abruptly, he stood. "It is not meet for us to speak of such things. No matter how much I revere you, you are a princess, and you will marry as the King bids. I am not even of noble birth. I – I will leave you now. Should you wish me to lead you in prayer, send word to my room and I will come, as always." He bowed deeply.

He was halfway out of the door when he turned back to say additional words of comfort, and his gaze met Celandine's. In shock, he realised she'd never left the room, but was still sitting in the corner. *How is that possible? She wasn't there!*

Aghast, he knew she must surely have heard everything they'd said. Her eyes – as grey as the rest of her – contemplated him with a complete lack of expression, as blank as a pane of window glass. Forgetting what he had been about to say, he left the room.

Va's teeth, he thought. *She does have glamour witchery.*

It had not been the lascar's dagger trying to bewitch him on board Juster's ship; it had been Celandine Marten.

Sorrel hid her anger. It wouldn't help Mathilda to know how enraged she was. But the thought was there nonetheless. *How dare they treat a woman, any woman, as if she was a commodity to be bargained for?*

She said, "It's not the witan's fault, milady. He has no power to alter this decision."

Mathilda, still seated by the window, did not bother to look her way. "Do you think me stupid? I know that."

Then why were you winding him up like a clockwork toy?

"And what of Ryce? He must have known the details of this for months! It doesn't even matter to any of them that the Horned Death is raging in Lowmeer as long as they get the kind of treaty they want," Mathilda said bitterly. "I so hate being in their power. Sometimes I want to seize a sword and chop off somebody's head." She took a calming breath, and added softly, "I will sabotage their plans if I can."

Va's teeth, what was the girl planning now? She knew better than to ask; she was not Mathilda's confidante. She had to wait to be told, which might or might not happen.

Mathilda glanced at her then. "Don't worry, Celandine. Sorrel. No matter who I marry, I'll take you with me. In another country, you'd be safer. You could even use your own face and name, for surely no one in Lowmeer will have heard tell of a common landsman's murder outside the petty little town of Melforn on the other side of Ardrone."

And it doesn't occur to you that I might have other wishes? She stifled a sigh. Once you'd lost control of your own life, it wasn't easy to get it back again.

The Princess stood up, and squared her shoulders. "One day I will have power. I will show them all what a woman can do."

Pox on all royals, Sorrel thought. *She's up to something.*

18

The Witan's Folly

There was no way he could sleep that night. He tossed and turned, then walked about the room until his feet were cold and he had to return to bed. It wasn't just thoughts of Mathilda's fate that tormented him; it was the mark he couldn't see on his hand.

A'Va had tainted him. There was only one reason he could think of to do that: he was marked for death. Sooner or later one of A'va's bootlickers would take it upon themselves to rid the world of a witan believed to be a threat. *And how am I supposed to be a threat anyway?*

When he heard someone tapping at his door around midnight, his immediate reaction was relief that he didn't need to pretend, even to himself, that he was going to have a good night's rest. Expecting it must be someone in need of his pastoral care – a dying member of the King's household, perhaps? – he rose, lit a candle from the coals still burning in the fireplace, and carried the holder to the door. At least he didn't have to beware of an assassin within the palace.

It was a woman. She'd pulled the hood of her grey cloak low to conceal her face. Her ringless fingers clutched at the folds of the mantle, but when she stepped forward, he saw she wore her plain grey gown beneath. Celandine. She was alone and the passage beyond was empty. She entered, almost treading on his toes, forcing him to step back.

He was so surprised, he gave way. "Mistress . . ." he began in protest, but before any further words, she was inside, shutting and barring the door. He tried again, speaking to her back. "Mistress, you really shouldn't be here. What if someone saw you? Your reputation! If you have a message from the Princess, then . . ."

She turned and flipped down her hood to reveal her identity. "I just borrowed Celandine's clothes. We're the same size."

"Milady!" Appalled thoughts tumbled through his mind, one after another. She was clay-brained. She could be destroyed by this, her whole life reduced to ruins. She might be confined to a cloister for the rest of her life. A scandal like this – dear Va, it could reverberate across nations! It was one thing for a married woman of lower rank to be careless with her assignations, but a virgin princess? And with *him*? He could be charged with treason. Beheaded, if they thought he'd shared her bed. *Oh, sweet Mathilda, what are you doing?*

He swallowed, searching for the right words, for a way not to hurt her. "This is unwise. Milady, you must leave. Just because I am a witan mentoring you does not mean we cannot be accused of behaviour that could wreck your marriage!"

"Maybe that's a good idea."

Appalled, he went cold. "Oh no. Milady—"

"Oh, pah! Stop 'miladying' me all the time! My name is Mathilda. Use it, at least while we are alone. And I'm not serious, of course, not about wrecking the nuptials. I will marry the Regal. I know my duty. I've known since I was five years old that this moment – or one like it – would come." She made no attempt to conceal her vexation. "I don't have a choice. But I do have a choice about who will be, um, the first."

She must surely have been blushing, although he couldn't see it in the candlelight. He took another step backwards, but the room was small and he bumped into his clothing chest. She took a step closer, twisting a hand into the cloth of his nightgown. He was forced to lift the candle holder high to avoid setting fire to her cloak.

Her upturned face was inches from his own as she whispered her next words. "I'm going to marry an old, wrinkled man." She undid the ties at the top of his nightgown with her free hand and touched his bare chest with her fingers. He started sweating. "I want to have a memory to take with me. Of what it's like to be cherished by someone who loves me, someone who will take, with gentleness and respect, what should be mine to freely bestow where I will. Someone who also has passion and desire."

Her hand slid up to his shoulder and then to the back of his neck. He stopped breathing.

"I've watched you, Saker. I've seen your duty turn to devotion, your respect replaced by love. I'm offering you all I have in return for a memory to last me a lifetime. A memory to see me through the horrors and the loneliness I will have to endure. Can you turn away?"

He opened his mouth to tell her again she must leave, choking on words he didn't know how to say without hurting her. Words that were becoming more impossible to voice with each passing minute. His heart thundered under his ribs.

When he still did not reply, she lowered her gaze, and continued, "Was that such a hard question?"

"Milady – Mathilda – what you ask is impossible. No matter how much I would value such a – such a perfect gift."

"I'm begging you." She raised her head, her words little more than a breath shivering against his skin.

"Please, Lady Mathilda . . ."

"Look, I humble myself before you." She slid to her knees in front of him. "A princess on her knees, beseeching you. Is it such a hard thing to ask you to love me tonight, to take me in your arms, to kiss my lips?"

His face flamed hot with embarrassment and desire. He groaned and grabbed her by the elbows and pulled her to her feet. "You mustn't kneel. Not you. Not before me. Milady, Mathilda, *please*." He wanted to tell her she'd been watching far too many of the court's romantic masques, but the depth of feeling in her voice told him she meant what she said.

She was holding him now, pressing her body to him, her mouth inches from his, whispering. "Do not fear for consequences. What court lady does not know how to ensure there is no child to explain away after an indiscretion?"

Embarrassed, he stuttered something incoherent. Mercifully, she changed the subject.

"Tell me this, Saker, dearest friend. If you were instructed to accompany me to the Regality as my mentor, how would you feel knowing you had to live out the rest of your years in Ustgrind, away from your friends and family? Never to worship again in the forests of Ardrone? You told me you've been to Ustgrind, and you thought their stone chapels cold, and their mists and their meres drear."

Every word she uttered was a blade of guilt into his soul. Torn, he knew he should offer to accompany her if it was allowed, to be her comfort in her lonely exile. She had just as good as told him she loved him. How could he say no? But the horror of drab Lowmeer and the comparative bleakness of its Way of the Flow, the idea of living for years at the Lowmian court, with its rigid protocols . . .

The words that came out of his mouth were not the ones he intended to say, but as he heard them, he knew they were right. "How can I go with you, feeling the way I do? If you hold me in equal affection, how could you look at me day after day and be loyal to your husband?"

She raised her eyes again then, to stare at him, her face so close, her breath a whisper against his cheek.

"Va save me, I would do it," he said. "I would do it, if I thought it was possible and if I thought it'd make you happier. But neither the Regal nor his clerics would ever allow an Ardronese witan at the Lowmeer court. And the Pontifect would never send me."

The moment dragged on, then she gave a slight nod. "Yes, you are right. Saker Rampion, always the wise mentor. Do not come with me, then. Instead . . ." She raised a hand and cupped the side of his face. His candle wobbled and shadows danced. Her next words were whispered. "As your beloved princess, I demand you give me my memory of love in your arms."

Without waiting for his answer, she drew his head down with one hand and ran her tongue over his lips. For a moment he resisted, but then her mouth was hard against his – and he was lost. His hips pressed against her, his desire swallowing him whole. He managed to place the candle on his clothing chest, but that was the last coherent thought he had.

He drew her into the vortex of his need, and she was there, matching it with her own. He tried to be gentle, to be cautious, but her response to his touch was so passionate and unrestrained that the last of his self-possession was devoured by desire. Afterwards he could never be sure how they ended up on the bed, sheened with perspiration, naked and in each other's arms.

Still later, when he lay sated at her side, she gave a low laugh. "And now you start to wonder," she said, "don't you? You doubt my virginity. Yet there is blood – see?" She touched the bed linen.

"You – you know much for an unschooled maiden," he said, careful not to sound condemnatory. He had no right to that. He was dazzled by what had happened. Sublimely happy, petrified with horror, all at the same time. He'd lain with a king's daughter. Broken her maidenhead. He could die for this. So, possibly, could she. Utter, irresponsible madness. Yet so glorious. With a finger he traced a line down her body from her neck, across a nipple, to the fuzz of her pubic hair, just to be sure she was real.

Her soft laugh made him nuzzle her neck for the sheer pleasure of her taste, her closeness and, yes, the danger. Anything not to think about the sublime stupidity of what they had done.

"We court women seek pleasure in each other's arms," she explained.

Blood rushed to his face. Glad she could not see the heat of his embarrassment in the dim light, he was nonetheless robbed of speech by the unabashed wantonness of her words. *Giddy hells, Mathilda, don't tell me anything more!*

She rolled over on to her stomach to look at him. "Oh, tush! What else is open to us before we marry? Our fathers demand we are chaste and ignorant until our husband is chosen for us. Our mothers and older sisters are wiser, and explain how to remain virginal and yet skilful in the ways of pleasure, so that we won't be cold in the arms of our husbands, nor ignorant of how to satisfy them."

He blushed yet again; before this night he hadn't even known he could. "I – I fear I am ignorant of, er, court . . . ways. But Mathilda, you've placed yourself in an impossible situation. You can only be a – a virgin once."

Va, he was suddenly having trouble managing his tongue. He took a deep breath and added, "You are about to marry a man of . . . experience. He will know, and your life could be endangered. Lowmeer is an unforgiving place and the Regal is an unforgiving man. You – no, *we* have been insanely unwise. It was my fault – I am the older and supposed to be the wiser, and I let this happen."

Va save us, how can I possibly undo this?

His renewed horror at what he had done seeped into his tone, yet she did not appear worried. She shrugged, indifferent, and placed his hand over her breast. "There are ways to deceive even a monarch. A sachet of blood, herbs that tighten the skin. My maid, Aureen, is the daughter of the palace midwife. She knows these things and she'll accompany me to Lowmeer. Don't fear for me, Saker. And never underestimate me, because you'll rue that day. Right now – I think I would like another memory to cherish. You see? I am wicked at heart."

"You are wonderful at heart. But I fear I have disappointed you. It has been a long while since I bedded a woman, and the result was by necessity, er, hasty."

"Then show me what it means when a man has bedded a woman less than an hour past."

Unable to refuse her anything, he obliged. He might as well be hung for a gold guildeen as for a brass bit.

Two hours before dawn, as she dressed again in the unattractive grey gown, he asked, suddenly panicked, "Does Celandine know you are here?"

"Yes, of course. How else could I be wearing her clothing?"

"What if she betrays you?"

She laughed. "Celandine would never do that."

"How can you be sure?" He started sweating again, with fear this time.

She shrugged. "I know her well. I saved her from an awful fate. She owes me everything, truly, and a word from me could send her to the gibbet."

Startled by the words, he paused, then reached for his shirt. "Do – do you trust her? She heard our conversation yesterday afternoon, and now you're going to ask her to help you fool a bridegroom!"

"She's the only one of my ladies I do trust."

"Everyone at court has a price."

"Do you think I don't know that? I'm a king's daughter. Everyone desires my favour, yet they'd throw me to the bears *and* the wolves if that would gain them my father's favour, or my brother's, instead. But Celandine? She's the mouse that gets her crumbs from *me,* and from me alone. And I know things about her that she doesn't want anyone else to know."

He was not reassured. "Be careful. The more dowdy the woman, the more easily she is seduced."

"You denigrate her." She pulled on her snood and began to tuck her hair up under it. "She's a very moral woman."

"Possibly. I do not know her. I've hardly spoken to her, or her to me. I'm just concerned for your welfare. You know she has a witchery. That's why you asked me about glamours, isn't it?"

She smiled and nodded. "Her talent has been useful to me."

He paused, searching for the right words. "Milady, Mathilda, what we did tonight gave us a moment of – of paradise, but even paradise is said to have its savage bears and cunning wolves. If you were hurt because of what happened here . . ." He couldn't express his dread and had to swallow back bile.

"Would you tie my bodice, please?"

It laced at the front, and his fingers fumbled as he obliged. She teased him, kissing his nose and chin and eyes as he tried to tie the bows. He could hardly breathe. Desire built in him again. And more: a deep anger against those who would treat her like a piece of merchandise to be bargained over.

When he bent to pick up her cloak from where it lay on the floor, she straightened her skirts and said, "No ill shall come to me."

Her calm put him to shame. Gone was the young girl he'd first known; this was a woman facing an unpleasant destiny with a courage that reproached him. As he placed the mantle around her shoulders, he said, his voice husky, "You gave me a precious memory too. I will never forget. And I'll always love you."

She stilled for a moment, regarding him. There was little in her expression to tell him what she was thinking. "You were right; that second time was better. A memory to last a lifetime. But as for the rest . . . You loved me enough to bed me, but not, I think, enough to sacrifice your life for me. You'd not come to Lowmeer even if you could."

The truth in her words seared more than he would have thought possible. He could have hunted for a way to be in her entourage. He could have begged the Pontifect to help him. But she was right. To go to Lowmeer, for an extended period of time? To watch her day after day married to a man like Regal Vilmar? To give up the adventure of his service to the Pontifect? He couldn't do it.

"It wouldn't be possible," he whispered at last.

"No," she agreed calmly. "Not for someone Shenat-born. I suspect I'll be lucky if I can say my prayers celebrating the Way of the Oak. They are very austere, are they not, with their water prayers?" She walked to the door. "Do not come with me now. It would seem strange if you accompanied Celandine anywhere at this time of night. Besides, the passage is secure."

He nodded. There were guards at every entrance to the royal section of the palace, so the passageways within it were safe.

Reluctant, he nodded his agreement. "Nor should this happen again. It's too risky." *Oh, Va take it. That didn't sound at all the way he meant it.*

He opened his mouth to try to explain, but she cut him short. "Indeed not." Just as he unlatched the door for her, she added, "If your life is changed by what happened tonight, I will regret it deeply – but I'd do the same again."

"Mathilda . . ." He wanted to kiss her one more time, he wanted to utter more words of love, of support, of regret, but she had already turned her back, and pulled her hood around her face. She stepped out into the passage and was gone.

The night's events should have made him the happiest man alive. Instead, he'd never felt more wretched, more guilty, more shamed.

And so certain that the two of them were teetering on the edge of disaster.

19

The Witan's Downfall

Prince Ryce ran downstairs to the King's chambers, wondering just what had prompted a peremptory royal summons not long after dawn. He was never normally up this early, a fact his father knew full well.

He was still fixing the ties on his doublet and adjusting the lace at his wrists when he arrived at the doors to the royal reception chamber. Va only knew what his hair looked like. He was fairly certain someone had spilled ale over his head the night before, although his memory was a little fuzzy about that.

The two pikemen on duty swung open the door without a word and Ryce marched straight in. King Edwayn was standing at the window, watching the lightening sky. The lines at the corners of his lips were grim furrows bracketing the straight line of his mouth.

Va help me. I didn't do anything really lackwitted last night, did I? Or was this going to be about Juster and that idiotic wager on the *Golden Petrel*?

It was obviously one of those times when a little formality would not go amiss. "Your Majesty," he said, and bowed. There was a pleasant smell of fresh bread in the air, wafting up from the kitchens, but he quelled his hunger. Now was not the time to think of food.

"Ryce." His father gave a terse nod. "Your spiritual adviser. Witan Saker Rampion." He spat the name out as though he were talking about a pestilence.

"Yes, sire?"

"What do you know about him?"

"Decent enough fellow, for a cleric. Although I'm not in the habit of, um, of sharing an ale or a lady or a night in the town with a witan."

The King stared at him, his eyebrows raised to signal his lack of comprehension.

"I meant, we're hardly *intimate* friends," Ryce said. This had to be even worse than he imagined.

"Hmph. That's good, because I want you to kill him."

What? He blinked, momentarily speechless. His knees wobbled and he wanted to sit, but Edwayn was standing, and not even he could sit before the King did.

"Not today, but soon," his father added, without looking his way.

"Ah . . ." He hunted for a suitable answer, but little came to mind. Finally he settled for: "I would have thought that you had other, more competent, er, blackguards for the occasional murder of an, er, inconvenient fellow, Father. I can't say I've had much . . . experience."

"No? I seem to remember a brawl in a tavern, a year ago."

"A low-class drunkard. And the man attacked me. Somehow I don't think Rampion is likely to do that. He's a very serious fellow. You do know he's a skilled swordsman? I spar with him, every so often. I'd hate to fight him in earnest, because I'm by no means sure I would come out alive." *A'Va take it, you don't want me dead, do you?*

"He's that good?" The King swung round to look at him. He appeared taken aback. "What's a witan doing with sword skills better than my son's?"

"He wears a Pashali sword," he replied, not wanting to admit that Saker practised much more than he could be bothered to do. "Rare as fish feathers, those. Good steel. He also swims across the Throssel river and back at Dunnock Pier every morning, after prayers. Even in winter!"

"Fortunately, I'm not asking you to fight him, or drown him, but to assassinate him! And you have to do it alone, and unobserved. I don't want the faintest whisper of this becoming either tavern gossip or a court rumour, understand? Which is why I want *you* to do it, and not someone I can't trust to keep their mouth shut when they're in their cups. There can be no hint that Ardrone's heir murdered a Va-Faith witan."

"Ah – no. Of course not. But Father, why is it . . . necessary? What's he done?" *Tell me this is a nightmare and I'm going to wake up soon. I* like *the man!*

"Oh, he deserves what's coming to him. I'm waiting for Valerian

Fox to arrive, then I'll explain. But this business of killing the varlet – that's just something to remain between you and me. The Prime is not to know."

"No, of course not." The idea of Fox knowing that the King had ordered the death of a cleric froze the blood in his veins. His father wasn't losing his grip on sanity, was he?

"Pox on that dog of a dastard!" Edwayn growled. "I've never heard of the Rampion family. They can't be all that important. I hope he's not influenced you to bad habits."

"Never seen him drunk. Doesn't seem to visit the port brothels or fancy houses." Ryce shrugged. "He's supposed to be my spiritual adviser, but we made a sort of agreement, right at the beginning. If I want advice, I'll tell him."

The King glowered at him.

"Well, that's true enough," he said defensively. "If I need advice on moral or religious matters, he's the person I'd ask, not Fox or whatsisname. Conrid Masterton."

The King looked alarmed. "Ryce, when it's your backside that sits on the throne, don't trust Shenat-born clerics. At least you can bribe a merchant, but one of them, or worse-still, a shrine-keeper?" He shook his head. "About them, you can never be certain. They hark back to past glories too much, to the old stories of earth magic and oak witchery."

"Pickles and hay, Father, we've got it better than Lowmians, dressed in black, being whipped for drunkenness, jailed for laying a bet on a cockfight, and listening to sermons three hours long telling us not to fornicate! I'd rather have Shenat-cleric piety than the puritanical austerity of a black-clad Lowmeer merchant."

The King snorted. "*You* would! But we shouldn't let hedge-born hayseeds keep our faith hooked to oak trees. I don't want to spend the rest of eternity looking out through the leaves of a hedge! I have my doubts about the teachings of the Way of the Oak. Lowmeer may have their water shrines, but at least they put more emphasis on the importance of obedience to Va, rather than the care of a few trees and soggy marshes."

Tush, he's serious! This is Fox's doing. Growing more and more curious about just what the witan had done, he said carefully, "Your Majesty,

I think you listen too much to Prime Valerian and his Lowmian attitude to Va. His sermons are as dry as ash from the hearth."

The King glared at him, but the retort he was about to utter was suppressed by a knock at the door and Prime Fox entered, his black gown sweeping the wooden floorboards.

Damn the fellow. Impeccably turned out, even at dawn. With a jaundiced eye, Ryce regarded the lacework on the Prime's collar and cuffs, and the bright gemstones in his clerical pendants and rings. The lower clergy might dress plainly, but as they rose to the higher levels they didn't stint on their baubles. *The man keeps his king waiting while he puts his rings on? Arrogant coxcomb.*

Fox inclined his head to the King rather than bowing.

King Edwayn switched his glare to him as the door closed. "Eminence," he said, "I wished to see you about one of your clerics. Witan Saker Rampion, to be exact."

The Prime raised an eyebrow in enquiry. "Sire? If it's about that affair on board Lord Juster's ship—"

"He ravished Lady Mathilda last night."

The words were so outrageous, it took a moment for Ryce to make sense of them. *Ravished?* No one would dare! Not Mathilda! In the *palace*? And above all, not the calm, controlled Rampion. He stared at his father in disbelief, wondering for a blink of an eye whether this was some sort of plot on the King's part to diminish the status of the Pontificate. *No, surely not.*

Valerian Fox was equally speechless. When he found his tongue, he sounded inane. "Are you *sure*?" he asked.

As if Father would make such an accusation without being sure. At any other time, Ryce might have laughed, but there was nothing humorous in this. He had to swallow before he could speak. "Is she all right?" he asked. The look the King gave him told him the question was just as stupid as Fox's.

"Of course I'm sure!" King Edwayn snapped, answering the Prime. He took a deep breath and began to explain. "Rampion spoke to her yesterday about her betrothal to Regal Vilmar. She was upset and could not sleep. She decided to go to the chapel to pray. This was about midnight. Foolish girl chose to go alone. Unfortunately, Rampion was there."

"I'll kill him!" Ryce said, his rage swamping his discretion.

King Edwayn shot a furious look in his direction. "Va defend me from your witless thinking, Ryce. You will do no such thing. We must avoid scandal at all cost! She's to marry the Regal and no wisp of a word of this must reach his ears."

"Forgive me," Fox said, bowing his head in contrition. "If Rampion truly did this – this *iniquitous* deed, it is my fault. The Pontifect herself recommended him and I acquiesced, even though he was not known to me personally. I should have investigated further. I was told he was a man of considerable learning . . ."

"And, it seems, no restraint on his filthy urges," Edwayn said from between gritted teeth, "and certainly no respect for the Crown. What I need to know is what is to be done now."

Ryce had never seen him in a rage like this one: deadly, white hot, yet controlled. He wasn't about to do anything without thinking through the consequences.

"You would be within your rights to charge him with treason," the Prime said slowly. "And have him executed."

"And just how would I do that and keep what happened quiet? A treason trial has to have three judges, at least one of them a senior cleric, and one a peer of the realm. No matter whom I chose, they could hold me to ransom with that secret – even if it was possible to hold a closed trial."

"I'm glad you don't have such a low opinion of *my* discretion."

"You have a lot to lose, Fox. I appoint primes: I can rid myself of primes."

"I would have kept counsel without the threat."

Ryce blinked, wondering if he'd heard correctly. Was the Prime *chiding* the King?

"Yes, yes, I know," Edwayn answered testily. "It hasn't escaped my notice that you hold a partnership in Viscount Sturvent's Spicerie Company. If this marriage to the Regal doesn't go ahead, and there's no bride price, you stand to lose almost as much as the Crown."

Ryce looked from one to the other, trying to absorb all that was said. *Oh, Va,* he thought. *Why do I always feel one step behind?* No matter how hard he tried, he seemed to miss half the nuances of conversation while it was in progress.

The Prime ignored Edwayn's statement. "Who else knows what Rampion has done?" he asked.

"Besides the man himself? I doubt *he* told anyone. So just the three of us here, plus Mathilda and her handmaiden. Mathilda ran straight back to her rooms afterwards, woke this one woman and came directly to my bedchamber. She seems to think this particular handmaiden of hers can be trusted."

"Then perhaps we can contain it," Fox said.

"How?"

"You want me to find some legal way to rid the world of Saker Rampion." The concept did not appear to worry Fox.

"Just so."

Ryce looked from one to the other, trying to puzzle out what his father was planning. Right now, his previous mention of murdering Rampion seemed irrelevant.

"Seeing as he's already committed a great evil," Fox continued, "I have no compunction about charging him with something equally heinous. He can then be arrested, charged, tried and nulled."

"Nulled?" Prince Ryce asked. "What's that?" From the brief flash of satisfaction across the King's face, he guessed this was the solution his father had been wanting Fox to propose all along.

"A rare punishment meted out to errant clerics by a combined crown and ecclesiastical court. It usually results in death," Valerian Fox replied.

Ryce took a deep breath. Perhaps he wouldn't have to murder the man after all. He breathed a little easier. The idea of killing someone in cold blood made him feel sick. Although if someone else did the deed . . . Rampion deserved to die. Sweet Va, how *dared* he? And in the royal *chapel* at that?

King Edwayn slumped into the nearest chair. "I blame Mathilda, too, in all this. She was foolish beyond measure, walking to the chapel at night alone!"

Ryce frowned. Foolish had never been a word he would have applied to his sister. In fact, even though he was two years older, she'd always been the bright one, the clever one. What was it their grandmother had called her when she was young? *The cunning scallywag* . . . Anyway, she had every right to have expected it safe to go to the chapel!

"What have you done so far, sire?" Fox asked.

"Confined Mathilda and the handmaiden, Celandine Marten, to my own retiring room." He nodded at the door on the far side of the chamber. "Through there. They've no access to anyone."

"And Rampion?" Fox asked.

"I've had him taken to the Keep, without explanation to anyone as yet. He was still in his room. I suppose he relied on Mathilda to be too ashamed to say anything. He miscalculated."

"Good. Then I shall handle this, if you so desire, sire. The more it is seen as a religious matter and the Prime's concern with a rogue witan, the better able we'll be to protect the Princess's good name."

The King nodded and waited for Fox to continue.

"I will have this Marten woman killed before she can talk."

Ryce blinked, his heart sinking still deeper. Only the day before, after being told of the identity of her bridegroom, Mathilda had made it clear to him how much she relied on both her handmaiden and her maid, Aureen. "I will not go to Lowmeer without them both," she'd told him. "I don't ask much of you, Ryce, but I want you to make sure that in this I have my way. Understand?"

And he had understood. Mathilda was quite capable of wreaking revenge on him, and she knew more than enough of his affairs to embarrass him.

"I don't think that would be a good idea," he said quickly, before his father could reply. "Mathilda is very dependent on her handmaiden, and we want her to be amenable to the marriage arrangements. If she thinks we murdered this woman . . ." He allowed the rest of the sentence to trail away, knowing that his father would be picturing one of Mathilda's rare but unforgettable tantrums.

The King nodded. "True. Ryce can put the fear of death by torture into Mistress Marten to keep her mouth shut. Think of something else, Fox."

"Ah. In that case, there are some nuns from the cloisters at Comfrey who have taken a vow of perpetual silence. I'll have several sent over here. We can put it about that Mathilda wishes to spend the time prior to her marriage in quiet prayer and contemplation. She can still have her dressmakers visit, or whatever she needs, but I'll instruct the nuns to supervise. Their job will be more to keep an eye on the Marten woman. I'll think of some plausible explanation for them. The handmaiden must not be permitted to leave the Princess's chambers, or to have private access to anyone."

"And Rampion?" King Edwayn asked.

"I'll spread the word that he's being charged with blasphemy. That's serious enough to warrant his incarceration in the Keep for a while. In the meantime, I shall find evidence enough to convict him on something more serious. Something that carries the penalty of nullification."

Fox's calm sent a shiver through Ryce.

"Excellent," the King said, in a voice that reminded Ryce of newly sharpened steel.

It was a further half-hour before the Prime left. In that time, the two men had refined their plan of action while Ryce listened and wondered. Everything was so . . . so devious. It wasn't that he disapproved; it was more that he found it hard to think things through the way his father did.

I'll never be a wise ruler, he thought morosely. *If I'd been king when this happened, I would just have ordered Rampion's head chopped off and been done with it.*

He shuddered. The religious ramifications would have been horrible and he would have spent the better part of his reign straightening it all out.

"What are you being so lily-livered about?" his father asked, after Fox had left. "You look as sick as a squashed frog! Rampion deserves everything he gets."

"Of course. What – what exactly is nullification?"

"Ah. Haven't seen that used since my father's day. It's punishment for clerics who sin against the Faith. First they are branded on the cheek. Then they are taken out on the high moors and chained to an unattended shrine, without money, or water, or food, as bare-arsed as they came into the world. Should anyone pass by, they see the branding and the chains, so they leave the mercy, or otherwise, for Va to decide. That's the whole idea: it's up to Va. The sinner usually dies of cold or starvation or wolves. In this case, with winter coming on . . ." He smiled.

"Then why do you want *me* to kill Saker?"

His eyebrows snapped together. "Because a ruler never takes chances. You're to make *sure* he dies once he's been abandoned, and you do it alone. Understand? No one is ever to know what Saker Rampion did to Mathilda. She only has value to us if she's assumed to be a virgin. I don't want the Regal to have the slightest suspicion his bride was ravished. We *need* this treaty, thanks to the stupidity of our merchants, arguing among themselves while Lowmeer steals the wealth from under their noses. Regal Vilmar could use her lack of virginity as an excuse to void the treaty. He must *never* find out."

"But – but won't he, um, realise anyway?"

The King gave an unpleasant laugh. "Ah, the innocence of a young man. You think court women don't know a dozen ways to cozen a man into believing she's a blushing virgin bride?"

Ryce glanced at the door to the retiring room, feeling uncomfortable. "And Mathilda . . .?"

"Ah, yes. Damned if I know what to do about crying womenfolk. You fix it."

He opened his mouth to protest, then realised there was no one they could ask to deal with this for them. He took a deep breath and opened the door to the adjacent room.

Somehow he'd been expecting to find Mathilda sobbing in agitation, and to see the Marten woman comforting her. Instead, the two women were standing on opposite sides of the room, both of them stony-faced and silent. If he hadn't known it was absurd, he'd have said they'd just had a vicious verbal exchange. Both of them had the kind of reddened cheeks he usually associated with anger.

"Well, about time," Mathilda snapped, crossing the room towards him. "What's happening?"

He gaped at her, confounded by the lack of hysterical grief he'd expected. "Are you, er, all right?" he asked, at a loss.

"No, of course I'm not all right!"

"I'm terribly sorry, Thilda, for what happened. I never expected anything like that from Saker Rampion. He seemed so – so *decent*."

Without warning, she flung herself into his arms and buried her face in his shoulder. "Oh, Ryce, it's been horrible!" The words were muffled, interspersed with sobs. He patted her back while looking over her head at Celandine, whose eyebrows were drawn together in a glower. Her mouth was a grim line across her face, and as he watched, she folded her arms and turned her back on them both.

"Tell me, quickly," Mathilda said, without raising her head. "What's Father going to do?"

"Rampion has been thrown in the Keep. He'll be tried for blasphemy or something. In due course, he'll end up dead. What he actually did will be kept a secret. That way, your marriage to the Regal will go ahead as planned. It will be up to you to convince the Regal you are still, er, pure."

He wasn't sure what reaction he'd expected, but it wasn't the one he received. The Marten woman turned abruptly to stare at him, with a sharp intake of breath.

Mathilda, still enfolded in his arms, jerked backwards to look up at him. "Oh no," she said. He knew that expression, although he hadn't seen it for years. She was working herself into a furious storm. "Father can't do that to me. He can't! I shan't go through with the marriage after this. I *won't*."

"I'm sorry, Thilda. I know it has been a terrible, terrible experience, but . . ."

Her glare indicated she thought him as low as a worm squashed under her slipper, and he knew he had somehow failed her. He floundered, miserably out of his depth, even as he wondered at her dry eyes. She hadn't been crying into his shoulder as he'd thought. He didn't understand that, but he banished the doubts skittering at the edge of his mind. He didn't want to consider them; they were far too dark.

"I will *not* marry a withered old man who probably can't father children, whose wives die surprisingly often and who presides over a court which seems to be as much fun as a funeral procession! For Va's sake, Ryce. *Pity* me in this!"

"I – well, of course, but Thilda—"

"No buts, Ryce. Talk to Father about it. I'm no longer a virgin; the Regal will have me killed on my wedding night if he finds out!"

With one last look, she swept past him into the reception room to talk to King Edwayn herself. He looked back at the Marten woman. She'd seated herself in the nearest chair, straight-backed and unmoving, staring at the floor. He cleared his throat. "The King's orders are that you're not to speak to anyone about this, on pain of . . ." He halted, not sure how to word it.

She looked up to regard him steadily, waiting for him to finish.

"Er, torture was mentioned. And death."

"I never doubted it," she said. "You can tell him I know who puts the bread on my plate."

He had never seen such bleak misery on a woman's face.

From the next room, he heard his father roar, "Ryce! Get in here and talk some sense into your sister's head!"

He obeyed, when what he really wanted to do was disappear in the direction of the nearest tavern and order himself a jeroboam of beer.

How can I have been such a fool?

After Mathilda left, Saker did not go back to sleep. As the first cold light of dawn crept in through an ill-fitted shutter that morning, the question echoed, over and over, at the forefront of his mind. *How can I have been such a fool?*

Cool, calm Saker Rampion. Swordsman, scholar, spy – and gold-plated, loggerheaded *lout*. What if someone found out? What if Celandine Marten betrayed them?

Betrayed? That was a joke – *he* was the one who'd betrayed Mathilda. And himself. He was older, supposedly wiser, a cleric. He was her spiritual adviser, dammit!

True, unlike the Way of the Flow of Lowmeer, the Way of the Oak did not promote the celibacy of the clergy, although they did emphasise the importance of constancy within marriage. But still, he was supposed to *guide* a pupil, not seduce her. Or assist her seduction of him.

And then, to compound his crime, by refusing to accompany her to Lowmeer, he'd walked away when she needed him most. He was in love – but not enough to make a sacrifice for her.

Useless to tell himself there was no way a Shenat witan would ever have been welcome at the court there; useless to tell himself that the Pontifect would never have allowed it either; useless to know it would have been an impossible situation for both Mathilda and himself anyway. He was as guilty as a hornswaggling pickpocket, and he knew it.

Earth and oak, how he loved her! Her compassion. Her quick wit. The way her smile lit up her face like the glow of a candle through frosted glass. The feel of her, the perfume of her body, the passion within, the absence of shame when she'd shown him her need . . .

Dear Va.

What have I done?

And how could he possibly undo any of it?

He was fully dressed, ready to go to the chapel for morning prayer, when a rapping at the door rattled the wooden planks. On opening it, he was surprised to see the sergeant of the Prince's personal guard standing there in uniform, with several others behind him. His greeting was a respectful, "Good morning, Witan Rampion."

"Yes, er, Sergeant Horntail, is it not? Good morning. What's the problem?"

"Here to detain you, I regret to say, witan. At the King's pleasure."

For a moment he stood, stunned. *They can't have found out already what we did last night, surely?* No, of course not. Maybe they knew about the night he eavesdropped from a window ledge on a meeting between the Secretary for the Navy and the Chancellor of the Exchequer. Or maybe the Prime had discovered that he'd broken into his office in Faith House . . .

Finding his voice, he asked, "On – on what charge?"

"I couldn't say, master witan," the Sergeant said.

"What are your instructions, Sergeant?"

"To deliver you to the Keep, witan."

The *Keep*? That wasn't good. For one mad moment he considered fleeing, but there was nowhere to run. He shook his head, as if that would bring clarity to his thoughts, but it didn't help. "Can I take anything with me?"

Dear Va, if someone knows about last night, I'm a dead man.

"Bit chilly down yonder, so bring a blanket. My men'll help you carry whate'er you want. No weaponry, of course."

Almost overcome by his sense of unreality – *Blister it, this couldn't be happening!* – he gathered as much as he could. Paper, ink, quill, a change of clothes, his prayer book, his cloak, the acorn he had taken from the King Oak shrine, money. He knew enough about jails to know he'd need all the coins he had for bribes, or to buy luxuries like decent food. He looked at his Pashali sword hanging in its scabbard behind the door and wondered if it would still be there when – if – he returned. There was no lock on the outside of his door.

You beef-witted fool. You deserve everything that happens to you . . .

Arriving at the Keep, Sergeant Horntail wished him luck and turned him over to the chief jailer, who apparently answered only to his title, Master Turnkey. The cell contained a table, a chair and a raised stone platform for a sleeping pallet. A slit through the thick outer wall, less than a hand-span wide, let in a little light and air. Unfortunately, the flagstoned floor was covered with filthy straw smelling of mould, rat droppings and roaches. The pallet hadn't been changed in years. The blanket was so ancient he thought it would disintegrate if it was washed.

After a glance around the tiny room, he turned to the turnkey and handed him the guildeen he'd just dug out of his purse. "Take this for you and your men, in appreciation. Would you be so kind as to tell one of your underlings that I would be mightily pleased if the cell were to be cleaner by nightfall? There'll be another guildeen in it . . ."

The turnkey, whose wizened face spoke of an age of experience just as much as his sizeable paunch announced his acquaintance with hearty meals and ample wine, glanced at the coin and smiled. They were both aware that jailers were largely dependent on contributions from their prisoners. "Sure and indeed, if it can be arranged, witan, 'twill be. I'm a reasonable cove, though a man with a large family and many expenses. For as long as the coinage dribbles in, I'll see to it that your stay will be comfortable, whether it be long or short. How it ends is – sadly – not up to me."

20

The Witan Betrayed

By nightfall, Saker's surroundings had vastly improved. The floor and walls had been washed with lye. Clean straw had been laid down. The pallet was replaced with a new one, freshly stuffed. Several clean blankets graced his bed. There was even a cushion for a pillow, a candlestick holder, several tallow candles and a tinder box with flint and steel to supply him with light. The slop bucket was scrubbed clean, and came with the promise that it would be emptied and scrubbed whenever he asked. He'd had a passable meal of bread, cheese, beef and carrots, served with a jug of cheap ale.

He had an idea the price he'd paid for the comforts would infuriate the Pontifect, when she heard about it. He wasn't sure she ever would, as the turnkey had informed him that no one was to be admitted to see him unless they were sent by King Edwayn or Prime Fox.

Saker spent most of the rest of the day trying to think of his next move. It was difficult to make a decision when he wasn't certain what his imprisonment was about. It was hard to think that it did not involve Mathilda, and agony to think that it did. The odds suggested that they had been betrayed, with breathtaking callousness, by Celandine Marten. He considered writing a letter to Fritillary, then decided it was pointless. If Valerian Fox wanted the Pontifect to know, he'd tell her – if he preferred her to be ignorant, there was no way he'd forward a letter.

He settled down to wait.

One good thing, he thought. *There's no way the lascar's kris will find a way back to me here.*

He dozed for a while that afternoon, only to waken abruptly with several apparently unrelated thoughts jostling for attention in the forefront of his mind.

Fritillary keeping secrets from him about his mother, and possibly his real father as well. Gerelda telling him about a pragmatic Regal not given to superstition, yet allowing the murder of twins. Fox telling him the present generation would oversee the death of the Way of the Oak. Juster saying, *Fox told you for a reason* . . . Fox using clerics for extensive information-gathering. The lists of names in groups of ten in one of Fox's ledgers. A ledger named "Resources". Penny-cress saying, *A'Va has a human face* . . . Another ledger named "Lances". There was a connection, he was sure of it, and now he had plenty of time to consider the problem.

He was still mulling over the idea of possible links when Prime Valerian Fox came to see him after sunset. After entering the cell, which Master Turnkey had just unlocked, Fox closed the door in the jailer's face.

Saker rose from the bed, expression schooled to bland calm. "Your eminence. Thank you for coming."

"You deserve no courtesy. I am not here to visit. I am here to offer you a bargain."

"Well, you'll have to explain to me first what this is all about. I do not know what the charge is, or who is accusing me."

Without warning, Fox lashed out with his arm and balled fist, catching him across the side of the face. Taken by surprise, he staggered against the table and went down on one knee. His head rang and he clutched at the table leg until the spinning settled down.

He staggered to his feet as Fox shouted, "How dare you, you cur of a Shenat mongrel! I might have known that someone of your parentage would behave in such a despicable fashion."

His mind went blank. What the blistering pox did the man mean? What could his parentage have to do with anything? Again he had a sensation of unreality, of the skewing of his world, as if Fox was playing a part he'd memorised and wasn't so much angry as delighted, revelling in his moment on the stage.

"My *parentage*?" he asked at last. "I – I fail to understand you, your eminence. I have no idea what any of this is about."

"You are being charged with blasphemy."

"*Blasphemy?* You must know that's ridiculous."

"Of course it is. It was the best I could think of to cover the iniquity of your real crime."

"And my real crime is . . .?" *Oh, Va save me, he knows about Mathilda . . .*

"How dare you act the innocent! After what you've done!"

"Suppose you explain, and then we'll both know what you are talking about?" For a moment he thought he was going to be struck again, and hastily stepped back.

"How could you possibly think that the Princess would not go to her father to tell him what you did to her? Did you think she would be too embarrassed? Too scared to tell him she'd been ravished?"

He stared, shocked. Panicked.

Mathilda said she'd been ravished?

No, of course she hadn't told the King that!

But someone must have. Which meant someone had betrayed them. The only person who knew besides himself and Mathilda: *Celandine.*

What in all the Va-cherished world was he going to do? Worse, what would the King do to Mathilda? Guilt swamped him, dragged him down to somewhere close to Va-less hell.

And then: *Rot it, I'm dead.*

Mathilda, poor Mathilda. He could picture what had happened. Cornered by Celandine's betrayal, knowing that if she denied the incident her virginity would be examined, Mathilda must have said that he'd raped her. Or maybe the King and the Prime had just jumped to conclusions.

He drew in a shuddering breath. Judging from the sneer on Fox's face, he guessed his reaction was taken as an admission of guilt. But what had it to do with his parentage?

"You misjudged your prey," Fox said. "The Princess is fearless and had the courage to describe her ravishment. Which brings me to why I am here."

I can't blame her. How can I? It was the only way out when Celandine decided to tell. A wave of relief subdued his fear. Mathilda had saved herself the only way possible, and he was glad. He must be glad. Maybe she wouldn't even have to marry the Regal.

He swallowed, took a deep breath. The penalty for any kind of attack on a member of the royal family was death. *My fault . . .* "You mention a reason for being here. I assume it is not just to abuse me."

"What you did is treason, and would normally bring you to the beheading block. But only after a trial, a trial judged by the nobility and clergy, in which the Princess's name would be brought down to the level of your stinking gutter. It's *unthinkable.* The King has asked for my intervention to save the good name of his daughter. I have suggested you be tried for blasphemy instead."

He thought back to his university studies. The penalty for blasphemy on the part of a cleric was to be unfrocked, fined and banished. Not such a bad fate, and he could still serve the Pontifect if she'd have him. A spy did not need to be a cleric.

Fortunately, the Prime can have no idea how close I am to Fritillary Reedling.

"Yes. I'm offering you a way out, Rampion," Fox continued. "One you don't deserve, in exchange for your silence and your agreement not to fight the case in court. You admit your guilt, throw yourself on the court's mercy, and you live. Not in Ardrone, and not as a cleric, but you'll be alive. If you do anything, in any way, now or in the future, to impugn the good name of the Princess, then King Edwayn will see to it that you die, unpleasantly. That's his promise to you."

His next thought was: *Wait. This is too good to be true.* If King Edwayn still wanted to marry off his daughter, to anyone at all, then would he risk having her supposed ravisher free in the world to talk about her lack of virginity?

How much of a fool do you think I am, Valerian Fox? We both know I have to die. "And if I don't agree, I am tried for treason for assaulting the King's daughter, found guilty and executed?"

"I doubt it will get as far as a law court." Fox smiled. "Do you?"

Of course not. As you've just said, that's unthinkable. The King would never allow his daughter's name to be dragged through such a procedure.

Fox folded his arms. "I'm offering you this one chance to live and to redeem your soul. Just one. Do this, and perhaps Va might forgive you for your sin."

"I agree, of course."

"The trial will start within the sennight."

Seven days. And I have no idea how you are going to kill me.

Just before he left, Fox added one last stab to his wounds. "By the way," he said, "those last three letters to the Pontifect you sent? The courier was very cooperative when I told him you were plotting treason, especially when I held one of his sons as hostage to ensure it. Clever of you to use a code. Pity they will never be read by her reverence. I do wonder, though, why you never told her about breaking into my offices."

The moment Fox was gone, Saker sat down abruptly. He was so stupefied, he didn't think his legs would hold him up.

You ninny.

He knew now why Fox had told him of his desire to rid the world of the Ways. The Prime had known the first thing he would do would be to send a message to the Pontifect. Fox had wanted to know who he used to send his private messages, so he could cut the line of communication.

Except I wasn't followed. Ever.

At least . . . not in the usual way. Fox had clasped his fingers tight, and not long afterwards he'd seen the black marks. What had Pennycress said? *It leaves a taint behind wherever you go.* And something about followers of A'Va seeing it any time.

And if Fox served A'Va, he might have seen the taint in his own office after Saker had broken in.

All of which meant that Fox had been after him long before he'd bedded Mathilda, and he, the Pontifect's oh-so-stupid spy, had as good as offered himself up as a cockerel for the Prime's feasting. Fritillary would boot him back to the Coldheart Pass on the northern border if – when – she found out. Except that he'd be dead.

He still didn't understand the bit about his parentage, though. Perhaps Fox had discovered something when he was in Shenat country? His half-brother's involvement with the Primordials? No, it had to be something more than that . . .

And where did the lascar's dagger fit into all this? Was it, too, an instrument of A'Va? An artefact from the Va-forsaken Hemisphere?

At least, he thought, trying to find something less dire to consider, that terse reply had not been from Fritillary. It must have been a forgery.

He saw no one but his jailers for the next three days. By that time he had memorised every one of their routines, scrutinised every corner of his cell, studied every stone of the floor, and still had not even the shadow of an idea how he could escape. He spent hours considering all he had learned, all he could guess, and all he could remember from the Prime's ledgers. Fox obviously thought it didn't matter if he'd seen them.

But Fox thinks you are bread-brained. With reason. Think, Saker, think. And he did. He resurrected the pages he'd seen, recalling names, numbers, amounts. Over and over. He looked for patterns. For clues. For anything he recognised.

The rest of the time he lived with the purgatory within his head. He'd become careless. He hadn't been suspicious enough of the Prime. Or of Celandine Marten. He'd behaved like a selfish, half-grown cockerel, instead of a man of responsibility. And because of him . . . only Va knew what was going to happen to Mathilda.

On the fourth day of his incarceration, Juster came to see him. Master Turnkey ushered him in, but didn't leave them alone. Instead the jailer lounged against the doorway, arms folded, watching while Juster placed a demijohn of wine on the table and then eased himself into the chair, his long legs sprawled. On the other side of the open door, two armed pikemen stood at ease.

"The Prime gave me permission to see you," Juster said, "after much pestering and a gift of considerable coinage to his favourite worthy cause. Got yourself into the bottom of a pickle barrel, didn't you?"

"You could say that." He'd been on the bed, flat on his back staring at the beams, wondering how he could get up to them so he could investigate the ceiling for weak spots. He rolled himself into a sitting position. "Almost as bad as attempting to castrate yourself with a hunk of tarred rope. How are the family jewels doing?"

"Let's just say that the cache was a lot bigger than usual for a few days. Bloody excruciating. Couldn't even sleep for the pain. Family leech says they'll polish up good as new eventually. Anyway, came to say thanks for saving my neck, which is perhaps marginally even more valuable than the jewellery."

Saker shrugged. "If it hadn't been me rescuing you, it would have been someone else. Your sailors were all over the rigging like rats."

"No one else would have got to me in time, and you know it. And you won the bet, you bastard. You did indeed beat me back to the deck. I'll pay up when I return to Throssel with a full cargo."

"Good. Do you have the letters of marque signed by the King yet?" He tried to layer the seemingly innocent question with a coating of warning, and was rewarded with an odd look from Juster. The nobleman had, after all, already told him that.

"Oh, yes," Juster replied. "All done."

"I assume it's common knowledge by now that Princess Mathilda is to marry?" He was hoping Juster would note the oddity of the juxtapositioning of the two questions.

"Talk of the city she's to become the new Regala," he said, dashing Saker's hopes that the marriage preparations might have been abandoned.

Fobbing damn. His reply had sounded casual enough, but Saker could tell he was alerted, wondering what was going on.

"The matrons are very annoyed the ceremony is to take place on board ship in Betany, not here," Juster added.

"I doubt that worries you too much, but be *warned*, everyone will be extremely busy in a few days' time, loading up the King's wedding gifts on to a ship, which will sail from Throssel. No one will be interested in your requirements. I'd get organised to leave now, if I were you." He dropped his left eyelid in an exaggerated wink, which the turnkey was unable to see from where he stood.

Juster's eyes widened a fraction. "Really?" he asked.

"I'd think about it," he replied with as much nonchalance as he could muster. *The Pontifect would kill me if she heard me giving this advice . . .* He wasn't even sure why he was doing it. *No, that's not true. I'm doing it because Juster has proved himself a friend.*

"Imagine: all the Princess's royal luggage and dowry, and the baggage of her entourage, gifts to the Regal, horses, saddlery and tackle, *bride price agreements* – all has to be properly packed and all of it assessed and loaded. Can you imagine the hubbub on the waterfront? You'd be *better off long gone with your letters of marque.* After all, I want my share of your privateering as soon as possible, don't I?"

This time Juster pursed his lips thoughtfully. "Oh. Never thought of that. You're right. Of course. But before I leave, what can I do to help you? And as you may have noticed, the only way I got in to see you was to promise Prime Fox that Master Turnkey here could listen in. No doubt he will quite rightly do his duty and relay the conversation to the Prime, so you'd better watch what you say. I don't want to be associated with any hint of treason. My family owes all to the King's line, and my loyalty is always to my liege."

The jailer grinned at the two of them and began to clean his fingernails with the point of his knife.

"Of course," Saker said. "Do you know when my trial will be?"

"Day after tomorrow, according to Fox."

"You could get me a decent advocate. I've asked Master Turnkey to hunt for someone who'll argue my case, but he tells me he can't persuade one of our learned pettifoggers to oblige for the amount of money I'm offering."

"Right. I shall dangle a heavier purse then. You hear that, Master Turnkey? Witan Rampion will be having a visit from an advocate tomorrow."

"Not for me to say," the jailer replied. "You got to ask his eminence first."

"I'll do that." He turned back to Saker. "Anything else?"

He shook his head. "I'll be fine, don't worry. If I don't see you before you leave: safe voyage and fair winds."

"Welcome to sail with me, you know, once you've been freed. Don't have a cleric on board. Won't be leaving until after your trial."

The invitation was clear: he was offering Saker a way out of Throssel, but they both knew it was unlikely, at least on this particular voyage. "I'll bear that in mind. And thanks for the wine, too." He nodded towards the demijohn on the table.

"Thought you'd appreciate it. Drink it to the last drop. From our best vines – the ones on the south slope that I showed you when you visited – and it would be a shame to waste any. If there's anything else you'd like, tell Master Turnkey here, and he'll send word to me, won't you?" He grinned at the jailer.

"I don't do nothing without the say-so of the Prime, m'lud. You know that. Not worth me job, it's not."

Juster sighed. "No, I don't suppose it is, at that. Scurvily lucrative position you've got here, if what you've been charging me is any indication."

The man smiled at him cheerfully. "If you say so, m'lud."

Juster stood. "Good luck with the trial, Saker. I was told I can't ask you about whatever it was you said to get you here, but I reckon it wouldn't make any difference to me. Unless of course it was treason. Owe you my neck, so take care of your own, right? And enjoy the wine."

Saker stood too. "Thank you. I never thought the best friend I'd ever have would be a buccaneer."

"*Privateer*. And I never thought I'd owe my life to a preacher!"

"A *witan*!" Saker rejoined.

They clasped hands for a moment, then Juster left with Turnkey, who locked the door behind them.

Saker waited a moment, then went to pick up the demijohn. He pulled the cork and smelled the bouquet. He took a sip. A very ordinary wine, as far as he could tell. Juster had once taken him to the family estate, so one thing he knew for sure: Juster's family did not grow grapes.

The door opened again, much later.

Saker awoke, startled. The person in the doorway was no more than a silhouette, thrown into relief by the lamp held by one of the two people behind him. He sat up hurriedly.

"So," the silhouette said, "you thought it was all right to ask Lord Juster to get you an advocate, did you?"

Blast. Valerian Fox.

"Well, just to make it quite clear – it was *not* all right, Rampion. This trial follows the pattern *I* design for it, not the path you think you can make it go. We had a bargain, and you seem to have forgotten it."

Saker stood. "I thought it would look better if I was represented by a man of legal letters."

The Prime moved aside and gestured one of the men behind him to enter. "Deal with him," he said. "But remember, not a mark on his face." Smiling, he turned to Saker. "Let this be a lesson to you. No one plays games with me and wins. Ever." He picked up the demijohn from the table and drank.

Oh, pickle it.

He knew what was coming. And he knew, no matter what, that he had to accept it. *Va, grant me courage.*

The man who had entered with Fox was huge, built like a

longshoreman used to lugging cargo. The first blow from his balled fist landed just above his waist, driving the breath out. The second punch cracked a rib. Saker, gasping, sank to the floor and curled himself up into a foetal position. Knowing the man had been forbidden to touch his face, he didn't bother to protect his head. Instead he wrapped his arms around his body.

Even so, several more ribs cracked under the onslaught of boots. A kick to the kidneys brought tears to his eyes. Somewhere far away, he heard himself grunt and groan at each impact. Pain drowned him, tore him to pieces, ripped his thoughts to an incoherent litany: *This will end, it willend, itwillend . . .*

And then silence, apart from his own moans. He opened his eyes.

Valerian Fox was smiling at him, his eyes alight with joy. He gestured the two other men out of the cell and bent down. Saker flinched. "I hate you Shenat," Fox whispered. Words meant for him, and him alone. "I will never rest until you are all gone from this world. Remember as you die, Rampion whoreson, that it will be my hand behind the blade, even if I am not the one to wield it. I shall enjoy telling Fritillary Reedling exactly how and why you died. And know this: one day I shall be Pontifect, and I shall rule all the Va-cherished Hemisphere. Kings and regals shall be my puppets, dancing a galliard to my flute. And the Shenat will crawl into holes in the hills – and die."

Fox straightened, only to aim his final insult. He heeled Saker from above, aiming for his privates. If he expected a scream, he was disappointed. The pain was so intense that Saker was robbed of all breath, of any ability to move, of any capacity to make a sound.

All he could do was watch through a red mist of agony as Fox grabbed the demijohn from the table and emptied the contents over his face and neck. Then he pulled the ceramic container from the wickerwork cover and threw it to the floor. It smashed, the shards bouncing up and scattering. The noise made Saker wince, and even wincing shafted him with pain.

Then the Prime was gone, and Saker was alone. The key rasped in the lock from the outside and he lay once more in blackness.

Every breath was a tortured ache to be endured.

Every beat of his heart pained him.

Pox on it, Juster. I know why you fainted.

The next coherent thought he had, a long time later, was how glad he was that he'd earlier swallowed the two perfectly polished rubies he'd found inside the wine.

Sometimes being overly cautious was wisdom.

The passages through the palace were largely deserted in the hours before dawn. Prince Ryce and his carousing companions, boisterously drunk, had returned from their foray into the town several hours earlier, and now all was quiet. The torchman had passed on his rounds a few minutes earlier, replacing the burned-out flambeaux.

Two of the King's Guards stood outside the door to the Princess's rooms. The only people with free access were the two cloister nuns, the King himself, Prince Ryce and the Prime – which was why, when one of the nuns came out of the apartment before dawn, the guards let her pass.

She was fully dressed in her shapeless habit, the white starched cornette-shaped coif sticking up like horns on her head, her long linen skirt scraping the floor. Over the top, the panels of the black scapular hung loosely from her shoulders.

She nodded to the guards but did not speak.

"Is there something we can do, sister?" one of the guards asked. He knew better than to expect a spoken answer. The nuns belonged to the silent order, and spoke to no one. The guards recognised her, though. This was the plumper one with the big nose.

The nun smiled and shook her head, put her hands together in a gesture of prayer, pointed in the direction of the chapel before walking away. She walked quickly, as if she knew exactly where she was going, looking neither to left nor right until she'd turned the corner.

"They give me the creeps," the guard said to his companion as she disappeared. "Never a word, an' with their funny hats an' all. Reckon they're virgins, Simmik?"

"Want to investigate?"

"Not likely!"

They laughed and settled down to wait out the rest of their watch.

The nun did not go to the royal chapel. She continued on her way until she came to the door of Saker's room. Plucking a burning torch from the sconce on the wall nearby, she lifted the latch and stepped inside. Closing the door behind her, she propped up the torch in the fireplace, where it continued to burn brightly while she looked around the room. As she relaxed, the nun's habit – and her face – faded away as if it had never been.

Methodically, Sorrel Redwing began to search. She ignored her reluctance to touch Saker's belongings, swallowed back her distaste at her invasion of his privacy. Instead, she collected his sword in its scabbard, and a selection of his clothing, including a pair of boots and a velvet hat.

She removed her outer clothing and pulled on a pair of his britches and a woollen tunic. After strapping on his scabbard and sword, she put on her own dress again, lacing it much looser to allow for the extra layers underneath. The boots went on over the top of her own flimsy slippers, his hat on her head. More clothing and a few other small items she stuffed into a cloth bag she'd found. Taking a deep breath, she carefully rebuilt the glamour of the nun's face and habit.

Back in the passage a moment later, she replaced the torch in its holder on the wall, and adjusted the cloth bag at her waist under the image of the scapular. She then walked briskly back to the royal wing of the palace apartments. She nodded politely to the two guards on duty and re-entered the solar.

As she tiptoed past the sleeping Mathilda on her way back to her own poky bedroom, she banished the glamour. Once in her room, she placed everything she had taken in the chest at the foot of her bed. It had all been simpler than she'd expected, but it was only the first part of her plan.

It was the next step that filled her with dread.

21

The Witan's Trial

The accused was not offered a chair.

Saker stood behind the U-shaped railing of the dock facing the three judges, headed by the elderly Earl of Fremont. He knew the Earl by sight, but he'd never seen the other two before, and no one bothered to tell him their names. They were both district Va-Faith arbiters; he could tell that much from their clerical robes. It didn't matter who they were anyway; their names would not make any difference to the outcome. They were just ciphers for Valerian Fox. Besides, Saker was far more preoccupied with the physical pain of standing, aware that he might have to do so for hours. Every joint throbbed, every muscle felt sore, every breath was a painful stab in the chest. His back ached and he'd been pissing blood ever since his beating.

Take shallow breaths. I won't let you see my pain, Master Prime. I won't give you that satisfaction. Not now, not ever.

He'd only just realised that Fox was assuming the role of prosecutor. No wonder the poxy bastard had wanted to make sure the prisoner didn't have an advocate.

Doing his best to disguise a real need to prop himself up, he leant against the railing, face impassive. He suspected the result was a false nonchalance that came across as a deliberate display of arrogance. He knew it would be taken as a subtle insult to the court, but what difference would it make? His case was pre-judged. He was guilty before it even began.

The Earl glowered at him, something his wild bushy eyebrows allowed him to do particularly well, and said, "The Prime informs me that you have refused an advocate."

Saker sighed, and bit back his protest. "Yes, my lord."

"This is your privilege, although it marks you as an imprudent young man. Let the trial proceed."

The first witness was a surprise, but his testimony wasn't. From the conviction with which he uttered his lies, it was clear Prince Ryce knew of the supposed rape and was out for revenge. He hardly needed the few leading questions from Fox before he launched into a damning description of a wholly mythical conversation he'd had with his witan spiritual adviser.

By the time he'd finished, everyone in the courtroom must have believed Saker had not only denied the existence of Va, but had outright stated that the only true faith was the worship in its oldest form, venerating the unseen shrine guardians.

Clever. So damned clever he knew it wasn't Ryce's idea. This had the mark of Fox's fingers on it, so much so that it made him want to smash a fist into the man's face. Fox didn't just want to brand him as a blasphemer; he wanted Saker identified as a Primordial apostate.

And if Fox means to find me guilty of apostasy, then I'm not going to escape with a rap over the knuckles and a fine. For a cleric, the punishment for apostasy was severe. *Blighted oak, I'm going to be nulled!*

At least he now knew just how he was going to be killed. Nullification was designed to be fatal. He'd never heard of a cleric who'd survived it.

He glanced at Ryce as he left the witness's podium, but the Prince ignored him. He felt ridiculously hurt by the testimony; he'd thought Ryce had known him well enough to know he would never have raped anyone, let alone Mathilda.

Celandine must have spun a good story. That betraying bitch; she was more rat than grey mouse.

The voice of conscience whispered inside his head: *But you did betray your position, Rampion. Mathilda was in your charge and you took her to bed . . .*

Even Juster's rubies wouldn't save him now. He'd guessed that any attempt to bribe his jailers with them would result in their confiscation, so he'd decided to see what he could achieve using the gems after the trial. Now he wondered if he'd left it too late.

On entering the courtroom, he'd seen Lord Juster in the seats reserved for people of rank, the only person present in that section. In contrast, the roped-off area for the clergy was full, as if every cleric within miles of the courtroom had been ordered to attend.

He wondered if the Prince would join Lord Juster once he'd completed his evidence, but Ryce turned the other way, to the spiral staircase that led up to the royal gallery. It was only then Saker realised several other people were seated above. One was a nun, her affiliation to a cloister made obvious by her cornette coif. She was seated beside a veiled woman, dressed all in grey.

Celandine . . .

He felt sick. Had Mathilda sent her to find out what happened? Did she realise Celandine must have betrayed the two of them? So many questions he couldn't answer.

It was my fault. I was the older one. The cleric. I should have been her guide, her mentor. Not her lover. Never her lover.

And now, how she must be suffering for it! How could that bitch of a grey widow have done this to her? Maybe *he'd* deserved it, but Celandine should have kept Mathilda's secrets. She'd known the Princess had planned a tryst, and instead of using her influence to stop her, she'd betrayed her.

Perhaps she'd been Fox's spy all along. Perhaps she was now Mathilda's guard.

The insufferable hellion. He'd always thought that folk granted witcheries were chosen for their virtuous piety and dedication to Va, whether through the Way of the Oak or the Flow. How did she ever come by a glamour? He looked away, face schooled to calm.

The Prime was calling the next witness. A young witan cleric with a Shenat name: Chub Saxifrage. Saker had never seen him before, yet there he was, recounting another conversation that had never taken place.

"And what did Witan Rampion tell you about your faith?" Fox asked him.

"He said we were both Shenat, both witans, and that meant more than being an ordinary cleric of Va. He said it was time the Shenat returned to their roots, to the old faith."

"Did he suggest you do that?"

"No, not exactly. He gave me some tracts to read and suggested I think about the contents as they portrayed a fundamental truth."

"And what did you do with those tracts?" Fox asked, his voice deceptively gentle.

"I gave them to you, your eminence."

"Are these the ones?" Fox approached the man where he stood and showed him a couple of sheets of flimsy bark paper.

The young witan glanced at them. "Yes, your eminence."

"Thank you. That will be all." Fox handed the papers to the Earl, who read them slowly, then handed them to the other two judges. Saker thought of asking to see the papers, but there wasn't any point. He could guess their message; he'd seen such writings before, usually poorly penned by semi-literate folk from some backwater village in the northern mountains. It would be a beautiful spot where the villagers hated to see the woodcutters come with their contracts from city merchants to fell the big forest oaks on Crown lands. Ignorant peasants, if you listened to people like Fox. Saker pitied them, and sympathised. But he didn't believe a return to the old Shenat ways would solve their problems.

His anger was building at the way he was being maligned, but he'd agreed to keep silent for Mathilda's sake. He had to find another way out of this mess, and accusing the witnesses of lying was not it.

The next piece of so-called evidence came from a report written by the arbiter of the ward where Saker had been born. Fox read out the relevant part of it with relish. It included a list of names of known Primordials in the area – and one of them was Gromwell Rampion.

"Your brother, I believe?" Fox asked him calmly.

"Half-brother," he amended, without comment. He had no doubt the report was accurate. There seemed no point in mentioning he had not spoken to Gromwell in seven or eight years.

The next witness was another surprise. Penny-cress, from the King Oak shrine. How did they know he'd been there recently? *Oh, of course. Tonias Pedding, Fox's secretary.* Va above, why had they dragged the ancient shrine-keeper all the way across the city to the court? One thing was for sure, they could never persuade her to utter a lie.

The Prime was solicitous, ordering one of the clerics to bring her a chair and a mug of water. While she was being settled, Penny-cress gazed around at the panelled walls in displeasure. Saker guessed she didn't like to see dead oak.

"You keep the witan shrine at a place called King Oak on the Throssel river, is that correct?" Fox asked gently.

"Ay. For more years than ye've been born."

"And five days ago, Witan Rampion came to the shrine, is that right?"

"Ay, he came to pray."

"What did you notice about one of his hands while he was there?"

"The black shadow was on his fingers."

"Black shadow? And in your opinion, what was that?"

"The mark o' A'Va as made by his minions, the devil-kin. Seen it too many times in my lifetime to have a doubt. Step into the shadow of the oak, and A'Va's mark will shine if a devil-kin's laid his hand on you."

"And you saw this mark on Witan Rampion."

"Ay. A black smear across his fingers."

"Thank you, mistress. One of the guards will escort you back to the shrine, unless of course Witan Rampion wishes to dispute your account?"

Saker looked towards the Earl. "No, but I'd like to ask the shrine-keeper a question, if I may, my lord."

"That is your right."

"Is the black shadow a sign of the evil of the man who wears it on his skin, or of the evil of the man who gave it to him?"

"Why, the man who gave it to him, to be sure."

"Thank you, mistress."

Penny-cress frowned, as if she didn't understand why all this was happening. He moved his hand in a gesture of calm, telling her not to worry, and she was escorted from the room.

"I would like to point out to the court," Fox said, "that the mark *is* proof that the recipient keeps the worst of company. I've even heard it said that it is A'Va himself that puts the mark there."

You slithering snake. So that's it. Twisting the truth to paint me as tainted by A'Va! He felt a wave of nausea. Penny-cress was far too canny to volunteer knowledge of his black mark, but if asked if she'd seen it, she'd never tell a lie. Fox had sent someone to ask because he knew about it beforehand, and he knew the black mark would appear under the canopy of the oak.

Fox. It always comes back to Fox.

You were *warned*, you fool. Fritillary warned you. Gerelda warned you. Juster warned you. Pus and pustules, maybe even the lascar's *dagger* warned you! But no, as a witan, you wanted your Prime to be above suspicion.

If they find me guilty of A'Va worship, I'll be hanging from a noose before the day ends. I have to fight this accusation.

The Earl frowned so deeply his eyebrows met in the middle of his brow. "Prime Fox, please explain to me this business of a devil-kin. Is it not just a mythical tale to scare children?"

"I fear we now have sufficient evidence that devil-kin exist," Fox said. "They're the human servants of A'Va in this world of ours, doing his bidding. The Pontifect has recently asked all clerics to watch for signs. I believe the black mark, which manifests itself to us only under the canopy of a sacred oak, is one indication that someone has had some kind of contact with one of the devil-kin. Or even with A'Va. Its precise significance is, alas, less clear."

"Ah. Proceed, then, your eminence."

"I have no fewer than five more witan clerics who are willing to present evidence against Witan Rampion. They all have the same story to tell – that the witan tried to influence them away from Va to the earlier form of the Shenat faith, the Primordial, now recognised as a heresy—"

"Your honour," Saker interrupted, "let me save the court some time. I am willing to plead guilty to all charges of blasphemy. Indeed, I shall plead guilty to apostasy too, while stating that I have made a sincere and humble return to the Faith, for Va has had the grace to show me the error of my ways." He had a slim hope his capitulation might be sufficient for the court, although he doubted Fox would be so lenient.

The Earl conferred briefly with his fellow judges, then turned back to Valerian Fox. "I think, under those circumstances, we do not need more evidence on the blasphemy and apostasy charges." His frown had lightened a shade as he addressed Saker once more. "Your repentance or otherwise does not change the nature of the crime, or its punishment."

Saker bowed. "I know, my lord. And I will take my punishment for blasphemy, and for flirting with apostasy."

"But the mark of the devil-kin? That is a much more serious matter," Fox protested.

"It is indeed," Fremont agreed. "I am assuming there is no such mark on the witan's hands now."

"No," Fox said, "but Saker Rampion is not under a sacred oak, either. We could take him to a shrine . . ."

Saker brightened. Outside in the open, he'd have a chance to escape. To bribe someone with Juster's rubies.

"No one would ever accuse Mistress Penny-cress of a lie," Fremont pointed out. "My family has supported her shrine ever since I remember, and I have known her since my childhood. She is renowned for her honesty and plain speaking. If she says she saw the mark, then she did." He glanced at his fellow judges, who both nodded in agreement.

Damn. No chance of getting outside, then. He said quickly, "My lord, if I may defend myself on this more serious charge . . .?"

Fox opened his mouth, obviously wanting to interject a protest, but the Earl held up his hand. "Go on, witan."

"The idea that I would countenance A'Va worship is baseless and deeply offensive to me. Moreover, it is contradictory to the very argument the Prime has been making: that I advocate a return to the pre-Va-Faith belief of the group called Primordials. No Primordial, or anyone else who believes in the importance of shrines and the Way, would ever voluntarily accept the taint of the devil-kin. A'Va is not just the antithesis of Va; he is also anathema to unseen guardians." He indicated the bark papers on the bench in front of the judges. "You have only to read those tracts."

"That's true," the Earl agreed, looking at his fellow judges once more to assess their accord.

"Do you accuse Mistress Penny-cress of lying, then, witan?" Fox asked him, mocking.

"It is my belief that the wearer of such a black mark has been targeted by evil. A victim, not a perpetrator. However, in my case I believe Mistress Penny-cress was mistaken, not lying," Saker said. "And with the court's approval, I will call a witness to prove that."

Fox shot him a disbelieving glance.

A-ha, you thought by denying me an advocate, you had me by the balls. Well, we will see, you slimy pulpiteer . . .

"And this person is in the court?" the Earl asked.

"Yes, your honour. There will be no delay."

"Then proceed."

"I would ask Lord Juster Dornbeck if he would answer a question or two about the day I visited the shrine. He will remember it well enough; it was the day of his celebration aboard the *Golden Petrel*."

Juster scrambled to his feet, startled. "Of course, if I can be of aid to the court . . ."

"Come forward, Lord Juster," the Earl said, "and reply to the accused's questions. Remember that all who give evidence here are under oath."

"Of course, my lord."

"Lord Juster, thank you," Saker said as Juster took his place before the court. "I think you'll find my questions easy enough. On that day, you and I were up in the rigging of your ship. Now, for the sake of the non-nautical people in the room, would you tell us the difference between the stay ropes – those ropes that anchor the masts – and the ordinary rigging?"

"The stays – well, they stay put, under tension. And they have to be stronger because they help to anchor the masts."

"Thank you. Now how do you ensure that a stay rope remains in good condition?"

"Why, we coat it with pitch. Tar."

"So the stays on your ship were tar-coated. Quite recently, I suspect?"

"Of course. The ship and the ropes are new."

"So the tar is not so very old and hard. And when two foolish men chose to slide down the stays from the mast to the deck – one of those men being myself – they were likely to get tar on their hands or clothes?"

"Yes, indeed. And elsewhere." Juster sounded rueful, and there was a titter around the court.

"Is it easy to remove?"

"No, it's the very devil. I feel certain you still had dirty hands by the time you reached the shrine."

"Thank you, my lord. That's all."

"Do you have any questions, your eminence?" Fremont asked Fox.

"Yes, just the one. I believe you met with a painful accident on that day, Lord Juster."

"Yes, that is correct."

"So may I assume you knew nothing of what happened to Witan Rampion after you were injured?"

Juster gave an amiable grin. "Yes, you may assume that."

The Earl sent Juster back to his seat, and Fox shot Saker an angry look before saying, "Penny-cress would know the difference between tarry hands and the mark of the devil-kin. Perhaps we can ask her to return . . ."

Before Fremont could reply, another voice entered the conversation, calling down from the balcony. Saker blinked in surprise as Celandine Marten scrambled to her feet, throwing off her veil. "That won't be necessary, your honour," she said. "I can shed light on this matter. The witan's palms were scraped raw by rope burns on board the ship. I was the person who bandaged them."

Saker's heart plummeted. *Va rot it, she's going to send me to the gallows. She's going to say she saw nothing black . . .*

He wasn't the only one alarmed by her statement; the consternation of the group in the gallery was easy to read. The Prince leapt to his feet, speaking to Celandine with inaudible urgency while waving his hands around in an agitated fashion. The nun grabbed her and tried to pull her back into her seat. Ryce signalled to the guard at the back of the balcony, who came forward, his stance indicating that he was prepared to intervene.

Saker looked from one to another, knowing now was not the time for him to say or do anything, but guessing his fate was about to be decided in the next few moments – either nullification, which he might survive, or hanging, which no bribe would halt. He gripped the railing in front of him tightly, welcoming the pain as a distraction.

Fox turned to address the judges. "Your honours, it is not meet that women should speak in an ecclesiastical court! They are not capable of answering difficult questions with appropriate gravitas."

The Earl of Fremont's mobile brows took on the appearance of a looming thundercloud. "You just this moment called a woman to the stand, Prime Fox."

"A shrine-keeper under Va's guidance, your grace. Not a mere court handmaiden too foolish to know right from wrong!"

"Are you, Prime Fox, about to tell me that a woman is foolish by nature and incapable of telling the truth in a court of law *simply because she is a woman*? Would your spiritual superior, the Pontifect, agree with you, I wonder?" His sarcasm cut like the honed edge of a new sword.

Nobility, Saker thought, momentarily distracted, even as his heart sank. *Can any commoner ever manage to achieve such a splendid level of imperious fury?*

Fox was at a loss. He opened his mouth, then closed it again.

"Do you *dare*, Master Prime?" the Earl persisted. "By virtue of your position, you defer to the Pontifect in ecclesiastical matters. Yet you think she would be an unacceptable witness in this court of law because she's a woman?"

A titter rippled through the clerics, many of whom were women.

Fox capitulated, his face now a deep shade of red. Rage, Saker guessed, not embarrassment. "My lord," he said, "I stand corrected."

"Good. Now if the lady in the gallery would be so kind as to identify herself to this court?"

Celandine, without a trace of nervousness, said, "I am Widow Celandine Marten, my lord, handmaiden to the Princess Mathilda. I assure the court that I know I speak under oath here, and I know the gravity of lying." Although she was addressing the Earl, the angle of her head suggested she was looking at the Prime.

Fremont nodded. "Very well. You need not descend, Mistress Marten. If you'd like to stand at the railing, it will be sufficient. Now tell us what you have to say on this matter, and please keep your statement relevant."

"Thank you, my lord." She stepped forward, and Ryce followed her, his face a picture of grim anger.

"On that day aboard the *Golden Petrel*, when I bandaged Witan Rampion's hands at the bidding of Princess Mathilda, they were streaked with tar from the ropes. I wiped the worst off, but there were still streaks of it on his fingers. I do not believe there would have been any easy way of ridding himself of it for several days."

Saker almost gaped. She was going to *save* him? He took a deep breath. Mathilda, of course. Mathilda had told her to do what she could, or face the consequences of a Princess's wrath.

"After you bandaged his hands, was all the tar covered by the binding?" the Earl asked.

"No, it was still visible."

"Would it be possible, do you think, that an elderly lady in a dimly lit shrine would be confused? That she'd think the tar was the touch of the devil-kin?"

"I think it very likely, especially as when I tried to scrub it off with my kerchief, it blurred into black smudges."

Saker hid his relief. Inside he was at war with himself over what to believe. Was she suffering an attack of conscience? Celandine knew that Mathilda had initiated their tryst that night, and perhaps she was suddenly awakening to the fact that he could *die* for it. Perhaps she was shocked to think that he could be unjustly accused of involvement with A'Va and his devil-kin. Or was it because she realised how appalling her own position was about to become if she didn't worm her way back into Mathilda's favour?

"Thank you, mistress," Fremont said. "Your eminence, do you have—"

"No questions," Fox said curtly. "Your honour, my apologies for taking up the court's time on this matter. The shrine-keeper was obviously mistaken in her belief. I'll revert to the two original charges against the accused. Blasphemy and apostasy concerning the supremacy of Va. He stands implicated by his association with members of his family, and condemned by the testimony we've heard, by the tracts he disseminated, which you have read, and by his own confession."

"Then you may be seated, Mistress Marten," the Earl said. He turned to confer with his fellow judges in low tones, and for a while they spoke only to one another. When the Earl sat straight up again, his face was stern.

"My fellow judges and I have decided there is no need to prolong this trial. In the light of what we've heard, we have reached a unanimous verdict on the grounds of blasphemy and apostasy. Saker Rampion, you have been found guilty of both charges and you are no longer entitled to be addressed as witan. Under the law of nullification you will be delivered to the mercy of Va exactly the way you came into the world, without possessions. If it please Va, you will survive. Your possessions are hereby granted to the Faith.

"You will wear the mark of nullification on your cheek, to show that even if you survive, you are neither permitted to live within the boundaries of Ardrone, nor to wear the robes or medallion of a cleric anywhere within the Va-cherished lands. The sentence is to be carried out by sunset tomorrow. Do you have anything you wish to say to this court?"

"My lord, the verdict is fair. I acquiesce to the justice of the court's punishment." He glanced up at the gallery. "If I have offended, I beg forgiveness. No one is to blame for this but myself." *And that last is true anyway.*

He bowed to the Earl, and allowed himself to be led away. As he passed the Prime, the man gave a smile full of promise.

Saker, chilled, averted his gaze. *Valerian bloody Fox isn't done with me yet, Va rot him. He's working out just how to have me murdered . . .*

"You know what to do." The King's expression was as tough and unforgiving as forged steel. "You wait until Rampion has been left at the shrine, then you move in to kill him. Alone. You leave your men back in the nearest town."

"Which shrine are they taking him to?" Prince Ryce asked.

"The one atop Chervil Moors. Va can forgive and save him for apostasy, but as far as we're concerned, he dies for the real crime. He defiled the Crown when he touched my daughter." His grim tone made it clear he didn't believe in the possibility of forgiveness. "The first snows should have fallen up there, and there'll be no one much on that road over the Spine. The shrine has no keeper. An easy kill for you."

"He will be unarmed," Ryce pointed out. The idea of murdering a chained and defenceless man, even one who had betrayed his trust, was a black storm cloud roiling through his mind.

"Not murder," his father snapped, as if he'd read the thought. "Execution. Remember your sister."

"I wonder if she wants him dead," he said. "I'm still puzzling over why she asked you for permission to send Celandine Marten to the court." Something about the whole matter didn't sit well with him.

"She said she wanted an account of the trial, seeing she couldn't attend it herself. None of us could have guessed the giddy woman would defend the witan! She's obviously not to be trusted. What's her family? Does she have any connections to the nobility or important landsmen or Shenat families?"

"She's the niece of a shrine-keeper in Melforn. Perhaps she didn't like the idea of Witan Rampion being charged with blasphemy and apostasy when that wasn't what he was guilty of."

"Pah! Couldn't stomach the idea of sending a man to his death, I suppose. Women of the lower classes are piss weak!"

Ryce considered the tavern wenches and skivvies and flower-sellers he knew. Weak was not a word he would have applied to any of them, but he wasn't about to contradict his father.

"Fox is right. We ought to have her killed," Edwayn muttered.

He was startled. "Who?"

"The Marten woman! Haven't you been listening? Did I breed a total fool? Think! She's the only other person, besides the Prime, who knows what really happened. The secret's safer if she dies. See to it."

"I'm not killing an innocent woman!" For a moment they stared at one another, then he added, as respectfully as he knew how, "Sire, Thilda's still begging not to be forced into this marriage. Not a day passes that she doesn't ask me to come and see her. And if I do, she does nothing but entreat me to speak to you on her behalf. Do we really have to give her to the Regal? Is it worth it?"

King Edwayn's glare was thunderous. "Have you learned *nothing* about being a king, Ryce? Marriages are for whatever advantages they bring. Even you will marry the girl of *my* choice, and I will choose someone who'll bring us something we want. It's as easy and as simple as that. If we have to tie Mathilda up in a sack and dispatch her to Regal Vilmar, we'll do it. We *need* that treaty port. Regal Vilmar is a fool to offer it, but he's aching for a pretty young thing in his bed to revive his flagging manhood and he's willing to pay the price. Mathilda *never* had a choice, not from the day she was born.

"Don't ever make the mistake of thinking a king hangs on to his throne by some divine right. Keeping your backside in the seat is all about money and influence and support. If you lack that, you'll find yourself bare-arsed and one of your second cousins wearing the crown.

"Now go and sharpen your sword for what you have to do tomorrow."

"Yes, sire. The witan cleric dies."

Edwayn stopped his pacing to face his son. There was nothing in his bearing that spoke of indecision or doubt. He looked every inch what he was – a monarch with the power of life and death over his subjects. "Don't fail me, Ryce. The Marten woman must also die."

"I can't just march into Thilda's apartments and kill her handmaiden."

"No. Her tongue is tied while only the cloister nuns and Mathilda can hear. Her demise can wait until the day Mathilda and her retinue set sail for the Regality. I'll put you in charge of getting the whole damn party and their luggage to the ship. Actually, you don't have to do this one yourself. You can arrange for someone to push her into Betany Bay if you can't think of anything else; the skirts women wear drag them under in a thrice and they can't swim. But, by Va, just choose someone who's already so indebted to you they'd never squeak a word, and of course, her death is never to be linked to Rampion in anyone's mind."

He felt ill just thinking of it. Murdering the rapist of his sister was going to be difficult enough, but to kill a woman who'd done nothing except obey her mistress's whims? *Oh Va above, I don't want to be king. I never want to be king if this is the sort of thing I have to order done.*

"One more thing," Edwayn said. "Make it quite clear to your sister that if she breathes a word to anyone of her broken maidenhead before she is safely tied to the Regal, I will see to it that she is locked away in that Comfrey nunnery, the Order of Perpetual Silence or whatever they call themselves. Now you may go."

He bowed and headed for the door, but his father's voice stopped him just as he put his fingers to the handle. "Son, when you are on the throne, you'll have to make many unpleasant decisions. People will die because of those decisions. You will perhaps send men to war, or women to the stake, or destroy whole families because of the treachery of a single man. It's time you learned what it is to be a monarch. It's time your hands were bloodied."

Ryce turned back to face his father. So, this was to be a test. *And what if I fail it, Father? What then?*

He couldn't bring himself to ask the question. He nodded and left the room.

22

The Branded Man

This is barbaric.

And it was part of a faith he'd followed and believed and preached . . .

Thoughts slipped and slid through his skull, hammering him like hailstones, even as pain battered his aching body. *I never thought to question its barbarism. I never thought about it at all.*

Perspiration ran down his face, trickled down his back. And it had nothing to do with the heat, though a brazier of glowing coals sat in the middle of the prison chamber, with the branding iron stuck deep into its glowing heart. ·

Fox had considerately shown him the brand while it was still cold. An oak leaf, symbol of the Way and one of the motifs on the royal flag, drawn here with a bar through its heart to signify banishment, and all of it wrought in iron.

They are going to brand me on my face. The cheek? The forehead? Dear Va . . .

Take deep breaths. Don't show them how scared you are.

How long since this had been done to a cleric? Most Ardronese would know what the brand meant, though, if they saw it: a cleric who had denied his faith and betrayed his calling, and was not to be aided in any way. It was up to Va to save the poor fellow. To save *him*.

Saker Rampion, witan no longer.

The Pontifect would hammer him flat and sell his hide to a shoemaker. Her past anger would be *nothing* compared to this. *And who are you anyway, Fritillary Reedling? In fact, I think I'm here partly because of you. You and your relationship with Valerian Fox. I'm just the pawn in the middle.* What was it Fox had said? "I shall enjoy telling Fritillary Reedling exactly how and why you died . . ." Fox, in all probability, had arranged for his fingers to be marked. Fox had found out that he spied for the Pontifect and had intercepted his letters. Fox might know more about his own parentage than he himself did. The vile man had enjoyed the trial because he knew it would upset the Pontifect.

Va damn you, Fritillary. You hog-tied me with all the secrets.

If he wanted to understand, then first he had to survive, and the odds were poor. Right then, he was chained upright against the roughness of the stone wall, bare to the waist, with his cleric's medallion taken from him, his wrists and ankles cuffed, his feet bare. He was awkwardly trussed, and as time went by, his discomfort had transformed into agony. And no one had done anything to him yet.

Fox had introduced the man stoking up the fire as Ash, the King's torturer. Saker had no idea if that was his real name and post, or whether it was just Fox's idea of humour. The Prime was certainly enjoying prolonging the lead-up to the branding. Superficially he was serious, but a closer look at his lean face revealed a fierce joy in the man's grey eyes, and amusement in the way the lines between his nose and mouth twitched.

Why did I not see that in him before? I never liked him, but I had no idea he was so . . . perverted as to enjoy another's pain. How far do his fingers stick into the dirt of Throssel, I wonder?

By the oak, Fritillary, was there no way you could have fought the appointment of this horror as Ardrone's Prime? He's not doing this because he believes I raped Mathilda; he's doing it because he hates you, or Shenat. Probably both.

No, wait a moment. I was marked with the black shadow because he fears me enough to warn others of his ilk that I'm dangerous, or because he wanted to be able to know where I went and what I did. He almost laughed. Here he was, chained to a wall, about to be branded and nulled, and someone *feared* him?

"Something amusing you, witan?" the Prime asked.

"You, Valerian Fox. It amuses me that I worry you."

"Worry me? No more than a gnat buzzing around that never manages to bite."

"You can't win this one. Whether I live or die matters little. Either way, I am your downfall." *If I don't bring you down one day, then the Pontifect will, once she learns what you have done.* That thought surprised him, springing into his mind unbidden, yet he knew the truth of it with unaccustomed certainty. Fritillary Reedling would avenge his death somehow or other.

But why would she? And why am I so certain she would? Another question he couldn't answer. Infuriating that there was a good chance he might die without getting the answers he wanted.

"We shall see about that, won't we?" The Prime turned to Ash, adding, "I think it's time for us to show this Shenat apostate how much the punishment for his crime is going to hurt."

"You sound like a schoolboy who torments kittens for fun," Saker said.

Ash seized the grip of the branding iron with a gloved hand and came across the room to where he was cuffed. "Sorry 'bout this, witan," he said. "Just my job, y'know."

"Shall we get on with it, then?" *And if I live through this, I swear I'll work to change things.*

"Look 'ee over there," Ash said, pointing. Saker turned his head before he realised the request was to make him present his cheek for the branding iron. The shock of its touch was so intense he couldn't breathe. Time stopped. He smelled the awful stench of burning meat in his nostrils, overpowering, obscene. His own flesh, cooked.

Ash emptied a bucket of cold water over his head.

The pain came, searing, obliterating, waves of it, first swelling, then ripping into his consciousness, serrated blades through his skin.

He gasped, dragging the air back into his lungs. The pain shattered his ability to think. He panted, hoping for control, but the agony was too great. He moaned.

"Not so much fun now, is it?" the Prime asked. He lowered his voice so that the torturer, now plunging the iron into a bucket of water in a cloud of hissing steam, would not hear. "Let me tell you something, you muck-worm. If I'd known your background when the Pontifect first foisted you on to me, I would have killed you on the spot, just because of the blood you inherited."

The words penetrated Saker's pain, but they only added another layer to a mystery that made no sense to him. He wanted to ask, *Whose blood?* But he'd get no answer, and he refused to give Fox the satisfaction of asking.

Teeth clenched, he said, "One day your crimes will catch up with you." *Stupid speech. Why are you wasting your breath? Va's teeth, talking made his face hurt as if the poker was still burning into him.*

Red waves of pain thundered into his skull.

The Prime ignored him, and spoke to Ash. "Shall we give him another brand on the other cheek? I rather like the idea of a matching pair."

Ash shook his head. "No, y'eminence. Can't do that. I do what Prince Ryce says. Or the King."

Fox stared at him, then capitulated. "Uncuff him from the wall," he said. He went to open the door and beckoned the officer waiting there. "Sergeant Horntail, get your men to strip this man naked."

"You want him naked *now*?" Horntail asked.

"Yes, now! He's to be taken from here to the shrine as bare-arsed as the day he was born."

Saker stared at Fox in shock. He was to be paraded naked through the city? *Nice touch, you maggot of a befouler.*

"I have to get him there alive, pleasing y'eminence," Horntail. "It's curdling cold out on the moor road."

"Then give him a horse blanket once you leave the city gates."

"Ay, y'eminence. That we can do." Horntail gestured to his men to set about the job.

Saker said nothing as he was stripped. Somewhere in the thinking part of his brain, he was glad Horntail had spoken up. It was already near freezing every night, and getting colder day by day as winter crept down from the north.

"Beware of him," Fox added. "He's clever. He'll invent any story to blacken the royal family. He'll utter any foul lie in an attempt to protest his innocence. Believe no word that passes his lips, and warn your men likewise."

"I will that, y'eminence."

"Cut off a piece of that rope over there and tie his hands behind him," the Prime continued, indicating a coil of cord hanging on the wall. "And keep him tied all the way to the shrine, understand? He's cunning, and he'll escape if you aren't alert."

"Yes, y'eminence," Horntail said. He plucked his knife out of his belt and began to saw off the rope.

"The King wants him paraded through the palace gardens before you take him into the city."

"Yes, your eminence. I was told." Horntail was still sawing at the rope, and finding it difficult.

"That's an interesting dagger. May I have a look?"

"Reckon it's not much good to me," Horntail said, handing it over. "Edges aren't sharp enough for a job like this. More a stabbing knife than a cutting one."

Fox turned it over and over in his hands. "Foreign, surely. Pashali, is it? Where did you get it?" He gave Saker a sharp look as he asked the question.

"Bought it off a mudlark who was hawking it around the guardhouse this morning. Said he'd picked it up on the mud at low tide."

"Strange. I saw something similar recently." Fox handed it back. "I'd get rid of it if I were you. No good can come out of the Va-forsaken Hemisphere."

Saker stared, disbelieving.

It was the lascar's kris he'd thrown into Throssel Water.

"What happened to the finch?" Princess Mathilda asked Sorrel petulantly. "The cage is empty!"

Sorrel looked up from her mending to where Mathilda sat with a disgruntled expression on her face and her embroidery frame on her lap in the midst of a tumble of coloured threads. As the days passed, the Princess had become increasingly irritable and frustrated with her enforced incarceration.

The reception room, once always crowded with chattering ladies and courtiers come to visit, was now too large and too silent. When the footmen brought in the meals, their footsteps on the wooden inlay of the floors would echo eerily in the emptiness. Prince Ryce came with his dogs occasionally, but never stayed long. Visits by the court dressmaker and her assistants were the highlight of Mathilda's day, but Sorrel wasn't permitted to be present.

"The bird died this morning," she replied. She knew she sounded curt, but she didn't care. "Once it couldn't fly, I don't think it ever recovered its joy in life. I threw the body into the garden from the balcony."

Mathilda gave up all pretence of sewing and flung the embroidery frame aside, scattering threads in its wake as it rolled across the floor. "You are cruel."

"For throwing away a dead bird? What else was I supposed to do with it – give it a state funeral?" *Oh, tush, things have come to a pretty pass when we can argue about the disposal of the corpse of a finch.* She bent to pick up the embroidery, smothering a sigh.

"I'm tired of needlework," Mathilda complained. "Why does the Prime not come to see me? I've asked Ryce *three* times to tell him I need his spiritual guidance!"

"I imagine there are many matters that demand his attention."

"But he told me I wouldn't have to marry the Regal if I agreed—" She stopped as if she was aware she'd said too much.

Sorrel was startled. "He did? If what?" Mathilda had been called to the Prime's office several times since the trial, escorted there and back by the nuns, but she had never explained why.

"Nothing. But he did promise me!"

"I doubt the Prime ever had that power, milady. It's the King who decides such things. Why would you think the Prime could make such a promise?"

"Don't be rude. I know things that you don't. You should pity me, anyway. You're so heartless!"

The Princess turned away, but not before Sorrel caught the oddest expression on her face, as if she suddenly understood something deeply unpalatable.

So, she thought, *Fox deceived you and you've just realised. I wonder what it was he tricked you into doing.* And then, the incredible thought: *It couldn't have been the Prime who asked you to seduce Saker, surely?*

No, that was too ridiculous. *Fiddle-me-witless, I'm losing my mind.*

She glanced across the expanse of the room to where the two cloister nuns were kneeling side by side on prayer stools, eyes closed and lips silently moving. Even though she was certain they were not listening, she lowered her voice but was unable to stop the savagery in her tone. "I can be a great deal more ill-mannered than this. I could perhaps tell milady that you should consider your own behaviour before you judge me heartless. As we speak, Saker is being branded. Within the next day or so, he's going to die of cold and hunger, his corpse torn to bits by wolves or bears. And all because you seduced him to avoid marrying the Regal!"

She wanted to scratch Mathilda's eyes out. How could she do that to Saker, who had been so kind to her? He'd *cared*. Sorrel had watched him fall in love and fight against it. And all the while, Mathilda had encouraged him. *Va-damn, if only she had guessed what Mathilda had intended that night . . .*

The Princess shrugged. "No, because of what *he* did. Anyway, it's too late now to do anything about it."

"Not entirely. If I could leave the palace for a day or two, I could save him." She held her breath. Everything she'd done over the past few days, she'd done to bring them both to this point. Everything depended on the next few moments.

Mathilda gave a harsh, cynical laugh. "*You?* How? You're a nobody. And why would you care anyway?"

"Why? Because I don't like the part I played in all this. If you'll help me, I think he can still be saved. But I need you to conceal my disappearance, at least in the beginning."

Mathilda's large blue eyes, wide with innocence, regarded her. "Why bother? Va will save Witan Saker, so we don't have to do anything! That's why they're leaving him at a shrine, so Va will intervene if he's innocent. And we know he is."

Does she really believe that? Perhaps. With her, I'm never sure. Perhaps she's even right, and I worry for nothing.

She curbed the beginnings of a sigh. "Milady, I don't think you've fully thought things through. This has little to do with Va's justice. It is King Edwayn who cannot allow Saker to live."

Mathilda's eyes widened still further. "Whatever makes you say that? Saker was found guilty by the court and he's being punished. Isn't that enough for everyone? Even my father?"

"Of course it's not enough! Milady, think!" She was still whispering, but the level of her urgency made her feel she was shouting. "The King believes you were raped. You and I know that's not the truth. What Saker did was reprehensible, but he doesn't deserve to die. The King, however, thinks he should. Worse, he will be afraid that the witan will speak of what happened."

Mathilda frowned. "Saker would never do that!"

"Of course not." *Although he might be tempted if he knew you were the one who betrayed him, who probably planned it that way from the first enticing flutter of your eyelashes.* "But King Edwayn doesn't know that and he can't take any chances." She resisted a temptation to grab Mathilda and shake her. "Someone is going to *kill* him. Or at the very least make sure he dies. Perhaps the soldiers who take him away. Although I think it more likely an assassin will be sent to the shrine once he is left alone to suffer his fate. However it is done, Saker Rampion is going to be dead and you and I will be guilty of his murder in the eyes of Va."

"Well, what would that matter to you? You're already a murderer, so what difference would one more make?"

Sorrel felt the blood leave her face. She gave a quick look at the nuns, but they were still praying, oblivious. "Believe me," she whispered, "it makes a difference." And for one fleeting moment, the scene, that horrible, ghastly moment in time she was always trying to flee, flashed before her. Nikard tumbling to his death.

The spoken words that were both liberating and shaming: *This is for Heather . . .*

She took a deep breath. "Milady, I need to know what shrine he's being taken to. Can you find out for me?" Her voice was remarkably steady, although she had to keep her hands locked together behind her back to stop her doing something she'd regret. Sweet cankers, what did a man like Saker ever see in such a – such a self-centred *flirt-skirt*?

The Princess pouted. "I think you're exaggerating."

"And what if I'm not?"

There was a long silence before Princess Mathilda replied. Then she said, "So what do you propose?"

"If I know where—" she began, then stopped as the door to the sitting room was flung open and Prince Ryce strode in with a couple of his fellhounds. The expression on his face was grim. With a gesture he dismissed the nuns to their bedroom and they scuttled away in silence.

"Thilda, Father wants you out on the balcony now."

"What the pox for? It's cold out there! Ryce, has he reconsidered his decision to insist on my marriage to Vilmar?"

"No. Thilda, accept its certainty. He believes we need the trade treaty and there's nothing you can say that will change his mind. And if you tell anyone what Saker did, and the marriage doesn't go ahead, well, I've already told you what Father will do."

She stared at him, her face hardening as if she was finally realising there was no way out for her.

"I'm sorry," he said, more gently. "I did try, truly. Not once, but several times. He was adamant. He puts Ardrone first, before either of us. That's who he is – the King."

She muttered, too low for him to hear, "It was all for nothing. Everything, for nothing."

Ryce waved his hand towards the balcony. "Saker Rampion is being brought up from the Keep and the King wants you to see him from out there."

Mathilda paled. "Why?"

"He wants you to see how Rampion was punished, and I suppose he wants to humiliate the hedge-born lout." He walked to the door that led to the balcony, opened it and gestured her out. She rolled her eyes, but did as she was told. "Come with me, Celandine," she ordered.

Sick to her stomach, Sorrel followed the royal siblings out on to the balcony, pausing only to grab a wrap for herself and another for Mathilda. She arranged the shawl over the Princess's shoulders and stepped back, effacing herself as usual, schooling her glamour into dull uniformity. The balcony was narrow, which meant that even standing behind Mathilda's copious skirts she had a good view.

She glanced at the King's balcony further along the palace facade. Edwayn and the Prime were both there, and fifteen or more courtiers. The formal garden below, with its rose-covered walls, neat flower beds and gravelled paths, was empty. There was still autumn colour in some of the bushes, but the last of the flowers was gone, and the fountains had been emptied. She shivered, feeling the first touch of winter as the wind gusted in from the north.

"Celandine says Father is going to have Rampion killed. Is that true?" Mathilda asked her brother.

Oh, Va rot her. Why did she have to say that to him? Sorrel shot a glance at the Prince. His look of startled shock was more profound even than the statement warranted.

Worse, he turned on her in barely controlled fury. "That's a vicious thing to say, mistress. Watch your tongue!" He glared at his sister. "I wouldn't repeat that kind of thing if I were you, Thilda. Your ladies should have more discretion!"

It's not me that should have more discretion, she thought. *It's Mathilda.*

"Here they come," the Prince said. "The soldiers are bringing him into the garden now."

"Sweet Va," Mathilda said. "He's naked."

"Milady, look at his face," Sorrel whispered. His face, so – so *damaged.* Her heart constricted in her chest, as if she was suddenly made small and helpless. A mouse against the hunger of a mastiff. Alone against the cruelty of the world. *I'm crazed. How can I possibly do anything to help him?*

"That's the branding," said Prince Ryce. His voice shook and she wondered why. It wasn't anger she could see on his face. He looked sick. *They were friendly*, she thought. *They must have been. They practised their swords together, they rode together. And often, in the evenings, when there were revels or music, or other entertainment at court, she'd seen them talking and laughing together.*

"Where are they taking him?" Mathilda asked the Prince. "Which shrine?"

"The one up at the top of Chervil Moors, near the pass to Crowfoot." His voice was tight with emotion. Perhaps there was anger there, but there were threads of so much more as well.

"They'll be lucky if they get that far by tomorrow night," Sorrel muttered. "He'll be dead by then if he's travelling naked. I thought the whole idea was to get him into a shrine where *Va* could make a judgement on him." *Oh, Saker . . .*

The Prince gave her a hard look. "I hope he *is* dead by tomorrow night," he said. "After what he's done, he deserves no better." He continued to regard her as if he was puzzled that a mere handmaiden would venture to have an opinion. "No thanks to you, mistress! Whoever gave you permission to defend that – that knave in court?"

"I was unaware that I had to seek permission to tell the truth before a court of law, your highness." She said the words steadily enough, but her heart was racing.

"You are both insolent and foolish," he snapped, and turned away, his dislike palpable.

He probably doesn't even remember my name, she thought. *A servant means nothing to these people. By the oak, how much longer do I have to live like this?* She turned her attention back to the small group of people now crossing the garden. A dozen guards under the leadership of a sergeant surrounded Saker Rampion.

She tried for dispassion as she gazed at him. Tall, broad across the shoulder, muscular too, in the way of a man used to an outdoor life rather than that of a more sedentary witan or scholar. His arms were pinioned behind his back. He stood tall as if not ashamed of his nakedness. *Courage*, she thought. *And honour too, I suppose. To save Mathilda's reputation, he's kept his mouth shut about her willingness.*

He looked up towards the King, his gaze neutral. One of the guards lost his temper, and kicked the back of his leg so that he fell to his knees. Instead of continuing to look at Edwayn, his gaze moved to Mathilda. It was only then that his eyes dropped to the ground.

"The arrogance of the hedge-born scallion! How dare he look at you like that," Ryce muttered to Mathilda. "It would be a pleasure to strike his head from his shoulders." To Sorrel's ears, there was something odd in his tone; it lacked the viciousness of his words.

She couldn't stand it any longer. She turned on her heel and went back inside. Curse them all, she *hated* feeling helpless. She was so sick of it. Too many years penniless under Nikard's thumb, and now under Mathilda's . . .

She squared her shoulders. The time had come for her to *do* something. Damn them all! If it was up to her to save Saker, she would. She bent to pat the fellhounds that had followed her inside, trying not to remember what she had just seen. The dogs fawned and wagged their tails in delight. "One day," she whispered to them. "One day soon, I swear I'll be free again."

Saker tried not to think about the humiliation. To stand there naked, and look up to see the faces staring down on him from the balcony . . . He shivered, and it wasn't entirely the cold. Rage. Contrition. Embarrassment. Shame. How was it possible to feel so many things at once and to be seared to the soul by them all? Somehow he managed it.

The King stood in front, outrage and scorn and hatred in the folded arms, in the glower of his brows. At his shoulder stood Valerian Fox, faintly smiling, that smug vulpine smirk of his. A whole array of courtiers were lined up behind them. Some laughing and chatting – he could imagine the jokes – but most just standing there, looking at him, which was worse.

He'd been so proud of himself. So sure no one would get the better of him, not him, not smart, skilled Saker. He was the Pontifect's best; the hunter after truth, the clever spy, the sharp-witted investigator. He was both the quiet man who noticed things other men didn't, and the fighter who could battle his way out of any corner.

And now humbled, disgraced, naked, a figure of fun.

Knocked to his knees, he took a deep breath and moved his gaze to the next balcony along. The one outside the Princess's apartments. Mathilda was there, and so was Celandine Marten, and Prince Ryce. He ignored Celandine. Mathilda's face was expressionless. She was holding on to the balustrade, looking down on him and the guards.

Oh, in the name of Va, I'm sorry, Mathilda.

And yet, and yet, it had been so perfect. It was hard to regret something that had been so wonderful.

He wished he could talk to her one more time.

Miserably, he thought of the Pontifect. She would never forgive what he'd done. He wasn't sure he would ever forgive himself. How could love be so wrong? And yet it had been. Of course it had.

Stupid. He should be thinking about survival. That was the only thing that counted now. He had to live and he had no idea of how he was going to do that. He looked back at the Prime.

One day, he thought, *I'm going to kill you, Valerian Fox. If that's the only thing I have to live for, then that's what is going to keep me alive.*

Sergeant Horntail ordered him back to his feet, and as he stood, he thought he saw pity in the man's eyes and wondered if he'd be able to turn that to his advantage. *Because I will not die.* As he was led away, his gaze met Mathilda's for one last brief moment. He'd never see her again and the grief he felt was the final coating on his misery.

He asked, "Tell me, Sergeant, where are we going?"

"Chervil Moors shrine. We won't get there until tomorrow afternoon, so we have a long ride ahead of us. We'll be camping out tonight."

Chervil Moors? Va grant the scurvy plague to whoever had chosen that particular shrine. The highest, most windswept place they could think of, at a guess.

He said neutrally, "It'll be a cold night, then."

Horntail didn't reply.

One of Fox's clerics went ahead of Horntail's mounted detachment of guards, ringing a bell to alert the townsfolk there was something afoot, and people came to see. He heard the whispered word that spread through the crowd: "Nullification." He saw several men shrug and mutter that it was Faith business, and no concern of theirs. Grubby children laughed and pointed, indulging their love of gutter language to poke fun at him. Women, he noted, were kinder, wincing at the mess of his face, although he did hear some ribald comments referring to his manhood. "Pity if they nullify that," one bawd yelled, bringing a flush to his cheeks.

A couple of youths threw muck from the street at him. When he ducked and a particularly malodorous clump sailed over his head and hit the mount of one of his escort, Horntail's men were quick to prevent any repeat.

His shame stayed with him, though, stinging him far more than the cold, to be felt long after they left the city. Several miles beyond the walls, Horntail gave him his clothes and told him to dress, muttering, "I'm damned if I'll let you die before we reach the shrine." Once Saker was clothed again, the Sergeant rebound his hands, but this time in front instead of behind his back. "And I have a horse for you too."

Mounted up, trying not to feel the ache of his broken ribs and bruised kidneys, or the agony of his face that was jabbing its damnable way into his skull to rot his brain, he forced himself to focus on the problem of Horntail's dagger.

He was certain it was Ardhi's Chenderawasi kris. He couldn't believe an arbitrary coincidence had brought it into Horntail's hands, either. It was *following* him.

Va-forsaken sorcery. That idea no longer scared him as much as it had. After all, anything that didn't like Valerian Fox must contain something of value.

23

Risk

Sorrel faced Mathilda across the expanse of the Princess's bed, her chin raised. The Princess was speaking, and on the surface she was being at her most imperious. Sorrel suspected that underneath she was terrified.

"You are far too disrespectful! I don't care what you know, I am still your princess and I deserve your loyalty."

For a moment she regarded Mathilda with dispassion, wondering how best to proceed. Threaten her? Blackmail her? Reason with her? *Sometimes I forget how young she is . . .* Young in years, young in experience, yet bred at court amid distrust and vicious rivalry, understanding that she was no more than a precious jewel to be bartered. She knew enough to be suspicious and bitter, and to use people.

Sorrel's initial rage at what the Princess had done to Saker faded. Mathilda had been dealt wealth and position at birth, but no one had ever loved her enough to fight for her. Even Ryce's defence had been half-hearted.

"Milady, we both know things about the other that could ruin us. I have trusted you with my secret for over a year; now it's up to you to trust me with yours. After all, neither of us can afford to betray the other, can we?"

Mathilda bit her lip, thinking. Then she said slowly, "I hold the best game piece. Everyone will believe me because of who I am. They believed me when I said I was ravished. No one will believe you if you say something different."

"You might have trouble convincing people I am Sorrel Redwing. Sorrel was blue-eyed and black-haired, and I'm just . . . grey and mousy. Besides, no one would believe you knowingly employed a murderess!"

"I'd tell them about how you use glamours!"

"Unwise. Imagine admitting to taking me into the royal household *knowing* I possess a witchery making it easy to spy on the court! I think your father's anger would be something to behold if he knew that."

She softened her tone, gentled her voice. "Mathilda, you saved my life. I owe you. I'll go to Lowmeer with you because you say you need me. I'll be on that ship when it leaves Betany, I promise. But right now, I have to save Saker Rampion, because if I don't, his death will haunt both of us for the rest of our lives."

"I don't want him to die. I thought Va would save him."

"I know."

"What guarantee have I you'll return?" She was tearful now; Sorrel could see the glisten in her eyes, hear the quaver in her voice. For the first time, she believed she was seeing a genuine emotion from the Princess. No artifice, no pretence.

"Where would I go? Here in Ardrone, one false step on my part could lead me to the gibbet. I *want* to go to Lowmeer. I'll be safer. Help me save Witan Saker, and I'll go with you, I swear."

"I warn you, if you betray me, or if you don't return, I will make you regret that you were ever born." She took a deep breath, and the tearful eighteen-year-old was gone. She was the Princess again, the royal daughter who was never allowed to be weak. "So what do I have to do?"

"Tell everyone my moon's bleed is upon me, I feel unwell and have taken to my bed. Tell the nuns I sleep a lot and eat little at this time of the month. Keep them out of my room. That should give me five or six full days to go and return. If someone *does* realise I'm missing, pretend amazement and say I was here last time you looked. If something goes wrong and I can't get back into the palace, I'll join you on the ship. Trust me. I'll be there."

"Swear it on the Way of the Oak. Swear it!"

"I swear," she said, and wondered if she'd live long enough to fulfil the vow.

Midnight, a night of deep dark. If there was a moon, clouds smothered its light. Outside in the palace grounds, the watchman called the hour. Sorrel walked to the door of the nuns' bedroom and listened with her ear to the panelling. One of the women was snoring. Apart from that, all was quiet.

"Ooh," Mathilda said, sounding awed as she watched. She clapped her hands, laughing softly. "You really do look like Ryce! I wish I could do that. It would be such *fun*."

It wasn't fun; it was hard work that left her exhausted, and she'd only just begun. The clothes she wore were Saker's, not Ryce's, so she'd glamoured them to rich lace and velvet and adorned herself with rings and brooches, none of which was real. She could glamour the way the Prince walked, the set of his shoulders, the swing of his arms, but there was nothing she could do disguise the fact that she was a hand span shorter than he was.

She picked up her cloak from where it lay on the bed, placed it over her shoulders and tied it at the neck. Lastly she put on Saker's velvet hat and sword, then glamoured both to fit Ryce's taste.

Mathilda was only satisfied after a number of adjustments, but in the end Prince Ryce was ready. He was a little smaller than usual, but nonetheless convincing, or so Mathilda said.

"Time to go." Sorrel sounded calmer than she felt.

Mathilda jumped. "Oh, Va above! It's so – so strange to hear your voice coming out of Ryce's lips. You – you will be careful, won't you?" For the first time in the two years since they'd met, the Princess looked genuinely woebegone. "I mean, it's night-time. You may look like a man, but it's dark out there and you'll have no escort and you don't know how to use that sword of Saker's and you can't fight and there are all sorts of cutpurses and fiends and horse thieves in the city and what about the midden-dwellers under the wall outside . . ."

Sorrel, touched, had opened her mouth to utter something kind and comforting when Mathilda added tearfully, "What will I do without you? I'll be *so* alone here! I can't speak to those nuns with their silly silence vows, and no one but Ryce is allowed to talk to me and he said he's going off hunting and it will be *so* lonely without him . . ."

"It will only be for a few days," Sorrel said brusquely. "You'll have the dressmakers in every day, and the shoemakers and the lacemakers and who knows who else. You may be about to marry far from your family, but you'll show everyone how you have the courage of Throssel kings and queens in your blood."

Mathilda sniffed, straightened and raised her chin. She held out her hand to be kissed, but Sorrel didn't take it. Instead she bent and brushed her lips against the Princess's cheek. "Be careful," she said and headed for the door.

Behind her, Mathilda didn't move. When Sorrel glanced back, she was raising her hand to her cheek, either astonished that a mere commoner could be so forward, or moved by the unbidden sign of affection. With Mathilda, there was no knowing which. And, being Mathilda, she wouldn't recognise that the kiss was born more of compassion than love.

Sorrel picked up the candle burning in its lantern near the door, and the bundle of things she was taking with her, and stepped out into the passage.

The two guards sprang to attention as soon as the door opened. They were the new watch detail, unaware that Prince Ryce had not come to see his sister that evening. She ignored them both and strode away, lengthening her stride and swinging the lantern so that shadows danced.

Perspiration trickled down her neck despite the cold of the passage. She'd stuffed the toes of Saker's large shoes with cloth, but it was hard to walk with any semblance of nonchalance when she felt so clumsy wearing them. She half expected to hear the guards shout an alarm, and resisted the almost overwhelming desire to look back over her shoulder.

You are a prince, confident that no one will question you . . .

She took the branching passage that led to the chapel, and once out of sight of the guards she leant against the wall. Shuddering in relief, she allowed the princely glamour to fall away.

Sounds of drunken laughter jerked her back to reality. The danger wasn't over yet. Pulling herself away from the wall, she walked on, building another glamour. It was easier this time around; she didn't change the appearance of her clothing at all, and left her hair and eyes their natural colour. All she did was make a few adjustments to her face to appear more masculine. This would be the face she'd keep on the journey.

A pair of drunken courtiers passed her by, and a little further on, two manservants on their way to bed, all of them scarcely noticing her presence. Buoyed by their lack of interest, she headed for the royal chapel.

It was eerily dark inside, and her footsteps echoed back at her from the cambered ceiling. She walked briskly to the side door, only to find it bolted, with a youth sound asleep on a straw pallet thrown across the threshold. She hadn't expected this. Perhaps it was something new; commenced as a result of Mathilda's supposed ravishment in the chapel. She shook the lad awake.

"Unbolt the door, my fellow," she said, pitching her voice several registers lower than usual. "I'm on royal business tonight, and in a hurry."

To her own ears she sounded like a woman trying unsuccessfully to imitate a man, but he didn't flinch or call her identity into question. His job was to prevent people entering the royal wing, not leaving it, and he didn't even bother to look at her properly. He had the door open before he was even fully awake. Blessing the fact that underlings were usually scared of upsetting those they assumed to be further up the hierarchy, she stepped outside.

You can do this. Keep calm, pretend. You are infinitely above a stable boy. Forget Celandine, handmaiden. Forget Sorrel. You are a man, your name is Burr Waxwing and you have legitimate business which is no concern of your inferiors.

Still swinging the lantern with a confidence she didn't feel, her heart pounding under her ribs, she briskly crossed the courtyard to the stables. She was oddly aware of the freedom trousers gave her, and the way she couldn't feel the roughness of the cobbles under her feet while wearing a man's boots.

A small brazier burned outside the stables. An ill-dressed stable lad smelling of horses was hunched over it to keep himself warm and awake.

"Messenger on royal business to the Prime," she said with all the peremptoriness she could muster. "I need a horse. Now."

"Y'own or a stable hack?" he asked, jumping up without suspicion.

"Is that dappled grey of the nulled witan still here?"

He nodded. "Ay."

"It should have been sent over to Faith Hall by now, tackle and all. Didn't you know that? It's all the property of the Prime's office."

He looked scared, so she added, more kindly, "Never mind, I'm going there now, so I'll take the animal for you. Saddle it up. I'll take the saddlebags and anything else that belonged to the witan."

If he thought her request odd, nothing of it showed in his face. He disappeared inside the stable with her lantern. She stayed outside, warming her hands at the brazier. When he reappeared, yawning, he was leading the dapple grey, already saddled and bridled.

"Keep the lantern," she said. "I'll pick it up when I return."

Suddenly at a loss, she stared at the horse. She hadn't ridden astride since she was a harum-scarum child of eight or nine, romping with her brother and his pony. As an adult woman wearing a riding habit, she'd grown used to using a mounting block on the few occasions she'd had reason to ride.

Fortunately, in the darkness the youth did not appear to notice her consternation. He handed her the reins and the crop, saying, "I've strapped on the witan's saddlebags for you," and went back to huddle over the brazier.

She spent a moment stroking the horse's nose, then stuffed the things she had with her into the saddlebags: food she'd hoarded, a few personal items for herself, the meagre amount of money the Princess had been able to scrounge, the rest of Saker's clothes and personal belongings. Reins in her hand, she reached up to the pommel and raised her foot to fit into the stirrup. It was a long way from the ground.

Don't be silly, Sorrel. You're not wearing a dress now. Of course you can do this.

She forgot she was wearing Saker's sword, and the scabbard tangled with her leg when she tried to swing herself up. The horse sidled. Hopping clumsily, she hauled herself into the saddle. Sitting astride felt all wrong. Skirtless, she felt naked and shameless. She took a deep breath. *You did this when you were a child; you can do it now.*

When the night sky began to spit rain as she turned the horse out of the stable yard, she muttered under her breath, "Saker, you'd better be suitably grateful."

At the palace gate, she told the guards she had a message for the Prime at Faith House in the city. One of them recognised her mount. "What are you doing riding the nullified witan's horse?" he asked, suddenly suspicious.

"He's a witan no longer. His belongings are the property of the Faith now, even if he survives the night."

The guard grunted and waved her through.

At night, the streets of the city were unrecognisable. Gone were the crowds, the carts and carriages, the hawkers and hustlers. Shadows melted away into the darkness at the sound of her horse's hooves. The occasional person out and about at that hour appeared just as nervous of her as she was of them. Nonetheless, her head swivelled this way and that in her anxiety. The dapple grey, taking its cue from her, was skittish. When a dog ran at its heels, barking, she was almost unseated. Her hands began to shake on the reins.

Va save me, calm down. You'll be a quivering heap of milk curds by the time you get to the main gate if you can't be braver than this. Remember what's at stake. You must have courage. You can do this.

She halted the horse and, wishing she'd asked the stable lad if it had a name, stroked its neck and uttered soothing noises until it stood quietly. Only then did she urge it on once more.

Her confidence grew. She'd forgotten how secure it felt to ride properly balanced. She was relearning all she'd known as a child about using her knees. Instead of missing her voluminous skirts, she was beginning to enjoy the freedom of their lack.

At the outer city wall, she altered her story to say she was taking a message from the Prime to the Pontifect. Once again the dapple grey was recognised. "Yes," she said before they could question her, "it was the witan's and was forfeited. The Prime is giving it to the Pontifect, I believe."

"Waste of good horse flesh," the guard complained as he opened the side gate for her. "When will *she* ever ride it?"

She urged her mount into a trot as it started to rain in earnest. The city continued in a huddle of hovels and ramshackle buildings inhabited by the desperately poor, diseased or dishonest. Many lived by sifting through the city's rubbish, or keeping pigs. Some worked in trades no longer welcome within the walls: the dyemakers and lyemakers, the slaughterers and tanners, the smelters and kiln-burners. Together they formed the midden-dwellers.

The rain, she decided, would be her protection. Luck was with her. So far. Nonetheless, she pulled Saker's sword out of its scabbard and laid it across the saddlebow. If someone made a grab for the horse's bridle, she knew what she was going to do, and there would be no hesitation.

She'd killed before and she'd do it again, if she must.

* * *

"Your breakfast. Sorry it's not more lavish, witan."

"Not witan any more, Sergeant," Saker said, not for the first time. Perversely, all the soldiers continued to address him that way. Apparently a guilty verdict for the crimes of apostasy and blasphemy did not rate high on the guards' list of wrongdoings, and their attitude towards him was more comradely than condemnatory.

Horntail shrugged, indifferent to his protest. He handed over a wooden bowl of hot porridge and a spoon.

With his hands tied, Saker had to take the bowl in both hands, then balance it on his knees while he ate. He looked around the clearing where they'd spent the night. The guards were attending to their chores, rounding up the hobbled horses and filling their water skins at the nearby stream. No one was close enough to overhear his conversation with Horntail.

"I don't suppose you'd be interested in being a wealthy man, Sergeant? It is within my ability to make you so." He still had Juster's rubies, safe somewhere in his gut.

The Sergeant frowned heavily. "Would you be offering me a bribe now, witan?"

"I would, if I thought you'd take it."

"Sorry. I'm a King's man, Witan Rampion. Like my da before me, and my grandpa before that, and my son after me. My family has little but our honour, and we keep what we have."

Saker sighed. "I thought as much. Pity."

"You're not the first offering money for your escape, neither. You've a friend in a certain seafaring lord as well."

"And you turned him down too? Alas, suddenly there are too many honest men in the world to please me." He finished the porridge and handed back the bowl.

"You're a cool one, I'll give you that. I'd've thought you'd too much stuffing in your noggin to have been charged with something like blasphemy."

"So would I," he said drily. "I wonder if you'll do something for me, nonetheless."

Horntail looked at him dubiously.

"Oh, it's nothing shifty this time. I just want you to hear me out."

"Words can't hurt lest I let 'em."

"Prime Valerian Fox keeps company with black-hearted men. Men who take orders from A'Va."

When he fell silent, Horntail's frown deepened. "Go on."

"That's it."

"That's all? And you expect me to believe it, just like that?"

"No, not really."

"Then why gab it?"

"Sergeant, you head the men who guard the Prince, and you are a man of honour. One day, the Prince will be king. And perhaps, at some crucial moment, when it might make a difference, you will remember those words of mine."

Horntail was silent, chewing on his lip.

Saker let him think, then said, "One more thing. That lascar dagger you bought from the mudlark?"

"What about it?"

"I don't think you'll have it much longer."

Horntail snorted. "You going to steal it from me, then?"

"When I have my hands tied day and night, and my feet hobbled when I'm not mounted? Hardly. But I stand by that prediction."

Horntail scrambled to his feet and threw his wooden bowl to one of his men. "Let's get on our way," he said grimly. "I want you left at the Chervil Moors shrine before nightfall, and I want us at least an hour back down the track by sunset. It'll be a cold night camped by the track."

24

The Reluctant Pilgrims

When the landward gates opened for business at dawn in Throssel city, and for an hour or so afterwards, the gateway was chaotic. Farmers and midden-pickers and hucksters wanted to enter with their produce; travellers and pilgrims and traders wished to leave as soon as it was light. Checks on those going in and out were perfunctory, but the traffic was slow nonetheless.

Prince Ryce told himself that was a good reason to delay an early start, but it was just an excuse. He was desperately hoping Saker was going to die a natural death, so he'd lingered on in the city until the morning after Horntail and his soldiers had left with the disgraced witan. It would take them well over a day to reach the shrine, and Ryce wanted to be sure Saker had at least one night naked and alone in the cold before he arrived on the scene.

One part of him was gnawed by the cowardice of his decision; another part justified it on the grounds of secrecy. *Father said no one must know, so I have to dodge Horntail and his escort. Saker, if we're both lucky, you'll die a quick death and I won't have to slit your throat.*

How had he, a prince who would one day be king, not realised what kind of man the witan was? He could have sworn that Saker was an honourable fellow. He'd spent more time with the man than he'd admitted to his father. They'd diced together and drunk too much and gone to see the latest plays. They'd shot arrows at the practice butt and fenced and played cards. How could he have been so *blind*? Damn the man! Va, he wanted to throttle the misbegotten son of a sow for what he'd done.

By the time he rode up to the landward gate of the city with his manservant and the four guards he'd chosen to accompany him on the early part of his journey, the morning crowd had cleared. Calling his two hunting hounds to stay with him, Ryce reined up in front of the Sergeant of the sentry detail. The hounds sniffed around the guardsmen's feet, then sat, regarding the men with suspicious eyes and twitching noses. "What's the latest word on the state of the road up towards Oakwood?" he asked.

"Good, your highness. But it's already started snowin' in the high country."

"Any banditry lately?"

"None I've heard of." The Sergeant smiled. "The most dangerous part is probably ridin' through them pox-marked foot-lickers in the midden fringe. There was some trouble there early this mornin'; I was worried it might have involved the Prime's messenger riding Rampion's dapple grey. Runnin' a risk he was, riding out alone after dark."

"What happened?"

"Oh, one of the worst miscreants of the midden-dwellers got run down by a rider. He reckoned the horseman was a demon with horns, or some such daft tale. Anyways, he got his leg broke for his trouble. The midden is laughing 'bout it this morn. I figure the fellow tried to rob the horseman, and got what he deserved. Must have been as drunk as a ship's rat that's got at a cask. The only rider we let through last night was the Prime's messenger, so I reckon he was the one who did the damage."

Ryce gathered up the reins, uninterested. All he wanted was to reach the small town of Chervil by nightfall. It had a wayside inn, and he'd heard their wine was excellent. He whistled to his dogs, but they were already through the gate, delighting in the stench of the midden fringe ahead of them.

By the time Sorrel rode into Chervil, nestled where the road to Oakwood met the track from the high moorland, she knew she'd never had a more miserable, uncomfortable journey. She'd ridden further in a single day than ever before; she'd been attacked, rained on, chased by dogs and doubled up with cramp. Every muscle screamed at her. She was tired and hungry and scared.

Worse, night was approaching and she was still far from the Chervil Moors shrine. Her first question when she rode into the stables of the single wayside inn was how far away the shrine was. The answer, another four hours' ride, was not encouraging. Afraid that Saker would not last the night without clothing, she asked to hire a hack, intending to continue on.

The stableman gave her a look that told her he doubted her sanity, and refused. He added sourly that there was no way anyone could ride the moorland track safely at night unless they wanted to kill either themselves or the horse, or both, and he was damned if he'd let her kill one of his jobbing mounts. She'd considered pushing on, but her horse was exhausted, and when the innkeeper told her she'd never find her way at night anyway, she gave up.

Saker is innocent of all the things they accused him of. Va and the unseen guardian will look after him, she thought, trying to convince herself. *They cared for me at a shrine . . .*

She pretended a competence she didn't feel as she organised the hiring of an additional horse for the next day, checked on the ostler's care of the dapple grey and arranged a room for the night. She forced herself to eat something, to order a ewer of hot water, to arrange with the cook for a packet of food to take with her the following morning, and finally to undress and wash away the dirt and dust – all before she fell into bed not long after sunset. As she pulled up the dingy feather-stuffed quilt, she barely noticed the absence of bedlinen and the scratchiness of the grubby straw pallet.

Heavily asleep within minutes, she dreamed, dark nightmares rooted in her recent past. In the midden fringe earlier that day, a man had jumped out of the shadows waving his arms to stop her. Terrified, she'd changed her glamour into an ugly mask and ridden him down to escape. In her nightmares, he caught her. Then, in this dream world, she was saved by a naked Saker, who immediately spoiled the heroism of his rescue by shaking her for not bringing a flintlock. She tried to tell him she couldn't afford to buy one, but he wouldn't listen. He yelled at her, saying that Sorrel Redwing had stolen his clothes, so why didn't she buy him some new ones.

The dream changed then, and she was surrounded by men shouting out for her to be hanged, accusing her of killing their children. They carried their battered offspring in their arms, dead, broken bodies held out to her, blaming her. Hunting dogs came to bare their teeth in her face, barking, snapping . . .

She woke to find herself sitting bolt upright. Outside, men shouted and dogs barked and growled. The room was cold. Shivering, she wrapped her cloak around her before going to the window. It had no glass, so when she opened the shutter, a blast of cold air swept in.

Directly below was the stable yard at the side of the inn. The smell of pitch rasped in her nostrils from a torch burning in a holder on the gatepost. The gate itself stood open. In the middle of the yard, two mounted men struggled to calm their horses amidst the yapping dogs and snarling hounds that milled around their feet.

One rider shouted over the top of the noise, demanding that someone get those scurvy curs under control or by Va he'd have the lot of them skinned. She thought she knew the voice, but couldn't place it. The other fellow, dressed sombrely in a servant's clothes, was mounted on a palfrey. Two of the dogs were fellhounds wearing collars, aristocrats compared to the mangy mongrels attacking them. Several more men, one of them the ostler and another she thought she recognised as the taproom boy, were nervously attempting to separate the animals, at risk to themselves. Dogs snapped, a horse shied, men shouted.

It was easy to guess the sequence of events. The two travellers had arrived with their own hounds, and the inn's guard dogs had set upon the intruding animals. The rider was furious at having his prized dogs threatened.

She watched for a moment, growing progressively colder, and was about to close the shutter and go back to bed when the light cast by the torch fell on the horseman's face.

At first she thought she must be mistaken. It *couldn't* be Prince Ryce, surely. She leaned out of the window a little further, staring. When the horse edged closer to the torch, she was certain: it *was* the Prince. No wonder the voice was familiar.

Prince Ryce? With only an unarmed servant?

Her thoughts raced. He'd told Mathilda he was going on a hunting trip, but if that was so, he would have had a bevy of noble friends and attendants with him, several of his best hunters, his huntmaster and a whole pack of hounds. And he wouldn't stay at a wayside inn. When a prince went hunting, he and his retinue stayed at some nobleman's manor.

Aghast, she wondered if he'd been following her. Had her theft of Saker's horse been discovered? No, that was ridiculous! Prince Ryce wouldn't follow a horse thief and he wouldn't follow Celandine Marten, either.

He wasn't here for her, or the horse. It had to be Saker who'd brought him to Chervil. Anything else was too great a coincidence. But why? Did he intend to rescue the witan too? She found that hard to believe, especially when he thought the man had raped his sister. She remembered his words: *It would be a pleasure to strike his head from his shoulders.*

So, not to rescue him. The opposite.

To kill him.

The Prince had come to avenge Mathilda.

She continued to stand there, heart and mind in turmoil as she watched. The men beat the inn mongrels off and shut them out in the street. Ryce dismounted to speak at length to the ostler, who then led the horses away. With his dogs at his heels and his servant trailing behind him carrying the saddlebags, the Prince entered the inn. Only then did she close the shutters and return to bed.

She tried to convince herself her reasoning was wrong. After all, the Prince might have had a hundred different reasons to be on the Oakwood road. But . . .

He'd *never* have a legitimate reason to stay at an inn like a commoner, and he couldn't possibly have come all the way from Throssel with only the servant; princes didn't travel without an escort. His guards must be camped somewhere nearby. The Prince obviously wanted – needed? – to be alone, apart from one trusted lackey. Which led her back to the only answer that made any sense. He was alone because he didn't want anyone else to know what he was going to do.

Sick at heart, she lay awake wondering how she could stop the Prince of Ardrone. Only one way: she had to get to Saker first and give him his horse so he could escape.

If he's still alive. Sweet Va above, she'd been shivering just standing at the window; what state would Saker be in after a night spent naked on the bleakness of the high moors? He might be dead by the time she arrived.

Huddled in bed and rubbing her arms to warm up, she considered all she knew about Ryce. He was a late riser who liked to start the day with a hearty breakfast before he went anywhere. She'd have a head start if she left at first light.

"Why are you doing this, Sorrel?" she whispered, and the question was for the woman she'd once been, so long ago. "Risking everything for a man who hardly knows you exist and wouldn't care if he never laid eyes on you again?"

She knew the answer. She'd always known.

There were some men who were worth fighting for, and dying for. Saker Rampion, in spite of his asinine infatuation with Mathilda, was one of them.

Still, she had not been so frightened since the day she'd murdered her husband.

"This is it," Horntail said. "We leave you here."

Saker looked around at the bleak landscape. In the distance, higher peaks had already disappeared under the grim grey of clouds promising snow. Gnarled vegetation, barely knee high, grew in continuous cover except where the narrow track ploughed a furrow through the heath. The only tree was an ageing oak, already leafless in the cold. He had no idea how it could ever have grown there. It would have taken three men linking arms to encircle the trunk, yet its height was stunted, no more than thrice his own. Branches stretched out in all directions, their deformed goblin limbs intertwining before drooping to brush the soil with crippled fingers of twigs.

There was no shrine building, and no sign of any other structure, not even a shepherd's hut.

"This is it?" he asked. "This is not a shrine; it's just a tree!"

"This is all there is," Horntail said.

One of the younger guardsmen, a man called Mole, spoke up. "This here's a holy place, witan," he said. "Witchery-strong. I was born near Chervil, and folk here say this was the very first shrine and the very first oak." His tone was a mixture of unease and awe. Saker hid his scepticism. They were nowhere near the Shenat Hills where the old religion of the oak had taken its first wobbly steps.

"Get down, witan," Horntail said. "And give me all your clothes. We need to be far away by dark."

Saker dismounted and held out his hands to one of the soldiers so they could be untied. He disrobed slowly, handing over his garments one at a time.

"Your shoes too," said Horntail. His face was grim with distaste. As Saker passed them to one of the men, the Sergeant nodded to Mole. "The shackles," he said.

Mole dug into his saddlebags and produced iron leg fetters linked by a chain no more than an arm's length long. Saker's mouth went dry. "Is that really necessary?" he asked Horntail. "I wasn't intending to go anywhere. Naked, I'd die out there. My only chance is to stay under the tree and trust in the unseen guardian and Va."

"Orders, m'lad. And as I got no doubt someone'll be checking on your corpse, I'll not be skimping on the shackles. Mole, thread the chain under that loop of root there, before you put 'em round his ankles."

Saker shuddered. He was going to be tethered to the tree itself, not far from the trunk. He stood still while Mole clicked the leg irons into place. A simple key or a set of lockpicks, neither of which he had, would have opened them.

"Va go with you, witan," Horntail said. There was compassion there, and sadness. He held no hope of his prisoner's survival. He patted the lascar's dagger, in its sheath at his side. "Still got it," he said, and turned his mount to ride away.

Entirely naked, Saker watched as they left. Mole was the last to depart. He lingered long enough to whisper, "Not Va, witan. Not here. This here's earth magic. Witchery. In this place, you look to the acorn and the Way of the Oak." He nodded at the moor. "I know this place. No soul out there. No shepherd huts, no folk, naught. The wind comes up like ice at night, and the cloud comes down like blindness. The tracks vanish in the blink of an eye. Only the unseen guardian can help you here." And then he too turned his horse and cantered after the others.

Saker was already shivering. He hauled on the chain, struggling to pull up the root, hoping to break it, but the wood was strong and deeply anchored.

He glanced around again. There wasn't any shelter, no dip in the ground that might have offered protection from the wind, no rocks either, nothing. He picked up a branch from under the tree and poked at the soil, wondering if he could dig a hole. The branch snapped. He tried elsewhere, with other branches and sticks, with desperate hacking and gouging, and each time with the same result. The ground was as hard as iron.

A bitter wind gusted from the north, not freezing yet, but it would be after nightfall. If he huddled on the leeward side of the oak, he'd have a little protection. He needed more of a barrier, he knew that. The ground under the tree was bare of plants, but the oak's protective branches – like a mother reluctant to let her children go – had prevented fallen leaves from scattering in the wind.

Desperation growing, he began to pile up as many of them as he could grasp. When he had cleared all he could reach with his hands, he used the longest stick he could find to gather more, and made a semicircle of them against the trunk on the leeward side. He worked in a fury, using precious energy and refusing to think about the cold. And yet it was already seeping into him. His shivers changed to a shuddering he could not halt.

When he had all he could gather, he wriggled deep into the pile, then lay on his side with his back to the trunk, his knees to his chest. He heaped the leaves on top until he was buried. It was damp in there, full of mould. He thought he felt crawling creatures. Worst of all, he was still chilled. The only good thing about that was it dulled the pain of his cheek, where the brand was still weeping blood and fluid.

Even if I survive the night, what then? Hugging himself for warmth, already half crazed with cold and pain, he thought, *Well, Va, earth-and-oak, forest-and-field, Mistress Oak, Master Forest, Va the Creator, it's just us here. If you have any purpose for me at all, this is the time to decide that I'm not going to die yet awhile.*

And then, *Mathilda, I'm sorry I couldn't help you.*

Fritillary, I'm sorry I let you down.

He began to pray.

He observed the ritual forms of prayer, giving thanks for all he had appreciated about his life, asking for mercy. After a while, he found it hard to focus, as the iciness and pain skewered his brain, changing his thoughts into dreams and his dreams into snatches of memory. The shuddering stopped, which scared him. He was weakening. How long had it been since the guards had left? He thought it must be dark already, but didn't put his head up to check. He stayed as still as he could, reluctant to waste energy in movement.

With every passing moment he grew colder and colder. His life was slipping away and he wanted to grasp it in his hands, pull it back, forbid it to leave him. He heard voices, voices he hadn't heard for years. His half-brothers mocking him. One of his early teachers telling him he was wasting his talents with his tomfoolery. His father, angry for no reason he could discern, yelling at him. What had he done to deserve that? Left a gate open? Not fully emptied the udder of one of the milch cows? He didn't know. He rarely did.

And then an older memory: his mother saying, "Don't ever forget me, Saker. Remember always that I love you and will watch over you."

And yet he *had* forgotten her. He wasn't even sure if she'd really said that. He'd never remembered it before. Maybe he was getting muddled. The cold did that to you.

Biting cold. It was at his centre now, soaking into the chambers of his heart. Placing frosty fingers into every bone, turning him to ice from the inside out. Somewhere he heard the Pontifect scolding him. "Fight it, fight the evil. Va needs you."

Va needs me? That's a laugh, Fritillary. Va just threw me to the wolves as unworthy. And this place here, it's the heart of the land, the oak, the natural. The wild.

Something crawled in the wound at his cheek. Several somethings. He wanted to scratch, to bat them away, but he couldn't move. He could still feel his cheek, feel it crawling with . . . ants? Oh, sweet Va, if you exist, not that, not that. Not while he was still alive . . . Hideousness that he could not alter. Or was it just imagination? The cold pinned him where he was, immobile, helpless.

What can I do anyway? I am no one. I will die here.

He thought of Mathilda. Remembered her lips on his. Her unexpected, adult passion.

And wondered if he was made of mist, because he no longer felt real.

The night was passing and he'd slipped into dream. And in his dream – no, not dream; in this phantasm, one small part of him was aware that all he saw did not exist in any reality, even as another part saw and felt and heard and touched.

His mother spoke to him again, faceless yet familiar, the perfume of her strong in his nostrils. *You may be of your lying father's blood,* she said, *but it's my family that's true Shenat.* He lay under the tree, free of the leaves, a child again lying in the warmth, and she was smiling down at him from the past. They were both dappled with sunlight and the false promise of happiness. She said, *I'm sorry for what I did to you. Forgive me.*

He had no idea what she meant.

When she faded, it was Mathilda who lay beside him, one hand to his shoulder and her lips trailing across his cheek towards his mouth. Just when she was about to kiss him, her face changed. Her blue eyes deepened to a darker shade, her hair no longer fair but a deep rich ebony. The smile she gave him was not hers but someone else's. Confused, he pushed her away, and her smile – no, Mathilda's smile – melted into petulance.

He stood up, still warm, still naked, and confused.

Another woman stood before him, dressed in a long, clinging garment of green that danced in the sun. Sun? There was something wrong about that. And the oak above him was green with fresh new leaves. That was wrong too. Nothing was real. She wasn't real. And yet he heard her words, spoken on the breeze . . .

A bargain, she said. *Your life for your life.*

Advice, she said. *Look to the twins of Lowmeer. They may be my salvation. Or my destruction.*

"I hate prophecies," he told her. He larded his tone with deliberate sarcasm as he added, "They are always worded so that no matter what happens, they appear to fit."

I cannot prophesy, she said. *I do not know the future. I offer you a bargain, and advice. The advice is perhaps a warning; I cannot tell its truth. I can only weigh all that you know, all that you have heard, all that you have observed from the day you were born.*

"How can I bargain when I don't know who you are?" he protested. "And when I don't know the nature of your bargain?"

You know, she said. *You know both. I can only affirm what you already know. I can only give lucidity to the thoughts and knowledge you already possess, though you may never have brought them to the fore. I have no voice, else. All creation is one entity. You, the land and the sea – you know in your heart they are all one, and therein lies duty and power and salvation.*

"And what of A'Va?"

You know he's real, yet a lie with no entity. He is lies and hate and temptation and fear and greed and indulgence. He hunts you down. You feel his presence. You fear him as you should. He has touched you. One day you may come face to face and recognise him for what he truly is . . .

He was back buried in the leaves, his body dying of bitter cold. With sudden clarity, he knew he had to make a decision. And he knew what it would mean. This was witchery, and if he accepted the offer dangled before him, he would be forever changed. If . . .

If he made it through the night.

"I've already given my life to the Faith," he said. "I am a witan. Was. Was a witan."

This time will be different. This time you will surrender your will, again and again. It is a harder road than you ever dreamed.

He shuddered. There was something implacable in the words, something without recourse to any manoeuvring. He gave it all, or he died.

My life for my life, he agreed. He thought he said the words aloud, but although his lips moved, his ears heard nothing. On his cheeks his tears flowed, warming his skin and washing away the pain of his wound.

Witchery, he thought. *The power of the oak. You'll never be free again.*

Just before he slept, he saw Ardhi's mocking grin. The lascar didn't speak; he didn't have to. The grin said it all.

Somewhere in the back of his mind he asked, *But why the lascar?*

And then he slept.

25

The Hunter and the Hunted

As she'd planned, Sorrel rose in the dark and was on the road the moment there was enough light to travel. She put the dapple grey on a lead and rode the roan she'd hired from the inn's stable. It was an irascible animal, fully prepared to take advantage of lack of experience. She suspected it would happily brush a rider against a fence or the low branch of a tree if it had the chance.

Fortunately, they left all trees and fences behind when they turned off the main road and began to climb steadily upwards. The track was narrow and rough, criss-crossed with ill-defined animal trails, but easy enough to follow as the mist thinned in the meagre morning warmth.

After the first hour, she crested a rise and looked back over the view of Chervil and the Oakwood road. There was no sign of Prince Ryce. She smiled grimly. She needed a good start. He was a fine rider with a better horse, and he'd soon catch up if her lead was not sufficiently great.

The track was less steep from there on, and she urged the horses to a better pace. A little later, the guards who had taken Saker from the palace passed her going in the opposite direction. She recognised their sergeant and pulled her mount to the side so they could pass. He nodded to her politely, but no one spoke. All they would have seen was an undistinguished middle-aged man on a horse. She kept the dapple grey close on her off-side, so the roan blocked a good view of it.

She rode on. When she estimated she was about an hour or less from the shrine, her mount faltered. Heart pounding in trepidation, she halted the horse and sat still to calm herself. Vex her toad-spotted luck, the wretched animal was limping. She was so *close*! And there was no one around to help her. Taking a deep breath, she slid to the ground. Just ahead, lying in the middle of the track, was a dagger.

It took her a moment to acknowledge that its presence must be pure coincidence; the horse hadn't trodden on it. Besides, it was still in its leather sheath. She picked it up and drew out the knife. It was Saker's wavy-bladed dagger, the one she'd used that day on the *Golden Petrel.* One of his guards must have dropped it. She shrugged, stuffed it into the dapple grey's saddlebags and tied the reins of both horses to furze bushes so they couldn't wander away.

Her first thought was that the roan might have cast a shoe, but she could see at a glance that was not the case. Then what? A sprain? She wasn't sure. When she studied the way it was standing, she could see it was favouring its left foreleg. She regarded it miserably. She'd watched other people pick up the hoof of a horse to look underneath, but she'd never done it herself. She had no idea what they expected to find, and this was the last animal she wanted to learn on anyway.

Positioning herself at its neck and facing its rump, she slid her hand down the foreleg as she'd seen grooms do. Its ears went back and its hindquarters sidled away from her. From the way it flung up its head, she knew this was not going to be easy.

In the next quarter of an hour, she had acquired a squashed big toe and a bruised shoulder, but still had no idea what was wrong with the hoof. Exasperated, she decided to mount the dapple grey, leave the roan behind and find Saker first.

She'd no sooner made the decision than Prince Ryce appeared over the nearest rise, heading towards her.

When he'd started from Chervil that morning, Ryce knew he was likely to meet up with Sergeant Horntail and his men returning from the shrine after having dumped Saker the night before, so it was no surprise when he saw them coming from a distance. He pulled his cloak around him, put up the hood and tucked his neckerchief over the lower part of his face. The horse he rode was not one from his personal stable, and the only thing that might have given him away were the two fellhounds, and he'd taken the precaution of removing their collars of distinctive royal red leather. He just had to hope Horntail and his men couldn't tell one hound from another.

They rode past at a trot, apparently oblivious to the fact that they'd just passed their prince.

He did not expect to meet other travellers on the track. With winter not far away, the first snows had already fallen on the high country and heavy mists were prevalent. The pass was a dangerous one to choose to travel to and from the coast.

A good place to leave a man you wanted to die of the cold.

How could Saker have done this? How could I have been so wrong about him?

Sometimes, remembering, he refused to believe it. Saker had been so helpful. His advice had always been good. The man hadn't made his life miserable with criticism of his carousing and whoring, nor had he tried to drag him off to the chapel every day as other clerics had done from time to time.

Yet the witan's own life had appeared beyond reproach.

Maybe Mathilda had misunderstood . . . Maybe Saker could explain what had happened. Maybe he should have asked the man, and interrogated Mathilda on the details.

Fobbing damn, why does life have to be so complicated? Despairing, he wondered how he was ever going to manage once he was king. Decisions were always so *difficult*.

From some distance away, he saw two horses tied to gorse bushes beside the trail, and a man with them. The fellow had dismounted and was attempting to look at the hoof of an unattractive roan. The horse, ears back, was shouldering him away and dancing sideways.

Ryce watched the battle of wills between horse and man as he approached, a conflict made worse by the appearance of his own two dogs to spook the roan further. As he was still hoping Saker would be dead by the time he reached the shrine, he was glad enough to stop.

"Can I help you?" he asked, giving the second horse a sidelong look. A dapple grey. *By the Oak, that's odd. It looks like Saker's*. It should now be the property of the Faith, surely. *Pickles 'n' pox, it* is *Saker's Greylegs.*

Thoughts started roiling in his head. This was the man the guards at the walls of the city had told him about. He felt his ire rising, along with his confusion. *The* Prime *sent someone up here? Why? To kill Saker too? To rescue him?* Who was this scut, and what was all this about?

The man was now standing by the roan's head, calming the animal as the hounds sniffed at its feet. Ryce summed him up with a glance: slightly built fellow, no rings or jewellery, well dressed, good-quality boots. A newly prosperous merchant, perhaps.

Calling his dogs back, he switched his gaze to the man's face. For a moment he could make no sense of what he was seeing. The man was the double of Mathilda's handmaiden, Celandine Marten. Her brother?

They stared at one another, wordlessly, for what seemed to be an age.

"I think perhaps you owe me an explanation," he said at last, his anger growing, his voice gravel in his ears. "Who the devil are you?"

"Celandine Marten," she replied, meeting his eyes without a scrap of discomfiture. "Who else?"

For a moment he was rendered speechless, appalled then embarrassed at seeing her without her skirts. Dressing as a man? Her hair tied at her neck like a lawyer's clerk? Had she taken leave of her senses? And what the pox was she doing here? Still mounted on his horse, he waved a hand at her clothing. "I thought you must be her brother. *Your* brother. If you have one." He was succeeding in sounding beef-witted, which riled him still further. "Have you no *shame* to dress like that? Not even a bawd from the midden fringe would be so – so disgustingly immodest!"

She shrugged, the gesture insolent in view of her knowledge of whom she was addressing. "If I'd tried to come all this way alone dressed as a woman, I would have been robbed at the very least. So easy for a man to be critical, isn't it? You don't have to think of your safety every moment you're alone! You have your dogs and your sword and your strength and your position. What do I have?" Her glare was fierce. "And what about you, your highness? Have you no shame, sneaking around alone like this, in order to kill a man in cold blood? The man who used to be your spiritual adviser?"

"How *dare* you!"

"Oh, I dare. Easily, because I don't think things could be much worse for me at the moment. We have much to discuss, you and I, Prince Ryce. But first, would you mind helping me find out what's wrong with this horse's hoof? No point in prolonging the suffering of an animal longer than necessary, is there?"

He gaped at her. The quiet handmaiden had turned into an impudent wench, speaking to him as if he was no more than a scullion in a taproom. He was having trouble believing what he was hearing. Had she taken leave of her senses?

"Well?" she asked. "Are you going to come down here and help fix this hoof?"

Raging with indignation, he dismounted, fumbling for his dagger.

When Saker woke in the morning, the sun was already in the sky. He couldn't believe he'd actually slept. Real sleep, not just dozing. Hours must have passed while he slumbered, because he'd missed the dawn. He pushed himself out of his pile of leaves, astonished to find himself still alive and, as far as he could see, with no frostbite. Even his cheek wasn't hurting. He touched it gingerly, to make sure it wasn't frozen, and his probing fingers snagged on the roughness of the scarring. Frowning in confusion and disbelief, he tried to remember everything that had happened.

He'd suffered some sort of phantasmagoria, obviously. He remembered that much. When he concentrated, he could even remember what had been said to him by the people he'd imagined. None of it made much sense.

"Think about it later, you maltworm," he muttered. *Right now I have to get out of here. I have to free myself somehow, and find somewhere safe and warm by nightfall, or I really will die.* The last meal he'd had, a generous one supplied by Horntail an hour or so before they'd reached the shrine, now seemed a lifetime ago. He was hungry, thirsty, dirty, cold and scared.

Everything he'd once been was indeed a lifetime ago . . .

He bent to take a look at his fetters.

They weren't around his ankles. They were lying next to him, opened.

He stared. And stared. Nothing could make sense of that. Nothing, so he didn't try. *Thank Va. Thank the unseen guardian. Think about it later.*

He had to get away, quickly.

Stepping out on to the track, he rubbed his arms in a desperate and futile attempt to keep warm, and started to walk towards the east, away from Chervil. He'd hardly gone three or four steps before he realised there was someone standing in front of him, ten or twelve paces away, blocking the track. His heart pounded furiously in shock. She'd appeared out of the air, and he'd seen it happen. One moment she hadn't been there; the next she was standing as solid as a statue on the path. Memories of his night came flooding back. This was the lady dressed in green. She was even more beautiful in reality, but her expression was stern. Wordlessly she raised her right arm and pointed back down the track towards Chervil.

He turned to look, but there was nothing to see that had not been there before. His shivering was shaking his whole body and he was no longer sure whether it was fear or cold.

"Who are you?" he asked, staring at her. "What do you want?"

She made no reply.

He continued to walk towards her. But when he was within five paces, he found he couldn't move. His feet felt leaden, almost as though they were tied down. All the while she pointed back the way he had come.

"What do you want?" he asked again. "Tell me who you are."

When she still didn't reply, he tried to walk around her. He thought he'd succeeded, but once again she was there, in front of him, blocking the way. He whirled and looked behind, but there was no one standing where she'd been before.

He turned back to face her again. She was still pointing towards Chervil. Refusing to give up, he tried several times more to leave, but each time she was there in front of him, and if he approached too close, he couldn't take the final steps, no matter how hard he tried.

At first he was afraid, then furious, then resigned. He returned to the oak to think. Seated on the pile of leaves, his back to the tree, his shivering stopped. He didn't feel warm, but at least he wasn't in danger of freezing. In some mystical way, the oak was warming him. Carefully, he thought back over all that had happened, or what he thought had happened, the night before. He'd heard and seen scenes from his past, either imagined or remembered. And then the lady had come to bargain with him, and to give him advice. The bargain, if he interpreted it correctly, was that she would save him now, if he gave his future life to her cause. Her advice had been to look to the twins of Lowmeer. And her cause? That depended on who she was, of course.

She'd said he must have the answer inside him. *She's not a person, or even a ghost of a person. She's the unseen guardian of this oak. Only she's not really unseen, is she? Or is it just me that's giving her a form and face? She can't really speak to me. All she can do is take something from my mind and fashion it into a truth I can recognise.*

The answer was there, clear in his head. *I thought I saw a goddess, but in truth she is nature, our land, our landscape, our living world, speaking to me.* It was all one. People, the land, the sea, Va. All one, and that was the only truth that mattered, because what mattered was to care for it all. To protect it. That was Va's desire – or creation's desire. Or just what was *right*.

With bemusement, he remembered that he had recognised that truth the night before. He'd agreed to her bargain. He'd already given his life away.

He chuckled ruefully and said, "All right, lady, you win. I'll walk back towards Chervil, to whatever my fate might be. I put my future, my destiny in the hands of guardian witchery. Or Va. Or whatever. I am yours, now and always."

He could think of plenty of worse fates, after all.

For a moment he glimpsed her again, shimmering in the wan sunlight at the edge of the tree canopy. Her smile was both sad and content. He thought he saw her lips move, but there was no sound.

Somewhere inside his head, though, he knew the truth she'd uttered the night before. If he – or someone else – didn't succeed, all that was most precious in the world would wither and die. And he didn't have the slightest idea why.

He started to walk towards Chervil, but away from the shelter of the oak he began to shiver. And so he ran, ignoring the pain of his bare feet on the rough path. Anything to keep warm.

When Prince Ryce came towards her, knife in hand, dogs at his side, Sorrel paled and skipped around to the other side of the horse, from where she eyed the blade with caution. "Why the knife, your highness?" she asked.

Prince Ryce felt himself colour up. He was supposed to kill her. "Your horse may have picked up one of the stones from the track, or need his foot cleaned," he said, more gruffly than he intended. "If my groom was here, we'd have the proper implement for the job. As it is, this is all I have." He added in freezing tones, just to show that he didn't appreciate her suspecting he was about to hurt her, "Now, if you wouldn't mind holding the horse's head and stroking its neck to keep it calm . . ."

His inner voice was more stripped of niceties. *You* are *going to have to kill her, you know that. You're just playing games.* Something inside his chest squeezed hard, paining him.

She did as he asked, once more the meek servant, at least for the moment. He still had trouble even beginning to understand how – or why – she had reached this spot, and how she had got hold of Saker's horse. He found it hard to believe her presence had anything to do with Prime Fox. No, she'd come on her own, to do . . . what? Save Saker? The dapple grey made sense if that was the reason. But why would she want to do that? Why help the man who'd ravished her mistress? And this was the second time she'd helped the wretch of a witan too, damn her eyes . . .

The hoof problem was caused by a small stone, which didn't seem to have done any long-term damage. He told her as much after he'd extracted it, and ended by saying, "Now you mount up and head back down to Chervil. Wait for me at the inn."

He had to kill her right here. *When she turns her back . . .*

He'd never have a better opportunity. Yet he hesitated. *Va above, how can I murder someone who never did me any harm? That's not the kind of prince I want to be.*

He knew what his father would say: now that she'd guessed what he was going to do to Saker, her death was even more imperative. Maybe he could slide his sword into her back if she turned around. Maybe he could take her two horses and leave her here, out on the heath, to die of cold. It would be easier that way.

Or so much easier to ask one of his guards to do it back in Chervil. But how long could you trust a guard to keep his mouth shut? A lifetime? Or just until he had a reason to talk?

She gave a tight little smile. "Turn back? And let you go on to kill an innocent man? I think not."

"Don't be ridiculous. Saker, innocent? Are you out of your mind? Weren't you there when the Lady Mathilda told the King what that rutting cleric did to her?"

"Indeed I was, and almost every word of it was a lie, told in the hope that the King would not send her away as a virgin bride when she patently was no such thing. Losing her virginity was her idea, not Saker's. And she certainly had no plans to lose her maidenhead by rape."

His mouth gaped foolishly open. It was a moment before he thought to snap it shut. Mathilda *lied*? He groped for words to deny what must be a calumny. "Have you no modesty, you – you – saucy . . ." Words failed him, until in the end he shouted, "You lying-tongued viper!"

He'd never been so furious. How dare this nobody, this servant from some unknown Shenat family, defile his sister with her words? He sprang at her, dagger still in his hand, and this time he did have murder on his mind. She dodged behind the roan again, but that placed her at a disadvantage because she was hemmed in by the dapple grey on the other side. There was nowhere to run except across the heath. He expected her to try, and yelled at his hounds to guard her. They approached her from behind, growling, but they were half-hearted about it. Va-damn, they knew her as someone likely to feed them titbits, rather than present a threat to him.

She ignored them and faced him instead, with surprising calm. "Think about it, your highness. Think about what the Lady Mathilda said. Consider what you know about your sister's character. Do you *really* think she would rise in the middle of the night to go to the chapel to *pray*? And if she did, do you think she'd go without me or one of her ladies-in-waiting? And consider what you know about Witan Saker. Is he really the kind of man to force himself on a woman? Let alone the Princess!"

She stood tall and proud in front of him, dressed in her ridiculous clothing, looking him directly in the eye. She didn't appear frightened, or embarrassed by her lack of skirts, or intimidated by his position. She didn't do any of the things he thought a normal woman would do under the circumstances. Instead, remarkably composed, she said, "So, would you like me to tell you the whole story?"

Nonplussed, he hesitated, aware that his moment of sheer rage had passed. "You can try," he said. "If you lie, I'll kill you."

She gave the faintest of smiles and said, "Oh, I suspect you'll be more likely to kill me if I tell the truth. Still, here's the true story of what happened that night. The Princess woke me about midnight. She told me she wanted to borrow a dress and my cloak in order to leave the solar, disguised as me. I wanted to know why. She wouldn't tell me. She ordered me to help her, and when I objected and called her behaviour foolish, she threatened me with dismissal. Your highness, I have nowhere to go. I have no money, no family who has any interest in my well-being, nothing except what Lady Mathilda gives me."

"So you're telling me that instead of performing your proper duties as a handmaiden and protecting your princess, instead of acting in her best interests, you allowed her to leave in the middle of the night dressed in your clothes, to go Va knows where?"

"Yes, that's exactly what I did do. I'm not proud of it."

"And as a result she was raped by a man we all trusted – her spiritual adviser."

"No, your highness. Her plans didn't include rape. I'm guessing she chose Saker to seduce because he's a very handsome man, and because he's in love with her. Any woman with her eyes open could see that. So she went to his room and knocked on his door."

"But you weren't there! How can you possibly know what happened?"

"I followed her, how could I not? Oh, I thought the passage was safe enough – there may not have been guards outside our door, not then, but the main entrances to all the corridors in the royal wing are guarded, after all. But I couldn't be sure where she was going, and I wanted to make certain she was safe. I saw her knock at Saker's door. I saw the door open. Va help me, I turned around and went away, leaving them alone."

She flushed. Colour filled her cheeks, suffused even her neck.

"And I do know what she told me afterwards," she added. "When she returned to our apartments I was sitting up waiting for her. She said she'd set out to seduce him, and succeeded. She came in with a smile on her face. She looked triumphant, not devastated by – by some sort of bestial attack."

His rage returned. He reached out, seized her shoulder with one hand and placed the point of the dagger to her breast. "You lie!"

"Do you want to hear the rest?"

He couldn't understand it. She still didn't seem to be afraid. She wasn't even trembling under his hand. She met his gaze fearlessly.

"Go on," he said, forcing the words out when he would rather have hit her. But even as he spoke, he pressed down on the knife until he felt it slip through the cloth of her clothing to break the skin beneath.

She flinched, but continued her story. "Lady Mathilda changed out of my clothes and into her own. While she dressed, she told me what she'd done. 'I'm no longer a maid,' she said, and she was *so* smug about it. 'Saker is an accomplished lover.' So I asked her why she'd done such a thing, when she was about to go to Lowmeer to marry. In truth, I was shocked. I know Lady Mathilda can be giddy at times, but I never dreamt she would do anything that dizzy-eyed. I never considered that Saker would . . ."

She stopped and took a deep breath. "That's when she told me she was going to the King. She thought that as she was no longer pure, he would not – could not – send her to the Regal for marriage."

Calmly she laid her hand over the top of his where it clasped the dagger, and said, "Would you mind not doing that? The point is hurting me."

Her cold serenity astonished him. He had control over her life or death, and the only person who could gainsay him was King Edwayn himself. So why wasn't this nondescript woman afraid of him? He poured his fury into his words. "Just who do you think you are to tell me what I can and cannot do?"

She did not move. "Are you going to kill me for telling the truth, your highness?"

"Why should I believe you instead of my royal sister?" He pushed the dagger in a little further. She gasped this time, and blood seeped out, staining her tunic. "So what do you have to say now, Mistress Marten?"

Her face was white, but she still didn't beg for her life. "If I must die in an attempt to save an innocent man, then I will. Perhaps you might also care to consider the well-being of Lady Mathilda's soul, so that on her death she can choose her place of rest for all eternity. If Saker dies, he'll die because of *her* lies. And think about this, Prince Ryce – could I have come on this journey without her help? Where would I have got the money from? Your sister sent me on this – this pilgrimage to save Saker's life. I suggest that you think twice before you stab me."

He felt ill. Nauseous, as if not only his assumptions had been turned upside down, but also his stomach. Thilda wouldn't have done this. She couldn't have. And then, heartbroken, *Mathilda, how could you? You shame us all!*

When she pushed his hand and the dagger away, he didn't resist. His mind was saying, *Tell me it's a lie. Sweet creation, tell me this is all a lie* . . . But his memory was of his grandmother calling Thilda a cunning scallywag. *She manipulates you so easily, Ryce. You must be more alert to her wiles.*

Oh, Va. It's true. *Thilda* betrayed Saker. She seduced him and then threw him away, knowing where he'd end up, as though he was a piece of offal.

He still had his hand on her shoulder, but he held the dagger loosely in his other hand now. Something had died inside him. *So this is what it is going to be like to be king.* "I'm not sure it makes any difference what Thilda did," he muttered. "Saker committed treason when he lay with her."

"Of course it makes a difference!"

"Mathilda has to marry the Regal. It's a – a concern of trade and commerce and Ardronese prosperity. So it's essential that no one knows of her lack of innocence. How it occurred is of no consequence. What matters is that you know and Saker knows. And so you both have to die. I'm sorry, mistress. I think Saker still deserves to die for what he did. It was his duty to advise his charge, not to take her to bed. And it was your duty to protect her. You both failed."

Yet I don't want to do this.

He took a deep breath, preparing himself to stab the knife upwards between her ribs and into her heart, knowing that this time there was no stepping away from his duty as Prince of Ardrone.

26

The Shattering of a Dream

Aren't princes supposed to be noble defenders of the Kingdom? Sorrel thought bitterly. *Protecting the people and upholding the law? Pox on this calf. He's forgotten he's supposed to have grown up.*

Well, she'd be cursed if she'd give up so easily. Besides, Ryce's determination had no more ice to it than summer snows. His hand quivered as he hesitated.

Sorrel allowed her face to appear to melt like butter in the sun. Under his horrified gaze, her skin sagged, then shifted into shapeless runnels. Eyes, nose, mouth flowed into the flux. He stumbled backwards away from her, appalled, then paralysed with shock.

She began to untie the horses, but kept a watchful eye on him. As soon as she saw he was beginning to regain his wits, she altered her appearance once more. This time she chose to become Mathilda. Perhaps he'd find it difficult to kill someone who was the image of his sister.

Smiling at him, she imitated the curve of Mathilda's lips, changing her dark hair to golden as it blew around her face. She even added the solitary freckle to her cheek, the blemish Mathilda hated so much. *There you are, your highness: your sister, blue eyes twinkling at you, wearing her favourite dress. And you should recognise that necklace; I believe it once belonged to your mother.*

Twice he tried to say something, but no words would come.

She had the grey untied, but the reins belonging to the roan had become hooked into the furze. Struggling with the thorns, she unsettled the roan, and that agitated Saker's horse in turn. Worse, it was so hard to maintain a smiling Mathilda while trying to deal with the horses and her own growing fear. *I don't want to die. And what happens to Saker if I do?*

"Thilda?" Ryce whispered, a tentative sound she hardly heard. Then, as if he realised that was nonsense, "Who – *what* are you?" His two hounds sniffed around her skirts, but without alarm.

"What does it matter?" She tried to sound like Mathilda.

"Witchery!" He spat the word at her.

"That's right," she agreed, tugging the reins free at last. "And witchery is granted by Va, remember. It's not an evil thing."

She stepped past him to mount the grey, but he grabbed her by the arm. "You can't trick me this way! I know who you are."

The hounds lost interest and disappeared as if they'd smelled something new. Pulling herself free, she flicked her appearance back to her Celandine face, but kept the blue dress. She plumped the imaginary material up into the full overskirt and kirtle, to disorientate him if he grabbed for her again.

The calm in her voice was at odds with the skipping of her heart, "Your highness, you can't kill me like this. You are an honourable man, and my death would haunt you. Besides, Lady Mathilda needs me, you know that. She's panic-stricken about her marriage and I can calm her. And think on this: I have the witchery of glamour, granted at the shrine that day you and the Princess met me in Melforn. I can spy for Mathilda at the court of the Regal. Think how useful I can be to the Princess of Ardrone."

"I can't trust you. Mathilda can't trust you! If you – or Saker – were to speak of what was done to her . . ."

"Nothing was done to her. And her secret is safe with me."

"Did I hear my name mentioned?" The new voice, coming from the other side of the horses, was so unexpected they both whirled in shock.

Saker stepped out from behind Ryce's horse, the two hounds indicating their enthusiasm at his arrival by leaping up, tails wagging. He winced as their paws landed on his naked skin.

"Well," he said, pushing the dogs off, "this *is* an interesting meeting. The last two people I expected to see standing around having a chat in the middle of a moor. Mind if I join you? Of course, I'm hardly dressed for company . . ."

Ryce, thunderstruck, jaw sagging, drew his sword.

"Mind? Of course not," Sorrel said, struggling to contain her relief. *He's alive! Va be thanked . . .* "Every conversation needs a naked man to add a touch of spice. You look cold." His chest rose and fell as if he had been running, but his lips were pinched and blue.

Thank you, Va, thank you, guardian of the oak, thank you for saving him. The relief she felt was so heartfelt, it destroyed all her carefully built barriers, all her carefully constructed self-delusions. Her heartbeat hammered at her ribs.

She cared about him. Damn him.

And there was nothing she could do about it. *Idiot.*

Saker twitched the Prince's cloak from where he'd left it on his saddle. Ryce said nothing, but there was no mistaking his look of consternation. He had no idea what to do.

He expected Saker to be dead, she thought. *Or close to it.*

Saker wrapped the cloak tight around himself. Sorrel stared at him, wondering at the rage she read in his expression, rage directed not at the Prince, but at her. She struggled to comprehend the lack of a wound on his face. His cheek should have been disfigured, horribly. Instead, it was smooth and untouched. She felt her own witchery recognise the existence of a witchery within him, where once there had been none. His burn had been healed and then concealed, but not by glamour magic. Whatever his witchery was, it was nothing like hers.

His gaze took in her clothing and the dapple grey. He said, in an apparent mix of puzzlement and outrage, "You're wearing my clothes! What in Va's name are you doing here? I can't think of a single reason for you to be up on this moor, in this weather, with Prince Ryce."

She didn't answer, unable to know where to start. She had pictured their meeting countless times, she'd planned the words, but now they didn't seem adequate. Or even appropriate. And she didn't understand why he was furious with her. He'd seen her come to his defence in the law court, risking much to do so. She didn't exactly expect gratitude, but even neutrality would have been preferable to this undercurrent of rage.

Ryce was holding his sword at the ready, but he didn't move and he still hadn't spoken, so she said, "I didn't come with the Prince. I came alone."

"Alone? From Throssel?" He was still staring at her, this time as if she'd taken leave of her senses. "Who brought Greylegs?"

That, she assumed, was his horse, so she said, "I did. Your things are here." She fetched the rear saddlebags and threw them down at his feet. "Some clothing, for a start."

He knelt to unbuckle them and haul out the contents. "I never expected to see these again." He pulled on his drawers and hose, then looked up to stare meaningfully at the sword she wore, still buckled at her side. "Especially not that Pashali blade. It's worth a small fortune."

She recognised the insult. The loggerheaded *lout*. He could have thanked her. As for the sword, she'd even forgotten she was wearing it. She undid the sword belt and was about to toss it to him, blade and all, when Prince Ryce grabbed at it, wrenching it out of her hands.

"The Prince is here to kill you," she warned. "In fact, he wants to kill us both, because he doesn't want the world to know you took Mathilda to bed. Of course, he thought you ravished her."

Saker said nothing to contradict that, but he eyed Ryce warily as he pulled on a shirt. "In that case, I hope you'll forgive me if I die fully dressed, your highness. It's fobbing cold up here, and I swear there's ice instead of blood in my veins. Besides, I am doubtless outraging the modesty of Mistress Celandine."

She winced at his sarcasm. "Indeed, you'd better get dressed before you freeze your pizzle off," she snapped.

He raised an eyebrow; at her language, she assumed.

A pox on you, Saker. I'm not going to be a sweetly demure lady to please your delicate ears. She took the second set of saddlebags from the front of the saddle and dropped them in front of him.

He said, pulling on his breeches, "While I can quite see why your highness would like to bring my miserable existence to an end, I must admit I fail to understand what crime Mistress Celandine has committed that is deserving of assassination. After all, was she not the informant who told you of my iniquity in this matter? As indeed she ought, as a loyal servant of the Crown."

She stared at him, unable at first to comprehend the enormity of what he was suggesting. Then, as the words sank in, she felt the pain right through to her backbone. *Oak-and-acorn, he thinks I not only betrayed Mathilda by going to the King in the first place, but that* I *told the lie about what happened!*

Her shock left her breathless.

Ryce spoke for the first time since Saker had arrived, his passion breaking through his shock. "Leak on you, you whoreson! I don't know what the rattling pox you mean, and I don't care. You are going to die here for what you did!"

"Oh, don't be such an idle-headed dewberry!" she snapped at the Prince. *Damn his loggerheaded stubbornness! He's trying to dredge up enough anger to murder us . . .* "You know now he didn't do anything to the Lady Mathilda that she didn't invite!"

But Ryce wasn't listening. He lunged at Saker with his blade, all his pent-up frustration bursting into action.

Saker moved as fast as a startled cat, flinging himself sideways into a head-roll. He rose to his feet in a half-crouch, arms raised at the ready, his stance balanced for either flight or fight. "Confound it, your highness, you do realise I'm not going to stand still and allow you to run me through, don't you?"

"You can't escape the King's justice!"

"Va has judged me, and then sent me here to you," Saker said quietly. "I cannot believe it was just so I may die on your sword."

"You *betrayed* my friendship. You betrayed your position in the royal household. You committed treason. You deserve the death coming to you."

"Deserve? Perhaps. But I will serve my country and my faith yet, Va willing." Even as he spoke, he was moving, grabbing Greylegs' reins, swinging himself into the saddle.

Ryce lunged forward again, but not for Saker. Instead, he grabbed Greylegs' bridle and swung his sword up to the horse's exposed throat. "Get down, or your horse dies."

Saker froze.

They stared at one another, prince and ex-witan, in a battle of wills. Sorrel knew she should be blurring herself into safety while their attention was on each other, but she was spelled into immobility, paralysed by the possibility that one of the men was going to die.

"You know me too well, my prince," Saker said at last. "And I think you have learned something about being a prince since last we spoke." He swung himself to the ground and moved to the mare's head, on the opposite side of the horse to Ryce. He patted Greylegs' neck.

Ryce lowered the sword. "It would have hurt to do it," he remarked. "She's a fine horse."

"And you chose her for me."

"Yes. I did." He regarded Saker thoughtfully. "Mistress Celandine says Mathilda went freely to you that night. That accusing you of ravishing her was all Mathilda's idea. Is that Va's truth?"

Saker looked at Sorrel in surprise. "Ah. So Mistress Celandine changed her mind." He looked at her, a penetrating gaze of contempt. "First you betray Lady Mathilda by telling the King his daughter was ravished, and then you betray her again by putting the blame on her. What is it you want here?"

Incandescent rage replaced her shock. How *dare* he! She groped for words adequate to express her fury.

Slowly Prince Ryce lowered his sword still further, until the point dug into the soil at his feet. He clasped his hands around the head of the hilt and stood regarding the two of them thoughtfully. "Mistress Celandine did not tell us anything. It was Mathilda. She came to the King with her tale of ravishment on her own volition. She put all the blame on you. If Mistress Celandine is guilty in this matter, it is for her loyalty to the Princess." He looked away from them both to gaze, unseeing, at the horizon. He added softly, "Mathilda planned the whole thing, right from the beginning, and cozened us all."

Saker whitened. Blindly, hands fumbling, he turned away to pick up his doublet and pull it on. "Nonsense!" he said. "If you were gulled, it was by Mistress Celandine, not Lady Mathilda."

Ryce shook his head. "No. I can see it now. I know Mathilda. And her woman's wiles hold no attraction to an elder brother. Careful where you tread now, Rampion. You come perilously close to calling both the King and me liars."

Saker looked as if he'd been slapped. He returned his gaze to Sorrel, appalled.

"It never occurred to me that you didn't realise who betrayed you," she said, and coated the words with all the contempt she could muster. "It was her futile attempt to find a way to prevent her marriage. She used you, from the beginning. In vain, because King Edwayn insists that this obscene union proceed."

The Prince gave her a sharp, angry glare. His sword swung up to point at her in threat. She stared back, unapologetic, even as she wondered at the reckless audacity of her words. "The truth can be unpalatable," she said, and refused to flinch. "But that doesn't make it a lie."

"Have a care, mistress," Ryce said. "What happens here need have no consequences for me."

They stared at each other, and finally he lowered the blade.

Saker turned away then, to pull his jacket out of the saddlebag and shrug it on. His face was chalk white, his mouth pinched, his look stricken. His composure wavered and he rested his forehead against Greylegs' saddle, his shoulders rising and falling as he inhaled deeply.

When he turned back to face them once more, it was with a bark of bitter laughter. "So we were all deceived. Va, but she is a woman fit to be a queen!" He took another long breath. "Your highness, I am not guiltless in this matter. I lay with a woman I should have protected and guided. I failed spectacularly to do so." He gave Sorrel a hard look. "You should have prevented her from such foolishness. And we should all remember that the Lady Mathilda is much to be pitied. Mistress Celandine is right about this union. It is one thing for a man to marry as he is told, and quite another for a maiden to be traded off to another land to bed an elderly monarch with a rancid reputation. We have not served her well, none of us."

Oh, sweet Va, he loves her still, the loggerheaded ninny.

"I should kill you both where you stand," Ryce said, but there was only resignation in his tone.

"My liege," Saker said, "you have my promise that nothing of this affair will ever cross my lips. I serve my faith and my king, as ever. If you wish to slit my throat with your blade, so be it. I do suggest, though, that you spare Mistress Celandine's life. A woman with a glamour can only be of great service to Lady Mathilda in the hell she has been sold into, and perhaps to Ardrone as well, should the Princess will it that way."

"A . . . a . . . glamour." The Prince took a deep breath. "Ah, I see. I trusted you once, Saker. Should I do so again?"

"The Oak warmed me last night. Without that, I would have died of the cold. The unseen guardian loosed the shackles that bound me to the tree. I – I believe there is a purpose in the life left to me."

Ryce cocked his head thoughtfully, then nodded. "You were branded. I saw the brand. Now it has vanished."

"It has?" In surprise, he raised his fingers to his cheek and ran them over the smoothness of his skin. "I feel it still, as roughness beneath my fingers."

"There's naught to see." Ryce paused to consider, then added, "You once told me there were things beyond the domain of a king or a prince. This is one of them. You are free to go. I pray it is Va's path you follow."

"That's not a decision the King would sanction."

Ryce sighed. "I know. But I made another decision here today: I do not wish to be my father. Take the road over the moors to the coast. Leave Ardrone and do not return, under pain of death." He turned to Sorrel. "And you – a witan once told me that glamours are the rarest of all Va's witcheries. That they are gifted only to Va's most trusted servants." He walked to his horse and gathered up the reins. "I don't like you, Mistress Marten," he added as he mounted. "I don't think you served my sister well. But you risked much to come here, and I bow to a greater power than mine. You too are free to go. Finish whatever business you have here with the witan, and then ride after me. I shall await you in the Chervil Inn, and will escort you back to Throssel. After that, doubtless your glamour will serve you to return to Lady Mathilda's side. If the King receives word of your presence, he would see you dead; never doubt it. If you are caught, I cannot protect you."

As he began to turn his mount away, Saker stayed him with a hand gesture. "A warning, your highness."

Ryce sighed. "Go on."

"Beware of Prime Fox."

"You're an addlepate, Saker Rampion. He was appointed by the King and serves at the King's pleasure."

"Perhaps. But I just saw the wisdom of a man who will one day be king. Such a man is wise enough to watch his back. Va go with you, my liege."

Sorrel waited until the Prince was out of sight and then said, "That last was patronising, coming from a foolish man not that much older than the Prince himself."

"Doubtless it's a fault of mine that the years will cure," he said, a dangerous edge to his tone. "Prince Ryce needs to believe in himself. Tell me, did Mathilda send you here?"

She gritted her teeth. Did he really think that Mathilda cared a withered acorn about his well-being? "Believe what you will, Master Rampion. Your self-esteem is doubtless in need of repair."

"I have to think there's no way you'd be here without the Princess's aid. You couldn't have taken my horse from the stable unless you had help. And someone obviously had access to my room and everything in it, so I assume the Lady Mathilda arranged it."

For a moment she just stared at him, rage and hurt so intertwined she didn't know what she wanted most: to weep, or to hit him, hard, right on the nose. She turned away so he wouldn't notice the tears pooling in her eyes. She didn't want him to see her cry. And vex it, she didn't like crying anyway. It was so – so *stupid*!

Drained of energy, she let all her witchery fade, until she was just herself, Sorrel Redwing, the woman who by rights should have been no more than bones and sinew hanging on a crossroads gibbet. She dragged air into her lungs, drowning in the pain of resignation.

She walked to the roan where it was grazing, picked up the loose reins and hauled herself into the saddle.

"You can drop your silly glamour," he said. "You don't have to appear beautiful to me. I'm not taken in by it. I already know what you look like."

She blinked at him in momentary bewilderment, wondering what he meant, and then realised. "This is not the glamour," she said. *Did he just say he thought I was beautiful?* She was no mouse, perhaps, but beautiful? The idea was ridiculous. Nikard had told her she had the coarse looks of a peasant, momentarily pleasing, soon faded.

He snorted. "Oh, I understand. You want me to believe you really are beautiful and Celandine the mouse was the glamour! Do you think me for a beef-witted fool to be taken in by a pretty face?"

The irony was too much. He believed she used a glamour to make herself more desirable? She began to laugh. "Yes," she said. "I think perhaps I do. A witan with his own witchery should know better!" She dredged up enough energy to bring back her glamour, to return the mouse to his sight. "Is this more to your taste?" she asked. *Not taken in by a pretty face, Saker? What about Mathilda's?* For all she'd done, he was still in love with Mathilda, and she – Celandine – was nothing more than the mouse beneath his feet.

"I'm sorry," he said, suddenly contrite. "I didn't mean to be insulting. Forgive me, it has been a . . . difficult day or two. I am grateful to you for making the journey from Throssel. It doesn't matter whose idea it was; it was bravely done, and I do thank you."

She turned her head to look down at him. *Dear Va, he's right. He's been to the dark of hell and back. Tortured, left to die, surviving – only to find out today that the woman he loved was the one who sacrificed him.* She nodded, recognising his apology. Glimpsing the despairing hurt in his eyes, she acknowledged that it wasn't easy to cease loving someone.

It doesn't stop, she thought bleakly, *just because you want it so.*

"You're a brave woman, Celandine Marten," he said. "I heard you stand up to Prince Ryce when he threatened to kill you just then. You were fearless in the face of death."

"No woman who has lost a child fears death, for she has already died once. And there is no woman called Celandine Marten. There never was." She flicked the reins, and the roan, without a trace of a limp, headed back down the track.

27

Picking Up the Pieces

Saker watched her go, his emotions in a muddle. It was hard to think because there were too many strands in the tangle, all begging to be considered.

Men weren't supposed to cry, but right then all he wanted to do was weep. Mathilda had used him, then thrown him to Fox and his hounds to be shredded. Had she ever even *liked* him? Had it *all* been lies? Perhaps she'd tried to save him by asking Celandine to go to the court to help his case, and then to bring him a horse and clothing when he needed it. Perhaps not. Perhaps that was just Celandine's doing. If so, *why*? He'd hardly ever spoken to the woman, and yet she'd risked her safety for him. She'd looked at him with such contempt, not once, but several times during the conversation they'd just had. And who the fobbing damn was she if there was no such person as Celandine Marten?

Thinking about all that had happened physically hurt. He was still wretchedly cold, so he flung Ryce's cloak over his shoulders, glad the Prince had ridden off without it. Greylegs nickered at him, so he went to pat the horse's neck, murmur soft words in its ear and check to see if the animal had picked up any injuries or strains. Then he turned to the saddlebags again, to see what else was in them. The first thing that caught his eye was the lascar's dagger.

He gave a dry chuckle.

I warned you, Horntail. It didn't take long for you to lose it, did it?

Not long ago, its unexpected appearance would have given him cold shivers. Now he smiled, oddly glad that it was back. It might have been exotic magic, out of place in the Va-cherished Hemisphere, but that didn't mean it couldn't be useful.

He laid the knife aside, and turned to the other items. A pair of his boots was quickly pulled on to his freezing feet. Food and watered wine – excellent. He gulped down some of the liquid and ate hungrily, but was careful to keep some for later.

At last he was beginning to feel human again. *But she said I had a witchery.* He fingered his cheek. He hadn't healed that, he was sure. That had been done by the unseen guardian. Or by Va. Did he have a witchery? He didn't think so. He didn't feel any different. Just chilled, and saddened. And utterly *stupid* to have made such a fool of himself over Mathilda. Furious too, with her. She'd played him, a lute player plucking all the right strings until he danced to her tune. She'd been prepared to send him to the block for treason.

The conniving, spoiled, treacherous little . . .

He stopped the thought. *We were the ones who planned to sell her to a man she didn't want to bed. By Va, who was without blame in all this?*

In the last of the saddlebag pockets he found a few odds and ends such as his drawstring purse, his penknife for trimming quills, his bottle of tooth powder, a small bound book of tales that he'd bought for a lot of money on Printers Street and, right at the bottom, a plain gold chain, wrapped in a piece of lace-edged linen. Scrawled across the paper enclosed with it were the words *Gifted by Mathilda, Princess of Ardrone.*

He rubbed his forefinger across the words, sadness welling up from a place of acid regret somewhere deep inside. Their moments of tenderness had been so beautiful, yet in retrospect, all he felt was a sour taste and scarring pain.

Va forgive her.

And yet – and yet . . .

Did he blame her? She had so few choices.

Oh, Mathilda. He didn't know whether to be heartbroken or enraged.

He rode in the direction of the coast, away from Chervil. He had to pass the oak shrine once more, but didn't stop. There was no sign of its green-clad guardian, no whisper of her voice. So much had happened there, yet he was still not sure of the significance of any of it. Saved by witchery? Certainly. But *granted* a witchery?

He had to get to Vavala as soon as possible. He had to tell the

Pontifect everything, even though his heart sank at the thought. She'd trusted him, and he'd made such a botch of things.

He'd need money for the journey, which meant he'd have to sell either one of Juster's rubies, which after repeated swallowings he still had, or the gold chain. He'd do that the moment he reached the coast, in the port of Crowfoot. From there he could buy a passage on a flat-boat for himself and Greylegs.

Rubies or gold? He considered it for only a moment. In a small town it would be easier to obtain the real value of the gold – and Mathilda owed him. He certainly wasn't going to be sentimental about a gift from her. The rubies he would give back to Juster one day.

Although he might keep Mathilda's kerchief . . .

Stupid dewberry. He'd sell that as well.

He rode on, decision made.

A little further down the track, before he'd even lost sight of the oak, he knew something was wrong. A flood of feelings jostled in his mind, none of which made much sense.

He was hungry, but he'd just eaten. Caterpillars. He needed caterpillars. There weren't any. Beetles. Beetles would do.

What the . . .? Not words, but pictures and weird emotions intruding into his head.

Someone was encroaching on his territory. Oh, that made him so *angry.* He puffed up, drew in breath. There, he'd gone, the interloper.

A worm. Good. Search for another. Hungry still.

Pox, he was going mad. His brain must have frozen last night! Fear, unease, contentment, belligerence, all piling up in an unrelated jumble, jabbering for attention, cluttering his mind.

Saker, stop thinking like a witless dunce. What's the matter with you? Concentrate on where you are going.

It was cold and windy up in the high country, a place where birds skulked low in bushes, hardly ever seen. Their calls were wispy, yet carried far on the wind. But now – not only were the birds keeping pace with his horse; they were noisy, chattering, piping, warbling. They flew from one side of the track to the other, in front, behind, over his head. Greylegs startled and shied until she finally settled into ignoring them.

No caterpillars in winter. Only worms.

Oh, pickle it! He was hearing the birds think. As if they were chattering inside his head. *Dear Va, what are you doing to me? Let me find myself again!*

He urged Greylegs into a canter and the horse responded. Together they left the birds behind, and he breathed steadily, reclaiming his thoughts.

Around the middle of the afternoon, after crossing the highest part of the mountain pass, he halted on the edge of the treeline. A stream and a patch of meadow grass gone to seed made it an ideal spot for Greylegs to graze, while he washed and filled his water skin. He rested with his back to a tree, watching the way the cloud teased along the crest of the mountains and drifted down into the folds, occasionally pouring into the pass like steaming milk into a pot. Sometimes, without warning, the mist would lift, revealing stark rock faces pocketed with snow.

As he watched, he glimpsed men and horses in the pass, dark outlines against a backdrop of mist. Immediately afterwards, birds shot out of the pass, thirty or forty bunched up in a compact flock. Just looking at them made him shudder with fear, and he knew – without knowing how he knew – that they were fleeing in terror. Alpine choughs. He'd seen them earlier in the pass, picking over the carcass of some small animal on a rock ledge.

He glanced up, expecting to see something in the blue sky above him, an eagle perhaps. There was nothing. The birds flew on, direct, silent, wings beating the air in remorseless desperation. They flew over his head, their fear as tangible to him as the yellow curve of their beaks and the red splash of their legs against the black of their feathers.

They passed on their agonising fear to him, until the drumming of his heart matched their wingbeats. His mouth went dry, his mind filled with a nameless terror. He grabbed up his water skin, snatched up the reins and pulled Greylegs off the grass and into the trees.

It's the horsemen, he thought. *Something to do with the horsemen.*

The trees were sparse, the undergrowth scanty. There was nowhere to hide. He placed Greylegs so that her outline was broken up by a few spare saplings, then flung Ryce's cloak over the horse's head to keep it still and calm under the dark of its cover. Holding the reins with one hand, he stroked Greylegs' neck with the other. The kris, alive again in its sheath, pressed hard against his thigh in warning.

Only half hidden behind a spindly young birch, he stood straight and still, and waited. The kris radiated warmth, a feeling of gentle heat surging upwards, flowing around his body, encasing him.

The horsemen, five of them, rode past at a fast trot. The riders, stony-faced, looked neither left nor right. All were men; all were dressed in dark grey clothing unalleviated by colour or decoration; each was armed with a lance and sword. As they passed, dread left him leaning weakly against the tree trunk. The warmth gradually faded. He had the disconcerting idea that maybe the kris had saved him from being seen.

Dear Va, what were they?

And he thought he heard the echo of something Fox had said to him. *I hate you Shenat. I will never rest until you are all gone from this world.*

Assassins, sent by Fox, gone to the shrine only to find him missing? Possible, but he'd never prove it.

He waited a while until he calmed, then removed the cloak from Greylegs. As he did so, he thought he glimpsed the momentary smudge of the black shadow on his fingers.

As if A'Va himself had passed by.

A man burst into Mathilda's bedroom, flinging the door wide. She woke in fright and confusion, unsure what was real and what were the tendrils of a lingering dream. She sat bolt upright, crying out in alarm.

"Is it true?" the man demanded. He grabbed her, shook her hard enough to make her bite her tongue.

Ryce's voice.

Aureen, awakening on the truckle at the foot of the four-poster, gave a shrill wail of shock.

Mathilda drew a deep breath, quietened the thunder of her heart. She stared at him, and wondered what he meant. He'd found out something to her detriment, obviously.

"Get out," he snapped at Aureen, just as the two nuns, clad in voluminous white nightgowns, hands waving in silent agitation, came to the door. "Out! Out! Out, the lot of you!"

They scuttled away, all three of them, and he slammed the door shut.

"This is *my* bedroom," Mathilda snapped back. "Pox on you, Ryce. What do you want?"

She used her anger to cover her consternation. In his whole life, he'd never threatened her, never really shouted at her, never done what he'd just done – shaken her awake hard enough to rattle her teeth. At dawn, what was more, for she glimpsed first light through the glassed window.

"You know fobbing well what I want!" he said. "An explanation! You've had me dancing to match your steps all your life, but that's over now. This time I can't be charmed by your smile. You told Father that Rampion raped you, but he didn't, did he? You went to his bed and *seduced* him! And we were all too blind to see it. You thought you could stop Father sending you to Lowmeer. It must've been a terrible shock when you realised your lack of a maidenhead wasn't going to change his mind. Thilda, you sent a man to be nullified for something *you* initiated!"

She shrugged and batted his hands away from her shoulders. "I was sold in exchange for the use of a port none of us are ever likely to see. What kind of a woman would I be if I took all that lying down? None of you cared, not even Witan Saker Rampion."

Arranging a shawl over her shoulders, she asked, "Were you up all night? You look awful and you smell of sweat and horses and ale." Before he could reply, she added, "Will you make me a promise, Ryce? If Regal Vilmar dies, bring me home."

He stared at her, astonished. "You're going there to get him an heir," he said at last. "If you come home a widow, you'd have to leave any children you have behind. You do realise that?"

"Do you think I'd care?"

"I'm beginning to think I don't know you at all."

"You've never tried."

"Too late to start now. The moment I arrived back, Father sent for me and kept me up half the night on this business of your wedding and how to treat the Regal. It seems Vilmar – a pox on the Lowmian swag-bellied haggard – is now off the coast of Betany. His ship has been sighted."

"*Already?*"

"He obviously wants to consummate the wedding as soon as he can."

She swayed, suddenly dizzy, and lay back against her pillows. "And what does Father say?"

"Father is sending me to represent him at your wedding. I will escort you and your ladies to Betany, perhaps leaving as early as tomorrow morning. Prime Fox will come to perform the ceremony."

"Consign Fox to a choiceless hell! I *hate* the man! He deceived me!" Abruptly she raised her hands to cover her face. "You treat your horses better than this," she said in a whisper.

"Va above, anyone would think we're sending you to the gallows! Think, Mathilda – you'll be the Regala! People will have to address you as 'your grace'. You'll have your own court. You can order everyone around to your heart's content."

It was a long time before she dropped her hands and spoke. "How did you know Saker didn't ravish me?"

"Father sent me to kill him."

The words were stark, points of steel driven into her flesh. *You pay a price when you play with men's lives,* she thought. *But then, they played with yours, didn't they?* "So Saker told you what happened?"

"No, he didn't. It was that grey woman of yours. Celandine Marten. Va's teeth, what did you think you were doing, sending her to help that whoreson of a witan? I was supposed to kill her too!"

Sweet nonce and hell's tomorrows! "Are – are they alive still?"

"Saker will never bother you again. Celandine, she tricked me, scared me halfway to death. She has a witchery – a glamour."

"I *need* her, Ryce, I need her glamour talents."

He stared at her, appalled. "You *knew* all along? That she had witchery?"

She patted him on the arm, smiling. "Of course! And I don't want anything at all happening to her. Do you understand me?"

"I brought her back with me. But I've been thinking. It may not be wise to take a Shenat witch to Lowmeer, especially one with a glamour. I've heard Lowmians see it as the witchery of deceit. Use it at court, and she could be accused of spying for Ardrone, and you could suffer as well, by association."

"They'll never know," she replied complacently.

He shrugged. "So be it. Your fate rests in your own hands when you leave our soil."

"Do you think I don't know that?" she asked bitterly. "Did you kill Saker?"

"What do you care?" He turned on his heel and left her.

"That was enlightening."

Sorrel let her glamour fall and stepped away from the corner of the room where she'd merged herself into the colours of the wood panelling. "As far as I know, Saker's still alive."

Mathilda gasped in shock. "When did you come in? How did you get in? How *dare* you listen to my conversation with my brother!"

She shrugged, indifferent. "You're the one who wanted me to be a spy. I arrived back in Throssel at dusk with the Prince. I sneaked in here a couple of hours later by following the older nun back from her evening prayer. You were already asleep, so I went straight to bed. I've spent the better part of five days on the back of a horse, you know. I'm exhausted."

"And you reached Saker in time?"

"No thanks to Prince Ryce, but yes, I did."

"You had no right to tell Ryce that Saker—"

"Was innocent? You have a strange idea of what's right and wrong."

"You impudent lightskirt! He wasn't exactly innocent. And you will treat me with respect."

"If your behaviour merits it. You call *me* a lightskirt? Milady, let's make one thing clear. I'm not your handmaiden any more, nor your maid, nor your lady-in-waiting, nor your friend. I'm not quite sure what I am. Your conscience, perhaps. You can do what you like to me, but if you do, there's always the chance I might bring you down with me. You can't ever be sure of me, any more than I can trust you. You asked me to come back, and I have. I've said I would help you, and I will. I was forced into an unpleasant marriage to someone I barely knew and didn't love. Believe me, you need someone at your side who understands what that means."

Mathilda was silent, considering. As her indignation drained away, she appeared younger, more vulnerable. "How can I get you to Lowmeer? The King wants you dead!"

"There's going to be chaos today. There'll be a hundred people in and out of here, packing your dresses and so on. The wardrobe mistress will be in charge, but she's too old and fat to be going with you to Betany. I'll make myself look different. You point me out to her, call me – oh, um, Jannis will do – call me Jannis and tell her I'm the person who's in charge of seeing that the wedding gown and your wardrobe reach the port and are loaded on to the Regal's ship. Tell her to make sure there's a place for me on the luggage coaches going to Betany.

"Once we're on board and Prince Ryce has left, Sorrel will suddenly reappear. You tell your Ardronese ladies she's your new attendant. No one knows the real me. No one has ever seen me before, not even Aureen. You were right. In Lowmeer, I can be Sorrel Redwing. And now, milady, you had better get out of bed, because any moment, there will be people knocking at the door. There's a lot to do today."

28

The Anger in the Aftermath

"The only reason I can see for you doing this was complete insanity. Raving, inane, juvenile *lunacy*."

Saker held himself ramrod straight. As was her norm when she was agitated, Fritillary Reedling strode up and down her sanctum as if it was too small to contain her passion. He'd assumed this meeting would not be easy, but he'd underestimated the full extent of her fury.

He could have coped if that had been all. Trouble was, she was so Va-damn *hurt*. And that swamped him with shame. At the same time, he was boiling with anger himself.

I didn't think I could feel any worse. I was wrong.

"Whatever made you think you could bed a princess? Are you so naive as to think you could get away with behaviour like that? And to think I sent you there as her *spiritual* adviser! I *trusted* you. You've shamed me. You've shamed the Faith, the clergy, yourself. You took advantage of a half-grown girl."

He stared resolutely at the floor, somewhere in the vicinity of her feet. Every word she said was true, which made any reply impossible. That was doubly annoying, because he had not yet had a chance to express his fury at her.

She hadn't finished, either. "I couldn't believe what I read in the Prime's report. I *didn't* believe it. Rape? That was out of the question! You can have no idea how shattered I was. I thought you'd be already dead and there was nothing I could do. I thought an innocent man had just died, the man I'd mentored. I – I *grieved* for you."

The pain in her voice startled him with its intensity. He raised his head to look at her. She was unnaturally pale, her mouth pinched.

She took a deep breath. "I suppose you imagined you were in love with one another! But how could you think that made it all right?"

"I – I don't believe I did much thinking at the time," he admitted.

She picked up a piece of parchment from the table and waved it at him. "Fox had a lot to say on the matter. Even after hearing your explanation, I don't think I've ever been so disappointed in anyone in my whole life as I am right now with you."

A slow flush started in his neck and suffused upwards. He felt the heat rise to brighten his cheeks.

"Have you nothing to say for yourself?"

"I can only say I'm sorry. Otherwise – otherwise everything you say is true."

"I suppose I shouldn't rail at you too much, in the light of her manipulation of you, and your subsequent fate."

He shrugged. "I'm trying not to blame her. She had a right to attempt to avoid marriage to a man almost three times her age with a reputation for unpleasantness and dead wives."

She ceased her pacing. To his astonishment and mortification, she had tears in her eyes, tears on her cheeks, and such profound sadness in her expression that he wanted to take her in his arms and pat her on the back.

He looked away, embarrassed.

She didn't dab at her tears, or try to hide them. Instead, she waved at the chairs at the other end of the room. "Let's sit down and discuss what is to be done. First, I want to know everything in detail. From court politics to how you got back here alive."

"I think – no, I *need* to put something else out into the open first. I've good reason to think you've lied to me."

She sat motionless, not even breathing. Then, "Go on."

"For a start, you didn't tell me all you knew, or guessed, or felt, about Prime Fox."

She dragged in a breath. "True. I didn't want to prejudice you before you'd met him. I wanted a fresh point of view from someone who hadn't been hearing the sort of things – albeit nebulous things – that I had."

"Well, fortunately I bumped into Gerelda Brantheld, who did have several things to say. But not even that warning was sufficient, because I'd heard nothing from *you* to indicate he might be a dangerous man. Dangerous to Shenat and the Way of the Oak. You sent me into a war I didn't even know was being fought."

"Ah. For that, I am sorry. I misjudged. I didn't think there was any way he would involve a mere spiritual adviser."

"I believe you also lied about something else. I went to see my father. He told me *you* forbade *him* to say anything about my mother to me. You told me it was the other way around. He also seemed to think he may not have been my father. Which would explain his irrational dislike of me as a child, and his determination to make sure I didn't inherit the farm. You said you bargained with him to let me go, but in fact, everything points to him being delighted to have me leave. You *lied* to me?"

"Yes, I did. What did he tell you about your mother?"

"Nothing, except that she left me *before* she died. I – I always believed I lost her *because* she died." He waited for her to say more, but she was silent. "Aren't you going to explain?" It was difficult to keep his rage to a simmer when he wanted to fill the room with it, to lash her with sarcasm and white-hot protest.

"Later." The words were calm enough, but the colour had drained from her face.

She feels what I'm thinking. She knows how angry I am. Well, it serves her right. Aloud he said, "Fox knows more about my parentage than I do, and something about it made him dislike me enough to want me dead. I have a right to know what it's all about. My ignorance hobbled me. I was always at a disadvantage with him, from the beginning. You have no right to keep secrets like that from me. Who was my mother? Did she really leave me? If so, why? *Is* Robin Rampion my father? What was your relationship with my mother? What is it about my birth that made Fox despise me so?"

She still didn't answer. Instead she said, "Tell me what happened between you and Fox. Everything."

"Your reverence, I want answers."

"And you'll have them. Later."

"I'll hold you to that. Before I leave this room."

"Very well."

It took him almost three hours to cover everything. Even then, he didn't mention the lascar's dagger or anything about his continuing trouble with birds, but they were the only two topics he dodged. She rarely interrupted, but when he'd finished his tale, her questions told him that nothing had escaped the sharpness of her mind. "This Celandine Marten. Do you trust her now?" she asked.

"I don't know. I don't know why she helped me, unless Lady Mathilda told her to do so. But I no longer make assumptions about the Princess's actions."

"Celandine's so-called attempt at a glamour just before she left you up there in the high country – it was pointless."

He digested that, knowing she was waiting for him to make sense of her statement. *Oh, pox.* "You mean that wasn't the glamour."

"Of course not. She showed you the real person, but you were so caught up in distrusting her, you didn't recognise the reality. The mouse was the glamour."

Blood rushed to his face. *Va rot you, Saker. When you're an idiot, you do a thorough job of it, don't you?* "She made herself hard to see. Why – why would she want everyone to think her such a nonentity when she's beautiful?"

"Perhaps because she was a spy for Mathilda. Or for someone else. Or maybe because her looks had previously brought her nothing but trouble."

"She as good as told me her name was not Celandine Marten. And when I overheard her talking to Prince Ryce, she said something about gaining her witchery at a shrine in Melforn, the day she met the Princess."

"I know the place. The oak there is truly a tree to behold." She paused, thoughtful. "I heard something about Melforn recently. Now what was it? Ask Secretary Barden to come inside, will you, Saker?"

He did as she asked, and when the man shuffled in, she said, "We need to poke into your memory for names and places, Barden. An incident at Melforn, within the past year or two? Concerning a runaway woman, I think."

Saker hurriedly offered the old man a chair to sit on. He was over seventy, by how many years no one was sure, and he'd outlasted some ten incumbents of the Pontifect throne. His knees might be troublesome, his teeth sparse and his hands gnarled, but there was nothing wrong with his memory. He'd soaked up fifty years of gossip and secrets during his tenure as secretary, and he wasn't going to forget one drop of it.

"Hmm," he murmured. "Not a good tale, I'm afraid. A Shenat woman, the wife of a landsman." He thought for a moment. "She murdered him. Pushed him down a set of stairs in front of witnesses. Now what was his name? Ferret. Weasel? No, Ermine. Nikard Ermine. Her name was Sorrel . . . and some kind of bird. Redpoll? Redstart? Redshank? Nikard's brother wanted to claim his estate because Nikard and Sorrel left no children. He had to have the local Va arbiter's permission to overrule any claim the missing widow could have, which is why we came to hear of it."

"That's it. I remember now. Considering the woman's crime and her subsequent disappearance, I told him to approve the man's petition," Fritillary said.

"Was there anything about a dead or missing child?" Saker asked.

"Not that I remember, master witan. Redwing, that was it. Sorrel Redwing."

After Secretary Barden left, Saker shook his head in disbelief. "That doesn't sound like Celandine Marten! That mouse? A killer?"

"How did she come to be the Princess's attendant?"

"I never asked." He felt shame yet again. He'd never been interested enough to ask. *I failed her as a witan.*

Fritillary said, "There's no proof Sorrel and Celandine are the same person. We may never know. But let's press on. What is your witchery?"

"My – my witchery? I don't have one!"

"Of course you do. I can feel it. Witcheries recognise one another. If you delve inside yourself, you'll feel mine. You haven't looked in the mirror lately, have you?"

"They don't have mirrors in the kind of hostelries I've been staying at." He fingered his cheek, saying, "I suppose you're referring to the scar having healed so quickly. But I didn't do that. It was part of what happened to me at the shrine."

"Ah." The look she was giving him now had a smidgeon of pity in it, and not a little mockery. "Come with me." She stood up and he followed her into the next room, which turned out to be her bedchamber. If he'd thought about it, he would have guessed it would be austere, in keeping with her monastic existence. The room was indeed small and plain, but there were touches of femininity, even luxury, that surprised him. Fresh roses on the washstand, paintings of bucolic scenes of country life and nature on the walls, a prettily embroidered bed cover with a lace fringe. There was also a mirror with a carved oak-wood frame.

"Take a look at your face," she said. "You told me you were branded. The Prime took great delight in telling me you were branded. You both said it was done on the cheek. Well, tell me why I can't see it."

He stared at his image. The picture reflected back at him was almost free of distortion, unlike the cheap looking-glasses he was accustomed to using. And that made what he was seeing all the more shocking. He expected to see a white or red puckering, something, to show where the brand had burned him. But his cheek had no scar at all. It was as if he had never been scarred, and yet he could *feel* the roughness of it.

He turned to look at the Pontifect, knowing that she must see how shaken he was. "This may be a glamour, a permanent one. But it's not mine," he said flatly. "And I don't have any healing power."

"So what is your witchery? Ask yourself what changed immediately after your night at the shrine."

The birds . . . He suppressed a shudder. "Birds," he said finally.

"*Birds?*"

"I know what they're thinking about. Well, they don't *think*, not really. They just . . . *feel* things. Which I sense. It's muckle-headed nonsense! Who wants to know when the local sparrows are hungry?" He was getting good at ignoring them now, though. Even the flocks of town pigeons that followed him around as if they were demented.

She stared at him, but he had nothing further to say. Shrugging, she led the way back into the main room to sit again. He felt exhausted and leant back against the cushions as if all energy had drained from him.

"We who draw on the power of the Oak have only one thing in common," she replied. "We have all endured something extreme. Extreme grief, or pain, or fear, or horror. And in the course of that experience, we surrendered ourselves. We gave up part of our life, part of our independence, to the service of the Way of the Oak. In return, we were granted the powers of witchery. If you don't truly understand yours, I suspect it's because you're holding something of yourself back. When you truly commit yourself, the full extent of your witchery will be revealed to you. And remember this: it comes with a terrible price."

"You mean something more then being unfrocked, branded and left for dead?"

"Oh yes, indeed. Part of your life belongs to the Faith now."

"It always did," he protested. "I am – was – a cleric, remember?"

"And can be again," she said. "After all, I'm the Pontifect, and it is ultimately my decision who serves the Faith as a cleric and who doesn't. Though I have no intention at this point of restoring your position. You can serve the Faith better as my spy."

His relief was immediate. *No more court life.*

Then, unexpectedly, she said, "I've always known this moment would come. I've been waiting for it."

He was appalled. "You can't possibly have known that I was going to be nullified!"

"No, no, of course not. But I did know that one day you would be offered witchery."

He pondered her words, exasperated because she didn't seem able to say anything clearly. "Has this something to do with my mother?"

"It has something to do with the blood you've inherited. Witcheries run in your family. But it's more to do with what I've sensed inside you. The potential."

At least he realised now the meaning of that feeling of expectation he'd sensed in the Pontifect from time to time; she'd been waiting for him to tell her that something like this had happened.

"I'm not sure that I want this."

"You have no choice. You have whatever it is already."

He said nothing. It was all so pointless. What good was it to know that a bird was enjoying a beetle? Was his mission in life to call up worms for them, perhaps?

He scowled. When she raised that querying eyebrow of hers, he said, "Fox wants you dead. And I think he would be happy to see that something fatal happens to you."

"I know. There have been several attempts on my life since you left. And I know he's already seeking supporters. And has found them." He looked up at her in surprise, and she added, "You aren't my only informant. Those ledgers in his office – what do you think they signify?"

"I've written down everything I can remember." He pulled out a sheaf of papers from his jacket and laid them in front of her on the desk. "You might get more from them than I did. I think he's raising his own force of armed men, lancers. I think ultimately he plans to use the resources of Ardrone's forests and lands to fund him after his seizure of power. I think some of the ledgers are his accounting of men and women he's recruited. He wants your job, and he wants the end of the Way of the Oak. And of the Flow too, I reckon. I believe those men I saw on the Chervil track across the mountains were after me, sent by Fox just to make sure I was dead. And I think it likely he's some kind of agent of A'Va."

She was dismissive, saying, "A'Va's power is always secondary to Va's."

What was it the shrine guardian had said? *A'Va is lies and hate and temptation and fear and greed and indulgence. He hunts you down . . . he's real, yet a lie with no entity.* He wasn't sure he understood that. A'Va was the antipodal of Va, of course, one positive, the other in opposition. But without entity? Was that the same as saying without body?

"Oh, one more thing. The Fox family tree I saw? There was something very odd about the dates on it. If they are correct, the whole lot of them seem to live to be well over a century old. Like shrine-keepers."

She snorted. "Unlikely. The rest is more worrying. I will send more cautionary words to King Edwayn about his Prime. It won't be the first warnings he's had. If anything does happen to me, make no assumption about my demise. I won't let Fox climb on to the Pontifect's chair without a fight."

"I'm glad to hear it." But the words chilled him. They made the danger more than just a possibility he'd considered. It was real, serious and close at hand. He waited for her to say more, to explain details, but she was silent. He forgot sometimes that although they had a special relationship, he was only a tiny part of the empire she headed. A minor cleric in a huge web of influence and connections.

He changed the subject.

"Now tell me about my parents. Tell me why you lied. And why they should have any relevance to Valerian Fox. Are you and I related?"

"No. Fox and I have a long history, from the days when we were rising through the clerical ranks of Ardrone. I met him often enough to know he has an evil, ambitious heart, and I thwarted his career whenever I could." She shrugged. "Naturally enough, he looked for my weaknesses. So when I rescued you from the kind of life you led with Robin Rampion, I wanted to hide my connection to you in order to keep you safe. I had no doubt then that if ever he found out he would hit at me through you. Hence the promise extracted from Robin Rampion, and the lies I told. I suppose, from what you just said, that he has discovered the connection. It's as simple as that."

Oh no, it's not. That's not the whole truth. Not by the length of an arrow shot.

"Why does my father – Robin Rampion – think I may not be his son?"

"Your mother was a farmer's daughter. She was beautiful, and wilful. Her parents arranged for her to marry Robin Rampion. She took one look at him and fled to Oakwood. She found a job working in a tavern frequented by students of the university. The three of us – Fox, myself and the man who was probably your father – we were all there at the time, all of an age more or less, and we all came to know Iris, your mother. She and I were friendly. She was very likeable, always laughing, popular with the students."

"Are you telling me Fox was part of your group?"

"No, Va forbid! We all disliked him, even then. Fox and the other man, they'd known each other since they were children, but they didn't like one another. Fox doesn't come into the story directly. I mention him merely because he might have known more of what happened then than I was aware of at the time.

"Anyway, we – Iris, the man who might have been your father and I – had a falling-out. It was the end of the university term. Iris went home. I believe she might have been pregnant with you, although she never told me that. She married Robin Rampion, so it is likely she saw him as a way out of her predicament. I think he made life unpleasant for her because he doubted your parentage. She ran away, leaving you behind. Shortly afterwards she died, back in Oakwood."

"She left me behind."

"Yes," Fritillary said. "She had no resources to care for a child."

"And the man who might have fathered me?"

"He'd moved on. Gone to another university."

"Did he know about me?"

"Perhaps. Iris loved him. I think she would have told him – if she was indeed having his child."

"Who was he?"

"Don't go there. It's not worth it. I don't know anything for sure, any more than Robin was sure. And you'll never know either. There was . . . gossip about your mother among the students. Leave it be."

His anger roiled, making him feel physically ill.

Worse still, the woman who'd cared, the one he'd "remembered" that night at the shrine? She hadn't existed. His mother had deliberately left him with a man who doubted the parentage of her child.

He looked at Fritillary. She said, "There are some things better left undisturbed, Saker. This is one of them. What matters is now, and the future. I want to keep you well out of Valerian Fox's reach. I don't want him to have another chance to hurt you in order to hurt me."

"How did he make the connection between us?"

She shrugged yet again. "A number of people have noted my mentorship of you over the years. I paid for your university fees, which would be a matter of record. Perhaps he investigated because I sent you to the court. Your death would grieve me, and he found that out."

He didn't answer that.

She said, "I want you to go to Lowmeer to investigate the incidences of the Horned Death."

His heart sank. "Are you trying to kill me?" he asked sourly. "Some sort of justice for my foolishness?"

"Don't be ridiculous. You'll be safer in Lowmeer. Saker Rampion is useless to me in Ardrone because he's not lawfully permitted back there. Change your name to a Lowmian one. They like fish. Call yourself Anchovy Stickleback. Or Thick-lip Mullet."

Damn, she wasn't going to let him forget his foolishness in a hurry. "Actually, I was thinking more about danger from the pestilence than from the law."

"Witchery gives you some power to protect yourself from A'Va's sorcery."

"Not true. In the Ardronese outbreaks, shrine-keepers died, and who ever heard of a shrine-keeper without at least one witchery?"

That reminder appeared to worry her, and she stirred uneasily. "It – it's a new development, and so far only in Ardrone. You are safer than most people I can send. I want you to investigate the Horned Death, anything you can find out about its connection to devil-kin, anything about the practice of twin murder. Anything relevant, in fact. I'll give you a letter to an old cleric friend of mine, Prelate Murram Loach, who now heads the Seminary of Advanced Studies on the outskirts of Ustgrind; he'll help you get started. Of course, you are never to cross the Princess's path again. You will steer well clear of the Regal's court."

"You didn't have to say that. I might have acted as a brainless fool once, but I do learn from my mistakes."

"Good."

"What are you going to do about Fox?"

"The Ardronese Prime is not your concern, Saker." She heaved a sigh. "He's been clever enough to win Shenat approval with his care of those suffering from the Horned Death, even as he stabs them in the back. You can have no idea how many epistles I've had from northern Ardrone praising him."

"Part of his plan, I imagine. Charm the people you want to make powerless into believing you are on their side . . ."

"I shall deal with it. You certainly cannot."

"There are other alternatives. Reverence, you need to watch for assassins. For poison in your food. For a stray arrow. A falling tile. If I stayed here, I could be responsible for your safety."

She smiled faintly. "No. You go to Lowmeer. Call it your penance, if you like. You leave as soon as you have replenished your kit, whatever you need. Oh, and I'd advise that you wear gloves. All the time."

"Did you tell him the truth?"

Fritillary, who had been standing at the window wondering just what Valerian Fox's next move would be, turned to face Secretary Barden. "Not entirely."

"Mistake." The old man leaned on his stick and shook his head sorrowfully at her. "He has a right to know."

"Yes, he does."

"But you still aren't going to tell him?"

"If I tell – no, *when* I tell him, I lose him for ever."

"Possibly you underestimate the young man."

"Underestimate his anger at my duplicity? I don't think so. Barden, I *need* him. I need his unquestioning loyalty. And if it takes a lie – or a prevarication – to get it, then that's what I'll do."

"Allies are those you trust, not those you deceive."

The truth of his words made her feel ill, but the old man didn't know what it was like to see into the head of a child and sense the nascent talent there, to know there was the possibility of a witchery within unlike any other the world had ever known. A witchery she would one day need at her side, no matter the price.

I am the Pontifect. Nothing else matters, only my duty to the Pontificate. And to Va, of course. "Right now he is a willing ally and a loyal servant *because* he doesn't know the depth of the deception. And that's exactly the way I want it."

She knew the price, though. In the end, Saker Rampion would walk away without a backward glance. There were some things that were indeed unforgivable.

Only when he'd left the Pontifect's palace and was sitting in a local hostelry did Saker remember that he'd intended to tell her all about the lascar's dagger. And yet he hadn't said a word.

He dropped his wooden spoon back into the bowl of potage he'd been eating, and drew the kris out of his sheath to lay it on the table. Thinking back to Throssel, he now remembered his earlier intention to write to her about it, and yet he never had.

You fobbing maggot-pie, he thought, addressing the dagger, *you made me forget.* More lascar witchery. *Ardhi, you'd better find me soon, before this thing curdles my brains.*

He ran a finger over the wrought metal of the blade. It seemed solid, inanimate. The times when it had been more fluid were either in its efforts to reach his side, or to warn him of danger.

You know what I think I'll do? I'm going to take you to a shrine, and see how you react.

The dirty smudge on his fingers came back the moment he stepped under the bare branches of the oak at the main Vavala shrine later that day. When he placed his hands flat to the bark of the trunk, he half expected something awful to happen, but nothing changed. He prayed, his forehead touching the tree, but found little solace. He fumbled for the dagger and touched it to the bark in turn. A stray shaft of wintry sun slipped down through the canopy to illuminate the blade and make the gold flecks shine, but apart from that, nothing happened. The dagger didn't move, the oak twigs hung still in the windless air, and the shrine-keeper noticed nothing.

Outside once again, standing near the edge of the tree's spread, a warbler chirped its friendliness and came down to perch on a branch only inches from his shoulder.

"Who asked you here, you saucy ball of fluff?" he growled. "You don't care enough to give me a single feather off your back, even if I asked!"

The warbler cocked its head, staring. Then it preened its back. When it had finished, it bent down towards him, offering up a single feather in its beak. He gaped at it, aghast.

No, oh no. That didn't just happen. He backed away, stumbling, then turned and fled.

A totally useless, boil-brained witchery. He could charm birds into giving him their feathers . . . Va above, was he mad? Had the whole fobbing world gone curdled crazy?

He began to laugh. There was Pontifect Fritillary Reedling thinking she was the one sending him to Lowmeer, when of course that wasn't it at all. It was Ardhi's doing, or the Chenderawasi kris, drawing him back to Ustgrind.

Part of him, the part that knew he was being manipulated by forces far greater than he, wanted to howl at the wind in frustration. In terror. The rest of him – the part that acknowledged he was going to Lowmeer to face whatever he must, whether it be Horned Death, or devil-kin, or A'Va, or just a life without ever seeing Mathilda again – knew that he had finally grown up.

Life, he thought, *is really about accepting that, in the end, you have to deal with whatever happens.*

29

Paying Another's Price

Mathilda sank into a deep curtsey, her skirts spread and her head bowed. She stayed that way, perfectly balanced, afraid to look up.

What if he's ugly? I wager he is. I wager he's repulsive. And old and wrinkled . . .

It wasn't entirely a guess. She'd seen his portrait, painted when he was at least ten years younger, and even then the Regal of Lowmeer had been an austere, grim-faced prune of a man. She'd heard rumours at court that he'd murdered his previous Ardronese noble wife because she'd proved barren.

"My lady, arise."

A hand wavered under her nose, thin-fingered, knobbled and swollen at the knuckles. She placed her hand on the palm offered to her, then raised her head to look.

"Your Grace," she whispered. Her sapphire-blue, pearl-studded wedding gown billowed around her, and her first impression was that she was the only splash of brightness on a ship draped in funereal colours. An awning, erected over the deck in case it rained, dimmed the sunlight and accentuated the sombre. Everyone within her range of vision was wearing black or grey, with white trimming. *Va save me, they're a congregation of pied auks!*

"Welcome on board," the Regal said. "We've been awaiting our royal bride with impatience."

He bent to kiss her fingers as she rose from her curtsey, and his dry lips lingered on her skin longer than was customary. She had a whiff of bad breath; the ruler of Lowmeer had rotting teeth. Her next impression was of a long face ending in a jowled jawline, and a paunch that obliterated his waistline. The rest of his figure was too thin. His neck was scraggy, his arms lacked flesh, and his thighs were as scrawny as those of an underfed rooster.

Sweet Va, she thought in revulsion. *I must bed a man who resembles a starveling fowl with a pot belly?* She fought a desire to scramble back on to the galley that had rowed her out to the anchorage. Instead, she said, "Your Grace is indeed kind." Her voice wobbled, more in horror then fright.

"Allow us to present our cousin, the Lady Friselda Drumveld. She will be milady's wards-dame."

Sweet Va, she had to be fifty. At least. A solid trunk of slate grey was finished with white cuffs at the wrists and topped with a white linen headdress. Her only adornment was a plain gold widow's band on her finger.

"It will be my honour," the woman said. Her voice rumbled like approaching thunder.

Mathilda inclined her head in acknowledgement. *What in Va's name is a wards-dame?*

"We are sure Lady Friselda will be of indispensible service to milady." Vilmar's gaze fell to the curve of Mathilda's breasts, pushed up by the tight bodice of her wedding gown, and lingered there. "Shall we proceed with the ceremony?" He offered her his arm, and she slipped her fingers through the crook of his elbow. He patted them with his other hand.

Prime Fox bowed and stepped forward to face them.

Sweet cankers, how she hated him!

She looked around the deck, desperately seeking a friendly face. In answer, Ryce moved forward until he was standing at her shoulder. She gave him a frantic look of entreaty, but he ignored the message.

Where's Celandine? I need Celandine. No . . . Sorrel. She must remember that. Celandine had ceased to exist. And Sorrel wanted to be unobtrusive until the ship sailed.

She was close to panic. Trapped. There was no way out, not now. The Prime spoke, something about the sanctity of marriage, but she didn't listen. The Regal was leaning heavily on her arm, as if his knees wouldn't hold him erect. She riveted her gaze on to his hand where it covered her own. Liver spots splotched his skin. She thought wildly of breaking free, of flinging herself over the railing into the cold waters of the Betany estuary. Her heavy gown would drag her under in seconds.

She shivered.

No. You are the daughter of a king. You are about to become the Regala. You will show the world what it is to be a queen . . .

She raised her chin and prepared herself to recite her wedding vows.

The festivities dragged on.

Festivities? *No,* Mathilda thought savagely, there was nothing festive in the way the Lowmians conducted themselves. Regal Vilmar ignored her and spent his time speaking to Ryce. Someone had brought him a chair, and he'd eased himself into it like an old man. When his glance did stray her way, it was to fixate on her neckline.

My husband.

Dear Va. I am truly married. Tonight he beds me; tomorrow morning we sail with the tide for Ustgrind.

As the afternoon wore on, and it grew colder up on deck, the wedding party dispersed. Most of the Ardronese guests departed for the shore and the town hall, where a banquet had been prepared to celebrate her marriage. The Regal, determined not to set foot on Ardronese soil because he believed it would show him to be the lesser monarch, ordered food to be ferried from there to the Lowmian banquet, planned for the lower deck of his own vessel.

Prince Ryce and several of their royal cousins stayed on, together with the four ladies-in-waiting who were to accompany her to Lowmeer. The only other Ardronese in attendance was the Prime. She couldn't see Sorrel anywhere, although she'd promised she'd be on board.

She won't break that promise. She won't.

Yet her handmaiden was tender-hearted and still so angry about what had happened to Saker. Which wasn't fair, really. Mathilda hadn't thought Saker would be *killed.* The idea that Ryce would be sent to murder him had never *occurred* to her. When he'd been nulled, she'd thought the shrine guardian would save him because he was innocent – and she must have been right to think so. He *hadn't* died. Ryce hadn't killed him. Sorrel knew that. She *needed* her. She *had* to be there.

"Would your grace like to adjourn to your quarters before the banquet begins?" Lady Friselda rumbled in her ear.

"Indeed I would," Mathilda replied, relieved. She'd being aching to use a privy and had been wondering how to ask. She signalled her ladies-in-waiting to follow her, and they all descended the narrow companionway to the lower deck, their dresses brushing the walls as they went.

When Lady Friselda stopped, she indicated a door on her right. "This is the Regal's cabin. Yours is the opposite one on the left."

She waved Mathilda in ahead of her, then closed the door behind her, shutting the four ladies-in-waiting outside in the companionway. Inside the cabin, Aureen and Sorrel, who had been unpacking Mathilda's cabin trunk, looked up from their task and hastily sank into curtseys.

Lady Friselda fixed them with an unfriendly stare. "There is no need to unpack her grace's Ardronese dresses. They are inappropriate for Lowmeer and will be sent ashore in the morning." Before Mathilda could protest, she added, waving her hand at a grey gown laid out across the bed, "That is a gift from me, and it is what you will wear to the banquet. I shall leave you to change."

"Wait!" Mathilda said, looking at the gown in dismay. "You want me to wear that? It looks like widow's weeds! My wedding gown was sewn especially for this occasion. You *cannot* mean me to change out of it now?"

"Indeed. It is the Regal's wish." Her eyes narrowed in irritation. "Your grace, you came on board an Ardronese princess, but you are now the Regala of Lowmeer. You will no longer be garbed in – *such* a way." With those words, uttered with dismissive contempt, she stepped out of the cabin and closed the door.

Mathilda gaped, rendered speechless. Then she picked up the charcoal-coloured high-necked gown and held it up against herself. "Oh, *no*."

"You knew this was possible," Sorrel pointed out with infuriating calm.

"She can't be serious. *All* my lovely dresses? And today, *now*?"

"I've been talking to some of the Lowmian servants," Sorrel said. "A wards-dame is a very powerful person whose task it is to initiate a new bride into the bridegroom's family. I wouldn't advise going against her wishes too much."

Mathilda grew more and more furious. "Aureen, go find my ladies and have them come here."

Aureen scuttled out the door.

"Be careful, your grace," Sorrel said. "You need to enchant your bridegroom *before* you challenge him."

"No. I need to challenge him *before* he gets what he craves. That is my power."

"That might work with many men, but Regal Vilmar is a monarch. Monarchs do not take kindly to direct challenges to their supremacy."

Va, but the woman was exasperating. Always so – so *prosaic*! She ignored her advice and demanded instead, "Is there a privy on this Va-forsaken boat?"

Sorrel waved her hand at a door on the other side of the cabin. "There's a commode in there."

"I need to use it, but first you may unlace me. If they want me to change my clothing, I will. Unpack my red gown."

Sorrel raised an eyebrow. "Isn't the bosom a little *low* on that dress? And the colour, er, a little too – *red*?"

"Exactly," Mathilda said, steely-voiced.

Aureen returned, flustered, just as Sorrel was about to lift the dress over Mathilda's petticoats.

"What is it?" Mathilda asked. The maid was white-faced, and Aureen was usually as phlegmatic as a well-fed cat.

"Milady – I mean, your grace – they've gone!"

"What has?"

"Your ladies. Lady Maris, Lady Annat . . ."

She couldn't absorb what Aureen was saying. "*Gone?* Gone where?"

"They've been sent back to shore. On the Regal's orders."

"That *can't* be right. It was agreed! I could bring four ladies-in-waiting, and two servants."

"Milady, I seen them being handed down into the longboat. With their luggage an' all. The Regal was there, watching them go. So I asked the Lady Friselda's maid what was happening. She said she'd overheard the Regal talking to her mistress, telling her to get rid of the four Ardronese wenches. Only Pashali peacocks should be that colourful, he said, and there weren't no place in his court for women who looked like tavern bawds."

Mathilda lowered herself slowly to sit on the edge of the bed. "Ryce," she whispered. "I must speak to Ryce. He's still on board, isn't he?"

Aureen nodded.

"He can't do anything for you," Sorrel said. "Your grace, you are now on your husband's ship. Neither Prince Ryce nor the King will risk abrogating the treaty for—" She halted.

"For me," Mathilda finished. "You think they won't do it for me."

Sorrel didn't answer that. Instead, she said, "Your grace, your greatest strength has always been your charm."

She regarded Sorrel, wondering what she *hadn't* said. Her mind began churning with ideas. She had charmed Saker, hadn't she? And he'd been a witan with strong ideas of right and wrong. She stood up and paced the room. Then she said, "You're right. I can choose my own jousting field."

Aureen looked from her to Sorrel, puzzled.

"Pack away my Ardronese gowns," Mathilda told her. "The Lowmians can send them back, if that's what they want."

"Shall we keep the nightdresses here?" Sorrel asked without expression, but it was a suggestion nonetheless.

She smiled, thinking of how pretty – and revealing – some of them were. "Yes, I think we'll keep those. Without letting the Lady Friselda see them. And one of my headdresses too."

Sorrel picked the grey dress up and shook out the creases.

Mathilda eyed her, wondering how the wretched woman managed to say so much without opening her mouth. "All right, I'll wear the horrible thing for the banquet. Oh, and one more thing. Don't call me 'your grace' when we're alone. Either of you. Call me 'milady', as you've always done. That will remind me that I'm still an Ardronese princess." She looked at Sorrel. "If I ever rule in my own right, *that* would be the time to call me 'your grace'."

She enjoyed seeing the perplexity on Sorrel's face. *Let her wonder.*

At least, Sorrel thought the following morning, *no one's said a word about the bride's virginity being suspect.*

When she came to help the Regala dress, all Mathilda said about her wedding night was, "I am so glad Saker was the first." Her expression was wooden, her tone bitter.

The crossing over the Ardmeer estuary was a rough one, and Mathilda appeared to be violently ill, although Sorrel had her doubts how much was real and how much feigned in order to avoid more advances from her husband.

Certainly when the ship edged into the Ustgrind's royal wharf, some days later, the Regala stood at the railing with the Regal as they docked, smiling and waving happily at the gathered crowd.

Sorrel observed them from a quiet corner at the stern, noting the way Mathilda had threaded her arm through her husband's, unobtrusively pressing herself to his side. Every now and then she looked up at his face with an adoring smile. When a strong gust of wind whipped away her white headdress, supplied by the Lady Friselda, she laughed delightedly. Her blonde curls blew about in the wind as the coif disappeared into the sea. She sent Sorrel to fetch a replacement. "The blue one," she whispered, "with the pearls."

Knowing that Aureen would never have tied the coif so loosely it would blow away, Sorrel guessed the incident was no accident. Mathilda had decided that the first glimpse the Lowmians had of her would be a memorable one, a pretty woman laughing with her hair loose in the wind. Their second glimpse would be of a lady wearing a coloured and beaded coif in a sea of white headdresses.

Oh, Va, she thought. *The minx might be overplaying her hand if she takes Vilmar or the Lady Friselda for a gullible fool.*

She couldn't help but wonder if the Regal had intended to part Mathilda from her ladies right from the beginning. She bit her lip, fearing that she and Aureen might be sent away too. *Va confound it, I don't know enough about the Regal and the Lowmian court. And I've no idea what I'll do if I'm dismissed!*

She pushed the thought away and turned her attention to the scenery. It was easy to be impressed by the port, with its many-fingered waterways, each lined with wharves and merchant warehouses. The hustle of boats and barges and wherries along the canals and channels, the bustling chandlers and laden carts on the wharves were all signs of a prosperous sea trade. It was the castle that hooked and held her gaze, though. An uncompromising pile of hewn stone, on its landward side it dominated the city, squinting down at the streets through glassless window slits. On the water side, the walls plunged straight down towards the estuary of the River Ust. At some point, stonework melded with the natural rock of the riverside cliff.

Her heart was leaden in her chest; this was no building she could enter and leave as easily as she had Throssel Palace. She now understood that anyone with a witchery could sense another's. Worse, she'd heard Lowmians didn't like glamours.

In Lowmeer, her use of witchery might destroy her.

"This place is always cold," Mathilda grumbled, looking around her bedchamber. "Even with fires burning in every room of the solar, the chill never leaves the walls. But will they put up tapestries? Or glass in the windows? No, of course not. They prefer to shiver than be so frivolous. And I hate the smell of peat! Why don't they use wood like Ardrone?"

"Perhaps because they don't have forests like Ardrone," Sorrel suggested drily. "This is a land of marshes and lakes, after all."

"Another reason to despise Lowmeer."

Sorrel muffled a sigh. This was only their second night in Ustgrind, and Mathilda had not ceased to complain. "There's glass in the windows that overlook the inner bailey."

"I know the Regal is going to call for me tonight," Mathilda said, ignoring her reply. "You should have seen the way he looked at me at dinner."

"I did." Sorrel had roamed the castle with her glamour that day, and she'd watched Regal Vilmar. "Come, Aureen will help you undress. If the Regal sends for you, you must be ready."

Mathilda pulled a face, but allowed the maid to help her change. A little later, with a warm robe over her thin cambric and lace nightgown, she was still restless and disgruntled. She wandered over to a hidden door in the wainscoting, clicked it open, looked inside, then closed it again.

On the other side of the door, a spiral staircase led directly down to the Regal's bedroom, and then on to another bedroom below his. The Princess had not yet used the staircase, but one of her new Lowmian ladies-in-waiting had related its history. Built as an escape route in the troubled times of a distant past, it had become a convenient way for a Regal to visit either his wife above, or his mistress below, without anyone knowing which way he'd gone. "Not, of course, that our beloved Regal Vilmar has a mistress," the lady had hastened to add. "Lady Friselda occupies that chamber now."

It was Friselda who told Mathilda that Regal Vilmar was no longer capable of climbing the narrow steps; such exertion pained him. His manservant would climb up to inform her when she was to descend to her husband's bedchamber.

Mathilda's instincts were correct. Not half an hour had passed before there was a knock on the hidden door and she was requested to appear below. She dimpled prettily, fixed an expression of eager anticipation on her face, and followed Torjen, the Regal's manservant, down the stairs.

Aureen watched soberly.

"You're very fond of her, aren't you?" Sorrel asked.

"I served her mother, Queen Amarys, from the time I was a lass of ten. Kind to me she was, the Queen. When she lay dying, she begged me to tend Lady Mathilda kindly. Poor lass, no mother to guide her as she grew."

"Aureen, I have something to tell you, which I think you ought to know. I have a witchery."

"You mean the glamour? Oh, I've known that these many months! You were Celandine Marten back in Throssel. 'Twas me mother told me she glimpsed a glamour on you. She's not got a witchery herself, but she's canny, and sees things others don't. She were fretful you might mean ill to the Princess, but I were soon able to set her straight. I got eyes in me head, not like some I might like to mention, and I could see you did what the Princess bid. Sorrel Redwing may not look like Celandine, but I knew 'twas you the moment you opened your mouth!"

Sorrel gave a rueful laugh. "Of course. I might have known you'd see through me! And I will continue to use my glamour in the service of the Princess. The Regala."

"I never doubted that." Aureen looked towards the concealed door. "Poor child."

"You go off to bed," Sorrel said. "I'll wait up for her."

* * *

Mathilda followed Torjen down the narrow circle of stairs. The candle he carried flickered, and shadows cavorted. Her heart fluttered with anxiety.

I can do this, she thought. *I can pretend. I can make him dance to my tune. He's old and besotted – and I am Mathilda of Ardrone.*

When she stepped out into his bedchamber, she held her head high and let her robe open up to give tantalising glimpses of the curve of her shoulder through the lace of her gown. The Regal was sitting in a padded chair in his nightgown, his feet encased in stockings and his head covered with a nightcap. He looked like a figure of fun, yet she feared him. Those watchful eyes of his held intelligence and calculation in every glance.

She dropped a curtsey, her robe gaping still further. "Your grace," she said, and lifted her gaze, smiling with her lips slightly parted. "You honour me," she purred.

He waved Torjen out of the room, and they were alone. "Come here, my dear," he said. "See what I have to show you." He gestured towards the table next to him.

She came to his side to look. Spread out on the polished wood was all her jewellery. Her eyes widened. It had been taken from her, along with her Ardronese gowns, and she'd assumed it had gone back to Throssel with Ryce. Instead, it was here. He picked up one of the pieces, a ruby necklace that had once belonged to her mother. With his thumb tip, he lovingly rubbed the largest stone.

"Beautiful, beautiful," he murmured. "Like a woman's wanton lips." He replaced it on the table and picked up another piece, only to stroke it too, sensually, as if it was an object of his love.

In growing amazement, she watched as he moved his fingers from one piece to the next. Not once did he ask her anything about them, nor did he glance at her. It was as if he was in a world of his own, rather like a child concentrating on his play.

She went to stand behind him and began to massage his back and neck with gentle strokes of her fingers. At first he hardly seemed to notice, so intent was he on the jewellery. She said, "I thought you'd sent it all back to Ardrone because it's not meet for a Lowmian lady to wear gaudy gems."

He turned to look at her then, and rubbed her cheek with his long dry fingers. "I collect beautiful things," he said. "I don't give them away, or send them back where they came from. And you are very beautiful, my dear. Take off your clothes and wear the jewellery."

"Which pieces?" she asked.

"All of them."

She kept her smile and, in a mix of assumed shyness and coquetry, played with the gems, holding them up against herself, sliding the necklaces over her bare breasts, entangling the rings in her pubic hair. By the time he bade her lie on the bed, she was adorned with jewellery from head to toe.

This could have been fun with someone like Saker, she thought. Instead, she felt sick.

He fumbled at the neck of his nightgown and drew out a key dangling from a chain. Using it, he unlocked a large wooden chest near the bed and reached inside. Unaccountably afraid of what he was about to do, she started to shiver. His breathing quickened as he drew out the contents.

At first she thought he held strips of burning cloth, flames licking into the air in spirals of red, orange and gold. She shrank away, trying to make sense of the sight.

No, not something on fire. Feathers. Huge feathers. Pickles 'n' hay, they were almost as long as she was tall! Three of them, not loose, but fitted into a gold handle to make a giant fan. Three plumes that shimmered and shivered like living fire.

She was both entranced and wary. "That is – magnificent. From what fowl did such feathers come?"

"One living on the Va-forsaken half of the world. A gift from the merchant Uthen Kesleer."

"Are they – are they bewitched?" She wasn't sure what had prompted the question, other than that the colours burned so bright.

He didn't answer. He pushed her down flat on her back and began to fan her where she lay. His eyes glittered, his smile took on an unworldly, faraway look. The cool air wafted across her body. She scented spice, tantalising perfumes. The plumes moved silently through the air and finally touched her skin. The hairs on her body stood up as fear suffused her. She looked through the feathers into another world. She glimpsed birds, an emerald sea, white sands and blood, streams of soaking blood. She heard the tinkling laughter of children fade into wrenching screams of devastation.

Terrified, she grabbed at the fan to push it away, but the Regal whisked it out of her reach.

"Never touch it. Never. *Do you understand?*"

His anger slammed into her and she sank back on to the pillows. He sounded like a man possessed, wild. She nodded dumbly. Shivers of ice tingled across her skin.

Slowly he stood up and took the fan back to the chest. When he reached it, he turned and said in a puzzled fashion, "Put the jewels away, and put on your nightgown. It is not meet to be thus undressed and adorned."

Not even in front of my husband, at his own request?

Once the chest was locked, he appeared more like his normal self, and she was back on the bed in her nightgown, still trying to keep the fear from her eyes. She gave him a weak smile.

"Let us make a Vollendorn heir tonight," he said, as if nothing untoward had happened. "That is your duty."

He knelt on the bed and lifted her gown.

Mathilda was in such a state when she returned several hours later that Sorrel knew something had shaken her to the core. When she heard the story, she couldn't make sense of it.

She's exaggerating, surely. Everything I've heard tells me Regal Vilmar is not the addle-pated fool she's just described.

"I tell you, Sorrel, it was as if he was a different person. Someone whose sense had been driven from his pate by a cudgel blow. And then, just as suddenly, he was normal again. Well, as far as Lowmians are ever normal," Mathilda added bitterly. "I'm married to a lackwit!"

"Perhaps he was just drunk?"

She shook her head. "He was quite sober at dinner."

"Milady, everything we've ever heard about Regal Vilmar tells us he's an astute ruler."

"Then he must be bewitched. There was something . . . uncanny about those feathers. That – that must be what it was. There's witchery afoot. And I don't mean a Va witchery. Those plumes never came from Va-cherished lands. We don't have birds as large as – as cows!"

"Don't repeat any of this, to anyone," Sorrel said. "Don't trust anyone with your secrets."

"Of course not! *I'm* not the one who's lackwitted," she said, yawning.

Sorrel tucked her in, and in moments the Regala was sound asleep.

30

Exiles in Lowmeer

Va-blast. The stench of a village caught in the grip of Horned Death, the putrid smell of people rotting *before* they died. It clung to his clothing, to his hair, to his skin. Soaked into his mind.

He'd never be able to erase the memory.

Children dying, their parents already dead. The words, the filth of language that poured from their mouths as though the disease was eating every shred of decency before it killed them. Saker had done what he could to ease their deaths, but it was precious little. Every piece of information he garnered, he recorded in the hope that it might make sense in the end, because it certainly didn't now.

He trudged up the only street in the village of Dortgren on the far southern coast of Lowmeer, heading away from the Juyrons house. When he'd first met the family, they'd numbered three: Tomas Juyrons; his wife Yosanda; their fourteen-year-old son Hannels.

Tomas had died earlier that night. Hannels was close to death, while Yosanda was yet in the early stages of the disease. When she'd asked to be alone with her son, he'd respected her wishes, even though he wondered if she meant to kill the lad. He'd nodded at her, and walked out into the night. What right had he to tell her she must watch the horns burrow through the bones of Hannels' skull, knowing all the while that cutting them off just prolonged the agony?

Walking up the hill towards his lodgings in the shrine, the horror of the night etched itself into his memory like acid into bronze. He'd never forget.

He took a deep breath, appreciating the freshness of the smell after the sour stench of the sickroom. Fog was rolling in from the port, and the tang of salt and seaweed and wet fish-baskets came with it. Birds cried into the night, gulls. He paused and turned back to look towards the ocean.

And the lascar's dagger flapped in his robe pocket like a stranded fish.

Oh, Va. What now?

Nervously, he looked around.

At first, they were just shadows in the mist. Then men, striding from the direction of the tiny fishing harbour, silent, grim, their faces wrapped in dark cloth, their lanternlight softened by the moisture in the air. They must have come by boat, slipping in on the tide.

Not fishermen, that was sure. The dagger wouldn't care about fishermen. Bandits, then? Hardly likely in a poor fishing village like this one. He stayed where he was, intending to warn them they risked their lives entering the village.

"Va's blessings," he said as they approached.

Their silence was unnerving. They surrounded him, swords drawn, but he felt no direct threat. Not yet.

"Good sirs," he said, "this is no place to linger. The Horned Death is on the prowl in Dortgren."

One of the men stepped forward. Like the others, his black velvet hat had a black rooster feather as a cockade, but it was an insignia that held no meaning for Saker. "That's why we're here," he said. For a moment Saker thought he recognised the voice, then realised it was more just his familiarity with the accent of the university-educated.

He held up his own lantern to see better, but the man had his lower face well wrapped against the chill of the night. Instinct made Saker stay in character; he'd come to the village in the guise of an itinerant assistant cleric, no one of much importance. "A poor reason," he drawled in the accent common to southern villagers. "You'd best not stay."

"Oh, we're not staying. We are – tax-gatherers here on the Throne's business. Who are you?"

The Regal's tax-gatherers? They were like no tax-gatherers he'd ever seen. Too alert, too grim, too anonymous, too well armed. "A man of the Way," he said. "Come from Grote to succour the dying."

The man did not reply immediately. His forehead creased in a frown and his gaze drifted from Saker's face to his cleric's clothes and back again. Then he said softly, "You're thus just the man we need, for surely you know the village and its tragedy. How many households have been affected?" As he spoke, he flicked his fingers at another of his group. Long, white fingers, ungloved even in the chill of night. "Record this, Bren."

One of the other men stepped forward, shook his cloak back over his shoulder on one side and readied what looked to be a schoolboy's slate and soapstone pencil.

"Eight," Saker said, trying to ignore his sense of the absurdity of the scene. A clerk tallying up the dead in the main street of a village in the middle of the night? "Thirty-eight dead."

"All buried?" the leader asked. His gaze never left Saker's face.

"Ay."

"Slaked with lime?"

"Ay."

"How many more will there be?"

He nodded towards the Juyrons house. "The last two are there, one close to death. No new cases in four days, so the contagion has probably run its course."

Once again a flick of the leader's fingers. This time it sent three of his followers to the Juyrons home with their lantern. "Walk with me," he said to Saker, "and show me the other seven households affected. We need to delete their names from the census sheets."

"At this hour o' the night?" He believed not a word of it.

"Better by darkness. What people don't see, they don't fear."

Saker glanced around the village. All the houses were shuttered against the wind and the cold. Not a beam of light showed through a crack anywhere. No one to witness what might occur in the middle of the night.

Down in the harbour, though, something had disturbed the sleeping gulls. They screamed and cawed, eerie sounds muffled and distorted by the fog. He shuddered, chilled not by the mist nor by the wailing cries, but by the coldness of the leader of the men, by the lack of emotion in his tone, by the uncanny silence of his cohort. For a moment he wondered whether he was dreaming, having a bizarre nightmare. Whether he might wake to find he could hardly remember any of it.

"The Federhorn house," he said, pointing. "The first to be emptied by death." He frowned as another two men peeled off in that direction.

"Don't look so worried," the leader said. "I need to check to see the houses are really empty."

"I've no cause to lie," Saker said mildly. They headed towards the empty pothouse, where the innkeeper and his family had succumbed. "My name's Zander Tench," he added, using the name he'd assumed for this mission. "Might I know yours?"

"What matters a name? But if you want one, you may call me Dyer."

That's not his name. His own skills as a liar made it easier for him to recognise another.

They walked on until he'd indicated all of the deserted houses. Of the twenty or so men who had come up from the harbour, only Bren and one other now remained with Dyer. "What d'your men want inside those houses?" he asked, knowing he could not trust the answer.

He was beginning to think they were raiders. Looters of the dead, following the rumours of pestilence to grab what they could. "They could be risking infection," he warned.

Behind them, a sound of splintering wood cut through the quiet. He jumped, and whirled. The door to the last house had evidently been barred and one of the men had just wielded a cudgel to break it open. Down the street, the Juyrons house burst into flames.

Without thought, he turned to run towards it. *Yosanda and Hannels, they'll burn to death.* He'd thought no more than that, moved no more than a pace, when Dyer grabbed his arm and spun him around to face him. His grip was tight. Saker raised his lantern to see him better; the man's muffler had slipped to display his lower face.

A handsome man, not young. Forty or fifty years old; lean, weather-beaten features. Piercing dark eyes that narrowed as they stared into his own, puzzled and thoughtful.

"No," the man said softly. "They are better off dead. You know that."

"No one is better off burning to death!"

"They are already dead, my supposedly Lowmian friend. My men, they kill quickly and mercifully."

Supposedly? Fear rippled through him. He dropped his lantern and slipped his gloved hand into his pocket for the dagger, cursing his decision to leave his sword behind at the shrine where he was lodging. *Oak-and-acorn, field-and-forest, save me. Somehow I gave myself away.*

"Now what would an Ardronese witan be doing here, posing as a man of the Way of the Flow?" Dyer asked softly.

As his fear built, the sound of the gulls grew louder. An owl flew low overhead, its wingbeat silent, wingtip so low it brushed Bren in passing. The man's slate disappeared under his cloak.

Dyer didn't appear to notice the birds. His grip on Saker's arm tightened. "You are another unlucky one tonight."

"I don't know what you mean . . ."

"I regret this is necessary, Witan Rampion. I don't know why you're here, or why you're pretending to be someone else, but the result is unfortunate for you." Once again those long white fingers fluttered. "Evann, dispatch this unfortunate cleric."

He knew his execution had just been sealed. And he had no idea why. No idea who Dyer was, or how he knew his name.

His dagger was in his hand and pressed to Dyer's ribs as swiftly as a smile could vanish. The Chenderawasi kris. The move offered nothing but a brief reprieve; he was surrounded by armed men, two of whom were only an arm's length away, and all he had was a single dagger. And his wits, plus a possible misconception. If they thought he was a cleric, they'd also think he was unused to a fight.

"Let me go," he said, addressing Dyer, "or this dagger goes into your chest."

Dyer released his arm, raised his hands in a gesture of surrender and took one step back. Bren and his companion, Evann, decided that was an invitation to approach, swords drawn. Fighting men, both, from their stance. Another house was burning now, and then another. The mist dissipated as the flames heated the air and sparks spiralled upwards in pinpricks of light. The villagers began to emerge from their houses, some of them already clutching buckets, ready to fight the fires. Dyer yelled at them, "The Dire Sweeper is here! Get back inside."

Dire. Dyer. Oh, merciful oak. Juster had mentioned them. The Regal's assassins . . .

He slung off his cloak and began to whirl it around. The men closing in were momentarily disconcerted. Another precious moment gained, to savour his life, to seek an escape route. At the edges of his vision, he saw the villagers obey the shouted command. Within moments, their doors were shut tight and their lamps extinguished. They were leaving the rest of the village to burn, and him to die. Dire Sweepers. The Regal's men. Better not to see anything.

They were going to kill him. Their leader knew him as an Ardronese, knew his name. Recognised him . . .

There was no time for wonder. He flung the cloak over Dyer's head and ran. A bare sword blade brushed his sleeve as he tore past Evann. His strides ate up the street, his feet winged by terror.

There's no way I can escape. Evann's bare blade was but a pace or two from his back. Perhaps if he turned, he could take the man by surprise and ram the dagger into him . . .

The kris ripped out of his hand. For one absurd moment, he thought Evann must have knocked it from him with his sword, but then he heard its distinctive whir through the air, which was even more unlikely. He looked over his shoulder to see Evann falling, clutching at his chest. His sword tumbled free.

He stopped short, gaping, as Evann died in front of his eyes, the lascar's dagger buried in his breast.

And then, like a bore tide from the sea, a line of gulls swooped out of the mist, their wingbeats swirling the fog into tendrils, their shrieks ripping the air apart. Men screamed in panic. Birds attacked them, up and down the street. Hundreds of winged assailants, clawing, pecking, slashing, screeching. Not just gulls, either. He saw owls and goatsuckers, a nighthawk and herons, even an eagle. A few died on sword blades, but not many, and still they came. Men began to fall under the onslaught of talons and beaks, the cries of eviscerated birds indistinguishable from those of blinded, bleeding men. Mercifully, the darkness swallowed much of the detail, because where flames illuminated the horror, he was beyond sickened.

Dear Va, so much blood.

Appalled, he shouted, "Stop it! No more!"

And as one, the birds lifted into the air, and were gone.

He turned and fled out of the village and up the hillside beyond, pushing his way through the scrub, tearing his skin and his clothes on brambles.

A dream. It had to be a dream.

But it wasn't.

He hid on the hillside, watching as the eight houses burned to ash, and silhouettes of men carried away their dead and injured. By the time dawn light stained the sky, the village was empty of the visitors. Out to sea, the dark shape of a ship edged away from the harbour, towed by its own longboat, its sails still hanging loosely in the morning stillness. No flag flew from the mast, and Saker suspected there was no name painted on the prow.

A sea eagle drifted over his head. He looked up, to see that it clutched something in its talons. He assumed it was a fish, until the bird dropped it. The object tumbled towards him. He watched, unmoving, as it fell to the ground barely a pace away, and buried its wavy blade in the ground as far as the hilt.

Shit.

Sorrel could always tell when Vilmar had been playing with his fan in the presence of the Princess. When Mathilda returned to her bedchamber, the expression on her face, a mixture of fear and bewilderment, said it all. Intrigue and schemes held no fear for a princess of Ardrone, but the Regal's bizarre behaviour left her disturbed and anxious.

One night, not quite three months after their arrival, Mathilda climbed back up the staircase and sat wearily on the edge of her bed. "He scares me," she said. "Every time it's the same. He appears to forget who I am, who he is – everything! Sorrel, he's ensorcelled."

"I wonder if we should speak to somebody about it. To Lady Friselda, perhaps. Or one of the other ladies-in-waiting. What about his manservant? Torjen might know something."

"He's never in the room when Vilmar brings the fan out of the chest." Mathilda shivered and pulled the covers up to her chin. "I don't want to say anything to Lady Friselda or any of the others. They're like a bunch of hawks waiting for me to make a mistake so they can fly in and rip me apart. Tattletales, just watching for the right time to tell the Regal something salacious about me. I stare at men too much, or laugh too loudly, or pray too little. There's always something about me that doesn't please them! How can I ever survive in this – this *prison*?"

Sorrel sat on the edge of Mathilda's bed. "Both Aureen and I think the time has come for you to tell the Regal you've not had a moon's bleed since arriving here. Once he knows you're breeding, he won't allow a word to be said to your detriment."

Mathilda nodded in agreement. "He'll notice I'm increasing soon anyway. But first, I want you to see the fan. I want you to tell me what it is and whether it is a danger to me, or to my child."

"Va above, what makes you think I can tell you anything about such an – an exotic thing?"

"Because you have a witchery, of course!"

"That doesn't mean a thing. Besides, how could I open the chest? I have no key!"

"Well, we know where it is, don't we?"

"If you think I'm going to steal it from around the Regal's neck, then I can only say that something has made mush of milady's brains."

Mathilda clutched her hand and said urgently, "It's not around his neck at the moment. He fell asleep before he put it back. It's on top of the chest where he keeps the fan. And what's more, he was still asleep when I came upstairs, so I left the door at the bottom ajar. We can go back, both of us."

"*What?* If I get caught in the Regal's bedchamber, I'll be dead tomorrow morning."

"But you won't *be* caught, will you? You have glamour. Please, Sorrel, for my sake."

She wavered. Va had gifted her the witchery for some reason. Was this it? *Oh, Va's teeth, why is it so hard to know the mind of a deity? Va, can't you ever make things simple?*

"I'm ordering you," Mathilda said, at her most imperious.

She sighed. "Very well. Let's go."

Mathilda's face lit up. "You'll come?" She sounded surprised.

"I just said so, didn't I? Besides, you just ordered me to."

"And since when has that meant anything to you? Usually an order just means you get more stubborn in your refusal."

Sorrel gave a falsely sweet smile and took up the candlestick. "Best be quick before I change my mind."

They crept down the spiral staircase. At the bottom step, Mathilda peeked out through the crack of the open door. There was no doubt the Regal was still asleep; they could both hear his snores. The room was dimly lit by several candles and the glow of firelight.

Mathilda led the way, her soft slippers making no sound on the wooden floor. She pointed to the chest under the window. Leaning close to Sorrel's ear, she whispered, "I'll go to the other side of the bed. If he wakes, I'll distract him."

He'd better not wake, Sorrel thought, gritting her teeth.

As she set the candlestick down on the floor beside the chest, she noticed the remains of the supper on a side table. Her eyes widened as she saw the leftover food: sweetmeats, honey and cream, pastries, buttered griddle cakes, pork sausage. None of them were dishes Mathilda preferred, and the Regal never partook of such rich dishes when in company.

She raised an eyebrow at Mathilda, who glared back and jabbed her forefinger at the chest.

The key was lying on top, just as she had said. Concentrating to adjust her glamour, Sorrel faded into her surroundings. Carefully, without a sound, she inserted the key into the lock and tried to turn it. It wouldn't move. She tried twisting it the other way and, with a loud click, it locked the chest.

Pox on it, it had been unlocked all along. She looked over her shoulder at Mathilda, who was biting her bottom lip in agitation. The Regal snuffled and moved restlessly in his sleep.

Sorrel waited until the snoring resumed before she turned the key again. Once more there was a loud click, this time as it unlocked. With infinite care, she raised the lid. It creaked. Loudly. She glanced back at the sleeping Regal.

Mathilda winced and clamped a hand over her mouth. Vilmar had stopped snoring. Sorrel froze, even stilled her breathing. When he didn't appear to be waking, she drew in a silent breath and turned her attention back to the chest.

Raising the candlestick to see inside, she only just stopped herself from gasping. The feathers filled the interior in glorious billows of liquid colour. For a moment she was spellbound, unable to move. Then, cautiously, she slipped her fingers in to pick up the fan.

The handle was metallic to her touch; nothing other-worldly there. But the plumes! So vibrant they appeared to glow, so alive she could have sworn they breathed. She touched her fingertips to the feathery end of one, and her arm prickled to her shoulder, a thousand tingling, delicate waves. For a sliver of time she was someone else, somewhere else, filled with fear, surrounded by beauty, washed by emotions not her own and memories she had never made.

Stung, confused, she dropped the fan back into the chest. The handle banged against the wood, and the Regal woke.

Instantly Sorrel's fingers closed over the candle wick, snuffing the flame and holding it tight to stop the smell of its smoking. She crouched where she was, terrified. The chest lid was still open and she couldn't glamour that.

"Husband," Mathilda said, "is all well? You mutter in your sleep. Perchance you require me again? Your loving wife is always willing."

The Regal sat up and swung his legs over the edge of the bed, with his back to Sorrel. Mathilda stood in front of him, her hands cupping his face.

Sorrel, sweating in spite of the cold, set the candlestick on the floor. Slowly, very slowly, she started to close the lid of the chest. *Please don't let it squeak this time.*

Inch by inch she lowered it.

The Regal said, "Twice tonight and you would make it thrice? Would you have me die in my bed from exhaustion, woman?"

"My desire for such a skilled lover is endless. Forgive me, my liege. I am no more than a foolish girl and feel myself complete only in your arms."

The lid shut without a sound. Sorrel took another breath. She closed her free hand over the key still in the lock and waited for the Regal to speak again.

"You are wanton," said Vilmar. He sounded more amused than angry.

"Only with you, my sweet lord. I can spare you much of the effort if you will but allow it. If I were to kneel humbly here, at your feet, could I not do all the work and my loving husband but appreciate the result?"

Sorrel winced. *Oh, dear Va, she's not going to . . .?* But she was. Mathilda had knelt and was already fumbling to lift the Regal's nightgown.

Wrapping herself tightly in her glamour and averting her face from the royal couple, she pulled the key out without locking the chest and laid it back on top where she'd found it. She couldn't prevent herself from hearing the Regal's rising excitement and Mathilda's intermittent giggles. Her cheeks radiating heat in her embarrassment, she headed for the door to the spiral staircase, only to realise she'd forgotten the candlestick on the floor. She forced herself to sneak back to retrieve it and place it on the table for Mathilda.

I am as imperceptible as a pane of delicate glass. I am as unnoticeable as a camouflaged moth lying flat to a wall. I am as invisible as a puff of wind passing through. I'm not here. You can't see me . . .

Her need for silence meant every step had to be slow and measured. Sweat ran from her forehead to the corners of her eyes. Each time she placed a foot to the floor she waited for a creak of the floorboards that would betray her, or a rustle from her gown.

At long last she reached the stairwell, and stepped inside. She eased the door partially closed and allowed her glamour to fade. For a moment she stood still, propped up against the wall, and bade her thudding heart calm.

The stairs were pitch dark. Slowly she felt her way up, one step at a time, until she reached the door to the Regala's bedchamber.

When Mathilda returned, Sorrel was pacing the floor, unable in her agitation to sit. She whirled on the Princess in a fury. "Don't you *ever* do anything like that to me again!"

Mathilda's eyes widened. "What do you mean? I have just saved your life!"

"I have never been so terrified! Or mortified. If the Regal ever realises, he'll – he'll have us both minced up to be fed to his dogs."

"Well, he's not going to find out, is he? What are you worrying about? Nothing happened."

"Nothing? Dear Va! I don't even know where to begin. You're trying to *murder* him, aren't you?"

"Oak-and-acorn, whatever do you mean?"

Mathilda's wide-eyed innocence was too much to stomach. Sorrel snorted. "We've come too far together for you to fool me. You think I didn't see all those pastries down there? You're encouraging him to eat food too rich for a man with a weak heart! The Regal is not well enough to walk up a set of stairs without pain and panting, and yet you're using him like he was—"

"Young and virile like Saker?" She gave a harsh laugh. "I didn't ask to be married to an old man. If he can't match me step for step, then he can always say no, can't he? If he dies from too much rich food and too much of a young wife, it's *his* fault, not mine. Anyway, you're the one who suggested I charm him to get what I want. I will lead my life as I will, and I will find power by whatever means is open to me. The men in my life so far have tried to strip me of control, and I won't tolerate it any longer."

"Saker wasn't like that! And what of me?" Sorrel asked. "Am I to be discarded too, when you're done with me, because I know too much? Because I see through you?"

Mathilda shrugged. "I like having you around. I like the fact that you know everything there is to know, just as I know what there is to know about you. We are two sides of a coin, you and I. Who is it who has the darker side? You killed the man who was your husband."

"And how is it you never asked me *why*?"

"I didn't need to. Va gave you witchery, so I know your reason was good and your husband deserved to die. Va has a plan for you and me; that's why we were brought together."

Is that true? I'm bound to her for the rest of my life? She only ever thinks of herself!

"So tell me," Mathilda asked, "what did you think of Vilmar's fan?"

She took a deep breath, calmer now. "There is witchery there. In the plumes, not the handle. And it's not a witchery that belongs here. It must come from the Va-forsaken Hemisphere. It made me see things I've never seen before."

"And should I fear it? Is it destined to harm me? Is it evil?"

"I don't think it's evil or good," she replied slowly. "It's just power, very strong power. In the hands of the wrong person, perhaps it could be used for evil."

"I don't think Vilmar knows how to use it. I think he's *succumbed* to it."

"Who gave it to him?"

"Uthen Kesleer, the spice merchant. His ships brought the plumes back from the Summer Seas and he had the fan made as a gift."

"He's the fellow with the growth on his face like a red onion, isn't he? I've seen him several times. He comes to see the Lord Treasurer."

Mathilda nodded. "He often dines in the Great Hall, at the Regal's table. He's the only merchant in all Lowmeer who has that privilege."

"Well, rest assured, Kesleer doesn't possess a witchery. If there's magic in the fan, I doubt he knows."

They exchanged a worried glance.

"Be careful, Mathilda. You play with the honed edge of an axe when you play with kings."

Mathilda shrugged. "Perhaps. But I just told Regal Vilmar I was having his child, so I suspect I'm safe for a little while longer."

She climbed into her bed and Sorrel, reverting to her role of handmaiden, removed the warming pan and tucked her in.

"Why *did* you kill your husband?" Mathilda asked sleepily.

"Because he murdered our child."

There was a long silence before Mathilda replied. Then she said, "I think that's a good reason to kill someone. And I think I'd kill for my child too."

"Let's hope you never have to."

31

Twins and Trepidation

"That'll be all," Mathilda said as Aureen finished braiding her hair. "You go off to bed now, Aureen. I need to talk to Sorrel."

Sorrel, who'd been putting away Mathilda's discarded clothing, looked over at her in surprise. Aureen bobbed a curtsy and disappeared into the servants' cuddy, where she shared a bed with Sorrel.

"I thought you were tired, milady," Sorrel said. Mathilda had pleaded the weariness of her pregnancy and retired early from the Great Hall that evening.

"Uncomfortable, not tired. Va, I *loathe* being with child. And I have another two moons of this to endure!" She clambered clumsily into the bed, tucking her feet under the covers to keep them warm, and sat there, contemplating the bulge of her abdomen with distaste. "Did you see who was sitting at the Regal's right hand tonight?"

Sorrel looked critically at the chemise in her hand and decided it was time it went to the washerwomen. "I saw. Mynster Uthen Kesleer."

"I don't understand why he's invited to court so often unless he has indeed ensorcelled the Regal. A man of trade and he sits next to the Regal at least once a sennight?"

"A very *rich* man of trade, milady. His Lowmian Spicerie Company has a monopoly of trade to the Summer Seas, which makes him one of the most powerful men in the Va-cherished Hemisphere."

"Perhaps, but the deference Regal Vilmar pays to him is odd. There's something *uncanny* about their relationship. I believe it makes others feel uncomfortable too. Prime Mulhafen was sitting wriggling like a schoolboy while he was listening to Regal Vilmar and Kesleer." She shook her head in puzzlement. "With everyone else Regal Vilmar is imperious and arrogant; with Kesleer he – he *grovels*. He's the Regal and he behaves like that to a *merchant*? It's – it's *undignified*."

"You think it has something to do with the fan?"

"Vilmar defers to no one else," Mathilda said, registering her contempt by dropping his title. "He takes no notice of the Prime. He listens to his advisers, but he doesn't necessarily do what they say. But when that repulsive Uthen Kesleer speaks, he's nodding his agreement before the sentences are even finished! The Chancellor was almost hysterical over something Vilmar agreed to yesterday. He was so worried, he came to me, and asked *me* to persuade Vilmar to turn down what Kesleer wanted. As if I have any influence over Vilmar! He treats me like a child of ten!"

Sorrel was silent, thinking.

Mathilda furrowed her brow. "The gift of a fan can't give Kesleer power over the Regal, surely?"

"It sounds unlikely. Witchery doesn't work that way. Didn't Saker once say that if someone misuses witchery to gain power or wealth, their gift disappears? There's no such thing as a rich shrine-keeper." *But what about a witchery from the Va-forsaken Hemisphere? Like . . . ensorcelled feathers.* "What did Kesleer want tonight?"

"Oh, something about exclusive rights to the sale of all spices landed at Lowmian ports, whether imported on his company ships or not."

"That can't be right, surely."

"Vilmar agreed to it."

"So did you speak to him about it?"

"Are you beef-witted? Of course not! He not only wouldn't listen, he'd be furious with me."

"I'm sure it's wise not to involve yourself." She held up the dress she'd been folding. "I don't think you can wear this any more. It's too tight."

Mathilda pouted. "That's the one with the prettiest lace, too. Va above, I'll be so glad when this wretched child is born!"

When Sorrel entered their cuddy a few minutes later, she expected to find Aureen already asleep. Instead, she was wide awake, sewing.

"You can't see very well there, surely?" she asked. As servants, they were only allowed the cheapest of tallow candles, and Aureen was almost setting her headdress on fire by sitting so close to the flame. "Aren't you going to bed?"

"I was waiting for you." She laid the sewing aside and wiped the back of her hand across her nose.

"What's wrong?" Something was, she could see that much.

"It's the baby."

"Everything seems normal to me." In fact, she thought Mathilda was having a relatively easy pregnancy. *Please don't tell me otherwise.*

"She's too big."

Her thoughts raced. *Too big. The pregnancy was further along than . . . Dear sweet Va above, please don't tell me this is Saker's child.*

Then: *If someone suspects it's not the Regal's, we'll all be dead.*

She lost her breath, and it was a moment before she was sure her heart was still beating. She held up a hand to halt Aureen's next words. "Wait. Let me think."

The day after Saker had bedded the Princess, Mathilda had sworn to her that she had taken every precaution. When Sorrel returned to the palace after rescuing him from the Chervil Moors shrine, Mathilda had casually said that her moon's bleed had come. There was no way this babe could be Saker's child.

Unless Mathilda had lied.

The room tilted, and she sat down hurriedly on the bed until her dizziness subsided. Desperately, she calculated. If it was Saker's child, she'd be . . . more than three weeks further along than she ought to be.

Long enough to make a noticeable difference in her size? Yes, of course.

Was it possible that Mathilda had lied to her? *Of course it is. She lies all the time, without a second thought.* Sorrel knew that Ardronese court women had knowledge of the best ways to prevent pregnancies, but there was no such thing as absolute assurance when it came to babies.

Aureen was staring at her. She gathered her wits enough to ask, "You were going to add something?"

"I wonder if them's twins inside."

Twins? She didn't know whether to be relieved or dismayed. "Well, if that's so, there's nothing we can do about it, and it's not a terrible disaster anyway, is it? Although – perhaps we shouldn't mention the possibility to Lady Mathilda yet. We don't want to worry her."

Aureen stood up, wringing her hands. Her sewing dropped to the floor unheeded. "You don't understand," she wailed.

"Hush, she'll hear you." She took hold of Aureen's hand and pulled her down on to the bed beside her. "Calm down. What don't I understand?"

"In Lowmeer, they kill twins at birth."

Sorrel stared at her in astonishment. "Tush, of course they don't! Whoever told you such a silly story?"

"Me ma. Being a midwife, she hear things. Some Lowmian mothers, told they have twins, 'scape to Ardrone to give birth. Because here, they kill twin babes. Drown them when they born."

Sorrel was speechless, shocked into silence. Finally she whispered, "I think – I think you'd better tell me everything you know."

The Regala pulled the bedclothes up over her head as Aureen opened the drapes around the massive four-poster bed in the morning. Sorrel, shivering, wished her own bed was surrounded by curtains. The damp wind that swept up the Ust estuary of a morning was chill.

She glanced over at Aureen. "Well, let's do it," she said.

Mathilda groaned, annoyed at being awoken earlier than usual. "What are you two whispering about?"

Bad temper, Sorrel reflected, was Mathilda's usual state now that she was so heavily pregnant. She said pleasantly, "Your health, milady. Aureen hasn't examined you since you were with child, yet she is an experienced midwife."

"What could she do anyway if she found out something was wrong?" Mathilda asked, her voice muffled by the bedclothes. "Dose me with more of that horrible tonic water the Regal's physicians are always delivering to my door?"

"It is time she checked to see if your pregnancy is proceeding well," Sorrel said firmly, and yanked the covers away. "Lie on your back, milady, and let Aureen do her job."

The Princess glared at her, but she folded her arms and glared back. *I wish I knew what was bothering her*. Perhaps it was no more than the normal fear of a first-time mother, knowing she had to give birth without the benefit of familiar physicians or any of her female relatives. Her own mother had died of infection after giving birth to a stillborn child.

She has every right to feel lonely and frightened. Yet Sorrel couldn't help suspecting there was more to it than that. Her stomach knotted. Perhaps the Princess was worried Aureen would realise her pregnancy could be further along than it was supposed to be . . .

Mathilda sighed, capitulated and turned over on to her back, saying, "Very well. I may as well get it over and done with, to silence you fidget-fussers."

Aureen stepped forward to arrange the Princess's nightgown and the bedcovers so that only the bulge of the pregnancy was exposed to the air. Her movements were precise and practised, but Mathilda continued to sulk. "Your hands are freezing," she complained. "There, did you feel that? Your cold fingers made the baby kick!"

Aureen continued her examination, then asked, "With milady's permission, I'd like to listen to the heartbeat of the baby."

Mathilda, startled, asked, "How can you do that?"

"I'll put my ear to your skin. With your permission?" she asked politely, but before Mathilda could protest, her ear was already resting against the Princess's abdomen.

Mathilda glowered in outrage, her hands digging into the covers. The longer Sorrel spent in the company of royalty, the more she was glad she'd been born an ordinary woman; what point was there in being a princess if your life was governed by what was proper for your elevated status, even if it was detrimental to your health?

When Aureen straightened up, there was a look of helpless panic on her face.

"What is it?" Mathilda cried, catching sight of her expression. "What's wrong?"

Aureen stuttered, "N-n-naught exactly, milady. Your grace. 'Cept them's two babies. Two heads, two heartbeats. Them's twins."

Mathilda sat bolt upright on the bed, clutching the bedclothes to her, staring from one to the other of them. "*Twins?* Are you *sure*?"

"Ay, surely. I've helped deliver twins before." She looked across at Sorrel. "Said she was too big."

There was a long silence while Mathilda knitted her brow and considered the news. "Well, isn't that good?" she asked tentatively at last. "I mean, there'll be two chances of having an heir to the throne."

"Please leave us, Aureen," Sorrel said quietly. "The Regala and I need to be alone for a while. When her ladies arrive, tell them her grace will not be appearing today. She'll rest in her chamber as she slept badly last night. Ask the chambermaid to see that breakfast is brought up for both of us."

Aureen, looking relieved, bobbed a curtsey and left, closing the door behind her.

Mathilda swung her legs over the edge of the bed. "Help me get dressed, Sorrel. And then have the goodness to explain to me just what is serious enough to have you give orders to my maid in front of me as if I do not exist." Her tone was as cold as the air.

In that moment, Sorrel could not help but be impressed with Mathilda. Her eyes might have been wild with fright, but she kept any tremor out of her voice as she gave orders about what she was going to wear. Only when Sorrel was tying the final laces on her kirtle did Mathilda say, "Now tell me why you think having twins is a bad thing – while you dress my hair. Which is your job today, seeing as you've sent Aureen away." She sat down in front of her looking-glass and waited, her face stony.

Sorrel picked up the hairbrush and began to tackle the tangles. "This is something that Aureen and I have wondered about for some time," she admitted. "Aureen felt you were larger then you should be, right from the beginning. She suspected twins, though we wanted to make sure before we told you. But you refused to let her examine you. If you were back in Ardrone, twins would doubtless be something to celebrate. Especially as Aureen knows that both of them are alive and well."

"So? Why did she look as if she'd seen a headless ghost? And why do you look so constipated?"

"Things are different here in Lowmeer. They don't like twins."

Mathilda met her gaze in the mirror. Her hands moved as if to smooth down her kirtle, but her fingers were trembling. Her eyes flashed warning. "You obviously know more than I do. I suggest you tell me whatever it is that has the two of you looking like you're walking to the executioner's block."

32

The Devil-Kin Dilemma

I've had a bellyful of grey days and rain, Saker thought. Grey skies, grey seas, grey clouds, miserable grey swamps and bogs. Was it any wonder that Lowmians were so dour?

Even now, as he stood looking out over the city from the library window of the Seminary of Advanced Studies, he could barely see the houses on the opposite side of the street. The fog had rolled up the Ust estuary at three o'clock in the afternoon and he doubted it would lift till morning.

He leaned his forehead against the cold of the window glass and thought again of Dortgren village. His memory retained its aura of a surreal dream, but the reality of its legacy was far sharper in his mind. The leader of those men had recognised him. Someone, he thought, from his university days. Maybe he'd decided to kill Saker because he realised that he must be a spy of some kind. Perhaps he'd just been afraid – needlessly – that Saker would remember him. Not a fellow student; the man had been too old for that.

And the birds?

I called them. Oh, not deliberately. But in his panic, he'd begged for help. He'd called not on Va, but to his Shenat roots. And with his witchery, the birds had come . . .

Va's teeth, I made a killing weapon out of a flock of birds. They stabbed and clawed men to death.

A pigeon landed on the sill. It cocked its head to stare at him with one round dark eye, then pecked at the glass, fluttering as if it wanted to enter.

"Go away," he snapped sourly.

"Chatting to birds now, Witan Zander?"

He shook his head ruefully as he turned to face the newcomer.

His gloomy mood lifted a little just to see her. When he'd first appeared at the seminary on the outskirts of Ustgrind seven months earlier, with the Pontifect's letter in his hand, Prelate Loach had assigned Witan Shanny Ide to assist him. A short, middle-aged woman, as broad as she was tall, she had a smile that made every recipient feel special. The Pontifect had been right about the naming conventions: shanny and ide and loach were all the names of fish, and they had chosen to disguise his Ardronese origins by calling him Zander Tench – both freshwater fish.

"Witan Shanny, it's good to see you again."

"Prelate Loach told me you were back, so here I am." She waved her hand at the pile of papers on the table of the library. "I see you didn't waste a moment getting back into your studies. What did you find out on this latest trip?"

"That I hate the Horned Death more than ever. Va rot it, it's a horrible way to die."

"The fishing village near Utmeer?"

He nodded. "Dortgren. Three already dead before I arrived. Too many more followed them to the grave." He swallowed at the memory. *The children, dear Va, why . . .?* "The sick *all* die. And all I could do was watch." In a fit of exasperated impotence, he slapped his palm down on the table. "Not anyone's prayer nor a witchery healer's skills makes one whit of difference."

She clicked her tongue in sympathy as she stooped to pick up a sheet of paper that had drifted to the floor.

Sighing, he took it from her. "Sorry." He unrolled one of the charts on the table, anchoring it with his dagger and his purse to stop it rolling up again. He pointed at one of the lake areas. "The last place I visited was this village. Barge folk, bordering a mere at the centre of the south-western barge network. Twenty-three people died there six months ago, all barge-owners and their bargees, men, women, children. In the month prior to the outbreak, one or another of the dead had been to every corner of that network. And yet no one else contracted the disease outside the village. There hasn't been a single case of Horned Death on *any* of those barge routes. So how is the disease carried? It's the same for almost all outbreaks. It's confined to a small area, usually people who are related or neighbours."

"You didn't find *anything* in common?"

"Apart from the fact that everyone who had it died? No. Except . . ."

She looked at him in hope, as though she thought he was capable of producing a miracle.

"The usual silly talk about devil-kin. When I ask about twins, though, nobody has anything tangible to say. Most are adamant that none of the affected families have twins. And yet still they believe it." He sighed. "I've scoured the country looking for some commonality, something that will explain these outbreaks, some reason that they never seem to spread very far, some reason that each outbreak comes to an end quite quickly.

"Here, look at the map." He tapped the chart with a finger. "I've marked every one of the twenty-four outbreaks for the past five years. Can you see *anything* any of these places could have in common? Because I can't. Villages and towns, coastal and inland, settlements in the marshes, and on the northern downs, and the high country on the northern border. Farmers, fishermen, noblemen, bargees, shopkeepers, peat-cutters, miners. Men, women, children, wealthy, poor, sinners and saints, drunks and clerics. Shrine-keepers here in Lowmeer seem to be immune as yet – while shrine-keepers were the ones most affected in Ardrone's lone outbreak."

She bent over the chart, looking at his latest additions. He watched as her eyes widened and her pink cheeks faded to ashen. She gave him a stricken look and then sat down heavily in the nearest chair. She opened her mouth to speak, then changed her mind. He was silent, sick to the stomach, both desiring and dreading answers.

Her plump cheeks working with suppressed emotion, she said, "Forgive me, witan. I think I need to talk to the Prelate about this first."

"You've seen a pattern," he said flatly.

"Not – not exactly. But those towns and villages . . . Oh, Va. They are all familiar to me." She levered herself up clumsily. "I'll talk to Prelate Loach." She left without another word.

Half an hour later, the Prelate arrived in the library flustered and frowning, Witan Shanny puffing behind, trembling like an oak leaf in a breeze. Loach was elderly, and thin with the scrawny fragility of the aged. He carried a ledger with him under one arm and slapped it down in front of Saker, saying, "In her letter, the Pontifect said I was to trust you, which is why I'm going to let you see this. Take a look while I consider this chart of yours."

Saker took the ledger, placed it on the other end of the table and began to turn the pages. There was no title, no indication of the significance of what it contained. Each page was divided into columns. The left-hand one was a list of dates: the first entry now fifty years in the past; the last entry was only several weeks ago. The other columns were names, of people and of towns.

Raising his gaze to stare at Prelate Loach, he found the man had already straightened up to look at him. "What is this list?" Saker asked quietly.

Instead of answering, Loach said, "The Basalt Throne and the Throne's assassins, known as the Dire Sweepers, have been killing twins in Lowmeer for generations. And why? Because they believe that one in every pair of twins is a servant of A'Va."

"As a witan with faith in Va's power, I cannot think there is any truth in such a notion."

"Which is why many of us Lowmian clerics have been trying to rescue twins for fifty years, by secretly spiriting away one – or even both – of the babies at birth and giving them to another family to raise."

"We missed many," Shanny whispered. "But our emphasis on secrecy has kept us safe. We find out about twin births by working closely with selected midwives. Of course, there have been rumours . . ."

Loach nodded. "The list in the ledger contains the names of towns and villages either where twins were born, or where one was placed with a local family. The birth family and the recipient family are all listed. The dates are the birth dates of the twins. In other words, Mynster Rampion, what you are looking at are all places connected in some way to twins *not* drowned at birth." He pointed to Saker's charts. "Every single town you've marked as having had an outbreak of the Horned Death is in that ledger."

Utterly appalled, Saker didn't know what to say. Pustules 'n' pox, for a moment he didn't even know what to *think*.

"Of course," Loach muttered, "there are many villages mentioned in the ledger that have had no pestilence." A breathless pause later, he added, "Yet. I am sure you realise that if these lists were leaked, everyone involved, be they twins or midwives or families, would die at the hands of the Dire Sweepers."

Saker nodded, but it was another implication that churned his thoughts into a whirlpool of horror. *Dear Va, Lowmian clerics have been rescuing twins believing in their innocence, and all along . . .?*

No, he couldn't think that. It couldn't be true.

No one spoke.

Devil-kin were real?

No, please not that. It was a savage superstition. An excuse for the murder of babies. A stinking, miserable lie that had brought untold misery to people for generations.

"We thought we were doing the right thing," the Prelate said in strangled tones. "We thought we were saving babies."

"We *were*," Shanny said. "We were. Only one in every set is . . ." Her voice trailed away.

Saker heard the words she didn't say: . . . *is a devil-kin. And one is innocent*. Which would account for the villages that had no Horned Death; they'd been blessed with innocent children.

No, please don't make this true. Don't make it true that to save an innocent baby, you must let a devil-kin free into the world.

"And in so doing, we killed how many other blameless people by loosing the Horned Death in their midst?" Loach asked, echoing his thought. "Shanny, we promised those good, pious folk that they were taking in an innocent babe. But it seems half the time we were giving them a child that would grow up to murder them horribly with a disease! We were planting a devil-kin in their households. We were giving A'Va a way to attack them in their own homes." He looked at Saker. "You wanted to know how this pestilence is spread? Well, now you know. The devil-kin are responsible."

Shanny clapped her hands over her mouth, as if that was the only way she could stop herself from screaming at the horror of their mistake. Prelate Loach looked at the ledger. "We need to compare the details in that" – he pointed at the book – "with your information."

Saker nodded, knowing what he was asking. They had to compare the names in the ledger with his own list of the dead. They had to find out how many of the twins were still alive. They had to find out just how ghastly the whole mess was. They had to be *sure* . . .

He had no idea how it would be possible to repair the damage. Or how the clerics could cope with the guilt.

The tears were already streaming down Shanny's cheeks. "Dear Va," she asked, "what have we done?"

No, Saker thought. *That's not the question to ask. The question is, how do we stop A'Va? Or maybe: how do we find out* why *this happened?*

Ardrone had no problem with twins. Nor had any of the Principalities. Why, then, did Lowmeer?

Bleary-eyed, Saker met Loach's grim gaze. They'd exchanged all the information they had.

Yet all any of them had now was more questions.

It's like walking in wet farmyard muck. You think your footing is secure, but it never is. You can fall any moment, and end up in the filth, without being sure how you got there.

They still sat around the library table, in the gloom now, for the single lighted candle and the coals in the fireplace did little to dispel the bleak dark of a foggy night.

"It's not just a Lowmian problem any more," Loach said. "After all, Ardrone has the Horned Plague too now."

Rage gripped him just thinking about that. "Pox on't, Loach, I want to know how a baby can become evil, *without* choice. This is a travesty of Va-Faith! If a person has no choice from birth about the nature of the path they choose through life, and the sort of afterlife they will have, what kind of world is it?"

To Saker's distress, Loach started weeping. To give the Prelate a chance to compose himself, he turned back to the ledger, studying the figures. Dortgren village was mentioned as having a childless couple named Juyrons who'd taken in a male baby thirteen years earlier. Saker winced, remembering. Hannels. He'd been angry, shouting that he wasn't supposed to die. He'd cursed Va . . .

A devil-kin.

He slumped in his chair.

He'd returned to the village after the Dire Sweepers had sailed away. Hannels' body was in the ruins of the burned house, with his mother's. One of the other villagers had remarked that the boy had recently become a problem to his parents, refusing to help his father, refusing to enter the local Oak shrine, fighting with other village lads.

But if the lad was a devil-kin, why did he contract the Horned Death? Saker had seen the horns . . . He'd suffered just as much as everyone else.

"The programme to save twins ends as of now," Loach said suddenly, stonily grim. "I will contact all the midwives and clerics and shrine-keepers involved, and tell them it is our duty to report to the Throne the birth of all twins. If midwives do not drown twins at birth, the law will do it for them."

Saker looked away, unable to condemn or to approve. Who was he to tell Lowmians to take the risk of further outbreaks of the Horned Death? What if the next outbreak emulated the one in Ardrone and killed shrine-keepers, thus striking at the Lowmian heart of Va-Faith as well?

A dilemma like this was an abomination. No solution sat well with him, none. And always there was the idea that he was missing something, something important. A piece of the puzzle that wasn't there yet.

"What are we going to do?" Shanny asked. Her hands had started shaking when she realised what Saker's charts meant and the trembling had never gone away. "I mean, about – about . . ." But she couldn't form the words.

Saker knew what she was trying to ask: what about the twins they had saved who were still living? He glanced at the Prelate, but Loach was silent, so he said slowly, "What happens here, in Lowmeer, it's not my decision."

"I fear it is mine," Loach said. "Mine and Prime Mulhafen's and the Pontifect's." When Saker glanced at him, the thought came that the man had aged twenty years.

Shanny finally found her tongue. "Are we to go out and kill those we saved because they might at some future date prove to be a devil-kin? In every single infected village Saker visited, the twin *died*. He died along with his family and neighbours. Why would he cause the Horned Death if it would kill him too?"

Loach turned his devastated gaze on her. "The only thing all outbreaks appear to have in common is a twin."

"But not all villages that had a twin also had the Horned Death," Saker pointed out, waving at the ledger.

"We have no *proof* of anything." Shanny was sobbing as she spoke.

"We need to gather more information from each affected village," the Prelate said, "but we have a problem right now that can't wait. There are still pairs of twins out there, both still alive. There could well be more deaths in more places because of one of them. There is no way we can tell who is the devil-kin twin and who the innocent one! It is a terrible thing that I contemplate, and I will pray deeply about it before making a decision, but I suspect that all the surviving twins will have to die."

Shanny shook her head violently. "No, you can't do that. You *can't* ask that of us!"

"I wouldn't ask it of you," Loach replied gently, "or any cleric. I would just tell the Regal's men where to find them."

I would have agreed with Shanny before I saw what the Horned Death can do. Now, I'm not so sure . . .

She was almost hysterical, so he intervened. "There is one thing I've noticed from the information we have. The twin involved in a Horned Death outbreak is always somewhere between ten and eighteen years old. Never younger, never older. I don't think you have to act at all yet on younger sets of twins, or on any who are already men and women. You have time to investigate, time perhaps to find a solution."

"And then we'll be sure?" Shanny asked. For once her voice was unpleasantly high-pitched and squeaky. "How can we ever be sure just by looking at someone whether they are devil-kin or some innocent child?"

"And how can we be sure that one of those living pairs of twins are not about to kill their families and their neighbours?" Loach asked in turn, his voice harsh in his pain.

"And, it seems, themselves," Saker added drily. There was something they were not understanding here. "Correlation of the kind we have is not proof that *anyone* is a devil-kin."

"You're right," Loach conceded. "We don't have to do anything about the very young or the older ones just yet."

Shanny sniffed and wiped her nose with the back of her hand. She straightened, transforming herself from a tearful, squat woman into someone of quiet dignity. "I keep remembering the baby girl I took from a mother here in Ustgrind. She was so pretty, and the mother was so grateful that I was saving the twins' lives by taking one of her babies away. She told me to choose which one, because she couldn't. She wept hard as I left, knowing she'd never see that twin again. She would never know who raised her little girl, or even her new name. But she'd always know what she looked like, because the twin left behind was identical."

She paused a moment before continuing. "I took that child all the way to a family in Umdorp. I had to feed her goats' milk to keep her alive, but she never complained. She had the loveliest hazel eyes, and curly brown hair. And that family in Umdorp? They were so grateful! They'd tried for years to have children of their own, but had never succeeded." She sniffed again. "And I told a lie, a horrible, beastly lie, as we always did. I told them her parents had died and she had no family to take care of her, to love her." She looked from one to the other. "Those people who took the babies in? They never knew they had a twin."

Without another word, she turned and left the room.

Saker and Murram Loach exchanged a glance, but neither said anything. Sometimes grief was too encompassing for words. But deep inside, Saker thought, *They shouldn't have lied. That wasn't right.* And then he felt contrite. Who was he to be critical of others faced with impossible choices?

He knew it would be a long while before he had another good night's sleep. Some things were just too hard to bear.

33

A Princess Awakening

Mathilda glared at Sorrel with an irritated frown. "What do you mean, they don't like twins in Lowmeer? They don't have any twins to dislike! That's what I've heard. For some reason, Lowmian women never have more than one baby at a time."

"I'm afraid they sometimes do," Sorrel replied, distressed and aware that she was failing to hide it. "But they drown them, because they think one of them is a devil-kin."

"Ridiculous," Mathilda scoffed. "No mother would agree to that!" She stood up, hands on hips, abdomen thrust forward to relieve an aching back.

Va above, she is huge, Sorrel thought, eyeing her figure. "I'm not sure they have much say in the matter. Some of the lucky ones, folk with means, who realise in time that they are bearing more than one child – they flee to Ardrone in secret, and give birth to perfectly ordinary babies. Most women, though, when they find out they're having twins, they're terrified. You see, they *believe* they'll give birth to a devil-kin. A servant of A'Va. A murderous, evil, vicious killer. So they surrender their babies."

"Surrender? To whom?"

"To a special cohort of the Regal's guardsmen. The Dire Sweepers, they're called."

Mathilda stared at her, silent, one eyebrow raised sceptically.

"If they try to hide such a birth," Sorrel continued, "their neighbours or the midwife might inform the Sweepers. That's what Aureen has heard, although others say the Sweepers have something to do with halting the spread of the Horned Death."

"In other words, all rumours." Mathilda turned on her in a fury. "You're frightening me! This can't be true. It's just superstition and gossip." She was pale, but a bright red spot in each cheek spoke of her rage.

"Milady, I questioned Aureen closely on this."

"She's my *maid*, by all that's holy! Why ever should I believe anything she says? And how do they account for the fact that Ardronese twins are perfectly normal people? My cousin had twin girls! They are in their thirties now, and they're just like anyone else."

"I don't know."

"Has anyone ever told you this, other than Aureen?"

"No, but—"

"I refuse to give credence to such talk. Shame on you both for maligning the Regal in such a way. You are talking treason and he'd see you both dead if he heard your words."

Beggar me speechless! How was she ever going to persuade Mathilda that Aureen would never lie – or exaggerate – about a subject like this? She took a deep breath. "What if I go into the city and visit a midwife? Someone with no connection to royalty. I'll tell her I'm worried about my sister's pregnancy and the size of her stomach girth. I'll say I'm anxious it may be twins and is it true what people say about them?"

Mathilda chewed at her lip. "Very well," she said after some thought. "Go tomorrow. Now leave me," she added, tone frosty. "I am out of patience with you. Go tell my ladies-in-waiting I require their presence – Lady Vonda and Lady Lotte, I think."

She bobbed and left the room with a sigh of relief. When Mathilda decided to be imperious, she would much rather be elsewhere.

Sorrel often left the castle on small errands for Mathilda, buying ribbons at the market, perhaps, or wandering down to the port to listen to gossiping sailors from Ardrone. The castle guards recognised her and she had no trouble coming and going, as long as she was back before the main gates closed at dusk. She tried to use her glamour skill as little as possible.

This time she risked it. She did not want it known that the Regal's handmaiden was asking midwives about twin births. Once she'd left the castle, she changed her appearance to that of a burgher's plump wife, a woman with a harelip to account for any oddity in her accent.

In that guise, she asked the hawkers in the nearest itinerant street market where she could find a midwife.

It was an easy task, and she came away with three separate recommendations. The first, after hearing about her fictitious sister, paled. "Twins are devil-kin," she said. "The work of A'Va. I'll have naught to do with such." She had invited Sorrel in; now she opened the house door indicating that the conversation was over.

"But what should I do?" Sorrel asked as she stood in the doorway.

The woman shrugged. "I can examine her. If she really is going to bear twins, then I must inform the Regal's Watch."

"And what happens then?"

"Naught to do with me. I know if I don't report it, I could end up in the Regal's dungeons."

"Are twins killed?"

"Lass, I don't ask."

"Have you ever *seen* twins again after they were birthed?"

She snorted. "What do *you* think? Now leave me be."

Sorrel headed for the second address she had. The woman there was even less welcoming. "I don't deliver twins," she said bluntly, and shut the door in Sorrel's face.

The third address belonged to a younger midwife with small children of her own. Her reaction was more guarded. "I'm not skilled with difficult cases," she said. "Your sister could just be having a large baby. I think you ought to go and see the shrine-keeper at Volfgard Shrine. I hear she's skilled in such birthings."

"Is it true that twins are drowned at birth because they are devil-kin?"

"Twins . . . never survive. But I really think you should go see the shrine-keeper. After all, you don't even know if your sister is going to have twins yet!"

She would say no more, so Sorrel left and returned to the castle, more convinced than ever that Aureen was right. Twins were not welcome in Lowmeer. Entering Mathilda's solar, she found the Regala lying down on a day bed in her morning room, complaining querulously about her fatigue while Lady Lotte and Lady Vonda, her youngest ladies-in-waiting, listened without comment.

On seeing Sorrel, the Regala dismissed the two women and

demanded Sorrel tell her all she had discovered. Once she had the information, she began to pace the room, her chest heaving, her fingers clawed as if she wanted to scratch someone's eyes out. "You're telling me," she said, "that when these babies are born, they will be taken from me and *drowned*? As if they were unwanted mongrel puppies?" Her chin wobbled, as she struggled not to cry.

"I suspect everything Aureen told us – as unbelievable as it is – is true. Mind you, you may be the exception. After all, your twins are also the Regal's."

"It's outrageous! If anyone thinks they are going to *murder* my children, slaughter the grandchildren of the King of Ardrone, then they'd better think again."

Sorrel blinked, torn between admiring Mathilda and worrying herself sick at her apparent inability to recognise this as a situation where being royal might not help.

"I shall return to Ardrone," Mathilda continued. "That's all there is to it."

Oh, pox. "Er, I'm not sure that would be so easy. Regal Vilmar would consider your departure a – a mortifying insult. I don't think he's the sort of man who takes kindly to public humiliation. He'll not let you go home. I'd be very cautious about telling him why you were asking to leave."

"I can hardly keep it a secret," she snapped. "This is a question of giving birth to an heir, and even in Ardrone that means there'll be several court physicians and probably the Lord Chamberlain as well, all ogling me to witness the birth. I have to endure the humiliation of that lack of privacy when I am at my most vulnerable. There is no way we can conceal a second baby!" She whirled to stand in front of Sorrel, shaking with rage. "We have to run away, back to Ardrone."

"How? Walk out of the castle one day, amble down to the port and ask a ship's captain to take us to Throssel?" She swallowed back her sarcasm and added more gently, "Milady, it wouldn't work. I'm sorry. The only thing I can suggest is that you ask the Ardronese Ambassador to call on you. Ask him to convey a letter to King Edwayn, telling him what you know. Maybe if your father puts pressure on the Regal . . ."

Mathilda stood still and silent for a long while, considering. When she lowered herself to sit on the window seat, Sorrel brought her a cup of water. She took it, but didn't drink. After a long silence, she said with quiet bitterness, "The King would not assist me."

"You don't know that."

"Oh yes, I do. He'd have to return my bride price, or risk outright war. And why should he? He sent me here with no expectation of ever seeing me again. He doesn't care much if his grandchild sits on this throne or not. Oh, he might take a little pride in his blood feeding the line of future monarchs in two countries, but any child of mine will be no one he ever knows, or loves. So what would he care if such a grandson died before ever being crowned?" A single tear rolled down each cheek. "No, he'd ignore any plea from me. He'd excuse his action by saying that the story of twin murder is a rumour. That no king would murder his own children. He'd say I was a woman made hysterical by her pregnancy. And he'd say it even if he knew they did kill twins here."

She looked up at Sorrel with surprising calm. "You *are* sure it is true?"

"I can't be sure, but *something* happens to twins. Something awful." Just thinking about it brought a feeling of sick nausea to the pit of her stomach.

"So what do you suggest I do?"

"I think we have to find out more before we make any decisions. It may well be that this law won't apply to you. The Regal is desperate for an heir! Royalty is usually exempt from the laws other people have to obey."

"I'll find out. I'll ask the Regal."

Pickle it. "Do – do you think you could question him about it without him knowing that you fear you're going to have twins?"

"Of course I can. I can do anything I put my mind to. And I will *not* allow any child of mine to be murdered."

"You must be careful. He's no fool." She picked up the water ewer to pour herself a drink.

"Isn't he?" Mathilda asked, the words laden with scorn. "Look at the way he behaves with that awful merchant Kesleer. Why, he's talking about giving him a title! A common tradesman! And as for giving his trading company a monopoly of the spice trade – there is not a person at court who thinks that was a good idea. Not for the country, and not for the Basalt Throne. And he did it because Kesleer gave him some *feathers*?"

"Tread carefully, milady."

"If need be, we'll kill Regal Vilmar, you and I."

Sorrel dropped the ewer. It smashed on to the floor and the water ran across the wooden boards. "You *can't* be serious!"

"It would be a better result than the murder of two innocent royal children." Mathilda's eyes glittered with angry determination. "And don't tell me you're squeamish. You killed *your* husband."

She was silenced, appalled. *Regicide?*

"First thing, I shall talk to Regal Vilmar," the Princess continued. "Then we'll decide what to do."

Sorrel nodded, torn between admiring this new Mathilda who was prepared to do anything to save her unborn children, and being scared senseless she'd do something impetuous and ill-considered. "Your ladies will be here shortly to escort you to the Great Hall for dinner," she said. "Shall – shall I call Aureen to help you dress?"

34

The Way of the Dagger

There are times, Saker thought, *when I prefer Lowmeer to Ardrone, in spite of its dismal weather.* He looked around at the bustle of the Ustgrind docks, comparing it to his memory of the undisciplined chaos of Throssel's unruly waterfront.

Lowmeer was such an *orderly* place. He laughed at himself then, acknowledging that he did not often appreciate orderliness. It was *boring*. Lately, though? Confronted with the horror of the Lowmian twins dilemma, he could have done with more boredom and fewer challenges. There was one thing he'd kept to himself, too, and it gnawed away at him like toothache.

There had been a page in one of Fox's ledgers that had included a list of Lowmian place names, followed by people's names . . . in pairs. Two people who shared the same surname, as twins would. Sometimes two women, sometimes two men, sometimes a man and a woman. Or maybe all children . . .

Fox. He seemed to have his finger in every pie.

Va-damn, Fritillary, I'm glad it's you and not me who has to make the hard decisions about Va-Faith and twin murder.

That morning, he'd told Prelate Loach he was returning to Vavala to report to the Pontifect, said his goodbyes to Witan Shanny Ide and proceeded to the port to make arrangements to catch a flat-boat up the Ardmeer estuary. Yet once he was dockside, he hesitated. For reasons he couldn't define, he didn't want to leave. Hints of unfinished business lingered at the edges of his mind, skittering away from definition when he tried to focus on them. All he knew for certain was that he wanted to remain in Ustgrind.

That fobbing kris. It had to be at the heart of his unease, of course.

Pox on you, Ardhi. Why in all Va's hemisphere did you choose me *to throw your dagger at?*

He took a room in a sailors' doss house, dressed himself in his most nondescript clothing, and ventured out to wander around the docks. Habit made him take note of all he observed: the cargoes being loaded and unloaded, the names of the ships, the flags they flew to indicate their owners and home ports.

When he came to the part of the quayside that had a view of Ustgrind Castle, he stopped to stare. The castle loomed over river and town, a cold, grim bastion. Jackdaws wheeled around weather-scarred ramparts, their yapping calls ricocheting from the stonework to be caught on the wind. He already knew the castle was accessed only through the town, where huge wooden gates built of logs and iron were guarded by armed men of the Regal's Watch. The rear wall of the keep was flush with the cliffs of the Ust river gorge, just before it opened up into the wider Ust estuary.

Saker shivered. *A prison, or a palace?* It certainly had the appearance of the former. And somewhere inside was Mathilda, Princess of Ardrone. Who had been prepared to see him dead without a qualm. *We all failed you, Mathilda, but by the Oak, you were remorseless in your revenge.*

Since he'd arrived in Lowmeer, almost the only thing he'd heard about her was that she was expecting a child. The Lowmians were ecstatic. He just tried not to think about it. When he did, the result was a strange mix of shame, forgiveness, grief and fury.

He wondered if that Celandine woman was with her in the palace, or whether she had chosen to go her own way. Celandine – or Sorrel? A murderess with her own reasons for serving the Princess? But then, she had a witchery.

And she saved your life. First at his trial, and then at the Chervil Moors' shrine. She'd ridden across the land several days alone, dressed as a man. Because Mathilda had asked her, or because she'd pitied him? He preferred not to think about that either, preferred not to dwell on his stupidity. Va above, though, Celandine had the courage of half a dozen men.

Don't think about the past. It's done. All three of us have different roads to travel, different burdens to carry.

He ripped his gaze away from the cold heap of stone and battlements and thought instead of Ardhi. Alive and well, of course he was. The man was still linked to him by the power of the Chenderawasi kris.

Pausing at the edge of a wooden wharf, he drew the weapon. The hilt was warm to his touch and the blade slithered sinuously out from its sheath, alive, a silvered snake.

Alive. His heart turned over, beat faster.

In the sunlight it slowly lost its fluidity and sank back into solid metal, sparkling with gold. Just a dagger once more.

Rot it, what was it? What fuelled it?

Gulls rose from the boardwalk, squawking and screaming, overwhelming him with their squabbling, with their blatant desire for food, with their warnings about him, the intruder into their world. He glared at them. More witchery, just as alien, yet Va-granted. More he didn't understand. More to turn his skin cold and his bowels to water.

"Oh, Va," he muttered in heartfelt prayer, "if you had to gift me a witchery, why this one? And if I had to bump into a lascar, why one with a bewitched blade?"

The dagger slithered across his hand, and it was all he could do to hold himself still. All he could do not to drop it and flee. Teeth clenched, he waited. The kris spun on his palm until it pointed towards a side alley. Then it stilled.

The blade had spoken.

Sighing, he resisted the temptation to toss it into the sea, and turned down the alley instead. With a sense of fatalistic destiny, he knew this was what he had been waiting for. He and Ardhi were coming together again.

The alley opened out on to another arm of the portside quays. An ornate two-storey building dominated this wharf, with a painted sign proclaiming it to be the Lowmian Spicerie Trading Company. The wrought-iron sign swinging in the stiff breeze displayed the company's sigils for those who could not read: a clove and a sliced-open nutmeg. The wooden building next door was the office of the Kesleer Trading Company.

He halted, taking it all in. A vessel was tied up at the quayside, a ship not yet completed. He guessed it had been recently launched, then towed from the shipyards. It was now undergoing the interior carpentry, the fitting of spars, the running of the rigging. Seamen and workmen swarmed over it, hammering, sawing, shouting orders. In all the noisy frenzy, he was unnoticed.

Even he could see the differences between Juster's galleon and this ship. Juster's had more gun ports, but the divergence was more in the subtle variations in shape, in the position of the masts.

A fluyt, he guessed. A ship designed for long journeys, big cargoes and smaller crews than usual. Part of Uthen Kesleer's new fleet, intended for the spice trade. He looked for any sign of the lascar, any lascar, but the artisans and sailors were all fair-skinned.

Seeking more information, he left the wharf to find a tavern. He didn't have to go far. Two tankards of beer and the heel of a crusty loaf later, and he'd ascertained from a ship's chandler and fellow customer that the return of the *Spice Dragon* from the Spicerie had been followed, six months later, by two more spice-laden Kesleer ships.

All had been badly infested with shipworm. The *Spice Dragon* had required a substantial overhaul and the other two had subsequently been scrapped. Three new fluyts had been constructed to make a fleet of four ships that would head for the Summer Seas again, under the protection of one of the Regal's fighting galleons as escort. "Have to give them Ardronese privateers a taste of their own grapeshot," the chandler explained. Nothing had yet been heard of the previous fleet; there were rumours that it might have been sunk by jealous Pashali traders or lost in a storm, but the chandler dismissed those as premature. "True, the ships are overdue, but that could just mean they took longer to set up their factor houses in the Spicerie than they anticipated."

"Factor houses?" Saker asked, feigning ignorance.

"Buildings for the company men who stay behind in the islands to trade."

"Mynster Uthen Kesleer's riding high," the tavern-keeper said, overhearing their conversation. "Some say he'll be made a lord if his fleet comes back, an' who ever heard of a shipping merchant lord? But then, if he's bringing back them spices, why not?"

"The new ships'll sail soon," the chandler said. "The orders for casks are already being filled."

"I heared them letters of marque are already gived out," the tavern-keeper said. "They can plunder an' sink any Ardronese they come across."

Saker winced. The Pontifect wouldn't like it. "They're boys," she'd fumed when he'd told her about King Edwayn's letters of marque to Lord Juster, "playing at games of pillage when it really is men's lives at stake. And on what excuse? Because they want to draw imaginary lines on a map and say that whole oceans are their private playground for plunder. They'll be lucky if this doesn't lead to outright war."

He wondered if the Pontifect was concerned because sea routes to the Va-forsaken Hemisphere would mean a loss in profits to the northern Principalities, where the traditional Pashali caravanner trade terminated.

At the close of the day, Saker thought with weary cynicism, *it's all about money.* "Tell me," he asked the tavern-keeper, "have you ever seen one of those brown-skinned seamen in the port? The ones they call lascars?"

"Oh, ay. There's one of them fellows teaching his heathenish tongue to ship's officers. Came in on the *Spice Dragon*, I believe."

Taken aback at the idea that Ardhi, after robbing Kesleer, might have then gone to *work* for him, he thought back to the morning they'd broken into the warehouse. The light had been dim, the merchants might not have seen the kris, or realised what it was even if they had, and later the guard outside had called the supposedly dead lascar a dark-skinned Pashali.

Saker recalled the cheerful mischievousness of Ardhi's smile. *Confound the man. That was exactly the sort of brazen thing he would do*. And then, *I wonder if I can risk going to see Kesleer? Dannis Kesleer was the only person who saw me properly, and he was a child.* Two years had passed since he'd broken into the warehouse, and in all probability the thing Dannis would remember most clearly was that he'd been a cleric. Well, he was a cleric no longer. There was no medallion around his neck.

After paying for his food and drink, he stepped back into the alley. He paused for a moment to reconsider, then shrugged and pulled out the kris. "This," he growled at it, "is your last chance. Take me to Ardhi, or I'll throw you away again. Into the most stinking midden I can find, what's more."

He laid the weapon on his palm, and the blade crawled across his hand, pointing. He allowed it to lead him up to the front door of the Lowmian Spicerie Trading Company.

He slipped it back into its sheath and stepped inside. There was no sign of Ardhi. "My name is Reed Heron," he told the clerk at the desk, making the name up on the spot. "Might I see Mynster Kesleer on a matter pertaining to the language of commerce in the Spicerie? I may be of assistance."

Uthen Kesleer filled the space around him with the potency of his personality, the way the aroma of a spice expanded to fill a room. He dominated simply by being himself.

"And you say Prelate Loach will vouch for you?" the merchant asked, leaning back in his chair and steepling his fingers over his rotund stomach. The gesture reeked of belief in his superiority. The wealth in the heavy gold rings he wore on both hands would have supported Saker for years.

"Yes, Mynster. We come from the same village north of Rutt," he lied. "The Prelate was acquainted with my father and gave me a job working on the books at the seminary." And with a little luck, Kesleer would not check with Loach before he had time to warn the prelate he had renamed himself.

Face to face, Saker began to doubt his temerity in coming to see Kesleer. He'd heard the rumours. The merchant, backed by the Regal, ruled all Lowmian commerce. A flick of Kesleer's fingers and an enemy could disappear. He was not only the richest man in Lowmeer; he was a merchant who treated the Regal as if they were equals.

"I have no need of another clerk." Kesleer's shrewd eyes lacked laughter lines and he made no attempt to conceal his contempt. "You told my chief clerk you had expertise that might aid me?"

"Yes. I am not offering myself as a clerk, but as a teacher of language."

"The only language that interests me is that of the Spicerie." Kesleer tapped the bulbous growth on the side of his nose. Another man might have been embarrassed by it; he drew attention to it, thus rendering it arresting, rather than ugly.

Clever, Saker thought. "I have it on good authority that there is not one language of the lascars, but many. There is, however, one tongue that all coastal traders and port officials understand." *And Iska, I hope you were telling me the truth.*

"And that is the tongue you speak, I suppose?" Kesleer's sarcastic tone made it clear he doubted Saker's assertion.

"It is, mynster. Pashali."

There was a long silence. When Kesleer spoke again, his tone was more neutral. "That's interesting. Who told you?"

"A lascar tar. I suppose he might have been lying, although he had no reason to do so."

"So you're telling me the language my lascar is teaching my company factors may be useless, and they should be learning Pashali?"

"I've heard your first two fleets to the Summer Seas brought Pashali interpreters from Javenka to negotiate the purchase of spices in the islands. They doubtless cheated your factors. They have reason to want you to pay high prices."

"In all probability. Which is why my lascar is teaching my factors and ship's officers the language of the Spicerie."

"Of the Spicerie – or of his own island?"

There was another long silence.

Kesleer rang the bell on his desk, and when a clerk entered, he asked the man to fetch "that bastard of a lascar".

"How good is your Pashali?" Kesleer asked as they waited.

"Fluent. I spent some time with Pashali caravanners," he added. A statement as vague as it was true.

A moment later Ardhi stepped into the room.

There was little left of the man Saker had first seen in the warehouse. His long hair was now cut level with his ears in the Lowmian style. He wore the black garb of a clerk, with detachable white collar and cuffs. A broad length of leather was belted around his waist with a cheap tin buckle. His feet were thrust into wooden clogs. He wore the outfit with an odd combination of dignity and discomfort that, to Saker's heightened senses, reeked of protest.

When they'd first met, Saker had thought him little more than a lad. Eighteen or nineteen, perhaps. Now, nearly two years later, he seemed to have aged more than those years warranted. Two years in a strange land, speaking a strange tongue, eating strange food, always the outsider, the exotic stranger to be stared at. *Va above, it can't have been easy.*

The only sign he gave that he recognised Saker was a slight narrowing of his eyes, followed by the faintest of quirks to the edge of his lips, as if to say: *Well, I won't give you away, if you don't betray me.* "Mynster?" he asked with a bow to Kesleer. "I am at your service." Both his accent and his delivery had improved.

Kesleer barely glanced at him. He stared at Saker instead. "Addy," he said, mispronouncing the name, "this man here tells me Pashali is the language used by traders and natives throughout the islands of the Summer Seas."

"Yes, mynster."

"You mean that's *true*?"

"Yes, mynster."

"Why did you not tell me?"

Kesleer's incredulous stare did not faze the lascar, who said levelly, "Mynster Kesleer not ask."

"Va preserve me from idle-headed dewberries! Are you from the Spicerie?"

"I not know that answer, mynster."

"What do you mean, you don't *know*? How can you not know where you live?"

"I know where I born, mynster. I not know what name you call my island."

"That's ridiculous!" Kesleer threw up his hands in frustration. "I suppose that's all one can expect of an ignorant savage from some outlandish jungle. What do *you* call this island of yours?"

"Chenderawasi, mynster," Ardhi replied with unruffled calm.

"And what language do you speak there?"

"Chenderawasi, mynster."

"Leak on you, you malt-worm! Why are you teaching my company factors to speak your wretched tongue?"

"Because you ask me, mynster. You say, 'Teach them the words of your island tongue', so I teach. Master Grobath the factor, he speaks very good Chenderawasi now."

Saker bit his lip hard to stop himself laughing. Ardhi may have looked as innocent as a daisy opening up to the sun, but Saker knew subtle impudence when he saw it.

"Do you speak Pashali?" Kesleer, eyes flashing, snapped the question at Ardhi.

"Of course, mynster."

"Well, you can stop teaching them your Va-damned language and teach them Pashali instead from now on!"

"As Mynster Kesleer wish."

"Now get out of here before I kick you out."

Ardhi dived for the door and was gone in a flash.

"And you, Master Heron, you can teach them as well. Some of them already have a smattering of Pashali from previous voyages to Javenka and the western shores of Pashalin. Come back tomorrow and speak to Clerk Zeeman in the front office about the terms. If you do well, I'll consider you for the position of company factor on the next voyage to the Spicerie."

He was dismissed. In the main office on his way out, he passed Ardhi. "I'm staying at Goffrey's doss house on Herring Street," he muttered. He didn't wait for an answer.

Outside on the boardwalk, he paused to gather his wits. *Company factor?* Sailing to the Summer Seas? He smiled at the thought. That was one post he wouldn't take. He was on his way back to report to the Pontifect. All he needed was an extra day so he could talk to Ardhi, and give that fobbing dagger back.

35

The Crime of the Vollendorns

Sorrel, wedged into a corner of the Regala's reception room between a prayer stool and a candelabra stand, was sick with apprehension. Mathilda was still incandescent with anger at Lowmeer in general and the Regal in particular, and there was no guarantee she could keep her ire reined in.

She's too volatile right now. Maybe we should have waited even longer . . . What if the Regal is suspicious? What if she is too obvious?

Sweat trickled down her neck. She'd spent days calming Mathilda before allowing her to tackle the Regal about Lowmian twins. "You have to curb your agitation," she'd said, until her words had penetrated Mathilda's fury enough for her to listen.

And now the moment had come. Regal Vilmar, hearing that his wife was unwell, had come alone to see her. And so Sorrel was blurred into her corner, while Mathilda reclined on a couch with the Regal seated beside her, close to a fire that struggled to warm the room.

Va's teeth, let's hope Mathilda forgets this insane idea of killing him.

"You must take care of yourself," Regal Vilmar was saying. "The doctors tell me you will not let them examine you."

Mathilda's reply was prim. "It is not meet for male physicians to touch the person of a royal woman." She then smiled sweetly to moderate the sting of her words. "My body is for my dear husband alone to see and touch. I will keep myself inviolate for him until he asks for me once more." It had been the Regal's decision to halt Mathilda's visits to his bed, out of concern for the child.

Sorrel rolled her eyes. Sometimes she couldn't believe he was so easily deceived by Mathilda's duplicity.

"Your grace will be glad to hear," Mathilda continued, "that the midwife" – she meant Aureen – "has listened to the baby's heartbeat.

She says the babe is big and strong enough to be a boy, a fitting heir for a noble monarch."

The Regal nodded complacently. "I am glad to hear it, but my dear, you must have the court physicians at the delivery."

"Oh, I know. Lady Friselda explained to me that the Lord Chamberlain must also be present in the birthing chamber. Some silly thing about making sure that no other baby is substituted for mine, although I cannot see how that could possibly happen! And also to make sure I am not having twins."

Sorrel held her breath.

Mathilda paused, tilting her head in a childlike pose. "I must admit I didn't understand *that* at all." Smiling with all her charm and coquetry, she leaned towards Regal Vilmar and enclosed his hand within hers. "You will have to explain it to me, my sweet husband, so that I do not make an inappropriate remark at some court function. I am the Regala and it would break my heart if I brought shame or embarrassment to the Basalt Throne because I am just a flighty Ardronese princess who lacks the advantage of being raised in the refinement of the Lowmian court." Another pause and another pleading smile. "Why is it that twins are unwelcome here, and not in Ardrone?"

Sorrel closed her eyes, unable to watch. Surely the Regal wouldn't fall for such – such a sickeningly rich cream of sycophancy and lies?

To her relief, when she opened her eyes again, he was patting Mathilda's hand with fatherly condescension. "You need not bother yourself with such matters."

"Oh, but I must! I have to bother my giddy head with these difficult subjects so I know what to say or not say the next time someone mentions it at court."

At this the Regal frowned. "They should not mention it at all! We should not speak of such things in public."

Mathilda nodded, but said nothing.

It was the Regal who broke the long silence. "It pains me to say this, but perhaps you are right in one respect. You are a Lowmian Regala now, and this will be a matter of grave importance to my heir. If I should die before my son is grown, you must pass on the knowledge of Bengorth's Law."

"Regal Bengorth was the first regal of the Vollendorn line, was he not? You see, I have learned my history!"

Bengorth's Law? Sorrel had never heard of it.

"Before I explain the details, I must swear you to secrecy." He pulled off the large gold signet ring on his finger. "This is the Vollendorn ring, which will be passed on to my son at his coronation." He placed it on the palm of her hand and closed her fingers over it. "Swear by this ring, and the future of your children, whose blood will continue the line of the Vollendorns. Swear by the blood of your son, who will sit on the Basalt Throne, that you will uphold the secrecy our family maintains pertaining to our adherence to Bengorth's Law."

Dear Va, if he finds out I'm here, I'm dead . . . Mathilda, don't look this way. Don't even think *about me!*

Mathilda swallowed. She tried to speak, but had to lick her lips before she could get the words out. "I swear."

The Regal slipped his ring back on to his finger. "Bengorth's Law applies to the heir when he first ascends the throne. A man will come to him, and ask for his oath. If he refuses to swear this oath, he will die and so will any person of the Vollendorn family who is in line to the throne. In other words, the Vollendorns will be wiped out."

Mathilda looked at him blankly. "I don't understand. By whom?"

"By A'Va and his devil-kin."

This time Mathilda was speechless. With a sudden movement that took her by surprise, he sprang at her, one hand outstretched to catch her in the throat. He pressed her against the high back of the couch, pinning her there.

Sorrel bit her lip, tasting blood. Dear Va, she couldn't stand by and watch the Princess of Ardrone *murdered* . . . She stepped away from the wall, ready to approach the Regal from behind.

"I will warn you now," he was saying, "just this once, that if I ever find out that you have told anyone what I am about to reveal, I'll see you skinned alive and hung on a gibbet while the birds peck out your eyes. A closed coffin will be buried here in the royal graveyard. So sad, the Regala, dead so young of a fever. Never speak of this to anyone but my heir. Do you understand me, Mathilda?"

She squeaked her assent, her eyes wild with terror. He released her abruptly, without apparent concern for her panic, or the bruises he'd caused.

Sorrel flattened herself against the wall again, careful not to make a sound or lose her hold on her glamour.

"You see, my dear," the Regal said, quietly yet savagely, "Bengorth's Law is an agreement made by Bengorth, and every regal since, with A'Va. A'Va swears to each regal that the Basalt Throne will be occupied by a Vollendorn, and that Lowmeer will prosper. There is a cost, of course. The man who comes to receive the price of this promise from each regal is a devil-kin. He represents A'Va. Before he demands this price of the Regal, he will do something to display his power, to prove whom he represents."

Mathilda stared at him, her pale face blank of any emotion but fear. Sorrel wondered if she was going to faint. "What – what powers were shown you?"

"He killed my favourite hound. With a glance, he forced it into the fireplace where, howling in agony, it burned to death."

Mathilda's eyes widened; her body shuddered.

The price, sweet Va, ask him the price!

"Bengorth wanted to start a dynasty," Vilmar continued. "A Vollendorn dynasty, with himself as the first Vollendorn monarch. But he was just an obscure nobleman without much of a following, so he made a bargain with A'Va. He offered A'Va dominion over certain newborn citizens of Lowmeer – one in every set of twins born on Lowmian soil – if he became regal. That twin, when grown, would become a vassal of A'Va, a dedicated devil-kin. In exchange, A'Va would not only aid Bengorth in his seizure of the throne, but would ensure that his line would continue, in direct descent, for as long as the bargain was upheld in each generation."

"I – I don't understand," Mathilda stuttered. "You – you aren't upholding the bargain. You're *killing* twins."

Sorrel froze. *The Regal hasn't told her that. She's not supposed to know it.* She waited for him to realise, her heart thumping, but when he continued, it was to say, "That's right. What monarch wants a country plagued with the horrors devil-kin can inflict? Like this damned Horned Death! Each Vollendorn regal, to ensure his reign, swears to uphold Bengorth's agreement. But Bengorth gave no guarantee that we would not try to kill those devil-kin once they are born."

Mathilda was looking confused, but he continued, oblivious. "The only way we can be sure they will never live to do anyone harm is to kill both twins after their birth. Which we always endeavour to do. I have a band of loyal, dedicated men who perform this task, as their fathers did before them, and their fathers before them, as far back as the Royal House of Vollendorn has occupied the Basalt Throne of Lowmeer. They are called the Dire Sweepers."

"That – that is horrible," Mathilda whispered, her eyes wide. Her bottom lip trembled. For once, there was no artifice. "You – you kill the *innocent* twin, too?"

Hold on, Mathilda. Don't break down now.

"It is the burden the regals of Lowmeer have borne for centuries and must bear into the future to keep our people safe. The burden our son must bear when his time comes. A burden that must never be forgotten, never neglected. The only reason I tell this to you is that it is also your burden, one that you must pass on to our son."

"Doesn't – doesn't killing the twins make A'Va, um, *angry*? Like – like it's cheating." Mathilda was trying hard to control her shaking.

Regal Vilmar gave a hard, unpleasant laugh. "A'Va appreciates a clever opponent. And alas, every now and then we miss a few twins. He makes do with those when they come into their power at maturity. They are the ones who cause the Horned Death. It is a deadly dance we do, A'Va and we regals of Lowmeer. Sometimes we are ahead, sometimes A'Va is. But what you have to understand, my dear, is this. If a regal repudiates the agreement, then he *and his line* dies out. Swiftly and horribly, I imagine. As long as I uphold the pact, I *know* that sooner or later I'll breed a healthy son. As long as A'Va upholds his side, he knows he will get a supply of devil-kin.

"What I *don't* know is whether I will live long enough to educate my son to adulthood and an understanding of what is expected of him. *That* may fall to you. I can trust no one else. *No one.* Only you will have a vested interest because you will want to see your son live to his coronation day. And you will see to it that our son understands and upholds the agreement at his coronation, because if he doesn't, he dies, and dies cruelly. Possibly you would too, in case you were breeding again. If a son of ours comes to the throne very young, then you will have to act as his proxy, and make the agreement for him until he is old enough to do it himself. *Do you understand?*"

Mathilda was looking at him, mesmerised by the horror of what he was telling her. "Do – do you mean that if my son doesn't agree with Bengorth's Law, he'll die?"

"Yes. That's exactly what I mean. I am sure you want him to live."

She nodded again. "Of course," she whispered. "Above everything."

"Then there will be no problem, will there?"

She shook her head.

"Good. Get plenty of rest, and eat well."

He took up her hand and kissed her palm, before he strode from the room. Mathilda couldn't see his face, but Sorrel could. His expression was a look of cold contempt.

She stayed where she was, still glamoured, afraid he might come back, or send someone else into the room. Mathilda staggered to her feet, reeling, her face pale and her neck still blotched with red fingerprints. She gasped, dragging air into her lungs as she lurched across the room to the door he had used. Once there, she shot the bolt.

Sorrel let her glamour fade and stepped away from the wall. They stared at one another in shock. It was Mathilda who spoke first. Her voice raw with emotion, she whispered, "A'Va – I saw A'Va in his eyes! Sorrel, he has been touched by A'Va. Such evil. I am so frightened. You must never leave me. I couldn't bear it if you were to go."

"We'll think about all that later. Right now we have to consider what to do about your babies."

"Is it possible, what he said? That a man can make a verbal agreement with A'Va that is so – so disgusting, and if he breaks it, he dies? Along with his children?"

She hesitated. "I think he believes it." *I'm not sure I do.*

"Which means he'll kill his own twins in order to save himself."

There's a paradox in that. Vollendorn regals make the bargain to ensure that they, and their sons after them, will rule. If Vilmar has to kill a twin son, then . . . Her head reeled under all the implications and possibilities. *Maybe the twins are girls. Women don't rule in Lowmeer.*

"It's hideous," Mathilda said at last. "And wrong. I will *never* let him kill my babies. He is evil, and my children will live. One day my son will sit on the throne of Lowmeer. I swear that."

But if you have a son – one of these twins, or another son from another birth – and he comes to sit on the Basalt Throne, he will have to make the same bargain with A'Va, or die.

Mathilda, however, wasn't thinking that far ahead. She said, "And you, you have to use your glamour to kill that man before he slaughters his own offspring."

Sorrel bit her lip in dismay. "Mathilda, it is not possible to use a witchery for evil, and murder is evil."

"You killed your husband."

"I did not do that in cold blood or with witchery. I was out of my mind with grief because I'd just learned that he had murdered our daughter."

"Well, I am out of my mind at the thought that he will kill *my* children!"

"I will not do it, so put that thought right out of your head. The only way out of this is to hide the fact that you are having two babies. Either Aureen or I must spirit away the firstborn of the children. Let's hope it's a girl."

There was a long pause while Mathilda continued to think things through. At last she whispered, "I'm going to give birth to one innocent baby and one vile spawn of A'Va, aren't I? And we won't know which is which until they are much, much older! Oh, Sorrel, I am so scared!" She leant her head on Sorrel's shoulder and started crying silently.

Sorrel patted her on the back. Her sympathy was real. Mathilda, for possibly the first time in her life, was putting others – her children – before herself. "Maybe it's not true," she said. "Maybe it's all just superstition. And why would A'Va not do anything to stop the death of his devil-kin as babies? Mathilda, look at your cousins in Ardrone! Neither of them is evil, right?"

"But he said it only applies to twins born in Lowmeer. Is there no way I can leave this wretched land?"

"Oh, Mathilda, can you risk telling him? And – and I'm not sure you'd get to Ardrone before they were born."

"Maybe – maybe I ought to let them die. But I *can't*! I can't!" Mathilda clamped a hand over her mouth and began to sob in earnest. "T-t-tell me all this is not true!" she wailed.

Sorrel said finally, "I can't believe a child is *born* evil."

Mathilda raised her tear-stained face. "Imagine a devil-kin on the Basalt Throne. Think of the terrible things that could happen . . ."

"If a devil-kin doesn't become a vassal of A'Va until they are grown, nothing will happen for maybe fourteen years or more. We have time to investigate. To stop it from happening."

"How?"

She made up her mind. "I'll take the first twin, girl or boy, to the Pontifect. This is a matter for the Faith to solve, not us."

"Do you really think so? We – we wouldn't be doing anything wicked if we saved both my babies?"

"Of course we wouldn't. We will do it, you and I together. Aureen will have to know, but no one else. She will keep the secret and so will I. I'll go and get her and the three of us will talk about this until we've worked out a way to do it."

For a moment Mathilda looked relieved. "Yes. We'll let Va-Faith take care of it. And my real baby will survive, won't it, even if the evil one dies?" Then her face changed again. "But what if the Regal finds out? What if you are caught? What if the one you leave with me is the devil-kin? What if the one you take is a boy and the one I'm left with is a girl? Oh Sorrel, what did I ever do to deserve this? I want to die! And what will I do if you aren't here? I just want to go home!"

And once again she burst into tears.

"Listen. Once we tell this story to the Pontifect, the Faith will have to do something. How can a monarch who acquiesced in his family's bargain with A'Va be tolerated on the Basalt Throne? He will be deposed. And you will become regent for the heir."

"Oh! Then I can do what I like, can't I?" The tears vanished. "Are you sure that's what will happen?"

"Yes, of course," said Sorrel, who hadn't the faintest idea of the truth of her words and wasn't about to point out the difficulty of keeping anyone in the Vollendorn family alive once the oath was not kept. "Unless you have girls, of course. Anyway, don't worry about things so far in the future. Our worst concern at the moment is how to get enough money to take me safely to Vavala."

"Oh, that's easy. You'll just have to steal some, using your glamour. After all, it will be in a good cause, won't it?"

Va, help me. Help us all.

36

The Man from Chenderawasi

Saker's room on the first floor of the doss house was small and poky and smelled of smoke, fish and heated lard. Cooking odours from the kitchens beneath had permeated the wood of the building for so many years they were an integral part of the establishment. He'd survived much worse on his numerous travels; even so, he preferred to wait for Ardhi in the taproom below. Here the smells were fresher and more enticing.

He'll come. I'm sure he'll come.

Around him the conversation was lively. These days the docklands of Ustgrind buzzed with optimism; prosperity was on its way as never before, if the scruffy tapboys and the dockyard customers were to be believed. And the reason? The Lowmian Spicerie Trading Company's monopoly over the spice trade was established and the city's commercial pre-eminence guaranteed, all thanks to the Regal's support. Other cities of Lowmeer had lost out, just as Ardrone and the Principalities had. The Ustgrind folk gloated.

"Things will be even better soon," the doss house owner predicted with a gap-toothed grin directed Saker's way. "We'll be riding high here in Ustgrind! Why, there's even a bit o' polish on our future prosperity: an heir to the Basalt Throne on the way!"

"The baby might be a girl," Saker pointed out, trying not to wince at the thought of Mathilda valued for her breeding ability like a brood mare.

The man winked. "Ah, but the Regal has proved he can still perform! And the Regala has showed she's fertile. If this babe's not a boy, there'll be others."

Saker felt an irrational desire to clobber the man with his fist in order to wipe the smirk from his face.

When there was a stir near the door, he was glad to have the fellow's interest diverted elsewhere, and he could concentrate on his tankard of beer. A moment later, however, Ardhi slipped into the empty space next to him on the bench. A dagger was slapped down on the boards of the table in front of him. He recognised it immediately. Once, it had been his.

"Swap you this fine steel for my kris," the lascar said. "My knife."

"I know what a kris is. And I know yours is a Chenderawasi dagger."

Ardhi raised a surprised eyebrow. "Aha! You show my kris to another man of the islands, eh?"

"I want some answers before I return it. I want to know why you threw it at me, why you were in that warehouse in the first place, why you stole the bambu, and what the Va-less hell that kris wants."

A broad grin lit up the young man's face. "Gives trouble, my blade, eh?" he asked. He tapped his forehead. "A Chenderawasi kris has mind. A will. It belongs to me. But its spirit? That has eaten the *sakti* of the Chenderawasi. That not mine. *Sakti,* the magic, the witchery, you understand? I not throw it at you, you know."

"I *saw* you throw it." There was something different about Ardhi, something more than his new maturity, and his increased familiarity with the language of the Va-cherished. An inner glow, but not one he could see. Rather something he *felt*. Something he'd seen in someone else, an elusive memory of – who? He dragged his thoughts back to the present.

"No, you saw wrong. I hanging on the beam outside warehouse, one hand only. Kris in other hand. I want put it away so I can climb on roof. Understand? Instead, it flies out of my hand, towards you. It chooses. You, me, we just servants of Chenderawasi kris. It plays with men. I look for you, but kris doesn't want. So I wait. I think maybe one day it come back, I know. And it has!"

He snorted. "After, what, almost two years?"

"Men are impatient. Not the kris. It bides its time. Now time comes. You and I, we dance its song."

Saker was silent, remembering all the dagger had done.

"You see now, eh?"

"Who or what does it serve?"

"The Chenderawasi."

Saker sighed in surrender. "I give up." He drew the kris out of its sheath and placed it beside his own.

Once again, it chose its own path. It spun across the tabletop and Ardhi just caught it before it dropped into his lap. "Wise decision, mynster. It knows where it wants to be."

Saker guessed the use of the honorific was ironic, rather than polite. Justifiably or not, Ardhi exuded the confidence of a man who knew himself to be an equal. He remembered how the lascar had subtly mocked Kesleer. *I'll be beggared. What manner of man is he?* He glanced at him, noting that although he was still dressed in the garb of a clerk, he was bare-footed again.

Ardhi stroked the hilt of the kris, and his lips curled in a smile. "Thank you for bringing it back. What is your name, mynster?"

"Reed Heron."

The kris flipped in his hand. "Ah. The blade says you lie."

"That's the name I am using right now. It will do. And you are Ardhi?"

"Yes."

"Do you have a family name?"

"Where I come from, one name is enough."

Saker said, "Tell me about the kris. Why would it have an interest in me in the first place?"

Ardhi shrugged. "I not know. Perhaps it leaves me because I fail." With a fingertip, he pushed at a pool of spilt liquid on the tabletop, obviously not really seeing it.

"Fail?"

"I fail my task. I steal the bambu, but find it empty."

"Are you trying to say the kris *threw itself* at me because you failed to steal something?"

"Yes. Something precious. Belongs to my people." He struggled for a moment, perhaps because he was having trouble finding the right words. "You speak Pashali, right?"

"Yes."

"Good. We speak Pashali." He switched languages. "The kris was made for me by the metalworker to the Raja, crafted especially for this task."

Saker blinked. With those few words, Ardhi had turned his own preconceptions on their head. The lascar spoke perfect, accentless Pashali, much better than his own. "Wait," he said, using the same language. "What – who – is a raja? Your ruler?"

"Yes. The Pashali use the word sultan. You would say regal. We say raja. Very few people are granted a kris like this one, certainly no one as young as I. It is a grave responsibility."

Saker struggled with the language, uncomfortably reminded how rusty his Pashali had become with disuse. "So you were given a Chenderawasi kris for this special task?"

"Do you understand the word you use? Chenderawasi?"

"Not – not really. The lascar I met said something about magic. And control." *He who holds Chenderawasi kris, he serves the Chenderawasi.*

There was a long silence. Saker remained quiet, while Ardhi considered what to say next. Finally he made a decision and said, "Chenderawasi is the name of my *pulauan.*"

When Saker looked blank, he translated the word into Pashali, but Saker didn't know that word either. He hazarded a guess. "Island group?"

"Yes. And it is *not* the Spicerie."

"And you were jerking Kesleer's leash. You're a braver man than I, Ardhi."

He grinned. "Chenderawasi Islands are further away from Pashalin than the Spicerie. Pashali traders not go there." He glanced around in a worried fashion to make sure no one was listening. His presence had aroused interest and there were many stares, some bright with interest, others frowning as if they disapproved of him on principle. No one was close enough to overhear their conversation.

"I am not Lowmian, you know," Saker said. "I was born in Ardrone." A secret for a secret.

That surprised him. "You *sound* Lowmian."

"A disadvantage in Ustgrind, to be Ardronese. I'm a good mimic of accents."

"Your Pashali accent is low-class. You learned the tongue from ill-educated Pashali caravanners?"

And university men from the Principalities, but he let that pass. Ardhi grinned yet again. Did the fellow ever just *smile*? "So," he said, now horribly conscious of his accent, "let's return to the kris. It was made for you because you must steal the thing inside the bambu?"

This time he was quick to correct Saker's use of words. "Not steal. To take back what belonged to my people in the first place."

Ah. So Fritillary had been right.

"The bambu and its contents were stolen by the crew of the *Spice Dragon*?" he guessed.

Ardhi glanced down at the table, where the tapboy, after taking note of a signal from Saker, had placed a mug of beer. He wrapped his fingers around the handle, but didn't drink. "Yes, when the Lowmian ship came to Chenderawasi. First time such a ship entered our waters." He shrugged. "They heard careless talk of Chenderawasi'mas and killed to obtain what they wanted. They slaughtered our raja." His eyes were sombre with grief. "The ones who did it died on the voyage back."

The gratification in his tone was clear. "You were on that ship then?" *Did he kill them? Toss their bodies overboard one stormy night?*

"Yes. I followed the *Spice Dragon* to Kotabanta on Serinaga Island, and signed on for the journey to Lowmeer. I did ask the ship's captain, Captain Lustgrader, to return the Chenderawasi'mas to our islands, but he refused."

"Chenderawasi'mas? Are you going to tell me what that is?"

"Of course! It's obvious you have been selected to help me return them."

"Obvious? Not obvious to me," he replied. "I don't want to help. Why should I?"

"The Chenderawasi kris chose you," Ardhi said, as if that explained everything. "I failed, and with my failure my chance of performing this task alone vanished. That day in the warehouse, Kesleer said he was sending the Chenderawasi'mas to the Regal. The spirit of the kris understood that intention. It decided that you are to be the person who will retrieve them. That's why it left my hand and flew to you."

"You're out of your mind. And what is it anyway, this Chenda . . . Chenderawasmas?"

"Two words. Chenderawasi emas. Although we usually, er, slide them together." Ardhi enunciated the words in full this time, then added the translation. "The Chenderawasi gold. The golden plumes from the Chenderawasi birds."

He took a moment to digest that. Then, incredulous, he blurted, "*Feathers?*"

Ardhi nodded. "Three plumes. Feathers of our guardians, the Chenderawasi, the paradise birds. The Pashali call them birds of heaven. The Lowmians say birds of paradise. Our *pulauan* – group of islands – is named for the birds."

"So . . . Chenderawasi is the name of the island chain. Chenderawasi is also the name of a type of bird. Chenderawasi'mas are bird feathers from the Chenderawasi birds that live in the Chenderawasi Islands. Simple enough to understand." He reverted to his own tongue, blurting, "What is clay-brained is that you want me to risk my life to retrieve some *feathers*."

Ardhi's eyes flashed with such fury, Saker found himself leaning away. His hand closed around the hilt of his own dagger, still on the table, but he didn't pick it up. "I have offended you," he said quietly, even as his body readied for attack.

The naked rage in the lascar was frightening. "You are an ignorant off-islander. You can be forgiven because you have never seen the Chenderawasi. You do not know our ways. But you might remember that the plumes were valuable enough to persuade the Regal to give the spice trade to the Lowmian merchant Mynster Kesleer."

Saker felt out of his depth. Ardhi's grasp of Pashali put his own to shame. It was idiomatic, fluent and erudite, whereas he, Saker, was having to revert to his own tongue whenever he was flustered. *Dear Va, how arrogant we are in the Va-cherished Hemisphere, to assume our superiority on so little evidence.*

He frowned, thinking back to the overheard conversation in the warehouse. He remembered the glimpse he'd had of something golden. Kesleer had put a high value on the contents of the bambu. *Feathers.* An astute merchant had thought they were enough to persuade Regal Vilmar to do something he'd never done before. And the Regal had indeed granted him his monopoly. Sweet heaven.

He recalled the court ladies back in Throssel, with their feathered headdresses. What wouldn't some of those ladies give to have golden plumes in their hair?

Ardhi said, more calmly, "The feathers are beyond price."

"I'm not interested in their monetary value. I want to keep hold of my *life*. And what you say about the kris is nonsense. If it wanted me to do something, then it failed, surely. I haven't stolen anything."

"Time means nothing to a Chenderawasi dagger. The older it grows, the more understanding it has, but from its birth it has the power of the Chenderawasi within. We call it Sri Kris, or Lord Dagger, and it possesses *sakti*. *Sakti* is like your witchery." He paused, then asked, puzzled, "Why do you believe in witchery, but not Chenderawasi magic?" He drew out the kris and put a finger on one of the gold filaments in the blade. "Look."

Saker almost laughed, but stopped himself in time. "Those gold flaws in the metal were Chenderawasi feathers?" he asked, stifling any expression of his scepticism. As if feathers would survive the heating of the forging!

Ardhi nodded, and the muted glow around him flared. *Oh Va, witchery. That's what I can see in him. It's because he has their equivalent of a witchery! It's the same thing I can now sense in Fritillary, and in Sorrel, and in shrine-keepers, since I became one of them.*

He went cold all over and had to clench his hands to stop them shaking. Chenderawasi witchery was akin to Va-granted witchery?

Aloud, he said in his own tongue, "All right. I'll believe in your kris magic. The curdling thing followed me everywhere I went, after all, but that doesn't alter my opinion. None of this is my business."

"I don't think you have a choice. You were chosen because of your possibility to become what you are now."

He raised an eyebrow, mystified, wondering if he'd understood correctly.

"When I first met you, you were an ordinary man. Since then, you've been gifted with *sakti*. Witchery. The kris sensed your potential. It must have done. And so it waited and nudged your witchery into the path it chose. I don't know what your *sakti* is, but I can sense you have it."

Dear Va. Birds. The kris had made sure that his witchery was some sort of stupid connection to birds? It had twisted his gift away from the usual witcheries into something it wanted? Blister that for a noxious joke! What about the unseen guardian? What about Va? What about the Way of the Oak? Had they no say? He felt sick enough to spew all over the floor, and it took an effort to swallow back bile. His hand went to his cheek, where the brand should be.

His witchery. His stupid witchery, an awareness of birds. *And this kris had chosen what it was to be . . .*

Birds. Feathers. A memory of golden feathers on the clerk's table back in Kesleer's warehouse. The gold streaks in the kris. *Sweet Va above. What the scabrous hell is going on?*

"Look," he said, scrambling to find some explanation that made sense, "all your kris did, for months, was follow me around. When I tried to get rid of it, it always came back. Oh, and it sometimes warned me of – of danger. That's *all*, until today, when it directed me to Uthen Kesleer's office."

"Perhaps it was waiting. For you to change. To come into your power. Then it brought you back to me."

"What power? I don't have any power!" Sensing a bird was hungry was not possessing power, dammit! And then that treacherous internal voice said, *Oh? Then what about having gulls and owls rescuing you from murderous assassins?*

Ardhi laughed, and sipped his beer. "Oh yes, you do. I can feel it."

"This is ridiculous. What's so special about a fobbing feather anyway?"

"I can show you."

"How?"

"I have my own Chenderawasi feather. In my room. Come, I'll show you."

Saker stood. His legs felt wooden. Throwing some coins on to the table, he followed Ardhi out.

The lascar's lodging was more comfortable than he expected, and surely cost more than a seaman's wages. His surprise must have been written on his face, because Ardhi shrugged, smiled and said, "I brought rare spices from home. Who thinks to look in a tar's dirty kitbag for such wealth? I sold them gradually for a small fortune."

"You should buy yourself a pair of boots." Ardhi – of course – just grinned. It would be a wonder if that damned grin didn't get him murdered one day. "So where's this feather of yours?"

The lascar eased out a piece of bambu from inside the stuffing of his pallet. Carefully he extracted the contents, saying, "This plume was gifted to me, in case I needed it."

With those words, the feather – no, never feather, for such a word was inadequate – the *plume* opened up in all its glory as it left the confines of the bambu. It puffed out in a cloud of colour, one of the loveliest things Saker had ever laid eyes on. Golden, and longer than his arm. No, not just gold: an almost liquid cascade of yellows, from pale lemon at the base to a rich, vivid orange-red at the tip. The hues shimmered and danced, even though the air was still. They glowed, casting a haze of ambient light. He reached out to stroke the barbules. They were soft, like warm water, and his hand tingled pleasantly.

He looked at Ardhi through a haze of affection. All his reservations deserted him. "It is beyond beauty," he said in wonder. He knew he had to see the bird that produced such a thing of glory. He stroked it again and could have sworn it vibrated under his hand. His fingertips sparkled with gold. For one crazed moment, he thought it spoke to him, a soft whisper of regret, like a foretelling of death.

"It's yours," said Ardhi. "I gift it to you."

He barely noticed the terrible pain in the lascar's tone. He abandoned all rational thought, all reservation, all caution. All he could think of was that this glorious creation was his for the taking. He could own it, look at it every day. With tender care, he took it from Ardhi's hands. "Thank you," he whispered. "I've never been given anything so – so superb."

He raised his gaze to look at the lascar, and Ardhi smiled. There were tears hesitating on his long dark lashes, but it was the curl of his lips that told Saker more. The quiet certitude of a task flawlessly performed. His heart contracted to a hard ball in his chest and he found it difficult to breathe. He looked down at the plume, then back at the lascar. "Dear Va," he whispered, "what have you done?"

"Not what I've done," the lascar said quietly. "What you've done, and what you cannot undo."

Saker thrust the feather at him. "Take it back," he said, overriding the immense desire to hug the glorious shimmer of orange and gold to his chest and never let anyone touch it again. "I don't want it! Take it back!"

Ardhi shook his head. "I can't. When I took it from the one who gifted it to me, I was sent here, to the other side of the world, to perform a task and never to return until it was done. And now I have passed the plume to you. It is yours, Mynster Reed Heron. And with it comes a command. You will help me with that task: you will help me find and steal the Chenderawasi'mas now in the hands of the Regal of Lowmeer. Three plumes. And you will then take all four to Pulauan Chenderawasi."

Saker went cold all over. He was in the grip of a magic so intense, so powerful, it left him helpless to refuse, or resist. Every breath, every thought, every instinct told him the enormity of the price he would pay for a treacherous moment of covetous craving. He had sold his future to the lascar, and put his thumbprint on the possibility of his own imminent death.

Steal something – anything – from Ustgrind Castle? *Suicidal madness.*

And there was no way he could ever say no.

"Damn your eyes!" He spat the words from between gritted teeth, his fury as useless as it was real. "Damn you to beggary. One day I'll put a blade through your heart for this, you – you bilge scut!"

37

The Chenderawasi Trap

It was odd how the days went by, seemingly normal. But nothing was normal, not really, not for Saker. He was under a compulsion and he knew it. It crawled under his skin, a relentless itch needing a scratch. It churned his gut until he wanted to spew. Every day he would look up at the walls of the castle, and feel the insidious pull of it.

Steal me. Take me away. Return me to my rightful place. Carry me home . . .

Pickles 'n' rot, home for a Chenderawasi plume was the other side of a heaving ocean!

For the first few days, he clung in desperation to a belief that he could overcome the coercion. It was just a matter of being strong. Of using his will. That delusion soon foundered on his increasing desire – his overwhelming *need* – to scale the castle walls.

There was no escape, not for him.

He went to work every day at the Lowmian Spicerie Trading Company, taught the factors and sailors every day, saw Ardhi every day, learned more about Kesleer and his company every day. What he couldn't do was leave. He should have gone back to Vavala to report to the Pontifect; instead he wrote her a letter, which he gave to Loach to send with his normal reports. This time, though, he told her about the dagger, about Ardhi, about the Chenderawasi plumes and how his moment of foolish acquisitiveness had imprisoned him in a future he didn't want. He used coded words the Pontifect would understand and couched it all so vaguely it wouldn't do much harm if the letter fell into the wrong hands, but even so, he didn't commit to paper his intention of robbing the Regal. He wasn't that boil-brained. Besides, it was better she learned that *after* the fact.

Five or six days after he'd accepted the wretched plume from Ardhi, he was leaving the offices of the Lowmeer Spicerie Trading Company when he realised Ardhi was right behind him. He looked over his shoulder and scowled.

Ardhi made a regretful face. "I'm sorry about what I did to you," he said in Pashali.

"No, you're not," he growled, making a point by using his own tongue to put the lascar at a disadvantage, then feeling petty and childish because he had. "You were sent to do something and you've handed the task over to me, so if anyone hangs for this, it'll be me. Blister you, why didn't you steal the fobbing feathers on board ship before you got here?"

Unfazed, Ardhi continued in Pashali, saying, "Rather hard to hide stolen goods on a ship, and even harder to leave the vessel carrying them. Forgive me, Mynster Heron, for catching you in the net of my problems, but I was manipulated into this just as much as you were. The *sakti* Chenderawasi is like that. We need to talk. Come with me."

He wanted to walk away before anger got the better of him, but Ardhi had asked him to follow, so he could do no less. *Damn his hide.* "This *sakti* of yours is an evil thing," he said as he caught up. This time he spoke Pashali. "I am your *slave.* Do you know how that makes me feel?"

"The *sakti* is not evil. Just as your witchery serves your people, mine serves the people of my islands. I won't give you any orders that don't further that aim."

"And if the interests of the Chenderawasi clash with the interests of the Va-cherished lands?"

"Does Ardronese witchery go to war with Lowmian witchery?"

He shook his head. "In self-defence, perhaps. You . . ." he searched for the correct Pashali word, "you equate your witchery with ours? Do you serve Va?"

Ardhi shrugged. "Va is just a name." They'd turned down a deserted wharf, bare of cargo and ships. Even the warehouse along the landward side was shuttered tight. Their footsteps rattled on the boards and the only other sounds were squabbling seabirds and the lap of wavelets on the pilings. "Let's sit here. No one can hear us," he said. He removed his clogs, then sat on the edge of the dock with his feet dangling.

For a moment Saker thought he was going to throw the wooden

shoes away into the shipping canal, but instead with a sigh he placed them at his side and said, "I think you must accept that what the kris and the *sakti* Chenderawasi want is the same as what the Way of the Oak and the Way of the Flow want."

"So my being hanged for theft would benefit the world?"

"You wouldn't have been chosen if your chances of success were not high."

"That's bilge rot!" He sat down on a coil of hawser rope, put his back to a bollard and rested his arms on his bent knees. Nearby, two small grey and white seagulls preened and watched him in an interested way. He scowled at them. They took no notice. Their stomachs were full, and they were content. *If they were cats*, he thought, *they'd be purring now.*

"I made a few enquiries," he continued, "through friends in the clergy. The castle guards check everyone who enters the outer wall. I may be able to penetrate that far, disguised as a tradesman. But then there's another layer of checks, a much stricter one, by different guards, for everyone entering the inner bailey. Then there's a gateway into the keep. After that, who knows? Worse, I have no idea where the plumes are kept and no idea how to find out."

When Ardhi said nothing, he added, "Was it Kesleer who gave the three plumes to the Regal?"

"Yes. When the men who killed the bird of paradise died on board ship, Captain Lustgrader took the feathers from their belongings. When the ship docked, Kesleer saw them and seized them. He gave them to the Regal to win his favour – not knowing the implications of what he was doing. He might have realised something was odd when he handed them over, though. Giving them away rips out your soul."

"That's ironic," Saker said drily, "because I felt I'd sold my soul to you when you gave yours to me. I wonder if Kesleer ever made the connection between the plume and the Regal acceding so readily to all his requests for commercial and trading concessions."

"Perhaps by now he has."

"These feathers are diabolical!" Saker resisted an urge to shake the lascar to rid himself of his pent-up anger.

"They aren't normally given to anyone, you know. I was the exception because three of them were stolen. Listen, at the moment it's possible the Regal doesn't understand what's happening to him. But he'll realise one day, and the result could be bad. He could, er, give the feathers to the King of Ardrone and tell him to do anything."

Like hand over his treasury to Lowmeer . . . or abdicate in favour of Mathilda's son . . . Or . . . Oh, pickle me sour, what if someone like Valerian Fox obtained the plumes?

Panic ripped through Saker. He stared at Ardhi, aghast. He'd been so riled by his own predicament, he hadn't thought of all the possible implications. He drew in a deep breath. "And with those words, you've just told me how to escape from under the spell myself."

"Yes. You could pass the plume on to another. You'd be free of me – and someone else would be enthralled to you, until they worked out how to enthral someone else."

"Why tell me that?"

"I think you're a decent man, and you'll see how important it is to get the plumes back, so we can return them to where they belong. You won't do to someone else what I did to you. You'll help me."

"You could have *asked*."

"Yes." A fleeting expression of anguish crossed the lascar's face. "I needed to be sure . . ."

"Damn your eyes. You could have passed the plume on to – oh, I don't know. Kesleer. You could have ordered him never to send another ship to the Summer Seas. You could have ordered him never to give the plume to anyone else. Or something!"

"And you think that would solve the problem – passing on power like that to a man like *Kesleer*? I'd be dead in a heartbeat, and he would think of a hundred ways to circumvent whatever commands I'd given. What would happen when he died? He could leave the plume to his son, with instructions on how to use its power."

"You're sure *I* won't use their power like that?"

"You have a witchery now, and I'm told that's only given to those who are deserving. You could have betrayed me in the warehouse the day we met, but you didn't. I believe you will want these plumes rescued and returned to their rightful owners, where they will do no more harm."

"And the rightful owner is your raja?"

"Yes. And his family."

"I *might* appreciate what you are doing more, if I knew more. I know you haven't told me one tenth of what I need in order to understand your world or your power or your history. I don't know who you are. Or why you were chosen for this task. Or why the feathers mean so much to your people. Why do you need them back? They will harm us, not your people."

"The plumes are sacred to us."

Not the whole truth, Saker decided. "Who was it who asked you – *forced* you – to come here? And why *you*? You can hardly have been more than a lad when you went up the gangplank of a Lowmian ship into a world you knew nothing about!"

"Just turned eighteen. And I knew more than you think. My people are not ignorant savages living in the forest. I was schooled in Javenka."

He was thunderstruck. "In Pashalin?"

"Yes. At the Javenka Library. I went there when I was fifteen, and stayed three years."

Dear Oak. The greatest centre of learning the world had ever seen, so some said. He almost choked. He would have given much to have had that privilege. "I've heard of it," he said drily.

"My people are mostly fishermen and hunters and farmers, it's true. But there are also scholars and traders and shipbuilders and explorers. The only reason you don't know of us is because we are a peaceable people. Until now, our *sakti* Chenderawasi has kept us safe. Now we are threatened as never before."

"By whom?"

"By your hemisphere's traders! Where do you think your spices come from?"

"From the Spicerie islands."

"Yes. But all nutmeg and mace comes from Chenderawasi."

"*All?*"

"All. Until the ship *Spice Dragon* came to our shores, our nutmeg crop was sent, by our sailors aboard our boats, to Kotabanta. That's a port on one of the Summer Seas islands. It's not one of our island group, or even in the group you call the Spicerie. There, we all sell our spices to Pashali traders." He heaved a sigh. "The trouble with you folk of the Va-cherished Hemisphere is that you think the Summer Sea islands are all the same. You even bundle us together and call us lascars

– that's a meaningless word to us. We are different islands, with different tongues, different customs."

"Oh! That's . . . very ignorant of us."

Ardhi sighed. "I suppose we are no better, if I am honest. If the Rani had understood that I'd have to come all the way to the Va-cherished Hemisphere, and that it was such a different place to Pashalin, I doubt she would have sent just me, alone."

"It does seem, um, overly optimistic, sending a mere lad on such an important quest to the other side of the world. And you sailed on the *Spice Dragon*, aboard the very ship responsible for the death of your ruler? Ardhi, if you want my unqualified help, tell me the whole story."

"You don't need to know everything. Just that I was arrogant and stupid."

For a moment Saker thought that was all he was going to hear, but then Ardhi said, "I was in Kotabanta. I was on my way home from my studies in Javenka, waiting for any boat from Chenderawasi that could take me the rest of the way. The *Spice Dragon* was in port and they heard that the only source of nutmeg was Chenderawasi. One of their factors learnt that I was from Chenderawasi, and he offered me a free passage home if I'd show him where the islands were. He said, why do we all pay Pashali traders when we could cut out the middleman and deal direct? I trusted him, and I guided them to our islands."

He sat very still, gazing out towards the Ust estuary, where ships and boats and wherries cut through the choppiness of the waves, but the faraway look on his face spoke of other oceans, other climes. Saker remained silent, afraid to break the thread of the story.

"One night on the voyage they plied me with grog. I wasn't used to it. They thought it was funny, laughed at me. I was drunk, and I told them – some of the sailors – about the beauty of the Chenderawasi plumes. The next morning when I woke up I didn't remember much. I didn't remember that I'd told them where to find the Chenderawasi. The birds.

"We sailed into the bay of our main port. Hardly more than a fishing village by your standards. But beautiful. Tranquil. My home. They bought our nutmeg and paid well for it. But there was trouble afterwards. The sailors went ashore, and they didn't respect our customs. Several women were hurt. A man was stabbed when he protested.

"The village elders were angry. Captain Lustgrader apologised, people were compensated and the ship sailed. He left some of his factors behind. That's what they do; did you know that? The factors stay and they build their warehouses to store the spices, so the next time their ships come back, they have the cargo ready.

"But my people were angry. And they were afraid the Raja would be angry too, because they had not consulted him. And now there were Lowmians living on our soil. They sent a man to ask the Raja what was to be done.

"My grandfather is one of the elders of my island, and he ordered me to speak to the factors to find out all I could. I knew them from the ship, you see, and I could talk to them in Pashali. The factors told me the *Spice Dragon* wasn't going straight back to Kotabanta. Captain Lustgrader had wanted to hunt wild pigs first to restock the ship's meat supply, and he was putting in to a bay I'd told the sailors about. That was when one of the factors laughed and said he had no doubt the sailors – the ones who had got me drunk – would go hunting there for Chenderawasi feathers . . .

"I felt as though I would never breathe again.

"I ran to my friend who had a boat. She sailed me to that part of the island, and then I ran some more. And ran and ran. I was too late."

There was a long silence. Saker waited, dreading what he was about to hear.

"Every afternoon," Ardhi said softly, "the Raja went to a forest pool to bathe. They'd found him there, alone, and they shot him for the feathered regalia he wore." He looked back at Saker then, pain pooled in his eyes. "It was my fault."

His grief hit Saker in the gut.

"And you went back to the *Spice Dragon*?"

"Not then. The kris had to be made first."

He pulled out the dagger and laid it on his palm. "The hilt was made from the Raja's body."

Saker swallowed. "It's *bone*? I thought – I thought it was horn."

"Raja Wiramulia's body is in the hilt, and his blood in the blade. The gold you see comes from part of the regalia the murderers left behind. After the kris was crafted, I sailed to Kotabanta on board a trading *korakora*. That's a Chenderawasi boat. I caught up with the *Spice Dragon* there, where she was loading other cargo. Those who sailed with me asked Captain Lustgrader to return the plumes. When he wouldn't, I signed on as a crew member."

Saker floundered for a moment, knowing he still wasn't hearing the whole truth. There might have been no lies, but there was something missing. It was annoying that they used the same word for their witchery, their island and their birds of paradise, and he wondered if he had the interactions clear. His mind boggled at the whole idea of a raja – who was like a king, if he understood correctly – wearing regalia that consisted of plumes almost as tall as Ardhi himself . . . to go bathing in a forest pool?

Perhaps the bathing was some sort of ritual cleansing?

He decided not to ask.

Ardhi said, "I may not live, but the mission will not fail, not if the Chenderawasi want its success." He shrugged. "If they don't, then nothing matters."

"You killed the sailors who were responsible for the death of your raja, didn't you?"

"One vanished while on watch. Another lost his footing aloft on a stormy night and fell to the deck. The third died in a knife fight ashore in Karradar on the way home." He shrugged. "Sailors die all the time. It was impossible to steal back the plumes, though. There's no private place on board a ship to hide anything."

He swung his legs up to sit cross-legged, facing Saker. "I'm sorry. I don't like what I have done to you. You know I can scale a wall like a – like a house lizard. That's my *sakti*. Climbing. Agility. Squeezing through small spaces. I can get you inside the castle over the wall."

"If I steal the feathers, will I be under anyone else's spell? Kesleer's? Regal Vilmar's? Because they once owned them?"

"No. The plumes have to be gifted for that to happen, not stolen or found."

"Let me make sure I have this quite straight. You're ordering me to steal the feathers back because the magic of your people, through the medium of the kris, chose me. Even though the only advantage I have is that I can pass for a Lowmian, and you can't. Then, assuming I'm successful, you don't want me to give you the feathers – because that would give *me* ascendancy over *you*. Instead, you want me to go to Chenderawasi with you so I can personally return the feathers – all four of them – to your new raja. I will do this, you assume, in order to rid myself of your power over me, and to ensure that the plumes don't wreak more havoc among the Va-cherished by being gifted to others."

"Er, yes."

"I have a better idea. If I steal the feathers, I give you all four, we call it quits, and I walk away. I won't use their power. My word as the Shenat witan I once was."

"I – I can't take back the one I gave away." He had paled, as if the idea of that made him sick. "I *gave* it to you. The feather would never stay with me. It would just find its way back to you."

"Like the dagger."

He nodded, subdued.

"And I can't give it to anyone else, because I am a decent fellow. Would it matter if I kept it for ever? Or maybe I could destroy all four."

Ardhi blanched. "You won't live for ever, Witan Heron. And on your death, then what? These feathers can't be destroyed. You can't burn them. Their potency lasts for generations. The only person who won't be affected by their power to enslave is the rightful owner. The new Raja."

"We've always been told that people with witcheries can't use them to commit crimes."

"What I'm asking you to do is not a crime. I am asking you to correct a terrible wrong that was done."

"Right now I don't feel like a decent fellow. I'm angry enough to murder you. I loathe this revolting witchery of yours."

"You are dying to see my islands, though, aren't you? Come, let me buy you an ale and we'll talk about the Summer Seas."

For one treacherous moment he pictured islands in an emerald sea; he savoured the perfume of nutmeg trees and imagined the taste of fresh coconut cut from the palm trees he'd heard about. Sailors' tales. Pashali stories.

And the story he'd never heard: of birds that must be impossibly beautiful.

His daydream didn't last long. Inside a taproom five minutes later, the conversation was all about an outbreak of the Horned Death in Ustgrind. Over in one of the tradesmen's districts along the River Ust . . .

Saker listened with a sinking heart.

Right then, all he wanted to do was go home. The trouble was, he had no idea of where home was, except that it wasn't some remote isle in the Summer Seas.

38

The Falcon and the Mouse

Saker lounged at the edge of the square outside the only gate to Ustgrind Castle. Makeshift stalls of the morning market cluttered the space in front of the looming grimness of the castle walls. Everything looked oddly wrong.

Colour, he thought. *There's no colour*. This was a society subscribing to the belief that a love of colour was intrinsically sacrilegious, a doctrine doubly absurd when it was obvious that so much of Va's creation was multicoloured. Poor Mathilda, with her love of pretty clothes and baubles and music, inside that ugly pile of stone . . . He tried to dredge up a spark of lingering anger towards her, and found only pity and guilt. The love was gone, if ever it had been real, and even the scars were fading. He shrugged and tossed the memory away. He was here to observe, to find some way to enter the castle without being caught, not to dwell on the past.

The Castle Watch kept the area immediately in front of the gate clear. They were easily identifiable by their pikes and their black tunics trimmed in dull red, and no one entered the outer bailey without their scrutiny. Their comrades patrolling the battlements were called the Castle Wardens. They wore a different uniform and some carried an arquebus in place of the pike.

Ardhi and I might as well be a couple of suicidal dewberries planning to be eaten alive, he thought miserably. *Fool-born idea to break into a royal castle. It looks as if we have to go over the wall in the dead of night . . . But then what? Wander around like a pair of purblind moles looking for worms?*

He scanned the crowd one more time, preparing to leave, when something made him hesitate. A nondescript woman, poorly dressed and elderly, weaving in and out of the crowd. She was hunched, bent over a walking stick, although several times she moved surprisingly fast through the crowd. Something about her momentarily puzzled him. He could *feel* her.

Witchery. She had a witchery.

She was not buying or selling anything, so her movements appeared purposeless. Every now and then she faded into the crowd like mist dissipating into the air.

Interested, he approached her more closely, only to see a much younger woman than her disguise suggested. No, not a disguise, a glamour. She was dark-haired, with long dark lashes framing deep blue eyes. He'd seen her before, twice. On board Juster's ship, and along the road to the Chervil shrine. Not the glamoured Celandine mouse, but the real woman, Sorrel Redwing. He watched as she sidled up unnoticed behind a wealthy merchant bargaining with a stallholder over some quills and ink. Taken by surprise, Saker could only gape as she deftly cut a gold button from the merchant's sleeve with a small-bladed knife. Both knife and button then disappeared into her clothing, her action blurred by her old-woman glamour.

Va's teeth, she's using her glamour to steal!

As he dithered, wondering what to do, she turned her attention to a burgher's wife, evidently tempted by a bulging pocket-purse hanging from her waist. He gaped, shocked, as her hand opened the drawstring.

He'd heard many tales of how witcheries vanished if someone tried to misuse them. Never had he heard of the successful use of a witchery to perpetrate a crime, and yet here he was, watching it happen.

Snapped out of his shocked immobility, he pushed his way through the crowd to her side. Seizing her by the elbow, he jerked her away from the burgher's wife, bending to mutter into her ear, "I know what you're doing. Stop it this instant or I'll call the guard."

Unaware until then that anyone had penetrated her glamour, she yelped, startled, wrenching her arm free even as she turned to look at him. Her walking stick fell to the ground unheeded. Her eyes widened in dawning recognition and disbelief. In her alarm, her glamour wavered.

He picked up the stick and hustled her away to the edge of the crowd, where they could have a more private conversation. By the time he had found a quiet spot, she had regained her composure.

"Hang me for a hedge-born flirt," she said. "If it isn't Saker Rampion."

"How in all Va's cherished world did Celandine Marten become a cutpurse in a street market? I thought you'd be living the pampered life in royal apartments!"

"Sorrel. Sorrel Redwing. No glamour, no Celandine, just me. Sorrel."

"Yes, I know. I'm an idiot. With a canker for a brain. And I owe you twenty thousand grovelling apologies for my idiocy about what was the glamour." He stared at her, trying to sort out the best way to handle her presence, and all he knew about her.

Sorrel Redwing murdered her husband.

She smiled faintly. "Ah, so you made some enquiries about me, then. I'm flattered you cared enough to bother."

He gritted his teeth. *Damn her for a harpy, she always managed to rile him.* "You murdered your husband."

"Yes, and you went to bed with a princess. We are a fine pair, aren't we? Although I had thought you might have given up hanging around Mathilda like a tomcat on the prowl."

He flushed, half in annoyance that she should think Mathilda was the reason he was in Ustgrind, half in embarrassment. Around them the disinterested crowd flowed, and life went on; he heard and saw none of it. Va rot it, he had no idea what to say.

When the silence threatened to become ridiculous she said, "If you want me to take a message to the Princess, I won't do it. I see no point in furthering your, er, idiocy."

"You – you . . ." He waved a hand ineffectually at the castle. "What the sweet acorns are you doing *stealing* in the street? Did the Regala throw you out? How can you use a guardian-granted witchery to steal? A common cutpurse! Shame on you!"

"There are no depths to which I will not sink," she agreed complacently. "Depraved, I am. But *never* common, surely."

His mind seethed with questions, but none of those were foremost in his thoughts now. Instead, he was thinking that this meeting was all too much of a coincidence. Pickles 'n' hay, was the damned Chenderawasi magic intervening to make things happen again? He needed to get into the palace, and lo and behold, here was someone who might be able to help. The Pontifect would say it was Va's work and he should have more faith. But he'd seen too much to believe in that kind of simplicity any more.

He took a painful breath. For all the control he had over his own life, he might as well have been an oarless rowing boat in a rip tide. Va, Chenderawasi, the Way of the Oak, A'Va – or just bizarre coincidence . . . When someone gifted with a witchery could use the gift to commit a crime, he no longer knew which way was forward, and which the path to the oblivion of hell.

He was still reeling from the implications of his thoughts when she said with a deadly seriousness, "We need to talk."

Unable to find the right words to say, he nodded.

"But not here," she added. "Somewhere we can be private."

"I know just the place. An abandoned shrine, not far from here." He offered her his arm and she slipped her fingers into the crook of his elbow. Her touch was firm, but her body maintained its distance as he guided her out of the square towards the river path. He was glad of that; she was far too alluring for him to be oblivious to the curves of her figure, or the shine of the curls that had escaped her coif. Mostly, though, it was her eyes that haunted him. So dark a blue, so intelligent, so scathing in their mockery of him.

She killed her husband.

And then, as if he was arguing with himself: *She must have had a reason.*

Ustgrind had no city wall, and he headed straight through the back streets towards the river upstream of the castle. She walked at his side, serenely composed now, all her glamour vanished. No one would ever call her pretty, yet he found her strong features had an attractive beauty all their own.

"Will you hear my apology?" he asked.

"Which one?"

Rot her, she didn't make anything easy. He ploughed on. "I accused you of using a glamour to cover your Celandine appearance in order to entice my interest. That was uncouth, incorrect and clay-brained."

"It was."

"I apologise. When I saw you near the Chervil Moors shrine, I ought to have realised, but I was not . . . not myself right then. I was not thinking clearly."

"When naked and blue with cold, doubtless it is hard to be rational."

He was silenced, thrown. She was laughing at him? Angry? He couldn't tell. He was off-kilter, trying to grasp the reality that the shadowy Celandine was no more than play-acting. She had never been real. This Sorrel Redwing, the woman he'd first met at the windswept moorland shrine, was the real person, and he didn't understand her. She didn't make *sense.* One thing he did know, she was no mouse, hiding in the corners because she was frightened. She was bold enough to disguise herself as a man and ride from Throssel to Chervil alone. Bold enough to steal on streets where the penalty was death.

Blister it, she was bold enough to have killed her husband. You need to be careful, Saker.

Lowmian shrines were always centred around water, not oak trees, but this one had the sad appearance of a place scarred by drought and neglect. The water that fed it and the shrine-keeper had died together, and now the charm and witchery of the shrine itself were fading.

Sorrel sat on a stone-carved seat and spread her skirts. He wondered if she was making certain he would not try to share her seat. He stood instead, although there was another seat opposite hers.

"Do you still serve the Princess?" he asked. "The Regala, I should say."

"Yes."

"Then why were you stealing?"

"I'm desperate for money, why else? No one has ever paid me coin for my service." His shock must have been apparent, because she added, "The Regal sent all Mathilda's ladies-in-waiting home. All her jewellery was taken from her. She has nothing more than a little pin money. Her access to the Ardronese Ambassador is limited. Her new Lowmian ladies spy for Vilmar and his courtier favourites. She couldn't give me anything to sell without someone calling attention to it being missing, so I must seek money where I can."

"That – that is inconceivable. To treat an Ardronese princess so?"

"Oh? And what about treating a servant so?"

He had no reply to that.

"To be fair to the Lowmians," she said, "if she asks for anything they consider reasonable, it is given to her without question. Nor do I believe her treatment is any different to that meted out to other regalas in the past. It's just the Lowmian way. What need has a regala for money when she has only to ask for what she wants? What need does someone as lowly as I have for coin?"

"Can she not seek an allowance from King Edwayn?"

"That would be insulting to the Regal, wouldn't it? All her letters are read by others, you know." She sighed. "Witan, the court here is not like the palace in Throssel. She is allowed no visitor except those chosen for her, and they would never dream of speaking to her without her ladies being present to overhear all that is said. Even her clerics are the Regal's choice. That is what is *normal.* I can come and go because I use the glamour, but I have no money and no access to anything I can legitimately sell."

"You should have lost your witchery after misusing it."

She shrugged. "If Va wanted it so, doubtless I would now be without. I saw no way out other than theft. My decision was to leave it up to Va. Perhaps your arrival is the answer." She looked him up and down. "Do you feel like the answer to a maiden's prayer?"

She *was* making fun of him. He was about to give a scathing reply about her being no maiden, but bit back the words. *By oak and acorn, how was it she could goad him so easily into losing his calm*? "Why do you need money?" he asked, as politely as he could. "Are you planning to abandon the Regala?"

"Ah, you always think the worst of me, don't you? I can trust you to do that." She looked away, her expression one of irritation. "I don't much like Mathilda, it's true. She blackmailed me to stay with her in the first place, because she wanted the use of my glamour skills. I stayed because I didn't know where else to go and I had no resources, no friends. Sorrel Redwing will always be wanted for a murder in Ardrone. My husband's brother is never likely to give up the hunt for me; he's not that kind of man. In the end I followed the Princess to Lowmeer partly because I pitied her, and because I'd made her a promise in exchange for—" She stopped. "Never mind about that. Yes, I am planning to leave her, but not for reasons you could ever imagine."

"You have no idea what I'm imagining."

"No? You always jump to the worst possible conclusion about my motives. Oddly enough, it's surprisingly difficult to walk away from someone who is in such a miserable position. However, I do intend to do so. Soon, and with her blessing. There is a baby to consider, you see. And for a child, I will do much. Which might surprise you, I suppose, but it's true, nonetheless."

"What child?"

"Mathilda's, of course. Unlike you, she trusted the guardian of the shrine who granted me my glamour, and now she's trusting me with her child. She has always trusted me, and she's always known I murdered my husband."

"Have you no shame about that?" *Trust Sorrel with her child? Trust her to do what?*

"Not really. He wasn't a pleasant man and he was about to kill me. As a witan, I'm sure you've heard similar stories. Have you no shame about sleeping with someone you were supposed to spiritually mentor?"

He felt his face turn scarlet.

"Oh, pah," she said. "We have to stop our dancing around one another, each trying to stamp on the other's feet. Let's put aside our antipathies and discuss the real problem here."

"Which is?"

"What are we going to do about the fact that Mathilda is going to have twins, and Lowmeer is going to slaughter them at birth?"

His knees were suddenly incapable of holding him upright. Slowly he lowered himself on to the stone seat opposite her, so confounded he could scarcely think.

"Is this some sort of cruel joke?" he asked at last.

"Of course, you would think that. You appear to imagine my whole life is devoted to telling you lies. I gather that you know the truth about one thing: what the Lowmians do to twins at birth."

"Yes," he whispered. *Oh no. Va could not be that cruel . . .* "I know all too well."

"Then listen carefully. Mathilda's Ardronese maid, Aureen, assisted her mother, who was the Throssel Palace midwife. Aureen told us that Mathilda is going to have twins, any time within this coming moon. We can't be sure when, because twins often come early. The Regal has no inkling she is having a double birth, of course, but he has made it quite clear there are never exceptions to the Lowmian policy on the matter. Her babies will die – both of them – if anyone from the court knows there are two."

He stared at her, appalled, trying to take it all in. "Are you – are you *certain* she will have twins?"

The look she gave him was exasperated. "There is much to be uncertain about. But not that. I have heard two heartbeats, and so has Aureen. We are making plans for me to take the firstborn one, no matter whether girl or boy, and escape from the castle before anyone knows it is born."

His horror at the possibilities spilled over into his words. Kidnapping? Stealing a royal child, possibly the heir to the Basalt Throne? The implications were so horrendous, so fraught with danger, he couldn't even think straight. "But – but what if the second one dies? Or if the first is a boy and the second a girl?"

"Under Lowmian law, a royal child's birth must be observed by at least three court officials. Obviously we can only let them observe the second birth."

While he absorbed the implications, she continued, "Mathilda and I agree that I must take the baby to the Pontifect. Only Va-Faith can handle the complications of this. But I'll need money. I'll need to hire a wet nurse. I'll need two berths on the flat-boat to Vavala. Saker Rampion, I don't care what you think of me, and I'm sure your affection for the Princess is not what it used to be, but this is a baby born of an Ardronese princess. Help us."

"Surely Mathilda must be returned to Ardrone, where she belongs! Where she will be loved and her twins will live."

She gave him a pitying look. "For a start, she is already huge with child, and in no condition to travel. Secondly, do you really think the Regal would permit that?"

His mouth went dry. Juster had intimated that Vilmar wasn't past murdering an unwanted wife. *Dear Va.*

"Thirdly," she continued, implacable, "King Edwayn sold her to Lowmeer in exchange for something he coveted. *He doesn't care about her*. He would care, though, deeply, if Regal Vilmar reneged on their treaty."

She meant the words to cut him, and they did. Was she right? Probably. The ramifications were beyond measure. "Forgive me if I sound inane. This is a – a shock." *And you've no idea how much of a shock. A devil-kin! And there is no way we can know which one of the twins it will be. Va above, what if a devil-kin ultimately sets his backside on the Basalt Throne?*

He took a deep breath as he made a decision. "Well, for a start, you can forget about stealing for a living." He dug into his hidden pocket and pulled out one of Juster's rubies. "This is a good-quality gem. I can change it for coins, sufficient for all your needs. You must not jeopardise yourself by stealing. If you are caught, you will hang . . . and the twins will die."

Which might be better for the fate of the world.

No, don't think like that, never think like that.

She gave a faint smile he could not interpret. "I will accept whatever you give with thanks – and relief that you believe me for a change."

"The moment I discovered that Va granted you a glamour witchery, I ought to have trusted you completely. Even today, I was far too quick to blame."

Her smile was faint. "A witan who doesn't trust Va enough?"

"A witan no longer. Can you come back here tomorrow, at the same time?"

"It's not usually a problem for me to sneak out and about. Can *you* take me and the child to Vavala?"

He didn't know what to say. He couldn't even begin to explain the compulsion he was under. "No," he said after a long pause. "I can't."

Her gaze was steady, but he read contempt there.

"I'll have the money for you from selling the ruby tomorrow. And some instructions on where to go and what to do to keep the child safe."

She nodded. "I'll meet you here at the same time. If something goes wrong, then I'll try again the next day, and the next." She stood up, looking down at him. "There's something else I haven't told you. The reason twins are killed in Lowmeer."

He looked at her in amazement. "How would you learn that?"

"The Regal told Mathilda," she said, and repeated all she had overheard.

He listened, sinking deep into a frozen horror as the story unfolded. When she finished, he could think of nothing to say.

She said flatly, "You knew this already."

"No. Well, only part of it. I didn't know it was the Vollendorn line that contrived this horror and foisted it on their own populace. Va rot it – if the Regal ever gets an inkling that you know this, you'll lose your head."

"That's the least of your concerns. Witan, if this is all true, then one of Mathilda's twins will be a devil-kin. He might become the Regal. Or he might be the one I save."

"Yes. And stop calling me witan. I'm not a cleric any more."

"So, are we doing the right thing?"

"I don't know. All I know is that I cannot kill babies, and I can't allow Lady Mathilda's child to be killed. You're right. The Pontifect is the person to deal with this. If anyone can work out how to solve it, she can. I'll write you a letter to take with you to give to her. And if it's any comfort, a devil-kin won't manifest their evil until he or she is at least half-grown."

She nodded, smoothing down her skirts. "The Regal said that too. Thank you, Saker. For offering to help."

Rising to face her, he said, "There – there is one other thing I'd like to ask you."

"Go ahead. Just try not to insult me."

She gave the ghost of a smile as she said the words, and he tried to reciprocate but knew his attempt was wan. "Have you heard about a gift given by the merchant Uthen Kesleer to Regal Vilmar? Three golden feathers from the Va-forsaken Hemisphere."

Her eyes widened in surprise. "Yes. In fact I've seen them. They are set into a fan."

"Where does the Regal keep them?"

"Near his bed. Inside a carved chest. Why do you want to know?"

"It doesn't matter. Come, let me walk you back to the city."

She didn't move to take his arm when he offered it to her. "Why do I get the impression that we are not really talking about ordinary feathers?"

"We aren't. They come from an island in the Summer Seas, I believe."

"But what can be special about *feathers*?"

He didn't answer.

She tilted her head to one side and regarded him thoughtfully. "I think you ought to tell me what you have so far avoided doing, and explain why you are in Ustgrind."

"What is there to explain? I had to leave Ardrone, as you know."

"There's something you're not saying. If you have no business here, then why not accompany me to Vavala? It would . . . be easier for me."

Oh, Va, if only I could. If only. But Ardhi would never let him go to Vavala for fear the fleet might sail without him. What a pilgarlic Sorrel must think him, turning his back on her and the baby like this.

Once again he could think of nothing to say.

"I would have thought you'd care more about the fate of Mathilda's children."

"There's nothing I'd rather do than escort you and the child, believe me. It's just that I'm not sure I'll be free to do so. I can't explain more than that. I'm sorry. I'll give you the name of someone who will help you, a woman cleric."

"You'd trust her?"

"Oh yes. Rescuing twins has been her life's work. Her name is Witan Shanny Ide, and she works at the Seminary of Advanced Studies. It's on the west side of Ustgrind, on the outskirts. I'll ask her to find a wet nurse who'll go with you to Vavala. I won't tell her exactly who you are, or whose baby you have."

Once again he offered her his arm, and this time she took it.

"You have really surprised me," she said. "I'd have thought nothing would have stopped you from saving Mathilda's child."

Oh, sweet Va. There was no mistaking her meaning, and his heart tightened painfully in his chest. "Celandine . . ."

"Sorrel."

"Sorrel. Are you trying to tell me this child – these children – could be *mine*?"

"I'd have thought you could have answered that better than I."

He floundered on, embarrassed, blushing, humiliated. "Lady Mathilda told me there'd be no problem and not to worry about it. I know – I knew court women have many ways to prevent unwanted children. She was not taken by surprise, you know."

"Oh, believe me, I was aware of that."

"I am sorry to embarrass you."

"Embarrassed?" Her voice was filled with laughter. "I thought it was you who was embarrassed. However, to answer your question, I don't know. Mathilda says she had her moon's bleed after her encounter with you, but I have my reservations about her honesty. Her indiscretion with you was more than three weeks prior to her wedding. If she gives birth soon, the baby could well be yours, or it could be an early delivery of twins. I don't see that there is any point in thinking about it. If you're worried about *my* discretion, there's no need."

Ashamed, growing redder and redder by the minute, he did not look at her, and they walked on in silence.

No need to worry? Oh, but he did. The possibility was slim, but it was there: he might have fathered a devil-kin.

Only Mathilda knew the truth. He never would.

39

The Reluctant Alliance

"So, you met a friend who works in the castle," Ardhi said, "and yet you didn't ask her how we can get in and out safely?" He was sitting cross-legged on Saker's bed, using Saker's dagger to whittle a piece of driftwood.

"She's hardly a friend." Saker paced, then sat on the bare boards of the floor. It was none too clean, but the room had no chair. He counted himself lucky it contained a bed.

"Oh, so you don't trust her. What did you do to the lady that she would be so ungallant as to betray us?" Ardhi asked, interested.

Va, how he *hated* the way Ardhi reworded things, twisted them to mean something else. Aloud, he said, "I trust her. I just don't want to endanger her." *Or Mathilda.*

"And you didn't think that perhaps meeting her was *sakti* Chenderawasi making itself felt again?" Ardhi looked up from his whittling. "Coincidences do happen, but we would be foolish to assume this is one of them." He fixed Saker with a steady gaze and said, "Tell me the whole story."

He opened his mouth to say that he would do no such thing, and then gagged. It hadn't been a request, but an order. Ardhi watched dispassionately as he struggled against the compulsion. In the end, he managed to say between gritted teeth, "Ardhi, really, there are some things it's wiser for you not to know. Don't ask me to do this. If you force me, I will never forgive you. Never."

The silence lengthened as Saker fought, biting through his lip until it bled, the blood trickling down his chin. He thought, anguished, *Can't I even keep my secrets?* He focused on the pain, biting deeper, concentrating. All thought directed away from Sorrel, away from Mathilda . . . into the stab of fire deep in his lip. He began to shudder with the effort.

And just when he knew he had to spill the words he didn't want to say, Ardhi capitulated. "Ah. You are right, and I am wrong. Just because one has the power does not mean one should use it. Not the whole story, then. Tell me what you will, and no more. It will go no further than this room."

He breathed again, his shoulders slumping, and wiped away the blood. "The woman, her name is Sorrel, is a servant to the Regala. I met her in Ardrone. I don't want to involve her, because it might mean bringing her, or the Regala, into danger."

"But you would trust her with your life?"

After the barest hesitation, he nodded.

Ardhi leaned towards him, meeting Saker's gaze with his own burning intensity, his normal good humour banished. "I'm sad you're caught in the middle of this and I know how unpleasant it is to be forced to do something by Chenderawasi magic. I want a partner, not a slave. I want to talk to this Sorrel woman tomorrow. I'm going to ask her how best we can get to the Regal's chamber. If we don't have that information, *we* may die. If I have to impose the coercion on you to help my cause, I will."

"I don't like being threatened."

"And I don't like bludgeoning you with magic. I want you on my side. I believe it's your side, too."

"Won't the kris *sakti* make sure we succeed anyway?" His sarcasm was deliberate. "We can just rely on it to manipulate our success!"

"The kris has limitations, as well you know. If it were all-powerful, I would have been able to steal the plumes the day we met." Ardhi threw up his hands, palms outwards, gesturing his own lack of understanding. "Besides, there are things that work against it here, surely you know that. There's evil in Lowmeer. Don't you feel the darkness? Can't you smell it creeping along the streets, lingering in dark corners? You're a witan; surely you're aware of bad magic used by evil men. What do you call bad magic in your tongue?"

"Sorcery. But the only sorcerers I've ever heard about were in myths. Legends. Stories. Not real."

"People have died in this city of the horror you call the Horned Death. Sorcery."

"No. That's the work of A'Va," he said. "A'Va is the antithesis of Va. Some call him A'Va the Devil."

"A sort of back-to-front god?" Ardhi shook his head, disbelieving. "So funny. Never mind. When do I meet this friend of yours?"

Sorrel stood among the trees and watched as Saker came up the hill path to the remains of the shrine. He moved the way she remembered, with cat-like litheness. She'd admired it back in Throssel Palace, and it stirred her now. Useless, though. A man who'd hankered after a woman like Mathilda would never be attracted to Sorrel Redwing.

With a cold determination, she slowed the quickening of her breath and shifted her gaze to his companion. A brown man, stocky, black-haired. He wore the normal Lowmian pantaloons, but without stockings or shoes. His calves were all muscle and sinew, his bare feet trod the rough path with confidence. Fascinated, she studied him. His skin had a deep tan that no amount of warm sun had caused. She'd never met anyone from the Va-forsaken Hemisphere before, but she knew that must have been his origin.

When she glanced back at Saker, it was to notice that he did not look well. There was tension in his frown, and unhappiness in his eyes. Her heart slipped a little in her chest, leaving a sick feeling behind. *Stupid ninnyhead, why should you care, after all he's said and done?* But she did, still, a little. A lot. It wasn't so easy to walk away from a man you'd once admired. *Time, it'll take time,* she told herself. *And every time he hurts you, you'll take another step on the road to recovery*. She smiled wryly, liking the idea of her attraction being some sort of disease that he was curing. One thing she knew for certain, she didn't want to go back there, to that vulnerability. He wasn't worth it.

She stood a little straighter, squared her shoulders. As the two men approached still closer, she raised her chin higher. And the dark man smiled at her.

A skitter of fear ran up her spine. He had some sort of witchery, and he was acknowledging that connection to her. She clasped her hands behind her back in an attempt to steady herself.

"I'm sorry to surprise you with someone else," Saker said without preamble as they walked up to her. "This is Ardhi. He's a lascar from an island beyond Pashalin."

The lascar bowed awkwardly over her hand. "Mistress."

"He wants to talk to you," Saker said. "But first, I have the money for you, and the letter." He took her by the arm and led her away where Ardhi couldn't hear. "I didn't name you in the letter; I thought it safer just to say 'the bearer'. It will open doors for you in Vavala. I've also told Witan Shanny to expect you. She'll have a wet nurse arranged."

Saker," she whispered, gesturing unobtrusively back at the lascar, "was this wise?"

"He knows nothing about the baby, don't worry. He needs your help on another matter. We both do."

Ardhi had been looking around the shrine while they talked. "This holy place, yes?" he asked. His accent was an odd mix of Lowmian and something else. "Witchery strong, like tide."

"Yes, a shrine," Saker replied. "Its keeper died."

She said, "Saker tells me you want to speak to me, Master Ardhi. How can I help you?"

His eyes twinkled at her, the corner of his lips twitching up, his mouth parting to show the gleam of his white teeth.

She couldn't help smiling back. *My,* she thought, *he's a very attractive man.*

"Forgive, Ardhi speak your tongue not so good."

"Better, I imagine, than I speak yours."

He laughed, but the laughter soon died. "I ask important thing. We want three feathers. Feathers belong to my people. With witchery, big witchery. Wrong person use witchery, very bad for everyone. Bad for Lowmian people, for my people."

This was about the *feathers*? "What could I possibly do?"

"We want steal these feathers," he said simply.

She sank down on to the stone seat, aghast. "I'm not going to do that!" she cried.

"No, no," he said in alarm. "*We* steal. Saker and me. But we not know house. Castle."

"You're mad! You can't rob the Regal! You'd be caught long before you even *got* to the Keep, let alone entered it. You'd have to cross both the outer and inner bailey to get to the main doors – with every gate guarded."

"My thoughts exactly," Saker said drily.

"Very important," Ardhi said. "Must do, or many people die in my land. Here too. Lady Sorrel help."

Appalled, she gaped at Saker.

He nodded, acknowledging the truth of Ardhi's words. "We need a plan of the Regal's solar, with all the entries and exits and where they lead."

"But without a glamour witchery, you'll never get into the Keep in the first place. It's not possible. It really isn't."

"Leave that up to us," Saker said. "Just tell us what entries there are to Regal Vilmar's solar."

She wanted to protest, but his expression was implacable. Reluctantly, she capitulated. "There's a narrow spiral staircase between the Regal's bedroom and Lady Mathilda's, used only by her and the Regal's servant. Her apartments are on the floor above his, but the door at his end is always locked from his side."

"We're not going to involve either you or Regala Mathilda," Saker said firmly. "What other ways in are there?"

"The main staircase, and the servants' staircase. Both are accessed via doors at either end of a gallery passage, each door guarded by pikemen who belong to the Castle Wardens. The men who wear that silly uniform with the peculiar-shaped hats."

"So, we'd have to pass those wardens to get either in or out."

"Yes. They may look silly, but I see them training in the bailey every day. Those pikes are not ornamental. And those who patrol the walls above have arquebuses."

"I have a sheet of parchment here. Can you give us a plan that will help us?" He spread the parchment out on the stone seat beside her, and handed her a graphite stick wrapped in twine.

She took it from him with a sigh and began to sketch, describing what she was drawing to them both. When she'd finished, she looked at Saker, wondering if he would notice the fear for him in her eyes. "I still don't see how you can get away with this. Even if you got in, there'll always be someone in the Regal's apartments, no matter what time of the day."

"When's the *best* time?"

She thought about that. "I suppose a night when the Regal entertains the city's notables. The Regal, the courtiers and most of the servants and wardens would be busy on the ground floor, probably until cock-crow." She straightened up to meet Saker's gaze. "Do you have to do this?"

He blinked, as if surprised she had bothered to ask. "Yes," he said. "I do." He folded her sketch and slipped it inside his tunic. "Thank you for your help, and tell – tell the Lady Mathilda . . ." He paused. "I hope and pray it will go well for her."

"Saker . . ."

"Yes?"

She wanted to scream at him, tell him not to be a fool. Risk his life for a feather fan? Then she remembered all that Mathilda had said about those feathers, and about Kesleer and Vilmar. "Never mind," she said.

"She's a brave lady," Ardhi said in Pashalin as they parted from Sorrel outside the castle gates. "She fears for you."

Saker looked at him in undisguised astonishment. "You have maggot-pie brains! She can't stand me. With good reason, I might add."

"Ah, there is none so blind as a man who has made up his mind. Let us talk of our plans. I think I need to know more about your witchery."

"I think I need a drink and something to eat. There's a good pothouse over there."

Ardhi brightened. "Cheese and a newly baked loaf. We don't have either of those things back in Pulauan Chenderawasi. So tasty!"

"No *bread*?"

He shook his head as they entered the pothouse. "And no ale, either. We drink rice wine, or cassava wine. Not so good."

Saker had no idea what cassava was, and had never seen rice, but he didn't pursue the topic. They ordered bread, cheese and ale, and when it arrived, Ardhi brought up the subject of witchery again. "Is it something that'll help us inside the castle?" he asked.

"Hardly." Should he explain? If he didn't, Ardhi might force him to do so, and he hated the thought of that more.

"We need to work together," Ardhi reminded him.

He sighed. "I seem to have some weird connection to birds. I know what they are thinking, sort of . . ." He stopped. Ardhi was staring at him as if he had performed a miracle. "What's the matter with you?"

"Nothing. It's just that everything begins to make sense. Why you, I mean, why you and not some other witchery-gifted person. Go on. What about your birds?"

"I didn't have my witchery when your reeky-damn dagger came sailing across the warehouse at me." He paused. "Wait – did you just confirm what I've been wondering: that your kris had something to do with the choice of this particular giddy-brained witchery of mine?"

Ardhi stared into his tankard, opened his mouth to say something, and closed it again. He shrugged.

Saker took a deep breath. "Others are gifted *sensible* witcheries. Healing. Enhanced talents and perceptions that are *helpful.* Skill with farm animals or crops or fishing. Something of *use.* And what do *I* get? An understanding of empty-headed bird twitter! People don't talk about bird-brains for nothing, you know!"

"Perhaps if you tell me what you can do with your birds . . ."

"They're not *my* birds. They're *any* birds. I sort of know what they're thinking. Though they don't think much at all, really. It's more – knowing how they feel. Angry, thirsty, scared, wanting to shit or fight or just plain hankering after the drab-feathered birdie in the next tree!"

"Is that all?"

He took a calming breath. "Well, they seem to do things that I want them to do. Sometimes. I don't know! It's certainly nothing that will help us enter the Regal's apartments undetected. No bird is going to tell me that. And if your – your foot-licking kris is to blame for the fact that I have this particular witchery . . ."

"Well, I don't know if that's exactly true," Ardhi said in a rush, "but I think we might be able to use such a witchery. Just as we can use mine. And the power of my kris, too. Remember those gold pieces in the blade?"

"Hmm. You said they are pieces of Chenderawasi feathers."

"It's true. I was there when the kris was made, remember. It will lead you to where the plumes are hidden, if you ask it."

Saker's mouth went dry. Va, how he hated things that he didn't understand. Things he couldn't control.

Besides, the deeper he became enmeshed in witchery, the closer he felt to the Ways of the Oak and the Flow, and the more remote Va seemed to be.

40

The Breaking Storm

A gusting storm wind sweeping up the estuary slanted rain against the stonework of the outer castle wall. The same wind drove icy needles into Saker's face. Dark, wet, cold. The stones beneath his feet slippery with slime. No moonlight penetrating the cloud cover.

Fitting weather for dicing with death.

The Regal was entertaining an ambassador from one of the Principalities, and a banquet was in full swing in the Great Hall. They'd waited twelve days for such a night, but now, as Saker watched Ardhi begin the climb up the wall on the windward side of the Keep in a blustery gale, he wondered if they'd made a disastrous mistake. The lascar had one end of a knotted rope tied around his waist as he made his way upwards. Impossible, surely. No one could climb a sheer wall in this weather . . .

Saker, his feet firmly planted on a narrow ledge of rock at the foot of the wall, paid out the rope through his gloved hands as Ardhi climbed. His foothold at the edge of the cliff was the length of his boot, and slick. Far below him, the river plunged through the rocky gorge in a roar of storm water. He worked hard at not looking down, at not thinking what would happen if Ardhi fell.

The wind tugged at his cloak, whipping the hood away from his head. The garment billowed, slapping him with sodden folds. Cold water trickled down his neck. The eerie wail of the wind squalled around the walls, as unsettling as Ardhi's climbing witchery.

"Look at how rough this is!" Ardhi had said earlier, running his hand over the stonework. "Salt winds have eaten it away and etched holes into the cracks between the stones. Those are my steps." And he'd started to climb with breathtaking assurance. Five or six paces up, he even looked down at Saker and waved.

Saker watched yet, almost unable to breathe. He couldn't see how it was possible. Battered by rain and wind, poorly clad, Ardhi was inching his way upwards using nothing but his fingers and bare toes.

If the lascar died, he – Saker – would be free. Instead of being glad, he feared. Anxiety gnawed at his stomach. He was haunted by the thought of Ardhi's quest, so important that a youth had made this lonely journey, friendless, to another land he could scarcely have been able to comprehend, let alone imagine.

The rope moved through his fingers, knot after knot. *He's a sailor*, he thought. *They do this all the time in the cold of storms on a rolling ship*. And he'd heard that some of them fell to their deaths, too. *Juster losing his grip on the rope . . .* No, he mustn't think of that. He must remember the witchery Ardhi possessed. He must remember there was a purpose to all this.

But was it a *worthy* purpose, an honourable cause?

You trust the Way of the Oak, you trust the Way of the Flow, but what about the way of a Chenderawasi dagger? What if the sorcery of the latter was working to destroy the witchery of the former?

The people of the Chenderawasi Archipelago don't worship Va. Ardhi feared the intrusion of the Va-cherished into his land. Saker was so far out of his depth, he felt himself to be drowning. Right then, there was nothing he would have liked more than to discuss this with the Pontifect.

Think of something else.

He lost sight of Ardhi when he was about halfway up. The night was too dark and the rain blinded him. He squinted against water-laden wind and waited while the minutes dragged by. A sudden jag of lightning briefly illuminated a black figure reaching a hand up towards the crenellations of the battlements, then left him dazzled and unable to see anything.

"Don't forget your birds," had been Ardhi's last words to him. He thought of gulls, the large ones with black wings and flanged yellow beaks. Argumentative, quarrelsome, with wingspans as wide as his outstretched arms, they were the seabirds the fishermen called "buccaneers of the air" because they raided their fishing nets.

He conjured up the thought of them, and bade them come. And they did. One after another, four of them all told. Huge things, swooping out of the darkness, sweeping over his head so close that even in the wind he could feel the downbeat of their wings moving the air. They cried out their welcome, and he sensed their acquiescence to his leadership. He pictured them standing on the battlements, and they wheeled away, climbing upwards.

Just then the rope jiggled, before moving several paces to the right. A moment later there were three tugs, the signal that Ardhi had reached the top safely and the rope was now tied securely to the battlements. Quickly he bundled up his cloak into his pack. His sword and the length of empty bambu Ardhi had given him already poked out of the top. He slung the pack on to his back and began to climb.

His hands moved upwards knot by knot, his knees and feet gripped the rope threaded between. The hemp was slippery with rain. *Blistering rattle-brained idiocy.* It'd be a Va-blessed miracle if he made it to the top. He'd tied a loop around his waist, hoping that if he slipped, at least he wouldn't fall all the way to the raging water and the black rocks . . .

He began to recite a litany to himself: *I will not let go. I will not let go. No matter what, I will not let go.* At first the words were silent, then spoken under his breath, then shouted into the air where the sound was snatched away into the wailing wind.

Just when he knew he could hold on no longer, words filled with laughter were spoken into his ear, "You can shut up now," and Ardhi was hauling him up and over the battlements.

For a moment he lay there on the wooden walkway, eyes closed, shuddering. When he did look, it was so dark on the roof he could only make out Ardhi's silhouette, and would not have recognised him if he hadn't spoken.

"Not a bad climb for a landlubber," Ardhi said.

Saker raised himself into a sitting position to undo his pack and pull out his cloak. "Any guards around?"

"No. You were right about that – no one wants to stand in the rain on a cold night to look for mythical attackers. And a couple of thieves is just *so* unthinkable, right?"

Va-damn. The man was *enjoying* this. Saker nodded towards the dark shape of a hut built on the flattest part of the roof. A sliver of light escaped from a window opening. "That the guardhouse?"

"Yes. I took a peek. The wardens are huddled around the fire. Four of them."

They sheltered under the walkway and Ardhi held the cloak over Saker while he lit their lantern, using the kris as a steel for the flint. When the oil-soaked wick caught, he adjusted the shutters so that only a narrow beam of light escaped.

Saker said, "Huddle beneath the walkway. Even if someone leaves the guardhouse, they won't see you. If I'm not back before first light, you scuttle down that rope."

Ardhi nodded as he handed his kris over. "Don't forget your birds."

The seagulls were lined up along the crenellations of the battlements, stoically facing into the wind with their heads hunkered in. *By the oaks, the mewlers were huge.*

Ardhi placed a hand on his shoulder. "May the protection of the Chenderawasi go with you."

He hesitated, wondering how to answer that. What did he mean: the islands? The paradise birds? The magic? Finally he said, "You forced this on me, but if you spake the truth, then this is the honest thing to do." With that, he walked away.

With Sorrel's map fixed firmly in his mind, he located the doorway in the corner turret and pushed the heavy wooden door open. Inside were the stairs descending to the kitchens and opening on to every floor between. Fixing his gaze on the row of seagulls still huddling in the rain, he called soundlessly to them.

One by one they took off and flew through the doorway to land at his feet on the flagstones of the stair landing. Four flying weapons, over which he had tenuous control. They shook their feathers, scattering water, and began to preen. He didn't know how he was controlling them. All he did was imagine what he wanted them to do.

They are no more free than I am. Ardhi coerces me, and I coerce fobbing gulls. Bemused and unsettled, he shook his head. *I don't care what Ardhi says, I don't like this Chenderawasi magic.*

He left the door open and by the meagre candlelight he descended, past the doors to the first two floors, towards the landing of the third. If Sorrel had given him the correct directions, he had just bypassed the servants' quarters and the upper royal solar where Mathilda had her apartments. She wouldn't be there, of course; she'd be down in the Great Hall somewhere, sitting beside the Regal.

He had no wish to see her, and the thought took him by surprise.

A line of poetry echoed in his memory. *When passion passes, lo, even the embers darken.*

Behind him, the birds followed, unhappily fluttering from step to step. They hated the dark and narrow stairwell. He could feel them rebelling against his will. He calmed them with thoughts of food and safety and warm sunlight. On the third landing, he halted and stroked them one by one with a gentle finger until he was sure he had their trust.

This floor was where the Regal had his private rooms as well as the chambers of his office. Sorrel had told him that on the other side of the closed door there were usually two wardens, each armed with a pike. She'd thought it more likely there'd only be one on duty on a banquet night, because extra guards were needed down on the lower floors.

He arranged the seagulls. Three of them he sent to the stairs below the landing, blocking the way down. The last bird he placed prominently at the foot of the stairs going up. The bird looked back at him, cocking its head, its round yellow eye fixing him with a bad-tempered glare. Saker positioned himself so that he would be hidden by the door when it swung open, then extinguished his lantern. He was shivering, and told himself it was because he was soaking wet and cold, nothing to do with the chill of his fear.

He rapped smartly on the panelling with his sword hilt and, using his will rather than words, bade the seagull on the upper stairs flap and caw angrily.

As he expected, the door was abruptly flung open. Through the crack of the hinges, he saw only one young man, blocking the way with his pike. Light illuminated the landing and the gull.

"What the slumbering whoreson . . .?" the warden muttered, in a mixture of surprise and annoyance. Without thinking, he plunged through the doorway, swinging his pike at the only bird he noticed.

At the same time, Saker forced his will on the mewler, sending it blundering up the stairs and out into the night. The warden hesitated, still on the landing. If he turned, he would be bound to see Saker incompletely concealed behind the door.

Saker ordered the other three birds into the air and they obeyed. Screaming their anger, they flew straight at the young warden. Their cries echoed, bouncing off the walls like the night-howlers of Lowmian legends. The narrow stairwell was filled with raucous cries and beating wings. The horrified man made an attempt to swing his pike at the first bird, but in the confines of the stairwell he caught the wall on his backswing instead. One gull slashed at him with its beak and opened up a cut on his forehead. Terrified, the warden stumbled, dropped his pike and tumbled down the steps.

Saker had intended to overpower him, but it was unnecessary; the man had knocked himself out cold. Quickly he sent the gulls on their way, their job done for the night. He closed the door to the roof, and half closed the door to the gallery, praying that no one noticed the guard was missing from his post. He stripped off his own outer clothes and began to do the same for the young warden. The unconscious body was awkwardly uncooperative, but finally he was wearing the uniform of a Castle Warden. The ridiculous many-tasselled hat was too small and perched on top of his head, but other than that the clothes were a good fit.

The warden, he was glad to see, was a good colour, and breathing steadily. With some difficulty, he dressed him again, using his own discarded clothing. Then he wrapped him tightly in his still wet cloak. That, he thought, might delay the discovery that the man was not wearing his uniform.

Picking up the fallen pike, he stepped out of the stairwell into the gallery. He was in a long, broad passageway with rooms opening on either side. And walking towards him was another warden. At a guess, he was the guard posted at the main staircase entry at the far end of the gallery, come to see why his counterpart was missing. Without giving him time to think, Saker placed the axe head of his pike so that it shaded his face from the torch burning nearby and snapped authoritatively, "Get back to your post! Quickly now, before anyone sees you've left it."

The man stopped. "What's up, then?" he asked.

"The youngster had the trots is all, and asked to be relieved." He grinned.

The man guffawed, turned on his heel and marched quickly back to his post. Saker followed, soft-footed, trusting the fellow wouldn't glance behind. He counted off the doors on the left until he came to the one that led – if Sorrel's information was correct – to the Regal's private chambers.

Breathing a sigh of relief, he pressed down on the door handle and eased his way inside. And then felt the familiar rush of exhilaration that accompanied the need for stealth. His senses heightened, his heartbeat quickened, his alertness sharpened. *This*, this was the kind of danger he enjoyed. The unknown, the challenge. Even if Sorrel had the right door, she was unfamiliar with the layout of the Regal's rooms. He smiled as he closed the door behind him and looked around.

He was in some kind of reception chamber. None of the candles were lit, but a fire burned in the large fireplace at one end, with chairs grouped around it. Treading softly, he crossed to the exit on the other side. He stood for a moment, ear to the panelling of the closed door. All was silent. When he stepped through, he found himself in what might have been a dressing room; there were certainly enough chests and cupboards to have concealed ample clothing for a royal personage. Two doors led into other rooms. From one, he heard the murmur of voices.

"I tell you, I heard a noise," a woman said, the words springing into clarity as she raised her voice. "Go and have a look. It might be a rat or something." The reply was a soothing murmur, then a man's low laugh.

Saker drew the kris and laid it across his palm. He had no idea what he would do if it swung towards the occupied room, but he was in luck. It settled on his hand with the point firmly indicating the other door. He eased it open a crack and listened. All was quiet within. He pushed it wider and stuck his head inside. It was the Regal's bedchamber, dominated by an enormous four-poster bed with elaborate drapes and tasselled ties. An open fire burned in here too, with an intricate metal fireguard protecting the hearth from rolling logs.

And, Va be thanked, no one was around.

He glanced down at the dagger on his palm again. It pointed to a wooden chest, strewn with cushions, occupying the space beneath a window embrasure. From the size of the window and the fact that it was glazed, it must have looked out over the inner bailey. As he walked to the chest, the kris vibrated on his palm like a leaf trembling in the wind.

Placing the dagger on the floor, he squatted to remove the cushions and open the lid. It was locked, so he dug in his pocket for his lock picks. The locking mechanism was a simple one and he soon had the lid open. The kris spun like a beetle on its back. Lying on top of a silken cloth were the Chenderawasi plumes, made into a gold-handled fan.

With care, he extracted the fan and pulled the feather quills out of their metalled sheaths, then returned the handle to the chest, closed the lid and replaced the cushions. Something about the plumes suffused him with reverential awe, and he was glad he was wearing gloves. He didn't want to touch the shafts with his bare hands, or sully the gloriousness of the wisping curls of the feathers.

He threaded the three plumes into the bambu with care. Once he'd stoppered the open end, he straightened up and took a final look around to make sure everything was as it should be, only to find he'd left the dagger on the floor. Grinning as he imagined what Ardhi would have said if he'd left *that* behind, he bent to pick it up.

Just before his fingers reached the handle, the blade moved – and the door behind him opened. Saker dropped to the floor, ducking down to put the bed between himself and the opening door. He had the briefest glimpse of a chambermaid carrying a warming pan, looking over her shoulder as she spoke to someone in the next room. "I tell you," she said, "I heard such a screeching! There's summat leery going on here, and you'd better find out what, Master Torjen, 'fore the Regal—"

The kris arrowed upwards, spinning as it went, and thunked into the wall to one side of the fireplace. It vibrated in the wood, but any sound it made was drowned in the high-pitched squeal of the chambermaid. He winced. She must have turned back in time to see it spin across the room.

"Master Torj! Help! There's some devil beastie flying . . ." The woman's voice faded as she fled.

Clutching the bambu tightly, he leapt across the room to pluck the kris out of the wall. His heart was pounding as possibilities rushed through his head . . . Fight? Flee? In which direction? Were they just servants? How many? He'd heard at least one man's voice . . .

Then he realised the question he should have asked first. What was the kris trying to tell him? The door. The door to the staircase Sorrel had mentioned. The blade had stuck itself into the centre of a camouflaged egress panelled to match the wall on either side. As he extracted the blade, a hidden latch clicked slightly and the door cracked open. Without a second thought, he pulled it open all the way and stepped inside. A narrow stone staircase spiralled both up and down.

Mathilda's bedroom was above.

He could already hear the excited conversation going on in the next room, something about flying bats and whirring wings. He pulled the door shut behind him. Instantly, he was plunged into utter darkness, such a profound lack of light that he couldn't even be sure he hadn't gone suddenly blind.

41

Thieves in the Night

"Perhaps you'll feel better if you sit over here by the fire," Sorrel suggested.

Mathilda was pacing the bedroom floor from door to window, occasionally stopping to arch her back. Impatience and exasperation and discomfort were written in every step and every pose.

"I can't! No matter what I do, I feel horrible. I can't stay still! I can't sleep. I can't sit. I'm miserably uncomfortable. I hate these babies! I hate them! Maybe they are both devil-kin. Maybe they'll kill me when they come into the world. Maybe that's what they wanted all along."

She slipped her arm around Mathilda's waist and smiled comfortingly. "My lady, you are a princess and a regala and you have your position to uphold. It's not like you to be hysterical. We all know you are *much* more sensible and brave than that."

Taking Mathilda's hand, she led her to the sofa to sit, but was distracted herself, all too aware that the combination of the banquet in the Great Hall and the rain outside would mean that Saker was likely to be somewhere in the castle. Risking his life. In danger. *Va protect him. And blast the man. Why should I care?*

Oblivious, Mathilda continued. "It's so *unfair*! Why am I not allowed to attend the banquet? Anyone would think I was ill, instead of being in a – a delicate condition."

Sorrel almost rolled her eyes. A couple of weeks back, Mathilda's complaint had been that she hated being required to sit at the Regal's side at every entertainment or dinner. "Well, quite apart from their peculiar idea that a heavily pregnant lady is more of a lady if she can avoid being seen in public, it is better from your point of view that not too many people see you," she pointed out. "We don't want any speculation about whether you are larger than normal at this stage."

"I'm *bored*! I have no friends, I can't do any of things I loved to do before, like – like riding, or theatricals, or dancing . . ."

"Your lying-in will be over before you know it."

Mathilda turned to regard her. "And then what?" she whispered. "You'll be gone, and I will have no one."

She had no answers. She could have pointed out that her own marriage had been little better, but it would have served no purpose. At least she'd had opportunities to run away; Mathilda would never have even that.

"You'll have more power once you have given the Regal an heir," she began, intending to offer her some hope, but stopped dead as the door to the spiral staircase was flung open without warning, and a warden with a pike stepped into the room, closing the door behind him.

Mathilda yelped in shock.

The first thing Sorrel noticed was that his hat was too small and his hair was wet. An appalled moment later, she realised it was Saker. He was breathing heavily, his usual cool calm in abeyance. She leapt to her feet, fear gripping her so tight she couldn't speak. Why had he used those stairs? What had gone wrong? *Dear Va, if he's caught in here, he'll be killed . . .*

At least she'd known he was likely to enter the castle; Mathilda had no such knowledge. Sorrel, deeming that the less the Regala knew the better, had not told her anything about his help.

Mathilda rose slowly to her feet, gaping. "*Saker?*" she whispered. "Saker, is it really you?"

He took one step forward, and halted. "Milady," he said. "Forgive the intrusion." He stopped there, at a loss for words.

Pox on him, he's still besotted with her, the lackwit. And he is indeed lacking wits to endanger her like this! Did he even have *the feathers?* He held an odd piece of wood as well as a pike, but that was all.

"Are you intending to behead us?" Mathilda asked him, eyeing the pike.

"What? No, of course not!" He turned to look at Sorrel. "How can I get out of here without anyone seeing me? I've got to get back to the roof . . ."

"Are you out of your mind? To involve us like this?" she asked, furious. "You said you wouldn't!"

"Oh, you came to help me," Mathilda cried. "You came to rescue me!" She flung herself at him, throwing her arms around his neck and burying her head in his shoulder, sobbing. "It's so awful here and I hate Vilmar so much and he is going to kill my babies!"

Saker, obviously aghast, with the pike in one hand and the round stick in the other, sent Sorrel a pleading look over the top of Mathilda's head.

Her mind raced. Saker must have been seen, or have been in danger of being seen. Either way, going back down the staircase was out of the question. The only way out was through the main doors of the solar into the gallery.

"Milady," Saker said, finally gathering his wits enough to speak soothingly to Mathilda, and disengage himself from her embrace, "you are the Regal's wife. That cannot be changed." His expression was horrified, and he firmly removed her arms from around his neck. "We'll do our best to save and care for both your children, I swear."

"And me?" Mathilda wailed.

"If anyone catches you here with Saker, we're all dead," Sorrel snapped at her. "Let's deal with the most important things first. Saker, did someone see you enter the spiral stair?"

"No, but they know something odd happened in the Regal's bedchamber. And sooner or later the feathers will turn up missing." He tapped the wood he carried. "They are inside this. I need to get to the door to the tower stairs on this level. Unseen."

"Not possible," she said flatly. "There will be at least two wardens out there in the gallery."

"Feathers? What are you talking about?" Mathilda asked. She looked from one to the other, her expression bewildered. "You mean the feathers from the Regal's fan? *Both* my children? *How did you know there are two?*"

Sorrel and Saker both ignored her. "Then I need a diversion," he said. "We have to entice the wardens into the Regala's solar in a way that allows me to slip out into an empty gallery, and so to the warden's stair."

"Diversion?" Sorrel asked, keeping a tight hold on her rage. "What sort of diversion is going to succeed in doing that? You want us to set fire to the place?"

Mathilda glared at her. "Are you out of your mind? Don't you dare!"

"No one is going to set fire to anything," Saker said in an attempt to soothe her. "Milady, your grace, the best thing you can do is get into your bed and stay there. Afterwards, you can tell people you slept through everything. No matter what you hear, stay where you are. Sorrel and I will fix this, but we have to be quick."

Sorrel was already bundling Mathilda into bed before he'd finished speaking. Mathilda began to protest, but Saker stopped her with a finger raised to his lips.

"Aren't you going to rescue me?" she asked instead.

He stared at her blankly, then drawled, "No, I rather think not."

This time Sorrel did roll her eyes as she yanked the curtains around the bed, forcing Mathilda to pull her head back or be enveloped in velvet hangings. "This way," she said, glaring at Saker.

She peeked into the reception room to make sure no one was there, then ushered him through and closed the door behind them. The fire had not been lit, and there were only three candles burning in a holder to give light. "Those are the main doors," she said, pointing to her left. "On the other side is the gallery corridor. Turn right, and you'll see the door to the tower at the end. The doors on the other side of the gallery belong to the rooms of the ladies-in-waiting. They will be gone, all but the Mistress of the Chamber and her maid. They remained to be of service to the Regala, should I call for them."

He nodded and glanced around the room they were in.

"If you want to hide in here, the only place is behind the Regala's chair." She indicated a high-backed winged seat placed close to the wall. All the other chairs were straight-backed and offered little cover. "The room through there on the right is the Regala's retiring room, which is more comfortable. It has a view over the inner bailey. And that door next to the fireplace leads to the Ladies' Hall, where the Regala can entertain a larger crowd."

"There's no one else here now?"

"There shouldn't be. All the servants are on duty downstairs, even Aureen."

He walked past her into the retiring room, which was in darkness, and flung open the casements. The rain had stopped, but everything outside still dripped.

"You can't jump," she protested. "You'd break your legs or kill yourself. And you'd still be deep inside the castle."

"I know."

He leaned out of the window. She looked over her shoulder anxiously, petrified that someone would come asking for Mathilda's permission to search the spiral staircase.

"What are you doing?" she asked, convinced something awful was going to happen any minute.

"I thought I could call up the gulls again, but there aren't any around. I think they've had the living daylights scared out of them. Do you mind chaws? They call them jackdaws here."

She stared at him blankly.

As he stepped away from the window, she saw a stream of birds approaching out of the darkness on silent wings. "You jest," she murmured.

"Er, no. You're about to find out what my witchery is." Quickly he outlined his plan.

When he finished, she nodded her acquiescence.

"I'm sorry about all this," he said. His apology sounded heartfelt, but she was in no mood to be mollified. He'd endangered them all, in order to steal some feathers.

The birds began to fly in through the window to land on the chairs and furniture within. They ruffled their feathers, shook their tails and sat regarding Saker with malicious grey eyes glistening in the dim light. Even though they ignored her, Sorrel had to suppress a shudder. The silence was unnatural. Everything about this was unnatural.

He took her by the elbow and escorted her to the main double entry doors. "Now," he said, and turned from her to crouch behind the Regala's chair.

She took a deep breath and put her hand to the doorknob. Behind her, the jackdaws began to stir and cluck.

Flinging open both doors at once, she dashed out, shrieking, "Help! Help!" A glance in either direction told her they were in luck. Each end of the gallery had only one warden. "Quickly!" she screamed at them. "We are being attacked!" She dived back into the reception room. "Only two," she said quietly to Saker. "Both with pikes."

The retiring room erupted into a cacophony of sound, a squawking and screaming that made the hair stand up on the back of her neck. She shrieked again, and it wasn't entirely forced. When the two men arrived at the door together, pikes at the ready, she pointed wordlessly in the direction of the noise. Even in her fear, she made sure she positioned herself so that when they regarded her, they'd be looking away from Saker. One of them ordered, "Bring the candles!"

She did as he asked, taking care to extinguish all but one as she carried the candelabra. When she entered the retiring room, she surreptitiously kicked the door to behind her. Both men were leaning out of the window and all the birds had gone.

"No problem, lady," one of them said. "Someone must've left the window open, and them chaws come in to get out of the rain. They've all gone, and not much damage done, barring a bit of birdshit."

"Oh! Was that all? I was all of a panic, truly. Never heard such a to-do! You were truly brave. I've heard it said they're birds of ill omen . . ."

"Nay, say not!" the second man interrupted. "All creatures are of Va's making, after all. 'Twas just the storm."

"Indeed, you must be right." She chatted on inanely, clutching at the arm of one of the wardens until he was forced to peel her off and gently lower her into the nearest chair.

Saker watched while Sorrel did everything he'd asked of her, and more. She even managed to snuff out two of the candles when she grabbed up the candelabra, dimming the room to near darkness. Dressed in her loose, plain retiring gown that swept the floor, her thick black hair flowing free, she deliberately made the shadows dance as she ran after the two wardens. She never looked his way and gave no sign he was there. He'd had to put his life – and Mathilda's – in her hands, and she had not wavered. He was still trusting her, trusting her with a royal child who could possibly be his. *Sweet Va, how did either of us come to this?*

As he crept out of the apartment and ran up the long, empty gallery, he wondered if he would ever see her again to thank her.

He had not yet reached the door to the tower stair when it was flung open and five or six pike-wielding wardens charged in, running towards him. He stopped dead, momentarily shocked into immobility.

Surreptitiously he edged his left hand with the bambu clutched in it behind him, at the same time as he gripped the pike in his right, ready to use.

"Any trouble here?" the officer of the wardens yelled at him, barely slackening pace. "There's an intruder somewhere in the Keep and he may have come upstairs to the Regala's rooms! One of the wardens is knocked out cold."

"Can't say I know aught about that," he replied calmly. "I came to shoo out a flock of chaws. Some addlepate maid left a window open. There're a couple of wardens attending to it now; mayhap they know something."

"What the pox is going on with birds tonight? Those buccaneers of the air attacked the warden on the roof like they were possessed! Scared him halfway to beggary." He was already on his way past Saker as he said this last, and his men jogged after him, exchanging apprehensive looks. One of them gave Saker a puzzled glance, obviously trying to place him.

He grinned to himself. Once the wardens were fixated on the birds, the more obvious questions they ought to ask were thrust into the background. He hurried on to the tower, before anyone wondered just who he was and why he was heading that way. The stairs were now lit with torches, so he had no problem running up to the roof. The young warden he'd left on the stairs was gone, and so was his cloak. To his dismay, the roof was well lit. The wardens, alerted to something amiss, had all emerged from the guardhouse to patrol the rooftop.

Oh, pox on them, he thought. *Disaster*. He glanced around to see if he could spot Ardhi, but there was no sign of him.

Without another thought, he took charge, and hoped no one would question his authority. "You, over there near the tower entry – you get down to the Regal's solar and help the guards find the intruder, if there is one. What the blistering blazes do you swag-bellied addlepates think you are doing anyway? Lighting up the roof so you can't see a damn thing out there in the dark? And providing a lighthouse for all the birds and their grannies to home in on? The Regala had chaws in her sitting room! Snuff those torches, you pickle-brains!"

As he'd hoped, every torch was seized and extinguished.

He continued to yell. "You three, line up along the wall overlooking the inner bailey, and keep an eye out for birds or a man that ought not to be there. I'll take the cliff side."

"Sir," one of the men said, agitated, "when we carried Konraad inside the guardhouse, we found he wasn't wearing his uniform!"

"It was stolen, you daft rabbits! There's a man in the Regal's solar pretending to be one of us. Look lively now, and make sure you're not taken unawares!"

The men scattered to do his bidding, and he strolled over to where he'd left Ardhi. To his relief, the lascar was huddled safely beneath the walkway. "All's well," he whispered. "I'm going over the side now."

"You have them?" Ardhi asked.

"Safe in the bambu."

Sitting astride the battlements, he reached for the rope and swung himself down. He cleared his mind of all thought of falling, or of being observed, or of having someone cut his lifeline. After all, if one was going to have an adventure, it was always best to enjoy it. Wrapping the rope over his shoulder and around his thigh, he began the long descent to the ground.

An age later, or so he felt, his feet hit the rock. He took one deep breath, then gave the agreed signal to Ardhi. In answer, his pack came tumbling down, tied to the rope. No sooner had he grabbed it than the whole length of rope followed. By the time Ardhi joined him, having happily climbed all the way down without aid, Saker had stowed the rope in his pack, and thrown the coat and hat of his stolen uniform into the river. He was shivering, and so was Ardhi.

"I know just where we can get a hot bath," Saker said as they trudged through the mud of the gorge track at the back of the castle.

"At this hour of the night?"

"In Lowmeer, whorehouses are banned. So they have bathhouses instead."

"I didn't think you would ever—"

"I don't. But I do know where to get a bath. We need to warm up in a hurry, and this is the best way I know of. And they'll have some dry clothes, too. For a price."

Half an hour later, soaking in a tub of warm soapy water and having his back massaged by a bathhouse bawd, Saker finally allowed himself to think of Mathilda. How had he never seen through her to the manipulating, self-serving woman beneath?

He didn't blame her, exactly, but by the sweet oak, he'd been as blind as a hedge-born mole.

Sorrel might have murdered someone, but he was sure she was a better woman than her mistress. He shrugged. Their paths were not likely to cross again.

42

Royal Twins

The night did not end for Sorrel after Saker was gone. The wardens left once they'd satisfied themselves no jackdaws remained hidden anywhere in the room, and once they'd made a few jokes about hysterical women who didn't know enough to close windows on a wet and windy night. Instead of uttering a scathing reply, she smiled sweetly and ushered them out with profuse thanks for rescuing them all from vicious birds.

When she returned to Mathilda, it was to find her sitting bolt upright in bed, her eyes wild with fear. She didn't ask about Saker. Instead, she clutched Sorrel, saying, "Oh, I am feeling pains! The babies are coming!"

Sorrel's heart sank. It was still too early, which might give rise to rumours about the length of the Regala's pregnancy.

"You've had pains before," she pointed out, "and they came to nothing."

"This is different! Go get Aureen!"

"Mathilda, nothing is going to happen for a while yet, I promise you. If I send for Aureen and your ladies-in-waiting find out, they're sure to come buzzing about to see if your confinement is upon you. Best we just wait for her to return."

"Oh! It hurts! How can you be so uncaring! You don't know what it's like."

Poignant memories lanced her. The pain. The fear. Heather's first cry, her tiny fist curling round her finger with surprising strength, the elation of the belief – later shattered – that her baby was perfect. She closed her mind to the remembrance. "Perhaps it will be better if you walk about for a while. If this is the beginning of your travail, it's too early yet for you to take to your bed."

Reluctantly Mathilda clambered out of the four-poster and began to pace the room, clutching at Sorrel every so often and moaning.

"Later, when the pain is more severe, you will have to muffle your cries," Sorrel warned. "It is important that no one hears. For the second baby you can scream all you want. But for this first one, we must not alert the wardens or your ladies-in-waiting." She smiled in encouragement. "You'll show us all what it is to be born of a long line of brave kings and courageous queens. Today you will show us what it is to be truly of royal blood."

After that, Mathilda's moaning was more subdued.

Aureen returned, bone-tired, an hour before dawn, to confirm that Mathilda was indeed on the way to delivery. "Tonight," she said. "All is well. The first twin has its head in the right place for the birth."

"Tonight?" Mathilda asked. "But the night is almost over!"

"She doesn't mean now," Sorrel said. "Perhaps you should try to sleep a while?"

"You mean I'll be in pain all *day*? Sleep? I can't sleep like this!"

However, after sipping some warm milk sent up from the kitchens, she did indeed sleep for several hours. Sorrel dozed as well, and dreamed of Saker, an unpleasant, restless dream about a man who ignored her in preference for a flock of orange-coloured birds the size of ponies. When she woke, she lay thinking about him. Why had she been so attracted? Perhaps because his lithe, muscular frame was so at variance with the usual cleric. Or because he lacked the unctuous rectitude she had come to associate with the clerics at court, or the ones who'd frequented Ermine Manor.

Maybe it was none of those things, she thought wryly. *Maybe it's merely because he is the exact opposite of Nikard.* Saker would never reject a child because she was born deaf. He'd be more likely to kill someone who'd sling their daughter down the stairs like unwanted garbage . . .

Tears pricked at her eyes, and that horrible lump returned, the one that came into her throat whenever she thought of Heather had died.

Mathilda called out to her then, and she left her pallet to see what she wanted. It was going to be a long day.

* * *

Several times people came to the outer door of the solar to see Mathilda, but Sorrel turned them away, saying the Regala was sleeping after an uncomfortable night.

The gossip up and down the gallery was that there had been at least one unauthorised person in the Keep during the evening, and the assumption by the servants was that he'd been one of the guests at the banquet. However, when the Sergeant of the Castle Wardens came to apologise for the disturbance by the jackdaws, it was clear he was more worried about a man he couldn't identify wearing a warden's uniform. He questioned Sorrel in detail about what had happened, but she said nothing to enlighten him.

Throughout the day, she kept waiting for the Regal to discover that the feathers in the fan were missing, but as the hours dragged by, nothing was said. Mostly, life in the castle dawdled on, as its occupants recovered from either overimbibing and overeating, or from overwork and lack of sleep.

Mathilda dozed and complained by turn. When each contraction came, she alternated between swearing that the Regal would never kill any baby of hers, and vowing that the twins she was about to deliver were devil-kin bent on ripping her innards out and she didn't care if they were thrown into the sea at birth. It took all Aureen and Sorrel's tact and cajoling to keep her on an even keel.

As the ferocity of the contractions increased, so did Mathilda's bad temper. "I'll kill him," she said, clutching her arm so tight Sorrel winced. "He said I wouldn't have to marry Vilmar! He promised me!"

"Hush, don't think about that, milady. Think about the babies." She didn't know who Mathilda was referring to, but it didn't seem important then.

The first baby slid into the world around midnight with a weak cry. A girl, to Sorrel's intense relief. She'd dreaded the thought that she would be leaving the castle with a male heir to the Regality in her arms. She was terrified enough of the night ahead, without that.

Mathilda had surprised her, displaying a courage she'd not expected, refusing to cry out, biting hard into a rolled-up towel, refusing to indicate her pain by anything other than grunts of exertion when expelling the child from her body.

Afterwards, bathed in perspiration, knowing she had to do the whole thing again, she sobbed and clutched Sorrel in a tight grip. "He swore it, Sorrel," she said between her sobs. "He did. He said everything would be all right. What if these are his children? He's an evil man. Sweet Va, what did I do?"

Appalled, Sorrel shot a glance to where Aureen was tying off the cord and wrapping the baby. "Hush, you don't know what you're saying."

"Aargh! Why am I getting pains still? Is the second one coming already?"

"It's just the afterbirth, milady," Aureen said. "Nothing to fret about."

The next few minutes were busy ones, and Sorrel had no time to think of Mathilda's words. Then Aureen was thrusting the tiny bundle of mewling baby at Mathilda, saying, "She's a bonny one. And not too small. You must feed her, milady."

Mathilda turned her head resolutely away. "No! I refuse! I won't touch her!"

"Ay, you will, milady," Aureen said, implacable. "Mistress Sorrel, you hold the babe to milady's breast. She must sup on the first milk 'fore you go. I'll start to clean up here."

"Milady, what will you call her?" Sorrel asked as she held the suckling newborn.

Mathilda, her head buried under her pillow, said, voice muffled, "Call her what you will, I don't care. She's the devil-kin."

You don't know that, Sorrel thought. *That's just what you want to believe.* Because if she wasn't, then the one about to be born was . . .

"The poor wee mite," Aureen said, whisking away the bloodied bedclothes. "'Tis an evil land to condemn a newborn with such dreadful words. You ask me, there bain't be such a thing as devil-kin! Va would ne'er be so cruel. And shame to the clerics who believe such things." She bustled off to hide the evidence of the birth in their cuddy.

"Don't you dare tell anyone what I said about Fox," Mathilda said to Sorrel. "If you do, I'll see you dead!"

"I don't know what you're talking about. Milady, you must calm yourself. Everything is going well. The babe's a girl, so she would never be the heir. Va has been kind. Look, she's fallen asleep. She's so beautiful . . ."

I don't want to ever see her again. Take her away!"

Aureen came back into the room then, shaking her head in sorrow at Sorrel as she caught those last words. "Time to be off, mistress," she said. "I'll clean up all that might betray us here, and call for them physicians. The other one might be along any time."

"Will Lady Mathilda be all right?" she asked, whispering.

"She's hardly tore at all, the babe being not so big. She'll be fine, poor lass."

Sorrel looked down at the tiny head peeking out from the woollen shawl. *An unwanted child.* Well, she could give it love, just the way she'd loved Heather in the face of Nikard's despising.

She grabbed up the bundle of items she was taking with her: the letter of introduction to the Pontifect, a change of clothes, Saker's money, her cloak, some of the swaddling and one of the warm shawls Mathilda had in readiness for the birth. A meagre accumulation.

"Milady," she said, "I will guard this child with my life, I promise you. I will beg the Pontifect for help and I will seek the blessing of Va upon you at the Great Shrine in Vavala."

Mathilda refused to look at her, or say goodbye. Sorrel touched her hand in farewell, and it was pity she felt, not hurt, or resentment. King Edwayn's daughter, indulged and spoiled when young, hadn't had much chance of happiness as an adult. At the very most, her future had always been to be the wife of a monarch who saw her bloodline as of more importance than her person.

Aureen kissed the top of the baby's head, then handed Sorrel a single lighted candle and opened the door to the spiral staircase. As Sorrel stepped through into the darkness, the midwife whispered, "All is well, so far. The other babe lives. I'm hoping it will be a while yet, an hour or two, mayhap. A little time for the Regala to rest."

She nodded, and squeezed the woman's hand. They both knew Aureen's life would be forfeit too if Sorrel was caught.

Although this was her favoured way of sneaking out of the castle, Sorrel had never done it in the middle of the night. She wound her way down the narrow treads of the staircase with care. She bypassed the door to the Regal's chamber, where loud snores indicated that his slumber was deep, and continued down to the next level, where the stair ended.

She cracked the door open a sliver, to see if there was a light in the room beyond. The darkness was softened a little by the glow of coals in the fireplace, but no candles were lit. Blowing out her own, she stood for a moment, concentrating on her creation of a glamour. Shapeless, colourless, just a dull formless blending into the background . . .

Please, little baby, don't cry, not yet. We have to slip past the dragon. The baby was small enough to be concealed by her glamour, but there would be no way she could disguise the mewling of a newborn as something else. Taking several deep breaths to calm herself, she stepped into the room and closed the camouflaged door behind her.

The curtains were drawn around the bed. More snoring, not quite as loud as the Regal's, indicated that the Lady Friselda was asleep. A maid lay on a straw pallet on the floor nearby, but she didn't stir. Sorrel crept past her in silence. The bedroom door was shut. When she opened it, the hinges squeaked.

She stopped dead, scarcely breathing. The maid rolled over and sleepily raised herself on one elbow to stare in her direction. There was no way she'd miss seeing the open door. Sorrel moved slightly to touch it again, and it swung open a little further, as if caught by a draught. The screech of unoiled hinges was appallingly loud. The maid flung off her coverlet and wandered, still half asleep, across the room in Sorrel's direction.

Sorrel gave the door one last push, opening it far enough for her to slip out. A moment later the maid had pushed the door to and latched it without seeing her.

She breathed again. Calmed her thudding heart. Crossed the anteroom to the servants' door leading into the kitchen maids' quarters. Here, pallets on a large wooden platform were occupied by five sleeping forms. Hurrying past, she reached the top of the narrow, dark stairway that led directly down to the kitchens. Without a light, she had to edge her way down, feeling with her feet and her free hand. Something scuttled away into the darkness ahead of her. Rats?

Don't think about them, they don't matter. They can't rat on you . . . She giggled, and wondered if she was losing her hold on her nerves. At last, the bottom stair.

She stepped into the empty scullery.

The room was still warm from the heat of the chimney in the neighbouring kitchen. Moonlight filtered through the cracks in the wooden shutter. She peeked at the crumpled face framed by a soft woollen shawl, touched a finger to the plump cheek – and remembered another child, another such moment. Suppressing the memory, she sat down on a sack of potatoes to wait. There was no point in leaving through the door to the outside; it led only to the inner bailey.

Until dawn, all the castle gates were closed.

Although she held on firmly to her precious bundle, she must have dozed, because the next thing she heard was the metallic scrape of someone cleaning out the ashes from the kitchen fireplaces. The baby stirred and whimpered in her arms, tiny sounds, but they alarmed her. Quickly she rose and unbarred the scullery door.

"Who's there?"

The tremulous tone of a scared kitchen boy. Some poor lad tossed out of bed early to riddle the grates and set the kindling for the ovens before the cooks arrived. "Just me," she called back unhelpfully. "Don't fash y'self, young'un."

She stepped outside and pulled the door shut behind her. It was still dark, and she had to feel her way along the wall towards the servants' gateway. When she arrived there, it was still closed, with two sleepy wardens on duty. She kept well back and blended herself into the wall. The baby began to cry, and she gave her the tip of her finger to suck. The child squirmed for a moment inside the swaddling, and then subsided, asleep again.

An hour later the sun came up and the gate was opened, but she waited until the first servants began moving between the two baileys before she slipped through to cross the outer bailey and make her way out of the main gate, unseen, on to the awakening streets of Ustgrind.

It was a long walk across the city to the seminary, but for the first time since her marriage, she was truly free, and there was a lightness to her step.

Soon, I shall be able to decide my own fate. Soon.

No one to tell her what to do, or where to go. Her only responsibility was to the baby in her arms. Mathilda had rejected the child, which wasn't all that surprising, and Saker had washed his hands of it, which puzzled her far more. What could be more important to him than the welfare of Mathilda's child?

She shrugged. She was unlikely ever to find out the reason, so she dismissed him from her mind and considered instead her own options. Right then, she had more money than she'd ever possessed for her own use in her whole life. It was more than she needed for the hire of the wet nurse and the journey to Vavala for the two of them and the baby. It would have set her up in her own household for a couple of years, if she wanted, together with the child and its nurse.

As if I had another daughter . . .

Not another Heather, no one would ever replace Heather, but another daughter to love and cherish. A tempting idea. Her heart speeded up even at the thought. But what if the child was truly a devil-kin?

I have to take her to the Pontifect. No silly dreams.

After an hour of walking, she was hungry and thirsty, and stopped at a stall for something to eat and drink. The smell of fresh buns seeded with marshberries was irresistible. She bought two, along with a hot mug of camomile tea. The woman behind the counter, who had been rocking a young baby to sleep when she arrived, immediately asked to see Sorrel's child.

"She's not mine," she said, and added glibly, "Her mother died at birth. I am taking her to a wet nurse over in Thorn Meadows."

On cue, the baby started to cry.

"Has she suckled yet?" the woman asked.

"Just first milk, before the mother bled to death."

"Oh, how sad. Give her here. I've plenty of milk! Though she won't take more than a sip yet a while."

While Sorrel ate and drank, the woman attended to Mathilda's child. "What's her name?" she asked.

"She doesn't have one yet," Sorrel replied, sipping the tea. "Her mother never said, and her father was not interested in a girl."

"Ah, that's even sadder. You could leave her here, if you like, with me. They call me Mother Odlenda round here. I've enough milk for two! I've birthed five of me own, though three died of the fever. I take in babes for a guildeen every moon. Safer here, anyways, than down in the hollow of Thorn Meadows; I heard there was the Horned Plague there. Elsewhere, too – even been a case or two down by the port wharves. Va save us from another plague!"

Sorrel shook her head. "She's family," she said firmly. "She stays with me."

"Then she's a lucky little darlin' to have such a fine-spoken aunt." Odlenda smiled down at the baby and touched her cheek with the back of her fingers. "Oh, look at the precious dear. Sucking so bravely!"

Just then bells started ringing in the distance, even though it was not a holy day. Odlenda cocked her head to listen. "I wonder what that's for?"

Sorrel felt a skitter of fear. "Warning of the Horned Death?"

"Why no, lass. Don't you know the bells ring like this only for celebration? For warning and death they toll a single note. You must be a country lass not to know that."

She nodded. "Yes, I am."

"Thought you must be. Explains the rattly way you sound." As more and more bells joined in from all over the city, she exclaimed, "Course! A new heir! A son of the Regal must have been born last night. Why did I not think of that?" Her face lit up. "After all these years, and past wives, finally a true son for the Basalt Throne. And here I was thinking we was about to be cursed by pestilence, when in truth Va has blessed the Regal and his bride!"

So the second baby was a boy. Good news, or bad? The idea that the next Regal might be an evil man serving A'Va sent shivers down her spine. *Sweet Va, someone has to make sure that doesn't happen.*

Once she was on her way again, with a contented baby in her arms, she considered her reaction to Odlenda's offer. *I promised Mathilda, I promised Saker, and now I promise you . . . little girl. I am your mother now. I will look after you as long as you need me.*

But first she would take her to the Pontifect, in case there was any truth in the legend of the twin devil-kin.

"Well?"

The query snapped from Regal Vilmar with the intensity of a loosed arrow. Lord Chancellor Yan Grussblat was used to the Regal's rages and replied calmly. In fact, he inwardly rejoiced to hear the return of some of Vilmar's old fire. It had been lacking too long.

"It seems the Regala's Ardronese handmaiden is missing, your grace. That can't be a coincidence. She must have been hand in glove with the man who stole the warden's uniform. She could have shown him how to enter your bedchamber while the banquet was in progress."

The Regal's eyes narrowed. "Was witchery involved?"

"It looks that way. All that strange behaviour of the birds? It can't have been normal, although it's hard to believe someone was able to misuse his witchery to steal. And my men have found out something more about this handmaiden. Seems she has the witchery of glamour."

"*Glamour?*"

For a moment Grussblat wondered if the limit of the Regal's equilibrium had been reached. Vilmar's face darkened, the pupils of his eyes contracted to pinpricks. "How is that possible? The Basalt Throne has *never* allowed glamoured witches to live! Glamours are not Va-granted!"

"Sorrel Redwing was Ardronese, sire. I assume she never told anyone here what she could do. The Regala didn't even know she had a witchery. Only reason we know now is that Frynster Annusel – she's the castle apothecary, sire, with that shop down in the outer bailey—"

"Yes, yes, I know who she is! Get on with it!"

"She told us she once saw Mistress Sorrel wearing a glamour to sneak out of the castle."

"*And she never mentioned it?*" The Regal drew in a deep breath. "If that haggard witch wasn't so blistering useful, I'd have her tied to a wheel! Put the fear of the Throne into Mistress Annusel, my lord Yan. I want her knock-kneed with fright for the next month, understand?" He leaned back in his chair, calming himself. "What about the man? Was he also glamoured?"

"I don't think so. His witchery was probably something to do with controlling birds. I have asked Prime Mulhafen to find out who has that kind of power."

"Offer a reward. How did this Redwing woman come to be in the Regala's service? Who was responsible for that?"

"The Regala says that when she arrived in Betany, the woman was already on board ship. She told the Regala that King Edwayn had arranged it. The Regala never thought to question her presence – why should she? The woman must have glamoured herself and no one saw her come on board in Betany."

"An Ardronese spy?"

"Seems likely, sire."

"A pox on their paunchy king! We shall have our revenge for that, Lord

Yan. I swear it. I want these thieves found. I want the city scoured until they are. I want every witchery-skilled man and woman looking for them with the Wardens and the Watch and the Dire Sweepers, night and day."

Grussblat was shocked. "The *Sweepers*? In the city, in broad daylight?" He hesitated, searching for a prudent way to couch his thoughts. "Sire, much of the Sweepers' success is due to the fear they arouse because people rarely see them. They are dark assassins in the night—"

"I gave you an order."

Astonished, the Lord Chancellor blurted, "And all this over the theft of some *feathers*, sire?"

The Regal eyed him with a look he knew he would never forget. "I am going to say this just once, Lord Yan. And then I want you to forget it was ever said. If you so much as whisper a word of this conversation, your bones will rattle next to those of all your children on a crossroads gibbet. Understand?"

"Sire." His mouth was suddenly so dry, his tongue stuck to the palate.

"Those feathers came from the Va-forsaken Hemisphere and were given to me by Uthen Kesleer. They were bewitched. They bewitched *me*, you understand? Those thieves did me a favour when they stole the plumes because they unwittingly lifted that witchery from me, but the fact that they took only the feathers also tells me they know too much and they have to die."

"Bewitched you? Kesleer dared?" *So much makes sense now. By the Flow, the merchant must be mad!*

"I can see you now understand much that was puzzling you."

"Forgive me, your grace, but you have not been yourself of late. It will be my personal pleasure to bring Kesleer to you in chains."

"Not yet. In fact, I don't want anyone to know about the theft of the feathers as yet, least of all Kesleer."

"I'm not sure I understand."

"Those feathers bewitched me. *Me*, the Regal! Think what power they must have. One day Kesleer will pay in ways that will make him regret he ever lived, but first I want those plumes back in our hands, without falling under their power again. When you find them, don't bring them back here. Put them in the keep on Bhor Island, and inform me, and me alone. Do not touch them. If anyone lays a hand to them, make sure that it is with thick gloves."

"I'll see it done."

"I want the whole of Ustgrind searched for these thieves. I want every road out of the city blocked, and every wharf patrolled. Offer a reward for their arrest. Understand?"

The Lord Chancellor blanched. His guess was that Ustgrind had fifty thousand households. He smiled weakly and said, "It is already being done, sire." *And if I find the bitch, I'll skin her alive myself for the trouble she's caused.*

"One more thing. I have written a letter of instruction to Captain Lustgrader of the *Spice Winds*, Kesleer's fleet commander, and also to Captain Russmon, who commands my royal galleon. I want these letters delivered into their hands before the fleet sails, with a verbal message. They are to be told that it is from me, but no one else is to hear that. They are to be told that they are to open the seal only once the fleet has left port, when they have a private moment." The Regal smiled. "As I do not usually ask my Lord Chancellor personally to attend to such mundane matters as my correspondence, I am sure you have an inkling how important it is that Kesleer does not get to hear of this. Your most trusted messenger, please, Lord Yan."

The Lord Chancellor bowed deeply in acquiescence. At least, he thought, the days were numbered for that scurvy varlet Uthen Kesleer.

When Sorrel arrived at the gates to the seminary, her way was blocked by several heavily armed men. They were all dressed in dark grey or black, not a scrap of colour on them anywhere. Each had his hair tucked up under a black velvet hat with a black rooster feather cockade pinned to the side. Each had his lower face muffled with a scarf.

"No entry here, mistress," one said as she approached. "The seminary is closed to all but the sick."

Her heart turned over. "Sick?"

"Have you not heard? Most of the clerics are dead. The Horned Plague. The Regal has ordered the seminary sealed. Enter here, you'll not come out again. Best you leave this place."

"I was supposed to meet Witan Shanny Ide," she said, thickening her accent to copy the country-born palace chambermaids.

"Ah, mistress, I'm sorry then. I heard she was the first to die."

No, oh no. Please tell me that's not so. Her knees buckled and she almost fell. Her dismay was overwhelming. Without the cleric's help, she had no idea of where she was going to find a wet nurse who would go with her to Vavala.

The man folded his arms over his chest, and there was something about his cold dark eyes that frightened her. Her arms tightened around the baby. "Is that a babe you have there?" he asked, and his tone was heavy with suspicion.

"Ay, indeed," she said quickly. "Poor wee mite has the spotted meazle, and frets like a nipped pup! I heared it said the witan had a fine physic for the meazle . . ."

"Not any more."

"Never mind. 'Tis only a fret, naught serious. Right sorry I am to hear 'bout the witan, though. A fine lady she were." She turned away then, sick at heart, and headed back. She would have to take up Mother Odlenda's offer while she searched for a wet nurse who would go to Vavala with her.

Only two hours or so had passed since she'd said goodbye to Odlenda, but the welcome she received on her return was no longer pleasant. Odlenda frowned when she saw her coming, and shook her head.

"Didn't think to see you again, girl. Not sure I want to, neither. The Regal's watchmen came by here while you were gone. Fact, they're all over the city looking for a black-haired lass with deep blue eyes and an odd way of speaking. You the one they were looking for? Name of Sorrel?"

Appalled, she tried not to show her fright. "That's an Ardronese name, isn't it? I'm from Lowmeer, up in the north," she said, as if indignant at the assumption. "Up near West Denva in the border country. What's she done, this Sorrel?"

The suspicion did not fade from Odlenda's eyes. "They say she was a servant in the castle and opened a door for someone to enter the royal apartments to steal."

"Well, that certainly weren't me. Wager they didn't mention a babe, did they? I've been staying with my brother-in-law and sister, and would be still, if my sis hadn't died. And here's my problem: the wet nurse who promised to suckle the child has died of the Horned Death. I just found out, which is why I came back to you."

"Well I'm not interested no more. I don't want no trouble, an' you look too much like this Sorrel they described."

"But the babe . . ."

"Not my business. You can't find a wet nurse, then get a nanny goat. Nothing like goat's milk for a babe that's lost her ma. Now be off with you!" With those words, Odlenda turned her back and went to serve another customer.

Sorrel turned away, her dismay fast changing to despair. If she didn't find a wet nurse before the day was over, then the baby would be in trouble. Once out of sight of Odlenda, she reverted to her Celandine persona, the grey mouse with wispy light hair and grey eyes.

Saker, she thought. *I have to find Saker*. But she had no idea where to start looking.

Ardhi, though . . .

A brown-skinned seaman from the Summer Seas was hardly common, even down on the wharves; everyone would know where to find Ardhi the lascar, surely. She glanced down at the baby. *You first, though. I have to find a way to feed you.*

43

The Company Factor

"So you wish to be one of my factors in the Spicerie?"

Mynster Uthen Kesleer raised a single eyebrow at Saker. This time he was seated at his table in the main office of the Lowmian Spicerie Trading Company, a position strategically placed to oversee, yet to be outside the earshot of, the scribes and bookkeepers and clerks so busily scratching in their ledgers. "I know I mentioned it, but you astonish me nonetheless, Heron. It seems you're a foolish man after all."

"Pardon?"

"A man who thinks being a company factor in the Summer Seas is a quick path to riches."

"I'm not looking for wealth, mynster." He struggled not to sneeze; the air in the room was saturated with the aroma of spices, even though he could see no cargo bales or sacks.

"Adventure, then?" The man's scorn was obvious. "Well, let me enlighten you. I have no fewer than thirty-five factors sailing in this fleet, and yet I really only have need of half that number." He placed his elbows on the desk and leaned forward with an anticipatory smile, reminding Saker of a hound that knew it was about to be fed. "You see, I expect half of them to die."

He then leaned back to observe the effect of his words. Saker sat expressionless. Or so he hoped.

"Certainly," Kesleer continued when Saker said nothing, "those who *do* return will be rich men. To earn the riches, they must stay five years working for the company on one of the islands. Those who don't return? Some will die of scurvy on the journey out, others of the fever or the bloody flux in a port of call. Some will die in a back alley with a knife in their guts, or have their head blown off by a privateer's cannonball at sea. And that's even before the ship reaches the islands.

So why would you want to take a risk like that, if not for a dream of wealth?"

"I have an earnest desire to see the Spicerie and the Va-forsaken Hemisphere for myself," Saker lied. Half lied. *Va rot Ardhi and his* sakti. All he really wanted to do right now was take Sorrel and the child to Vavala. And to make sure there was no devil-kin heir to the Basalt Throne. Instead, he had to go halfway round the world as an errand boy delivering feathers. He struggled to keep a bland expression of deference pasted on his face as he added, "I know how to keep books, my handwriting is excellent and I am scrupulously honest. I do not suffer from seasickness and I am in good health."

Kesleer leaned back in his chair, laced his fingers together and folded them over the rotundity of his stomach. "Add up these figures," he said. "Fourteen, two hundred and eight, one thousand seven hundred and sixty-five. What's the answer?"

"One thousand nine hundred and eighty-seven."

"If one measure of cloves costs six guildeens, you buy four measures, then the price goes up to eight guildeens before you buy more. I have given you one hundred guildeens to spend, so how many measures can you buy?"

"Thirteen, with four guildeens to spare."

"Is there anyone who can speak for your good name?"

"The Prelate of the Witan Seminary of Advanced Studies, Murram Loach."

Kesleer frowned. "Ah, yes, we made enquiries with him and he was high in his praise. Did you know the seminary has since been quarantined and most of the seminarians have died of the Horned Plague? The gossip is that A'Va is now targeting clerics and shrine-keepers."

Saker stared at him and felt the blood drain from his face. "I – I didn't know that." *Shanny*. And he'd told Sorrel to go there with the first baby when it was born. His mouth went dry. *Oak-and-acorn . . . what can I do*?

"Well, you can have the job if you want it. Most of your salary will be paid on your return, one per cent of the profit on cargo sold in Ustgrind which you *personally* negotiated to buy in the islands and saw loaded on board. Your advance now will be sufficient to buy personal items such as new clothing, a hammock, shoes, bedding and so forth. You will be under the orders of the senior factor on board the *Spice Winds*, Mynster Yonnar Cultheer. Oh, and I expect you to continue to teach the Pashali language to officers and factors throughout the voyage, is that clear?"

He scribbled a payment voucher and handed it to Saker.

Wonderful. A small investment on your part, and a good chance that I'll never collect what is owed me because I'll be dead. You're a mean bastard, Kesleer. Aloud he said, "Thank you, mynster. That's very generous."

"Settle your affairs now. Make plenty of use of your wife tonight, if you have one, or tickle the bawds, because the ship sails out of here on the evening tide tomorrow. So you don't have much time left on land."

His stomach lurched. "I thought the sailing date was still several weeks away!"

Kesleer gave a humourless superior smile as he scribbled a note of appointment for him to show the ship's captain. "I want the fleet out of here as soon as possible because the Horned Death has its grip on the city, at least for those who don't have access to the spices that keep it at bay." He opened a wooden box on his desk and took out a pomander the size of an apple. It was stuck through with cloves, cinnamon sticks and slivers of nutmeg. From the colour, it had also been soaked in honeyed mace-water. "Take this and use it. Hang it around your neck and it will protect you – but don't hang it where it will be seen. These are selling for well over fifty guildeens now."

He didn't believe it had any value at all against the Horned Death, but he thanked Kesleer profusely anyway.

"No thanks needed. Now that you're a company factor, I can't have you dying of the pestilence, can I? Give it back to me tomorrow when you come to embark. There were cases of the Death today on wharf number eight, which is perilously close by. I sent my wife and children out to the country several days back and I intend to follow them as soon as the fleet sails."

Saker raised the pomander to his nose and inhaled the glorious concoction. "Was that what all the bells were about earlier? Warning of the Horned Death?"

"No, indeed. In fact the Basalt Throne is wisely trying to underplay the situation to keep the commerce of the city running as long as possible. The bells were to announce the birth of a male heir to the Basalt Throne. Now off you go, and do what you have to. Be on board two hours before sundown tomorrow. We leave before sunset."

Ardhi was waiting for him in the street when he left the office. "Well?" he asked. "Did you get a berth?" He didn't look at all anxious.

"Yes, I'm sailing with you." He grabbed Ardhi by the arm and turned him to walk at his side down the wooden boardwalk. "As if you ever doubted it," he added sourly. "Your sodding Chenderawasi magic – was there ever a chance Kesleer would say no?"

Ardhi grinned.

"Wipe that weasel smile off your face. I have a problem. It's about Sorrel. She had to run away from the castle and she'll have gone to the seminary – but it's under quarantine. She won't get the help I arranged. I have to look for her."

Ardhi glanced at him curiously. "I think there is a something, a very long story, you have not told me."

"And I don't have the time or the inclination to tell you right now. I should be with her; I *would* have been with her if it hadn't been for you and your damned Chenderawasi *sakti*. I must find her."

Ardhi's smile changed to a frown. "We're sailing with the tide tomorrow evening."

"I know!" His rage almost overwhelmed him. "Do you think I'd have committed myself to that if you hadn't twisted me into the fobbing service of your Chenderawasi magic? You left me no choice but to follow you!" He took a calming breath, pushed down the horror of his thoughts. "Sorrel has a child with her. They're both in danger and won't know where to go for help."

"Ah, so it's the babe, not the mother, eh?"

Saker winced. Hang the scut, and his way of putting his finger on matters he didn't want to think about. "I don't have time to get the things I'll need to take with me on this Va-forsaken voyage. You have a better idea of what to buy. A hammock? Clothing?" He pressed a generous handful of guildeens into Ardhi's palm, then added, after glancing at the lascar's feet, "Don't bother about shoes for me. And remember I'm a good hand-span taller than you are."

Ardhi nodded. "All right. I'll take them on board today. I have to sleep on the ship tonight."

"Hey, you two, wait right there!"

They had been so intent on their conversation that they almost bumped into the man standing with his underlings to block the way off the quayside boardwalk. Saker looked up and his heart turned over, leaving a sick feeling behind. The man, dressed all in black, with a black velvet hat and the lower part of his face muffled, could have been one of the same Dire Sweepers he'd met in Dortgren.

"Yes?" he asked, trying to still the thudding of his heart. He kept his tone carefully neutral, but his hand lingered near his sword hilt and he stood a little straighter.

"Who are you and where are you going?"

"By whose authority do you ask?"

"The Regal's, you wharf-rat!"

"I'm a factor for the Lowmeer Spicerie Trading Company. This man is a sailor on the *Spice Winds*. He's off to the market to make some purchases for me. I am returning to my lodging to pack my kit. The ship sails tomorrow. If you have a problem with any of that, may I suggest you take it up with Mynster Kesleer?" He waved his letter of appointment under the man's nose.

The man glanced at it, then waved him on. "Not necessary," he said.

As they walked on, Ardhi sent a sidelong glance at Saker. "What was all that about?"

"If I'm not mistaken, those fellows are part of a grim bunch of aristocratic assassins called the Dire Sweepers. They work for the Regal. If they're the least bit suspicious of a fellow, they'd rather kill him than talk. I'm not sure, but I have a nasty idea this might have something to do with some missing feathers. Cankers and curs, Ardhi, my gut is curdling with worry about Sorrel."

They left the wharf area and headed towards the market stalls. There they were accosted by several members of the Castle Watch, accompanied by a cleric. The guard in charge held up his hand to stop them.

"State your names and your business here," he ordered.

Saker repeated the information he'd given before.

"Witan here says you got a witchery. That right?"

"Yes," Saker said, with a smile in the direction of the cleric. *Interesting. I wonder why he doesn't see that Ardhi has one too?* "And so has the witan." His heart sped up as he realised why the cleric was with the guards. Sweet heavens, they'd realised the thief of the feathers had a witchery. And that meant Sorrel, who must be out on the streets by now, would be in danger if she used her glamour.

"What's your witchery skill?" the guard asked.

Saker's mind raced. He certainly didn't want to admit that he had power over birds, not after what he'd done inside the castle. "Keeping vermin out of warehouses, sir," he said. "Rats and roaches." *There, disprove that if you can.* "What's all this about? If you're looking for someone in particular, perhaps I can be of assistance. Do you have a description? If I see them, I can inform you."

"A woman. Black hair, dark blue eyes," the head of the guards said. "Wearing a white snood and widow's weeds. By all reports, a pretty squeeze. Your age or thereabouts. Probably in the company of a young man who possibly has a witchery as well."

"I'll keep a lookout for them," Saker replied. It was an effort to maintain his bland expression.

"She might be using a glamour," said the cleric.

"And she used it to steal from the castle," the guard said grimly. "A hanging offence."

Sweet Va-less hell.

When they were alone again, Saker said, "He didn't notice you had a witchery."

Ardhi laughed. "He didn't look at me! I'm only a dark-skinned lascar to him. A Va-forsaken nobody. Certainly no one who would have a witchery, or the audacity to steal from the Regal."

"Does that sort of thing happen often?"

"What?"

"People not – not *seeing* you."

"All the time. Do they think *Sorrel* stole the feathers? Why would they think that?"

"She's in trouble and it's all the fault of your Va-damned Chenderawasi magic," he said, his anger bubbling. "It's trying to take the danger away from us and push it on to her. Leak on its manipulative mongrel sorcery!"

"Why should that matter to you?"

"Of course it matters! She doesn't deserve to be hanged for our theft."

"If she'd stayed in the castle, they would never have suspected her. And it wasn't theft."

"Stop being so blithering pedantic! They'll hang whoever they blame, and at the moment that's Sorrel. Worse, they'll have every cleric who possesses a witchery talent looking for her because they can see right through a glamour. And she doesn't know the danger she's in."

"You'd better tell me exactly why you're itching to plant your fist into my face," Ardhi said quietly. "I thought you knew how important my mission is, for your land, as well as mine."

He reined in his urge to slam Ardhi up against the nearest wall. "You tell me it's for the good of us all," he muttered, his fury barely contained as he clutched the lascar's shoulder, "but when I see something like this – a blameless woman heading for castle dungeons, to be tortured and killed for a theft she didn't commit – then I'm guessing that whoreson dagger of yours is manipulating it. Protecting us at her expense!"

"We don't know that."

"Your slubbering Chenderawasi magic is a botch of nature! It's self-serving, and its master is your island nation, not our Va-cherished lands! Every time I help you, I'm being a traitor to my country, to my faith, to the Pontifect and to my king. I cannot stand by and see Sorrel blamed for my complicity in your schemes." Panting, he let go of the lascar and his rage drained away. "This is killing me," he whispered. To his mortification, he felt tears collect in the corners of his eyes as his frustration and grief sought an outlet.

Ardhi appeared unmoved. "Tomorrow you'll board the ship and sail with me, Saker. And you won't kill me either, however much you want to."

"Blister your tongue, you bilge rat!"

"And just to be sure we understand each other, if I seem a cheerful sort of fellow, often smiling, it's not because life amuses me. I smile because the alternative is to weep." The look he gave Saker contained no hint of amusement. "I'll buy what you need." With that, he turned on his heel and walked away.

For a moment Saker stood still in the middle of the street, shaking as he tried in vain to break free of the compulsion. He knew in his heart he would be on board that vessel. And he would sail for the Summer Seas. He could no more have resisted the magic than he could have sprouted wings and flown.

Slave.

Saker hired a hack and rode out to the seminary. He was refused entry by more of the Dire Sweepers. Fortunately, none of them were men from the group in Dortgren, but he was wary of them anyway. And puzzled, too; they seemed to be obvious in their presence, rather than the secretive assassins he'd been led to believe they were.

One of them told him that both Shanny Ide and Murram Loach had died the day before. His knowledge of the long, slow process of the disease made him think they were lying. If they'd contracted the Horned Plague and they were already dead, it was the Sweepers who had killed them, and it would have been a mercy. He didn't dare ask them if anyone with a baby had been there asking for Shanny.

Sick with worry, he returned to the city. Sorrel's most immediate problem would have been to find a wet nurse, any wet nurse, so he set off on the same quest. By nightfall, he had spoken to a number of wet nurses and nursing mothers, but he'd not found Sorrel, nor any trace of her. She'd vanished.

He returned to his rented lodging after dark, flung himself on to his cot, hands behind his head, and stared at the sagging ceiling. *I'm to blame for this*, he thought. *I should have told her how to contact me other than through the seminary.* He had to work out where she'd go.

And the babies: oh, dear Va.

Part of him wished the world would open up and swallow him whole. They had been born three weeks early. Which made it perfectly possible that the next Regal to sit on the Basalt Throne would be his own son, bastard-born without a drop of Lowmian blood, a fact that would break Bengorth's Law. Which ought to be impossible.

44

On the Run

Sorrel was walking across a cobbled street following a lead to a wet nurse, confident that her glamour made her look nothing like Sorrel Redwing, when she came face to face with three guards and a shrine-keeper. The latter pointed at her, crying, "She has a glamour witchery!"

For a split second Sorrel stared at her as thoughts jostled and sorted themselves. She had no idea how they knew to look for someone with a witchery, but they did.

The guards leapt towards her at the same moment as she turned and fled. She was burdened by the child and the bundle of things she carried. They'd have her in their clutches within twenty paces, and she knew it.

Desperation made her act without thought: she changed her appearance into something inhuman and sprang at a group of schoolboys about to pass her by as they poured out of a chapel school with their slates and chalks. A raging boar, complete with tusks, raced into their midst on its hind legs with a bundle on its back and a snarl on its ugly face. The glamour was ill-contrived, tending to break up and re-form as she lost her hold on what it was supposed to look like, but it served its purpose. The boys scattered in twenty different directions, screaming in terror and shock. The baby started to wail, her thin cry adding to the bedlam. The panic spread to others in the street.

She banished the glamour of the boar and switched to join the boys, becoming one of them. She pounded after them, the baby clutched to her chest, the bundle bouncing on her back.

The shrine-keeper wasn't deceived. She pointed, yelling, "That's her, that's her!"

The guards, however, had no idea which boy she was singling out. They dithered, shouted contradictory orders at one another, then split up. None of them followed Sorrel, who swung around the nearest corner and didn't stop until she was well away from the area. When she could run no more, she sank to her heels in a quiet corner of a side street and calmed herself with shuddering breaths. The panicked baby fell silent, gasping for air. Sorrel rocked her and crooned until she fell into an exhausted sleep.

Oak-and-acorn, she couldn't walk the streets as herself, and yet she was probably almost as much at risk if she used a glamour.

In the next hour or so, she was left aghast by the number of people apparently mobilised just to look for her. Not only men of the watch, but Castle Wardens, strange men dressed in black with muffled faces, men in the Regal's livery and even men from the Lowmian Spicerie Trading Company. She maintained a glamour, though, thinking that there couldn't be nearly as many witchery-alert folk as there were guards.

And the irony appeared to be that it wasn't a twin they were after, but missing feathers. *Sweet Va, they've organised the whole city to look for me because of the plumes from a fan? If ever I meet Saker again, I'll wring his neck for involving me! He risked my life and Mathilda's life and the babies' for something plucked from a bird on the other side of the world?*

The thought was beyond terrifying. By the Oak, *why*? Her life had spun out of control into a nightmare. She couldn't even seek out a shrine for help because a shrine-keeper might betray her. *Damn you to a Lowmian bog, Saker! This is all your fault.*

By nightfall, she felt as if she'd been stretched to breaking point. Every unusual sound made her jump, every loud voice filled her with fear, and every time the baby whimpered she felt like crying. The lead she'd followed had led to nothing. The poor nameless babe hadn't been fed since Odlenda had suckled her that morning and she wouldn't stop fretting.

As the sun set, Sorrel headed towards the house of a wet nurse she'd spoken to earlier. The woman had a family and she certainly hadn't wanted to journey to Vavala, but perhaps she could be persuaded to feed the baby. She knew it was a risk; the woman had probably heard about the search by now. But her choices had vanished. The child needed to be fed and her mewls were more and more frequent and anguished.

She was still ten minutes away from where the woman lived when she noticed an alley, narrow and dark, on her left. And somewhere deep down that shadowed lane, another child was crying. Turning her head to look, she halted and stared. The sound was reedy and unhappy; an older baby, she guessed. She took a few hesitant steps into the dimness of the alley.

A faint flickering danced in the shadows on the brick wall at the end of the lane; somewhere a fire had been lit, but the flames were hidden from sight around a corner. She hesitated, telling herself it was none of her business. She already had a child to look after and she certainly didn't need another. Yet the cry was haunting, not so much from the quality of the sound, but from the idea that any child should be crying in an alley in the dark at this time of night.

She was still dithering, wondering what to do, when a voice a few paces away on her right, said, "In a pickle, sister?"

Startled, ready to run, she turned to face the speaker. A raggedly dressed man, middle-aged, stood in a recessed doorway. The door had long since been bricked up, but the recess offered a good lookout post for someone not wanting to be noticed. *He's on guard,* she thought.

There was nothing threatening about him. He didn't move towards her and his words were more enquiry than menace.

"You could say that," she said.

He stepped out of the doorway then, with the aid of a crutch, but came no closer. He smelled of dirt, sweat and unwashed clothing, and he was missing a leg, now replaced by a wooden peg. "You got a hungry littl'un there, methinks."

She turned, intending to leave, but he halted her with his next words. "You're the thief they're hunting, right? The Ardronese spy who robbed the castle using a glamour. The talk's all o'er the town 'bout you."

It was a moment before she could gather her wits enough to face him once more, choked by her despair.

He said gently, "We're all bleeding poor here. Gutter scum. Varmints, living on the streets of Ustgrind, stealing to eat 'cause we had hard luck. Look at me, a bosun on a Regal's ship, laid off after an accident, got no leg and no future. We stick together to 'elp one 'nother. There's one thing we don't do, not our lot, anyways. We don't betray our own. Heard you got a Shenat name fer a start."

"Sorrel Redwing."

"An' you got a witchery, an' we respect them gifted with witcheries. We don't turn away no child, neither. With a babe in arms you're safe here."

Desperate, weary and afraid, she whispered, "She's newborn. Her mother died and I was looking for a wet nurse."

"Then Va got yer to the right place." Pointing to the end of the alley, he said, "Go on down to the end of the lane. There's folk there who'll look after yer." He coughed then, the chronic cough of a sick man. "Tell 'em Salamander sent yer."

Had she been less desperate or more frightened, she would have walked away. Instead, she did as he suggested. When she reached the end of the alley, she saw that it turned sharply to the left into a dead end. The blank-eyed windows of gutted buildings stared sightlessly on a huddle of people warming their hands at a small fire on the cobbles. A motley group of people, she thought. Some fifteen or so adults and a number of ragged children with besmirched faces. The crying baby had been hushed.

As she stepped up to the fire, they all fell silent. She said, faltering in her courage, "I heard the crying. I was wondering if any of you can feed the child I have here. Salamander said to come. My name's Sorrel, and the Regal's men are hunting me."

The silence stretched until she wanted to scream at them to say something, anything. One of the older women stood up to see her better. She had a black patch over one eye, and her clothing looked more like the contents of a ragpicker's bag than anything that had ever been sewn into a garment. After careful scrutiny, she apparently approved of Sorrel because she said, "Minnow here has milk. There are them offering a reward for turning in the glamoured bit-picker, but here we don't never turn away a babe."

A younger woman, hardly more than a girl, who had been sitting on a heap of fallen brickwork stood up. "I'm Minnow," she said, and held her arms out offering to take the baby. She had a waif-like face, but her eyes were old with experience. "You got no sap in your tits?"

"She's not mine. Her mother died."

"Give 'er here. Whasser name?"

"She hasn't got a name yet." She handed the baby over to Minnow, who peeled back the blanket to uncover her face.

"Oh," the girl said, and her face softened with wonder as she loosened her clothing to offer her breast. "She's polished new. Be blest in the world, littl'un!"

"Her name's Piper." It was the older woman who'd spoken. "I'm Bitterling and I read the waters. And she is Piper, born to travel far on the winds. She is a child of summer and spice."

Piper. The sandpipers and windpipers that flew to the coasts from far-off lands every summer, to bob and dip along the beaches where sand met sea . . .

She smiled. "Yes," she said. "That shall be her name. Piper."

For the first time since she'd left the seminary gates, she felt safe.

In the morning Saker was on the wharves early. They were already chaotic and crowded. The newly built *Spice Winds*, fully laden, was at anchor in the middle of the Ust estuary, side by side with the galleon of the fleet, *Sentinel.* The ageing carrack *Spice Dragon* and two more new fluyts were tied up at the wharf. Workmen were still putting the finishing touches to the superstructure, polishing and varnishing. Longshoremen were loading barrels and butts of food and water in a continuous stream.

A drayman screeched his outrage as both he and a muleteer tried to manoeuvre their beasts close to the gangplank. "I were here first, you misbegotten son of a bawd!"

"An' I got more to deliver, you pizzle of an ass!"

For a moment Saker wondered if the two men would come to blows, but a ship's officer intervened and a line of dock-hefters quickly formed to lug the provisions on board. The moment of order was short-lived. Tempers frayed, carters fought over who had precedence, company clerks counted and recorded, ships' officers disputed the tallies.

Ensuring even greater tumult were the families of those about to depart. They gathered on the quayside to snatch a final farewell with the loved ones they could, at best, expect to see again about two years hence. Tears were shed, children wailed, couples wept or argued.

Piled on the dock, blocking free access to the ships, was all the cargo not yet loaded. Some of the first arrivals that morning had been the farm animals, and as these were mostly deck cargo, they were also going to be the last on board. Saker saw goats, pigs and sheep, all bleating their distress, but it was the chickens in their coops that overwhelmed him with their distressed inanity.

He groaned. For Va-sake, this fobbing bird witchery could make him as miserable as a wet winter's day. And how in all Va's marvels was he ever going to find Sorrel in all this? If she was here. If she had thought to seek out Ardhi.

He worked his way from one end of the docks to the other, pushing his way through the throng. Twice he was stopped and questioned about his own witchery; twice he escaped real scrutiny by showing his letter of appointment. The worst of the hubbub was at the several access roads, where castle guards, Kesleer officials and men of the Dire Sweepers were trying to regulate entry to the wharves. They wanted to question everyone and have them passed by a witchery-gifted cleric or shrine-keeper. When Uthen Kesleer decided they were slowing down the smooth flow of carts in and out, he descended on those responsible with all the ire and fury of a powerful man for obstructionist underlings.

The result was a shambles, but at least Saker thought it'd be relatively easy for a glamour-gifted woman to slip through on to the docks. He still thought his best chance of finding Sorrel was somewhere portside. If she wasn't looking for Ardhi, she'd be trying to book a berth on the flat-boat to Borage.

As the day wore on, however, he became more and more unsettled, because there was no sign of her.

By all the acorns on an oak, where was she? The only hope he had that she was still alive was the knowledge that the Dire Sweepers and the other guards were still looking for her. Well, looking for someone, anyway. It could have been him they were after . . .

Around mid-afternoon he did catch a glimpse of the glow of a witchery-gifted person. A disreputable family group was pushing their way through the crowd with scant manners and much vulgar language and raucous laughter. They were grubby folk, with unkempt hair, ragged clothing and dirty bare feet. There was a man with a peg leg, another who was blind and a woman with a black patch over her eye. They seemed to be accompanied by innumerable children running in all directions, and he thought he saw a boy with a knife fingering a purse hanging from a man's belt, but lost sight of what happened as people jostled, and the crowd ebbed and flowed like the tide.

Among them was someone with a witchery. He thought it was the one-eyed woman, but it was hard to tell because of the constant mingling and merging of people.

He pushed past some sailors who'd blocked his view, only to find the group had moved on and he could no longer see them. A cart drove past, and then another, forcing him to step back. By the time he had extricated himself from the dock-hefters swarming over the new deliveries, he had no idea where the band had gone. Baffled, he headed back to where the Borage flat-boat normally berthed.

The crowd there was irate, and the person on the receiving end of the ire was the unfortunate clerk from the ship's chandler who sold the berths. The flat-boat was due in, but there was no ship there, and none to be seen beating its way up the estuary. Of course, it was always hard to keep to a schedule; any ship was at the mercy of the wind, so it was not the vessel's tardiness that irritated the crowd.

"Sorry," the clerk was saying, shouting to make himself heard. "That's just what we've heared from a fisher – the flat-boat's not coming."

"It's not coming today?" someone cried.

"Not coming at all. Captain won't risk himself or his crew here 'cause of the Horned Death."

"We want to leave the city!" someone shouted. "We don't want to die neither!"

"Do I git my money back?"

"When will the flat-boat come again?"

"How can we get to Gort?"

"To Fluge?"

"To Borage?"

Just when it looked as it was going to get ugly, someone laid a hand on Saker's arm. He jumped, startled, and turned to see who had accosted him. A ragged woman clutched at him, her clothes thick with dirt, a baby on her arm and a bundle on her back. She held out a hand palm up, saying, "Spare a brass bit, sorr? For the babe, like?"

Appalled, Saker blanched at her smell. "*Sorrel?*" he hissed. "What in Va's name . . .? By the Oak, you're *filthy*!"

"Ay, sorr. The poor don't get to bathe much. 'Specially them that's accused of theft, and chased by the Regal's assassins. What did you do, betray me to the Basalt Throne so they wouldn't come after you?" She was whispering, and her sarcasm eventually overpowered her assumed accent.

"You can't possibly think that." Nearby, an angry middle-aged man launched a missile at the chandler's clerk and a fight broke out. Saker grabbed her by the arm and pulled her to the back of the crowd.

She glared as she shook his hand off. "No, I suppose not. I'm not as dizzy-eyed as you are."

He flushed. "I think we'd better get out of here. This crowd is getting ugly." He strode away, leaving her to follow or not. She came after him, running to catch up. "I've been looking for you all day," he said.

"Those people in black – I'm sorry, but they said your friend at the seminary is dead."

"I know. I went there too, but I guess you'd already gone." His gaze dropped from her face to seek out the child in the bundle she carried in her arms. "Is it a girl or a boy?"

"A girl. Her name is Piper." They had reached the stone steps down to the water-level dock, where the launches from the ships at anchor were tied up. It was quieter there. He stopped and turned to her. "Is – is she all right? How have you been feeding her?"

"I made some friends among Lowmeer's lowlife. People always say it's the poor who help the poor, don't they? It's true."

She glanced over her shoulder and nodded to someone. He turned to look, and found that a man and a young woman from the band of thieves had been following them at a distance. The woman had an older baby in her arms. The man with her was the one with the peg leg. He was leading a nanny goat on a rope. They were standing by the crates of livestock yet to be loaded on to one of the fluyts and the goat was gazing at the others of its kind.

Sorrel continued, "I'm now the proud owner of that goat and a baby-feeder, which is a sort of jug with a tiny spout. I was intending to catch the flat-boat, along with the goat. Now it seems I must walk to Vavala. With the nanny goat."

He stared at her, open-mouthed. She was serious. "You'd do that?"

She shrugged. "What else? Actually, I don't really think I'd have to walk all the way. I could take the flat-boat from Gort."

"Oh, pox on it. I – I'm truly sorry you've been caught up in this business of the feather. I've no idea why they decided you were involved."

"Well, there was that matter of the jackdaws . . ." She shrugged. "And the coincidence that I disappeared around the same time. It doesn't matter. I do wonder if the best thing I could do for us all is leave this child with a wet nurse and just walk away. If they find me, and therefore the child, they might start to question where it came from. If there is any gossip within the castle about . . ." She let the words trail away.

"Is – is she all right? Mathilda?"

"I suspect she's a lot better off than I am right now," she snapped.

"Look, I don't have much time. I have to go on board any moment now." He nodded out at the anchored ships. The Regal's galleon was already hoisting its sails to catch a favourable wind. It would be the first to sail, but the others wouldn't be far behind. On the wharf beside them, the last of the cargo was being shifted on to the decks of the two fluyts. They'd be casting off any minute.

"I can see the launch from the *Spice Winds* heading this way," he said, "and I suspect one of the men rowing it will be Ardhi, making sure I'm on board before the ship sails. We have to get you out of the city safely. If I can find a fishing vessel, I might be able to persuade them to take you to Borage."

She looked at him with hope, but before she could say anything, there was a sudden surge through the crowd on the wharf and someone was yelling, "That's her!"

They whirled to see who was shouting. A cleric. He was pointing at Sorrel and yelling back to several wardens and a black-clad Dire Sweeper.

The first person to react was the man with the peg leg. He kicked at the catch on the chicken coop beside him, knocking the lid open and spilling the coop on to its side. The hens, in a swirl of feathers and cackling hysteria, shot out of their prison. Some flew, some ran off, flapping their wings and squawking.

Saker pushed Sorrel behind him and called up as many birds as he could, not just the chickens, to attack the wardens and the man in black. Other people on the wharf – and there was still crowds of onlookers come to see the ships sail – squealed and scattered.

Within a blink, the air was thick with estuary birds: gulls, terns, cormorants, herons, even a sea eagle. The latter, at Saker's instigation, plunged at the cleric, who took one horrified look and jumped off the wharf into the water. Sorrel's band of thieves melted away.

The only person who didn't appear to be intimidated, who hardly seemed to notice the birds, was the Dire Sweeper.

"I might have known the birds were your doing in Dortgren," he said as he drew his sword. His face was still muffled, but Saker knew he was smiling. "A witchery, eh? Hello again, Saker. This time I'm going to make sure of you."

It was the man who had called himself Dyer.

Saker already had his sword in one hand and his dagger in the other. "Oh? So certain?" He flexed his knees slightly, ready for the man's first move. Behind him, the birds had already put the wardens to flight. He debated whether to bring them in for an attack on Dyer, but hesitated. There was something about the amusement in the man's eyes that told him he would relish such a move.

"Send your birds away," Dyer said. "Let's fight this man to man, skill to skill."

"How would that be fair?" he asked. "An assassin versus a cleric? Hardly an even fight!"

"I've made some enquiries about you." They were circling each other and Dyer's gaze never left Saker's. "And you know what I think? You're a spy for the Pontifect. A master swordsman, a worthy opponent. And of course, an Ardronese witan with a witchery."

Saker was still trying to place him. No one he'd known well, he was sure of that, but he was just as certain they'd met some time in the past. At one of the Lowmian universities when he'd been a student. Grundorp, if he wasn't mistaken. This man hadn't been a student, though, or a tutor.

"I've already made sure that you won't use those birds against me," the man said. "You Shenat folk have a weakness . . . Bren! You there?"

"Yes, m'lud!"

Saker's gaze didn't shift. The answer came from somewhere near one of the warehouses abutting on to the boardwalk. Bren, the Dire Sweeper who'd kept the accounts for Dyer. Accounts of who'd died of the Horned Death, and who'd lived.

M'lud?

"Bren, tell my friend here what my orders are with regard to birds, if he sends his feathered friends my way right now."

"We are to wipe out all birds within twenty miles of Ustgrind, destroy every heronry, every gull colony, every eagle nest, every rookery, every roost, every year for the next ten years until there are no birds . . ."

Dyer, still watching Saker, added, "Your weakness: you care."

Blast the haggardly lout, he was right. He did care. Inwardly cursing, he sent the birds on their way. *It's not a weakness, you leprous worm. It's my strength. The love of a Shenat witan for our world.* "All right," he said. "Let's fight."

They clashed, disengaged, and clashed again. Dyer was a head taller, with a longer reach and a heavier sword. Pox on't, this wasn't a match of equals, but a meeting of two different styles. It wasn't going to be enough to be fast and clever, attacking swiftly with speedy retreats. *Not enough to be lighter and quicker on my feet. I've got to get under his guard, or he'll wear me down.*

And time would be on Dyer's side. The man's lunges were strong and dangerous, his parries vicious. Hell, his right arm was aching already. When he blocked Dyer's attacks, the heavy blows rattled up his arm to his shoulder. It was like trying to wrestle a bull.

He dared a quick lunge and tore a hole in Dyer's tunic over his ribs, then brought his dagger up unnoticed to slice a thin red line across the man's forearm on the underside. Pinpricks, dammit. And what if he defeated the fellow? He'd be up for murder! If he lasted that long. The scurvy scut's friends were watching like vultures, ready to run him through if he won the fight. Blister this for a battle lost before it began!

Another lunge from Dyer.

He stepped back to dodge and tripped over the remains of the chicken coop. Dyer's sword whistled past in a slashing swing, missing his chest by a whisker. He somersaulted away and snatched a brief look around.

The launch from the *Spice Winds* had already reached the quayside. Ardhi was in the stern, holding the boat steady by clutching the metal ring on the lower landing. The two other seamen had shipped the oars, but were still seated. All three men were gazing up at him. A goat stood in the prow and a chicken was perched on the gunwale. The wet and bedraggled cleric was hauling himself up on to the steps of the landing, struggling to overcome the weight of his sodden robes. On the fluyt, sailors were lined up along the railing to watch the fight, some yelling encouragement.

His swift glance failed to find Sorrel anywhere.

In Va's name, where had she gone? His mouth went dry. They didn't get her, did they?

Out of the corner of his eye, all he could see on the boardwalk were the wardens, scratched and bloodied, regrouping now that the birds had gone. There was no way he could emerge the victor here.

He had to flee, and there was only one way to go.

But what about Sorrel and the baby?

Nothing suggested itself. Dyer attacked again. This time they went into a clinch, swaying back and forth as each fought for the upper hand. The cloth over Dyer's face dislodged and he saw the man's full face in good light for the first time. He remembered him then. One of the university's patrons, a nobleman's son and rumoured to be rich enough to buy the university several times over. His father was a lord . . . and his name was certainly not Dyer.

His extra weight won the day, and he pushed Saker away, sweeping upwards with his dagger in his left hand.

Saker staggered backwards towards the wardens; no way to flee, no way he could escape the wicked jab that was going to push through his ribs. There was no time to feel anything: not terror, not regret, not despair. Just an inward cry of denial that burst inside his chest, that only he could hear. *Noooo . . . not like this. Va, not like this.*

Then sheer amazement. Not only was he still alive and unhurt, but it was Dyer who was staggering, Dyer who dropped his sword with a grunt of pain, Dyer who fell to the ground on all fours with a dagger in the back of his right shoulder.

Ardhi's Chenderawasi kris.

No time to wonder. With one fluid movement he dropped his own dagger, yanked out the kris, booted Dyer in the backside and raced for the launch. At the bottom of the steps he took a flying leap to clear the cleric, now on all fours on the landing. He alighted precariously on the gunwale. The hen squawked, panicked and flew back to the wharf. Ardhi pushed the boat away from the steps with a boat hook, and Saker wobbled alarmingly, arms flailing. One of the seamen pulled him into the launch, just saving him from a ducking.

He plonked himself down next to Ardhi, dropped the kris on the seat and sheathed his sword. The seamen put their oars in the water and began to stroke towards the *Spice Winds*. "You missed," he said to the lascar. "You should have got the bastard in the jugular." He hoped the seamen did not understand Pashali.

Ardhi shrugged. "Next time."

"There will be a next time. That fellow is trouble. You owe me a dagger, by the way, dammit. What the fobbing hells happened to Sorrel? Did you see where she went? Did they get her? Is she hurt? What happened to the baby?"

"The goat," muttered Ardhi. "Take a look at the goat."

He did, and it wasn't Sorrel's goat. It was Sorrel, glamoured, crouching in the bow of the boat, clutching Piper to her chest. The look she gave him would have soured a cask of beer.

45

Spice Winds

"Get – me – off – this – ship!"

Saker winced as Sorrel growled at him, emphasising every word as she glared from him to Ardhi.

"I can't stay here! Piper is going to want to eat any time soon, and I can hardly milk an imaginary goat. Nor glamour away a baby's howls, either."

They had managed to get Sorrel up on the weather deck undetected as anything except a nanny goat, but were now left with the problem of what to do next. Ardhi wasn't supposed to be there, doing nothing, and it was only a matter of time before one of the officers noticed and took exception to his idleness. Sorrel had banished the goat and blurred herself into her surroundings instead. Saker appreciated her problem, but was at a loss to know how to deal with it. He didn't even know how to explain to the bosun the absence of the extra goat that had apparently come aboard.

"*Spice Winds* got she-goats," Ardhi remarked, abandoning Pashali to include Sorrel in the conversation. "Two. Tie up on deck near chicken. Ship officers drink milk." He pointed, then looked around uneasily. "I go aloft soon or big trouble. No one send boat to shore now. *Spice Winds* sail soon."

Sorrel looked close to weeping. "Saker, *please*. I can't sail all the way to the Va-forsaken Hemisphere! The only woman on the ship, with a baby that's only a couple of days old!"

"The only way to get you ashore now would be to tell the captain we have a stowaway," he said, worried, "but that would mean being rowed back to the same wharf and into the hands of the wardens or worse, the Dire Sweepers."

"More big problem," Ardhi said, pointing. "Look! They come!"

Saker forgot himself long enough to swear richly. A pinnace had put out from the wharf and was already halfway to the *Spice Winds*. It was easy enough to make out the uniforms of the Castle Wardens, interspersed with people in black. "Oh, Va," he whispered, "they mean business.

"Listen, Sorrel, there's only one way we can save us both. And it means you have to stay on board when the ship weighs anchor. We can get you off later when we're sailing down the Ardmeer estuary, but for now you have to stay here. We're going to see the captain, but first I have to pick up something from my luggage. Stay here; I'll be back in a minute."

"Saker do what?" Ardhi asked, a look of alarm on his face.

He reverted to Pashali, to make sure the lascar understood what he intended to do. "I'm going to gift the captain my feather."

"No! No! You can't!"

Saker grabbed him by the arm. "Show me where my luggage is, right now." He dragged Ardhi away from Sorrel towards the companionway, speaking urgently into his ear. "Listen. If those men on the boat persuade Captain Lustgrader to surrender us to them, which they will, you won't get me to go to Chenderawasi, because I'll be dead. You need me alive. And this is the only way to keep me alive." He gave Ardhi an unpleasant smile. "This, I think, is the one thing that you can't force me to do, or not to do. That plume you gave me is mine, and whom I gift it to is my choice and there's not a damned thing you can do about it, is there?"

Ardhi stared at him, his dismay comical.

When Saker returned to the deck, the ship was like a waking behemoth; the closer to the moment of sailing, the more the activity. Sorrel, blurred into little more than a shadow near the mast, was the only person doing nothing.

Ardhi, following Saker up the companionway, was blasted with a roar from one of the ship's officers the moment his feet hit the deck. "Hey you, you scurvy son of a cur! Get your skinny arse aloft *now*!"

He fled up the shrouds.

"He thinks his precious fobbing magic will solve all our problems," Saker muttered to Sorrel. "A pox on it, it's more likely to kill us."

"I don't understand what you're going to do!" If Sorrel was trying to contain her trepidation and curb her rage, she'd failed.

"We gamble everything. We can't hide you and the baby, not on board a ship. Not even with a glamour." His piece of bambu containing the feather in his hand, he seized her by the elbow and propelled her towards the quarter deck at the stern, where Captain Lustgrader was standing with several of his officers behind the two helmsmen, eyeing the activity aloft as the sail unfurled from the spars in a slap of canvas. Around them were all the sounds of a ship about to get under way: the groan of the anchor chain being winched through the hawse pipe, the grunting of sailors as they hauled on ropes, orders repeated the length of the ship like an echo.

Before approaching the Captain, Saker drew Sorrel into the shelter of one of the deck cannons, eyeing her critically. The ragged garments she wore were more those of a homeless ruffian than a woman of substance. He said, "Glamour up some decent clothing. A woman's. Neat, good quality. Make yourself look respectable and clean."

"There might be someone on board with a witchery who can see through a glamour."

"I haven't seen anyone yet."

"Do you know what you're doing, Saker? Because it doesn't sound like it," she said as she adjusted her appearance.

"I think a sailor would say making any port in a storm is better than hitting the rocks. I think I'm doing the only thing that will save us both." He paused to look her over. "That's better. Now let's present ourselves to Lustgrader."

He marched past the helmsmen, pulling Sorrel behind him, and bowed to the Captain. "Sir," he said, "Factor Reed Heron reporting. I've found a stowaway on board. A lady." He indicated Sorrel and before Lustgrader could react, he added, "And this is for you. Both a personal gift and a matter of considerable urgency, sir." He thrust the bambu at him and Lustgrader took it without thinking.

"Captain," a midshipman said, interrupting them, "pinnace off the portside, a Castle Warden requesting permission to come aboard. Flying the Regal's standard, sir."

"Before you grant them permission, sir," Saker said hurriedly, "please look inside the bambu."

Lustgrader directed a thunderous frown at Saker, then switched his attention to the midshipman. "Find out who they are and what they want. And it had better be urgent before they can come aboard a vessel about to sail." He looked back at Saker. "What the fobbing blazes is a *woman* doing here?" he demanded. "How did she get on board?" He inserted his fingers into the end of the bambu to draw out the contents. "Is this what I think it is? And is that female holding a *child*?"

"A plume, sir," Saker said, ignoring the last question, "given to me by a lascar, which I wish to present to you. It will be of value to you in the Spicerie. I wouldn't pull it out here, if I were you. The wind . . ."

The captain had his fingers gripped around the end of the quill, and they were shaking. Saker knew what he was feeling. Desire, gratitude, longing. And an odd sense of inevitability.

He wanted to snatch the feather away from Lustgrader, tell him he hadn't meant it, it was *his*, dammit. He bit his lip to halt the words and tasted blood.

"That's – that's very kind of you. I accept," Lustgrader said. The look he turned to Saker was obsequious, almost lover-like. Saker felt sick. Pain welled up to choke him. He wanted to howl with the agony of letting go. At the repulsiveness of enslaving another. Instead he said, "Ask your second to take command of the sailing. It's important you attend to the pinnace. Deal with the stowaway later."

The Captain looked at him in a puzzled way. "Yes, of course. You heard, Mynster Tolbun? You have the ship."

The man standing behind the captain looked shocked, but stuttered, "Ay, ay, sir."

As Saker and Lustgrader left the poop deck, Sorrel trailing behind, Saker spoke softly into the Captain's ear. "You will get rid of this pinnace. No one is to come aboard. Some of them are Dire Sweepers. You know, the assassins who hunt out and kill those with the Horned Plague."

Lustgrader nodded. "There's no plague on board," he said. He sounded as if he was having trouble focusing. "I'll stop that nonsense immediately!"

Saker was relentless. "The woman and the baby are to be given a cabin to themselves for as long as they're on board. You will tolerate no discussion of this among the crew. Just tell them you've received instructions that they are to be regarded as privileged, um, supernumeraries. Do you understand?"

"Yes, of course." Lustgrader strode off without a backward glance to where the midshipman was calling down to the pinnace. "Refuse them permission, Mynster Bachold! If they insist, fire that wheel-lock pistol of yours at them . . ."

Saker let him go and drew in a deep breath. "Don't go near the railing," he murmured to Sorrel. "We don't want anyone on the pinnace to be certain we're on board."

She turned to him, her face a picture of utmost horror. "That – that was *hideous*! How could you *do* that?"

"Easily enough, if it was the only way to save your life and mine. And Piper's." He sighed. "I think if anything it's worse this way than the other way around, with me on the receiving end."

"I don't understand."

"There were four bewitched feathers. Ardhi gifted me one, which meant I had to do everything he asked of me. And what he asked was that I steal the other plumes from Regal Vilmar. I had no choice."

Her jaw dropped as she began to understand. "And now you've done that to someone else?" She took a step away from him in revulsion. "You just used the same witchery on Captain Lustgrader? A ghastly magic from the Va-forsaken Hemisphere! How *could* you?"

"Would you rather be returning to the shore, with Piper in your arms?"

She stared at him. "This is vile, Saker, and you know it. How can you not, when it was done to you? How long will this – this witchery last?"

"Long enough to save us, I hope. Look, the good thing is you'll have a cabin of sorts to yourself, with Piper, which means you'll both be safe. Later, I'll tell you everything we know about . . . about all this. About why I am on board this ship. Everything."

"I'll hold you to that," she said.

She wasn't smiling.

Saker was up on the deck at first light, watching the sky beyond the coast of Ardrone. Angry anvil-shaped storm clouds glowered, promising stormy seas. The ship was scudding down the Ardmeer estuary with a strong following wind from the north-east. Looking up, he noticed the mainsails had been reefed some time during the night in anticipation of bad weather.

Sorrel, with Piper sleeping in her arms, came to stand next to him at the railing. She was wearing a real dress this time instead of a glamoured one, and she'd obviously had an opportunity to wash.

"What happened to the rags you were wearing?" he asked.

"I kept them. They'll do for swaddling once they're clean. Fortunately I had my own clothes in my bundle."

"I'll order the captain to put you ashore in Ardrone," he said. "He'll have to do it if I ask. Port Teal, or Port Sedge, perhaps. I hope the strong winds won't be a problem. Did you sleep?"

"Not much." She laughed. "A woman with a young baby rarely sleeps much. But I felt . . . safe. The ship's boy milked the goats for Piper." She grimaced. "I was worried I might be sick, the wind is so strong, but it seems I'm a good sailor."

"Piper?"

"She's fine."

"Can I hold her?"

She transferred Piper to his arms and he stood for a long time in silence, looking down on her. Then he said quietly, "She might have lied to me." It wasn't a question and he knew she'd understand who he meant. "She lied about a lot of things. She lied to King Edwayn. She planned it all." He looked up from the sleeping baby. "Vilmar's first wife was also from the Ardronese royal family. There was some suggestion she was murdered because she didn't give him a son. Mathilda might have heard that story."

He drew in a deep breath, feeling he needed more air before he could continue. "Perhaps she took me to bed hoping it would put an end to her marriage. But maybe, just maybe, she had a second plan if the first one didn't work. Maybe she wanted to make sure she was increasing *before* she was married."

"And if the wedding had been called off and she was already bearing a child?"

"There are ways to get rid of an unwanted child early on. Maybe she thought it was worth the risk."

She thought about that. "You'll never know. Even if she were to tell you, you've no way of knowing what's truth and what's lie."

"No. I'll never know." He touched Piper's cheek. "What an empty-headed ninny you must have thought me."

"Yes, I did." Her honesty was brutal. "There is something else you don't know. To be truthful, I'm not sure I know it either."

He looked at her, curious. "Go on."

"Prime Fox called Princess Mathilda to Faith House several times after you were arrested. Both times she came back crying, but also strangely . . . buoyant. Later she kept asking to see him again, but he never would. I didn't think much about it. But then, when she was delivering Piper here, half out of her mind with pain, and not being able to scream . . . she blamed someone for not helping her. Said he was an evil man who'd promised she wouldn't have to marry Vilmar. I thought she might have meant you. After the birth, she said, 'What if these are his children?' She calmed down a bit after that, but I don't think she remembered exactly what she'd said. She threatened me with death if I told anyone what she'd said about Fox. But she hadn't mentioned the Prime at all. So then I thought, she wasn't talking about you at all. She meant Fox."

He stared at her, shocked. "Va above, you think *Valerian Fox* bedded her, promising to help prevent her marriage if she agreed?"

"She might have been muddled. She'd been in pain, with no sleep. But yes, that's what I think."

He stood in silence for a long time, looking down on the face of the sleeping child. Then he said quietly, "I loved her, you know. Or I thought I did."

"That doesn't excuse your actions."

"No. I've spent every day since then wishing I could undo it, but I can't." He looked away from her, unable to meet her gaze. "Afterwards, the only thing I held on to, tenaciously, was that we'd loved one another. That was my justification. And then I realised the person I thought she was . . . doesn't really exist. Never did exist."

He bent and brushed his lips to Piper's head. The milky, baby smell of her made his chest feel tight. "It was your idea wasn't it? Coming to my trial, defending me, taking that dangerous ride to the Chervil Moors. Your idea, not hers. You wanted to make things right. I didn't deserve it, but you did it anyway, because she'd wronged a foolish witan. Va above, you must despise me."

She cocked her head to regard him with a serious expression. "Despised? No. I've only ever despised one man, and believe me, he deserved it. And died for it, too. You were just clay-brained."

"Dizzy-eyed was the expression you used, I believe."

She smiled then, a playful twitch of the lips. "Extremely."

Piper stirred in his arms and he wrapped her blanket a little tighter. Her mouth blew a kiss and he felt as if his knees had turned to sand. "I seem to have ruined your life, and I never meant to. We can still undo some of the knots, partly. You can still get to Vavala from the Ardronese coast on one of the coastal boats. Once in Vavala, the Pontifect will help you. You – you'll like her."

"You can come with me now. Ardhi can't force you to do anything any more, can he?"

"No, he can't."

"So come ashore with me. We'll both go to the Pontifect."

"I could do that," he admitted, and smiled at Piper. "There's nothing I would like better than to take the problem to her and dump it in her lap. To say: 'You fix it. This is a problem for the Va-Faith, not me.'"

"But you hesitate."

He decided to be honest with her. She deserved that much. *And telling someone might clarify my own thoughts on it.* "When I was granted a witchery, it was an odd one. I've never heard of someone being able to talk to birds. Well, sort of talk to them. And then along comes Ardhi and tells me things about bird feathers and witchery and birds of paradise."

"So?"

"You remember Ardhi's kris? The one you saw on Juster's ship."

She nodded.

"Those gold flecks – they are part of bird of paradise plumes. Feathers that don't burn when metal is forged."

"That's impossible, surely."

He didn't speak.

She said, "Oh. Apparently not."

"Everywhere I look there is a connection to birds. So that's the first oddity that gives me pause. Then there's something deeply wrong in Lowmeer, and it's spreading to Ardrone. The Horned Death. The Dire Sweepers. The devil-kin, the murder of twins. The unholy pact made by a regal so long ago . . . That's the second thing. The wrongness."

Why in all Va's cherished world had Dyer remembered an unimportant student called Saker Rampion, and recognised him five or six years later on a dark night in Dortgren? He needed to think about that too.

"And you think the answer to *that* is on the other side of the world?" She was incredulous.

He ploughed on, remorseless. "I believe the magic of Ardhi's kris has been manipulating my life for the past year or more. I need to find out why. That's the third reason. And the fourth . . . the fourth is more nebulous. It's about what the plumes can do. You said it was diabolical, and you are right. I want them out of this hemisphere, and back where they belong."

She waited for him to say something more, but he was silent. Frowning, she said, "Would it be correct to say that Kesleer doesn't have that power over Regal Vilmar any more?"

He nodded.

"Will the Regal know he was duped?"

"By now? Oh yes. He'll know *how*, too."

"Then I think Regal Vilmar would love to get more of those plumes. For himself."

"And where there was one bird with plumes that can bewitch, there will be others . . ." His hold tightened instinctively around the sleeping child. *You have no rights to her, Saker,* he told himself. *None.*

"You need to go to the Summer Seas."

He nodded. "There's a final reason, Sorrel, something else you don't know – I'm the Pontifect's spy. I always have been. Since I was a lad in the lowest school of the university, learning my letters. Not a very good spy, not half as good as I thought I was, but my duty is to her, to the Pontificate and Va-Faith, to the whole of the Va-cherished Hemisphere. It is what I am: an agent of the Faith. And that might be something even more important to all of us."

She shivered, and he moved closer to her, putting his back between her and the wind, sheltering the baby between them. "If this fleet raids the Chenderawasi Islands for the plumes, they'll have a potent weapon of domination when they return here. Even if people were warned about the outcome of accepting, resisting the lure of a gift of a plume is not easy." He shuddered. "The Regal probably doesn't realise how the power can be passed on either . . . I think it's my duty to stay here on board. I'm sorry, Sorrel. You'll have to go to the Pontifect on your own."

She shrugged, smiling slightly. "Never mind. I'm a capable woman with a glamour. I can travel the length of the Va-cherished Hemisphere alone, if I want."

He believed her. "Tell the Pontifect everything you know. Everything. I've written to her as well, and my letter is already on its way."

She nodded wordlessly.

Gently he transferred Piper into her arms and then watched her walk away. *Perhaps it's just as well. I could get far too fond of her.*

He meant Piper. Of course he did.

Up in the rigging, Ardhi was checking all the reefs made by one of the tyro sailors. As he moved along the sail testing the ties, his dagger twisted in its sheath. He halted, heart lurching. *What now?*

Still balanced on the footrope, one hand holding tight to the spar, he pulled out the blade and looked at it. The metal was a dark and angry slate-grey, churning, alive. The gold flecks within flashed and streaked like lightning in the sky, only to die and reappear elsewhere in the metal.

He raised his eyes to the storm clouds along the distant coast of Ardrone. Lightning flickered through the billows. Gusting around him, the wind strengthened until the ropes and pulley rings rattled and slapped against the mast.

Oh, pigshit.

With a wind like that blowing offshore, and a storm brewing, there'd be no way they could make landfall on the coast of Ardrone – and there was no doubt in his mind what was to blame. He shoved the kris back into its sheath and glanced down to where Sorrel and the baby stood with Saker.

Tears gathered at the corners of his eyes.

His fault. All his fault.

Ah, Chenderawasi . . . which one is it you want now? The woman or the child?

Postscript

To Gunrad Lustgrader, Commander of the fleet of the Lowmeer Spicerie Trading Company, Captain of the Spice Winds.

Greetings.

Herewith are the direct orders from the undersigned, your Liege Lord, Regal Vilmar Vollendorn, Monarch. These orders are to supersede any others given to you by Mynster Uthen Kesleer or by directors of the Lowmian Spicerie Trading Company.

On your first voyage to the Spicerie, you obtained orange plumes of the creature named the "paradise bird", which you then presented to Mynster Kesleer.

You are instructed to make the procurement of more of these plumes your primary concern on this present voyage, taking precedence over your secondary concern, the procurement of spice cargo.

Any plumes obtained from henceforth are to be considered the property of the Basalt Throne, and the Lowmeer Spicerie Trading Company will be reimbursed accordingly.

Once reaching the Summer Seas, you are to proceed immediately to make every endeavour to locate, buy or seize as many of said feathers as possible. They are to be kept in good order under lock and key in your possession, away from the prying eyes of anyone else in the fleet. No other member of this expedition, whether crew, supernumerary or company employee, is to be permitted to own or keep such plumes, on pain of summary execution by you in your capacity as commander of the fleet.

On your return to Ustgrind you are to deliver the plumes collected directly to the Regal. It is recommended that such plumes are handled at all times with gloved hands.

By order of
His Grace, Regal Vilmar Vollendorn,
Lord and Monarch of the Regality of Lowmeer.
Signed, dated and sealed, the seventeenth day of Va year 902.

Acknowledgements

When I look back on my career as a published writer, I see many, many people who have helped me along the way. You are all special to me, but let me name just a few of you:

- my very special agent, Dorothy Lumley who has never wavered in her support or in her faith in me as a writer;
- Kay Hashim and all my friends in the Kuala Lumpur bookgroup, which has to be one of the longest lasting book clubs in the world, having been founded in the 1950s;
- Karen Miller, fantasy writer *par excellence*, who can always be relied on to tell me the truth when I need it;
- Alena Sanusi, very special friend, neighbour and fellow reader – I miss you so much;
- my other first readers: Phillip Berrie, Jo Wake, Nicole Murphy and Donna Hanson;
- my editor Jenni Hill and everyone at Orbit UK;
- and last but never least, members of my family, especially my husband the nuclear scientist, who really doesn't "get" fantasy. Maybe he'll read this one; after all, one of his ancestors might just have been a lascar . . .

extras

meet the author

Glenda Larke was born in Australia and trained as a teacher. She has taught English in Australia, Vienna, Tunisia, and Malaysia. Glenda has two children and lives in Erskine, Western Australia, with her husband.

Find out more about Glenda Larke and other Orbit authors by registering for the free monthly newsletter at www.orbitbooks.net.

introducing

If you enjoyed
THE LASCAR'S DAGGER,
look out for

THE LAST STORMLORD

Book One in the Stormlord Trilogy

by Glenda Larke

***Shale** is the lowest of the low—an outcast from a poor village in the heart of the desert. In the desert water is life, and currency, and Shale has none. But he has a secret. It's the one thing that keeps him alive and may save all the cities of Quartern in the days to come. If it doesn't get him killed first...*

***Terelle** is a slave fleeing a life as a courtesan. She finds shelter in the home of an elderly painter, but as she learns the strange and powerful secrets of his art she fears she may have traded a life of servitude for something far more perilous...*

***THE LAST STORMLORD** is dying in his tower and there are none, by accident or design, to take his place. He brings the rain from the distant seas to his people. Without a Stormlord, the cities of the Quartern will wither and die.*

Their civilization is at the brink of disaster. If Shale and Terelle can find a way to save themselves, they may just save them all. Water is life and the wells are running dry...

Chapter One

Scarpen Quarter
Scarcleft City
Opal's Snuggery, Level 32

It was the last night of her childhood.

Terelle, unknowing, thought it just another busy evening in Opal's Snuggery, crowded and noisy and hot. Rooms were hazed with the fumes from the keproot pipes of the addicted and fuggy with the smell of the resins smouldering in the censers. Smoky blue tendrils curled through the archways, encouraging a lively lack of restraint as they drifted through the air.

Everything as usual.

Terelle's job was to collect the dirty plates and mugs and return them to the kitchen, in an endless round from sunset until the dark dissolved under the first cold fingering of a desert dawn.

Her desire was to be unnoticed at the task.

Her dream was to escape her future as one of Madam Opal's girls.

Once she'd thought the snuggery a happy place, the outer courtyard always alive with boisterous chatter and laughter as friends met on entry, the reception rooms bustling with servants fetching food from the kitchens or amber from the barrels in the cellar, the stairs cluttered with handmaidens as they giggled and flirted and smiled, arm in arm with their clients. She'd thought the snuggery's inhabitants lived each night adrift on laughter and joy and friendship. But she had only been seven then, and newly purchased. She was twelve now, old enough to realize the laughter and the smiles and the banter were part of a larger game, and what underlay it was much sadder. She still didn't understand everything, not really, even though she knew now what went on between the customers and women like her half-sister, Vivie, in the upstairs rooms.

She knew enough to see the joy was a sham.

She knew enough to know she didn't want any part of it.

And so she scurried through the reception rooms with her laden tray, hugging the walls on her way to the kitchen. A drab girl with brown tunic, brown skin, brown hair so dark it had the rich depth of rubies, a timid pebblemouse on its way back to its lair with a pouch-load of detritus to pile around its burrow entrance, hoping to keep a hostile world at bay. She kept her gaze downcast, instinctively aware that her eyes, green and intelligent, told another story.

The hours blurred into one another. Laughter devoid of subtlety drowned out the lute player's strumming; vulgar banter suffocated the soft-sung words of love. As the night wore on, Scarcleft society lost its refinement just as surely as the desert night lost its chill in the packed reception rooms.

Out of the corner of her eye, Terelle noted Vivie flirting with one of the younger customers. The man had a sweet smile, but he was no more than an itinerant seller of scent, a street peddler. Madam Opal wanted Vivie to pay attention to Kade the waterlender instead, Kade who was fat and had hair growing out of his nose. He'd come all the way downhill from the twentieth level of the city because he fancied the Gibber woman he knew as Viviandra.

Behind the peddler's slender back, Terelle made a face at Vivie to convey her opinion of her sister's folly with the peddler, then scurried on.

Back in the main reception room a few moments later, she heard nervous laughter at one of the tables. A man was drunk and he'd lost some sort of wager. He wasn't happy and his raised voice had a mean edge to it.

Trouble, she thought. Rosscar, the oil merchant's son. His temper was well known in the snuggery. He was jabbing stiffened fingertips at the shoulder of one of his companions. As she gathered mugs onto her tray, Terelle overheard his angry accusation: "You squeezed the beetle too hard!" He waved his mug under the winner's nose and slopped amber everywhere. "Cheat, you are, Merch Putter—"

Hurriedly one of the handmaidens stepped in and led him away, giggling and stroking his arm.

Poor Diomie, Terelle thought as she wiped the stickiness of the alcohol from the agate inlay of the stone floor. *He'll take it out on her. And all over a silly wager on how high a click beetle can jump.* As she rose wearily to her feet, her gaze met the intense stare of a Scarperman. He sat alone, a hungry-eyed, hawk-nosed man dressed in a blue tunic embroidered with the badge of the pedemen's guild.

"This is empty," he growled at her, indicating the brass censer in the corner of the room. "Get some more resin for it, girl, and sharp about it. You shouldn't need to be told."

She ducked her head so that her hair fell across her face and mumbled an apology. Using her laden tray as a buffer, she headed once more for the safety of the kitchens, thinking she could feel those predatory eyes sliding across her back as she went. She didn't return to replenish the censer; she sent one of the kitchen boys instead.

Half the run of a sandglass later, she saw Vivie and Kade the fat waterlender heading upstairs, Madam Opal nodding her approval as she watched. The sweet-smiling, sweet-smelling peddler was nowhere in evidence. Terelle snorted. Vivie had sand for brains if she'd thought Opal would allow her to dally with a scent seller when there was a waterlending upleveller around. A waterlender, any waterlender, was richer than Terelle could even begin to imagine, and there was nothing Opal liked better than a rich customer.

Terelle stacked another tray and hurried on.

Some time later the bell in Viviandra's room was ringing down in the kitchen, and Madam Opal sent Terelle up to see what was needed. When she entered the bedroom, Vivie was reclining on her divan, still dressed. The waterlender was not there.

"Where's the merch?" Terelle asked.

"In the water-room," Vivie said and giggled. "Sick as a sand-flea that's lost its pede. Drank too much, I suspect. I was bored, so I rang down to the kitchen. Now you can have a rest, too." She patted the divan and flicked her long black hair over her shoulder. "And Kade's not a merchant, you know. He lends people water tokens. Which means you should address him as Broker Kade. Terelle, you *have* to learn that sort of thing. It's important. Keeps the customers happy."

"Vivie, if Opal catches us doing nothing, she'll be spitting sparks."

"Don't call me Vivie! You *know* I hate it. It's not a proper name for a Scarpen snuggery girl."

"It's your name. And you're not Scarpen. You're Gibber, like me."

"Not any more. Opal's right when she says 'Viviandra' has class and 'Vivie' doesn't. And why shouldn't we be lazy occasionally? I deserve a rest! You think it's easy pandering to the tastes of the men who come here? You'll find out when your turn comes."

"I'm not going to be a handmaiden," Terelle said. "I'm going to be an arta. A dancer, like the great Arta Amethyst. In fact, I am going to be greater than Amethyst." To demonstrate her skill, she bounced to her feet, undulated her hips in a slow figure of eight and then did the splits.

Vivie groaned. "You are *such* a child! You won't have any choice in the matter, you know. Why in all the Sweepings do you think Madam Opal paid Pa for the two of us? So as you could be a dancer? Not weeping likely!"

All hope vanished as Terelle glimpsed the darkness of her future, crouching in wait just around a corner not too far away. "Oh, Vivie! What sort of handmaiden would I make? Look at me!"

She hadn't meant to be literal, but Vivie sat up and ran a critical gaze over her. "Well," she said, "it's true that you're nothing much to look at right now. But you're only twelve. That will change. Look at how scrawny Diomie was when she first came! And now..." She sketched curves with her hands. "That jeweller from Level Nine called her luscious last night. A plum for the picking, he said."

"Even if I burst out of my dresses like Diomie, my face will still be the same," Terelle pointed out. "*I* think I have nice eyes, but Madam Opal says green is unnatural. And my skin's too brown, even browner than yours. And my hair's too straight and ordinary, not wavy and black like yours. No load of powder and paint is going to change any of that." She was not particularly upset at the thought. "I can dance, though. Or so everyone says. Besides, I don't *want* to be a whore."

"Opal will stick a pin in your backside if you use that word around here. Whores sell their bodies on the street for water. We are trained snuggery handmaidens. We are Opal's girls. We do much more than—well, much more than whores do. We are, um, *companions*. We speak prettily, and tell stories and sing and recite and dance, and we listen to the men as though they are the wisest sages in the city. We entertain and make them laugh. Do it properly, like I do, and no one cares if we don't have fair skin and blue eyes and straw hair like Scarpen Quarter folk."

"Opal says I'm the best fan dancer she's seen for my age."

"Maybe, but she can't teach you, not properly, you know that. You'd have to go to a professional dancer for lessons, and that'd cost tokens we don't have. Opal's not going to pay for it. She doesn't want a dancer, or a musician, or a singer—she just wants handmaidens who can also dance and sing and play the lute. There's a difference. Forget it, Terelle. It's not going to happen. When your bleeding starts, the law says you are old enough to be a handmaiden and Opal will make sure that's what happens."

Terelle lifted her chin. "I won't be a whore, Vivie. I *won't*."

"Don't say things like that, or Opal will throw you out."

"I wish she would. Ouch!"

Vivie, irritated, had leaned across and yanked a lock of her hair. "Terelle, she's given you water for more than five whole years, just on the strength of what you will become after your bleeding starts. You *know* that. Not to mention what she paid Pa. She *invested* in you. She will spit more than sparks if she thinks she's not going to get a return on her investment. She won't let you get away with it. Anyway, it's not such a bad life, not really."

But the crouching shape of her unwanted future grew in Terelle's mind. "It's—it's horrible! Like slavery. And even barbarian Reduners don't own slaves any more. We were *sold*, Vivie. Pa sold us to those men knowing we would end up in a brothel." The bitterness spilled over into her voice.

"This is *not* a brothel. It's a snuggery. A house for food and entertainment and love. We have style; a brothel is for lowlifes with hardly any tokens. And I am not a slave—I am paid, and paid well. One day I shall have enough to retire." She picked up her hand mirror from the divan and fluffed up her hair. The reddish highlights in the black gleamed in the lamplight. "I think I need another ruby rinse."

"I'll do it tomorrow."

"Thanks." Vivie smiled at her kindly. "Terelle, you're not a slave, either. For the odd jobs you do, you have water and food and clothes and a bed, not to mention the dancing and singing lessons. You've been taught to read and write and recite. When you start working properly, you'll be paid in tokens like the rest of us. You can leave any time you want, once you pay back what you owe."

"Leave? How can I leave unless I have somewhere else to go? I'd die of thirst!"

"Exactly. Unless you save enough tokens first."

Terelle slumped, banging her heels against the legs of the divan in frustration.

Vivie laid her mirror aside. "Terelle, Terelle, don't you remember what it was like in the Gibber Quarter before we came here? I do. It was *horrid*." She shuddered. "The only time we had enough water was when we stole it. I was *glad* when Pa sold us to the Reduner caravanners—"

She broke off as they heard footsteps in the passageway outside. Terelle jumped off the divan and grabbed up her tray. When the waterlender entered, she was picking up the empty mugs on the low table. She bobbed and scuttled past him. When she glanced back from the doorway, she saw Vivie smile shyly at Kade from under her lashes. One bare shoulder, all invitation, had slipped from the confines of her robe.

Terelle pulled the door shut.

* * *

Back in the main reception room, the crowd had thinned. Most of the handmaidens had gone upstairs with their first customers of the night. Men who had not secured a girl waited their turn. Opal, plump and painted, flirted shamelessly as she bargained prices with latecomers. Servants brought more amber, keproot and pipes. The air was thicker now, yet there was an edginess to the atmosphere. Terelle scanned the crowd, seeking the cause.

The pedeman in the blue tunic sat alone, and his eyes, still sheened with feral hunger, sought her—but he wasn't causing any trouble. On the other side of the room, Merch Rosscar glowered at Merch Putter, the man he had earlier called a cheat. He began another drunken tirade, his speech slurred, his words threatening, his nastiness growing more and more overt. Putter stirred uneasily. Terelle glanced at Opal, who gave the merest of nods. Terelle dumped her tray and slipped out of the room. She went straight to the unroofed courtyard where Garri the steward and Donnick the doorman controlled entry to the snuggery via a gate to South Way.

"Trouble," she told them. "Madam Opal wants Merch Rosscar removed."

"Drunk again, I s'pose," Garri said. "Look after the gate a moment, Terelle. Anyone comes, they'll have to wait a bit till we get back. Come on, Donnick."

Terelle sat down on the doorman's stool next to the barred gate. Outside in the street all seemed quiet; at this late hour, not too many people were still up and about. The city of Scarcleft tumbled down the slope known as The Escarpment in stepped levels and South Way was one of three roads that descended from the highlord's dwelling, on Level Two, to the southern city wall, on Level Thirty-six. During the day it was usually one of the busiest thoroughfares in the city.

She leaned back against the courtyard's mud-brick wall so she could look up at the sky. On those nights when Opal's was closed, once every ten days, she would take her quilt up to the flat roof so she could fall asleep watching the stars as they slid, oh so slowly, across the black depth of the sky. She liked not being surrounded on all sides by walls. She liked the feel of the wind gusting in from the gullies of the Skirtings in unpredictable eddies. She even liked it during the day when the air was so hot it crackled the hair on her head, and she had to rub rendered pede fat onto her lips to stop them drying out.

Whenever Terelle tried to explain such things to Vivie, the older girl would throw her hands up in incomprehension and remark that talking to her sister was as unsettling as having a stone in your sandal. So Terelle didn't try any more. She learned to accept the fact that she was odd and Vivie was the one who fitted in. Terelle wasn't comfortable in the snuggery; Vivie revelled in it like a birthing cat that had found silk cushions. Terelle sometimes cried real tears—and Vivie had never shed a tear in grief in her whole life.

Now, though, the oil lamps around the walled courtyard dulled the sky and made it hard to see the stars. A flame sputtered and shadows danced. Once more she saw the dark lump of a future crouching just out of reach, waiting to smother her.

I'm trapped, she thought. It had been her fate from the moment she had been included in the deal made with the caravanners passing through their settle. Her father had his tokens, enough for a year or two's water, and she had this. She took a deep breath, inhaling the scent of citrus flowers, a hint of perfume, the stale smoke of burned keproot.

She had to get out. She wasn't Vivie, and she never would be. Yet how to escape?

Garri and Donnick returned, hustling an irate Rosscar

between them. Outside in the fresh air, he appeared less drunk and more dangerous. "I'll be back, Merch Putter!" he shouted over his shoulder, even though the merchant was nowhere in sight. "You'll regret the day you cheated me!"

Terelle opened the gate, but when the steward attempted to guide the man through it, he lashed out with a kick, catching the older man in the knee. Terelle winced. Garri had swollen joints at the best of times. Donnick, a hulking youth of eighteen with few wits but a good heart, gently levered the drunken man through the gateway and closed the gate.

Terelle stepped back into the passage leading to the main reception room. Light flickered as some of the lamps guttered. There was someone coming the opposite way, and she politely flattened herself against the wall to let him pass. But he didn't pass. He stopped: the pedeman in the blue tunic. She turned to hurry on, but he barred her way, his arm braced against the wall at chest height.

Her heart scudded; fear broke through on her skin in goose bumps. She did not look at him but kept her head lowered. "Excuse me, pedeman. I have work to do."

He did not move the arm but lowered his head to whisper close to her cheek. "How much is your first-night price, child?" The tip of his tongue thrust into her ear, seeking to know her.

She tilted her head away, reminded of the forked tongue of a snake questing after prey. "I'm not a handmaiden. I'm a servant." Her voice sounded thin and frightened to her ears. Her terror was out of all proportion to her danger; after all, one way lay the security of Garri and Donnick, the other way Opal and her servants. No one would allow him to touch her. Not this night. Yet she shivered as if the cold of a desert night wind brushed her skin.

Madam Opal won't sell my first-night before my bleeding starts, will she?

"You're a lying Gibber child," he whispered. "And you should not try to deceive your betters. I will buy your firstnight, and you'll pay for that lie." He placed a hand on the bud of her breast and squeezed, the touch a promise of horror. "It won't be long now, will it, sweetmeat?" She pushed him away, ducked under his arm and ran for the safety of the reception room at the end of the passage.

But the safety was illusory, her danger only postponed.

She was crying when she entered the room, and dipped her head to hide the tears.

The night was unending. The man in the blue tunic did not come back, but from one of the handmaidens she learned his name: Huckman. Pedeman Huckman, and worse still, he was a relative of Opal's. He owned a train of packpedes and ran cargoes from the coast to Scarcleft, bringing pressed seaweed briquettes to fuel the ovens and fireplaces and smelters of the city.

A wealthy man, and wealthy men bought what they wanted.

Fear fluttered at the edges of Terelle's thoughts for the rest of the evening. She still felt his hand on her breast, bruising her as he enjoyed her shock. Just thinking about him made her stomach churn.

At last the final dirty dishes and mugs were delivered to the kitchen and Opal indicated she could go to bed. Feet dragging with fatigue, she walked down the passage to the courtyard once more, on her way to the servants' stairs. Merch Putter was walking in front of her, on his way out after his time upstairs with one of the handmaidens.

Donnick opened the gate for the merchant, but before the man stepped through, he turned to press a tinny token into the youth's palm. And that was when they all heard it: a shrill keening, like a fingernail being dragged down a slate. No, more than that, a screech so horrible it shrieked of danger, of death on the move. Terelle had never heard such a sound before. She was terror-struck, rendered motionless. The merchant flung himself back into the courtyard, plunging sideways into the potted pomegranates.

Garri, on the other side of the courtyard, yelled "Zigger!" He dropped the bundle of dirty tablecloths he had been carrying and ran towards Donnick. "Close the gate! Close the blasted gate!"

But Donnick stood rooted, his mouth gaping foolishly at Garri, as if the danger was coming from his direction.

And the zigger flew into his mouth.

Terelle glimpsed it as a black blur the size of a man's thumb. The keening stopped abruptly, replaced by the shriek of Donnick's agony. He clutched at his throat and a gush of blood spewed from his mouth like water from an opened spigot. His screams faded into a choking gurgle. He fell to his knees, staring at Terelle, begging her for help she could not render. He clawed at his face, jammed his hand into his mouth, clutching for something he could not reach. She stared, appalled. His blood was splattered over her feet but she couldn't move.

Time slowed. She saw past Donnick through the gate to where a man stood on the opposite side of the street, his face muffled in a scarf. He held a zigger cage in one hand and a zig-tube in the other.

She thought, her calm at odds with her shock, *I suppose it's Rosscar and he meant to kill Putter.* Her terror dissipated into numbing vacuity. Donnick fell sideways, his body twitching uncontrollably.

She moved then, to kneel at his side and stroke his arm, as if she could bring comfort.

Garri came to stand beside her, patting her shoulder in clumsy sympathy. "Go inside, Terelle. Nothing you can do here."

She stammered an irrelevance that suddenly seemed important: "He's from the Gibber, like Vivie and me. He tells me stuff. About the settle where he was born. His family." She started to tremble. "We must be able to do *something*—"

The steward shook his head. "Lad's already dead. His body just don't know it yet."

As if he heard the words, Donnick gave one last shuddering spasm that arched his back from the ground. His gaze fixed on Terelle's face, speaking his horror, his terror, his pain. When he collapsed it was with brutal finality. His eyes glazed, blank with death. The zigger crawled out through his open mouth and paused. Terelle hurled herself backwards, half sprawling as she levered herself away on her bottom, whimpering in fear.

The zigger sat on the plumpness of Donnick's lip, blood-covered and sated, purring softly while it used its back legs to clean its jagged mouthparts and brush the human flesh from its wing cases. Terelle's trembling transformed to shudders, racking her whole body.

"Kill it!" she begged, clutching at Garri's ankles. *Do something, anything, please...*

"I dare not, lass. That there beetle is a trained zigger, worth more tokens than I earn in a year, and someone'd blame me, sure as there's dust in the wind. 'S all right, though," he said, lifting her to her feet. "Won't hurt us. It's eaten now and won't want to feed again. In a while it'll fly back to its cage. That's what they're trained to do." He glared out through the gate to where the zigger's owner still waited, but didn't challenge him. With a sigh he turned back to her. "Go wash, child. Use the water in Donnick's day jar."

She looked down at her feet. Blood ran stickily down her legs and into her slippers. Shuddering, she kicked them off. Mesmerised, unable to stop herself, she stared at the zigger again.

She wanted to flee, but couldn't bring herself to turn her back on it. Next to the gate, Merch Putter vomited messily into the pomegranate bushes.

"Remember that whining sound," Garri said, "and if you ever hear it again, take cover and hide your face. It's the wing cases sawing 'gainst each other in flight. Makes the victim turn his head, so all his soft bits and holes—eyes, nose, throat, ears—are facing the bleeding little bastard." He glanced at Merch Putter. "Go, Terelle. I'll take care of this, and tomorrow I'll report it to the highlord's guard. That's all I dare do."

"Would it—would it have made a difference if Donnick had closed the gate?" she asked.

He drew in a heavy breath. "No, I don't suppose so. It would've flown over the wall, wouldn't it?"

Just then the zigger spread its brightly veined wings and flew off, heading straight towards the cage held by the muffled figure on the other side of the street. Garri bolted the gate behind it, as if it was a departing guest.

Terelle fled towards the servants' rooms, leaving a line of bloody footprints across the courtyard.

introducing

If you enjoyed
THE LASCAR'S DAGGER,
look out for

ICE FORGED

Book One of the Ascendant Kingdoms Saga

by Gail Z. Martin

Condemned as a murderer for killing the man who dishonored his sister, Blaine "Mick" McFadden has spent the past six years in Velant, a penal colony in the frigid northern wastelands. Harsh military discipline and the oppressive magic keep a fragile peace as colonists struggle against a hostile environment. But the supply ships from Dondareth have stopped coming, boding ill for the kingdom that banished the colonists.

Now, as the world's magic runs wild, McFadden and the people of Velant must fight to survive and decide their fate...

Prologue

"This has to end." Blaine Mcfadden looked at his sister Mari huddled in the bed, covers drawn up to her chin. She was sobbing hard enough that it nearly robbed her of breath and was leaning against Aunt Judith, who murmured consolations. Just sixteen, Mari looked small and lost. A vivid bruise marked one cheek. She struggled to hold her nightgown together where it had been ripped down the front.

"You're upsetting her more." Judith cast a reproving glance his way.

"I'm upsetting her? Father's the one to blame for this. That drunken son of a bitch..." Blaine's right hand opened and closed, itching for the pommel of his sword.

"Blaine..." Judith's voice warned him off.

"After what he did...you stand up for him?"

Judith McFadden Ainsworth raised her head to meet his gaze. She was a thin, handsome woman in her middle years; and when she dressed for court, it was still possible to see a glimpse of the beauty she had been in her youth. Tonight, she looked worn. "Of course not."

"I'm sick of his rages. Sick of being beaten when he's on one of his binges..."

Judith's lips quirked. "You've been too tall for him to beat for years now."

At twenty years old and a few inches over six feet tall, Blaine stood a hand's breadth taller than Lord McFadden. While he had his mother's dark chestnut hair, his blue eyes were a match in color and determination to his father's. Blaine had always been secretly pleased that while he resembled his father enough to avoid questions of paternity, in build and features he took after his mother's side of the family. Where his father was short and round, Blaine was tall and rangy. Ian McFadden's features had the smashed look of a brawler; Blaine's were more regular, and if not quite handsome, better than passable. He was honest enough to know that though he might not be the first man in a room to catch a lady's eye, he was pleasant enough in face and manner to attract the attention of at least one female by the end of the evening. The work he did around the manor and its lands had filled out his chest and arms. He was no longer the small, thin boy his father caned for the slightest infraction.

"He killed our mother when she got between him and me. He took his temper out on my hide until I was tall enough to fight back. He started beating Carr when I got too big to thrash. I had to put his horse down after he'd beaten it and broken its legs. Now this... it has to stop!"

"Blaine, please." Judith turned, and Blaine could see tears in her eyes. "Anything you do will only make it worse. I know my brother's tempers better than anyone." Absently, she stroked Mari's hair.

"By the gods... did he..." But the shamed look on Judith's face as she turned away answered Blaine's question.

"I'll kill that son of a bitch," Blaine muttered, turning away and sprinting down the hall.

"Blaine, don't. Blaine—"

He took the stairs at a run. Above the fireplace in the parlor hung two broadswords, weapons that had once belonged to his grandfather. Blaine snatched down the lowest broadsword. Its grip felt heavy and familiar in his hand.

"Master Blaine..." Edward followed him into the room. The elderly man was alarmed as his gaze fell from Blaine's face to the weapon in his hand. Edward had been Glenreith's seneschal for longer than Blaine had been alive. Edward: the expert manager, the budget master, and the family's secret-keeper.

"Where is he?"

"Who, m'lord?"

Blaine caught Edward by the arm and Edward shrank back from his gaze. "My whore-spawned father, that's who. Where is he?"

"Master Blaine, I beg you..."

"Where is he?"

"He headed for the gardens. He had his pipe with him."

Blaine headed for the manor's front entrance at a dead run. Judith was halfway down the stairs. "Blaine, think about this. Blaine—"

He flung open the door so hard that it crashed against the wall. Blaine ran down the manor's sweeping stone steps. A full moon lit the sloping lawn well enough for Blaine to make out the figure of a man in the distance, strolling down the carriage lane. The smell of his father's pipe smoke wafted back to him, as hated as the odor of camphor that always clung to Lord McFadden's clothing.

The older man turned at the sound of Blaine's running footsteps. "You bastard! You bloody bastard!" Blaine shouted.

Lord Ian McFadden's eyes narrowed as he saw the sword in Blaine's hand. Dropping his pipe, the man grabbed a rake that leaned against the stone fence edging the carriageway. He held its thick oak handle across his body like a staff. Lord McFadden might be well into his fifth decade, but in his youth he had been an officer in the king's army, where he had earned King Merrill's notice and his gratitude. "Go back inside, boy. Don't make me hurt you."

Blaine did not slow down or lower his sword. "Why? Why Mari? There's no shortage of court whores. Why Mari?"

Lord McFadden's face reddened. "Because I can. Now drop that sword if you know what's good for you."

Blaine's blood thundered in his ears. In the distance, he could hear Judith screaming his name.

"I guess this cur needs to be taught a lesson." Lord McFadden swung at Blaine with enough force to have shattered his skull if Blaine had not ducked the heavy rake. McFadden gave a roar and swung again, but Blaine lurched forward, taking the blow on his shoulder to get inside McFadden's guard. The broadsword sank hilt-deep into the man's chest, slicing through his waistcoat.

Lord McFadden's body shuddered, and he dropped the rake. He met Blaine's gaze, his eyes wide with surprise. "Didn't think you had it in you," he gasped.

Behind him, Blaine could hear footsteps pounding on the cobblestones; he heard panicked shouts and Judith's scream. Nothing mattered to him, nothing at all except for the ashen face of his father. Blood soaked Lord McFadden's clothing, and gobbets of it splashed Blaine's hand and shirt. He gasped for breath, his mouth working like a hooked fish out of water. Blaine let him slide from the sword, watched numbly as his father fell backward onto the carriageway in a spreading pool of blood.

"Master Blaine, what have you done?" Selden, the groundskeeper, was the first to reach the scene. He gazed in horror at Lord McFadden, who lay twitching on the ground, breathing in labored, slow gasps.

Blaine's grip tightened on the sword in his hand. "Something someone should have done years ago."

A crowd of servants was gathering; Blaine could hear their whispers and the sound of their steps on the cobblestones. "Blaine! Blaine!" He barely recognized Judith's voice. Raw from screaming, choked with tears, his aunt must have gathered her skirts like a milkmaid to run from the house this quickly. "Let me through!"

Heaving for breath, Judith pushed past Selden and grabbed Blaine's left arm to steady herself. "Oh, by the gods, Blaine, what will become of us now?"

Lord McFadden wheezed painfully and went still.

Shock replaced numbness as the rage drained from Blaine's body. *It's actually over. He's finally dead.*

"Blaine, can you hear me?" Judith was shaking his left arm. Her tone had regained control, alarmed but no longer panicked.

"He swung first," Blaine replied distantly. "I don't think he realized, until the end, that I actually meant to do it."

"When the king hears—"

Blaine snapped back to himself and turned toward Judith. "Say nothing about Mari to anyone," he growled in a voice low enough that only she could hear. "I'll pay the consequences. But it's for naught if she's shamed. I've thrown my life away for nothing if she's dishonored." He dropped the bloody sword, gripping Judith by the forearm. "Swear to it."

Judith's eyes were wide, but Blaine could see she was calm. "I swear."

Selden and several of the other servants moved around them, giving Blaine a wary glance as they bent to carry Lord McFadden's body back to the manor.

"The king will find out. He'll take your title... Oh, Blaine, you'll hang for this."

Blaine swallowed hard. A knot of fear tightened in his stomach as he stared at the blood on his hand and the darkening stain on the cobblestones. *Better to die avenged than crouch like a beaten dog.* He met Judith's eyes and a wave of cold resignation washed over him.

"He won't hurt Mari or Carr again. Ever. Carr will inherit when he's old enough. Odds are the king will name you guardian until then. Nothing will change—"

"Except that you'll hang for murder," Judith said miserably.

"Yes," Blaine replied, folding his aunt against his chest as she sobbed. "Except for that."

* * *

"You have been charged with murder. Murder of a lord, and murder of your own father." King Merrill's voice thundered through the judgment hall. "How do you plead?" A muted buzz of whispered conversation hummed from the packed audience in the galleries. Blaine McFadden knelt where the guards had forced him down, shackled at the wrists and ankles, his long brown hair hanging loose around his face. Unshaven and filthy from more than a week in the king's dungeon, he lifted his head to look at the king defiantly.

"Guilty as charged, Your Majesty. He was a murdering son of a bitch—"

"Silence!"

The guard at Blaine's right shoulder cuffed him hard. Blaine straightened, and lifted his head once more. *I'm not sorry and I'll be damned if I'll apologize, even to the king. Let's get this over with.* He avoided the curious stares of the courtiers and nobles in the gallery, those for whom death and punishment were nothing more than gossip and entertainment.

Only two faces caught his eye. Judith sat stiffly, her face unreadable although her eyes glinted angrily. Beside her sat Carensa, daughter of the Earl of Rhystorp. He and Carensa had been betrothed to wed later that spring. Carensa was dressed in mourning clothes; her face was ashen and her eyes were red-rimmed. Blaine could not meet her gaze. Of all that his actions cost him—title, lands, fortune, and life—losing Carensa was the only loss that mattered.

The king turned his attention back to Blaine. "The penalty for common murder is hanging. For killing a noble—not to mention your own father—the penalty is beheading."

A gasp went up from the crowd. Carensa swayed in her seat as if she might faint, and Judith reached out to steady her.

"Lord Ian McFadden was a loyal member of my Council. I

valued his presence beside me whether we rode to war or in the hunt." The king's voice dropped, and Blaine doubted that few aside from the guards could hear his next words. "Yet I was not blind to his faults.

"For that reason," the king said, raising his voice once more, "I will show mercy."

It seemed as if the entire crowd held its breath. Blaine steeled himself, willing his expression to show nothing of his fear.

"Blaine McFadden, I strip from you the title of Lord of Glenreith, and give that title in trust to your brother, Carr, when he reaches his majority. Your lands and your holdings are likewise no longer your own. For your crime, I sentence you to transportation to the penal colony on Velant, where you will live out the rest of your days. So be it."

The king rose and swept from the room in a blur of crimson and ermine, followed by a brace of guards. A stunned silence hung over the crowd, broken only by Carensa's sobbing. As the guards wrestled Blaine to his feet, he dared to look back. Judith's face was drawn and her eyes held a hopelessness that made Blaine wince. Carensa's face was buried in her hands, and although Judith placed an arm around her, Carensa would not be comforted.

The soldiers shoved him hard enough that he stumbled, and the gallery crowd awoke from its momentary silence. Jeers and catcalls followed him until the huge mahogany doors of the judgment chamber slammed shut.

Blaine sat on the floor of his cell, head back and eyes closed. Not too far away, he heard the squeal of a rat. His cell had a small barred window too high for him to peer out, barely enough to allow for a dim shaft of light to enter. The floor was covered with filthy straw. The far corner of the room had a small drain for him to relieve himself. Like the rest of the dungeon, it stank. Near the iron-bound door was a bucket of brackish water and an empty tin tray that had held a heel of stale bread and chunk of spoiled cheese.

For lesser crimes, noble-born prisoners were accorded the dignity of confinement in one of the rooms in the tower, away from the filth of the dungeon and its common criminals. Blaine guessed that his crime had caused scandal enough that Merrill felt the need to make an example, after the leniency of Blaine's sentencing.

I'd much prefer death to banishment. If the executioner's blade is sharp, it would be over in a moment. I've heard tales of Velant. A frozen wasteland at the top of the world. Guards that are the dregs of His Majesty's service, sent to Velant because no one else will have them. Forced labor in the mines, or the chance to drown on board one of the fishing boats. How long will it take to die there? Will I freeze in my sleep or starve, or will one of my fellow inmates do me a real mercy and slip a shiv between my ribs?

The clatter of the key in the heavy iron lock made Blaine open his eyes, though he did not stir from where he sat. *Are the guards come early to take me to the ship? I didn't think we sailed until tomorrow.* Another, darker possibility occurred to him. *Perhaps Merrill's "mercy" was for show. If the guards were to take me to the wharves by night, who would ever know if I didn't make it onto the ship? Merrill would be blameless, and no one would be the wiser.* Blaine let out a long breath. *Let it come. I did what I had to do.*

The door squealed on its hinges to frame a guard whose broad shoulders barely fit between the doorposts. To Blaine's astonishment, the guard did not move to come into the room. "I can only give you a few minutes. Even for another coin, I don't dare do more. Say what you must and leave."

The guard stood back, and a hooded figure in a gray cloak rushed into the room. Edward, Glenreith's seneschal, entered behind the figure, but stayed just inside the doorway, shaking his head to prevent Blaine from saying anything. The hooded visitor slipped across the small cell to kneel beside Blaine. The hood fell back, revealing Carensa's face.

"How did you get in?" Blaine whispered. "You shouldn't have come. Bad enough that I've shamed you—"

Carensa grasped him by the shoulders and kissed him hard on the lips. He could taste the salt of her tears. She let go, moving away just far enough that he got a good look at her face. Her eyes were red and puffy, with dark circles. Though barely twenty summers old, she looked careworn and haggard. She was a shadow of the vibrant, glowing girl who had led all the young men at court on a merry chase before accepting Blaine's proposal, as everyone knew she had intended all along.

"Oh, Blaine," she whispered. "Your father deserved what he got. I don't know what he did to push you this far." Her voice caught.

"Carensa," Blaine said softly, savoring the sound of her name, knowing it was the last time they would be together. "It'll be worse for you if someone finds you here."

Carensa straightened her shoulders and swallowed back her tears. "I bribed the guards. But I had to come."

Blaine shifted, trying to minimize the noise as his heavy wrist shackles clinked with the movement. He took her hand in both of his. "Forget me. I release you. No one ever comes back from Velant. Give me the comfort of knowing that you'll find someone else who'll take good care of you."

"And will you forget me?" She lifted her chin, and her blue eyes sparked in challenge.

Blaine looked down. "No. But I'm a dead man. If the voyage

doesn't kill me, the winter will. Say a prayer to the gods for me and light a candle for my soul. Please, Carensa, just because I'm going to die doesn't mean that you can't live."

Carensa's long red hair veiled her face as she looked down, trying to collect herself. "I can't promise that, Blaine. Please, don't make me. Not now. Maybe not ever." She looked up again. "I'll be there at the wharf when your ship leaves. You may not see me, but I'll be there."

Blaine reached up to stroke her cheek. "Save your reputation. Renounce me. I won't mind."

Carensa's eyes took on a determined glint. "As if no one knew we were betrothed? As if the whole court didn't guess that we were lovers? No, the only thing I'm sorry about is that we didn't make a handfasting before the guards took you. I don't regret a single thing, Blaine McFadden. I love you and I always will."

Blaine squeezed his eyes shut, willing himself to maintain control. He pulled her gently to him for another kiss, long and lingering, in lieu of everything he could not find the words to say.

The footsteps of the guard in the doorway made Carensa draw back and pull up her hood. She gave his hand one last squeeze and then walked to the door. She looked back, just for a moment, but neither one of them spoke. She followed the guard out the door.

Edward paused, and sadly shook his head. "Gods be with you, Master Blaine. I'll pray that your ship sails safely."

"Pray it sinks, Edward. If you ever cared at all for me, pray it sinks."

Edward nodded. "As you wish, Master Blaine." He turned and followed Carensa, leaving the guard to pull the door shut behind them.

* * *

"Get on your feet. Time to go."

The guard's voice woke Blaine from uneasy sleep. He staggered to his feet, hobbled by the ankle chains, and managed to make it to the door without falling. Outside, it was barely dawn. Several hundred men and a few dozen women, all shackled at the wrists and ankles, stood nervously as the guards rounded up the group for the walk to the wharves where the transport ship waited.

Early as it was, jeers greeted them as they stumbled down the narrow lanes. Blaine was glad to be in the center of the group. More than once, women in the upper floors of the hard-used buildings that crowded the twisting streets laughed as they poured out their chamber pots on the prisoners below. Young boys pelted them from the alleyways with rotting produce. Once in a while, the boys' aim went astray, hitting a guard, who gave chase for a block or two, shouting curses.

Blaine knew that the distance from the castle to the wharves was less than a mile, but the walk seemed to take forever. He kept his head down, intent on trying to walk without stumbling as the manacles bit into his ankles and the short chain hobbled his stride. They walked five abreast with guards every few rows, shoulder to shoulder.

"There it is—your new home for the next forty days," one of the guards announced as they reached the end of the street at the waterfront. A large carrack sat in the harbor with sails furled. In groups of ten, the prisoners queued up to be loaded into flat-bottomed rowboats and taken out to the waiting ship.

"Rather a dead man in Donderath's ocean than a slave on Velant's ice!" One of the prisoners in the front wrested free from the guard who was attempting to load him onto the boat. He twisted, needing only a few inches to gain his freedom, falling from the dock into the water where his heavy chains dragged him under.

"It's all the same to me whether you drown or get aboard the boat," shouted the captain of the guards, breaking the silence as the prisoners stared into the water where the man had disappeared. "If you're of a mind to do it, there'll be more food for the rest."

"Bloody bastard!" A big man threw his weight against the nearest guard, shoving him out of the way, and hurtled toward the captain. "Let's see how well you swim!" He bent over and butted the captain in the gut, and the momentum took them both over the side. The captain flailed, trying to keep his head above water while the prisoner's manacled hands closed around his neck, forcing him under. Two soldiers aboard the rowboat beat with their oars at the spot where the burly man had gone down. Four soldiers, cursing under their breath, jumped in after the captain.

After considerable splashing, the captain was hauled onto the deck, sputtering water and coughing. Two of the other soldiers had a grip on the big man by the shoulders, keeping his head above the water. One of the soldiers held a knife under the man's chin. The captain dragged himself to his feet and stood on the dock for a moment, looking down at them.

"What do we do with him, sir?"

The captain's expression hardened. "Give him gills, lad, to help him on his way."

The soldier's knife made a swift slash, cutting the big man's throat from ear to ear. Blood tinged the water crimson as the soldiers let go of the man's body, and it sank beneath the waves. When the soldiers had been dragged onto the deck, the captain glared at the prisoners.

"Any further disturbances and I'll see to it that you're all put on half rations for the duration." His smile was unpleasant. "And I assure you, full rations are little enough." He turned to his second in command. "Load the boats, and be quick about it."

The group fell silent as the guards prodded them into boats. From the other wharf, Blaine could hear women's voices and the muffled sobbing of children. He looked to the edge of the wharf crowded with women. Most had the look of scullery maids, with tattered dresses, and shawls pulled tight around their shoulders. A few wore the garish colors and low-cut gowns of seaport whores. They shouted a babble of names, calling to the men who crawled into the boats.

One figure stood apart from the others, near the end of the wharf. A gray cloak fluttered in the wind, and as Blaine watched, the hood fell back, freeing long red hair to tangle on the cold breeze. Carensa did not shout to him. She did not move at all, but he felt her gaze, as if she could pick him out of the crowded mass of prisoners. Not a word, not a gesture, just a mute witness to his banishment. Blaine never took his eyes off her as he stumbled into the boat, earning a cuff on the ear for his clumsiness from the guard. He twisted as far as he dared in his seat to keep her in sight as the boat rowed toward the transport ship.

When they reached the side of the *Cutlass*, rope ladders hung from its deck.

"Climb," ordered the soldier behind Blaine, giving him a poke in the ribs for good measure. A few of the prisoners lost their footing, screaming as they fell into the black water of the bay. The guards glanced at each other and shrugged. Blaine began to climb, and only the knowledge that Carensa would be witness to his suicide kept him from letting himself fall backward into the waves.

Shoved and prodded by the guards' batons, Blaine and the other prisoners shambled down the narrow steps into the hold of the ship. It stank of cabbage and bilgewater. Hammocks were strung side by side, three high, nearly floor to ceiling. A row of portholes, too small for a man to crawl through, provided the only light, save for the wooden ceiling grates that opened to the deck above. Some of the prisoners collapsed onto hammocks or sank to the floor in despair. Blaine shouldered his way to a porthole on the side facing the wharves. In the distance, he could see figures crowded there, though it was too far away to know whether Carensa was among them.

"How long you figure they'll stay?" a thin man asked as Blaine stood on tiptoe to see out. The man had dirty blond hair that stuck out at angles like straw on a scarecrow.

"Until we set sail, I guess," Blaine answered.

"One of them yours?"

"Used to be," Blaine replied.

"I told my sister not to come, told her it wouldn't make it any easier on her," the thin man said. "Didn't want her to see me, chained like this." He sighed. "She came anyhow." He looked Blaine over from head to toe. "What'd they send you away for?"

Blaine turned so that the seeping new brand of an "M" on his forearm showed. "Murder. You?"

The thin man shrugged. "I could say it was for singing off-key, or for the coins I pinched from the last inn where I played for my supper. But the truth is I slept with the wrong man's wife, and he accused me of stealing his silver." He gave a wan smile, exposing gapped teeth. "Verran Danning's my name. Petty thief and wandering minstrel. How 'bout you?"

Blaine looked back at the distant figures on the wharf. Stripped of his title, lands, and position, lost to Carensa, he felt as dead inside as if the executioner had done his work. *Blaine*

McFadden is dead, he thought. "Mick," he replied. "Just call me Mick."

"I'll make you a deal, Mick. You watch my back, and I'll watch yours," Verran said with a sly grin. "I'll make sure you get more than your share of food, and as much of the grog as I can pinch. In return," he said, dropping his voice, "I'd like to count on some protection, to spare my so-called virtue, in case any of our bunkmates get too friendly." He held out a hand, manacles clinking. "Deal?"

With a sigh, Blaine forced himself to turn away from the porthole. He shook Verran's outstretched hand. "Deal."